WILBUR
SMITH

WILBUR SMITH

EAGLE IN THE SKY
THE DIAMOND HUNTERS

CHANCELLOR
PRESS

Eagle in the Sky first published in Great Britain in 1974
by William Heinemann Ltd
The Diamond Hunters first published in Great Britain in 1971
by William Heinemann Ltd

This collected volume first published in Great Britain
in 1987

This edition published in 1992 by Chancellor Press an imprint of
Reed International Books Ltd
Michelin House
81 Fulham Road
London SW3 6RB

ISBN 1 85152 188 7

Printed in Great Britain by The Bath Press

CONTENTS

EAGLE IN
THE SKY

While writing this story I had valuable help from a number of people. Major Dick Lord and Lieutenant Peter Cooke gave me advice on the technique and technicalities of modern fighter combat. Dr Robin Sandell and Dr David Davies provided me with the medical details. A brother angler, the Rev. Bob Redrup, helped with the choice of the title. To them all I am sincerely grateful. While in Israel many of the citizens of that state gave help and hospitality in generous measure. It grieves me that I may not mention their names.

As always my faithful research assistant gave comfort, encouragement and criticism when it was most needed. This book is dedicated to her son – my stepson – Dieter Schmidt.

There was snow on the mountains of the Hottentots' Holland and the wind came off it, whimpering like a lost animal. The instructor stood in the doorway of his tiny office and hunched down into his flight jacket, thrusting his fists deeply into the fleece-lined pockets.

He watched the black chauffeur-driven Cadillac coming down between the cavernous iron-clad hangars, and he frowned sourly. For the trappings of wealth Barney Venter had a deeply aching gut-envy.

The Cadillac swung in and parked in a visitors' slot against the hangar wall, and a boy sprang from the rear door with boyish enthusiasm, spoke briefly with the coloured chauffeur, then hurried towards Barney.

He moved with a lightness that was strange for an adolescent. There was no stumbling over feet too big for his body, and he carried himself tall. Barney's envy curdled as he watched the young princeling approach. He hated these pampered darlings, and it was his particular fate that he must spend so much of his working day in their company. Only the very rich could afford to instruct their children in the mysteries of flight.

He was reduced to this by the gradual running down of his body, the natural attrition of time. Two years previously, at the age of forty-five, he had failed the strict medical on which his position of senior airline captain depended, and now he was going down the other side of the hill, probably to end as a typical fly-bum, steering tired and beaten-up heaps on unscheduled and shady routes for unlicensed and unprincipled charter companies.

The knowledge made him growl at the child who stood before him. 'Master Morgan, I presume?'

'Yes, sir, but you may call me David.' The boy offered his hand and instinctively Barney took it—immediately wishing he had not. The hand was slim and dry, but with a hard grip of bone and sinew.

'Thank you, David.' Barney was heavy on irony. 'And you may continue to call me "sir".'

He knew the boy was fourteen years old, but he stood almost level with Barney's five-foot-seven. David smiled at him and Barney was struck almost as by a physical force by the boy's beauty. It seemed as though each detail of his features had been wrought with infinite care by a supreme artist. The total effect was almost unreal, theatrical. It seemed indecent that hair should curl and glow so darkly, that skin should be so satiny and delicately tinted, or that eyes possess such depth and fire.

Barney became aware that he was staring at the boy, that he was falling under the spell that the child seemed so readily to weave—and he turned away abruptly.

'Come on.' He led the way through his office with its flyblown nude calendars and handwritten notices carrying terse admonitions against asking for credit, or making right-hand circuits.

'What do you know about flying?' he asked the boy as they passed through the cool gloom of the hangar where gaudily coloured aircraft stood in long rows, and out again through the wide doors into the bright mild winter sunshine.

'Nothing, sir.' The admission was refreshing, and Barney felt his mood sweeten slightly.

'But you want to learn?'

'Oh, yes sir!' The reply was emphatic and Barney glanced at him. The boy's eyes were so dark as to be almost black, only in the sunlight did they turn deep indigo blue.

'All right then—let's begin.' The aircraft was waiting on the concrete apron.

'This is a Cessna 150 high-wing monoplane.' Barney began the walk-around check with David following attentively, but when he started a brief explanation of the control surfaces and the principle of lift and wing-loading, he became aware that the boy knew more than he had owned up to. His replies to Barney's rhetorical questions were precise and accurate.

'You've been reading,' Barney accused.

'Yes, sir,' David admitted, grinning. His teeth were of peculiar whiteness and symmetry and the smile was irresistible. Despite himself, Barney realized he was beginning to like the boy.

'Right, jump in.'

Strapped into the cramped cockpit shoulder to shoulder, Barney explained the controls and instruments, then led into the starting procedure.

'Master switch on.' He flipped the red button. 'Right, turn that key—same as in a car.'

David leaned forward and obeyed. The prop spun and the engine fired and kicked, surged, then settled into a satisfying healthy growl. They taxied down the apron with David quickly developing his touch on the rudders, and paused for the final checks and radio procedure before swinging wide on to the runway.

'Right, pick an object at the end of the runway. Aim for it and open the throttle gently.'

Around them the machine became urgent, and it buzzed busily towards the far-off fence markers.

'Ease back on the wheel.'

And they were airborne, climbing swiftly away from earth.

'Gently,' said Barney. 'Don't freeze on to the controls. Treat her like—' he broke off. He had been about to liken the aircraft to a woman, but realized the unsuitability of the simile. 'Treat her like a horse. Ride her light.'

Instantly he felt David's death-grip on the wheel relax, the touch repeated through his own controls.

'That's it, David.' He glanced sideways at the boy, and felt a flare of disappointment. He had felt deep down in his being that this one might be bird, one of the very rare ones like himself whose natural element was the blue. Yet here in the first few moments of flight the child was wearing an expression of frozen terror. His lips and nostrils were trimmed with marble white and there were shadows in the dark blue eyes like the shape of sharks moving beneath the surface of a summer sea.

'Left wing up,' he snapped, disappointed, trying to shock him out of it. The wing came up and held rock steady, with no trace of over-correction.

'Level her out.' His own hands were off the controls as the nose sank to find the horizon.

'Throttle back.' The boy's right hand went unerringly to the throttle. Once more Barney glanced at him. His expression had not altered, and then with a sudden revelation Barney recognized it not as fear, but as ecstasy.

'He is bird.' The thought gave him a vast satisfaction, and while they flew on through the basic instruction in trim and attitude, Barney's mind went back thirty years to a battered old yellow Tiger Moth and another child in his first raptures of flight.

They skirted the harsh blue mountains, wearing their mantles of sun-blazing snow, and rode the tail of the wild winds that came down off them.

'Wind is like the sea, David. It breaks and swirls around high ground. Watch for it.' David nodded as he listened to his first fragment of flying lore, but his eyes were fixed ahead savouring each instant of the experience.

They turned north over the bleak bare land, the earth naked pink and smoky brown, stripped by the harvest of its robes of golden wheat.

'Wheel and rudder together, David,' Barney told him. 'Let's try a steep turn now.' Down went the wing and boldly the nose swept around holding its attitude to the horizon.

Ahead of them the sea broke in long lines of cream on the white beaches. The Atlantic was cold green and ruffled by the wind, flecked with dancing white.

South again, following the coastline where small figures on the white sand paused to look up at them from under shading hands, south towards the great flat mountain that marked the limit of the land, its shape unfamiliar from this approach. The shipping lay thick in the bay and the winter sunshine flashed from the windows of the white buildings huddling below the steep wooded sides of the mountain.

Another turn, confident and sure, Barney sitting with his hands in his lap, and his feet off the rudder bars, and they ran in over the Tygerberg towards the airfield.

'Okay,' said Barney. 'I've got her. And he took them in for the touch-down and taxied back to the concrete apron beside the hangars. He pulled the mixture control fully lean and let the engine starve and die.

They sat silent for a moment, neither of them moving or speaking, both of them unwinding but still aware that something important and significant had happened and that they had shared it.

'Okay?' Barney asked at last.

'Yes, sir,' David nodded, and they unstrapped and climbed down on to the concrete stiffly. Without speaking they walked side by side through the hangar and office. At the door they paused.

'Next Wednesday?' Barney asked.

'Yes, sir.' David left him and started towards the waiting Cadillac, but after a dozen steps he stopped, hesitated, then turned back.

'That was the most beautiful thing that has ever happened to me,' he said shyly. 'Thank you, sir.' And he hurried away leaving Barney staring after him.

The Cadillac pulled off, gathering speed, and disappeared round a bend amongst the trees beyond the last buildings. Barney chuckled, shook his head ruefully and turned back into his office. He dropped into the ancient swivel chair and crossed his ankles on the desk. He fished a crumpled cigarette from the pack, straightened and lit it.

'Beautiful?' he grunted, grinning. 'Crap!' He flicked the match at the waste bin and missed it.

The telephone woke Mitzi Morgan and she crept out from under her pillows groping blindly for it.

"'Lo.'

'Mitzi?'

'Hi, Dad, are you coming up?' She came half-awake at her father's voice, remembering that this was the day he would fly up to join the family at their holiday home.

'Sorry, baby. Something has broken here. I won't be up until next week.'

'Oh, Dad!' Mitzi expressed her disappointment.

'Where's Davey?' her father went on quickly to forestall any recriminations.

'You want him to call you back?'

'No, I'll hold on. Call him, please, baby.'

Mitzi stumbled out of bed to the mirror, and with her fingers tried to comb some order into her hair. It was off-blonde and wiry, and fuzzed at the first touch of sun or salt or wind. The freckles were even more humiliating, she decided, looking at herself disapprovingly.

'You look like a Pekinese,' she spoke aloud, 'a fat little Pekinese—with freckles,' and gave up the effort of trying to change it. David had seen her like this a zillion times. She pulled a silk gown over her nudity and went into the passage, pass the door to her parents' suite where her mother slept alone, and into the living area of the house.

The house was stacked in a series of open planes and galleries, glass and steel and white pine, climbing out of the dunes along the beach, part of sea and sky, only glass separating it from the elements, and now the dawn filled it with a strange glowing light and made a feature of the massive headland of the Robberg that thrust out into the sea across the bay.

The Playroom was scattered with the litter of last night's party, twenty house guests and as many others from the big holiday homes along the dunes had left their mark—spilled beer, choked ashtrays and records thrown carelessly from their covers.

Mitzi picked her way through the debris and climbed the circular staircase to the guest rooms. She checked David's door, found it open, and went in. The bed was untouched, but his denims and sweat shirt were thrown across the chair and his shoes had been kicked off carelessly.

Mitzi grinned, and went through on to the balcony. It hung high above the beach, level with the gulls which were already dawn-winging for the scraps that the sea had thrown up during the night.

Quickly Mitzi hoisted her gown up around her waist, climbed up on to the rail of the balcony and stepped over the drop to the rail of the next balcony in line. She jumped down, drew the curtains aside and went into Marion's bedroom.

Marion was her best friend. Secretly she knew that this happy state of affairs existed chiefly because she, Mitzi, provided a foil for Marion's petite little body and wide-eyed doll-like beauty—and was a source of never-ending gifts and parties, free holidays and other good things.

She looked so pretty now in sleep, her hair golden and soft as it fanned out across David's chest. Mitzi transferred all her attention to her cousin, and felt that sliding sensation in her breast as she looked at him. He was seventeen years old now, but already he had the body of a grown man.

He was her most favourite person in all the world, she thought. He's so beautiful, so tall and straight and beautiful, and his eyes can break your heart.

The couple on the bed had thrown aside their covering in the warmth of the night, and there was hair on David's chest now, thick and dark and curly, there was muscle in arm and leg, and breadth across the shoulders.

'David,' she called softly, and touched his shoulder. 'Wake up.'

His eyes opened, and he was awake instantly, his gaze focused and aware.

'Mitz? What is it?'

'Get your pants on, warrior. My papa's on the line.'

'God.' David sat up, dropping Marion's head on to the pillow. 'What time is it?'

'Late,' Mitzi told him. 'You should set the alarm when you go visiting.'

Marion mumbled a protest and groped for the sheets as David jumped from the bed.

'Where's the phone?'

'In my room—but you can take it on the extension in yours.'

She followed him across the balcony railing, and curled up on David's bed while he picked up the receiver and with the extension cord trailing behind him began pacing the thick carpet restlessly.

'Uncle Paul?' David spoke. 'How are you?'

Mitzi groped in the pocket of her gown and found a Gauloise. She lit it with her gold Dunhill, but at the third puff David turned aside from his pacing, grinned at her, took the cigarette from between her lips and drew deeply upon it.

Mitzi pulled a face at him to disguise the turmoil that his nakedness stirred within her, and selected another cigarette for herself.

'He'd die if he knew what I was thinking,' she told herself, and derived a little comfort from the thought.

David finished his conversation and cradled the receiver before turning to her.

'He's not coming.'

'I know.'

'But he is sending Barney up in the Lear to fetch me. Big pow-wow.'

'It figures,' Mitzi nodded, then began a convincing imitation of her father. 'We have to start thinking about your future now, my boy. We have to train you to meet the responsibilities with which destiny has entrusted you.'

David chuckled and rummaged for his running shorts in the drawer of his bureau.

'I suppose I'll have to tell him now.'

'Yes,' Mitzi agreed. 'You sure will have to do that.'

David pulled up his shorts and turned for the door.

'Pray for me, doll.'

'You'll need more than prayer, warrior,' said Mitzi comfortably.

The tide had swept the beach smooth and firm, and no other feet had marked it this early. David ran smoothly, long strides leaving damp footsteps in a chain behind him.

The sun came up casting a soft pink sheen on the sea, and touching the Outeniqua mountains with flame—but David ran unseeing. His thoughts were on the impending interview with his guardian.

It was a time of crisis in his life, high school completed and many roads open. He knew the one he had chosen would draw violent opposition, and he used these last few hours of solitude to gather and strengthen his resolve.

A conclave of gulls, gathered about the body of a stranded fish, rose in cloud as he ran towards them, their wings catching the low sun as they hovered then dropped again when he passed.

He saw the Lear coming before he heard it. It was low against the dawn, rising and dropping over the towering bulk of the Robberg. Then swiftly, coming in on a muted shriek, it streaked low along the beach towards him.

David stopped, breathing lightly even after the long run, and raised both arms above his head in salute. He saw Barney's head through the Perspex canopy turned towards him, the flash of his teeth as he grinned and the hand raised, returning his salute as he went by.

The Lear turned out to sea, one wingtip almost touching the wave crests, and it came back to him. David stood on the exposed beach and steeled himself as the long sleek nose dropped lower and lower, aimed like a javelin at him.

Like some fearsome predatory bird it swooped at him and at the last possible instant David's nerve broke and he flung himself on the wet sand. The jet blast lashed him as the Lear rose and turned inland for the airfield.

'Son of a bitch,' muttered David as he stood up brushing damp sand from his bare chest, and imagined Barney's amused chuckle.

'I taught him good,' thought Barney, sprawled in the co-pilot's seat of the Lear as he watched David ride the delicate line of altitude where skill gave way to chance.

Barney had put on weight since he had been eating Morgan bread, and his paunch peeked shyly over his belt. The beginning of jowls bracketed the wide down-turned mouth that gave him the air of a disgruntled toad, and the cap of hair that covered his skull was sparser and speckled with salt.

Watching David fly, he felt the small warmth of his affection for him that his sour expression belied. Three years he had been chief pilot of the Morgan group and he knew well to whose intervention he owed the post. It was security he had now, and prestige. He flew great men in the most luxuriously fitted machines, and when the time came for him to go out to pasture he knew the grazing would be lush. The Morgan group looked after its own.

This knowledge sat comfortably on his stomach as he watched his protégé handle the jet.

Extended low flying like this required enormous concentration, and Barney watched in vain for any relaxation of it in his pupil.

The long golden beaches of Africa streamed steadily beneath them, punctuated by rock promontories and tiny resorts and fishing villages. Delicately the Lear followed the contours of the coastine, for they had spurned the direct route for the exhilaration of this flight.

Ahead of them stretched another strip of beach but as they howled low along it they saw that this one was occupied.

A pair of tiny feminine figures left the frothy surf and ran panic-stricken to where towels and discarded bikinis lay above the high-water mark. White buttocks constrasted sharply with a coffee-brown tan, and they laughed delightedly.

'Nice change for you to see them running away, David,' Barney grinned as they left the tiny figures far behind and bore onwards into the south.

From Cape Agulhas they turned inland, climbing steeply over the mountain ranges, then David eased back on the throttles and they sank down beyond the crests towards the city, nestling under its mountain.

As they walked side by side towards the hangar, Barney looked up at David who now topped him by six inches.

'Don't let him stampede you, boy,' he warned. 'You've made your decision. See you stick to it.'

David took his British racing green M.G. over De Waal Drive, and from the lower slopes of the mountains looked down to where the Morgan building stood four-square amongst the other tall monuments to power and wealth.

David enjoyed its appearance, clean and functional like an aircraft's wing—but he knew that the soaring freedom of its lines was deceptive. It was a prison and fortress.

He swung off the freeway at an interchange and rode down to the foreshore, glancing up at the towering bulk of the Morgan building again before entering the ramp that led to the underground garages beneath it.

When he entered the executive apartments on the top floor, he passed along the row of desks where the secretaries, hand-picked for their looks as well as their skill with a typewriter, sat in a long row. Their lovely faces opened into smiles like a garden of exotic blooms as David greeted each of them. Within the Morgan building he was treated with the respect due the heir apparent.

Martha Goodrich, in her own office that guarded the inner sanctum, looked up from her typewriter, severe and business-like.

'Good morning, Mister David. Your uncle is waiting—and I do think you could have worn a suit.'

'You're looking good, Martha. You've lost weight and I like your hair like that.' It worked, as it always did. Her expression softened.

'Don't you try buttering me up,' she warned him primly. 'I'm not one of your floozies.'

Paul Morgan was at the picture window looking down over the city spread below him like a map, but he turned quickly to greet David.

'Hello, Uncle Paul. I'm sorry I didn't have time to change. I thought it best to come directly.'

'That's fine, David.' Paul Morgan flicked his eyes over David's floral shirt open to the navel, the wide tooled leather belt, white slacks and open sandals. On him they looked good, Paul admitted reluctantly. The boy wore even the most outlandish modern clothes with a furious grace.

'It's good to see you.' Paul smoothed the lapels of his own dark conservatively-cut suit and looked up at his nephew. 'Come in. Sit down, there, the chair by the fireplace.' As always, he found that David standing emphasized his own lack of stature. Paul was short and heavily built in the shoulders, thick muscular neck and square thrusting head. Like his daughter, his hair was coarse and wiry and his features squashed and puglike.

All the Morgans were built that way. It was proper course of things, and David's exotic appearance was outside the natural order. It was from his mother's side, of course. All that dark hair and flashing eyes, and the temperament that went with it.

'Well, David. First off, I want to congratulate you on your final results. I was most gratified,' Paul Morgan told him gravely, and he could have added—'I was also mightily relieved.' David Morgan's scholastic career had been a tempestuous affair. Pinnacles of achievement followed immediately by depths of disgrace from which only the Morgan name and wealth had rescued him.

There had been the business with the games master's young wife. Paul never did find out the truth of the matter, but had thought it sufficient to smooth it over by donating a new organ to the school chapel and arranging a teaching scholarship for the games master to a foreign university. Immediately thereafter David had won the coveted Wessels prize for mathematics, and all was forgiven—until he decided to test his housemaster's new sports car, without that gentleman's knowledge, and took it into a tight bend at ninety miles an hour. The car was unequal to the test, and David picked himself up out of the wreckage and limped away with a nasty scratch on his calf. It had taken all Paul Morgan's weight to have the housemaster agree not to cancel David's appointment as head of house. His prejudices had finally been overcome by the replacement of his wrecked car with a more expensive model, and the Morgan group had made a grant to rebuild the ablution block of East House.

The boy was wild, Paul knew it well, but he knew also that he could tame him. Once he had done that he would have forged a razor-edged tool. He possessed all the attributes that Paul Morgan wanted in his successor. The verve and confidence, the bright quick mind and adventurous spirit—but above all he possessed the aggressive attitude, the urge to compete that Paul defined as the killer instinct.

'Thank you, Uncle Paul,' David accepted his uncle's congratulations warily. They were silent, each assessing the other. They had never been easy in the other's company, they were too different in many ways—and yet in others too much alike. Always it seemed that their interests were in conflict.

Paul Morgan moved across to the picture windows, so that the daylight back-lit him. It was an old trick of his to put the other person at a disadvantage.

'Not that we expected less of you, of course,' he laughed, and David smiled to acknowledge the fact that his uncle had come close to levity.

'And now we must consider your future.' David was silent.

'The choice open to you is wide,' said Paul Morgan, and then went on swiftly to narrow it. 'Though I do feel business science and law at an American University is what it should be. With this obvious goal in mind I have used my influence to have you enrolled in my old college–'

'Uncle Paul, I want to fly,' said David softly, and Paul Morgan paused. His expression changed fractionally.

'We are making a career decision, my boy, not expressing preferences for different types of recreation.'

'No, sir. I mean I want to fly—as a way of life.'

'Your life is here, with the Morgan group. It is not something in which you have freedom of action.'

'I don't agree with you, sir.'

Paul Morgan left the window and crossed to the fireplace. He selected a cigar from the humidor on the mantel, and while he prepared it he spoke softly, without looking at David.

'Your father was a romantic, David. He got it out of his system by charging around the desert in a tank. It seems you have inherited this romanticism from him.' He made it sound like some disgusting disease. He came back to where David sat.

'Tell me what you propose.'

'I have enlisted in the air force, sir.'

'You've done it? You've signed?'

'Yes, sir.'

'How long?'

'Five years. Short service commission.'

'Five years—' Paul Morgan whispered, 'well, David, I don't know what to say. You know that you are the last of the Morgans. I have no son. It will be sad to see this vast enterprise without one of us at the helm. I wonder what your father would have thought of this—'

'That's hitting low, Uncle Paul.'

'I don't think so, David. I think you are the one who is cheating. Your trust fund is a huge block of Morgan shares, and other assets given to you, on the unstated understanding that you assume your duties and responsibilities—'

'If only he would bawl me out,' thought David fiercely, knowing that he was being stampeded as Barney had warned him. 'If only he would order me to do it—so I could tell him to shove it.' But he knew he was being manipulated by a man skilled in the art, a man whose whole life was the manipulation of men and money, in whose hands a seventeen-year-old boy was as soft as dough.

'You see, David, you are born to it. Anything else is cowardice, self indulgence—' the Morgan Group reached out its tentacles, like some grotesque flesh-eating plant, to suck him in and digest him, '—we can have your enlistment papers annulled. It will be the matter of a single phone call—'

'Uncle Paul,' David almost shouted, trying to shut out the all-pervasive flow of words. 'My father. He did it. He joined the army.'

'Yes, David. But it was different at that time. One of us had to go. He was the younger—and, of course there were other personal considerations. Your mother—' he let the rest of it hang for a moment then went on, '—and when it was over he came back and took his rightful place here. We miss him now, David. No one else has been able to fill the gap he left. I have always hoped that you might be the one.'

'But I don't want to.' David shook his head. 'I don't want to spend my life in here.' He gestured at the mammoth structure of glass and concrete that surrounded them. 'I don't want to spend each day poring over piles of paper—'

'It's not like that, David. It's exciting, challenging, endlessly variable—'

'Uncle Paul.' David raised his voice again. 'What do you call a man who fills his belly with rich food—and then goes on eating?'

'Come now, David.' The first edge of irritation showed in Paul Morgan's voice, and he brushed the question aside impatiently.

'What do you call him?' David insisted.

'I expect that you would call him a glutton,' Paul Morgan answered.

'And what do you call a man with many millions—who spends his life trying to make more?'

Paul Morgan froze into stillness. He stared at his ward for long seconds before he spoke.

'You become insolent,' he said at last.

'No, sir. I did not mean it so. You are not the glutton—but I would be.'

Paul Morgan turned away and went to his desk. He sat in the high-backed leather chair and lit the cigar at last. They were silent again for a long time until at last Paul Morgan sighed.

'You'll have to get it out of your system, the way your father did. But how I grudge you five wasted years.'

'Not wasted, Uncle Paul. I will come out with a Bachelor of Science degree in aeronautical engineering.'

'I suppose we'll just have to be thankful for little things like that.'

David went and stood beside his chair.

'Thank you. This is very important to me.'

'Five years, David. After that I want you,' then he smiled slightly to signal a witticism, 'at least they will make you cut your hair.'

Four miles above the warm flesh-coloured earth, David Morgan rode the high heavens like a young god. The sun visor of his helmet was closed, masking with its dark cyclops eye the rapt, almost mystic expression with which he flew. Five years had not dulled the edge of his appetite for the sensation of power and isolation that flight in a Mirage interceptor awoke in him.

The unfiltered sunlight blazed ferociously upon the metal of his craft, clothing him in splendour—while far below the very clouds were insignificant against the earth, scattered and flying like a sheep flock before the wolf of the wind.

Today's flight was tempered by a melancholy, a sense of impending loss. The morrow was the last day of his enlistment. At noon his commission expired and if Paul Morgan prevailed he would become Mister David—new boy at Morgan Group.

He thrust the thought aside, and concentrated on the enjoyment of these last precious minutes; but too soon the spell was broken.

'Zulu Striker One, this is Range Control. Report your position.'

'Range Control, this is Zulu Striker One holding up range fifty miles.'

'Striker One, the range is clear. Your target-markers are figures eight and twelve. Commence your run.'

The horizon revolved abruptly across the nose of the Mirage, as the wing came over and he went down under power, falling from the heights, a controlled plunge, purposeful and precise as the stoop of a falcon.

David's right hand moved swiftly across the weapon selector panel, locking in the rocket circuit.

The earth flattened out ahead, immense and featureless, speckled with a low bush that blurred past his wing-tips as he let the Mirage sink lower. At this height the awareness of speed was breathtaking, and as the first marker came up ahead it seemed at the same instant to flash away below the silvery nose.

Five, six, seven—the black numerals on their glaring white grounds flickered by.

A touch of left rudder and stick, both adjustments made without conscious effort—and ahead was the circular layout of the rocket range, the concentric rings shrinking in size around the central mound—the 'coke' of flight jargon, which was the bull's-eye of the target.

David brought the deadly machine in fast and low, his mach meter recording a speed that was barely sub-sonic. He was running off the direct line of track, judging his moment with frowning concentration. When it came he pulled the Mirage's nose in to the 'pitch up' and went over on to the target with his gloved right finger curled about the trigger lever.

The shrieking silver machine achieved her correct slightly nose-down attitude for rocket launch at the precise instant of time that the white blob of 'coke' was centred in the diamond patterns of the reflector sight.

It was an evolution executed with subtle mastery of many diverse skills, and David pressed against the spring-loaded resistance of the trigger. There was no change in the feel of the aircraft, and the hiss of the rocket launch was almost lost beneath the howl of the great jet, but from beneath his wings the brief smoke lines reached out ahead towards the target, and in certainty of a fair strike David pushed his throttle to the gate and waited for the rumbling ignition of his after-burners, giving him power for the climb out of range of enemy flak.

'What a way to go,' he grinned to himself as he lay on his back with the Mirage's nose pointed into the bright blue, and gravity pressing him into the padding of his seat.

'Hello, Striker One. This is Range Control. That was right on the nose. Give the man a coke. Nice shooting. Sorry to lose you, Davey.' The break in hallowed range discipline touched David. He was going to miss them—all of them. He pressed the transmit button on the moulded head of his joystick, and spoke into the microphone of his helmet, 'From Striker One, thanks and farewell,' David said. 'Over and out.'

His ground crew were waiting for him also. He shook hands with each of them, the awkward handshakes and rough jokes masking the genuine affection that the years had built between them. Then he left them and went down the vast metal-skinned cavern, redolent with the smell of grease and oil along which the gleaming rows of needle-nosed interceptors stood, even in repose their forward lines giving them speed and thrust.

David paused to pat the cold metal of one of them, and the orderly found him there peering up at the emblem of the Flying Cobra upon the towering tailplane.

'C.O.'s compliments, sir, and will you report to him right away.'

Colonel 'Rastus' Naude was a dried-out stick of a man, with a wizened monkey face, who wore his uniform and medal ribbons with a casually distracted air. He had flow Hurricanes in the Battle of Britain, Mustangs in Italy, Spitfires and Messerschmitt 109's in Palestine and Sabres in Korea—and he was too old for his present command—but nobody could muster the courage to tell him that, especially as he could out-fly and out-gun most of the young bucks on the squadron.

'So we are getting rid of you at last, Morgan,' he greeted David.

'Not until after the mess party, sir.'

'Ja,' Rastus nodded. 'You've given me enough hardship these last five years. You owe me a bucket of whisky.' He gestured to the hard-backed chair beside his desk. 'Sit down, David.'

It was the first ime he had used David's given name, and David placed his flying helmet on the corner of the desk and lowered himself into the chair, clumsy in the constricting grip of his G-suit.

Rastus took his time filling his pipe with the evil black Magaliesberg shag and he studied the young man opposite him intently. He recognized the same qualities in him that Paul Morgan had prized, the aggressive and competitive drive that gave him a unique value as an interceptor pilot.

He lit the pipe at last, puffing thick rank clouds of blue smoke as he slid a sheaf of documents across the desk to David.

'Read and sign,' he said. 'That's an order.' David glanced rapidly through the papers, then he looked up and grinned.

'You don't give in easily, sir,' he admitted.

One document was a renewal of his short service contract for an additional five years, the other was a warrant of promotion—from captain to major.

'We have spent a great deal of time and money in making you what you are. You have been given an exceptional talent, and we have developed it until now you are—I'll not mince words—one hell of a pilot.'

'I'm sorry, sir,' David told him sincerely.

'Damn it,' said Rastus angrily. 'Why the hell did you have to be born a Morgan. All that money—they'll clip your wings, and chain you to a desk.'

'It's not the money.' David denied it swiftly. He felt his own anger stir at the accusation.

Rastus nodded cynically. 'Ja!' he said. 'I hate the stuff also.' He picked up the documents David had rejected, and grunted. 'Not enough to tempt you, hey?'

'Colonel, it's hard to explain. I just feel that there is more to do, something important that I have to find out about—and it's not here. I have to go look for it.'

Rastus nodded heavily. 'All right then,' he said. 'I had a good try. Now you can take your long-suffering commanding officer down to the mess and spend some of the Morgan millions on filling him up with whisky.' He stood up and clapped his uniform hat at a rakish angle over his cropped grey head. 'You and I will get drunk together this night—for both of us are losing something, I perhaps more than you.'

It seemed that David had inherited his love of beautiful and powerful machines from his father. Clive Morgan had driven himself, his wife, and his brand new Ferrari sports car into the side of a moving goods train at an unlit level crossing. The traffic police estimated that the Ferrari was travelling at one hundred and fifty miles an hour at the moment of impact.

Clive Morgan's provision for his eleven-year-old son was detailed and elaborate. The child became a ward of his uncle Paul Morgan, and his inheritance was arranged in a series of trust funds.

On his majority he was given access to the first of the funds which provided an income equivalent to that of, say, a highly successful surgeon. On that day the old green M.G. had given way to a powder-blue Maserati, in true Morgan tradition.

On his twenty-third birthday, control of the sheep ranches in the Karroo, the cattle ranch in South West Africa and Jubulani, the sprawling game ranch in the Sabi-Sand block, passed to him, their management handled smoothly by his trustees.

On his twenty-fifth birthday the number two fund interest would divert to him, in addition to a large block of negotiable paper and title in two massive urban holdings—office and supermarket complexes, and a high-rise housing project.

At age thirty the next fund opened for him, as large as the previous two combined, and transfer to him of the first of five blocks of Morgan stock would begin.

From then onwards, every five years until age fifty further funds opened, further blocks of Morgan stock would be transferred. It was a numbing procession of wealth that stretched ahead of him, daunting in its sheer magnitude; like a display of too much rich food, it seemed to depress appetite.

David drove fast southwards, with the Michelin metallics hissing savagely on the tarmac, and he thought about all that wealth, the great golden cage, the insatiable maw of Morgan Group yawning open to swallow him so that, like the cell of a jelly fish, he would become part of the whole, a prisoner of his own abundance.

The prospect appalled him, adding a hollow sensation in his belly to the pulse of pain that beat steadily behind his eyes—testimony to the foolhardiness of trying to drink level with Colonel Rastus Naude.

He pushed the Maserati harder, seeking the twin opiates of power and speed, finding comfort and escape in the rhythms and precision of driving very fast, and the hours flew past as swiftly as the miles so it was still daylight when he let himself into Mitzi's apartment on the cliffs that overlooked Clifton beach and the clear green Atlantic.

Mitzi's apartment was chaos, that much had not changed. She kept open house for a string of transitory guests who drank her liquor, ate her food and vied with each other as to who could create the most spectacular shambles.

In the first bedroom that David tried there was a strange girl with dark hair curled on the bed in boys' pyjamas, sucking her thumb in sleep.

With the second room he was luckier, and he found it deserted, although the bed was unmade and someone had left breakfast dishes smeared with congealed egg upon the side table.

David slung his bag on the bed and fished out his bathing costume. He changed quickly and went out by the side stairs that spiralled down to the beach and began to run—a trot at first, and then suddenly he sprinted away, racing blindly as though from some terrible monster that pursued him. At the end of Fourth beach where the rocks began, he plunged into the icy surf and swam out to the edge of the kelp at Bakoven point, driving overarm through the water and the cold lanced him to the bone, so that when he came out he was blue and shuddering. But the hunted feeling was gone and he warmed a little as he jogged back to Mitzi's apartment.

He had to remove the forest of pantihose and feminine underwear that festooned the bathroom before he could draw himself a bath. He filled it to the overflow, and as he settled into it the front door burst open and Mitzi came in like the north wind.

'Where are you, warrior?' She was banging the doors. 'I saw your car in the garage—so I know you're here!'

'In here, doll,' he called, and she stood in the doorway and they grinned at each other. She had put on weight again, he saw, straining the seam of her skirt, and her bosom was bulky and amorphous under the scarlet sweater. She had finally given up her struggle with myopia and the metal-framed spectacles sat on the end of her little nose, while her hair fuzzed out at unexpected angles.

'You're beautiful,' she cried, coming to kiss him and getting soap down her sweater as she hugged him.

'Drink or coffee?' she asked, and David winced at the thought of alcohol.

'Coffee will be great, doll.'

She brought it to him in a mug, then perched on the toilet seat.

'Tell all!' she commanded and while they chatted the pretty dark-haired girl wandered in, still in her pyjamas and bug-eyed from sleep.

'This is my coz, David. Isn't he beautiful?' Mitzi introduced them. 'And this is Liz.'

The girl sat on the dirty linen basket in the corner and fixed David with such an awed and penetrating gaze that Mitzi warned her. 'Cool it, darling. Even from here I can hear your ovaries bouncing around like ping-pong balls.'

But she was such a silent, ethereal little thing that they soon forgot her and talked as if they were alone. It was Mitzi who said suddenly, without preliminaries, 'Papa is waiting for you, licking his lips like an ivy-league ogre. I ate with them Saturday night—he must have brought your name up one zillion times. It's going to be strange to have you sitting up there on Top Floor, in a charcoal suit, being bright at Monday morning conference—'

David stood up suddenly in the bath, cascading suds and steaming water, and began soaping his crotch vigorously. They watched him with interest, the dark-haired girl's eyes widening until they seemed to fill her face.

David sat down again, slopping water over the edge.

'I'm not going!' he said, and there was a long heavy silence.

'What do you mean—you're not going?' Mitzi asked timorously.

'Just that,' said David. 'I'm not going to Morgan Group.'

'But you have to!'

'Why?' asked David.

'Well, I mean it's decided—you promised Daddy that when you finished with the airforce.'

'No,' David said, 'I made no promise. He just took it. When you said a moment ago—being bright at Monday morning conference—I knew I couldn't do it. I guess I've known all along.'

'What you going to do, then?' Mitzi had recovered from the first shock, and her plump cheeks were tinged with excitement.

'I don't know. I just know I am not going to be a caretaker for other men's achievements. Morgan Group isn't me. It's something that Gramps, and Dad and Uncle Paul made. It's too big and cold—'

Mitzi was flushed, bright-eyes, nodding her agreement, enchanted by this prospect of rebellion and open defiance.

David was warming to it also. 'I'll find my own road to go. There's more to it. There has to be something more than this.'

'Yes,' Mitzi nodded so that she almost shook her spectacles from her nose. 'You're not like them. You would shrivel and die up there on executive suite.'

'I've got to find it, Mitzi. It's got to be out there somewhere.'

David came out of the bath, his body glowing dull red-brown from the scalding water and steam rising from him in light tendrils. He pulled on a Terry robe as he talked and the two girls followed him through to the bedroom and sat side by side on the edge of the bed, eagerly nodding their encouragement as David Morgan made his formal declaration of independence. Mitzi spoiled it, however.

'What are you going to tell Daddy?' she asked. The question halted David's flow of rhetoric, and he scratched the hair on his chest as he considered it. The girls waited attentively.

'He's not going to let you get away again,' Mitzi warned. 'Not without a stand-up, knock-down, drag-em-out fight.'

In this moment of crisis David's courage deserted him. 'I've told him once, I don't have to tell him again.'

'You just going to cut and run?' Mitzi asked.

'I'm not running,' David replied with frosty dignity as he picked up the pigskin folder which held his thick sheaf of credit cards from the bedside table. 'I am merely reserving the right to determine my own future.' He crossed to the telephone and began dialling.

'Who are you calling?'

'The airline.'

'Where are you heading?'

'The same place as their first flight out.'

'I'll cover for you,' declared Mitzi loyally, 'you're doing the right thing, warrior.'

'You bet I am,' David agreed. 'My way—and screw the rest of them.'

'Do you have time for that?' Mitzi giggled, and the dark-haired girl spoke for the first time in a husky intense voice without once taking her eyes off David. 'I don't know about the rest of them, but may I be first, please?'

With the telephone receiver to his ear David glanced at her, and realized with only mild surprise that she was in deadly earnest.

David came out into the impersonal concrete and glass arrivals hall of Schipol Airport, and he paused to gloat on his escape and to revel at this sense of anonymity in the uncaring crowd. There was a touch at his elbow, and he turned to find a tall, smiling Dutchman quizzing him through rimless spectacles.

'Mr David Morgan, I think?' and David gaped at him.

'I am Frederick Van Gent of Holland and Indonesian Stevedoring. We have the honour to act on behalf of Morgan Shipping Lines in Holland. It is a great pleasure to make your acquaintance.'

'God, no!' David whispered wearily.

'Please?'

'No. I'm sorry. It's nice to meet you.' David shook the hand with resignation.

'I have two urgent Telex messages for you, Mr Morgan.' Van Gent produced them with a flourish. 'I have driven out from Amsterdam especially to deliver same.'

The first was from Mitzi who had sworn to cover for him.

'Abject apologies your whereabouts extracted with rack and thumbscrew stop be brave as a lion stop be ferocious as an eagle Love Mitzi.'

David said, 'Traitorous bitch!' and opened the second envelope.

'Your doubts understood, your action condoned stop confident your good sense will lead you eventually on to path of duty stop your place here always open affectionately Paul Morgan.'

David said, 'Crafty old bastard,' and stuffed both messages into his pocket.

'Is there a reply?' Van Gent asked.

'Thank you, no. It was good of you to take this trouble.'

'No trouble, Mr Morgan. Can I help you in any way? Is there anything you require?'

'Nothing, but thanks again.' They shook hands and Van Gent bowed and left him. David went to the Avis counter and the girl smiled brightly at him.

'Good evening, sir.'

David slipped his Avis card across the desk. 'I want something with a little jump to it, please.'

'Let me see, we have a Mustang Mach I?' She was pure blonde with a cream and pink unlined face.

'That will do admirably,' David assured her, and as he began filling the form in, she asked, 'Your first visit to Amsterdam, sir?'

'They tell me it's the city with the most action in Europe, is that right?'

'If you know where to go,' she murmured.

'You could show me?' David asked and she looked up at him with calculating eyes behind a neutral expression, made a decision and resumed her writings.

'Please sign here, sir. Your account will be charged,' then she dropped her voice. 'If you have any queries on this contract, you can contact me at this number—after hours. My name is Gilda.'

Gilda shared a walk-up over the outer canal with three other girls who showed no surprise, and made no objection when David carried his single Samsonite case up the steep staircase. However, the action that Gilda provided was in a series of discotheques and coffee bars where lost little people gathered to talk revolution and guru babble. In two days David discovered that pot tasted terrible and made him nauseous, and that Gilda's mind was as bland and unmarked as her exterior. He felt the stirrings of uneasiness when he studied the others that had been drawn to this city by the news that it was wide open, with the most understanding police force in the world. In them he saw symptoms of his own restlessness, and he recognized them as fellow seekers. Then the damp chill of the lowlands seemed to rise up out of the canals like the spirits of the dead on doomsday, and when you have been born under the sun of Africa the wintry effusions of the north are a pale substitute.

Gilda showed no visible emotion when she said goodbye, and with the heaters blasting hot air into the cab of the Mustang, David sent it booming southwards. On the outskirts of Namur there was a girl standing beside the road. In the cold her legs were bare and brown, protruding sweetly from the short faded blue denim pants she wore. She tilted her golden head and cocked a thumb.

David hit the stick down, and braked with the rubber squealing protest. He reversed back to where she stood. She had flat-planed slavic features and her hair was white blonde and hung in a thick plait down her back. He guessed her age at nineteen.

'You speak English?' he asked through the window. The cold was making her nipples stand out like marbles through the thin fabric of her shirt.

'No,' she said. 'But I speak American—will that do?'

'Right on!' David opened the passenger door, and she threw her pack and rolled sleeping bag into the back seat.

'I'm Philly,' she said.

'David.'

'You in show biz?'

'God, no—what makes you ask?'

'The car—the face—the clothes.'

'The car is hired, the clothes are stolen and I'm wearing a mask.'

'Funny man,' she said and curled up on the seat like a kitten and went to sleep.

He stopped in a village where the forests of the Ardennes begin and bought a long roll of crisp bread, a slab of smoked wild boar meat and a bottle of Möet Chandon. When he got back to the car Philly was awake.

'You hungry?' he asked.

'Sure.' She stretched and yawned.

He found a loggers' track going off into the forest and they followed it to a clearing where a long golden shaft of sunlight penetrated the green cathedral gloom.

Philly climbed out and looked around her. 'Keen, Davey, keen!' she said.

David poured the champagne into paper cups and sliced the meat with a penknife while Philly broke the bread into hunks. They sat side by side on a fallen log and ate.

'It's so quiet and peaceful–not at all like a killing ground. This is where the Germans made their last big effort–did you know that?'

Philly's mouth was full of bread and meat which didn't stop her reply. 'I saw the movie, Henry Fonda, Robert Ryan–it was a complete crock.'

'All that death and ugliness, we should do something beautiful in this place,' David said dreamily, and she swallowed the bread, took a sip of wine, before she stood up languidly and went to the Mustang. She fetched her sleeping bag and spread it on the soft bed of leaf mould.

'Some things are for talking about–others are for doing,' she told him.

For a while in Paris it looked as though it might be significant, as though they might have something for each other of importance. They found a room with a shower in a clean and pleasant little pension near the Gare St Lazare, and they walked through the streets all that day, from Concorde to Etoile, then across to the Eiffel Tower and back to Notre Dame. They ate supper at a sidewalk café on the 'Boul Mich', but half-way through the meal they reached an emotional dead end. Suddenly they ran out of conversation, they sensed it at the same time, each aware that they were strangers in all but the flesh and the knowledge chilled them both. Still they stayed together that night, even going through the mechanical and empty motions of love, but in the morning, when David came out of the shower, she sat up in the bed and said, 'You are splitting.'

It was a statement and not a question, and it needed no reply.

'Are you all right for bread?' he asked, and she shook her head. He peeled off a pair of thousand-franc notes and put them on the side table.

'I'll pay the bill downstairs.' He picked up his bag. 'Stay loose,' he said.

Paris was spoiled for him now, so he took the road south again towards the sun for the sky was filled with swollen black cloud and it rained before he passed the turn-off to Fontainebleau. It rained as he believed was only possible in the tropics, a solid deluge that flooded the concrete of the highway and blurred his windscreen so that the flogging of the wipers could not clear it swiftly enough for safe vision.

David was alone and discomforted by his inability to sustain communication with another human being. Although the other traffic had moderated its pace in the rain, he drove fast, feeling the drift and skate of his tyres on the slick surface. This time the calming effect of speed was ineffective and when he ran out of the rain south of Beaune it seemed that the wolf pack of loneliness ran close behind him.

However, the first outpouring of sunshine lightened his mood, and then far over the stone walls and rigid green lines of the vineyards he saw a wind-sock floating like a soft white sausage from its pole. He found the exit from the highway half a mile farther on, and the sign 'Club Aeronautique de Provence'. He followed it to a neat little airfield set among the vineyards, and one of the aircraft on the hard-stand was a Marchetti Aerobatic type F260. David climbed out of the Mustang and stared at it like a drunkard contemplating his first whisky of the day.

The Frenchman in the club office looked like an unsuccessful undertaker, and even when David showed him his logbook and sheafs of licences, he resisted the temptation of hiring him the Marchetti. David could take his pick from the others–but the Marchetti was not for hire. David added a 500-franc note to the pile of documents, and it disappeared miraculously into the Frenchman's pocket. Still he would not let David take the Marchetti solo, and he insisted on joining him in the instructor's seat.

David executed a slow and stately four-point roll before they had crossed the boundary fence. It was an act of defiance, and he made the stops crisp and exaggerated. The Frenchman cried 'Sacré bleu!' with great feeling and froze in his seat, but he had the good sense not to interfere with the controls. David completed the manœuvre and then immediately rolled in the opposite direction with the wing-tip a mere fifty feet above the tips of the vines. The Frenchman relaxed visibly, recognizing the masterly touch, and when David landed an hour later he grinned mournfully at him.

'*Formidable!*' he said, and shared his lunch with David—garlic polony, bread and a bottle of rank red wine. The good feeling of flight and the aroma of garlic lasted David all the way to Madrid.

In Madrid suddenly it began to happen, almost as though it had been arranged long before, as though his frantic flight across half of Europe was a pre-knowledge that something of importance awaited him in Madrid.

He reached the city in the evening, hurrying the last day's journey to be in time for the first running of the bulls that season. He had read Hemingway and Conrad and much of the other romantic literature of the bullring. He wondered if there might not be something for him in this way of life. It read so well in the books—the beauty, the glamour and excitement—the courage and trial and the final moment of truth. He wanted to evaluate it, to see it here in the great Plaza Des Torros, and then, if it still intrigued him, go on to the festival at Pamplona later in the season.

David checked in at the Gran Via with its elegance faded to mere comfort, and the porter arranged tickets for the following day. He was tired from the long drive and he went to bed early, waking refreshed and eager for the day. He found his way out to the ring and parked the Mustang amongst the tourist buses that already crowded the parking lot so early in the season.

The exterior of the ring was a surprise, sinister as the temple of some pagan and barbaric religion, unrelieved by the fluted tiers of balconies and encrustations of ceramic tiles—but the interior was as he knew it would be from film and photograph. The sanded ring smooth and clean, the flags against the cloud-flecked sky, the orchestra pouring out its jerky, rousing refrain—and the excitement.

The excitement amongst the crowd was more intense than he had known at prize fights or football internationals, they hummed and swarmed, rank upon rank of white eager faces and the music goaded them on.

David was sitting amongst a group of young Australians who wore souvenir sombreros and passed goat-skins of bad wine about, the girls squealing and chittering like sparrows. One of them picked on David, leaning forward to tug his shoulder and offer him the wine-skin. She was pretty enough in a kittenish way and her eyes made it clear that the offer was for more than cheap wine, but he refused both invitations brusquely and went to fetch a can of beer from one of the vendors. His chilly experience with the girl in Paris was still too fresh. When he returned to his seat the Aussie girl eyed the beer he carried reproachfully and then turned brightly and smiling to her companions.

The late arrivals were finding their seats now and the excitement was escalating sharply. Two of them climbed the stairs of the aisle towards where David sat. A striking young couple in their early twenties, but what first drew

David's attention was the good feeling of companionship and love that glowed around them, like an aura setting them apart.

They climbed arm in arm, passed where David sat, and took seats a row behind and across the aisle. The girl was tall with long legs clad in short black boots and dark pants over which she wore an apple-green suède jacket that was not expensive but of good cut and taste. In the sun her hair glittered like coal newly cut from the face and it hung to her shoulders in a sleek soft fall. Her face was broad and sun-browned, not beautiful for her mouth was too big and her eyes too widely spaced, but those eyes were the colour of wild honey, dark brown and flecked with gold. Like her, her companion was tall and straight, dark and strong-looking. He guided her to her seat with a brown muscled arm and David felt a sharp stab of anger and envy for him.

'Big cocky son of a gun,' he thought. They leaned their heads together and spoke secretly, and David looked away, his own loneliness accentuated by their closeness.

The parade of the toreadors began, and they came out with the sunlight glittering on the sequins and embroidery of their suits, as though they were the scales of some flamboyant reptile. The orchestra blared, and the keys to the bull pens were thrown down on to the sand. The toreadors' capes were spread on the *barrera* below their favourites and they retired from the ring.

In the pause that followed David glanced at the couple again. He was startled to find that they were both watching him and the girl was discussing him. She was leaning on her companion's shoulder, her lips almost touching his ear as she spoke and David felt his stomach clench under the impact of those honey golden eyes. For an instant they stared at each other and then the girl jerked away guiltily and dropped her gaze—but her companion held David's eyes openly, smiling easily, and it was David who looked away.

Below them in the ring the bull came out at full charge, head high, and hooves skidding in the sand.

He was beautiful and black and glossy, muscle in the neck and shoulder bunching as he swung his head from side to side and the crowd roared as he spun and burst into a gallop, pursuing an elusive flutter of pink across the ring. They took him on a circuit, passing him smoothly from cape to cape, letting him show off his bulk and high-stepping style, and the perfect sickle of his horns with their creamy points, before they brought in the horse.

The trumpets ushered in the horse, and they were a mockery—a brave greeting for the wretched nag, with scrawny neck and starting coat, one rheumy old eye blinkered so he could not see the fearsome creature he was going to meet.

Clownish in his padding, seeming too frail to carry the big armoured man on his back, they led him out and placed him in the path of the bull—and here any semblance of beauty ended.

The bull went into him head down, sending the gawky animal reeling against the *barrera* and the man leaned over the broad black back and ripped and tore into the hump with the lance, worrying the flesh, working in the steel with all his weight until the blood poured out in a slick tide, black as crude oil, and dripped from the bull's legs into the sand.

Raging at the agony of the steel, the bull hooked and butted at the protective pads that covered the horse's flanks. They came up as readily as a theatre curtain and the bull was into the scrawny roan body, hacking with the terrible horns, and the horse screamed as its belly split open and the purple and pink entrails spilled out and dangled into the sand.

David was dry-mouthed with horror as around him the crowd blood-roared, and the horse went down in a welter of equipment and its own guts.

They drew the bull away and flogged the fallen horse, twisting its tail and prodding its testicles, forcing it to rise at last and stand quivering and forlorn. Then beating it to make it move again they led it from the ring stumbling over its own entrails.

Then they went to work on the bull, slowly, torturously, reducing it from a magnificent beast to a blundering hunk of sweating and bleeding flesh, splattered with the creamy froth blown from its agonized lungs.

David wanted to scream at them to stop it, but sick to the stomach, frozen by guilt for his own part in this obscene ritual, he sat through it in silence until the bull stood in the centre of the ring, the sand about him ploughed and riven by his dreadful struggles. He stood with his head down, muzzle almost touching the sand and the blood and froth dripped from his nostrils and gaping mouth. The hoarse sawing of his breathing carried to David even above the crazed roaring crowd. The bull's legs shuddered and he passed a dribble of loose liquid yellow dung that fouled his back legs. It seemed to David that this was the final humiliation, and he found he was whispering aloud.

'No! No! Stop it! Please, stop it!'

Then the man in the glittering suit and ballet shoes came to end it, and the point of the sword struck bone and the blade arced then spun away in the sunlight, and the bull heaved and threw back thick droplets of blood, before he stood again.

They picked up the sword from the sand and gave it to the man and he sighted over the quiescent, dying beast and again the thrust was deflected by bone and David found that at last he had power in his voice, and he screamed:

'Stop it! You filthy bastards.'

Twelve times the man in the centre tried with sword, and each time the sword flicked out of his hand, and then at last the bull fell of its own accord, weak from the slow loss of much blood and with its heart broken by the torture and the striving. It tried to rise, lunging weakly, but the strength was not there and they killed it where it lay, with a dagger in the back of the neck, and they dragged it out with a team of mules—its legs waggling ridiculously in the air and its blood leaving a long brown smudge across the sand.

Stunned with the monstrous cruelty of it, David turned slowly to look at the girl. Her companion was leaning over her solicitously, whispering to her, trying to comfort her.

She was shaking her head slowly, in a gesture of incomprehension, and her honey-coloured eyes were blinded with weeping. Her lips were apart, quivering with grief, and her cheeks were awash, shiny with her tears.

Her companion helped her to her feet, and gently took her down the steps, leading her away blindly like a new widow from her husband's grave.

Around him the crowd was laughing and exhilarated, high on the blood and the pain—and David felt himself rejected, cut off from them. His heart went out to the weeping girl, she of all of them was the only one who seemed real to him. He had seen enough also, and he knew he would never get to Pamplona. He stood up and followed the girl out of the ring, he wanted to speak to her, to tell her that he shared her desolation, but when he reached the parking lot they were already climbing into a battered old Citroen CV.100, and although he broke into a run, the car pulled away—blowing blue smoke and clattering like a lawn-mower, and turned into the traffic leading east.

David watched it go with a sense of loss that effectively washed away the good feeling of the last few days, but he saw the old Citroen again two days later, when he had abandoned all idea of the Pamplona Festival and headed south. The Citroen looked even sicker than before, under a layer of pale dust and with the canvas showing on a rear tyre. The suspension seemed to have sagged on the one side, giving it a rakishly drunken aspect.

It was parked at a filling station on the outskirts of Zaragoza on the road to Barcelona, and David pulled off the road and park beyond the gasoline pumps. An attendant in greasy overalls was filling the tank of the Citroen under the supervision of the muscular young man from the bullring. David looked quickly for the girl–but she was not in the car. Then he saw her.

She was in a *cantina* across the street, haggling with the elderly woman behind the counter. Her back was turned towards him, but David recognized the mass of dark hair now piled on top of her head. He crossed the road quickly and went into the shop behind her. He was not certain what he was going to do, acting only on impulse.

The girl wore a short floral dress which left her back and shoulders bare, and her feet were thrust into open sandals. But in concession to the ice in the air she wore a shawl over her shoulders. Close to, her skin had a plastic smoothness and elasticity, as though it had been lightly oiled and polished, and down the back of her naked neck the hair was fine and soft, growing in a whorl in the nape.

David moved closer to her as she completed her purchase of dried figs and counted her change. He smelt her, a light summery perfume that seemed to come from her hair. He resisted the temptation to press his face into the dense pile of it.

She turned smiling and saw him standing close behind her. She recognized him instantly, his was not a face a girl would readily forget. She was startled. The smile flickered out on her face and she stood very still looking at him, her expression completely neutral, but her lips slightly parted and her eyes soft and glowing golden. This peculiar stillness of hers was a quality he would come to know so well in the time ahead.

'I saw you in Madrid,' he said, 'at the bulls.'

'Yes,' she nodded, her voice neither welcoming nor forbidding.

'You were crying.'

'So were you.' Her voice was low and clear, her enunciation flawless, too perfect not to be foreign.

'No,' David denied it.

'You were crying,' she insisted softly. 'You were crying inside.' And he inclined his head in agreement. Suddenly she proffered the paper bag of figs.

'Try one,' she said and smiled. It was a warm friendly smile. He took one of the fruits and bit into the sweet flesh as she moved towards the door, somehow conveying an invitation for him to join her. He walked with her and they looked across the street at the Citroen. The attendant had finished filling the tank, and the girl's companion was waiting for her, leaning against the bonnet of the weary old car. He was lighting a cigarette, but he looked up and saw them. He evidently recognized David also, and he straightened up quickly and flicked away the burning match.

There was a soft whooshing sound and the heavy thump of concussion in the air, as fire flashed low across the concrete from a puddle of spilled gasoline. In an instant the flames had closed over the rear of the Citroen, and were drumming hungrily at the coachwork.

David left the girl and sprinted across the road.

'Get it away from the pumps, you idiot,' he shouted, and the driver started out of frozen shock.

It was happy fifth of November, a spectacular pyrotechnic display—but David got the handbrake off and the gearbox into neutral, and he and the driver pushed it into an open parking area alongside the filling station while a crowd materialized, seeming to appear out of the very earth, to scream hysterical encouragement and suggestions while keeping at a discreet distance.

They even managed to rescue the baggage from the rear seat before the flames engulfed it entirely—and belatedly the petrol attendant arrived with an enormous scarlet fire extinguisher. To the delighted applause of the crowd, he drenched the pathetic little vehicle in a great cloud of foam, and the excitement was over. The crowd drifted away, still laughing and chattering and congratulating the amateur firefighter on his virtuoso performance with the extinguisher—while the three of them regarded the scorched and blackened shell of the Citroen ruefully.

'I suppose it was a kindness really—the poor old thing was very tired,' the girl said at last. 'It was like shooting a horse with a broken leg.'

'Are you insured?' David asked, and the girl's companion laughed.

'You're joking—who would insure that? I only paid a hundred U.S. dollars for her.'

They assembled the small pile of rescued possessions, and she spoke quickly to her companion in foreign, slightly guttural language which touched a deep chord in David's memory. He understood what she was saying, so it was no surprise when she looked at him.

'We've got to meet somebody in Barcelona this evening. It's important.'

'Let's go,' said David.

They piled the luggage into the Mustang and the girl's companion folded up his long legs and piled into the back seat. His name was Joseph—but David was advised by the girl to call him Joe. She was Debra, and surnames didn't seem important at that stage. She sat in the seat beside David, with her knees pressed together primly and her hands in her lap. With one sweeping glance, she assessed the Mustang and its contents. David watched her check the expensive luggage, the Nikon camera and Zeiss binoculars in the glove compartment and the cashmere jacket thrown over the seat. Then she glanced sideways at him, seeming to notice for the first time the raw silk shirt with the slim gold Piaget under the cuff.

'Blessed are the poor,' she murmured, 'but still it must be pleasant to be rich.'

David enjoyed that. He wanted her to be impressed, he wanted her to make a few comparisons between himself and the big muscular buck in the back seat.

'Let's go to Barcelona,' he laughed.

David drove quietly through the outskirts of the town, and Debra looked over her shoulder at Joe.

'Are you comfortable?' she asked in the guttural language she had used before.

'If he's not—he can run behind,' David told her in the same language, and she gawked at him a moment in surprise before she let out a small exclamation of pleasure.

'Hey! You speak Hebrew!'

'Not very well,' David admitted. 'I've forgotten most of it,' and he had a vivid picture of himself as a ten-year-old, wrestling unhappily with a strange and mysterious language with back-to-front writing, an alphabet that was squiggly tadpoles and in which most sounds were made in the back of the throat, like gargling.

'Are you Jewish?' she asked, turning in the seat to confront him. She was no longer smiling; the question was clearly of significance to her.

David shook his head. 'No,' he laughed at the notion. 'I'm a half-convinced non-practising monotheist, raised and reared in the Protestant Christian tradition.'

'Then why did you learn Hebrew?'

'My mother wanted it,' David explained, and felt again the stab of an old guilt. 'She was killed when I was a kid. I just let it drop. It didn't seem important after she had gone.'

'Your mother—' Debra insisted, leaning towards him, '—she was Jewish?'

'Yeah. Sure,' David agreed. 'But my father was a Protestant. There was all sorts of hell when Dad married her. Everyone was against it—but they went ahead and did it anyway.'

Debra turned in the seat to Joe. 'Did you hear that—he's one of us.'

'Oh, come on!' David protested, still laughing.

'Mazaltov,' said Joe. 'Come and see us in Jerusalem some time.'

'You're Israeli?' David asked, with new interest.

'Sabras, both of us,' said Debra, with a note of pride and deep satisfaction. 'We are only on holiday here.'

'It must be an interesting country,' David hazarded.

'Like Joe just said, why don't you come and find out some time,' she suggested offhandedly. 'You have the right of return.' Then she changed the subject. 'Is this the fastest this machine will go? We have to be in Barcelona by seven.'

There was a relaxed feeling between them now, as though some invisible barrier had been lowered, as though she had made some weighty judgement. They were out of the city and ahead the open road wound down into the valley of the Ebro towards the sea.

'Kindly extinguish cigarettes and fasten your seat belts,' David said, and let the Mustang go.

She sat very still beside him with her hands folded in her lap and she stared ahead when the bends leapt at them, and the straights streamed in a soft blue blur beneath the body of the Mustang. There was a small rapturous smile on her mouth and the golden lights danced in her eyes, and David was moved to know that speed affected her the way it did him.

He forgot everything else but the girl in the seat beside him and the need to keep the mighty roaring machine on the ribbon of tarmac.

Once when they went twisting down into a dry dusty valley in a series of tight curves and David snaked the Mustang down into it with his hands darting from wheel to gear lever, and his feet dancing heel and toe on the foot pedals—she laughed aloud with the thrill of it.

They bought cheese and bread and a bottle of white wine at a village *cantina* and ate lunch sitting on the parapet of a stone bridge while the water swirled below them, milky with snow melt from the mountains.

David's thigh touched Debra's, as they sat side by side. He could feel the warmth and resilience of her flesh through the stuff of their clothing and she made no move to pull away. Her cheeks were flushed a little brighter than seemed natural, even in the chill little wind that nagged at them.

David was puzzled by Joe's attitude. He seemed to be completely oblivious of David's bird dogging his girl, and he was deriving a childlike pleasure out of tossing pebbles at the trout in the waters below them. Suddenly David wished he would put up a better resistance, it would make his conquest a lot more enjoyable—for conquest was what David had decided on.

He leaned across Debra for another chunk of the white, tangy cheese and he let his arm brush lightly against the tantalizing double bulge of her bosom. Joe seemed not to notice.

'Come on you big ape,' David thought scornfully. 'Fight for it. Don't just sit there.'

He wanted to test himself against this buck. He was big, and strong, and David could tell from the way he moved and held himself that he was well co-ordinated and self-assured. His face was chunky and half ugly, but he knew that some women liked them that way, and he was not fooled by Joe's slow and lazy grin—the eyes were quick and sharp.

'You want to drive, Joe?' he asked suddenly, and the slow grin spread like a puddle of spilled oil on Joe's face—but the eyes glittered with anticipation.

'Don't mind if I do,' said Joe, and David regretted the gesture as he found himself hunched in the narrow back seat. For the first five minutes Joe drive sedately, touching the brakes to test for grab and pull, flicking through the gears to feel the travel and bite of the stick, taking a burst of power through a bend to establish stability and detect any tendency for the tail to break out.

'Don't be scared of her,' David told him, and Joe grunted with a little frown of concentration creasing his broad forehead. Then he nodded to himself and his hands settled firmly, taking a fresh grip, and Debra whooped as he changed down to get the revs peaking. He slid the car through the first bend and David's right foot stabbed instinctively at a non-existent brake pedal and he felt his breathing jam in his throat.

When Joe parked them in the lot outside the airport at Barcelona and switched off the engine, all of them were silent for a few seconds and then David said softly,

'Son of a gun!'

Then they were all laughing. David felt a tinge of regret that he was going to have to take the girl away from him, for he was beginning to like him, despite himself, beginning to enjoy the slow deliberation of his speech and movements that was so clearly a put on and finding pleasure in the big slow smile that took so long to reach its full bloom. David had to harden his resolve.

They were an hour early for the plane they were meeting and they found a table in the restaurant overlooking the runways. David ordered an earthen-ware jug of Sangria, and Debra sat next to Joe and put her hand on his arm while she chatted, a gesture that tempered David's new-found liking for him.

A private flight landed as the waiter brought the Sangria, and Joe looked up.

'One of the new executive Gulfstreams. They tell me she is a little beauty.' And he went on to list the aircraft's specifications in technical language that Debra seemed to follow intelligently.

'You know anything about aircraft?' David challenged him.

'Some,' admitted Joe, but Debra took the question.

'Joe is in the airforce,' she said proudly, and David stared at them.

'So is Debs,' Joe laughed, and David switched his attention to her. 'She's a lieutenant in signals.'

'Only the reserve,' Debra demurred, 'but Joe is a flier. A fighter pilot.'

'A flier,' David repeated stupidly. He should have known from Joe's clear and steady gaze that was the peculiar mark of the fighter pilot. He should have known by the way he handled the Mustang. If he was an Israeli flier—then he would have flown a formidable number of operations. Hell, every time they took off, they were operational. He felt a vast tide of respect rising within him.

'What squadron are you on—Phantoms?'

'Phantoms!' Joe curled his lip. 'That isn't flying. That's operating a computer. No, we really fly. You ever heard of a Mirage?'

David blinked, and then nodded.

'Yeah,' said David, 'I've heard of them.'

'Well, I fly a Mirage.'

David began to laugh, shaking his head.

'What's wrong?' Joe demanded, his smile fading. 'What's funny about that?'

'I do too,' said David. 'I fly a Mirage.' It was no use trying to get hot against this buck, he decided. 'I've got over a thousand hours on Mirages.' And it was Joe's turn to stare, then suddenly they were both talking at once—Debra's head turning quickly from one to the other.

David ordered another jug of Sangria, but Joe would not let him pay. He repeated for the fiftieth time, 'Well, that beats all,' and punched David's shoulder. 'How about that, Debs?'

Half-way through the second jug, David interrupted the talk which had been exclusively on aviation.

'Who are we meeting, anyway? We've driven across half of Spain and I don't even know who the guy is.'

'This guy is a girl,' Joe laughed, and Debra filled in.

'Hannah,' and she grinned at Joe, 'his fiancée. She is a nursing sister at Hadassah Hospital, and she could only get away for a week.'

'Your fiancée?' David whispered.

'They are getting married in June.' Debra turned to Joe. 'It's taken him two years to make up his mind.'

Joe chuckled with embarrassment, and Debra squeezed his arm.

'Your fiancée?' asked David again.

'Why do you keep saying that?' Debra demanded. David pointed at Joe, and then at Debra.

'What,' he started, 'I mean, who—what the hell?'

Debra realized suddenly and gasped. She covered her mouth with both hands, her eyes sparkling. 'You mean—you thought—? Oh, no,' she giggled. She pointed at Joe and then at herself. 'Is that what you thought?' David nodded.

'He is my brother,' Debra hooted. 'Joe is my brother, you idiot! Joseph Israel Mordecai and Debra Ruth Mordecai—brother and sister.'

Hannah was a rangy girl with bright copper hair and freckles like sovereigns. She was only an inch or two shorter than Joe but he lifted her as she came through the customs gate, swung her off her feet and then engulfed her in an enormous embrace.

It seemed completely natural that the four of them should stay together. By a miracle of packing they got all their luggage and themselves into the Mustang with Hannah perched on Joe's lap in the rear.

'We've got a week,' said Debra. 'A whole week! What are we going to do with it?'

They agreed that Torremolinos was out. It was far south, and since Michener had written *The Drifters*, it had become a hangout for all the bums and freaks.

'I was talking to someone on the plane. There is a place called Colera up the coast. Near the border.'

They reached it in the middle of the next morning and it was still so early in the season that they had no trouble finding pleasant rooms at a small hotel off the winding main street.

The girls shared, and David insisted on a room of his own. He had certain plans for Debra that made privacy desirable.

Debra's bikini was blue and brief, hardly sufficient to restrain a bosom that was more exuberant than David had guessed. Her skin was satiny and tanned to a deep mahogany, although a strip of startling white peeped over the back of her costume when she stooped to pick up her towel. She was long in the waist, and leg, and a strong swimmer—pacing David steadily through the cool blue water when they set out for a rocky islet half a mile off shore.

They had the tiny island to themselves and they found a pitch of flat smooth rock out of the wind and full in the sun. They lay side by side with their fingers entwined and the salt water had sleeked Debra's hair to her shoulders, like the coat of an otter.

They lay in the sun and they talked away the afternoon. There was so much they had to learn about each other.

Her father had been one of the youngest colonels in the American Airforce during World War II, but afterwards he had gone on to Israel. He had been there ever since, and was now a Major-General. They lived in a house in an old part of Jerusalem which was five hundred years old, but was a lot of fun.

She was a senior lecturer in English at the Hebrew University in Jerusalem and, this shyly as though it were a rather special secret, she wanted to write. A small volume of her poetry had already been published. That impressed David, and he came up on one elbow and looked at her with new respect, and a twinge of envy, for someone who saw the way ahead clearly.

She lay with her eyes closed against the sun, and droplets of water sparkling like gems on her thick dark eyelashes. She wasn't beautiful, he decided carefully, but very handsome and very, very sexy. He was going to have her, of course. There was no doubt in David's mind about this, but there seemed little urgency in it now. He was enjoying listening to her talk, she had a quaint way of expressing herself, once she was in full flight, and her accent was strangely neutral—although there were faint echoes of her American background now he knew to look for them. She told him that the poetry was merely a beginning. She was going to write a novel about being young and living in Israel. She had the outline worked out, and it seemed like a pretty interesting story to David. Then she started to talk about her land and the people who lived in it. David felt something move within him as he listened—a nostalgia, a deep race memory. Again his envy stirred. She was so certain where she was from and where she was going—she knew where she belonged, and what her destiny was, and this made her strong. Beside her he felt suddenly insignificant and without purpose.

She opened her eyes suddenly, squinting a little in the sunlight and looked up at him.

'Oh dear,' she smiled. 'We are so sad, David. Do I talk too much?' He shook his head but did not answer her smile, and she became solemn also.

She studied his face carefully, with minute attention. The sun had dried his hair and fluffed it out, and it was soft and fine and very dark. The bone of his cheek and jaw was sculptured and finely balanced, the eyes very clear and slightly Asiatic in cast, the lips full and firm, and the nose delicately fluted with wide nostrils and a straight graceful line.

She reached up and touched his cheek.

'You are very beautiful, David. You are the most beautiful human being I have ever seen.'

He did not move, she ran the finger down his neck on to his chest, twirling it slowly in the dark body hair.

Slowly he leaned forward and placed his mouth over hers. Her lips were warm and soft and tasted of sea salt. Her arms came up around the back of his head and folded around him. They kissed until he reached behind her and unfastened the clasp of her costume between the smooth brown shoulder blades. She stiffened immediately and tried to pull away from him.

David held her gently but firm, murmuring little soothing noises as he kissed her again. Slowly she relaxed and he went on gentling her until her hands went to the back of his neck again, and she sighed and shuddered.

His hands were skilled and expert, masterful enough to prevent rebellion, not rough enough to panic her. He pushed up the thin material of her costume top and was surprised and enchanted with the firm rubbery weight of her breasts and the big husky rose-brown nipples which were pebble hard to his touch.

It was shocking, completely foreign to his experience, for David was not accustomed to check or denial, but Debra placed her hands on his shoulders and shoved him with such force that he lost his balance and slid down the rock, grazing his elbow and ending in a heap at the water's edge.

He scrambled angrily to his feet as Debra came up with a fluid explosive movement, fastening her costume as she did so. A single bound of her long brown legs carried her to the edge of the rocks and she dived outwards, hitting the water flat and surfacing to call back to him.

'I'll race you to the beach.'

David would not accept the challenge and followed her at his own dignified pace. When he emerged unsmilingly from the low surf, she studied his face a moment and then grinned.

'When you sulk you look about ten years old,' she told him, which was no great exercise of tact and David stalked back to his room.

He was still being extremely dignified and aloof that evening when they discovered a discotheque named '2001 A.D.' run by a couple of English boys down on the sea-front. They crowded round a table at which there were already two B.E.A. hostesses and a couple of raggedy-looking beards. The music was loud enough and the rhythm hard enough to jar the spine and loosen the bowels, and when the two hostesses gazed at David with almost religious awe Debra forsook her attitude of cool amusement and suggested to David that they dance. Mollified by this little feminine by-play, David dropped his impersonation of the Ice King.

They moved well together, sharing the gut rhythms of the harsh music, executing the primeval movements that reeked of Africa with a grace that drew the attention of the other dancers.

When the music changed Debra came to him and lay her body against his. David felt some force flowing from her that seemed to charge every nerve of his body—and he knew that no relationship he had with this woman would ever run calmly. It was too deeply felt for that, too volatile and triggered for momentary explosion.

When the record ended they left Joe and Hannah huddled over a carafe of red wine and they went out into the silent street and down to the beach.

There was a moon in the sky that lit the dark cliffs crowding in above the beach, and reflected off the sea in multiple yellow images. The low surf hissed and coughed on the pebble beach and they took off their shoes and walked along it, letting the water wash around their ankles.

In an angle of the cliff, they found a hidden place amongst the rocks and they stopped to kiss again, and David mistakenly took her new soft mood as an invitation to continue from where he had left off that afternoon.

Debra pulled away again, but this time with determination and said angrily, 'Damn you! Don't you ever learn? I don't want to do that. Do we have to go through this every time we are alone?'

'What's the matter?' David was immediately stung by her tone, and furious with this fresh check. 'This is the twentieth century, darling. The simpering virgin is out of style this season—hadn't you heard?'

'And spoilt little boys should grow up before they come out on their own,' she flashed back at him.

'Thanks!' he snarled. 'I don't have to stay around taking insults from any professional virgin.'

'Well, why don't you move out then?' she challenged him.

'Hey, that's a great idea!' He turned his back on her and walked away up the beach. She had not expected that, and she started to run after him—but her pride checked her. She stopped and leaned against the rock.

He shouldn't have rushed me, she thought miserably. I want him, I want him very much, but he will be the first since Dudu. If he will just give me time it will be all right, but he mustn't rush me. If he could only go at my speed, help me to do it right.

It is funny, she thought, how little I remember about Dudu now. It's only three years, but his memory is fading so swiftly, I wonder if I really did love him. Even his face is hazy in my mind, while I know every detail of David's—every plane and line of it.

Perhaps I should go after him and tell him about Dudu, and ask him to be patient and to help me a little. Perhaps I should do that, she thought, but she did not and slowly she walked up the beach, through the silent town to the hotel.

Hannah's bed across the room was empty. She would be with Joe, lying with him, loving with him. I should be with David also, she thought. Dudu is dead, and I'm alive, and I want David and I should be with him—but she undressed slowly and climbed into the bed and lay without sleeping.

David stood in the doorway of '2001 A.D.' and peered through the weirdly flashing lights and the smog, the warm palpable emanation from a hundred straining bodies. The B.E.A. hostesses were still at the table, but Joe and Hannah had gone.

David made his way through the dancers. The one hostess was tall and blonde, with high English colour and china-doll eyes. She looked up and saw David, glanced around for Debra, made sure she was missing before she smiled.

They danced one cut of the record without touching each other and then David leaned close to her and placed both hands on her hips. She strained towards him with her lips parting.

'Have you got a room?' he asked, and she nodded, running the tip of her tongue lewdly around her lips.

'Let's go,' said David.

It was light when David got back to his own room. He shaved and packed his bag, surprised at the strength of his residual anger. He lugged the bag down to the proprietor's office and paid his bill with his Diners Club card.

Debra came out of the breakfast room with Joe and Hannah. They were all dressed for the beach with Terry robes over their bathing gear, and they were gay and laughing—until they saw David.

'Hey!' Joe challenged him. 'Where are you going?'

'I've had enough of Spain,' David told them. 'I'm taking some good advice, and I'm moving out,' and he felt a flare of savage triumph as he saw the quick shadow of pain in Debra's eyes. Both Joe and Hannah glanced at her, and quickly she controlled the quiver of her lips. She smiled then, a little too brightly and stepped forward, holding out her hand.

'Thank you for all your help, David. I'm sorry you have to go. It was fun.' Then her voice dropped slightly and there was a tiny quaver in it. 'I hope you find what you are looking for. Good luck.'

She turned quickly and hurried away to her room. Hannah's expression was steely, and she gave David a curt nod before following Debra.

'So long, Joe.'

'I'll carry your bag.'

'Don't bother.' David tried to stop him.

'No trouble.' Joe took it out of his hand and carried it out to the Mustang. He dumped it on the rear seat.

'I'll ride up to the top of the hills with you and walk back.' He climbed into the passenger seat and settled comfortably. 'I need the exercise.'

David drove swiftly, and they were silent as Joe deliberately lit a cigarette and flicked the match out the window.

'I don't know what went wrong, Davey, but I can guess.'

David didn't reply, he concentrated on the road.

'She's had a bad time. These last few days she has been different. Happy, I guess, and I thought it was going to work out.'

Still David was silent, not giving him any help. Why didn't the big bonehead mind his own business.

'She's a pretty special sort of person, Davey, not because she's my sister. She really is, and I think you should know about her—just so you don't think too badly about her.'

They had reached the top of the hills above the town and the bay. David pulled on to the verge but kept the engine running. He looked down on the brilliant blue of the sea, where it met the cliffs and the pine-covered headlands.

'She was going to be married,' said Joe softly. 'He was a nice guy, older than she was, they worked together at the University. He was a tank driver in the reserve and he took a hit in the Sinai and burned with his tank.'

David turned and looked at him, his expression softening a little.

'She took it badly,' Joe went on doggedly. 'These last few days were the first time I've seen her truly happy and relaxed.' He shrugged, and grinned like a big St Bernard dog. 'Sorry to give you the family history, Davey. Just thought it might help.' He held out a huge brown hand. 'Come and see us. It's your country also, you know. I'd like to show it to you.'

David took the hand. 'I might do that,' he said.

'Shalom.'   ·

'Shalom, Joe. Good luck.' Joe climbed out of the car and when David pulled away he watched him standing on the side of the road with his hands on his hips. He waved and the first bend in the road hid him.

There was a school for aspiring Formula I racing drivers on a neglected concrete circuit near Ostia, on the road from Rome. The course lasted three weeks and cost $500 U.S.

David stayed at the Excelsio in the Via Veneto, and commuted each day to the track. He completed the full course, but after the first week knew it was not what he wanted. The physical limitation of the track was constricting after flying the high heavens, and even the crackling snarling power of a Tyrell Ford could not match the thrust from the engine of a jet interceptor. Although he lacked the dedication and motivation of others in his class his natural talent for speed and his co-ordination brought him out high in the finishing order—and he had an offer to drive on the works team of a new and struggling company that was building and fielding a production team of Formula I racing machines. Of course, the salary was starvation, and it was a measure of his desperation that he came close to signing a contract for the season, but at the last moment he changed his mind and went on.

In Athens he spent a week hanging around the yacht basins of Piraeus and Glyfada. He was investigating the prospects of buying a motor yacht and running it out on charter to the islands. The prospect of sun and sea and pretty girls seemed appealing and the craft themselves were beautiful in their snowy paint and varnished teakwork. In one week he learned that charter work was merely running a sea-going boarding house for a bunch of bored, sunburned and seasick tourists.

On the seventh day the American Sixth Fleet dropped anchor in the bay of Athens. David sat at a table of one of the beach-front cafés and drank *ouzo* in the sun, while he studied the anchored aircraft carriers through his binoculars. On the great flat tops the rows of Crusaders and Phantoms were grouped with their wings folded. Watching them he felt a consuming hunger, a need that was almost spiritual. He had searched the earth, it seemed, and there was nothing for him upon its face. He laid the binoculars aside, and he looked up into the sky. The clouds were high, a brilliant silver against the blue.

He picked up the glass of milky *ouzo* that the sun had warmed and rolled its sweet liquorice taste about his tongue.

'East, west, home is best.'

He spoke aloud, and had a mental image of Paul Morgan sitting in his high office of glass and steel. Like a patient fisherman he tended his lines laid across the world. Right now the one to Athens was beginning to twitch. He could imagine the quiet satisfaction as he began to reel it in, drawing David struggling feebly back to the centre. What the hell, I could still fly Impalas as a reserve officer, he thought, and there was always the Lear—if he could get it away from Barney.

David drained the glass and stood up abruptly, feeling the fading glow of his defiance. He flagged a cab and was driven back to his room at the Grande Bretagne on Syndagma Square.

His defiance was dying so swiftly that one of his companions for dinner that night was John Dinopoulos, Morgan Group's agent for Greece, a slim elegant sophisticate with an unlined sun-tanned face, silver wings in his hair and an elegantly casual way of dressing.

John had selected for David's table companion the female star of a number of Italian spaghetti westerns. A young lady of ample bosom and dark flashing eye whose breathing and bosom had become agitated when John introduced David as a diamond millionaire from Africa.

Diamonds were the most glamorous, although not the most significant of Morgan Group's interests.

They sat upon the terrace of Dionysius, for the evening was mild. The restaurant was carved into the living rock of the hill-top of Lycabettus, under the church of St Paul.

Down the zig-zag path from the church, the Easter procession of worshippers unwound in a flickering stream of candle flames through the pine forest below them, and the singing carried sweetly on the still night air. On its far hill-top the stately columns of the Acropolis were flood-lit so that they glowed as creamily as ancient ivory, and beyond that again on the midnight waters of the bay the American fleet wore gay garlands of fairy lights.

'The glory that was Greece—' murmured the star of Italian westerns, as though she voiced the wisdom of the ages, and placed one heavily jewelled hand on David's thigh while with the other she raised a glass of red Samos wine to him and cast him a look under thick eyelashes that was fraught with significance.

Her restraint was impressive, and it was only after they had eaten the main course of savoury meats wrapped in vine leaves and swimming in creamy lemon sauce that she suggested that David might like to finance her next movie.

'Let's find some place where we can talk about it—' she murmured, and what better place than her suite?

John Dinopoulos waved them away with a grin and a knowing wink, a gesture that annoyed David for it made him see the whole episode for the emptiness that it was.

The star's suite was pretentious, with thick white carpets and bulky black leather furniture. David poured himself a drink while she went to change into clothing more suitable for a discussion of high finance. David tasted the drink, realized that he did not want it and left it on the bar counter.

The star came out of the bedroom in a bedrobe of white satin which was cut back from arm and bosom, and was so sheer that her flesh gleamed with a pearly pink sheen through the material. Her hair was loose, a great wild mane of swirling curls—and suddenly David was sick of the whole business.

'I'm sorry,' he said. 'John was joking—I'm not a millionaire, and I really prefer boys.'

He heard his untouched glass shatter against the door of the suite as he closed it behind him.

Back at his own hotel he ordered coffee from room service, and then on an impulse he picked up the telephone again and placed a Cape Town call. It came through with surprising speed, and the girl's voice on the other end was thickened with sleep.

'Mitzi,' he laughed. 'How's the girl?'

'Where are you, warrior? Are you home?'

'I'm in Athens, doll.'

'Athens–God! How's the action?'

'It's a drag.'

'Yeah! I bet,' she scoffed. 'The Greek girls are never going to be the same again.'

'How are you, Mitzi?'

'I'm in love, Davey. I mean really in love, it's far out. We are going to be married. Isn't that just something else?' David felt a spur of anger, jealous of the happiness in her voice.

'That's great, doll. Do I know him?'

'Cecil Lawley, you know him. He's one of Daddy's accountants.' David recalled a large, pale-faced, bespectacled man with a serious manner.

'Congratulations,' said David. He felt very much alone again. Far from home, and aware that life there flowed on without his presence.

'You want to talk to him?' Mitzi asked. 'I'll wake him up.' There was murmur and mutter on the other end, then Cecil came on.

'Nice work,' David told him, and it really was. Mitzi's share of Morgan Group would be considerably larger than David's. Cecil had drilled himself an oil well in a most unconventional manner.

'Thanks, Davey.' Cecil's embarrassment at being caught tending his oil well carried clearly over five thousand miles of telephone cable.

'Listen, lover. You do anything to hurt that girl, I'll personally tear out your liver and stuff it down your throat, okay?'

'Okay,' said Cecil, and his alarm was brittle in his tone. 'I'll put you back to Mitzi.'

She prattled on for another fifty dollars' worth before hanging up. David lay on the bed with his hands behind his head and thought about his dumpy soft-hearted cousin and her new happiness. Then quite suddenly he made the decision which had been lurking at the edge of his consciousness all these weeks since leaving Spain. He picked up the phone again and asked for the porter's desk.

'I'm sorry to trouble you at this time of the morning,' he said, 'but I should like to get on a flight to Israel as soon as possible, will you please arrange that.'

The sky was filled with a soft golden haze that came off the desert. The gigantic T.W.A. 747 came down through it, and David had a glimpse of dark green citrus orchards before the solid jolt of the touch-down. Lod was like any other airport in the world but beyond its doors was a land like no other he had ever known. The crowd who fought him for a seat in one of the big black sheruts, communal taxis plastered with stickers and hung with gew-gaws, made even the Italians seem shining towers of restrained good manners.

Once aboard, however, it was as though they were on a family outing–and he a member of that family. On one side of him a paratrooper in beret and blouse with his winged insignia on the breast and an Uzzi submachine-gun slung about his neck offered him a cigarette, on the other a big strapping lass also in khaki uniform and with the dark gazelle eyes of an Israeli, which became even darker and more soulful when she looked at David, which was often, shared a sandwich of unleavened bread and balls of fried chick-peas, the ubiquitous pita and falafel, with him and practised her English upon him. All the occupants of the front seat turned around to join the conversation, and this included the driver who nevertheless did not allow his speed to diminish in the slightest and who punctuated his remarks with fierce blasts of his horn and cries of outrage at pedestrians and other drivers.

The perfume of orange blossom lay as heavily as sea mist upon the coastal lowlands, and always afterwards it would be for David the smell of Israel.

Then they climbed into the Judaean hills, and David felt a sense of nostalgia as they followed the winding highway through pine forests and across the pale shining slopes where the white stone gleamed like bone in the sunlight and the silver olive trees twisted their trunks in graceful agony upon the terraces which were the monuments to six thousand years of man's patient labour.

It was so familiar and yet subtly different from those fair and well-beloved hills of the southern cape he called home. There were flowers he did not recognize, crimson blooms like spilled blood, and bursts of sunshine-yellow blossoms upon the slopes—then suddenly a pang that was like a physical pain as he glimpsed the bright flight of chocolate and white wings amongst the trees, and he recognized the crested head of an African hoopoe—a bird which was a symbol of home.

He felt a sense of excitement building within him, unformed and undirected as yet but growing, as he drew closer to the women he had come to see—and to something else of which he was as yet uncertain.

There was, at last, a sense of belonging. He felt in sympathy with the young persons who crowded close to him in the cab.

'See,' cried the girl, touching his arm and pointing to the wreckage of war still strewn along the roadside, the burned-out carapaces of trucks and armoured vehicles, preserved as a memorial to the men who died on the road to Jerusalem. 'There was fighting here.'

David turned in the seat to study her face, and he saw again the strength and certainty that he had so admired in Debra. These were a people who lived each day to its limit, and only at its close did they consider the next.

'Will there be more fighting?' he asked.

'Yes,' she answered him without hesitation.

'Why?'

'Because—if it is good—you must fight for it,' and she made a wide gesture that seemed to embrace the land and all its people, 'and this is ours, and it is good,' she said.

'Right on, doll,' David agreed with her, and they grinned at each other.

So they came to Jerusalem with its tall, severe apartment blocks of custard-yellow stone, standing like monuments upon the hills, grouped about the massive walled citadel that was its heart.

T.W.A. had reserved a room at the Intercontinental Hotel for David while on board the inward flight. From his window he looked across the garden of Gethsemane at the old city, at its turrets and spires and the blazing golden Dome of the Rock—centre of Christianity and Judaism, holy place of the Moslems, battleground for two thousand years, ancient land reborn—and David felt a sense of awe. For the first time in his life, he recognized and examined that portion of himself that was Jewish, and he thought it was right that he should have come to this city.

'Perhaps,' he said aloud, 'it's just possible that this is where it's all at.'

It was early evening when David paid off the cab in the car park of the University and submitted to a perfunctory search by a guard at the main gate. Here body search was a routine that would soon become so familiar as to pass unnoticed. He was surprised to find the campus almost deserted, until he remembered it was Friday—and that the whole tempo was slowing for the Sabbath.

The red-bud trees were in full bloom around the main plaza and the ornamental pool, as David crossed to the admin block and asked for her at the inquiries desk where the porter was on the point of leaving his post.

'Miss Mordecai—' the porter checked his list. 'Yes. English Department. On the second floor of the Lauterman building.' He pointed out through the glass doors. 'Third building on your right. Go right on in.'

Debra was in a students' tutorial, and while he waited for her, he found a seat on the terrace in the warmth of the sun. It was as well, for suddenly he felt a breath of uncertainty cooling his spine. For the first time since leaving Athens, he wondered if he had much cause to expect a hearty welcome from Debra Mordecai. Even at this remove in time, David had difficulty in judging his own behaviour towards her. Self-criticism was an art which David had never seriously practised; with a face and fortune such as his, it was seldom necessary. In this time of waiting he found it novel and uncomfortable to admit that it was just possible that his behaviour may have been, as Debra had told him, that of a spoiled child. He was still exploring this thought, when a burst of voices and the clatter of heels upon the flags distracted him and a group of students came out on to the terrace, hugging their books to their chests, and most of the girls glanced at him with quick speculative attention as they passed.

There was a pause then before Debra came. She carried books under her arm and a sling bag over one shoulder, and her hair was pulled back severely at the nape of her neck; she wore no make-up, but her skirt was brightly coloured in big summery whorls of orange. Her legs were bare and her feet were thrust into leather sandals. She was in deep conversation with the two students who flanked her, and she did not see David until he stood up from the parapet. Then she froze into that special stillness he had first noticed in the *cantina* at Zaragoza.

David was surprised to find how awkward he felt, as though his feet and hands had grown a dozen sizes. He grinned and made a shrugging, self-deprecatory gesture.

'Hello, Debs.' His voice sounded gruff in his own ears, and Debra stirred and made a panicky attempt to brush back the wisps of hair at her temples, but the books hampered her.

'David—' She started towards him, a pace before she hesitated and stopped, glancing at her students. They sensed her confusion and melted, and she swung back at him.

'David—' she repeated, and then her expression crumbled into utter desolation. 'Oh God, and I haven't even a shred of lipstick on.'

David laughed with relief and went towards her, spreading his arms, and she flew at him and it was all confusion with books and sling bag muddled, and Debra making breathless exclamations of frustration before she could divest herself of them. Then at last they embraced.

'David,' she murmured with both arms wound tightly around his neck. 'You beast—what on earth took you so long? I had almost given you up.'

Debra had a motor scooter which she drove with such murderous abandon that she frightened even the Jerusalem taxi-drivers who crossed her path—men with a reputation for steel nerves and disregard for danger.

Perched on the pillion David clung to her waist and remonstrated with her gently as she overtook a solid line of traffic and then cut smartly across a stream coming in the opposite direction with her exhaust popping merrily.

'I'm happy,' she explained over her shoulder.

'Fine! Then let's live to enjoy it.'

'Joe will be surprised to see you.'

'If we ever get there.'

'What's happened to your nerve?'

'I've just this minute lost it.'

She went down the twisting road into the valley of Ein Karem, as though she was driving a Mirage, and called a travelogue back to him as she went.

'That's the Monastery of Mary's Well where she met the mother of John the Baptist—according to the Christian tradition in which you are a professed expert.'

'Hold the history,' pleaded David. 'There's a bus around that bend.'

The village was timeless amongst the olive trees, dug into the slope with its churches and monasteries and high-walled gardens, an oasis of the picturesque, while the skyline above it was cluttered with the high-rise apartments of modern Jerusalem.

From the main street Debra scooted into the mouth of a narrow lane, where high walls of time-worn stone rose on each hand, and braked to a halt outside a forbidding iron gate.

'Home,' she said, and wheeled the scooter into the gatehouse and locked it away before letting them in through a side gate hidden in a corner of the wall.

They came out into a large garden court enclosed by the high rough plastered walls which were lime-washed to glaring white. There were olive trees growing in the court with thick twisted trunks. Vines climbed the walls and spread their boughs overhead; already there were bunches of green grapes forming upon them.

'The Brig is a crazy keen amateur archaeologist,' Debra indicated the Roman and Greek statues that stood amongst the olive trees, the exhibits of pottery amphorae arranged around the walls, and the ancient mosaic tiles which paved the pathway to the house. 'It's strictly against the law, of course, but he spends all his spare time digging around in the old sites.'

The kitchen was cavernous with an enormous open fireplace in which a modern electric stove looked out of place, but the copper pots were burnished until they glowed and the tiled floor was polished and sweet-smelling.

Debra's mother was a tall slim woman with a quiet manner, who looked like Debra's older sister. The family resemblance was striking and, as she greeted them, David thought with pleasure that this was how Debra would look at the same age. Debra introduced them and announced that David was a guest for dinner, a fact of which he had been unaware until that moment.

'Please,' he protested quickly, 'I don't want to intrude.' He knew that Friday was a special night in the Jewish home.

'You don't intrude. We will be honoured,' she brushed aside his protest. 'This house is home for most of the boys on Joe's squadron, we enjoy it.'

Debra fetched David a Goldstar beer and they were sitting on the terrace together when her father arrived. He came in through the wicket gate, stooping his tall frame under the stone lintel and taking off his uniform cap as he entered the garden.

He wore uniform casually cut, and open at the throat with cloth insignia of rank and wings at the breast pocket. He was slightly round-shouldered, probably from cramming his lanky body into the cramped cockpits of fighter aircraft, and his head was brown and bald with a monk's fringe of hair and a fierce spiky moustache through which a gold tooth gleamed richly. His nose was big and hooked, the nose of a biblical warrior, and his eyes were dark and snapping with the same golden lights as Debra's. He was a man of such presence that he commanded David's instant respect. He stood to shake the General's hand and called him 'sir' completely naturally.

The Brig subjected David to a rapid, raking scrutiny and reserved his judgement, showing neither pleasure nor disdain.

Later David would learn that the nickname 'The Brig' was a shortened version of 'The Brigand', a name the British had given him before 1948 when he was smuggling warplanes and arms into Palestine for the *Haganah*. Everyone, even his children called him that and only his wife used his given name, Joshua.

'David is sharing the Sabbath meal with us tonight,' Debra explained to him.

'You are welcome,' said the Brig, and turned to embrace his women with love and laughter, for he had seen neither of them since the previous Sabbath, his duties keeping him at air bases and control rooms scattered widely across the land.

When Joe arrived, he was also in uniform, the casual open-necked khaki of summer, and when he saw David he dropped his slow manner and hurried to him, laughing, and enfolded him in a bear hug, speaking over his shoulder to Debra.

'Was I right?'

'Joe said you would come,' Debra explained.

'It looks like I was the only one who didn't know,' David protested.

There were fifteen at dinner, and the candlelight gleamed on the polished wood of the huge refectory table and the silver Sabbath goblets. The Brig said a short prayer, the satin and gold embroidered *yamulka* looking slightly out of place on his wicked bald head, then he filled the wine goblets with his own hand murmuring a greeting to each of his guests. Hannah was with Joe, her copper hair glowing handsomely in the candlelight, and she greeted David with reserve. There were two of the Brig's brothers with their wives and children and grandchildren, and the talk was loud and confusing as the children vied with their elders for a hearing and the language changed at random from Hebrew to English. The food was exotic and spicy, although the wine was too sweet for David's taste. He was content to sit quietly beside Debra and enjoy the sense of belonging in this happy group. He was startled then when one of Debra's cousins leaned across her to speak to him.

'This must be very confusing for you—your first day in such an unusual country as Israel, and not understanding Hebrew, you not being Jewish—'

The words were not meant unkindly, but all conversation stopped abruptly and the Brig looked up, frowning swiftly, quick to sense an unkindness to a guest at his board.

David was aware of Debra staring at him intently, as if to will words from him, and suddenly he thought how three denials finalized any issue—in the New Testament, in Mohammedan law, and perhaps in that of Moses as well. He did not want to be excluded from this household, from these people. He didn't want to be alone again. It was good here.

He smiled at the cousin and shook his head. 'It's strange, yes—but not as bad as you think. I understand Hebrew, though I don't speak it very well. You see, I am Jewish also.'

Beside him Debra gave a soft gasp of pleasure and exchanged quick glances with Joe.

'Jewish?' the Brig demanded. 'You don't look it,' and David explained, and when he was through the Brig nodded. It seemed that his manner had thawed a little.

'Not only that, but he is a flier also,' Debra boasted, and the Brig's moustache twitched like a living thing so that he had to soothe it with his napkin while he reappraised David carefully.

'What experience?' he demanded brusquely.

'Twelve hundred hours, sir, almost a thousand on jets.'

'Jets?'

'Mirages.'

'Mirages!' The Brig's gold tooth gleamed secretly.

'What squadron?'

'Cobra Squadron.'

'Rastus Naude's bunch?' The Brig stared at David as he asked.

'Do you know Rastus?' David was startled.

'We flew in the first Spitfires from Czechoslovakia together—back in '48. We used to call him Butch Ben Yok—Son of a Gentile—in those days. How is he, he must be getting on now? He was no spring chick even then.'

'He's as spry as ever, sir,' David answered tactfully.

'Well, if Rastus taught you to fly—you must be half good,' the Brig conceded.

As a general rule the Israeli Airforce would not refuse foreign pilots, but here was a Jew with all the marks of a first-class fighter pilot. The Brig had noticed the marvellous *élan* and thrust which that other consummate judge of young men, Paul Morgan, had recognized also and valued so highly. Unless he had read the signs wrongly, something he seldom did, then here was a rare one. Once more he appraised the young man in the candlelight and noticed that clear and steady gaze that seemed to seek a distant horizon. It was the eye of the gunfighter, and all his pilots were gunfighters.

To train an interceptor pilot took many years and nearly a million dollars. Time and money were matters of survival in his country's time of trial—and rules could be bent.

He picked up the wine bottle and carefully refilled David's goblet. 'I will place a telephone call to Rastus Naude,' he decided silently, 'and find out a bit more about this youngster.'

Debra watched her father as he began to question David searchingly on his reasons, or lack of them, for coming to Israel—and on his future plans.

She knew precisely how the Brig's mind was working, for she had anticipated it. Her reasons for inviting David to dinner and for exposing him to the Brig were devious and calculated.

She switched her attention back to David, feeling the tense warm sensation in the pit of her stomach and the electric prickle of the skin upon her forearms as she looked at him.

'Yes, you big cocky stallion,' she thought comfortably, 'you aren't going to find it easy to escape again. This time I'm playing for keeps, and I've got the Brig on to you also.'

She lifted her goblet to him, smiling sweetly at him over the rim.

'You're going to get exactly what you're after, but in trumps and with bells on,' she threatened silently, and aloud she said, '*Lechaim!* To life!' and David echoed the toast.

'This time I'm not going to be put off so easily,' he promised himself firmly as he watched the candlelight explode in tiny golden sparks in her eyes. 'I'm going to have you, my raven-haired beauty, no matter how long it takes or what it costs.'

The telephone beside his bed woke David in the dawn, and the Brig's voice was crisp and alert, as though he had already completed a day's work.

'If you have no urgent plans for today, I'm taking you to see something,' he said.

'Of course, sir.' David was taken off balance.

'I will fetch you from your hotel in forty-five minutes, that will give you time to breakfast. Please wait for me in the lobby.'

The Brig drove a small nondescript compact with civilian plates, and he drove it fast and efficiently. David was impressed with his reaction time and co-ordination—after all the Brig must be well into his fifties, and David allowed himself to contemplate such immense age with awe.

They took the main highway west towards Tel Aviv, and the Brig broke a long silence.

'I spoke with your old C.O. last night. He was surprised to hear where you were. He tells me that you were offered promotion to staff rank before you left—'

'It was a bribe,' said David, and the Brig nodded and began to talk. David listened to him quietly while he watched with pleasure the quickly changing landscape as they came down out of the hills and turned southwards through the low rolling plains towards Beersheba and the desert.

'I am taking you to an airforce base, and I might add that I am flouting all sorts of security regulations to do so. Rastus assured me that you can fly, and I want to see if he was telling me the truth.'

David looked at him quickly.

'We are going to fly?' and he felt a deep and pleasurable excitement when the Brig nodded.

'We are at war here, so you will be flying a combat sortie, and breaking just about every regulation in the book. But you'll find we don't go by the book very much.'

He went on quietly, explaining his own particular view of Israel, its struggle and its chances of success, and David remembered odd phrases he used.

'—We are building a nation, and the blood we have been forced to mix into the foundations has strengthened them—'

'—We don't want to make this merely a sanctuary for all the beaten-up Jews of the world. We want the strong bright Jews also—'

'—There are three million of us, and one hundred and fifty million enemies, sworn to our total annihilation—'

'—If they lose a battle, they lose a few miles of desert, if we lose one we cease to exist—'

—We'll have to give them one more beating. They won't accept the others. They believe their ammunition was faulty in 1948, after Suez the lines were restored so they lost nothing, and in '67 they think they were cheated. We'll have to beat them one more time before they'll leave us alone—'

He talked as to a friend or an ally and David was warmed by his trust, and enlivened by the prospect of flying again.

A plantation of eucalyptus trees grew as a heavy screen alongside the road, and the Brig slowed to a gate in the barbed wire fence and a sign that proclaimed in both languages: 'Chaim Weissmann Agricultural Experimental Centre.'

They turned on to the side road through the plantation, and there was a secondary fence and a guard post amongst the trees.

A guard at the gate checked the Brig's papers briefly, they clearly knew him well. Then they drove on, emerging from the plantation into neatly laid-out blocks of different cereal crops. David recognized oats, barley, wheat and maize—all of it flourishing in the warm spring sunshine. The roads between each field were surveyed long and straight and paved with concrete that had been tinted to the colour of the surrounding earth. There was something unnatural in these smooth two-mile-long fairways bisecting each other at right angles, and to David they were familiar. The Brig saw his interest and nodded, 'Yes,' he said, 'runways. We are digging in—not to be taken by the same tactics we used in '67.'

David pondered it while they drove rapidly towards a giant concrete grain silo that stood tall in the distance. In the fields, scarlet tractors were at work, and overhead irrigation equipment threw graceful glittering ostrich feathers of spray into the air.

They reached the concrete silo and the Brig drove the compact through the wide doors of the barn-like building that abutted it. David was startled to see the lines of buses and automobiles parked in neat lines along the length of the barn. There was transport here for many hundreds of men—and yet he had noticed less than a score of tractor-drivers.

There were guards here again, in paratrooper uniform, and when the Brig led David to the rounded bulk of the silo, he realized suddenly that it was a dummy. A massive bomb-proof structure of solid concrete, housing all the sophisticated communications and radar equipment of a modern fighter base. It was combined control tower and plot for four full squadrons of Mirage fighters, the Brig explained briefly as they entered an elevator and sank below the earth.

They emerged into a reception area where again the Brig's papers were examined, and a paratrooper major was called to pass David through, a duty he performed reluctantly and at the Brig's insistence. Then the Brig led David along a carpeted and air-conditioned underground tunnel to the pilots' dressing-room. It was tiled and spotless, with showers and toilets and lockers like a country club changing-room.

The Brig had ordered clothing for David, guessing his size and doing so accurately. The orderly corporal had no trouble fitting him out in overalls, boots, G-suit, gloves and helmet.

The Brig dressed from his own locker and both of them went through into the ready room, moving stiffly in the constricting grip of the G-suits and carrying their helmets under their arms.

The duty pilots looked up from chess games and magazines as they entered, recognized the general and stood to greet him, but the atmosphere was easy and informal. The Brig made a small witticism and they all laughed and relaxed, while he led David through into the briefing-room.

Swiftly, but without overlooking a detail, he outlined the patrol that they would fly, and checked David out on radio procedure, aircraft identification, and other parochial details.

'All clear?' he asked at last, and when David nodded, he went on, 'Remember what I told you, we are at war. Anything we find that doesn't belong to us we hit it, hard! All right?'

'Yes, sir.'

'It's been nice and quiet the last few weeks, but yesterday we had a little trouble down near Ein Yahav, a bit of nastiness with one of our border patrols. So things are a little sensitive at the moment.' He picked up his helmet and map case then turned to face David, leaning close to him and fixing him with those fierce brown and golden eyes.

'It will be clear up there today, and when we get to forty thousand, you will be able to see it all, every inch of it from Rosh Hanikra to Suez, from Mount Hermon to Eilat, and you will see how small it is and how vulnerable to the enemies that surround us. You said you were looking for something worthwhile—I want you to decide whether guarding the fate of three million people might not be a worthwhile job for a man.'

They rode on a small electric personnel carrier down one of the long underground passages, and they entered the concrete bunker dispersed at one point of a great star whose centre was the concrete silo, and they climbed down from the cart.

The Mirages stood in a row, six of them, sleek and needle-nosed, crouching like leashed and impatient animals, so well remembered in outline, but vaguely unfamiliar in their desert brown and drab green camouflage with the blue Star of David insignia on the fuselage.

The Brig signed for two machines, grinning as he wrote 'Butch Ben Yok' under David's numeral.

'As good a name as any to fly under,' he grunted. 'This is the land of the pseudonym and alias.'

David settled into the tiny cockpit with a sense of homecoming. In here it was all completely familiar and his hands moved over the massed array of switches, instruments and controls like those of a lover as he began his pre-flight check.

In the confined space of the bunkers the jet thunder assaulted the eardrums, their din only made bearable by the perforated steel baffles set into the rear of the structure.

The Brig looked across at David, his head enclosed in the garishly painted helmet, and gave him the high sign. David returned it and reached up to pull the Perspex canopy closed. Ahead of them, the steel blast doors rolled swiftly upwards, and the ready lamps above them switched from red to green.

There was no taxiing to take-off areas; no needless ground exposure. Wing-tip to wing-tip they came up the ramp out of the bunker into the sunlight. Ahead of them stretched one of the long brown runways, and David pushed open his throttle to the gate, and then ignited his afterburners, feeling the thrust of the mighty jet through the cushioning of his seat. Down between the fields of green corn they tore, and then up, with the swooping sensation in the guts and the rapier nose of the Mirage pointed at the sapphire of the sky that arched unbroken and unsullied above them, and once again David experienced the euphoria of jet-powered flight.

They levelled out a little under forty thousand feet avoiding even altitudes or orderly flight patterns, and David placed his machine under the Brig's tail and eased back on the throttles to cruising power, his hands delighting in the familiar rituals of flight which his helmeted head revolved restlessly in the search routine, sweeping every quarter of the sky about him, weaving the Mirage to clear the blind spot behind his own tail.

The air had an unreal quality of purity, a crystalline clarity that made even the most distant mountain ranges stand out in crisp silhouette, hardly shaded with the blue of distance. In the north the Mediterranean blazed like a pool of molten silver in the sunlight, while the sea of Galilee was soft cool green, and farther south the Dead Sea was darker, forbidding in its sunken bed of tortured desert.

They flew north over the ridge of Carmel and the flecked white buildings of Haifa with its orange gold beaches on which the sea broke in soft ripples of creamy lacework. Then they turned together easing back on the power and sinking slowly to patrol altitude at twenty thousand feet as they passed the peak of Mount Hermon where the last snows still lingered in the gullies and upon the high places, streaking the great rounded mountain like an old man's pate.

The softly dreaming greens and pastels delighted David who was accustomed to the sepia monochromes of Africa. The villages clung to the hill-tops, their white walls shining like diamonds above the terraced slopes and the darker areas of cultivated land.

They turned south again, booming down the valley of the Jordan, over the Sea of Galilee with its tranquil green waters enclosed by the thickets of date palm and the neatly tended fields of the Kibbutzim, losing altitude as the land forsook its gentle aspect and the hills were riven and tortured, rent by the wadis as though by the claws of a dreadful predator.

On the left hand rose the mountains of Edom, hostile and implacable, and beneath them Jericho was a green oasis in the wilderness. Ahead lay the shimmering surface of the Dead Sea. The Brig dropped down, and they thundered so low across the salt-thickened water that the jet blast ruffled the surface behind them.

The Brig's voice chuckled in David's earphones, 'That's the lowest you are ever going to fly—twelve hundred feet below sea level.'

They were climbing again as they crossed the mineral works at the southern end of the sea, and faced the blasted and mountainous deserts of the south.

'Hello, Cactus One, this is Desert Flower,' again the radio silence was broken, but this time David recognized the call sign of command net. They were being called directly from the Operation Centre of Airforce Command, situated in some secret underground bunker at a location that David would never learn. On the command plot their position being accurately relayed by the radar repeaters.

'Hello, Desert Flower,' the Brig acked, and immediately the exchange became as informal as two old friends chatting, which was precisely what it was.

'Brig, this is Motti. We've just had a ground support request in your area,' he gave the co-ordinates quickly, 'a motorized patrol of border police is under sneak low-level attack by an unidentified aircraft. See to it, will you.'

'Beseder, Motti, okay.' The Brig switched to flight frequency. 'Cactus Two, I'm going to interception power, confirm to me,' he told David, and they turned together on to the new heading.

'No point in trying a radar scan,' the Brig grumbled aloud. 'He'll be down in the ground clutter. We'll not pick the swine off amongst those mountains. Just keep your eyes open.'

'Beseder.' David had already picked up the word. The favourite Hebrew word in a land where very little was really 'okay'.

David spotted it first, a slim black column of smoke beginning to rise like a pencil line drawn slowly against the windless and dazzling cobalt blue of the horizon.

'Ground smoke,' he said into his helmet microphone. 'Eleven o'clock low.'

The Brig squinted ahead silently, searching for it, and then saw it on the extreme limit of his vision range. He grunted, Rastus had been right in one thing at least. The youngster had eyes like a hawk.

'Going to attack speed now,' he said and David acked and lit his afterburners. The upholstery of the seat smacked into his back under the mighty increase in thrust and David felt the drastic alteration in trim as the Mirage went shooting through the sonic barrier.

Near the base of the smoke column, something flashed briefly against the drab brown earth, and David narrowed his eyes and made out the tiny shape, flitting as a sunbird, its camouflage blending naturally into the backdrop of desert, so it was ethereal as a shadow.

'Bandit turning to port of the smoke,' he called the sighting.

'I have him,' said the Brig, and switched to command net.

'Hello, Desert Flower, I'm on an intruder. Call strike, please.' The decision to engage must be made to command level, and the answering voice was laconic, and flat.

'Brig, this is Motti. Hit him!'

While they spoke they were rushing down so swiftly that the details of the little drama being played out below sprang into comprehension.

Along a dusty border track three patrol vehicles of the border police were halted. They were camouflaged half tracks, tiny as children's toys in the vastness of the desert.

One of the half tracks was burning. The smoke was greasy black and rose straight into the air, the beacon that had drawn them. Lying spread-eagled in the road was a human body, flung down carelessly in death, and the sight of it stirred in David a deeply bitter feeling of resentment such as he had last felt in the bullring at Madrid.

The other vehicles were pulled off the track at abandoned angles, and David could see their crews crouching amongst the scrub and rock. Some of them were firing with small arms at their attacker who was circling for his next run down upon them.

David had never seen the type before, but knew it instantly from the recognition charts that he had studied so often. It was a Russian MIG 17 of the Syrian airforce. The high tailplane was unmistakable. The dappled brown desert camouflage was brightened by the red, white and black roundels with their starred green centres on the fuselage and the stubby swept wings.

The MIG completed its turn, settling swiftly down and levelling off for its next strafing run upon the parked vehicles. The pilot's attention was concentrated on the helpless men cowering amongst the rocks and he was unaware of the terrible vengeance that was bearing down upon him from on high.

The Brig lined up for his pass, turning slightly to bring himself down on the Syrian's tail, attacking in classic style from behind and above, and David dropped back to weave across his rear, covering him and backing up to press in a supporting attack if the first failed.

The Syrian opened fire again and the cannon bursts twinkled like fairy lights amongst the men and trucks. Another truck exploded in a dragon's breath of smoke and flame.

'You bastard,' David whispered as he levelled out behind the Brig, and saw the havoc that was being wrought amongst his people. It was the first time he had thought of them as that, his people, and he felt the cold anger of the shepherd whose flock is under attack.

A line of poetry popped up in his mind 'The Assyrian came down like a wolf on the fold,' and his hands went purposefully to the chore of locking in his cannons-selectors and flicking the trigger forward out of its recess in the moulded grip of the joystick. The soft green glow lit his gunsight as it came alive and he squinted through it.

The Brig was pressing his attack in to close range, rapidly overhauling the slower clumsy-looking MIG, and at that moment that he knew he would open fire David saw the Syrian's wing-shape alter. At the fatal instant he had become aware of his predicament, and he had done what was best in the circumstances. He had pulled on full flap and while his speed fell sharply he dropped one wing in a slide towards the earth a hundred feet below.

The Brig was committed and he loosed his salvo of cannon fire at the instant that the Syrian dropped, ducking under it like a boxer avoiding a heavy punch. David saw the blaze of shot pass high, rending the air above the sand-coloured aircraft. Then the Brig was through, missing with every shell, spiralling up and around in a great flashing circle, raging internally at his failure.

At the instant that David recognized the MIG's manoeuvre, he reacted with a rapidity that was purely reflexive. He closed down his power, and hit his air brakes to punch a little of the speed off the Mirage.

The MIG turned steeply away to port, standing on one wing-tip that seemed to be pegged into the bleak desert earth. David released his air brakes, to give his wings lift for the next evolution, and then he dropped his own wing-tip and went sweeping round to follow the Syrian's desperate twists with the Mirage hovering on the edge of the stall.

The Syrian was turning inside him, slower and more manoeuvrable; David could not bring his sights to bear, his right forefinger was curled around the trigger but always the dark shape of the MIG was out of centre in the illuminated circle of the sight as the aiming pipper dipped and rose to the pull of gravity.

Ahead of the two circling aircraft rose a steep and forbidding line of cliffs, rent by deep defiles and gullies.

The MIG made no attempt to climb above them, but selected a narrow pass through the hills and went into it like a ferret into its run, a desperate attempt to shake off the pursuit.

The Mirage was not designed for this type of flying, and David felt the urge to hit his afterburners and ride up over the jagged fangs of rock–but to do so was to let the MIG escape, and his anger was still strong upon him.

He followed the Syrian into the rock pass, and the walls of stone on either hand seemed to brush his wing-tips, the gully turned sharply to starboard and David dropped his wing and followed its course. Back upon itself the rock turned, and David swung the needle nose from maximum rate turn starboard to port, and the stall warning device winked amber and red at him as he abused the Mirage's delicate flying capabilities.

Ahead of him the MIG clawed its way through the tunnel of rock. The pilot looked back over his shoulder and he saw the Mirage following him, creeping slowly up on him, and he turned back to his controls and forced his machine lower still, hugging the rugged walls of stone.

The air in the hills was hot and turbulent, and the Mirage bucked and fought against restraint wanting to be free and high, while ahead of it the Syrian drifted tantalizingly off-centre in David's gunsight.

Now the valley turned again and narrowed, before climbing and ending abruptly against a solid dark purple wall of smooth rock.

The Syrian was trapped, he levelled out and climbed steeply upwards, his flight path dictated by the rocks on each side and ahead.

David pushed his throttle to the gate and lit his afterburners, and the mighty engine rumbled, thrusting him powerfully forward, up under the Syrian's stern.

The eternal micro-seconds of mortal combat dragged by, as the Syrian floated lazily into the circle of the gunsight, expanding it to fill it as the Mirage's nose seemed to touch the other's tailplane and David felt the buffeting of the Syrian's slip-stream.

He pressed the cannon trigger and the Mirage lurched as she hurled her deadly load into the other machine in a clattering double stream of cannon fire and an eruption of incendiary shells.

The Syrian disintegrated, evaporating in a gush of silvery smoke, rent through with bright white lightning, and the ejecting pilot's body was blown clear of the fuselage. For an instant it was outlined ahead of David's screen, cruciform in shape with arms and legs thrown wide, the helmet still on the head, and the clothing ballooning in the rush of air. Then it flickered past the Mirage's canopy as David climbed swiftly up out of the valley and into the open sky.

The soldiers were moving about amongst their vehicles, tending their wounded and covering their dead, but they all looked up as David flew back low along the road. He passed so close that he could see their faces clearly. They were sun-browned, some with beards or moustaches, strong young faces, their mouths open as they cheered him, waving their thanks.

My people, he thought. He was still high on the adrenalin that had poured into his blood, and he felt a fierce elation. He grinned wolfishly at the men below him and lifted one gloved hand in salute before climbing up to where the Brig was circling, waiting for him.

The artificial lights of the bunkers were dim after the brilliance of the sun. An engineer helped David from the cockpit as his mates swarmed over the Mirage to refuel and rearm it. This was one of the vital skills of this tiny airforce, the ability to ready a warplane for combat in a fraction of the time usually required for the task. Thus in emergency the machine could return to the battle long before its adversary.

Moving stiffly from the confines of the cockpit, David crossed to where the Brig was already in conversation with the flight controller.

He stood with the gaudy helmet tucked under one arm as he stripped off his gloves, but as David came up he turned to him and his wintry smile exposed the gold tooth in its nest of fur.

Lightly he punched David's arm 'Ken! Yes!' said Major-General Joshua Mordecai. 'You'll do.'

David was late to fetch Debra for dinner that evening, but she had already learned the reason from her father.

They went to the Select behind David's Tower, inside the Jaffa Gate of the old city. Its unpretentious interior, decorated with patterns of rope upon the walls, did not fully prepare David for the excellent meal that the Arab proprietor served them with the minimum of delay—mousakha chicken, with nuts and spices on a bed of kouskous.

They ate almost in silence, Debra quickly recognizing and respecting David's mood. He was in the grip of post-combat *tristesse,* the adrenalin hangover of stress and excitement, but slowly the good food in his belly and the heavy Carmel wine relaxed him, until over the thimble-sized cups of Turkish coffee, black and powerfully reeking of cardamom seed, Debra could ask, 'What happened today, David?'

He sipped the coffee before replying.

'I killed a man.' She set down her cup and studied his face solemnly, and he began to speak, telling her the details of it, the chase and the kill, until he ended lamely, 'I felt only satisfaction at the time. A sense of achievement. I knew I had done what was right.'

'And now?' she prompted him.

'Now I am sad,' he shrugged. 'I am saddened that I had to do it.'

'My father, who has always been a soldier, says that only those who do the actual fighting can truly know what it is to hate war.'

David nodded. 'Yes, I understand that now. I love to fly, but I hate to destroy.'

They were silent again, both of them considering their own personal vision of war, both of them trying to find words to express it.

'And yet it is necessary,' Debra broke the silence. 'We must fight—there is no other way.'

'There is no other way—with the sea at our backs and the Arabs at our throats.'

'You speak like an Israeli,' Debra challenged him softly.

'I made a decision today—or rather I was press-ganged by your father. He has given me three weeks to brush up my Hebrew, and complete the immigration formalities.'

'And then?' Debra leaned towards him.

'A commission in the airforce. That was the only point I scored on, I had just enough strength to hold out for the equivalent rank I would have had back home. He haggled like a secondhand clothes dealer, but I had him, and he knew it. So he gave in at last. Acting major, with confirmation of rank at the end of twelve months.'

'That's wonderful, Davey, you'll be one of the youngest majors in the service.'

'Yeah,' David agreed, 'and after I've paid my taxes I'll have a salary a little less than a bus-driver back home.'

'Never mind,' Debra smiled for the first time. 'I'll help you with your Hebrew.'

'I was going to talk to you about that,' he answered her smile. 'Come on, let's get out of here. I'm restless tonight—and I want to walk.'

They strolled through the Christian quarter. The open stalls on each side were loaded with garish and exotic clothes, and leather work and jewellery, and the smell of spices and food and drains and stale humanity was almost solid in the narrow lanes where the arches met overhead.

Debra drew him into one of the antique stores in the Via Dolorosa, and the proprietor came to them, almost wriggling with pleasure.

'Ah, Miss Mordecai—and how is your dearly esteemed father?' Then he rushed into the back room to brew more coffee for them.

'He's one of the half-honest ones, and he lives in mortal fear of the Brig.'

Debra selected an antique solid gold Star of David on a slim golden neck chain, and though he had never before worn personal jewellery, David bowed his head and let her place it about his neck. The golden star lay against the coarse dark curls of his chest.

'That's the only decoration you'll ever get—we don't usually give medals,' she told him laughingly. 'But welcome to Israel anyway.'

'It's beautiful,' David was touched and embarrassed by the gift, 'thank you.' And he buttoned his shirt over it and then reached awkwardly to kiss her—but she drew away and warned him.

'Not in here. He's a Moslem, and he'd be very offended.'

'All right,' said David. 'Let's go and find some place where we won't hurt anybody's sensibilities.'

They went out through the Lion Gate in the great wall and found a stone bench in a quiet place amongst the olive trees of the Moslem cemetery. There was half a moon in the sky, silver and mysterious, and the night was warm and waiting, seemingly as expectant as a new bride.

'You can't stay on at the Intercontinental,' Debra told him, and they both looked up at its arched and lighted silhouette across the valley.

'Why not?'

'Well, first of all it's too expensive. On your salary you just can't afford it.'

'You don't really expect me to live on my salary?' David protested, but Debra ignored him and went on.

'And what is more important, you aren't a tourist any more. So you can't live like one.'

'What do you suggest?'

'We could find you an apartment.'

'Who would do the housework, and the laundry, and the cooking?' he protested vehemently. 'I haven't had much practice at that sort of thing.'

'I would,' said Debra, and he froze for an instant and then turned slowly on the seat to look at her.

'What did you say?'

'I said, I would,' she repeated firmly, and then her voice quavered. 'That's if you want me to.' He was silent for a long moment.

'See here, Debs. And you talking about living together? I mean, playing house-house on a full-time basis—the whole bit?'

'That's precisely what I am talking about.'

'But—' He could think of nothing further to say. The idea was novel, breathtaking, and alive with enchanting possibilities. All David's previous experiences with the opposite sex had been profuse rather than deep, and he found himself on the frontiers of unexplored territory.

'Well?' Debra asked at last.

'Do you want to get married?' his voice cracked on the word, and he cleared his throat.

'I'm not sure that you are the finest marriage material in the market, my darling David. You are as beautiful as the dawn, and fun to be with—but you are also selfish, immature and spoiled stupid.'

'Thank you kindly.'

'Well, there is no point in me mincing words now, David, not when I am about to throw all caution aside and become your mistress.'

'Wow!' he exclaimed, with all the frost thawing from his voice. 'When you say it straight out like that—it almost blows my mind.'

'Me too,' Debra confessed. 'But one condition is that we wait until we have our own special place, you may recall that I'm not so high on public beaches or rocky islands.'

'I'll never forget,' David agreed. 'Does this mean that you *don't* want to marry me?' He found his mortal terror of matrimony fading under this slur on his potential marriage worth.

'I didn't say that either,' Debra demurred. 'But let's make that decision when both of us are ready for it.'

'Right on, doll,' said David, with an almost idiot grin of happiness spreading over his face.

'And now, Major Morgan, you may kiss me,' she said. 'But do try and help me remember the conditions.'

A long while later, they drew a little apart to breathe and a sudden thought made David frown with worry.

'My God,' he exclaimed, 'what will the Brig say!'

'He won't be joining us,' she told him, and they both laughed together, excited by their own wickedness.

'Seriously, what will you tell your parents?'

'I'll lie to them graciously, and they'll pretend to believe me. Let me worry about that.'

'Beseder,' he agreed readily.

'You are learning,' she applauded. 'Let's just try that kiss again—but this time in Hebrew, please.'

'I love you,' he said in that language.

'Good boy,' she murmured. 'You are going to make a prize pupil.'

There was one more doubt to be set at rest, and Debra voiced it at the iron gate to the garden, when at last he took her home.

'Do you know what the Bris, the Covenant, is?'

'Sure,' he grinned, and made scissors out of his fist and second finger. It seemed in the uncertain light that she blushed, and her voice was only just audible.

'Well, what about you?'

'That,' David told her severely, 'is a highly personal question, the answer to which little girls should find out for themselves,' and his expression became lascivious, 'the hard way.'

'All knowledge is precious as gold,' she said in a small voice, 'and be sure that I will seek the answer diligently.'

David discovered that the acquisition of an apartment in Jerusalem was a task much like the quest for the Holy Grail. Although the high-rise blocks were being thrown up with almost reckless energy, the demand for accommodation far outweighed the supply.

The father of one of Debra's students was an estate agent and the poor man took their problem to his heart; the waiting-list for the new blocks was endless, but an occassional apartment in one of the older buildings fell vacant, and he used all his influence for them.

At unexpected moments of the day, Debra would send out an urgent signal, and David would fetch her in a taxi at the University and they would hell across town, urging on the driver, to inspect the latest offering.

The last of these reminded David of a movie set from *Lawrence of Arabia* complete with a dispirited palm tree out front, a spectacular display of bright laundry hanging from every balcony and window, and all the sounds and smells of an Arab camel market and a nursery-school playground at recess from the courtyard.

There were two rooms and an alleged bathroom. The roses and wreaths of the wallpaper had faded, except in patches where hangings had protected their original pristine virulent colouring.

David pushed open the door of the bathroom and, without entering, inspected the raggedy linoleum floor-covering and the stained and chipped bath tub; then pushing the door further he discovered the toilet bowl festering quietly in the gloom with its seat at a rakish angle like the halo of a drunken angel.

'You and Joe could work on it,' Debra suggested uncertainly. 'It's not really *that* bad.'

David shuddered, and closed the door as though it were the lid of a coffin.

'You're joking—of course,' he said, and Debra's determinedly bright smile cracked and her lip quivered.

'Oh, David, we are never going to find a place.'

'And I can't wait much longer.'

'Nor can I,' admitted Debra.

'Right,' David rubbed his hands together briskly' 'It's time to send in the first team.'

He was not sure what form the presence of Morgan Group would take in Jerusalem, but he found it listed in the business directory under 'Morgan Industrial Finance' and the Managing Director was a large mournful-looking gentleman named Aaron Cohen who had a suite of offices in the Leumi Bank building opposite the main post office. He was overcome with emotion to discover that one of the Morgan family had been ten days in Jerusalem without his knowledge

David told him what he wanted, and in twenty hours he had it signed and paid for. Paul Morgan picked his executives with care, and Cohen was an example of this attention. The price David must pay for this service was that Paul Morgan would have a full report of David's transaction, present whereabouts and future plans on his desk the next morning—but it was worth it.

Above the Hinnom canyon, facing Mount Zion with its impressive array of spires, the Montefiore quarter was being rebuilt as an integrated whole by some entrepreneur. All of it was clad in the lovely golden Jerusalem stone, and the designs of the houses were traditional and ageless. However, the interiors were lavishly modernized with tall cool rooms, mosaic-tiled bathrooms, and ceilings arched like those of a crusader church. Most of them had their own walled and private terraces. The one that Aaron Cohen procured for David was the pick of those that fronted Malik Street. The price was astronomical. That was the first question that Debra asked, once she had recovered her voice. She stood stunned upon the terrace beneath the single olive tree. The stone of the terrace had been cut and polished until it resembled old ivory, and she ran her fingers lightly over the carved front door. Her voice was hushed and her expression bemused.

'David! David! How much is this going to cost?'

'That's not important. What is important is whether you like it.'

'It's too beautiful. It's too much, David. We can't afford this.'

'It's paid for already.'

'Paid for?' She stared at him. 'How much, David?'

'If I said half a million Israeli pounds or a million, what difference would it make? It's only money.'

She clapped her hands over her ears. 'No!' she cried. 'Don't tell me! I'd feel so guilty I wouldn't be able to live in it.'

'Oh, so! You are actually consenting to live in it.'

'Try me,' she said with emphasis. 'You just try me, lover!'

They stood in the central room that opened on to the terrace, and although it was light and airy enough for the savage heat of summer that was coming, it smelled of new paint and varnished woodwork.

'What are we going to do about furniture?' David asked.

'Furniture?' Debra repeated. 'I hadn't thought that far ahead.'

'For what I have in mind, we'll need at least one king-size bed.'

'Sex maniac,' she said, and kissed him.

No modern furniture looked at home under the domed roof, or upon the stone-flagged doors. So they began to furnish from the bazaars and antique shops.

Debra solved the main problem with the discovery in a junk yard of an enormous brass bedstead from which they scraped the accumulated dirt; they polished it until it glowed, fitting it with a new inner-spring mattress, and covered it with a cream-coloured lace bedspread from Debra's bottom drawer.

They purchased *kelim* and woven woollen rugs by the bale from the Arab dealers in the old city, and scattered them thickly upon the stone floors, with leather cushions to sit upon and a low olive-wood table, inlaid with ebony and mother of pearl, to eat off. The rest of the furniture would come when they could find it for sale, or, failing that, have it custom-made by an Arab cabinet-maker that Debra knew of. Both the bed and the table were enormously heavy, and they needed muscle to move them, so they called for Joe. He and Hannah arrived in his tiny Japanese compact, and after they had recovered from the impact of the Morgan palace they fell to work enthusiastically with David supervising. Joe grunted and heaved, while Hannah disappeared with Debra into the modern American kitchen to exclaim with envy and admiration over the washing-machine, dryer, dish-washer and all the other appliances that went with the house. She helped to cook the first meal.

David had laid in a case of Goldstar beer, and after their labours they all gathered about the olive-wood table to warm the house and wet the roof.

David had expected Joe to be a little reserved, after all it was his baby sister who was being set up in a fancy house; but Joe was as natural as ever and enjoyed the beer and the company so well that Hannah had to intervene at last.

'It's late,' she said firmly.

'Late?' asked Joe. 'It's only nine o'clock.'

'On a night like tonight, that's late.'

'What do you mean?' Joe looked puzzled.

'Joseph Mordecai, diplomat extraordinary,' Hannah said with heavy sarcasm, and suddenly Joe's expression changed as he glanced from Debra to David guiltily, swallowed his beer in a single gulp, and hoisted Hannah to her feet by one arm.

'Come on,' he said. 'What are we sitting here for?'

David left the terrace lights burning, and they shone through the slats of the shuttered windows, so the room was softly lit, and the sounds from the outside world were so muted by distance and stone walls as to be a mere murmur that drifted from afar, and seemed rather to accentuate their aloneness than to spoil it.

The brass of the bedstead gleamed softly in the gloom, and the ivory lacework of the bedspread smelled of lavender and moth balls.

He lay upon the bed and watched her undress slowly, conscious of his eyes upon her and shy now as she had never been before.

Her body was slim and with a flowing line of waist and leg, young and tender-looking, with a child's awkward grace, and yet with womanly thrust of hip and bosom.

She came to sit upon the edge of the bed, and he marvelled once again at the lustre and plasticity of her skin, at the subtlety of colouring where the sun had darkened it from soft cream to burned honey, and at the contrast of her dusky rose-tipped breasts and the dark thick bush of curls at the base of her softly curving stomach.

She leaned over him, still shyly, and touched his cheek with one finger, running down his throat on to his chest where the gold star lay upon the hard muscle.

'You are beautiful,' she whispered, and she saw it was true. For he was tall and straight with muscled shoulders and lean flanks and belly. The planes of his face were pure and perfect, perhaps its only fault lying in its very perfection. It was almost unreal, as though she were lying with some angel or god from out of mythology.

She twisted her legs up on to the bed, stretching out beside him upon the lace cover, and they lay on their sides facing each other, not touching but so close that she could feel the warmth of his belly upon her own like a soft desert wind, and his breath stirred the dark soft hair upon her cheek.

She sighed then, with happiness and contentment, like a traveller reaching the end of a long lonely journey.

'I love you,' she said for the first time, and reaching out she took his head, her fingers twining in the thick springing hair at the nape of his neck, and drew it tenderly to her breast.

Long afterwards the chill of night oozed into the room, and they came half-awake and crept together beneath the covers.

As they began drifting back into sleep she murmured sleepily, 'I'm so glad that surgery won't be necessary, after all,' and he chuckled softly.

'Wasn't it better finding out for yourself?'

'Much better, lover. Much, much better,' she admitted.

Debra spent one entire evening explaining to David that a high-performance sports car was not a necessity for travel between his base and the house on Malik Street, for she knew her man's tastes by then. She pointed out that this was a country of young pioneers, and that extravagance and ostentation were out of place. David agreed vehemently, secure in the knowledge that Aaron Cohen and his minions were scouring the country for him.

Debra suggested a Japanese compact similiar to Joe's, and David told her that he would certainly give that his serious consideration.

Aaron Cohen's henchman tracked down a Mercedes Benz 350 SL belonging to the German Charge d'Affaires in Tel Aviv. This gentleman was returning to

Berlin and wished to dispose of his auto, for a suitable consideration in negotiable cash. A single phone call was sufficient to arrange payment through the Crédit Suisse in Zurich.

It was golden bronze in colour, with a little under twenty thousand kilometres on the clock, and it had clearly been maintained with the loving care of an enthusiast.

Debra, returning on her motor scooter from the University, found this glorious machine parked at the top end of Malik Street, where a heavy chain denied access by all motor-driven vehicles to the village.

She took one look at it, and knew beyond all reasonable doubt who it belonged to. She was really quite angry when she stormed on to the terrace, but she pretended to be angrier than that.

'David Morgan, you really are absolutely impossible.'

'You catch on fast,' David agreed amiably; he was sun-bathing on the terrace.

'How much did you pay for it?'

'Ask me another question, doll. That one is becoming monotonous.'

'You are really–' Debra paused and searched frantically for a word of sufficient force. She found it and delivered it with relish, 'decadent!'

'You don't know the meaning of the word,' David told her gently as he rose from the cushions in the sun and drifted lazily in her direction. Though she had been his lover for only a mere three days she recognized the look in his eye and she began backing away.

'I will teach you the meaning,' he said. 'I am about to give you a practical demonstration of decadence in such a sensitive spot that you are likely to remember it for a long time.'

She ducked behind the olive tree as he lunged, and her books spilled across the terrace.

'Leave me! Hands off, you beast.'

He feinted right, and caught her as she fell for it. He picked her up easily across his chest.

'David Morgan, I warn you, I shall scream if you don't put me down this instant.'

'Let's hear it. Go ahead!' and she did, but in a ladylike fashion so as not to alarm the neighbours.

Joe, on the other hand, was delighted with the 350. The four of them took it on a trial run down the twisting road through the Wilderness of Judaea to the shores of the Dead Sea. The road challenged the car's suspension and David's driving skill, and they whooped with excitement through the bends. Even Debra was able to overcome her initial disapproval, and finally admitted it was beautiful–but still decadent.

They swam in the cool green waters of the oasis of Ein Gedi where they formed a deep rock pool before overflowing and running down into the thick saline water of the sea itself.

Hannah had brought her camera and she photographed Debra and David sitting together on the rocks beside the pool.

They were in their bathing costumes, Debra's brief bikini showing off her fine young body as she half-turned to laugh into David's face. He smiled back at her, his face in profile and the dark sweep of his hair falling on to his forehead. The desert light picked out the pure features and the boldly stated facets of his beauty.

Hannah had a print of the photograph made for each of them, and later those squares of glossy photographic paper were all they had left of it, all that remained of the joy and the laughter of those days, like a lovely flower taken from the growing tree of life and pressed and dried, flattened and desiccated, deprived of its colour and perfume.

But the future threw no shadow over their happiness on that bright day, and with Joe driving this time they ran back for Jerusalem. Debra insisted that they stop for a group of tank corps boys hitch-hiking home on leave, and although David protested it was impossible, they squeezed three of them into the small cab. It was Debra's sop to her feelings of guilt, and she sat in the back seat with her arms around David's neck and they all sang the song that was that year a favourite with the young people of Israel, 'Let there be peace'.

In the last few days while David waited to enter the airforce, he loafed shamelessly, frittering the time away in small chores like having his uniforms tailored. He resisted Debra's suggestion that if regulation issue were good enough for her father, a general officer, then they might be good enough for David. Aaron Cohen supplied him with an introduction to his own tailor. Aaron was beginning to develop a fine respect for David's style.

Debra had arranged membership for David at the University Athletic Club, and he worked out in the first-class modern gym every day, and finished with twenty lengths of the Olympic-size swimming pool to keep himself in shape.

However, at other times, David merely lay sunbathing on the terrace, or fiddled with electrical plugs or other small tasks Debra had asked him to see to about the house.

As he moved through the cool and pleasant rooms, he would find an item belonging to Debra, a book or a brooch perhaps, and he would pick it up and fondle it briefly. Once a robe of hers thrown carelessly across the foot of the bed and redolent of her particular perfume gave him a physical pang as it reminded him sharply of her, and he held the silkiness to his face and breathed the scent of her, and grudged the hours until her return.

However, it was amongst her books that he discovered more about her than years of study would have revealed. She had crates of these piled in the unfurnished second bedroom which they were using as a temporary store-room until they could find shelves and cupboards. One afternoon David began digging around in the crates. It was a literary mixed grill—Gibbon and Vidal, Shakespeare and Mailer, Solzhenitsyn and Mary Stewart, among other strange bedfellows. There was fiction and biography, history and poetry, Hebrew and English, softbacks and leather-bound editions—and a thin green-jacketed volume which he almost discarded before the author's name caught his attention. It was by D. Mordecai and with a feeling of discovery he turned to the flyleaf. *This year, in Jerusalem,* a collection of poems, by Debra Mordecai.

He carried the book through to the bedroom, remembering to kick off his shoes before lying on the lace cover—she was very strict about that—and he turned to the first page.

There were five poems. The first was the title piece, the two-thousand-year promise of Jewry 'Next year in Jerusalem' had become reality. It was a patriotic tribute to her land and even David, whose taste in writing ran to Maclean and Robbins, recognized that it had a superior quality. There were lines of startling beauty, evocative phrasing and penetrative glimpses. It was good, really good, and David felt a strange proprietary pride—and a sense of awe. He had not guessed at these depths within her, these hidden areas of the mind.

When he came to the last poem, he found it was the shortest of the five, and it was a love poem—or rather it was a poem to someone dearly loved who was gone—and suddenly David was aware of the difference between that which was good and that which was magic.

He found himself shivering to the music of her words, felt the hair on his forearms standing erect with the haunting beauty of it, and then at last he felt himself choking on the sadness of it, the devastation of total loss, and the words swam as his eyes flooded, and he had to blink rapidly as the last terrible cry of the poem pierced him to the heart.

He lowered the book on to his chest, remembering what Joe had told him about the soldier who had died in the desert. A movement attracted his attention and he made a guilty effort to hide the book as he sat up. It was such a private thing, this poetry, that he felt like a thief.

Debra stood in the doorway of the bedroom watching him, leaning against the jamb with her hands clasped in front of her, studying him quietly.

He sat up on the bed and weighed the book in his hands. 'It's lovely,' he said at last, his voice was gruff with the emotions that her words had evoked.

'I'm glad you like it,' she said, and he realized that she was shy.

'Why did you not show it to me before?'

'I was afraid you might not like it.'

'You must have loved him very much?' he asked softly.

'Yes, I did,' she said, 'but now I love you.'

Then, finally, his posting came through and the Brig's hand was evident in it all, though Joe admitted that he had used his own family connections to influence the orders.

He was ordered to report to Mirage squadron 'Lance' which was a crack interceptor outfit based at the same hidden airfield from which he had first flown. Joe Mordecai was on the same squadron, and when he called at Malik Street to tell David the news, he showed no resentment that David would out-rank him, but instead he was confident that they would be able to fly together as a regular team. He spent the evening briefing David on squadron personnel, from 'Le Dauphin' the commanding officer, a French immigrant, down to the lowest mechanic. In the weeks ahead David would find Joe's advice and help invaluable, as he settled into his niche amongst this tightly-knit team of fliers.

The following day the tailor delivered his uniforms, and he wore one to surprise Debra when she backed in through the kitchen door, laden with books and groceries, using her bottom as a door buffer, her hair down behind and her dark glasses pushed up on top of her head.

She dropped her load by the sink, and circled him with her hands on her hips, her head cocked at a critical angle.

'I should like you to wear that, and come to pick me up at the University tomorrow afternoon, please,' she said at last.

'Why?'

'Because there are a few little bitches that lurk around the Lauterman Building. Some of them my students and some my colleagues. I want them to get a good look at you—and eat their tiny hearts out.'

He laughed. 'So you aren't ashamed of me?'

'Morgan, you are too beautiful for one person, you should have been born twins.'

It was their last day together, so he indulged her whimsy and wore his uniform to fetch her at the English Literature Department, and he was surprised to find how the dress affected the strangers he passed on the street—the girls smiled at him, the old ladies called *shalom*, even the guard at the University gates waved him through with a grin and a joke. To them he was a guardian angel, one of those that had swept death from the very sky above them.

Debra hurried to meet and kiss him, and then walked beside him, her hand tucked proudly and possessively into the crook of his elbow. She took him to eat an early dinner at the staff dining-room in the rounded glass Belgium building.

While they ate, a casual question of his revealed the subterfuge she had used to protect her reputation.

'I'll probably not get off the base for the first few weeks, but I'll write to you at Malik Street—'

'No,' she said quickly, 'I won't be staying there. It would be too lonely without you in that huge bed.'

'Where then? At your parents' home?'

'That would be a dead give-away. Every time you arrive back in town, I leave home! No, they think I am staying at the hostel here at the University. I told them I wanted to be closer to the department—'

'You've got a room here?' He stared at her.

'Of course, Davey. I have to be a little discreet. I couldn't tell my relatives, friends and employers to contact me care of Major David Morgan. This may be the twentieth century, and modern Israel, but I am still a Jewess, with a tradition of chastity and modesty behind me.'

For the first time David began to appreciate the magnitude of Debra's decision to come to him. He had taken it lightly compared to her.

'I'm going to miss you,' he said.

'And I you,' she replied.

'Let's go home.'

'Yes,' she agreed, laying aside her knife and fork. 'I can eat any old time.'

However, as they left Belgium House she exclaimed with exasperation: 'Damn, I have to have these books back by today. Can we go by the library? I'm sorry, Davey, it won't take a minute.'

So they climbed again to the main terrace and passed the brightly-lit plate-glass windows of the Students' Union Restaurant, and went on towards the solid square tower of the library whose windows were lighted already against the swiftly falling darkness. They had climbed the library steps and reached the glass doors when a party of students came pouring out, and they were forced to stand aside.

They were facing back the way they had come, across the plaza with its terraces and red-bud trees, towards the restaurant.

Suddenly the dusk of evening was lit by the searing white furnace glare of an explosion, and the glass windows of the restaurant were blown out in a glittering cloud of flying glass. It was as though a storm surf had burst upon a rock cliff, flinging out its shining droplets of spray, but this was a lethal spray that scythed down two girl students who were passing the windows at that moment.

Immediately after the flash of the explosion the blast swept across the terrace, a draught of violence that shook the red-bud trees and sent David and Debra reeling against the pillars of the library veranda. The air was driven in upon them so that their eardrums ached with the blow, and the breath was sucked from their lungs.

David caught her to him and held her for the moments of dreadful silence that followed the blast. As they stared so, a soft white fog of phosphorus smoke billowed from the gutted windows of the restaurant and began to roll and drift across the terrace.

Then the sounds reached them through their ringing eardrums, the small tinkle and crunch of glass, the patter and crack of falling plaster and shattered furniture. A woman began to scream, and it broke the spell of horror.

There were shouts and running feet. One of the students near them began in a high hysterical voice, 'A bomb. They've bombed the cafe.'

One of the girls who had fallen under the storm of glass fragments staggered up and began running in small aimless circles, screaming in a thin passionless tone. She was white with plaster dust through which the blood poured in dark rivulets, drenching her skirt.

In David's arms Debra began to tremble. 'The swine,' she whispered, 'oh, the filthy murdering swine.'

From the smoking destruction of the shattered building another figure shambled with slow deliberation. The blast had torn his clothing from his body, and it hung from him in tatters, making him a strange scarecrow figure. He reached the terrace and sat down slowly, removed from his face the spectacles that were miraculously still in place and began fumbling to clean them on the rags of his shirt. Blood dripped from his chin.

'Come on,' grated David, 'we must help.' And they ran down the steps together.

The explosion had brought down part of the roof, trapping and crushing twenty-three of the students who had come here to eat and talk over the evening meal.

Others had been hurled about the large low hall, like the toys of a child in tantrum, and their blood turned the interior into a reeking charnel house. Some of them were crawling, creeping, or moving spasmodically amongst the tumbled furniture, broken crockery and spilled food. Some lay contorted as though in silent laughter at death's crude joke.

Afterwards they would learn that two young female members of El Fatah had enrolled in the university under false papers, and they had daily smuggled small quantities of explosive on to the campus until they had accumulated sufficient for this outrage. A suitcase with a timing device had been left under a table and two terrorists had walked out and got clean away. A week later they were on Damascus television, gloating over their success.

Now, however, there was no reason nor explanation for this sudden burst of violence. It was as undirected, and yet as dreadfully effective as some natural cataclysm. Chilling in its insensate enormity, so that they, the living, worked in a kind of terrified frenzy, to save the injured and to carry from the shambles the broken bodies of the dead.

They laid them upon the lawns beneath the red-bud trees and covered them with sheets brought hurriedly from the nearest hostel. The long white bundles in a neat row upon the green grass was a memory David knew he would have for ever.

The ambulances came, with their sirens pulsing and roof-lights flashing, to carry away death's harvest and the police cordoned off the site of the blast before David and Debra left and walked slowly down to where the Mercedes was parked in the lot. Both of them were filthy with dust and blood, and wearied with the sights and sounds of pain and mutilation. They drove in silence to Malik Street and showered off the smell and the dirt. Debra soaked David's uniform in cold water to remove the blood. Then she made coffee for them and they drank it, sitting side by side in the brass bed.

'So much that was good and strong died there tonight,' Debra said.

'Death is not the worst of it. Death is natural, it's the logical conclusion to all things. It was the torn and broken flesh that still lived which appalled me. Death has a sort of dignity, but the maimed are obscene.'

She looked at him with almost fear in her eyes. 'That's cruel, David.'

'In Africa there is a beautiful and fierce animal called the sable antelope. They run together in herds of up to a hundred, but when one of them is hurt–wounded by a hunter or mauled by a lion–the lead bulls turn upon him and drive him from the herd. I remember my father telling me about that, he would say that if you want to be a winner then you must avoid the company of the losers for their despair is contagious.'

'God, David, that's a terribly hard way to look at life.'

'Perhaps,' David agreed, 'but then, you see, life *is* hard.'

When they made love, there was for the first time a quality of desperation in it, for it was the eve of parting and they had been reminded of their mortality.

In the morning David went to join his squadron and Debra locked the house on Malik Street.

Each day for seventeen days David flew two, and sometimes three, sorties. In the evenings, if they were not flying night interceptions, there were lectures and training films, and after that not much desire for anything but a quick meal and then sleep.

The Colonel, le Dauphin, had flown one sortie with David. He was a small man with a relaxed manner and quick, shrewd eyes. He had made his judgement quickly.

After that first day, David and Joe flew together, and David moved his gear into the locker across from Joe in the underground quarters that the crews on standby used.

In those seventeen days the last links in an iron friendship were forged. David's flare and dash balanced perfectly with Joe's rock-solid dependability.

David would always be the star while Joe seemed destined to be the accompanist, the straight guy who was a perfect foil, the wingman without personal ambition for glory whose talent was to put his number one into the position for the strike.

Quickly they developed into a truly formidable team, so perfectly in accord that communication in the air was almost extra-sensory, similar to the instantaneous reaction of the bird flock or the shoal of fish.

Joe sitting out there behind him was for David like a million dollars in insurance. His tail was secure and he could concentrate on the special task that his superior eyesight and lightning reactions were so suited to. David was the gunfighter, in a service where the gunfighter was supreme.

The I.A.F. had been the first to appreciate the shortcomings of the air-to-air missile, and to revert to the classic type of air combat. A missile could be induced to 'run stupid'. It was possible to make its computer think in a set pattern and then sucker it with a break in the pattern. For every three hundred missile launches in air-to-air combat, a single strike could be expected.

However, if you had a gunfighter coming up into your six o'clock position with his finger on the trigger of twin 30-mm. cannons, capable of pouring twelve thousand shells a minute into you, then your chances were considerably lighter than three hundred to one.

Joe also had his own special talent. The forward scanning radar of the Mirage was a complicated and sophisticated body of electronics, that required firstly a high degree of manual dexterity. The mechanism was operated entirely by the left hand, and the fingers of that hand had to move like those of a concert pianist. However, more important was the 'feel' for the instrument, a lover's touch to draw the optimum results from it. Joe had the 'feel', David did not.

They flew training interceptions, day and night, against high-flying and low-altitude practice targets. They flew low-level training strikes, and at other times they went out high over the Mediterranean and engaged each other in plane-to-plane dog-fights.

However, Desert Flower steered them tactfully away from any actual or potential combat situation. They were watching David.

At the end of the period, David's service dossier passed over Major-General Mordecai's desk. Personnel was the Brig's special responsibility and although each officer's dossier was reviewed by him regularly, he had asked particularly to see David's.

The dossier was still slim, compared to the bulky tomes of some of the old salts and the Brig flicked quickly over his own initial recommendation and the documents of David's acting commission. Then he stopped to read the later reports and results. He grinned wolfishly as he saw the gunnery report. He could pick them out of a crowd, he thought with satisfaction.

At last he came to le Dauphin's personal appraisal:

'Morgan is a pilot of exceptional ability. Recommended that acting rank be confirmed and that he be placed on fully operational basis forthwith.'

The Brig picked up the red pen that was his own special prerogative and scrawled 'I agree' at the foot of the report.

That took care of Morgan, the pilot. He could now consider Morgan, the man. His expression became bleak and severe. Debra's sudden desire to leave home almost immediately David arrived in Jerusalem had been too much of a coincidence for a man who was trained to search for underlying motives and meanings.

It had taken him two days and a few phone calls to learn that Debra was merely using the hostel room at the University as an accommodation address, and that her real domestic arrangements were more comfortable.

The Brig did not approve, very definitely not. Yet he knew that it was beyond his jurisdiction. He had learned that his daughter had inherited his own iron will. Confrontations between them were cataclysmic events, that shook the family to its foundations and seldom ended in satisfactory results.

Although he spent much of his time with young people, still he found the new values hard to live with—let alone accept. He remembered the physical agony of his long and chaste engagement to Ruth with pride, like a veteran reviewing an old campaign.

'Well, at the least she has the sense not to flout it, not to bring shame on us all. She has spared her mother that.' The Brig closed the dossier firmly.

Le Dauphin called David into his office and told him of his change in status. He would go on regular 'green' standby, which meant four nights a week on base.

David would now have to undergo his paratrooper training in unarmed combat and weapons. A downed pilot in Arab territory had a much better chance of survival if he was proficient in this type of fighting.

David went straight from le Dauphin's office to the telephone in the crewroom. He caught Debra before she left the Lauterman Building for lunch.

'Warm the bed, wench,' he told her, 'I'll be home tomorrow night.'

He and Joe drove up to Jerusalem in the Mercedes, and he wasn't listening to Joe's low rumbling voice until a thumb like an oar prodded his ribs.

'Sorry, Joe, I was thinking.'

'Well, stop it. Your thoughts are misting up the windows.'

'What did you say?'

'I was talking about the wedding—Hannah and me.'

David realized it was only a month away now, and he expected the excitement amongst the women was heavy as static on a summer's day before the rain. Debra's letters had been filled with news of the arrangements.

'I would be happy if you will stand up with me, and be my witness. You fly as wingman for a change, and I'll take on the target.'

David realized that he was being honoured by the request and he accepted with proper solemnity. Secretly he was amused. Like most young Israelis David had spoken to, both Debra and Joe claimed not to be religious. He had learned that this was a pose. All of them were very conscious of their religious heritage, and well versed in the history and practice of Judaism. They followed all the laws of living that were not oppressive, and which accorded with a modern and busy existence.

To them 'religious' meant dressing in the black robes and wide-brimmed hats of the ultra-orthodox Mea Shearim, or in following a routine for daily living that was crippling in its restrictions.

The wedding would be a traditional affair, complete with all the ceremony and the rich symbolism, complicated only by the security precautions which would have to be most rigorously enforced.

The ceremony was to take place in the Brig's garden, for Hannah was an orphan. Also the secluded garden and fortress-like walls about it, were easier to protect.

Amongst the guests would be many prominent figures in the government and the military.

'At the last count we have five generals and eighteen colonels on the list,' Joe told him, 'to which add most of the cabinet, even Golda has promised to try and be there. So you see, it's going to make a nice juicy target for our friends in Black September.' Joe scowled and lit two cigarettes, passing one to David. 'If it wasn't for Hannah, you know how women feel about weddings, I would just as soon go down to a registry office.'

'You are fooling nobody,' David grinned. 'You are looking forward to it.'

'Sure,' Joe's scowl cleared. 'It's going to be good to have our own place, like you and Debs. I wish Hannah had been sensible. A year of pretending,' he shook his head. 'Thank God it's nearly over.'

He dropped Joe in the lane outside the Brig's house in Ein Karem.

'I won't bother to invite you in,' Joe said. 'I guess you've got plans.'

'Good guess,' David smiled. 'Will we see you and Hannah? Come to dinner tomorrow night.'

Joe shook his head again. 'I'm taking Hannah down to Ashkelon to visit her parents' graves. It's traditional before a wedding. Perhaps we'll see you Saturday.'

'Right then, I'll try and make it. Debra will want to see you. *Shalom*, Joe,'

'*Shalom, shalom*,' said Joe and David pulled away, flicking the gears in a racing change as he put the Mercedes at the hill. Suddenly he was in a hurry.

The terrace door stood open in welcome, and she was waiting for him. Debra was vibrant and tense with expectation, sitting in one of the new leather chairs with her legs curled under her. Her hair was freshly washed and shimmering like a starling's wing. She was dressed in a billowing kaftan of light silk and subtle honey colours that picked out the gold in her eyes.

She came out of the chair in a swirl of silk, and ran bare-footed across the rugs to meet him.

'David! David!' she cried and he caught her up and spun on his heels, laughing with her.

Afterwards she led him proudly about the rooms and showed him the changes and additions that had turned it into a real home during his absence. David had convinced her that cost was not fundamental and they had chosen the designs for the furniture together. These had been made and delivered by Debra's tame Arab and she had arranged them as they had planned it. It was all in soft leather and dark wood, lustrous copper and brass, set off by the bright rugs. However, there was one article he had never seen before—a large oil-painting on canvas, and Debra had hung it unframed on the freshly painted white wall facing the terrace. It was the only decoration upon the wall, and any other would have been insignificant beside it. It was a harsh dominant landscape, a desert scene which captured the soul of the wilderness; the colours were hot and fierce and seemed to pour through the room like the rays of the desert sun itself.

Debra held his hand and watched David's face anxiously for a reaction as he studied it.

'Wow!' he said at last.

'You like it?' She was relieved.

'It's terrific. Where did you get it?'

'A gift from the artist. She's an old friend.'

'She?'

'That's right. We are driving up to Tiberias tomorrow to have lunch with her. I've told her all about you, and she wants to meet you.'

'What's she like?'

'She's one of our leading artists, and her name is Ella Kadesh, but apart from that I can't begin to describe her. All I can do is promise you an entertaining day.'

Debra had prepared a special dish of lamb and olives and they ate it on the terrace under the olive tree. Again the talk turned to Joe's wedding, and in the midst of it David asked abruptly, 'What made you decide to come with me—without marrying?'

She replied after a moment. 'I discovered that I loved you, and I knew that you were too impatient to play the waiting game. I knew that if I didn't, I might lose you again.'

'Until recently, I didn't realize what a big decision it was,' he mused, and she sipped her wine without replying.

'Let's get married, Debs,' he broke the silence.

'Yes,' she nodded. 'That's a splendid idea.'

'Soon,' he said. 'Soon as possible.'

'Not before Hannah. I don't want to steal her day from her.'

'Right,' David agreed, 'but immediately afterwards.'

'Morgan, you have got yourself a date,' she told him.

It was a three-hour drive to Tiberias so they rose as soon as the sun came through the shutters and tiger-striped the wall above the brass bed. To save time, they shared one bath, sitting facing each other, waist-deep in suds.

'Ella is the rudest person you'll ever meet,' Debra warned him. She looked like a little girl this morning with her hair piled on top of her head and secured with a pink ribbon. 'The greater the impression you make on her, the ruder she will be, and you are expected to retaliate in kind. So please, David, don't lose your temper.'

David scooped up a dab of suds with a finger and smeared it on the tip of her nose.

'I promise,' he said.

They drove down to Jericho, and then turned north along the valley of the Jordan, following the high barbed-wire fence of the border with its warning notice boards for the minefields, and the regular motorized patrols grinding deliberately along the winding road.

It was hot in the valley and they drove with the windows open and Debra pulled her skirts high around her waist to cool her long brown legs.

'Better not do that if you want to be in time for lunch,' David warned her, and she smoothed them down hurriedly.

'Nothing is safe with you around,' she protested.

They came at last out of the barren land into the fertile basin of the Kibbutzim below Galilee, and again the smell of orange blossom was so strong on the warm air that it was difficult to breathe.

At last they saw the waters of the lake flashing amongst the date palms and Debra touched his arm.

'Slow down, Davey. Ella's place is a few miles this side of Tiberias. That's the turn-off, up ahead.'

It was a track that led down to the lake shore and it ended against a wall of ancient stone blocks. Five other cars were parked there already.

'Ella's having one of her lunch parties,' Debra remarked and led him to a gate in the wall. Beyond was a small ruined castle. The tumbled walls formed weird shapes and the stone was black with age; over them grew flamboyant creepers of bougainvillaea and the tall palms clattered their fronds in the light breeze that came off the lake. Other exotic flowering shrubs grew upon the green lawns.

Part of the ruins had been restored and renovated into a picturesque and unusual lakeside home, with a wide patio and a stone jetty against which a motor-boat was moored. Across the green waters of the lake rose the dark smooth whale-back of the Golan Heights.

'It was a crusader fortress,' Debra explained. 'One of the guard posts for traffic across the lake and part of the series leading up to the great castle on the Horns of Hittem that the Moslems destroyed when they drove the crusaders out of the Holy Land. Ella's grandfather purchased it during the Allenby administration, but it was a ruin until she did it up after the war of independence.'

The care with which the alterations had been made so as not to spoil the romantic beauty of the site was a tribute to Ella Kadesh's artistic vision, which was completely at odds with the woman herself.

She was enormous; not simply fat or tall, but big. Her hands and feet were huge, her fingers clustered with rings and semi-precious stones and her toenails through the open sandals were painted a glaring crimson, as if to flaunt their size. She stood as tall as David, but the tent-like dress that billowed about her was covered with great explosive designs that enhanced her bulk until she seemed to make up for two of him. She wore a wig of tiered curls, flaming red in colour and dangling earrings. It seemed she must have applied her eye make-up with a spade, and her rouge with a spray gun. She removed the thin black cheroot from her mouth and kissed Debra before she turned to study David. Her voice was gravelly, hoarse with cheroot smoke and brandy.

'I had not expected you to be so beautiful,' she said, and Debra quailed at the expression in David's eyes. 'I do not like beauty. It is so often deceptive, or inconsequential. It usually hides something deadly–like the glittering beauty of the cobra–or like the pretty wrapper of a candy bar, it contains cloying sweetness and a soft centre.' She shook the stiffly lacquered curls of her wig, and fixed David with her shrewd little eyes. 'No, I prefer ugliness to beauty.'

David smiled at her with all his charm upon display. 'Yes,' he agreed, 'having met you, and seen some of your work, I can understand that.'

She let out a cackle of raucous laughter, and clapped the cheroot back in her mouth. 'Well now, at the very least we are not dealing with a chocolate soldier.' She placed a huge masculine arm about David's shoulders and led him to meet the company.

They were a mixed dozen, all intellectuals–artists, writers, teachers, journalists–and David was content to sit beside Debra in the mild sunshine and enjoy the beer and the amusing conversation. However, Ella would not let him relax for long and when they sat down to the gargantuan *alfresco* meal of cold fish and poultry, she attacked him again.

'Your martial airs and affectations, your pomp and finery. A plague on it I say, a pox on your patriotism, and courage–on your fearlessness and your orders of chivalry. It is all sham and pretence, an excuse for you to stink up the earth with piles of carrion.'

'I wonder if you will feel the same when a platoon of Syrian infantry break in here to rape you,' David challenged her.

'My boy, I find it difficult to get laid these days that I should pray for such a heaven-sent opportunity.' She let out a mighty hoot of laughter and her wig slipped forward at an abandoned angle. Nothing was safe from her, and she pushed the wig back into place and streamed straight into the attack again.

'Your male bombast, your selfish arrogance. To you this woman–' and she indicated Debra with a turkey leg, '–to you she is merely a receptacle of your seething careless sperm. It matters not to you that she is a promise for the future, that within her are the seeds of a great writing talent. No, to you she is a rubbing block, a convenient means to a–'

Debra interrupted her. 'That definitely is enough, I will not allow a public debate on my bedroom,' and Ella turned towards her with the battle lust lighting her eyes.

'Your gift is not yours to use as you wish. You hold it in trust for all mankind, and you have a duty to them. That duty is to exercise your gift, to allow it to grow and blossom and give forth fruit.' She used the turkey leg like a judge's gavel, banging the edge of her plate with it, to silence Debra's protests.

'Have you written a word since you took young Mars to your heart? What of the novel we discussed on this very terrace a year ago? Have your animal passions swamped all else? Has the screeching of your ovaries—'

'Stop it, Ella!' Debra was angry now, her cheeks flushed and her brown eyes snapping.

'Yes! Yes!' Ella tossed the bone aside and sucked her fingers noisily. 'Ashamed you should be, angry with yourself—'

'Damn you,' Debra flared at her.

'Damn me if you will—but you are damned yourself if you do not write! Write, woman, write!' She sat back and the wicker chair protested at the movement of her vast body. 'All right, now we will all go for a swim. David has not seen me in a bikini yet—much he will care for that skinny little wench when he does!'

They drove back to Jerusalem in the night, flushed with the sun, and although the Mercedes seats had not been designed for lovers, Debra managed to sit close up against him.

'She's right, you know,' David broke a long contented silence. 'You must write, Debs.'

'Oh, I will,' she answered lightly.

'When?' he persisted, and to distract him she snuggled a little closer.

'One of these days,' she whispered as she made her dark head comfortable on his shoulder.

'One of these days,' he mimicked her.

'Don't bug me, Morgan.' She was already half-asleep.

'Stop being evasive.' He stroked her hair with his free hand. 'And don't go to sleep while I'm talking to you.'

'David, my darling, we have a lifetime—and more,' she murmured. 'You have made me immortal. You and I shall live for a thousand years, and there will be time for everything.'

Perhaps the dark gods heard her boast, and they chuckled sardonically and nudged each other.

On Saturday Joe and Hannah came to the house on Malik Street, and after lunch they decided on a tourist excursion for David and the four of them climbed Mount Zion across the valley. They entered the labyrinth of corridors that led to David's tomb, covered with splendid embroidered cloth and silver crowns and Torah covers. From there it was a few steps to the room of Christ's last supper in the same building, so closely interwoven were the traditions of Judaism and Christianity in this citadel.

Afterwards they entered the old city through the Zion gate and followed the wall around to the centre of Judaism, the tall cliff of massive stone blocks, bevelled in the fashion of Herodian times, which was all that remained of the fabulous second temple of Herod, destroyed two thousand years before by the Romans.

They were searched at the gate and then joined the stream of worshippers flocking down towards the wall. At the barrier they stood for a long time in silence. David felt again the stirring of a deep race memory, a hollow feeling of the soul which longed to be filled.

The men prayed facing the wall, many of them in the long black coats of the

Orthodox Jew with the ringlets dangling against their cheeks as they rocked and swayed in religious ecstasy. Within the enclosure on the right-hand side, the women seemed more reserved in their devotions.

Joe spoke at last, a little embarrassed and in a gruff tone. 'I think I'll just go say a *sh'ma.*'

'Yes,' Hannah agreed. 'Are you coming with me, Debra?'

'A moment.' Debra turned to David, and took something from her handbag. 'I made it for you for the wedding,' she said. 'But wear it now.'

It was a *yamulka*, an embroidered prayer cap of black satin.

'Go with Joe,' she said. 'He will show you what to do.'

The girls moved off to the women's enclosure and David placed the cap upon his head and followed Joe down to the wall.

A *shamash* came to them, an old man with a long silver beard, and he helped David bind upon his right arm a tiny leather box containing a portion of the Torah.

'So you shall lay these words upon your heart and your soul, and you shall bind them upon your right arm—'

Then he spread a *tallit* across David's shoulders, a tasselled shawl of woven wool, and he led him to the wall, and he began to repeat after the *shamash*:

'Hear, O Israel, the Lord our God, the Lord is one—'

His voice grew surer as he remembered the words from long ago, and he looked up at the wall of massive stone blocks that towered high above him. Thousands of previous worshippers had written down their prayers on scraps of paper and wedged them into the joints between the blocks, and around him rose the plaintive voices of spoken prayer. It seemed to David that in his imagination a golden beam of prayer rose from this holy place towards the heavens.

Afterwards they left the enclosure and climbed the stairs into the Jewish quarter, and the good feeling remained with David, glowing warmly in his belly.

That evening they sat together on the terrace drinking Goldstar beer and splitting sunflower seeds for the nutty kernels, and naturally the talk turned to God and religion.

Joe said, 'I'm an Israeli and then a Jew. First my country, and a long way behind that comes my religion.'

But David remembered the expression on his face as he prayed against the wailing wall.

The talk lasted until late, and David glimpsed the vast body of his religious heritage.

'I would like to learn a little more about it all,' he admitted, and Debra said nothing but when she packed for him to go on base that night she placed a copy of Herman Wouk's *This is my God* on top of his clean uniforms.

He read it and when next he returned to Malik Street, he asked for more. She picked them for him, English works at first but then Hebrew, as his grip upon the language became stronger. They were not religious works only, but histories and historical novels that excited his interest on this ancient centre of civilization which for three thousand years had been a crossroads and a battle ground.

He read anything and everything that she put into his case, from Josephus Flavius to Leon Uris.

This led to a desire to see and inspect the ground. It became so that much of the time they were free together was spent in these explorations. They began with the hill-top fortress of Herod at Masada where the zealots had killed each other rather than submit to Rome, and from there they moved off the tourist beat to the lesser-known historical sites.

In those long sunlit days they might eat their basket lunch sitting on the ruins of a Roman aqueduct and watching a falcon working the thermals that rose off the floor of the desert, after they had searched the bed of a dry wadi for coins and arrowheads brought down by the last ruins.

Around them rose the tall cliffs of orange and golden stone, and the light was so clean and stark that it seemed they could see for ever, and the silence so vast that they were the only living things in the world.

They were the happiest days that David had ever known, and they gave point and meaning to the weary hours of squadron standby, and when the day had ended there was always the house on Malik Street with its warmth and laughter and love.

Joe and David arranged leave of absence from the base for the wedding. It was a time of quiet, and le Dauphin let them go without protest, for he would be a guest.

They drove up to Jerusalem the day before and were immediately conscripted to assist with arrangements. David laboured mightily as a taxi-driver and trucker. The Mercedes transported everything from flowers to musical instruments and distant relatives.

The Brig's garden was decorated with palm leaves and coloured bunting. In the centre stood the *huppah*, a canopy worked with religious symbols in blue and gold, the Star of David and the grapes and ears of wheat, the pomegranates and all the other symbols of fertility. Beneath it, the marriage ceremony would take place. Trestle tables covered with gay cloths set with bowls of flowers and dishes of fruit were arranged beneath the olive trees. There were places for three hundred guests, an open space for the dancing, a raised timber stand hung with flags for the band.

The catering was contracted out to a professional firm and the menu had been carefully decided upon by the chef and the women. It would have two high points—an enormous stuffed tuna, again a symbol of fertility, and a lamb dish in the bedouin style served upon enormous copper salvers.

On the Sunday of the wedding, David drove Debra to the home of the chief surgeon of Hadassah Hospital. Hannah was one of his theatre sisters and he had insisted that she use his home to prepare for the wedding. Debra was to assist her, and David left them and drove on to Ein Karem. The lane leading to the house was cordoned off and thick with secret service men and paratroopers.

While he watched Joe dressing, losing and finding the ring, and sweating with nerves, David lay on Joe's bed and gave him bad advice. They could hear the guests gathering on the garden below, and David stood up and went to the window. He watched an airforce colonel being carefully scrutinized and searched at the gates, but taking it all in good part.

'They are being pretty thorough,' David remarked.

'Hannah has asked to have as few as possible of the guards in the garden. So they are being damned careful about who they let in.' Joe had at last completed dressing and already he was beginning to sweat through the armpits of his uniform.

'How do I look?' he asked anxiously.

'God, you handsome beast,' David told him.

'Piss off, Morgan,' Joe grinned at him, crammed his cap on to his head and glanced at his watch. 'Let's go,' he said.

The Chief Rabbi of the army was waiting with the Brig and the others in the Brig's study. The Rabbi was the mild-mannered man who had personally liberated the Tomb of the Patriarchs in the war of '67. During the advance on Hebron, he had driven a jeep through the disintegrating Arab lines, shot open the door to the tomb with a submachine-gun and chased the Arab guards screaming over the rear wall.

Joe sat at the Brig's desk and signed the *ketubbah*, the marriage contract, then the Rabbi handed him a silken cloth which Joe lifted in a formal act of acquisition to a chorus of congratulatory *'Mazal tovs'* from the witnesses.

The bridegroom's party trooped out into the crowded garden now to await the arrival of the bride, and she came accompanied by the chief surgeon standing in for her dead father, and a party of festively dressed women, including Debra and her mother. They all carried lighted candles.

To David, Hannah had never been particularly attractive, she was too tall and severe in body and expression; however, in her white bridal dress and veil she was transformed.

She seemed to float cloudlike upon the billowing white skirts, and her face was softened by the veil and by the inner happiness that seemed to glow through her green eyes. Red-gold hair framed her cheeks, and the freckles were disguised under make-up applied by Debra's cunning hand. She had used it to mute the rather harsh lines of Hannah's bony nose, and the result was as near to beautiful as she would ever come.

Joe, looking big and handsome in his airforce tans, went forward eagerly to meet her at the gate to the garden and to lower the veil over her face in the ceremony of *bedeken dikalle*.

Joe moved to the *chuppah* canopy where the Rabbi waited with a *tallit* over his shoulders. After Joe the women led Hannah, each of them still carrying a burning candle, and the Rabbi chanted a blessing as the women and the bride circled Joe seven times in a magical circle which in olden times would serve to ward off evil spirits. At last bride and groom stood side by side, facing towards the site of the Temple with the guests and witnesses pressed closely about them and the ceremony proper began.

The Rabbi spoke the benediction over a goblet of wine from which bride and groom both drank. Then Joe turned to Hannah, her face still veiled, and he placed the plain gold ring upon her right forefinger.

'Behold you are consecrated unto me by this ring, according to the law of Moses and Israel.'

Then Joe broke the glass under his heel and the sharp crunch was a signal for an outburst of music and song and gaiety. David left Joe's side and worked his way through the joyous crowd of guests to where Debra waited for him.

She wore a gown of yellow and she had fresh flowers in the dark sheen of her hair. David smelled their perfume as he hugged her surreptitiously about the waist and whispered in her ear, 'You next, my beauty!' and she whispered back, 'Yes, please!'

Joe took Hannah on his arm, and they went to the improvised dance floor. The band began with a light bouncy tune and all the younger ones flocked to join them – while the elders spread out at the tables beneath the palm-decked trellis.

Yet amongst all the laughter and the gaiety, the uniforms added a sombre touch; almost every second man was adorned with the trappings of war, and at the golden gate and the entrance to the kitchens were uniformed paratrooper guards each with a Uzzi submachine-gun slung at his shoulder. It was easy to pick out the secret service men. They were the ones in civilian clothes who moved without smiling, alert and vigilant, amongst the guests.

David and Debra danced together, and she was so light and warm and strong in his arms that when the band paused for breath he resented it. He led her to a quiet corner, and they stood together, discussing the other guests in the most disrespectful terms until Debra giggled at some particularly outrageous remark and struck his arm lightly.

'You are terrible.' She leaned against him. 'I'm dying of thirst, won't you get me something to drink?'

'A glass of cold white wine?' he suggested.

'Lovely,' she said, smiling up into his face. For a moment they studied each other, and suddenly David felt something dark welling up from within him, a terrible despair, a premonition of impending loss. It was a physical thing and he could feel the chill of it enclose his chest and squeeze out all the happiness and the joy.

'What is it, David?' Her own expression altered in sympathy with his, and she tightened her grip on his arm.

'Nothing.' Abruptly he pulled away from her, trying to fight off the feeling. 'It's nothing,' he repeated, but it was still strong in his belly, and he felt a wave of nausea from it. 'I'll get you the wine,' he said and turned away.

He made his way towards the bar, pushing gently through the throng. The Brig caught his eye and smiled bleakly across the garden at him. Joe was with his father and he called to David, laughing, with one arm around his bride. Hannah had her veil pushed up and her freckles were beginning to emerge from under the make-up, glowing vividly against the snow-white lace. David waved at them but went towards the open-air bar at the end of the garden, the mood of sadness was still on him and he didn't want to talk to Joe now.

So he was cut off from Debra at the moment when, with a flourish, a procession of white-jacketed waiters came in through the iron gate of the garden. Each of them carried a huge copper salver from which, even in the warm sun, rose tendrils of steam, and the odour of meat and fish and spices filled the garden. There were gasps and cries of appreciation from the guests.

A way opened for them towards the high table on the raised terrace which led to the kitchen doors and the house.

The procession of waiters passed close to David, and suddenly his attention was drawn from the display of fine food to the face of the second waiter in line. He was a man of medium height and dark complexion, a mahogany face with a thickly drooping moustache.

He was sweating. That was what had drawn David's attention, his face was shiny with sweat. Droplets clung in his moustache and slid down his cheeks. The white jacket was sodden at the armpits as he lifted the gigantic platter on high.

At the moment that he drew level with David their eyes met for an instant. David realized that the man was in the grip of some deep emotion—fear, perhaps, or exhilaration. Then the waiter seemed to become aware of David's scrutiny and his eyes slid nervously away.

David felt suspicion begin to chill his arms as the three figures climbed the stone stairs, and filed behind the table.

The waiter glanced again at David, saw that his gaze was still locked upon his face, and then he said something out of the corner of his mouth to one of his companions. He also glanced at David, and caught his stare, and his expression was sufficient to send alarm flaring urgently through David's chest and brain. Something was happening, something dangerous and ugly, he was certain of it.

Wildly he looked about for the guards. There were two of them on the terrace behind the line of waiters, and one near David beside the gate.

David shoved his way desperately towards him, mindless of the outraged comments of those in his way. He was watching the three waiters and so he saw it begin to happen.

It had obviously been carefully rehearsed for as the three waiters placed the salvers upon the table to the laughter and applause of the guests crowded in the garden below them, so they drew the sheets of plastic on which a thin display of food had been arranged to cover the deadly load that each copper salver carried.

The brown-faced waiter lifted a machine pistol from under the plastic sheet, and turned swiftly to fire a traversing burst into the two paratroopers behind him at point-blank range. The clattering thunder of automatic fire was deafening in the walled garden, and the stream of bullets slashed through the bellies of the two guards like a monstrous cleaver, almost cutting them in half.

The waiter on David's left was a wizened monkey-faced man, with bright black berries for eyes. He, too, lifted a machine pistol from his salver, and he crouched over it and fired a burst at the paratrooper by the gate.

They were going for the guards, taking them first. The pistol shook and roared in his fists, and the bullets socked into human flesh with a rubbery thumping sound.

The guard had cleared his Uzzi, and was trying to aim as a bullet hit him in the mouth and snapped his head back, his paratrooper beret spinning high into the air. The machine-gun flew from his arms as he fell, and it slid across the tiles towards David. David dropped flat below the stone steps of the terrace as the Arab gunner turned their pistols on the wedding crowd, hosing the courtyard with a triple stream of bullets, and unleashing a hurricane of screams and shouts and desperate cries to join the roar of the guns.

Across the yard, a security agent had the pistol out of his shoulder holster and he dropped into the marksman crouch, holding the pistol with both arms extended as he aimed. He fired twice and hit the monkey-faced gunman, sending him reeling back against the wall, but he stayed on his feet and returned the agent's fire with the machine pistol, knocking him down and rolling him across the paving stones.

The yard was filled with a panic-stricken mob, a struggling mass of humanity, that screamed and fell and crawled and died beneath the flail of the guns.

Two bullets caught Hannah in the chest, smashing her backwards over a table of glasses and bottles that shattered about her. The bright blood spurted from the wounds, drenching the front of her white wedding gown.

The centre gunman dropped his pistol as it emptied, and he stooped quickly over the copper salver and came up with a grenade in each hand. He hurled them into the struggling, screaming throng and the double blast was devastating, twin bursts of brightest white flame and the terrible sweep of shrapnel. The screams of the women rose louder, seeming as deafening as the gunfire—and the gunman stooped once more and his hands held another load of grenades.

All this had taken only seconds, but a fleeting moment of time to turn festivity into shocking carnage and torn flesh.

David left the shelter of the stone steps. He rolled swiftly across the flags towards the abandoned Uzzi, and he came up on his knees, holding it at the hip. His paratrooper training made his actions automatic.

The wounded gunman saw him, and turned towards him, staggering slightly, pushing himself weakly away from the wall. His one arm was shattered and hung loosely in the tattered, blood-soaked sleeve of his jacket, but he lifted the machine pistol and aimed at David.

David fired first, the bullets struck bursts of plaster from the wall behind the Arab and David corrected his aim. The bullets drove the gunman backwards, pinning him to the wall, while his body jumped and shook and twitched. He slumped down leaving a glistening wet smear of blood down the white plaster.

David swivelled the gun on to the Arab beside the kitchen door. He was poised to throw his next grenade, right arm extended behind him, both fists filled with the deadly steel balls. He was shouting something, a challenge or a war cry, a harsh triumphant screech that carried clearly above the screams of his victims.

Before he could release the grenade, David hit him with a full burst, a dozen bullets that smashed into his chest and belly, and the Arab dropped both grenades at his feet and doubled over clutching at his broken body, trying to stem the flood of his blood with his bare hands.

The grenades were short fused and they exploded almost immediately, engulfing the dying man in a net of fire and shredding his body from the waist down. The same explosion knocked down the third assassin at the end of the terrace, and David came to his feet and charged up the steps.

The third and last Arab was mortally wounded, his head and chest torn by grenade fragments, but he was still alive, thrashing about weakly as he groped for the machine pistol that lay beside him in a puddle of his own blood.

David was consumed by a terrible rage. He found that he was screaming and raging like a maniac, and he crouched at the head of the stairs and aimed at the dying Arab.

The Arab had the machine pistol and was lifting it with the grim concentration of a drunken man. David fired, a single shot that slapped into the Arab's body without apparent effect, and then suddenly the Uzzi in David's hands was empty, the pin falling with a hollow click on an empty chamber.

Across the terrace, beyond range of a quick rush, the Arab's face was streaked with sweat and blood as he frowned heavily, trying to aim the machine pistol as it wavered. He was dying swiftly, the flame fluttering towards extinction, but he was using the last of his strength.

David stood frozen with the empty weapon in his hand, and the blank eye of the pistol sought him out, and fastened upon him. He watched the Arab's eyes narrow, and his sudden murderous grin of achievement as he saw David in his sights, and his finger tightening on the trigger.

At that range the bullets would hit like the solid stream of a fire hose. He began to move, to throw himself down the stairs, but he knew it was too late. The Arab was at the instant of firing, and at the same instant a revolver shot crashed out at David's side.

Half the Arab's head was cut away by the heavy lead slug, and he was flung backwards with the yellow custard contents of his skull splattering the white-washed wall behind him, and his death grip on the trigger emptied the machine pistol with a shattering roar harmlessly into the grape vines above him.

Dazedly David turned to find the Brig beside him, the dead security guard's pistol in his fist. For a moment they stared at each other, and then the Brig stepped past him and walked to the fallen bodies of the other two Arabs. Standing over each in turn he fired a single pistol shot into their heads.

David turned away and let the Uzzi drop from his hands. He went down the stairs into the garden.

The dead and the wounded lay singly and in piles, pitiful fragments of humanity. The soft cries and the groans of the wounded, the bitter weeping of a child, the voice of a mother, were sounds more chilling than the screaming and the shouting.

The garden was drenched and painted with blood. There were splashes and gouts of it upon the white walls, there were puddles and snakes of it spreading and crawling across the paving, dark slicks of it sinking into the dust, ropes of it dribbling and pattering like rain from the body of a musician as he hung over the rail of the bandstand. The sickly sweetish reek of it mingled with the smell of spice food and spilled wine, with the floury taste of plaster dust and the bitter stench of burned explosive.

The veils of smoke and dust that still drifted across the garden could not hide the terrible carnage. The bark of the olive trees was torn in slabs from the trunks by flying steel, exposing the white wet wood. The wounded and dazed survivors crawled over a field of broken glass and shattered crockery. They swore and prayed, and whispered and groaned and called for succour.

David went down the steps, his feet moving without his bidding; his muscles were numb, his body senseless and only his finger-tips tingled with life.

Joe was standing below one of the torn olive trees. He stood like a colossus, with his thick powerful legs astride, his head thrown back and his face turned to the sky, but his eyes were tight-closed and his mouth formed a silent cry of agony—for he held Hannah's body in his arms.

Her bridal veil had fallen from her head, and the bright copper mane of her hair hung back—almost to the ground. Her legs and one arm hung loosely, also, slack and lifeless. The golden freckles stood out clearly on the milky-white skin of her face—and the bloody wounds bloomed like the petals of the poinsettia tree upon the bosom of her wedding-gown.

David averted his eyes. He could not watch Joe in his anguish, and he walked on slowly across the garden, in terrible dread of what he would find.

'Debra!' he tried to raise his voice, but it was a hoarse raven's croak. His feet slipped in a puddle of thick dark blood, and he stepped over the unconscious body of a woman who lay, face down, in a floral dress, with her arms thrown wide. He did not recognize her as Debra's mother.

'Debra!' He tried to hurry, but his legs would not respond. He saw her then, at the corner of the wall where he had left her.

'Debra!' He felt his heart soar. She seemed unhurt, kneeling below one of the marble Grecian statues, with the flowers in her hair and the yellow silk dress gay and festive.

She knelt, facing the wall, and her head was bowed as though in prayer. The dark wind of her hair hung forward screening her and she held her cupped hands to her face.

'Debra.' He dropped to his knees beside her, and timidly he touched her shoulder.

'Are you all right, my darling?' And she lowered her hands slowly, but still holding them cupped together. A great coldness closed around David's chest as he saw that her cupped hands were filled with blood. Rich red blood, bright as wine in a crystal glass.

'David,' she whispered, turning her face towards him. 'Is that you, darling?'

David gave a small breathless moan of agony as he saw her blood-glutted eye sockets, the dark gelatinous mess that congealed in the thick dark eyelashes and turned the lovely face into a gory mask.

'Is that you, David?' she asked again, her head cocked at a blind listening angle.

'Oh God, Debra.' He stared into her face.

'I can't see, David.' She groped for him. 'Oh David–I can't see.'

And he took her sticky wet hands in his, and he thought that his heart would break.

The stark modern silhouette of Hadassah Hospital stood upon the skyline above the village of Ein Karem. The speed with which the ambulances arrived saved many of the victims whose lives were critically balanced, and the hospital was geared to sudden influxes of war casualties.

The three men–the Brig, Joe and David–kept their vigil together all that night upon the hard wooden benches of the hospital waiting-room. When more was learned of the planning behind the attack, a security agent would come to whisper a report to the Brig.

One of the assassins was a long-term and trusted employee of the catering firm, and the other two were his 'cousins' who had been employed as temporary staff on his recommendation. It was certain that their papers were forged.

The Prime Minister and her cabinet had been delayed by an emergency session, but had been on their way to the wedding when the attack was made. A fortunate chance had saved them, and she sent her personal condolences to the relatives of the victims.

At ten o'clock, Damascus radio gave a report in which El Fatah claimed responsibility for the attack by members of a suicide squad.

A little before midnight, the chief surgeon came from the main theatre, still in his theatre greens and boots, with his mask pulled down to his throat. Ruth Mordecai was out of danger, he told the Brig. They had removed a bullet that had passed through her lung and lodged under her shoulder blade. They had saved the lung.

'Thank God,' murmured the Brig and closed his eyes for a moment, imagining life without his woman of twenty-five years. Then he looked up. 'My daughter?'

The surgeon shook his head. 'They are still working on her in the small casualty theatre.' He hesitated. 'Colonel Halman died in theatre a few minutes ago.'

The toll of the dead was eleven so far, with four others on the critical list.

In the early morning the undertakers arrived for the bodies with their long wicker baskets and black limousines. David gave Joe the keys of the Mercedes, that he might follow the hearse bearing Hannah's body and arrange the details of the funeral.

David and the Brig sat side by side, haggard and with sleepless bruised eyes, drinking coffee from paper cups.

In the late morning the eye surgeon came out to them. He was a smooth-faced, young-looking man in his forties, the greying of his hair seeming incongruous against the unlined skin and clear blue eyes.

'General Mordecai?'

The Brig rose stiffly. He seemed to have aged ten years during the night.

'I am Doctor Edelman. Will you come with me please?'

David rose to follow them, but the doctor paused and looked to the Brig.

'I am her fiancé,' said David.

'It might be best if we spoke alone first, General.' Edelman was clearly trying to pass a warning with his eyes, and the Brig nodded.

'Please, David.'

'But−' David began, and the Brig squeezed his shoulder briefly, the first gesture of affection that had ever passed between them.

'Please, my boy,' and David turned back to the hard bench.

In the tiny cubicle of his office Edelman hitched himself on to the corner of the desk and lit a cigarette. His hands were long and slim as a girl's, and he used the lighter with a surgeon's neat economical movements.

'You don't want it with a sugar coating, I imagine?' He had appraised the Brig carefully, and went on without waiting for a reply. 'Neither of your daughter's eyes are damaged,' but he held up a hand to forestall the rising expression of relief on the Brig's lips, and turned to the scanner on which hung a set of X-ray plates. He switched on the back light.

'The eyes were untouched, there is almost no damage to her facial features−however, the damage is here−' he touched a hard frosty outline in the smoky grey swirls and patterns of the X-ray plates, '−that is a steel fragment, a tiny steel fragment, almost certainly from a grenade. It is no larger than the tip of a lead pencil. It entered the skull through the outer edge of the right temple, severing the large vein which accounted for the profuse haemorrhage, and it travelled obliquely behind the eye-balls without touching them or any other vital tissue. Then, however, it pierced the bony surrounds of the optic chiasma,' he traced the path of the fragment through Debra's head, 'and it seems to have cut through the canal and severed the chiasma, before lodging in the bone sponge beyond.' Edelman drew heavily on the cigarette while he looked for a reaction from the Brig. There was none.

'Do you understand the implications of this, General?' he asked, and the Brig shook his head wearily. The surgeon switched off the light of the X-ray scanner, and returned to the desk. He pulled a scrap pad towards the Brig and took a propelling pencil from his top pocket. Boldly he sketched an optical chart, eyeballs, brain, and optical nerves, as seen from above.

'The optical nerves, one from each eye, run back into this narrow tunnel of bone where they fuse, and then branch again to opposite lobes of the brain.'

The Brig nodded, and Edelman slashed the point of his pencil through the point where the nerves fused. Understanding began to show on the Brig's strained and tired features.

'Blind?' he asked, and Edelman nodded.

'Both eyes?'

'I'm afraid so.'

The Brig bowed his head and gently massaged his own eyes with thumb and forefinger. He spoke again without looking at Edelman.

'Permanently?' he asked.

'She has no recognition of shape, or colour, of light or darkness. The track of the fragment is through the optic chiasma. All indications are that the nerve is severed. There is no technique known to medical science which will restore that.' Edelman paused to draw breath, before going on. 'In a word then, your daughter is permanently and totally blinded in both eyes.'

The Brig sighed, and looked up slowly. 'Have you told her?' and Edelman could not hold his gaze.

'I was rather hoping that you would do that?'

'Yes,' the Brig nodded, 'it would be best that way. Can I see her now? Is she awake?'

'She is under light sedation. No pain, only a small amount of discomfort, the external wound is insignificant—and we shall not attempt to remove the metal fragment. That would entail major neurosurgery.' He stood up and indicated to the door. 'Yes, you may see her now. I will take you to her.'

The corridor outside the row of emergency theatres was lined along each wall with stretchers, and the Brig recognized many of his guests laid out upon them. He stopped briefly to speak with one or two of them, before following Edelman to the recovery room at the end of the corridor.

Debra lay on the tall bed below the window. She was very pale, dry blood was still clotted in her hair and a thick cotton wool and bandage covered her eyes.

'Your father is here, Miss Mordecai,' Edelman told her, and she rolled her head swiftly towards them.

'Daddy?'

'I am here, my child.'

The Brig took the hand she held out, and stooped to kiss her. Her lips were cold, and she smelled strongly of disinfectant and anaesthetic.

'Mama?' she asked anxiously.

'She is out of danger,' the Brig assured her, 'but Hannah—'

'Yes. They told me,' Debra stopped him, her voice choking. 'Is Joe all right?'

'He is strong,' the Brig said. 'He will be all right.'

'David?' she asked.

'He is here.'

Eagerly she struggled up on to one elbow, her face lighting with expectation, the heavily bound eyes turned blindly seeking.

'David,' she called, 'where are you? Damn this bandage. Don't worry, David it's just to rest my eyes.'

'No,' the Brig restrained her with a hand on her arm. 'He is outside, waiting,' and she slumped with disappointment.

'Ask him to come to me, please,' she whispered.

'Yes,' said the Brig, 'in a while, but first there is something we must talk about—something I have to tell you.'

She must have guessed what it was, she must have been warned by the tone of his voice for she went very still. That peculiar stillness of hers, like a frightened animal of the veld.

He was a soldier, with a soldier's blunt ways, and although he tried to soften it, yet even his tone was roughened with his own sorrow, so that it came out brutally. Her hand in his was the only indication that she had heard him, it spasmed convulsively like a wounded thing and then lay still, a small tense hand in the circle of his big bony fist.

She asked no questions and when he had done they sat quietly together for a long time. He spoke first.

'I will send David to you now,' he said, and her response was swift and vehement.

'No.' She gripped his hand hard. 'No, I can't meet him now. I have to think about this first.'

The Brig went back to the waiting-room and David stood up expectantly, the pure lines of his face seemingly carved from pale polished marble, and the dark blue of his eyes in deep contrast.

The Brig forestalled him harshly. 'No visitors.' He took David's arm. 'You will not be allowed to see her until tomorrow.'

'Is something wrong? What is it?' David tried to pull away, but the Brig held him and steered him towards the door.

'Nothing is wrong. She will be all right—but she must have no excitement now. You'll be able to see her tomorrow.'

They buried Hannah that evening in the family plot on the Mountain of Olives. It was a small funeral party attended by the three men and a mere handful of relatives, many of who, had others to mourn from the previous day's slaughter.

There was an official car waiting to take the Brig to a meeting of the high command, where retaliatory measures would certainly be discussed, another revolution in the relentless wheel of violence that rolled across the troubled land.

Joe and David climbed into the Mercedes and sat silently, David making no effort to start the engine, Joe lit cigarettes for them, and they both felt drained of purpose and direction.

'What are you going to do now?' David asked him.

'We had two weeks,' Joe answered him. 'We were going down to Ashkelon—' his voice trailed off. 'I don't know. There isn't anything to do now, is there?'

'Shall we go and have a drink somewhere?'

Joe shook his head. 'I don't feel like drinking,' he said. 'I think I'll go back to the base. They are flying night interceptions tonight.'

'Yes,' David agreed quickly, 'I'll come with you.' He could not see Debra until tomorrow, and the house on Malik Street would be lonely and cold. Suddenly he longed for the peace of the night heavens.

The moon was a brightly curved Saracen blade against the soft darkness of the sky, and the stars were fat and silver and gemlike in their clarity.

They flew high above the earth, remote from its grief and sorrow, wrapped in the isolation of flight and lost in the ritual and concentration of night interception.

The target was a Mirage of their own squadron, and they picked it up on the scanner far out over the Negev. Joe locked on to it and called the track and range while David searched for and at last spotted the moving star of the target's jet blast, burning redly against the velvety blackness of the night.

He took them in on a clean interception creeping up under the target's belly and then pulling steeply up past its wing-tip, the way a barracuda goes for the lure from below and explodes out through the surface of the sea. They shot past so close that the target Mirage broke wildly away to port, unaware of their presence until that moment.

Joe slept that night, exhausted with grief, but David lay in the bunk beneath him and listened to him. In the dawn he rose and showered and left Joe still asleep. He drove into Jerusalem and reached the hospital just as the sun came up and lit the hills with its rays of soft gold and pearly pink.

The night sister at the desk was brusque and preoccupied. 'You shouldn't be here until visiting hours this afternoon,' but David smiled at her with all the charm he could muster.

'I just wanted to know if she was doing well. I have to rejoin my squadron this morning.'

The sister was not immune either to his smile or the airforce uniform, and she went to consult her lists.

'You must be mistaken,' she said at last. 'The only Mordecai we have is Mrs Ruth Mordecai.'

'That's her mother,' David told her, and the sister flipped the sheet on her clipboard.

'No wonder I couldn't find it,' she muttered irritably. 'She was discharged last night.'

'Discharged?' David stared at her uncomprehendingly.

'Yes, she went home last night. I remember her now. Her father came to fetch her just as I came on duty. Pretty girl with eye bandages–'

'Yes,' David nodded. 'Thank you. Thank you very much,' and he ran down the steps to the Mercedes, his feet light with relief, freed at last from the gnawing doubt and dread.

Debra had gone home. Debra was safe and well.

The Brig opened the door to him, and let him into the silent house. He was still in his uniform, and it was wilted and rumpled. The Brig's face was fine-drawn, the lines crudely chiselled around his mouth, and his eyes were swollen and bloodshot from worry and sorrow and lack of sleep.

'Where is Debra?' David demanded eagerly, and the Brig sighed and stood aside for him to enter.

'Where is she?' David repeated, and the Brig led him to his study and waved him to a chair.

'Why don't you answer me?' David was becoming angry, and the Brig slumped into a chair across the large bare room, with its severe monastic furnishings of books and archaeological relics.

'I couldn't tell you yesterday, David, she asked me not to. I'm sorry.'

'What is it?' David was fully alarmed now.

'She had to have time to think–to make up her mind.' The Brig stood up again and began to pace, his footsteps echoing hollowly on the bare wooden floor, pausing every now and then to touch one of the pieces of ancient statuary, caressing it absently as he talked, as though to draw comfort from it.

David listened quietly, occasionally shaking his head, as though to deny that what he was hearing was the truth.

'So you see it is permanent, final, without hope. She is blind, David, totally blind. She has gone into a dark world of her own where nobody else can follow her.'

'Where is she? I want to go to her,' David whispered, but the Brig ignored the request and went on steadily.

'She wanted time to make her decision–and I gave it to her. Last night, after the funeral, I went back to her and she was ready. She had faced it, come to terms with it, and she had decided how it must be.'

'I want to see her,' David repeated. 'I want to talk to her.'

Now the Brig looked at him and the bleakness in his eyes faded, his voice dropped, becoming gruff with compassion.

'No, David. That was her decision. You will not see her again. For you she is dead. Those were her words. Tell him I am dead, but he must only remember me when I was alive–'

David interrupted him, jumping to his feet. 'Where is she, damn you?' His voice was shaking. 'I want to see her now.' He crossed swiftly to the door and jerked it open, but the Brig went on.

'She is not here.'

'Where is she?' David turned back.

'I cannot tell you, I swore a solemn oath to her.'

'I'll find her–'

'You might, if you search carefully–but you will forfeit any respect or love she may have for you,' the Brig went on remorselessly. 'Again I will give you her exact words. "Tell him that I charge him on our love, on all we have ever been to each other, that he will let me be, that he will not come looking for me."'

'Why, but why?' David demanded desperately. 'Why does she reject me?'

'She knows that she is altered beyond all hope or promise. She knows that what was before can never be again. She knows that she can never be to you again what you have a right to expect–' he stopped David's protest with an angry chopping gesture of his hand. 'Listen to me, she knows that it cannot endure. She can never be your wife now. You are too young, too vital, too arrogant–' David stared at him. '–she knows that it will begin to spoil. In a week, a month, a year perhaps, it will have died. You will be trapped, tied to a blind woman. She doesn't want that. She wants it to die now, swiftly–mercifully, not to drag on–'

'Stop it,' David shouted. 'Stop it, damn you. That's enough.' He stumbled to the chair and fell into it. They were silent for a while, David crouched in the chair with his face buried in his hands. The Brig standing before the narrow window casement, the early morning light catching the fierce old warrior's face.

'She asked me to make you promise–' he hesitated, and David looked up at him, '–to promise that you would not try to find her.'

'No.' David shook his head stubbornly.

The Brig sighed. 'If you refused, I was to tell you this–she said you would understand, although I don't–she said that in Africa there is a fierce and beautiful animal called the sable antelope, and sometimes one of them is wounded by a hunter or mauled by a lion.'

The words were as painful as the cut of a whiplash, and David remembered himself saying them to her once when they were both young and strong and invulnerable.

'Very well,' he murmured at last, 'if that's what she wants–then I promise not to try and find her, though I don't promise not to try and convince her she is wrong.'

'Perhaps it would be best if you left Israel,' the Brig told him. 'Perhaps you should go back to where you came from and forget all of this ever happened.'

David paused, considering this a moment, before he answered, 'No, all I have is here. I will stay here.'

'Good.' The Brig accepted the decision. 'You are always welcome in this house.'

'Thank you, sir,' said David and went out to where the Mercedes was parked. He let himself into the house on Malik Street, and saw instantly that someone had been there before him.

He walked slowly into the living-room; the books were gone from the olive-wood table, the Kadesh painting no longer hung over the leather couch. In the bathroom he opened the wall cabinet and all her toilet articles had been removed, the rows of exotic bottles, the tubes and pots, even the slot for her toothbrush beside his was empty.

Her cupboard was bare, the dresses gone, the shelves blank, every trace of her swept away, except the lingering scent of her perfume on the air, and the ivory lace cover upon the bed.

He went to the bed and sat upon it, stroking the fine lacework, remembering how it had been.

There was the hard outline of something thin and square upon the pillow, beneath the cover. He turned back the lace and picked up the thin green book.

This year, in Jerusalem. It had been left there as a parting gift.

The title swam and went misty before his eyes. It was all he had left of her.

It seemed as though the slaughter at Ein Karem was the signal for a fresh upsurge of hostility and violence throughout the Middle East. A planned escalation of international tensions, as the Arab nations rattled their impressive, oil-purchased, array of weaponry and swore once more to leave not a single Jew in the land they still called Palestine.

There were savage and merciless attacks on soft targets, ill-protected embassies and consulates around the world, letter bombs, and night ambushes on school buses in isolated areas.

Then the provocations grew bolder, more directly aimed at the heart of Israel. Border infringements, commando-style raids, violations of air space, shellings and a threatening gathering and massing of armed might along the long, vulnerable frontiers of the wedge-shaped territories of the tiny land.

The Israelis waited, praying for peace—but girt for war.

Day after day, month after month, David and Joe flew to maintain that degree of expertise, where instinct and instantaneous reaction superseded conscious thought and reasoned action.

At those searing speeds beyond sound, it was only this training that swung the advantage from one combat to another. Even the superior reaction times of these carefully hand-picked young men were unequal to the tasks of bringing their mighty machines into effective action, where latitudes of error were measured in hundredths of a second, until they had attained this extra-sensory perfection.

To seek out, to recognize, to close, to destroy, and to disengage—it was a total preoccupation that blessedly left little time for brooding and sorrow.

Yet the sorrow and anger, that David and Joe shared, seemed doubly to arm them. Their vengeance was all-consuming.

Soon they joined that select half-dozen strike teams that Desert Flower called to undertake the most delicate of sorties. Again and again they were ordered into combat, and each time the confidence that Command had in them was strengthened.

As David sat in his cockpit, dressed from head to foot in the stiff constricting embrace of a full-pressure suit, breathing oxygen from his closed face mask, although the Mirage still crouched upon the ground, there were four black, red and white miniature roundels painted on the fuselage below his cockpit. The scalps of the enemy.

It was a mark of Desert Flower's trust that Bright Lance flight had been selected for high altitude 'Red' standby. With the starter lines plugged ready to blow compressed air into the compressors and whirl the great engines into life, and the ground crew lounging beside the motors, the Mirages were ready to be hurled aloft in a manner of seconds. Both David and Joe were suited to survive the almost pressureless altitudes above sixty thousand feet where an unprotected man's blood would fizzle like champagne.

David had lost count of the weary uncomfortable days and hours he had sat cramped in his cockpit on 'Red' standby with only the regular fifteen-minute checks to break the monotony.

'Checking 11.15 hours—fifteen minutes to stand-down,' David said into the microphone, and heard Joe's breathing in his ears before the reply.

'Two standing by. Beseder.'

Immediately after stand-down, when another crew would assume the arduous waiting of standby, David would change into a track suit and run for five or six miles to get the stiffness out of his body and to have his sweat wash away the staleness. He was looking forward to that, afterwards he would—

There was a sharp crackle in his earphones and a new voice.

'Red standby—Go! Go!'

The command was repeated over loudspeakers in the underground bunker, and the ground crew boiled into action. With all his pre-flight checks and routine long ago completed, David merely pushed his throttle to starting position, and the whine of the starters showed immediate results. The engine caught and he ran up his power to one hundred per cent.

Ahead of him the blast doors were lifting.

'Bright Lance Two, this is leader going to take off power.'

'Two conforming,' said Joe and they went screaming up the ramp and hurled themselves at the sky.

'Hallo, Desert Flower, this is Bright Lance airborne and climbing.'

'Bright Lance, this is the Brig,' David was not surprised to find that he was in charge of command plot. Distinctive voices and the use of personal names would prevent any chance of the enemy confusing the net with false messages. 'David, we have an intruder approach at high level that should enter our air space in four minutes, if it continues on its present course. We are tracking him at seventy-five thousand feet which means it is either an American U.2, which is highly unlikely, or that it is a Russian spy plane coming over to have a look at our latest dispersals.'

'Beseder, sir,' David acked.

'We are going to try for a storm-climb to intercept as soon as the target becomes hostile in our air space.'

'Beseder, sir.'

'Level at twenty thousand feet, turn to 186 and go to maximum speed for storm-climb.'

At twenty thousand, David went to straight and level flight and glanced into his mirror to see Joe's Mirage hanging out on his tail.

'Bright Lance Two, this is leader. Commencing run now.'

'Two conforming.'

David lit his tail and pushed the throttle open to maximum afterburn position. The Mirage jumped away, and David let the nose drop slightly to allow the speed to build up quickly. They went blazing through the sound barrier without a check, and David retrimmed for supersonic flight, thumbing the little top-hat on the end of his stick.

Their speed rocketed swiftly through mach 1·2, mach 1·5.

Their Mirages were stripped of all their essentials, there were no missiles dangling beneath them, no auxiliary fuel tanks to create drag, the only weapons they carried were their two 30 mm. cannons.

Flying lightly, they drove on up the mach scale, streaking from Beersheba to Eilat in the time it would take a man to walk a city block. Their speed stabilized at mach 1·9, just short of the heat barrier.

'David, this is the Brig. We are tracking you. You are on correct course and speed for interception. Prepare to commence climb in sixteen seconds.'

'Beseder, sir.'

'Counting now. Eight, seven, six . . . two, one. Go! Go!'

David tensed his body and as he pulled up the nose of the Mirage, he opened his mouth and screamed to fight off the effects of gravity. But despite these precautions and the constricting grip of his pressure suit, the abrupt change of direction crammed him down into his seat and the blood drained out of his head so that his vision went grey and then black.

The Mirage was standing on her tail flying at very nearly twice the speed of sound and, as his vision returned, David glanced at the G-meter and saw that he had subjected his body to nearly nine times the force of gravity to achieve this attitude of climb without loss of speed.

Now he lay on his back and stared up at the empty sky while the needle of his altimeter raced upwards, and his speed gradually eroded away.

A quick sweep showed Joe's Mirage rock steady in position below him, climbing in concert with him, and his voice came through calm and reassuring.

'Leader, this is Two. I have contact with target.'

Even under the stress of storm-climb, Joe was busy manipulating his beloved radar, and he had picked up the spy plane high above them.

In this manoeuvre they were trading speed for height, and as one increased so the other drained away.

They were like a pair of arrows aimed directly upwards. The bowstring could throw them just so far and then they would hang there in space for a few moments, until they were drawn irresistibly back to earth. In those few moments they must find and kill the enemy.

David lay back in his seat and watched with fresh wonder as the sky turned darker blue and then slowly became the midnight black of space, shot through with the fiery prickings of the stars.

They were at the top edge of the stratosphere, high above the highest clouds or signs of weather as known to earth. Outside the cockpit the air was thin and weak, insufficient for life, hardly sufficient to keep the jets of the Mirage's engines burning—and the cold was a fearsome sixty degrees of frost.

The two aircraft slowly ran out of energy, and they came out together at the top of a mighty parabola. The sensation of flight was gone, they swam through the dark forbidding oceans of space and far below them the earth glowed strangely, with a weird unnatural light.

There was no time to admire the view, the Mirage was wallowing in the thin and treacherous air, her control surfaces skidding and sliding without bite.

Joe was on the target, tracking quietly and steadily and they came round carefully on to the heading, with the aircraft staggering mushily and beginning to fall away from these inhospitable heights.

David stared ahead, holding the Mirage's nose up for sustained altitude but already the stall warning device was flicking amber and red at him. He was running out of time and height.

Then suddenly he saw it, seeming startlingly close in the rare air, ghosting along on its immense wings, like a black manta-ray through the sable and silent sea of space–ahead and slightly below them–calmly and silently, it drifted along, its height giving it a false sense of invulnerability.

'Desert Flower, this is Bright Lance visual on the intruder and requesting permission for strike.' David's cool tone hid the sudden gust of his anger and hatred that the sighting had released.

'Report your target,' the Brig was hedging, it was a dangerous decision to call the strike on an unknown target.

'Desert Flower, it's an Ilyushin Mark 17-11. No apparent markings.'

It needed no markings, it could only belong to one nation. David was closing fast, he could fly no slower than this, and he was rapidly overhauling the other machine. Those huge wings were designed to float upon the feeble air of the stratosphere.

'Closing fast,' he warned Desert Flower. 'Opportunity for strike will pass in approximately ten seconds.'

The silence in his headphones hummed quickly, and he readied his cannons and watched the spy plane blowing up rapidly in size as he dropped down upon it.

Suddenly the Brig made the decision, perhaps committing his country to heavy retaliation, but knowing that the spy plane's cameras were steadily recording vital details of their ability to resist aggression, information that would be passed quickly to their enemies.

'David,' his voice was curt and harsh, 'this is the Brig. Hit him!'

'Beseder.' David let the Mirage's nose drop a fraction, and she responded gratefully.

'Two, this is leader attacking.'

'Two conforming.'

He went down on the Ilyushin so fast, that as she came into his sights he knew he had time for only a few seconds of fire.

He pressed the trigger with the aiming pipper on the spy plane's wing roots, and he saw her rear up like a great fish struck by the steel of the harpoon.

For three seconds he poured his cannon shells into her, and watched them flash and twinkle against the massive black silhouette. Then he was through, falling away below the giant's belly, with his power spent, dropping away like the burned-out shell of a rocket.

Joe came down astern of him, backing up the attack, and in his sights the spy plane hung helplessly on its wide wings, its long rounded nose pointing to the black sky with its cold uncaring stars.

He pressed the trigger and the plane broke up amidst the bright flashes of exploding cannon shells. One wing snapped off at its root and the carcass began its long slow tumble down the heavens.

'Hello, Desert Flower, this is Bright Lance leader. Target destroyed.' David tried to keep his voice level, but he found his hands were trembling and his guts were aching cold from the spill-over of his hatred that not even the enemy's death could expunge.

Again he pressed the button to open the flight net. 'Joe, that's one more for

Hannah,' he said, but for once there was no reply, and after he had listened in vain to the throb of the carrier beam for a few seconds he closed it, and activated his doppler gear for a homing signal, and silently Joe followed him back to base.

Debra had been a steadying and maturing influence, but now David reacted so wildly to her going that Joe had to continue his role of wing man, even when they were off base.

They spent much of their leisure time together, for although they seldom mentioned their loss, yet the sharing of it drew them closer.

Often Joe slept over at Malik Street, for his own home was a sad and depressing place now. The Brig was seldom there in these troubled times, Debra gone and his mother was so altered by her terrible experience that she was grey and broken, aged beyond her years. The bullet wound in her body had closed, but there was other damage that would never heal.

David's wildness was a craving for the forgetfulness of constant action. He was only truly at peace when he was in the air, and on the ground he was restless and mercurial. Joe moved, big and calm beside him, steering him tactfully out of trouble with a slow grin and an easy word.

As a consequence of the downed spy plane, the Syrians began a policy of provocative patrols, calculated infringement of Israeli air space, which was discontinued as soon as retaliation was drawn. As the interceptors raced to engage they would swing away, declining combat, and move back within their own borders.

Twice David saw the greenish luminous blur of these hostile patrols on the screen of his scanning radar, and each time he had surprised himself with the icy feeling of anger and hatred that had lain heavy as a rock upon his heart and lungs as he led Joe in on the interception. Each time, however, the Syrians had been warned by their own radar and they had turned away, increasing speed, and withdrawn discreetly and mockingly.

'Bright Lance, this is Desert Flower. Target is no longer hostile. Discontinue attack pattern.' The Syrian MIG21's had crossed their own frontier, and each time David had answered quietly, 'Two, this is leader. Discontinuing attack pattern and resuming scan.'

The tactics were designed to wear on the nerves of the defenders, and in all the interceptor squadrons the tension was becoming explosive. The provocation was pushing them to the edge of restraint. Incidents were only narrowly being averted, as the hot-bloods crowded their interceptions to the very frontiers of war. Finally, however, there had to come intervention from above as Desert Flower tried to hold them on a tighter leash. They sent the Brig to talk to his crews and as he stood on the dais and looked about the crowded briefing room, he realized that it was unfair to train the hawk and then keep the hood over his eyes and the thong upon his leg, to hold him upon the wrist, when the wild duck were flighting overhead.

He started at a philosophical level, taking advantage of the regard that he knew his young pilots had for him.

'–the object of war is peace, the ultimate strategy of any commander is peace–' There was no response from his audience. The Brig caught the level scrutiny of his own son. How could he talk of placation to a trained warrior who had just buried the mutilated body of his bride? The Brig ploughed on manfully.

'Only a fool allows himself to be drawn on to a field of the enemy's choosing,' he was reaching them now, 'I won't have one of you young pups pushing us into something we are not ready for. I don't want to give them an excuse. That is what they want–' They were thawing now, he saw a head nod thoughtfully and heard a murmur of agreement.

'Any of you looking for big trouble, you don't have to go to Damascus, you know my address,' he tried for his first laugh, and got it. They were chuckling now. 'All right, then. We don't want trouble. We are going to lean right over backwards to prevent it–but we are not going to fall on our arses. When the time comes, I'll give you the word and it won't be the soft word, or the other cheek–' they growled then, a fierce little sound, and he ended it, '–but you wait for that word.'

Le Dauphin stood up and took over from the Brig.

'All right, while I've got you all together, I've a little news for you that may help to cool the hot-heads who want to follow the MIGs over the border.' He motioned to the projection box at the end of the briefing-room, the lights went down and there was a shuffling of feet, and an outburst of coughing. A voice protested resignedly.

'Not *another* film show!'

'Yes,' the colonel took it up. '*Another* film show.' Then as the images began to flash upon the screen he went on, 'This is a military intelligence film, and the subject is a new ground-to-air missile system that has been delivered by the Soviet Army to the armies of the Arab Union. The code name for the system is "Serpent" and it updates the existing "Sam III" system. As far as we know, the system has been installed and is operative in the Syrian defensive perimeter, and will shortly be installed by the Egyptians. It is manned at present by Russian instructors.' As the colonel went on talking, the Brig sat back in his chair and watched their faces in the silver reflection from the screen. They were intent and serious, men looking for the first time on the terrible machines that might be the instrument of their own deaths.

'The missile is fired from a tracked vehicle. Here you see aerial reconnaissance shots of a mobile column. Notice that each vehicle carries a pair of missiles, and you will realize that they constitute an enormous threat–'

The Brig picked out the marvellously pure profile of David Morgan as he leaned forward to study the screen, and he felt a pang of sympathy and sorrow for him–and yet this was underlined by a new respect, a realignment of judgement. The boy had proved himself to be constant, capable of embracing an ideal and remaining loyal to it.

'The improvements in design of the "Serpent" are not certain, but it is believed that the missile is capable of greater speeds, probably in the order of mach 2·5, and that the guidance system is a combination of both infra-red heat seeker and computerized radar control.'

Watching the handsome young face, he wondered if Debra had not misjudged his reserves. It was possible that he would have been capable of–no, the Brig shook his head and groped for a cigarette. He was too young, too greedy for life, spoiled by good looks and riches. He would not be capable of it. Debra was right, as so often was the case. She had chosen the correct course. She could never hold him, she must set him free.

'It is expected that the "Serpent" is capable of engaging targets at altitudes between 1,500 ft. and 75,000 ft.'

There was a stir amongst the listeners, as they assessed the threat of this new weapon.

'The warhead delivers a quarter of a ton of explosive and it is armed with a proximity fuse which is set to fire if the target is passed at range less than 150 feet. Within these limits the "Serpent" is lethal.'

The Brig was still watching David. Ruth and he had not seen the boy at their home for many months. He had come with Joe to spend the Sabbath evening with them twice after the outrage. However, the atmosphere had been stiff and artificial, everybody carefully avoiding mention of Debra's name. He had not come again after the second time, nearly six months ago.

'Evasive tactics at this stage will be the same as for "Sam III".'

'Prayer and good luck!' Someone interjected and that raised a laugh.

'–a maximum-rate turn towards the missile, to screen the radiation from your jet blasts, and attempt to force the "Serpent" to overshoot. In the event that the missile continues to track, you should climb into the sun and then make another maximum-rate turn. The missile may then accept the sun's infra-red radiation as a more tempting target–'

'And if that doesn't work?' a voice called, and another answered flippantly, 'Repeat the following: "Hear O Israel, the Lord our God, the Lord is one."' But this time nobody laughed at the old blasphemy.

The Brig timed his departure from the briefing room to fall in beside David.

'When are we going to see you, David? It's been a long time.'

'I'm sorry, sir. I hope Joe made my apologies.'

'Yes, of course. But why don't you come with Joe this evening? God knows, there will be enough food.'

'I'll be very busy tonight, sir,' David declined lamely.

'I understand.' And as they reached the door of the O.C.'s office the Brig paused, 'Remember you are always welcome,' and he turned away.

'Sir!' the Brig stopped and looked back at him. David spoke rapidly–almost guiltily.

'How is she, sir?' and then again, 'how is Debra? Have you seen her–I mean, recently?'

'She is well,' the Brig answered heavily. 'As well as she can be.'

'Will you tell her I asked?'

'No,' answered the Brig, ignoring the pleading in the dark blue eyes. 'No. You know I can't do that.'

David nodded and turned away. For a moment the Brig looked after him and then with a frown he went on into the colonel's office.

David dropped Joe in Ein Karem, at the entrance to the lane, and then he drove on into the main shopping area of East Jerusalem and parked outside the big new supermarket in Melech George V to do his shopping for the weekend ahead.

He was hanging over the freezer tray pondering the delicate choice between lamb cutlets and steak, when he became aware that he was being watched.

David looked up quickly and saw that she was a statuesque woman with a thick mane of blonde curls. She stood beside the shelves farther down the aisle. Her hair was dyed, he could see the dark shadow of the roots, and she was older than he was, with a womanly heaviness in her hips and bosom and tiny lines at the corners of her eyes. She was eyeing him, a steady appraisal so unashamedly sensual that he felt the check in his breathing and the quick stirring of his loins. He looked back at the meat in the freezer, guilty and angry with the treachery of his body. It had been so long, so very long since he had experienced sexual awareness. He had believed that he never would again. He wanted to throw the pack of steak back into the freezer and leave, but he stood rooted with the breathless feeling squeezing his lungs, and he was aware of the woman's presence at his side. He could feel the warmth of her on his arm, and smell her—the flowery perfume mingled with the natural musky odour of the sexually aroused female.

'The steak is very good,' she said. She had a light sweet voice and he recognized the same breathless quality as his own. He looked at her. Her eyes were green, and her teeth were a little crooked but white. She was even older than he had thought, almost forty. She wore her dress low in front, he could see the crêpe effect of the skin between her breasts. The breasts were big and motherly, and suddenly David wanted to lay his head against them. They looked so soft and warm and safe.

'You should cook it rare, with mushrooms and garlic and red wine,' she said. 'It's very good that way.'

'Is it?' he asked hoarsely.

'Yes,' she nodded, smiling. 'Who will cook it for you? Your wife? Your mother?'

'No,' said David. 'I will cook it myself. I live alone,' and she leaned a little closer to him, her breast touching his arm.

David was dizzy and hot with the brandy. He had bought a bottle of it at the supermarket, and he had drunk it mixed with ginger ale to mask the spiritous taste. He had drunk it fast, and now he leaned over the basin in the bathroom and felt the house rock and sway about him. He steadied himself, gripping the edge of the basin.

He splashed cold water on to his face and shook off the drops, then he grinned stupidly at himself in the mirror above the basin. His hair was damp and hung on to his forehead; he closed one eye and the wavering image in the mirror hardened and squinted back at him.

'Hi there, boy,' he muttered and reached for the towel. He had dripped water down his tunic and this annoyed him. He threw the towel over the toilet seat and went back into the living-room.

The woman was gone. The leather couch still carried the indentation of her backside, and the dirty plates were on the olive-wood table. The air was thick with cigarette smoke and her perfume.

'Where are you?' he called thickly, swaying slightly in the doorway.

'Here, big boy.' He went to the bedroom. She lay on the bed, naked, plump and white with huge soft breasts and swelling belly. He stared at her.

'Come on, Davey.' Her clothing was thrown across the dressing-table, and he saw that her corsets were grey and unwashed. Her hair was yellow against the soft ivory lacework.

'Come to Mama,' she whispered hoarsely, opening her limbs languidly in invitation. She was spread upon the brass bed, upon the lace cover which had been Debra's—and David felt his anger surge within him.

'Get up,' he said, slurring the words.

'Come on, baby.'

'Get off that bed,' his voice tightened and she heard the tone and sat up with mild alarm.

'What is it, Davey?'

'Get out of here,' his voice was rising sharply. 'Get out, you bitch. Get out of here!' He was shaking now, his face pale and his eyes savage blue.

Quivering with panic, she climbed hurriedly from the bed, the great white breasts and buttocks wobbling with ridiculous haste as she stuffed them into the grey corset.

When she had gone, David went through into the bedroom and vomited into the toilet bowl. Then he cleaned the house, scouring pans and plates, polishing the glasses until they shone, emptying the ashtrays, opening the shutters to blow out the stench of cigarette and perfume—and finally, going through into the bedroom, he stripped and remade the bed with fresh sheets and smoothed the lace cover carefully until not a crease or wrinkle showed.

He put on a clean tunic and his uniform cap, and drove to the Jaffa gate. He parked the car in the lot outside the gate and walked through the old city to the reconstructed sephardic synagogue in the Jewish quarter.

It was very quiet and peaceful in the high-domed hall and he sat a long time on the hard wooden bench.

Joe sat opposite David with a worried expression creasing his deep forehead as he studied the board. Three or four of the other pilots had hiked their chairs up and were concentrating on the game also. These chessboard conflicts between David and Joe were usually epics and attracted a partisan audience.

David had been stalking Joe's rook for half a dozen moves and now he had it trapped. Two more moves would shatter the kingsize defence, and the third must force a resignation. David grinned smugly as Joe reached a decision and moved a knight out.

'That's not going to save you, dear boy,' David hardly glanced at the knight, and he hit the rook with a white bishop. 'Mate in five,' he predicted, as he dropped the castle into the box, and then—too late—he realized that Joe's theatrical expression of anguish had slowly faded into a beatific grin. Joseph Mordecai used any deception to bait his traps, and David looked with alarm at the innocuous-seeming knight, suddenly seeing the devious plotting in which the castle was merely bait.

'Oh, you bastard,' David moaned. 'you sneaky bastard.'

'Check!' Joe gloated as he put the knight into a forked attack, and David had to leave his queen exposed to the horseman.

'Check,' said Joe again with an ecstatic little sigh as he lifted the white queen off the board, and again the harassed king took the only escape route open to him.

'And mate,' sighed Joe again as his own queen left the back file to join the attack. 'Not in five, as you predicted, but in three.' There was a loud outburst of congratulation and applause from the onlookers and Joe cocked an eye at David.

'Again?' he said, and David shook his head.

'Take on one of these other patsies,' he said. 'I'm going to sulk for an hour.' He vacated his seat and it was filled by another eager victim as Joe reset the board. David crossed to the coffee machine, moving awkwardly in the grip of his G-suit, and drew a mug of the thick black liquid, stirred in four spoons of sugar and found another seat in a quieter corner of the crewroom beside a slim curly-headed young kibbutznik, with whom David had become friend!y. He was reading a thick novel.

'*Shalom*, Robert. How you been?'

Robert grunted without looking up from his book, and David sipped the sweet hot coffee. Beside him, Robert moved restlessly in his seat and coughed softly, David was lost in his own thoughts, for the first time in months thinking of home, wondering about Mitzi and Barney Venter, wondering if the yellowtail were running hot in False Bay this season, and remembering how the proteas looked upon the mountains of the Helderberg.

Again Robert stirred in his chair and cleared his throat. David glanced at him, realizing that he was in the grip of a deep emotion as he read, his lips quivering, and his eyes too bright.

'What you reading?' David was amused, and he leaned forward to read the title. The picture on the dust jacket of the book was instantly familiar. It was a deeply felt desert landscape of fierce colours and great space. Two distant figures, man and woman, walked hand in hand through the desert and the effect was mystic and haunting. David realized that only one person could have painted that—Ella Kadesh.

Robert lowered the book. 'This is uncanny,' his voice was muffled with emotion. 'I tell you, Davey, it's beautiful. It must be one of the most beautiful books ever written.'

With a strange feeling of pre-knowledge, with a sense of complete certainty, of what it would be, David took the book out of his hands and turned it to read the title, *A Place of Our Own.*

Robert was still talking. 'My sister made me read it. She works for the publisher. She cried all night when she read it. It is very new, only published last week, but it's got to be the biggest book ever written about this country.'

David hardly heard him, he was staring at the writer's name in small print below the title.

'Debra Mordecai.'

He ran his fingers lightly over the glossy paper of the jacket, stroking the name.

'I want to read it,' he said softly.

'I'll let you have it when I'm finished,' Robert promised.

'I want to read it now!'

'No way!' Robert exclaimed with evident alarm, and almost snatched the book out of David's hands.

'You wait your turn, comrade!'

David looked up. Joe was watching him from across the room, and David glared at him accusingly. Joe dropped his eyes quickly to the chessboard again, and David realized that he had known of the publication. He started up to go to him, to challenge him, but at that moment the tannoy echoed through the bunker.

'All flights Lance Squadron to "Red" standby,' and on the readiness board the red lamps lit beside the flight designations.

'Bright Lance.'

'Red Lance.'

'Fire Lance.'

David snatched up his flying helmet and joined the lumbering rush of G-suited bodies for the electric personnel carrier in the concrete tunnel outside the crew-room door. He forced a place for himself beside Joe.

'Why didn't you tell me?' he demanded.

'I was going to, Davey. I really was.'

'Yeah, I bet,' David snapped sarcastically. 'Have you read it?'

Joe nodded, and David went on, 'What's it about?'

'I couldn't begin to tell you. You'd have to read it yourself.'

'Don't worry about that,' David muttered grimly, 'I will,' and he jumped down as they reached their hangar and strode across to his Mirage.

Twenty minutes later they were airborne and Desert Flower sent them hastening out over the Mediterranean at interception speed to answer a Mayday call from an El Al Caravelle who reported that she was being buzzed by an Egyptian MIG 21 J.

The Egyptian sheered off and raced for the coast and the protection of his own missile batteries as the Mirages approached. They let him go and picked up the airliner. They escorted her into the circuit over Lod before returning to base.

Still in his G-suit and overalls, David stopped off at le Dauphin's office and got himself a twenty-four-hour pass.

Ten minutes before closing time he ran into one of the bookstores in Jaffa Road.

There was a pyramid display of *A Place of Our Own* on the table in the centre of the store.

'It's a beautiful book,' said the salesgirl as she wrapped it.

He opened a Goldstar, and he kicked off his shoes before stretching out on the lace cover of the bed.

He began to read, and paused only once to switch on the overhead lights and fetch another beer. It was a thick book, and he read slowly—savouring every word, sometimes going back to re-read a paragraph.

It was their story, his and Debra's, woven into the plot she had described to him that day on the island off the Costa Brava, and it was rich with the feeling of the land and its people. He recognized many of the secondary characters, and he laughed aloud with the pleasure and the joy of it. Then at the end, he choked on the sadness as the girl of the story lies dying in Hadassah Hospital, with half her face torn away by a terrorist's bomb, and she will not let the boy come to her. Wanting to spare him that, wanting him to remember her as she was.

It was dawn then, and David had not noticed the passage of the night. He rose from the bed, light-headed from lack of sleep, and filled with a sense of wonder that Debra had captured so clearly the way it had been—that she had seen so deeply into his soul, had described emotions for which he had believed there were no words.

He bathed and shaved and dressed in casual clothes and went back to where the book lay upon the bed. He studied the jacket again, and then turned to the flyleaf for confirmation. It was there. 'Jacket design by Ella Kadesh.'

So early in the morning he had the road almost to himself and he drove fast, into the rising morning sun. At Jericho he turned north along the frontier road, and he remembered her sitting in the seat beside him with her skirts drawn high around her long brown legs and her thick dark hair shaking in the wind.

The whisper of the wind against the body of the Mercedes seemed to urge him, 'Hurry, hurry.' And the urgent drumming of the tyres carried him up towards the lake.

He parked the Mercedes beside the ancient crusader wall and went through into the garden on the lake shore.

Ella sat upon the wide patio before her easel. She wore a huge straw hat the size of a wagon wheel adorned with plastic cherries and ostrich feathers, her vast overalls covered her like a circus tent and they were stiff with dried paint in all her typically vivid colours.

Calmly she looked up from her painting with her brush poised.

'Hail, young Mars!' she greeted him. 'Well met indeed, and why do you bring such honour on my humble little home?'

'Piss on it, Ella, you know damn well why I'm here.'

'So sweetly phrased,' she was shifty, he could see it in her bright little eyes. 'Shame on it that such vulgar words pass such fair lips. Would you like a beer, Davey?'

'No, I don't want a beer. I want to know where she is?'

'Just who are we discussing?'

'Come on, I read the book. I saw the cover. You know, damn you, you know.'

She was silent then staring at him. Then slowly the ornate head-dress dipped in acquiescence.

'Yes,' she agreed. 'I know.'

'Tell me where she is.'

'I can't do that, Davey. You and I both made a promise. Yes, I know of yours, you see.'

She watched the bluster go out of him. The fine young body with the arrogant set of shoulders seemed to sag, and he stood uncertainly in the sunlight.

'How about that beer now, Davey?' She heaved herself up from her stool and crossed the terrace with her stately tread. She came back and gave him a tall glass with a head of froth and they took a seat together at the end of the terrace out of the wind, in the mild winter sunlight.

'I've been expecting you for a week now,' she told him. 'Ever since the book was published. I knew it would set you on fire. It's just too damned explosive—even I wept like a leaky faucet for a couple of days,' she giggled shyly. 'You'd hardly believe it possible, would you?'

'That book was us—Debra and me,' David told her. 'She was writing about us.'

'Yes,' Ella agreed, 'but it does not alter the decision she has made. A decision which I think is correct, by the way.'

'She described exactly how I felt, Ella. All the things I felt and still feel—but which I could never have put into words.'

'It's beautiful and it's true, but don't you see that it confirms her position.'

'But I love her, Ella—and she loves me,' he cried out violently.

'She wants it to stay that way. She doesn't want it to die, she doesn't want it to sicken.' He began to protest, but she gripped his arm in a surprisingly powerful grip to silence him. 'She knows that she can never keep pace with you now. Look at you, David, you are beautiful and vital and swift—she must drag you back, and in time you must as certainly resent it.'

Again he tried to interrupt, but she shook his arm in her huge fist. 'You would be shackled, you could never leave her, she is helpless, she would be your charge for all your life—think on it, David.'

'I want her,' he muttered stubbornly. 'I had nothing before I met her, and I have nothing now.'

'That will change. Perhaps she has taught you something and young emotions heal as swiftly as young flesh. She wants happiness for you, David. She loves you so much that her gift to you is freedom. She loves you so much that for your sake she will deny that love.'

'Oh, God,' he groaned. 'If only I could see her, if I could touch her and talk to her for a few minutes.'

She shook her massive head, and her jowls wobbled dolefully.

'She would not agree to that.'

'Why, Ella, tell me why?' His voice was rising again, desperate with his anguish.

'She is not strong enough, she knows that if you came near her, she would waver and bring even greater disaster upon you both.'

They sat silently together then and looked out across the lake. High mountains of cloud rose up beyond the heights of Golan, brilliant white in the winter sunlight, shaded with blue and bruised grey, and range upon range they bore down upon the lake. David shivered as an icy little wind came ferreting across the terrace and sought them out.

He drank the rest of his beer, and then revolved the glass slowly through his fingers.

'Will you give her a message from me, then?' he asked.

'I don't think–'

'Please, Ella. Just one message.'

She nodded.

'Tell her that what she wrote in the book is exactly how much I love her. Tell her that it is big enough to rise above this thing. Tell her that I want the chance to try.'

She listened quietly, and David made a groping gesture with his hands as though to pluck words from the air that might convince her.

'Tell her–' he paused, then shook his head. 'No, that's all. Just tell her that I love her, and want to be with her.'

'All right, David. I'll tell her.'

'And you will give me her answer?'

'Where can I reach you?'

He gave her the number of the telephone in the crew ready room at the base.

'You'll ring me soon, Ella? Don't keep me waiting.'

'Tomorrow,' she promised. 'In the morning.'

'Before ten o'clock. It must be before ten.'

He stood up, and then suddenly he leaned forward and kissed her sagging and raddled cheek.

'Thank you,' he said. 'You are not a bad old bag.'

'Away with you, you and your blarney. You'd have the sirens of the Odyssey themselves come arunning to your bidding.' She sniffed moistly. 'Get away with you now, I think I'm going to cry, and I want to be alone to enjoy it.'

She watched him go up across the lawns under the date palms and at the gate in the wall he paused and looked back. For a second they stared at each other and then he stepped through the gate.

She heard the engine of the Mercedes whirr and pull away slowly up the track, then the note of it rose as it hit the highway and went racing away southwards. Ella rose heavily and crossed the terrace, went down the steps towards the jetty and its stone boathouses screened from the house by part of the ancient wall.

Her speedboat rode at its mooring, restless in the wind and the chop of the lake. She went on down to the farthest and largest of the boathouses and stood in the open doorway.

The interior had been stripped and repainted with clean white. The furniture was simple and functional. The rugs on the stone floor were for warmth, plain woven wool, thick and rough. The large bed was built into a curtained alcove in the wall beside the fireplace.

On the opposite wall was a gas stove with a double cooking ring above which a number of copper cooking pots hung. A door beyond led through to a bathroom and toilet which Ella had added very recently.

The only decoration was the Ella Kadesh painting from the house on Malik Street, which hung on the bare white wall, facing the door. It seemed to lighten and warm the whole room; below it the girl sat at a working table. She was listening intently to her own voice speaking in Hebrew from the tape recorder. Her expression was rapt and intent, and she stared at the blank wall before her.

Then she nodded her head, smiling at what she had just heard. She switched off the recorder and turned in the swivel chair to the second recorder and punched the transmit button. She held the microphone close to her lips as she began to translate the Hebrew into English.

Ella stood in the doorway and watched her work. An American publisher had purchased the English-language rights of *A Place of Our Own*. They had paid Debra an advance of thirty thousand American dollars for the book, and an additional five thousand for her services as translator. She had almost completed the task now.

From where she stood, Ella could see the scar on Debra's temple. It was glazed pinkish white against the deeply tanned skin of her face, a dimple like a child's drawing of a seagull in flight; V-shaped and no bigger than a snowflake, it seemed to enhance her fine looks, almost like a beauty spot, a tiny blemish that gave a focus point for her strong regular features.

She had made no attempt to conceal it for her dark hair was drawn back to the nape of her neck and secured there with a leather thong. She wore no make-up, and her skin looked clean and glowing, tanned and smooth.

Despite the bulky fisherman's jersey and woollen slacks her body appeared firm and slim for she swam each day, even when the snow winds came down from the north.

Ella left the doorway and moved silently closer to the desk, studying Debra's eyes as she so often did. One day she would paint that expression. There was no hint of the damage that lay behind, no hint that the eyes could not see. Rather their calm level gaze seemed to penetrate deeper, to see all. They had a serenity that was almost mystic, a depth and understanding that Ella found strangely disquieting.

Debra pressed the switch of the microphone, ending the recording, and then she spoke again without turning her head.

'Is that you, Ella?'

'How do you do it?' Ella demanded with astonishment.

'I felt the air move when you walked in, and then I smelt you.'

'I'm big enough to blow up a storm, but do I smell so bad?' Ella protested, chuckling.

'You smell of turpentine, and garlic and beer,' Debra sniffed, and laughed with her.

'I've been painting, and I was chopping garlic for the roast, and I was drinking beer with a friend.' Ella dropped into one of the chairs. 'How does it go with the book?'

'Nearly finished. It can go to the typist tomorrow. Do you want some coffee?' Debra stood up and crossed to the gas stove. Ella knew better than to offer her help, even though she gritted her teeth every time she watched Debra working with fire and boiling water. The girl was fiercely independent, utterly determined to live her life without other people's pity or assistance.

The room was laid out precisely, each item in its place where Debra could put her hand to it without hesitation. She could move confidently through her little world, doing her own house-work, preparing her own food and drink, working steadily, and paying her own way.

Once a week, a driver came up from her publisher's office in Jerusalem to collect her tapes and her writing was typed out along with her other correspondence.

Weekly also she would go with Ella in the speedboat up the lake to Tiberias to do their shopping together, and each day she swam for an hour from the stone jetty. Often an old fisherman with whom she had become friendly would row down the lake to fetch her and she would go out with him, baiting her own lines and taking her turn at the oars.

Across the lawns from the jetty, in the crusader castle, there was always Ella's companionship and intelligent conversation–and here in her little cottage there was quietness and safety and work to fill the long hours. And in the night there was the chill of terrible aloneness and silent bitter tears into her solitary pillow, tears which only she knew about.

Debra placed a mug of coffee beside Ella's chair and carried her own back to her work bench.

'Now,' she said, 'you can tell me what is keeping you fidgeting around in your seat, and drumming your fingers on the arm of the chair,' she smiled towards Ella, sensing the surprise. 'You have got something to tell me, and it's killing you.'

'Yes,' Ella spoke after a moment. 'Yes, you are right, my dear.' She took a deep breath and then went on. 'He came, Debra. He came to see me, as we knew he must.'

Debra set the mug down on the table, her hand was steady and her face expressionless.

'I didn't tell him where you were.'

'How is he, Ella? How does he look?'

'He is thinner, a little thinner, I think, and paler than when I last saw him, but it suits him. He is still the most beautiful man I have ever seen.'

'His hair,' Debra asked, 'has he let it grow a little?'

'Yes, I think so. It's soft and dark and thick around his ears and curly down the back.'

Debra nodded, smiling. 'I'm glad he didn't cut it.' They were silent again, and then almost timidly Debra asked, 'What did he say? What did he want?'

'He had a message for you.'

'What was it?'

And Ella repeated it faithfully in his exact words. When she had finished, Debra turned away to face the wall above her desk.

'Please go away now, Ella. I want to be alone.'

'He asked me to give him your reply. I promised to speak to him tomorrow morning.'

'I will come to you later–but please leave me now.' And Ella saw the drop of bright liquid that slid down the smooth brown curve of her cheek.

Mountainously Ella came to her feet and moved towards the door. Behind her she heard the girl sob, but she did not turn back. She went across the stone jetty and up to the terrace. She sat before her canvas and picked up her brush and began to paint. Her strokes were broad and crude and angry.

David was sweating in the stiff shiny skin of his full pressure suit and he waited anxiously beside the telephone, glancing every few minutes at the crew-room clock.

He and Joe would go on high-altitude 'Red' standby at ten o'clock, in seven minutes' time, and Ella had not called him.

David's depression was thunderous and there was black anger and despair in his heart. She had promised to call before ten o'clock.

'Come on, Davey,' Joe called from the doorway and he stood up heavily and followed Joe to the electric carrier. As he took his seat beside Joe he heard it ring in the crew-room.

'Hold it,' he told the driver, and he saw Robert answer the telephone and wave through the glass panel at him.

'It's for you, Davey,' and he ran back into the crew-room.

'I'm sorry, David,' Ella's voice was scratchy and far away. 'I tried earlier but the exchange here—'

'Sure, sure,' David cut her short, his anger was still strong. 'Did you speak to her?'

'Yes, Davey. Yes, I did. I gave her your message.'

'What was her reply?' he demanded.

'There was no reply.'

'What the hell, Ella. She must have said something.'

'She said—' Ella hesitated, '—and these are her exact words—"the dead cannot speak with the living. For David, I died a year ago."'

He held the receiver with both hands but still it shook. After a while she spoke again.

'Are you still there?'

'Yes,' he whispered, 'I'm still here.'

They were silent again, but David broke it at last.

'That's it, then,' he said.

'Yes. I'm afraid that's it, Davey.'

Joe stuck his head around the door.

'Hey, Davey. Cut it short, will you. Time to go.'

'I have to go now, Ella. Thanks for everything.'

'Goodbye, David,' she said, and even over the scratchy connection he could hear the compassion in her tone. It heightened the black anger that gripped him as he rode beside Joe to the Mirage bunker.

For the first time ever, David felt uncomfortable in the cockpit of a Mirage. He felt trapped and restless, sweating and angry, and it seemed hours between each of the fifteen-minute readiness checks.

His ground crew were playing backgammon on the concrete floor below him, and he could see them laughing and joshing each other. It made him angrier than ever to see others happy.

'Tubby!' he barked in to the microphone, and his voice was repeated by the overhead loudspeakers. The plump, serious young man, who was chief engineer for Lance squadron, climbed quickly up beside his cockpit and peered anxiously through the canopy at him.

'There is dirt on my screen,' David snapped at him. 'How the hell do you expect me to pick up a MIG, when I'm looking through a screen you ate your bloody breakfast off?'

The cause of David's distress was a speck of carbon that marred the glistening perfection of his canopy. Tubby himself had supervised the polishing and buffing of it, and the carbon speck was wind-carried since then. Carefully he removed the offending spot, and lovingly he polished the place where it had been with a chamois leather.

The reprimand had been public and unfair, very unlike their top boy Davey. However, they all made allowances for 'Red' standby nerves—and spots on a canopy played hell with a pilot's nerves. Every time it caught his eye it looked exactly like a pouncing MIG.

'That's better,' David gruffed at him, fully aware that he had been grossly unfair. Tubby grinned and gave a high sign as he climbed down.

At that moment there was a click and throb in his earphones and the distinctive voice of the Brig.

'"Red" standby—Go! Go!'

Under full reheat and with the driving thrust of the after-burners hurling him aloft David called, 'Hello, Desert Flower, Bright Lance airborne and climbing.'

'Hello, David, this is the Brig. We have a contact shaping up for intrusion on our air space. It looks like another teaser from the Syrians. They are closing our border at twenty-six thousand and should be hostile in approximately three minutes. We are going to initiate attack plan Gideon. Your new heading is 42° and I want you right down on the deck.'

David acked and immediately rotated the Mirage's nose downwards. Plan Gideon called for a low-level stalk so that the ground clutter would obscure the enemy radar and conceal their approach until such time as they were in position to storm-climb up into an attack vector above and behind the target.

They dropped to within feet of the ground, lifting and falling over the undulating hills, so low that the herds of black Persian sheep scattered beneath them as they shrieked eastwards towards the Jordan.

'Hello, Bright Lance, this is Desert Flower—we are not tracking you.' Good, thought David, then neither is the enemy. 'Target is now hostile in sector'—the Brig gave the co-ordinates—'Scan for your own contact.'

Almost immediately Joe's voice came in. 'Leader, this is Two. I have a contact.'

David dropped his eyes to his own radar screen and manipulated his scan as Joe called range and bearing. It was a dangerous distraction when flying in the sticky phase of high subsonic drag at zero feet, and his own screen was clear of contact.

They raced onwards for many more seconds before David picked up the faint luminous fuzz at the extreme range of his set.

'Contact firming. Range figures nine six nautical miles. Parallel heading and track. Altitude 25,500 feet.'

David felt the first familiar tingle and slither of his anger and hatred, like the cold of a great snake uncoiling in his belly.

'Beseder, Two. Lock to target and go to interception speed.'

They went supersonic and David looked up ahead at the crests of the thunderheads that reared up from the solid banks of cumulo nimbus lower down. These mountainous upthrusts of silver and pale blue were sculptured into wonderful shapes that teased the imagination—towers and turrets embattled and emblazoned, heroic human shapes standing proud or hunched in the attitude of mourning, the rearing horsemen of the chessboard, a great fleecy pack of wolves, and other animal shapes of fantasy—with the deep crevasses between them bridged in splendour by the rainbows. There were hundreds of these, great blazes of colour, that turned and followed their progress across the sky, keeping majestic station upon them. Above them, the sky was a dark unnatural blue, dappled like a Windsor grey by the thin striation of the cirro cumulus, and the sunlight poured down to shimmer upon the two speeding warplanes. As yet there was no sight of the target. It was up there somewhere amongst the cloud mountains. He looked back at his radar screen. He had taken his radar out of scan and locked it into the target, and now as they closed rapidly he could appraise their relative positions.

The target was flying parallel to them, twenty miles out on their starboard side, and it was high above them and moving at a little more than half their speed. The sun was beyond the target, just short of its zenith, and David calculated his approach path to bring him into an attack vector from above and into the target's starboard quarter.

'Turning to starboard now,' he warned Joe, and they came around together, crossing the target's rear to put themselves in the sun. Joe was calling the range and bearing, it showed a leisurely patrol pattern. There was no indication as yet that the target was aware of the hunters behind and far below.

'Two, this is leader. Arm your circuits.'

Without taking his eyes from the radar screen, David pressed the master switch on his weapon console. He activated the two air-to-air sidewinder missiles that hung under each wing-tip, and immediately heard the soft electronic tone cycling in his earphones. That tone indicated that the missiles were dormant, they had not yet detected an infra-red source to excite them. When they did they would increase the volume and rate of cycle, growling with anticipation, clamouring like hunting dogs on the leash. He tuned them down so he could no longer hear them.

Now he selected his cannon switch, readying the twin 30-mm. weapons in their pods just below his seat. The trigger flicked forward out of its recess in the head of the joystick and he curled his forefinger about it to familiarize himself with the feel of it.

'Two, this is leader. I am commencing visual.' It was a warning to Joe to concentrate all his attention on the screen and feed David with directional data.

'Target is now ten o'clock high, range figures two seven nautical miles.'

David searched carefully, raking the billowing walls of blinding white, breaking off the search to look away at a ground point or a pinnacle of cloud to prevent his eyes focusing short, and to sweep the blind spot behind them, lest the hunters become the hunted.

Then he saw them. There were five of them, and they appeared suddenly out of cloud high above and were immediately outlined against it like tiny black fleas on a newly ironed bedsheet. Just then Joe called the range again.

'Figures one three nautical miles,' but the targets were outlined so crisply against their background that David could make out the delta-winged dart shape, and the high tailplane that identified them beyond all doubt as MIG 21 J.

'I have target visual,' he told Joe. 'Five MIG 21's J.' His tone was flat and neutral, but it was a lie, for now at last his anger had something on which to fasten, and it changed its shape and colour, it was no longer black and aching but cold and bright and keen as a rapier's blade.

'Target is still hostile,' Joe confirmed that they were within Israeli territory, but his tone was not as well guarded as David's. David could detect the huskiness in it, and knew that Joe was feeling that anger also.

It would be another fifteen seconds before they had completed their turn across the enemy's stern, and David assessed the relative positions and saw that so far it had been a perfect approach. The formation sailed on serenely, unaware of the enemy beneath their tail, creeping up in the blind spot where the forward scanning radar could not discover them and rapidly moving into a position up sun. Once there, David would go to attack speed and climb steeply up into a position of superior height and tactical advantage over the enemy formation. Looking ahead now, he realized that chance had given him an added bonus; one of the huge tower blocks of cloud was perfectly placed to screen his climb into the sun. He would use it to cover his stalk, the way the Boer huntsman of Africa stalked wild buffalo from behind a herd of domestic oxen.

'Target is altering course to starboard,' Joe warned him. The MIGS were turning away, edging back towards the Syrian border. They had completed their taunting gesture, they had flaunted the colours of Islam in the face of the infidel, and were making for safety.

David felt the blade of anger in his guts burn colder, sting sharper, and with an effort of restraint he waited out the last few seconds before making his climb. The moment came and his voice was still flat and without passion as he called to Joe, 'Two, this is leader, commencing storm-climb.'

'Two conforming.'

David eased back on the controls and they went up in a climb so vicious that it seemed to tear their bowels from their bellies.

Almost immediately, Desert Flower picked up the radar images as they emerged from the ground clutter.

'Hullo both units Bright Lance. We are now tracking you. Show friend or foe.'

Both David and Joe were lying on their backs in the thrust of storm-climb, but at the order they punched in the I.F.F. systems. Identification Friend or Foe would show a distinctive pattern, a bright halo, around their radar images on command plot identifying them positively even while they were locked with the enemy in the close proximity of the dogfight.

'Beseder—we are tracking you in I.F.F.,' said the Brig, and they went plunging into the pillar of cloud and raked upwards through it. David's eyes darted between the boulé that contained his blind-flying instruments and the radar screen on which the enemy images shone bright and with hard outline, so close now that the individual aircraft in the enemy formation stood out clearly.

'Target is increasing speed and tightening starboard turn,' Joe intoned and David compensated for the enemy's manœuvre.

David was certain that they had not detected his approach, the turn away was coincidental. Another glance at the screen showed that he had achieved his height advantage. He was now two miles off their quarter above them, with the sun at his back. It was the ideal approach.

'Turning now into final leg of attack pattern,' he alerted Joe to his intention and they began the pitch in. The last-second strike which would send their speed rocketing as they closed.

The target centred dead ahead, and the gunsight lit up, glowing softly on the screen ahead of him. The sidewinder missiles caught the first faint emanations of infra-red rays from their victims, and they began to growl softly in David's earphones.

Still blinded by thick grey cloud they raced in, and suddenly they burst out into the clear. Ahead and below them opened a deep trough of space, a valley between cloud ranges and close below them the five MIGs sparkled silvery in the sunlight, pretty and toylike, their red, white and green markings festive and gay, the clean geometrical sweeps of wing and tail nicely balanced and the shark-like mouths of the jet intakes gaping, as they sucked in air.

They were in loose V-formation, two stacked back on each flank of the leader and in the fleeting seconds that David had to study them, he had assessed them. The four wingmen were Syrians, there was an indefinable sloppiness in their flying, a looseness of control. They flew with that lack of polish and confidence of the pupil. They were soft targets, easy pickings.

However, it did not need the three red rings about the leader's fuselage to identify him as a Russian instructor. Some leery old veteran with hawk's blood in his veins, tough and canny, and dangerous as an angry black mamba.

'Engage two port targets,' David ordered Joe, reserving the MIG leader and the starboard echelon for his attack. In David's headphones the missiles were growling their anxiety, they had sniffed out the massed jet blasts below them and already they were tracking, howling their eagerness to kill.

David switched to command net. 'Hello, Desert Flower, this is Bright Lance on target and requesting strike.'

Almost instantly the voice came back. 'David, this is the Brig–' he was speaking rapidly, urgently, '–discontinue attack pattern. I repeat, disengage target. They are no longer hostile. Break off attack.'

Shocked by the command, David glanced down the deep valley of cloud and saw the long brown valley of the Jordan falling away behind them. They had crossed over a line on the earth and immediately their roles had changed from defender to aggressor. But they were closing the target rapidly. It was a fair bounce, they were still unaware.

'We are going to hit them,' David made the decision through the cold bright thing that burned within him and he closed command net and spoke to Joe.

'Two, this is leader attacking.'

'Negative! I say again negative!' Joe called urgently. 'Target is no longer hostile!'

'Remember Hannah!' David shouted into his mask. 'Conform to me!' and he curled his finger about the trigger and touched left rudder, yawing fractionally to bring the nearest MIG into the field of his sights. It seemed to balloon in size as he shrieked towards it.

There was a heart-beat of silence from Joe, and then his voice strangled and rough.

'Two conforming.'

'Kill them, Joe,' David yelled and pressed against the spring-loaded tension of the trigger. There was a soft double hiss, hardly discernible above the jet din, and from under each wing-tip the missiles unleashed, they skidded and twisted as they aligned themselves on the targets, leaving darkly etched trails of vapour across David's front, and at that moment the MIGs became aware.

At a shouted warning from their leader, the entire formation burst into its five separate parts, splintering silvery swift like a shoal of sardines before the driving charge of the barracuda.

The rearmost Syrian was slow, he had only just begun to turn away when one of the sidewinders flicked its tail, followed his turn and united with him in an embrace of death.

The shock wave of the explosion jarred David's machine, but the sound of it was muted as the MIG was enveloped in the greenish-tinted cloud of the strike and it shattered into fragments. A wing snapped off and went whirling high and the brief blooming flower of smoke blew swiftly past David's head.

The second missile had chosen the machine with the red rings, the formation leader, but the Russian had reacted so swiftly and pulled his turn so tight that the missile slid past him in an overshoot, and it lost the scent, unable to follow the MIG around. As David hauled the Mirage round after the Russian, he saw the missile destroy itself in a burst of greenish smoke, far out across the valley of clouds.

The Russian was in a hard right-hand turn, and David followed him. Staring across the imaginary circle that separated them, he could see every detail of the enemy machine; the scarlet helmet of the pilot, the gaudy colours of its roundels, the squiggle of Arabic script that was its identification markings—even the individual rivets that stitched the polished metal skin of the MIG.

David pulled back with all his strength against his joystick, for gravity was tightening the loading of his controls, opposing his efforts to place additional stress on the Mirage lest he tear its wings off the fuselage.

Gravity had hold of David also, its insidious force sucked the blood away from his brain so that his vision dimmed, the colour of the enemy's pilot's helmet faded to dull brown, and David felt himself crushed down into his seat.

About his waist and legs his G-suit tightened its coils squeezing brutally like a hungry python, attempting to prevent the drainage of blood from his upper torso.

David tensed every muscle in his body, straining to resist the loss of blood, and he took the Mirage up in a sliding, soaring yo-yo, up the side of an imaginary barrel. Like a motor-cyclist on a wall of death he whirled aloft, trying once more for the advantage of height.

His vision narrowed, greyed out, until his field was reduced to the limits of his cockpit, and he was pinned heavily to his seat, his mouth sagging open, his eyelids dragging downwards; the effort of holding his right hand on the control column was Herculean.

In the corner of his vision the stall indicator blinked its little eye at him, changing from amber to red, warning him that he was on the verge of catastrophe, courting the disaster of supersonic stall.

David filled his lungs and screamed with all his strength, his own voice echoing through the grey mist. The effort forced a little blood back to his brain and his vision cleared briefly, enough to let him see that the MIG had anticipated his yo-yo and had come up under him, sliding up the wall of death towards his unprotected flank and belly.

David had no alternative but to break out of the turn before the MIG's cannons could bear. He rolled the Mirage out, and went instantly into a tight climbing left-hander, his afterburners still thundering at full power, consuming fuel at a prodigious rate and placing a limit upon these desperate manœuvres.

Neatly and gracefully as a ballet dancer, the Russian followed him out of the turn and locked into his next manœuvre. David saw him coming up into an attack position in his rear-view mirror and he rolled out again and went up and right, blacking out with the rate of turn.

Roll and turn, turn for life, David had judged the Russian fairly. He was a deadly opponent, quick and hard, anticipating each of David's turns and twists, riding always within an ace of strike. Turn, and turn again, in great winging parabolas, climbing always, turning always, vapour trails spinning out from their wing-tips in silky arabesque patterns against the hard blue of the sky.

David's arms and shoulders ached as he fought the control dampers and the weight of gravity, sickened by the drainage of blood and the adrenalin in his system. His cold battle rage turned gradually to icy despair as each of his efforts to dislodge the Russian were met and countered, and always the gaping shark's maw of the MIG hung and twisted a point off his shoulder or belly. All David's expertise, all the brilliance of his natural flying gifts were slowly being discounted by the store of combat experience upon which his enemy could draw.

At one stage, when for an instant they flew wing-tip to wing-tip, David glanced across the gap and saw the man's face. Just the eyes and forehead above the oxygen mask; the skin was pale as bone and the eyes were deep socketed like those of a skull—and then David was turning again, turning and screaming and straining against gravity, screaming also against the first enfolding coils of fear.

He rolled half out of the turn and then without conscious thought, reversed the roll. The Mirage shuddered with protest and his speed bled off. The Russian saw it and came down on him from high on his starboard quarter. As David pushed the stick fully forward and left he kicked on full left rudder, ducking under the blast of cannon fire, and the Mirage went down in a spiralling dive. The blood which gravity had sucked from his head was now flung upwards through his body, filling his head and his vision with bright redness, the red-out of inverted gravitational force. A vein in his nose popped under the pressure and suddenly his oxygen mask was filled with a flood of warm choking blood.

The Russian was after him, following him into the dive, lining him up for his second burst.

David screamed with the metallic salty taste of blood in his mouth and hauled back on the stick with all his strength, the nose came up and over, climbing out of the dive, and again the blood drained from his head—going from red-out to black-out in the fraction of a second and he saw the Russian following him up, drawn by the ploy. At the top David kicked it out in a breakaway roll. It caught the Russian, he was one-hundredth of a second slow in countering and he swung giddily through David's gunsight, an almost impossible deflection shot that sluiced cannon fire wildly across the sky, spraying it like water from a garden hose. The MIG was in David's sights for perhaps one-tenth of a second, but in that time David saw a flash of light, a bright wink of it below the pilot's canopy, and then David rolled and turned out, coming around hard and finding the Russian still hanging in the circuit, but losing air space, swaying out with a feather of white vapour streaming back from below his cockpit canopy.

'I've hit him, David exulted, and his fear was gone, become anger again, a fierce triumphant anger. He took the Mirage up in another soaring yo-yo and this time the MIG could not hold station on him and David flick-rolled off the top and came out with the Russian centred in his gunsight.

He fired a one-second burst and saw the incendiary shells lace in and burst in quick little stabbing stars in the silver fuselage of the MIG.

The Russian came out of his turn, in a gentle dive, flying straight, no longer taking evasive action, probably dead at his controls, and David sat on his tail, and settled the pipper of his gunsight.

He fired another one-second burst and the MIG began to break up. Small unidentifiable pieces of wreckage flew back at David, but the Russian stayed with his machine.

Again David hit him with a two-second burst, and now the MIG's nose sank until she was in a vertical dive still under full power and she went down like a silver javelin. David could not follow her without tearing off his own wings. He pulled out and watched the Russian fly into the earth at a speed that must have exceeded mach 2. He burst like a bomb in a tall tower of dust and smoke that stood for long seconds on the brown plains of Syria.

David shut down his afterburner and looked to his fuel gauges. They were all showing only a narrow strip above the empty notch, and David realized that the last screaming dive after the MIG had taken him down to an altitude of five thousand, he was over enemy territory and too low—much too low.

Expending precious fuel he came around on a westerly heading and went to interception speed, climbing swiftly out of range of flak and searching the heavens above him for sign of either Joe or the other MIGs—although he guessed that the Syrians were either with Allah in the garden of the Houris, or back home with mother by this time.

'Bright Lance Two, this is leader. Do you read me?'

'Leader, this is Two,' Joe's voice answered him immediately. 'I have you visual. In the name of God, get out of there!'

'What is my position?'

'We are fifty miles within Syrian territory, our course for base is 250° '

'How did you go?'

'I took out one of mine. The other one ran for it, after that I was too busy keeping an eye on you—'

David blinked his eyes and was surprised to find that sweat was pouring down his forehead from under his helmet and his mask was slick and sticky with blood from his nose-bleed. His arms and shoulders still ached, and he felt drunken and light-headed from the effects of gravity and combat and his hands on the control column were shaky and weak.

'I got two,' he said, 'two of the swines—one for Debra, and one for Hannah.'

'Shut up, Davey,' Joe's voice was stiff with tension. 'Concentrate on getting out of here. You are within range of both flak and ground missiles. Light your tail—and let's go.'

'Negative,' David answered him. 'I'm low on fuel. Where are you?'

'Six o'clock high at 25,000.' As he answered, Joe sat up in his seat, leaning forward against his shoulder straps to watch the tiny wedge shape of David's machine far below. It was climbing slowly to meet him, slowly—too slowly, and low—too low. David was vulnerable and Joe was afraid for him, frowning heavily into his face mask and searching restlessly, sweeping heaven and earth for the first hint of danger. Two minutes would see them clear, but they would be two long, slow minutes.

He almost missed the first missile. The ground crew must have allowed David to overfly their launch pad before they put it up in pursuit—for Joe picked up its vapour trail as it streaked in from behind David, closing rapidly with him.

'Missile, break left,' Joe yelled into his mask. 'Go! Go! Go!' and he saw David begin his turn instantly, steeply, side-stepping the sizzling attack of the missile.

'It's lost you!' Joe called, as the missile continued its crazy career through space, beginning to yaw from side to side as it hunted for a target and at last bursting in self-destruction.

'Keep going, Davey,' Joe encouraged him, 'but keep awake, there will be more.'

They both saw the next one leave the ground from its camouflaged vehicle. There was a nest of them on a rocky ridge above a sun-blasted plain. The Serpent slid off the rock and lifted into the sky, climbed rapidly towards David's little machine.

'Light your tail,' Joe told him, 'and wait for it!' He watched the missile boring in, converging with dazzling speed on David's Mirage.

'Break right! Go! Go! Go!' Joe yelled and David twisted violently aside. Again the Serpent slid past him, over-shooting, but this time not losing contact and coming around to attack again, its seekers locked on David's machine.

'He's still on you,' Joe was screaming now. 'Go for the sun, Davey. Try for the sun,' and the Mirage pointed its nose at the great blazing orb that burned above the mountain ranges of dark cloud. The Serpent followed him upwards, hunting him with the dreadful single-mindedness of the automaton.

'He's on to you, Davey. Flip out now! Go! Go! Go!'

David flicked the Mirage out of her vertical climb, and fell like a stone—while the Serpent fastened its attention upon the vast infra-red output from the sun and streaked on towards it, losing the Mirage.

'You've lost it. Get out, Davey, get out!' Joe pleaded with him, but for the moment the Mirage was helpless. In her desperate climb for the sun she had lost manœuvring speed and was wallowing clumsily now. It would be many seconds before she became agile and lithe once more—and by then it would be too late—for Joe saw the third missile become airborne and dart upwards on its feather of flame and smoke aiming at David's Mirage.

Joe did not consciously realize what he was going to do until he had winged over and commenced his dive under full power. He came down with his mach meter indicating twice the speed of sound, and he levelled across David's tail, cutting obliquely across his track under the nose of the oncoming Serpent.

The Serpent saw him with its little cyclops radar eye, and it sensed the heat of his exhausts—fresher, more tantalizing than David's, and it accepted him as an alternative target and swung away after him, leaving David to fly on unscathed.

David saw Joe's aircraft flash past his wing-tip at searing speed, and but an instant behind him followed the Serpent. It took him only a second to realize that Joe had deliberately pulled the missile off him, had accepted the attack that must surely have destroyed David.

He watched with fascinated horror as Joe pulled out of his dive, and used his speed to climb into the sun. The missile followed him smoothly, angling upwards, overhauling Joe's Mirage with effortless ease. Joe was watching the missile in his mirror, and at the last instant he flipped out of the climb—but this time the Serpent was not deceived; as Joe dropped so it swivelled also, and as earlier David had wallowed helplessly now Joe was in the same predicament. He had taken his chance and it had not worked for him. The missile found him, and in a brusque burst of flame, Joe and his Mirage died together.

David flew on alone, his Mirage once more at manœuvring speed and his throat dry with horror and fear and grief. He found himself talking aloud.

'Joe, no, Joe. Oh God no! You shouldn't have done it.'

Ahead of him through the gaps in the massive cloud bases he saw the Jordan.

'It should be you that's going home, Joe,' he said. 'It should be you, Joe,' and felt the hard ball of sorrow in his throat.

But the instinct of survival was still strong and David yawed and glanced back to clear his blind spot—and he saw the last missile coming in on him. It was just a small black speck far behind, with a little frill of dark smoke around it, but it was watching him hungrily with its wicked little eye.

As he saw it, he knew beyond doubt that this one was his, the one that the fates had reserved for him. The attacks he had evaded so far had worn his nerves and strained his judgement, he felt a sense of fatalistic dismay as he watched the attacking missile gaining on him, nevertheless he gathered his scattered reserves for one more supreme effort.

His eyes narrowed to slits, the sweat sliding down his face and drenching his mask, his left hand holding the throttle fully open and his right gripping the control column with the strength, of despair, he judged his moment.

The missile was almost upon him and he screamed with all his might and hurled the Mirage into the turn, but he had misjudged it by the smallest part of a second. As he turned away the missile slid past him and it was close enough to pick up the shadow of the Mirage in the photo-electric eye of its fusing device. The eye winked at him and the missile exploded.

The Mirage was in the critical attitude of its turn, and the cockpit canopy was exposed entirely to the centre of the blast. It hit the plane with a blow that sent it tumbling; like a running man tripping it went over, and it lost lift and flying capability.

The canopy was penetrated by flying steel. A piece struck David's armoured seat with a clang and then it glanced off and struck his left arm above the elbow, snapping the bone cleanly so that the arm dropped uselessly and hung into his lap.

An icy wind raged through the torn canopy as the Mirage hurled itself through space with suicidal force, whipping its nose through the vicious motions and flat plane of high-speed spin. David was thrown against his straps, his ribs bruised and his skin seared from his shoulders, and the broken arm flailing agonizingly.

He tried to hold himself upright in his seat as he reached up over his head, caught hold of the handle of the ejector mechanism and hauled the blind down over his face. He expected to have the charge explode beneath his seat and hurl him free of the doomed Mirage—but nothing happened.

Desperately he released the handle and strained forward to reach the secondary firing mechanism under his seat between his feet. He wrenched it and felt despair as there was no response. The seat was not working, the blast had damaged some vital part of it. He had to fly the Mirage out of it, with one arm and very little altitude left to him. He fastened his right fist on to the moulded grip of the stick, and in the crazy fall and flutter and whirl, David began to fight for control, flying now by instinct alone, for he was badly hurt, and sky and horizon, earth and cloud spun giddily across his vision.

He was aware that he was losing height rapidly, for every time the earth swayed through his line of vision it was closer and more menacing, but doggedly he continued his attempts to roll against the direction of spin.

The earth was very close before he felt the first hint of response, and the ferocity of her gyrations abated slightly. Stick and rudder together, he tried again and the Mirage showed herself willing at last. Gently, with the touch of a lover, he wooed her and suddenly she came out and he was flying straight and level, but she was hard hit. The blast of the missile had done mortal damage, and she was heavy and sick in his hands. He could feel the rough vibration of the engine shaking her, and he guessed that the compressor had thrown a blade and was now out of balance. Within minutes or seconds she would begin to tear herself to pieces. He could not try for climbing power on her.

David looked quickly about him and realized with a shock how far he had fallen in that terrible tumble down the sky. He was only two or three hundred feet above the earth. He was not sure of his direction, but when he glanced at his doppler compass, he found with mild surprise that he was still heading in the general direction of home.

The engine vibration increased, and he could hear the shrill screech of rending metal. He wasn't going to make it home—that was certain, and there was insufficient height to jettison the canopy, release his straps and attempt to scramble out of the cockpit. There was only one course still remaining, he must fly the Mirage in.

Even as he made the decision his one good hand was busy implementing it. Holding the stick between his knees, he let down his landing gear; the nose wheel might hold him up long enough to take some of the speed off her and prevent her cartwheeling.

He looked ahead, and saw a low ridge of rocky ground and sparse green vegetation. Disaster lurked for him there—but beyond it were open fields, ploughed land, orderly blocks of orchard, neatly laid-out buildings. That in itself was cheering. Such order and industry could only mean that he had returned across the border to Israel.

David skimmed over the ridge of broken rocks, sucking in his own belly as though to lift the Mirage bodily over the hungry teeth of granite, and ahead of him lay the fields. He could see women working in one of the orchards, stopping and turning to look at him. So close that he could clearly see the expression of surprise and apprehension on their faces.

There was a man on a blue tractor and he jumped from his seat and fell to the earth as David passed only feet above his head.

All fuel cocks closed, all switches off, master switch off—David went into the final ritual for crash-landing.

Ahead of him lay the smooth brown field, open and clear. He might just be lucky enough, it might just come off.

The Mirage was losing flying speed, her nose coming up, the airspeed needle sinking back, 200 miles per hour, 190, 180, dropping back to her stalling speed of 150.

Then suddenly David realized that the field ahead of him was latticed with deep concrete irrigation channels. They were twenty feet wide, and ten deep, a deadly hazard—enough to destroy a Centurion tank.

There was nothing David could do now to avoid their gaping jaws. He flew the Mirage in, touching down smoothly.

'Smooth as a tomcat pissing on a sheet of velvet,' he thought bitterly, aware that all his skill was unavailing now. 'Even Barney would have been proud of me.' The field was rough, but the Mirage settled to it, pitching and lurching, shaking David ruthlessly about the cockpit, but she was up on all three wheels, losing speed handily, her undercart taking the strain. However, she was still travelling at ninety miles an hour when she went into the irrigation ditch.

It snapped her undercart off like pretzel sticks and she nosed in, struck the far bank of concrete that sheered through metal like a scythe, and sent the fuselage cartwheeling across the field with David still strapped within it. The wings broke away and the body slid on across the soft earth to come to rest at last, right way up like a stranded whale.

The whole of David's left side was numb, no feeling in his arm or leg, the straps had mauled him with their rude grasp, and he was stunned and bewildered in the sudden engrossing silence.

For many seconds he sat still, unable to move or think. Then he smelled it, the pervasive reek of Avtur jet fuel from the ruptured tanks and lines. The smell of it galvanized him with the pilot's deadly fear of fire.

With his right hand he grabbed the canopy release lever and heaved at it. He wasted ten precious seconds with it, for it was jammed solid. Then he turned his attention to the steel canopy breaker in its niche below the lever. This was a tool specially designed for this type of emergency. He lifted it, lay back in his seat and attacked the Perspex dome above his head. The stink of jet fuel was overpowering, filling the cockpit, and he could hear the little pinging and tinkling sound made by white-hot metal.

His left arm hampered him, he had no feeling or use in it. The straps bound him tightly to his seat and he had to pause in his assault upon the canopy to loosen them.

Then he began again. He tore an opening in the Perspex, the size of a hand, and as he worked to enlarge it, a ruptured fuel pressure line somewhere in the shattered fuselage sprayed a jet of Avtur high in the air. it fell in a heavy drizzle upon the canopy like a garden sprinkler, poured down the curved sides and dribbled through the hole David was cutting. It fell into his face, icy cold on his cheeks and stinging his eyes, it drenched his shoulders and the front of his pressure suit, and David began to pray. For the first time ever in his life the words took on meaning and he felt his terror receding.

'Hear O Israel, the Lord our God, the Lord is one.'

He prayed aloud, striking up at the softly yielding Perspex and feeling the soft rain of death in his face. He tore at the opening with his hands, bringing away slabs of transparent material, but ripping his gloves and leaving his blood smearing the jagged edges of the opening.

'Blessed be His name, whose glorious kingdom is for ever—'

The opening was large enough. He hauled himself up in the seat, and found himself caught by the oxygen and radio lines attached to his helmet. He could not reach them with his crippled left arm. He stared down at the offending limb, and saw the blood welling out of the torn sleeve of the suit. There was no pain but it was twisted at a comical angle from the elbow.

'You shall love the Lord your God with all your heart—' he whispered, and with his right hand he tore loose the chin strap and let his helmet drop to the floor-boards. The Avtur soaked into the soft dark mop of his hair and ran down his neck behind his ears, and he thought about the flames of hell.

Painfully he dragged himself out through the opening in the canopy, and now not even prayer could hold off the dark hordes of terror that assaulted his soul.

'–For the anger of God will kindle against you–'

Laboriously he crawled across the slippery sleek metal of the wing root and fell to the ground. He fell face-down and lay for a moment, exhausted by fear and effort.

'–remember all the commands of God–'

He heard voices then as he lay with his face against the dusty earth, and he lifted his head and saw the women from the orchard running towards him across the open field. The voices were shrill but faint and the words were in Hebrew. He knew that he was home.

Steadying himself against the shattered body of the Mirage, he came to his feet with the broken arm dangling at his side, and he tried to shout to them.

'Go back! Beware!' but his voice was a throaty croak, and they ran on towards him. Their dresses and aprons were gay spots of colour against the dry brown earth.

He pushed himself away from the aircraft and staggered to meet the running women.

'Go back!' he croaked in his own terrible distress, with the grip of his G-suit strangling his movements and the evaporating fuel cold as ice in his hair and down his face.

Within the battered hull of the Mirage a puddle of Avtur had been heated by the white-hot shell of the jet compressor. Its low volatility at last was raised to flash point and a dying spark from the electronic equipment was enough to ignite it.

With a dull but awful roar, the Mirage bloomed with dark crimson flame and sooty black smoke, the wind ripped the flames outwards in great streamers and pennants that engulfed all around them, and David staggered onwards in the midst of the roaring furnace that seemed to consume the very air.

He held his breath–if he had not, the flame would have scorched his lungs. He closed his eyes tightly against the agony and ran on blindly. His body and his limbs were protected by the fireproof pressure suit and boots and gloves–but his head was bare and soaked with fuel.

As he ran his head burned like a torch. His hair frizzled off, in a stinking puff of flame and the skin of his scalp and neck and face was exposed. The flames burnt his ears off and most of his nose, they flayed off his skin in a blistering sheet and then they ate into the raw flesh, they burnt away his lips and exposed his teeth and part of the bone of his jaw. They ate through his eyelids and stripped the living meat from his cheeks.

David ran on through the burning air and smoke, and he did not believe that such pain was possible. It exceeded all his imaginings and swamped all the senses of his body and mind–but he knew he must not scream. The pain was a blackness and the vivid colours of flame in his tightly closed eyes, it was a roaring in his ears like all the winds of the world, and in his flesh it was the goads and whips and burning hooks of hell itself. But he knew he could not let this terrible fire enter his body and he ran on without screaming.

The women from the orchard were brought up short by the sudden forest of flame and black smoke that rose up in front of them, engulfing the squashed-insect body of the aircraft, and closing around the running figure of the pilot.

It was a solid impenetrable wall of heat and smoke that blotted out all ahead of them, and forced them to draw back, awed and horrified, before its raging hot breath. They stood in a small group, panting and wild-eyed.

Then abruptly a freak gust of wind opened the heavy oily curtains of smoke, and out of them stumbled a dreadful thing with a scorched and smoking body and a head of flame.

Blindly it came out of the smoke, one arm hanging and its feet dragging and staggering in the soft earth. They stared at this thing in horror, frozen in silence, and it came towards them.

Then a strapping girl, with a strong brown body and a mane of dark hair, uttered a cry of compassion—and raced to meet him.

As she ran, she stripped off her heavy voluminous skirt of thick wool, leaving her strong brown legs bare. She reached David and she swirled the skirt over his head, smothering the flames that still ate into his flesh. The other women followed her, using their clothing to wrap him as he fell and rolled on the earth.

Only then did David begin to scream, from that lipless mouth with the exposed teeth. It was a sound that none of them would ever forget. As he screamed the eyes were open, with the lashes and brow and most of the lids burned away. The eyes were dark indigo blue in the glistening mask of wet scorched meat, and the little blood vessels, sealed by the heat, popped open and dribbled and spurted. As he screamed, the blood and lymph bubbled from the nostril holes where his nose had been, and his body writhed and heaved and convulsed as spasm after spasm of unbearable agony hit him.

The women had to hold him down to control his struggles, and to prevent him tearing with clawed fingers at the ruins of his face.

He was still screaming when the doctor from the kibbutz slashed open the sleeve of his pressure suit with a scalpel and pressed the morphine needle into the twitching jumping muscles of his arm.

The Brig saw the last bright radar image fade from the plot and heard the young radar officer report formally. 'No further contact.' And a great silence fell on the command bunker.

They were all watching him. He stood hunched over the plot and his big bony fists were clasped at his sides. His face was stiff and expressionless, but his eyes were terrible.

It seemed that the frantic voices of his two pilots still echoed from the speakers above his head, as they called to each other in the extremes of mortal conflict.

They had all heard David's voice, hoarse with sorrow and fear.

'Joe! No, Joe! Oh God, no!' and they knew what that meant. They had lost them both, and the Brig was still stunned by the sudden incalculable turn that the sortie had taken.

At the moment he had lost control of his fighters he had known that disaster was unavoidable—and now his son was dead. He wanted to cry out aloud, to protest against the futility of it. He closed his eyes tightly for a few seconds, and when he opened them, he was in control again.

'General alert,' he snapped. 'All squadrons to "Red" standby–' he knew they faced an international crisis. 'I want air cover over the area they went down. They may have ejected. Put up two Phantom flights and keep an umbrella over them. I want helicopters sent in immediately, with paratrooper guards and medical teams–'

Command bunker moved swiftly into general alert procedure.

'Get me the Prime Minister,' he said, he was going to have to do a lot of explaining, and he spared a few vital seconds to damn David Morgan roundly and bitterly.

The airforce doctor took one look at David's charred and scorched head and he swore softly.

'We'll be lucky to save this one.'

Loosely he swathed the head in Vaseline bandages and they hurried with David's blanket-wrapped body on the stretcher to the Bell 205 helicopter waiting in the orchard.

The Bell touched down on the helipad at Hadassah Hospital and a medical team was ready for him. One hour and fifty-three minutes after the Mirage hit the irrigation canal David had passed through the sterile lock into the special burns unit on the third floor of the hospital–into a quiet and secluded little world where everybody wore masks and long green sterile robes and the only contact with the outside world was through the double-glazed windows and even the air he breathed was scrubbed and cleaned and filtered.

However, David was enfolded in the soft dark clouds of morphine and he did not hear the quiet voices of the masked figures as they worked over him.

'It's third degree over the entire area–'

'No attempt to clean it or touch it, sister, not until it stabilizes. I am going to spray with Epigard, and we'll go to intra-muscular Tetracycline four-hourly against infection–'

'It will be two weeks before we dare touch it.'

'Very well, doctor.'

'Oh, and sister, fifteen milligrams of morphine six-hourly. We are going to have a lot of pain with this one.'

Pain was infinity, an endless ocean across which the wave-patterns marched relentlessly to burst up the beaches of his soul. There were times when the surf of pain ran high and each burst of it threatened to shatter his reason. Again there were times when it was low, almost gentle in its throbbing rhythm and he drifted far out upon the ocean of pain to where the morphine mists enfolded him. Then the mists parted and a brazen sun beat down upon his head, and he squirmed and writhed and cried out. His skull seemed to bloat and swell until it must burst, and the open nerve-ends screamed for surcease.

Then suddenly there was the sharply beloved sting of the needle in his flesh, and the mists closed about him once more.

'I don't like the look of this at all. Have we taken a culture, sister?'

'Yes, doctor.'

'What are we growing?'

'I'm afraid it's strep.'

'Yes. I thought so. I think we'll have to change to Cloxacillin–see if we get a better response with that.'

With the pain, David became aware of a smell. It was the smell of carrion and things long dead, the smell of vermin in dirty blankets, of vomit and excreta, and the odour of wet garbage festering in dark alleys–and at last he came to know that the smell was the rotting of his own flesh as the bacteria of Streptococcus infection attacked the exposed tissue.

They fought it with the drugs, but now the pain was underlined with the fevers of infection and the terrible burning thirsts which no amount of liquids could slake.

With the fever came the nightmares and the fantasies to plague and goad him even further beyond the limits of his endurance.

'Joe–' he cried out in his agony, 'try for the sun, Joe. Break left now–Go! Go!' And then he was sobbing from the ruined and broken mouth. 'Oh, Joe! Oh God, no! Joe.'

Until the night-sister could no longer bear it and she came hurrying with the syringe, and his screams turned to babbling and then into the low whimper and moan of the drug sleep.

'We'll start with the acriflavin dressings now, sister.'

When they changed the dressings every forty-eight hours it was under general anaesthetic for the entire head was of raw flesh, a bland expressionless head, a head like a child's drawing, crude lines and harsh colours, hairless, earless, streaked and mottled with yellow runs and patches of soft pus and corruption.

'We are getting a response from the Cloxacillin, it's looking a lot healthier, sister.'

The naked flesh of his eyelids had contracted, pulling back like the glistening petals of a pink rose, exposing the eyeballs to the air without respite. They had filled the eyes' sockets with a yellow ointment to soothe and moisten them, to keep out the loathsome infection that covered his head. The ointment prevented vision.

'I think we'll go for an abdominal pedicel now. Will you prep for afternoon theatre, please, sister?'

Now it was time for the knife, and David was to learn that the pain and the knife lived together in terrible sin. They lifted a long flap of skin and flesh from his belly, leaving it still attached at one end, and they rolled it into a fat sausage, then they strapped his good arm, the one without the plaster cast, to his side and they stitched the free end of the sausage to his forearm, training it to draw its blood supply from there. Then they brought him back from theatre and left him trussed and helpless and blind with the pedicel fastened to his arm, like a remora to the belly of a shark.

'Well, we have saved both eyes,' the voice was proud, fond almost, and David looked up and saw them for the first time. They were gathered around his cot, a circle of craning heads, mouths and noses covered by surgical masks, but his vision was still smeary with ointment and distorted by the drip irrigation that had replaced it.

'Now we will go for the eyelids.'

It was the knife again, the contracted and bunched-up eyelids split and re-shaped and stitched, the knife and pain and the familiar sickly tissue taste and stink of anaesthetic that saturated his body and seemed to exude from the very pores of his skin.

'Beautiful, really lovely–we have cleaned up the infection nicely. Now we can begin.'

The head was cleansed of its running rivers of pus, and now it was glistening and wet, bald and bright red, the colour of a cocktail cherry as granulation tissue formed. There were two gnarled and twisted flaps for ears, the double row of teeth startlingly white and perfect where the lips had been eaten away, a long white blade of exposed bone outlined the point of the jaw, the nose was a stump with the nostrils like the double muzzles of a shotgun, and only the eyes were still beautiful–dark indigo and flawlessly white between the lids of shocking crimson and neatly laid black stitches.

'We'll begin at the back of the neck. Will you prep for this afternoon's theatre, please, sister?'

It was a variation on the theme of the knife. They planed sheets of live skin from his thighs and meshed them to allow a wider spread, then they laid them over the exposed flesh, covering a little at each session, and evaluating each attempt while David lay in his cot and rode the long swells of pain.

'That one is no good. I'm afraid we will have to scrap it and try again.'

While his thighs grew a new crop of skin, they planed fresh sheets from his calves, so that each donor-site became a new source of pain.

'Lovely! An edge-to-edge take with that graft.'

Slowly the cap of skin extended up across the nape of his neck and over his scalp. The meshing of the skin grafts gave them a patterned effect, regular as the scales of a fish, and the new grafts were hard-looking and raised.

'We can move the pedicel up now.'

'This afternoon's theatre, doctor?'

'Yes, please, sister.'

David came to know that they operated every Thursday in the burns unit. He came to dread the Thursday morning rounds when the consultant and his staff crowded around his cot and touched and prodded and discussed the restructuring of his flesh with an impersonal candour that chilled him.

They freed the fat sausage of flesh from his belly and it dangled from his arm like some grotesque white leech, seeming to have a life of its own, drawing blood and sustenance from its grip upon his forearm.

They lifted his arm and strapped it across his chest, and the raw end of the pedicel they split and stitched to his jaw and to the stump of his nose.

'It's taken very nicely. We will begin shaping it this afternoon. We'll have him at the head of the theatre list. Will you see to that please, sister?'

With the living flesh that they had stolen from his belly they fashioned a crude lump of a nose, taut, narrow lips and a new covering for his jaw-bone.

'The oedema has settled. This afternoon I will go for the bone-graft on the jaw.'

They opened his chest and split his fourth rib laterally, robbing it of a long sliver of bone and they grafted this to the damaged jaw-bone, then they spread the flesh of the pedicel over it and stitched it all into place.

On Thursdays it was the knife and the stink of anaesthetic, and for the days between it was the ache and pain of abused and healing flesh.

They fined down the new nose, piercing it with nostrils, they finished the reconstruction of his eyelids. They laid the last grafts behind his ears, they cut a double zig-zag incision around the base of his jaw where the contracting scar tissue was trying to draw his chin down on to his chest. The new lips took firm hold on the existing muscles and David gained control of them so he could form his words again and speak clearly.

The last area of raw flesh was closed beneath the patchwork of skin grafts, flesh grafts and stitches. David was no longer a high-infection risk and he was moved from a sterile environment. Once again he saw human faces, not merely eyes peering over white surgical masks. The faces were friendly, cheerful faces. Men and women proud of their achievement in saving him from death and refleshing his ravaged head.

'You'll be allowed visitors now, I expect you'll welcome that,' said the consultant. He was a distinguished-looking young surgeon who had left a highly paid post at a Swiss Clinic to head this burns and plastic surgery unit.

'I don't think I will be having any visitors,' David had lost contact with the reality of the outside world during the nine months in the burns unit.

'Oh, yes, you will,' the surgeon told him. 'We've had regular inquiries on your progress from a number of people. Isn't that correct, sister?'

'That's right, doctor.'

'You can let them know that he is allowed visitors now.'

The consultant and his group began to move on.

'Doctor,' David called him back. 'I want a look at a mirror,' and they were silent, immediately embarrassed. This request of his had been denied many times over the last months.

'Damn it,' David became angry. 'You can't protect me from it for ever.'

The consultant gestured for the others to leave and they filed out of the ward, while he came back to David's bed.

'All right, David,' he agreed gently. 'We'll find you a mirror–though we don't have much use for them around here.' For the first time in the many months he had known him, David glimpsed the depths of his compassion, and he wondered at it. That a man who lived constantly amongst great pain and terrible disfigurement could still be moved by it.

'You must understand that how you are now is not how you will always be. All I have been able to do, so far, is heal your exposed flesh and make you functional again. You are once more a viable human being. You have not experienced the loss of any of your faculties–but I will not pretend that you are beautiful. However, there remains much that I can still do to change that. Your ears, for example, can be reconstructed with the material I have reserved for that purpose–' He indicated the stump of the pedicel that still hung from David's forearm '–There is much fine work still to be done about the nose and mouth and eyes.' He paced slowly the length of the ward and looked out into the sunlight for a moment before turning back again and coming forward to face David.

'But let me be truthful with you. There are limitations to what I can do. The muscles of expression, those delicate little muscles around the eyes and mouth have been destroyed. I cannot replace those. The hair follicles of your lashes and brows and scalp have been burned away. You will be able to wear a wig, but–'

David turned to his bedside locker and took from the drawer his wallet. He opened it and drew out a photograph. It was the one which Hannah had taken so long ago of Debra and David sitting at the rock-pool in the oasis of Ein Gedi and smiling at each other. He handed it to the surgeon.

'Is that what you looked like, David? I never knew.' The regret showed like a quick shadow in his eyes.

'Can you make me look like that again?'

The surgeon studied the photograph a moment longer, the young god's face with the dark mop of hair and the clean pure lines of the profile.

'No,' he said. 'I could not even come close.'

'That's all I wanted to know.' David took the photograph back from him. 'You say I'm functional now. Let's leave it at that, shall we?'

'You don't want further cosmetic surgery? We can still do a lot–'

'Doctor, I've lived under the knife for nine months. I've had the taste of antibiotics and anaesthetics in my mouth, and the stink of it in my nostrils for all that time. Now all I want is a little escape from pain–a little peace and the taste of clean air.'

'Very well,' the surgeon agreed readily. 'It is not important that we do it now. You could come back at any time in the future.' He walked to the door of the ward. 'Come on. Let's go find a mirror.'

There was one in the nurses' room beyond the double doors at the end of the passage. The room itself was empty and the mirror was set into the wall above the wash basin.

The surgeon stood in the doorway and leaned against the jamb. He lit a cigarette and watched as David crossed towards the mirror and then halted abruptly as he saw his own image.

He wore the blue hospital dressing-gown over his pyjamas. He was tall and finely proportioned. His shoulders were wide, his hips narrow, and he had the same lithe and beautiful man's body.

However, the head that topped it was something from a nightmare. Involuntarily he gasped out loud and the gash of a mouth parted in sympathy. It was a tight lipless mouth, like that of a cobra, white-rimmed and harsh.

Drawn by the awful fascination of horror, David drew closer to the mirror. The thick mane of his dark hair had concealed the peculiar elongation of his skull. He had never realized that it jutted out behind like that, for now the hair was gone and the bald curve was covered with meshed skin, thickened and raised.

The skin and flesh of his face was a patchwork, joined by seams of scar tissue drawn tightly over his cheekbones, giving him a vaguely Asiatic appearance, but the eyes were round and startled, with clumsy lids and puffed dead-looking flesh beneath.

His nose was a shapeless blob, out of balance with his other coarsened features and his ears were gnarled excrescences, seemingly fastened hap-hazardly to the sides of his head. The whole of it was bland and bald and boiled-looking.

The gash of a mouth twisted briefly in a horrid rictus, and then regained its frozen shape.

'I can't smile,' said David.

'No,' agreed the surgeon. 'You will have no control of your expressions.'

That was the truly horrifying aspect of it. It was not the twisted and tortured flesh, with the scarring and stitch marks still so evident—it was the expressionlessness of this mask. The frozen features seemed long dead, incapable of human warmth or feeling.

'Yeah! But you should have seen the other guy!' David said softly, and the surgeon chuckled without mirth.

'We'll have those last few stitches behind your ears out tomorrow—I shall remove what remains of the pedicel from your arm—and then you can be discharged. Come back to us when you are ready.'

David ran his hand gingerly over the bald patterned skull.

'I'm going to save a fortune in haircuts and razor blades,' he said, and the surgeon turned quickly away and walked down the passage, leaving David to get to know his new head.

The clothes that they had found for him were cheap and ill-fitting—slacks and open-neck shirt, a light jacket and sandals—and he asked for some head covering, anything to conceal the weird new shape of his scalp. One of the nurses found him a cloth cap, and then told him that a visitor was waiting for him in the hospital superintendent's department.

He was a major from the military provost marshal's office, a lean grey-haired man with cold grey eyes and a tight hard mouth. He introduced himself without offering to shake hands and then opened the file on the desk in front of him.

'I have been instructed by my office to ask for the formal resignation of your commission in the Israeli Air Force,' he started, and David stared at him. In the long pain-filled, fever-hot nights, the thought of flying once more had seemed like a prospect of paradise.

'I don't understand,' he mumbled, and reached for a cigarette, breaking the first match and then puffing quickly as the second flared. 'You want my resignation—and if I refuse?'

'Then we shall have no alternative other than to convene a court martial and to try for dereliction of duty, and refusing in the face of the enemy to obey the lawful orders of your superior officer.'

'I see,' David nodded heavily, and drew on the cigarette. The smoke stung his eyes.

'It doesn't seem I have any choice.'

'I have prepared the necessary documents. Please sign here, and here, and I shall sign as witness.'

David bowed over the papers and signed. The pen scratched loudly in the silent room.

'Thank you.' The major gathered his papers, and placed them in his briefcase. He nodded at David and started for the door.

'So now I am an outcast,' said David softly, and the man stopped. They stared at each other for a moment, and then the major's expression altered slightly, and the cold grey eyes became ferocious.

'You are responsible for the destruction of two warplanes that are irreplaceable and whose loss has caused us incalculable harm. You are responsible for the death of a brother officer, and for bringing our country to the very brink of open war which would have cost many thousands more of our young people's lives—and possibly our very existence. You have embarrassed our international friends—and given strength to our enemies.' He paused and drew a deep breath. 'The recommendation of my office was that you be brought to trial and that the prosecution be instructed to ask for the death penalty. It was only the personal intervention of the Prime Minister and of Major-General Mordecai that saved you from that. In my view, instead of bemoaning your fate, you should consider yourself highly fortunate.'

He turned away and his footsteps cracked on the stone floor as he strode from the room.

In the bleak impersonal lobby of the hospital, David was suddenly struck by a reluctance to walk on out into the spring sunshine through the glass swing doors. He had heard that long-term prisoners felt this way when the time came for their release.

Before he reached the doors he turned aside and went down to the hospital synagogue. In a corner of the quiet square hall he sat for a long time. The stained-glass windows, set high in the nave, filled the air with shafts of coloured light when the sun came through, and a little of the peace and beauty of that place stayed with him and gave him courage when at last he walked out into the square and boarded a bus for Jerusalem.

He found a seat at the rear, and beside a window. The bus pulled away and ground slowly up the hill towards the city.

He became aware that he was being watched, and he lifted his head to find that a woman with two young children had taken the seat in front of him. She was a poorly dressed, harassed-looking woman, prematurely aged and she held the grubby younger infant on her lap and fed it from a plastic bottle. However, the second child was an angelic little girl of four or five years. She had huge dark eyes and a head of thick curls. She stood on the seat facing backwards, with one thumb thrust deeply into her mouth. She was watching David steadily over the back of the seat, studying his face with that total absorption and candour of the child. David felt a sudden warmth of emotion for the child, a longing for the comfort of human contact, of which he had been deprived all these months.

He leaned forward in his seat, trying to smile, reaching out a gentle hand to touch the child's arm.

She removed her thumb from her mouth and shrank away from him, turning to her mother and clinging to her arm, hiding her face in the woman's blouse.

At the next stop David stepped down from the bus and left the road to climb the stony hillside.

The day was warm and drowsy, with the bee murmur and the smell of the blossoms from the peach orchards. He climbed the terraces and rested at the crest, for he found he was breathless and shaky. Months in hospital had left him unaccustomed to walking far, but it was not that alone. The episode with the child had distressed him terribly.

He looked longingly towards the sky. It was clear and brilliant blue, with high silver cloud in the north. he wished he could ascend beyond those clouds. He knew he would find peace up there.

A taxi dropped him off at the top of Malik Street. The front door was unlocked, swinging open before he could fit his key to the lock.

Puzzled and alarmed he stepped into the living-room. It was as he had left it so many months before, but somebody had cleaned and swept, and there were fresh flowers in a vase upon the olive-wood table–a huge bouquet of gaily coloured dahlias, yellow and scarlet.

David smelled food, hot and spicy and tantalizing after the bland hospital fare.

'Hello,' he called. 'Who is there?'

'Welcome home!' There was a familiar bellow from behind the closed bathroom door. 'I didn't expect you so soon–and you've caught me with my skirts up and pants down.'

There was a scuffling sound and then the toilet flushed thunderously and the door was flung open. Ella Kadesh appeared majestically through it. She wore one of her huge kaftans, it was a blaze of primary colours. Her hat was apple-green in colour, the brim pinned up at the side like an Australian bush hat by an enormous jade brooch and a bunch of ostrich feathers.

Her heavy arms were flung wide in a gesture of welcome, and the face was split in a huge grin of anticipation. She came towards him, and the grin persisted long after the horror had dawned in her bright little eyes. Her steps slowed.

'David?' Her voice was uncertain. 'It is you, David?'

'Hello, Ella.'

'Oh God. Oh, sweet holy name of God. What have they done to you, my beautiful young Mars–'

'Listen, you old bag,' he said harshly, 'if you start blubbering I'm going to throw you down the steps.'

She made a huge effort to control it, fighting back the tears that flooded into her eyes, but her jowls wobbled and her voice was thick and nasal as she enfolded him in her huge arms and hugged him to her bosom.

'I've got a case of cold beers in the refrigerator—and I made a pot of curry for us. You'll love my curry, it's the thing I do best—'

David ate with enormous appetite, washing down the fiery food with cold beer, and he listened to Ella talk. She spouted words like a fountain, using their flow to cover her pity and embarrassment.

'They would not let me visit you, but I telephoned every week and kept in touch that way. The sister and I got very friendly, she let me know you were coming today. So I drove up to make sure you had a welcome—'

She tried to avoid looking directly at his face, but when she did the shadows appeared in her eyes, even though she made a convincing effort at gaiety. When he finished eating at last, she asked, 'What will you do now, David?'

'I would have liked to go back and fly. It's the thing I like to do best—but they have forced me to resign my commission. I disobeyed orders, Joe and I followed them across the border, and they don't want me any more.'

'There was nearly open war, David. It was a crazy thing that you and Joe did.'

David nodded. 'I was mad. I wasn't thinking straight that day—after Debra—'

Ella interrupted quickly. 'Yes, I know. Share another beer?'

David nodded distractedly. 'How is she, Ella?' It was the question he had wanted to ask all along.

'She is just fine, Davey. She has begun the new book, and if anything it's better than the first. I think she will become a very important writer—'

'Her eyes? Is there any improvement?'

Ella shook her head. 'She has come to terms with that now. It doesn't seem to bother her any longer, just as you will come to accept what has happened—'

David was not listening. 'Ella, in all that time, when I was in hospital, every day I hoped—I knew it was useless, but I hoped to hear from her. A card, a word—'

'She didn't know, Davey.'

'Didn't know?' David demanded and leaned across the table to grip Ella's wrist. 'What do you mean?'

'After Joe—was killed, Debra's father was very angry. He believed that you were responsible.'

David nodded, the blank mask of his face concealing his guilt.

'Well, he told Debra that you had left Israel, and gone back to your home. We were all sworn to silence—and that's what Debra believes now.'

David released Ella's wrist, picked up his beer glass and sipped at the head of froth.

'You still haven't answered my question, David. What are you going to do now?'

'I don't know, Ella. I guess I'll have to think about that.'

A harsh warm wind came off the hills and ruffled the surface of the lake, darkening it to black and flecking it with white crests. The fishing boats along the curve of the shore tugged restlessly at their mooring ropes, and the fishing nets upon their drying racks billowed like bridal veils.

The wind caught Debra's hair and shook it out in a loose cloud. It pressed the silk dress she wore against her body, emphasizing the heavy roundness of her breasts and the length of her legs.

She stood on the battlements of the crusader castle, leaning both hands lightly on the head of her cane and she stared out across the water, almost as though she could see beyond it.

Ella sat near her, on a fallen block of masonry out of the wind, but she pinned her hat down with one hand as he spoke, watching Debra's face intently to judge her reactions.

'At the time it seemed the kindest thing to do. I agreed to keep the truth from you, because I did not want you to torture yourself—'

Debra spoke sharply. 'Don't ever do that again.'

Ella made a moue of resignation and went on. 'I had no way of knowing how bad he was, they would not let me see him, and so I suppose I was a coward and I let it drift.'

Debra shook her head angrily, but she remained silent. Ella wondered again that sightless eyes could contain so much expression, for Debra's emotions blazed clearly in the honey-coloured sparks as she turned her head towards Ella.

'It was not the time to distract you. Don't you see, my dear? You were adjusting so nicely—working so well on your book. I did not see that we could gain anything by telling you. I decided to co-operate with your father—and see how things turned out later.'

'Then why are you telling me all this now?' Debra demanded. 'What has happened to change your mind—what has happened to David'

'Yesterday at noon David was discharged from Hadassah Hospital.'

'Hospital?' Debra was puzzled. 'You don't mean he has been in hospital all this time, Ella. Nine months—it's impossible!'

'It's the truth.'

'He must have been terribly hurt,' Debra's anger had changed to concern. 'How is he, Ella? What happened? Is he healed now?'

Ella was silent a moment, and Debra took a pace towards her. 'Well?' she asked.

'David's plane flamed out and he was very badly burned above the head. He has recovered completely now. His burns have healed—but—'

Ella hesitated again, and Debra groped for her hand and found it. 'Go on, Ella! But—?'

'David is no longer the most beautiful man I have ever seen.'

'I don't understand?'

'He is no longer swift and vital and—any woman who sees him now will find it difficult to be near him, let alone love him.'

Debra was listening intently, her expression rapt and her eyes soft-focused.

'He is very conscious of the way he looks now. He is searching for some place to hide, I think. He talks of wanting to fly as though it is some form of escape. He knows he is alone now, cut off from the world by the mask he wears—'

Debra's eyes had misted, and Ella made her gravelly voice gentler and she went on.

'But there is somebody who will never see that mask.' Ella drew the girl closer to her. 'Somebody who remembers only the way he was before.' Debra's grip tightened on Ella's hand, and she began to smile—it was an expression that seemed to radiate from deep within her.

'He needs you now, Debra,' Ella said softly. 'That is all there is left for him.

Will you change your decision now?'

'Fetch him to me, Ella,' Debra's voice shook. 'Fetch him to me as soon as you can.'

David climbed the long line of steps towards Ella's studio. It was a day of bright sunlight and he wore open sandals and light silk slacks of a bronze colour and a short-sleeved shirt with a wide V-neck. His arms were pale from lack of sun, the dark hair of his chest contrasting strongly against the soft cream—and upon his head he wore a wide-brimmed white straw hat to guard the cicatrice from the sun and to soften his face with shadow.

He paused, and he could feel the break of sweat under the shirt and the pumping of his lungs. He despised the weakness of his body and the quivering of his legs as he came out on the terrace. It was deserted, and he crossed to the shuttered doors and went into the gloom.

Ella Kadesh sitting on a Samarkand carpet in the centre of the paved floor was an astonishing sight. For she was dressed in a brief bikini costume adorned with pink roses that almost disappeared under the rolls of ponderous flesh that hung over it from belly and breast. She was in the yoga position of Padmasana, the sitting lotus, and her massive legs were twisted and entwined like mating pythons. Her hands were held before her palm to palm and her eyes were closed in meditation; upon her head her ginger wig was set four square like that of a judge.

David leaned in the doorway and before he could recover his breath he began to laugh. It began as a wheezy little chuckle, and then suddenly he was really laughing, from deep down—great gusts of it that shook his helpless body, and flogged his lungs. It was not mirth but a catharsis of the last dregs of suffering, it was the moment of accepting life again, a taking up once more of the challenge of living.

Ella must have recognized it as such, for she did not move, squatting like some cheerful buddha on the brilliant carpet, and she opened one little eye. The effect was even more startlingly comic, and David reeled away from the door, and fell into one of the chairs.

'Your soul is a desert, David Morgan,' said Ella. 'You have no recognition of beauty, all loveliness would wither on the dung heap which—' But the rest of it was lost as she also began to giggle and the yoga pose broke down, melting like a jelly on a hot day, and she traded him hoot for hoot and bellow for bellow of laughter.

'I'm stuck,' she gasped at last. 'Help me, Davey, you oaf—' And he staggered to her, knelt and struggled to help her unlock her interwoven legs. They came apart with little creaking and popping sounds and Ella collapsed face down on the carpet groaning and giggling at the same time.

'Get out of here,' she moaned. 'Leave me to die in peace. Go and find your woman, she is down on the jetty.'

She watched him go quickly, and then she dragged herself up and went to the door. The laughter dried up and she whispered aloud, 'My two poor little crippled kittens—I wonder if I have done the right thing.' The shadows of doubt crossed her face, and then faded. 'Well, it's too damn late for worry now, Kadesh, you interfering old bag, you should have thought about that before.'

A gaudily coloured towel and beach jacket were spread upon the jetty and a transistor radio, with its volume turned high, blared out a heavy rock tune. Far out in the bay Debra was swimming alone, a steady powerful overarm crawl. Her brown arms flashed wetly in the sun at each stroke and the water churned to froth at the beat of her legs.

She stopped to tread water. Her bathing cap was plain white, and he could see that she was listening for the sound of the radio for she began to swim again, heading directly in towards the jetty.

She came out of the water, pulling off the cap and shaking out her hair. Her body was dark, sun-browned and bejewelled with drops, the muscles looked firm and hard and her tread was confident and sure as she came up the stone steps and picked up her towel.

As she dried herself David stood near and watched her avidly, seeming to devour her with his eyes, trying to make up in that first minute for all those many months. He had pictured her so clearly, and yet there was much he had forgotten. Her hair was softer, cloudier than he remembered. He had forgotten the plasticity and lustre of her skin, it was darker also than it had been before -almost the colour of her eyes—she must have spent many hours each day in the sun. Suddenly and unaffectedly she threw her towel down and adjusted the top of her brief costume, pulling open the thin fabric and cupping one fat breast in her hand to settle it more comfortably, David felt his need of her so strongly that it seemed he could not contain it all within the physical bounds of his chest. He moved slightly and the gravel crunched softly under his shoes.

Instantly the lovely head turned towards him and froze in the attitude of listening. The eyes were wide open, intelligent and expressive, they seemed to look slightly to one side of him—and David had a powerful impulse to turn and glance behind him, following their steady gaze.

'David?' she asked softly. 'Is that you, David?'

He tried to answer her, but his voice failed him and his reply was a small choking sound. She ran to him, swiftly and long-legged as a roused foal, with her arms reaching out and her face lighting with joy.

He caught her up, and she clung to him fiercely, almost angrily—as though she had been too long denied.

'I've missed you, David.' Her voice was fierce also. 'Oh, God, you'll never know how I have missed you,' and she pressed her mouth to the stark gash in his mask of flesh.

This was the first human being who had treated him without reserve—without pity or revulsion—in all those months, and David felt his heart swell harder and his embrace was as fierce as hers.

She broke at last, leaning back to press her hips unashamedly against his, exulting in the hard thrustingness of his arousal, proud to have evoked it—and quickly, questioningly she ran her hands over his face, feeling the new contours and the unexpected planes and angles.

She felt him begin to pull away, but she stopped him and continued her examination.

'My fingers tell me that you are still beautiful—'

'You have lying fingers,' he whispered, but she ignored his words, and pushed forward teasingly with her hips.

'And I'm getting another very powerful message from further south.' She gave a breathless little laugh. 'Come with me, please, sir.'

Holding his hand, she ran lightly up the steps, dragging him after her. He was amazed at the agility and confidence with which she negotiated the climb.

She drew him into the cottage and as he looked about him, quickly taking it all in, she closed and bolted the door. Immediately the room was cool and dim and intimate.

On the bed her body was still damp and cold from the lake, but her lips were hot as she strained against him urgently. The two beautiful young bodies meshed hungrily, almost as if they were attempting to find sanctuary within each other, desperately flesh sought haven within flesh, within each other's encircling arms and legs they searched for and found surcease from the loneliness and the darkness.

The physical act of love, no matter how often repeated, was insufficient for their needs; even in the intervals between they clung desperately to each other; sleeping pressed together, they groped drowsily but anxiously for each other if the movements of sleep separated them for even an instant. They talked holding hands, she reaching up to touch his face at intervals, he staring into her golden eyes. Even when she prepared their simple meals, he stood close beside or behind her so that she could sway against him and feel him there. It was as though they lived in momentary dread of being once more separated.

It was two days before they left the sanctuary of the cottage and walked together along the lake shore or swam from the jetty and lay in the warm sun. But even when Ella looked down at them from the terrace and waved, David asked, 'Shall we go up to her?'

'No,' Debra answered quickly. 'Not yet. I'm not ready to share you with anybody else yet. Just a little while more, please, David.'

And it was another three days before they climbed the path to the studio. Ella had laid on one of her gargantuan lunches, but she had invited no other guests and they were grateful to her for that.

'I thought I'd have to send down a party of stretcher-bearers to carry you up, Davey,' Ella greeted him, with a lecherous chuckle.

'Don't be crude, Ella,' Debra told her primly, flushing to a dark rose brown, and Ella let fly with one of her explosive bursts of mirth that was so contagious they must follow it.

They sat beneath the palm trees and drank wine from the earthenware jugs, and ate hugely, laughing and talking without restraint, David and Debra so involved with each other that they were not aware of Ella's shrewdly veiled appraisal.

The change in Debra was dramatic, all the coolness and reserve were gone now, the armour in which she had clad her emotions was stripped away. She was vital and eager and blooming with love.

She sat close beside David, laughing with delight at his sallies, and leaning to touch and caress him, as though to reassure herself of his presence.

Ella glanced again at David, trying to smile naturally at him, but guiltily aware of the sneaking sensation of repulsion she still felt—repulsion and aching pity—when she looked at that monstrous head. She knew that if she saw it every day for twenty years, it would still disturb her.

Debra laughed again at something David had said and turned her face to him, offering her mouth with a touching innocence.

'What a terrible thing to say,' she laughed. 'I think a gesture of contrition is called for,' and responded eagerly as the great ravaged head bent to her and the thin slit of a mouth touched hers.

It was disquieting to see the lovely dark face against that mask of ruined flesh, and yet it was also strangely moving.

'It was the right thing. For once I did the right thing,' Ella decided, watching them, and feeling a vague envy. These two were bound together completely, made strong by their separate afflictions. Before it had been a mutual itching of the flesh, a chance spark struck from two minds meeting, but now it was something that transcended that.

Ella recalled regretfully a long line of lovers stretching back to the shadowy edges of her memory, receding images which seemed unreal now. If only there had been something to bind her to one of those, if only she had been left something more valuable than half-remembered words and faded memories of brief mountings and furtive couplings. She sighed, and they looked to her questioningly.

'A sad sound, Ella, darling,' Debra said. 'We are selfish, please forgive us.'

'Not sad, my children,' Ella denied hotly, scattering the old phantoms of her memory. 'I am happy for you. You have something very wonderful—strong and bright and wonderful. Protect it as you would your life.'

She took up her wine glass. 'I give you a toast. I give you David and Debra—and a love made invincible by suffering.' And they were serious for a moment while they drank the toast together in golden yellow wine, sitting in golden yellow sunlight, then the mood resumed and they were gay once more.

Once the first desperate demands of their bodies had been met, once they had drawn as close together as physical limits would allow, then they began a coupling of the spirit. They had never really spoken before, even when they had shared the house on Malik Street, they had used only the superficial word symbols.

Now they began learning really to talk. Some nights they did not sleep but spent the fleeting hours of darkness in exploring each other's minds and bodies, and they delighted to realize that this exploration would never be completed—for the area of their minds were boundless.

During the day the blind girl taught David to see. He found that he had never truly used his eyes before, and now that he must see for both of them he had to learn to make the fullest use of his sight. He must learn to describe colour and shape and movement accurately and incisively, for Debra's demands were insatiable.

In turn, David, whose own confidence had been shattered by his disfigurement, taught confidence to the girl. She learned to trust him implicitly as he grew to anticipate her needs. She learned to step out boldly beside him, knowing that he would guide or caution her with a light touch or a word. Her world had shrunk to the small area about the cottage and jetty within which she could find her way surely. Now with David beside her, her frontiers fell back and she was free to move wherever she chose.

Yet they ventured out together only cautiously at first, wandering along the lakeside together or climbing the hills towards Nazareth, and each day they swam in the green lake waters and each night they made love in the curtained alcove.

David grew hard and lean and sun-tanned again, and it seemed they were complete for when Ella asked, 'Debra, when are you going to make a start on the new book?' she laughed and answered lightly.

'Sometime within the next hundred years.'

A week later she asked of David this time:

'Have you decided what you are going to do yet, Davey?'

'Just what I'm doing now,' he said, and Debra backed him up quickly. 'For ever!' she said. 'Just like this for ever.'

Then without thinking about it, without really steeling themselves to it, they went to where they would meet other people in the mass.

David borrowed the speedboat, picked up a shopping list from Ella, and they planed down along the lake shore to Tiberias, with the white wake churning out behind them and the wind and drops of spray in their faces.

They moored in the tiny harbour of the marina at Lido Beach and walked up into the town. David was so engrossed with Debra that the crowds about him were unreal, and although he noticed a few curious glances they meant very little to him.

Although it was early in the season, the town was filled with visitors, and the buses were parked in the square at the foot of the hill and along the lake front, for this was full on the tourist route.

David carried a plastic bag that grew steadily heavier until it was ready to overflow.

'Bread, and that's the lot,' Debra mentally ticked off the list.

They went down the hill under the eucalyptus trees and found a table on the harbour wall, beneath a gaily coloured umbrella.

They sat touching each other and drank cold beer and ate pistachio nuts, oblivious of everything and everybody about them even though the other tables were crowded with tourists. The lake sparkled and the softly rounded hills seemed very close in the bright light. Once a flight of Phantoms went booming down the valley, flying low on some mysterious errand, and David watched them dwindle southward without regrets.

When the sun was low they went to where the speedboat was moored, and David handed Debra down into it. On the wall above them sat a party of tourists, probably on some package-deal pilgrimage, and they were talking animately—their accents were Limehouse, Golders Green and Merseyside, although the subtleties of pronunciation were lost on David.

He started the motor and pushed off from the wall, steering for the harbour mouth with Debra sitting close beside him and the motor burbling softly.

A big red-faced tourist looked down from the wall and, supposing that the motor covered his voice, nudged his wife.

'Get a look at those two, Mavis. Beauty and the beast, isn't it?'

'Cork it, Bert. They might understand.'

'Go on, luv! They only talk Yiddish or whatever.'

Debra felt David's arm go rigid under her hand, felt him begin to pull away, sensing his outrage and anger—but she gripped his forearm tightly and restrained him.

'Let's go, Davey, darling. Leave them, please.'

Even when they were alone on the safety of the cottage, David was silent and she could feel the tension in his body and the air was charged with it.

They ate the evening meal of bread and cheese and fish and figs in the same strained silence. Debra could think of nothing to say to distract him for the careless words had wounded her as deeply. Afterwards she lay unsleeping beside him. He lay on his back, not touching her, with his arms at his sides and his fists clenched. When at last she could bear it no longer, she turned to him and stroked his face, still not knowing what to say. It was David who broke the silence at last.

'I want to go away from people. We don't need people—do we?'

'No,' she whispered. 'We don't need them.'

'There is a place called Jabulani. It is deep in the African bushveld, far from the nearest town. My father bought it as a hunting lodge thirty years ago—and now it belongs to me.'

'Tell me about it.' Debra laid her head on his chest, and he began stroking her hair, relaxing as he talked.

'There is a wide plain on which grow open forests of mopani and mohobahoba, with some big fat old baobabs and a few ivory palms. In the open glades the grass is yellow gold and the fronds of the ilala palms look like beggars' fingers. At the end of the plain is a line of hills, they turn blue at a distance and the peaks are shaped like the turrets of a fairy castle with tumbled blocks of granite. Between the hills rises a spring of water, a strong spring that has never dried and the water is very clear and sweet—'

'What does Jabulani mean?' Debra asked when he had described it to her.

'It means the "place of rejoicing",' David told her.

'I want to go there with you,' she said.

'What about Israel?' he asked. 'Will you not miss it?'

'No,' she shook her head. 'You see, I will take it with me—in my heart.'

Ella went up to Jerusalem with them, filling the back seat of the Mercedes. She would help Debra select the furniture they would take with them from the house and have it crated and shipped. The rest of it she would sell for them. Aaron Cohen would negotiate the sale of the house, and both David and Debra felt a chill of sadness at the thought of other people living in their home.

David left the women at it and he drove out to Ein Karem and parked the Mercedes beside the iron gate in the garden wall.

The Brig was waiting for him in that bleak and forbidding room above the courtyard. When David greeted him from the doorway he looked up coldly, and there was no relaxation of the iron features, no warmth or pity in the fierce warrior eyes.

'You come to me with the blood of my son upon your hands,' he said, and David froze at the words and held his gaze. After a few moments the Brig indicated the tall-backed chair against the far wall, and David crossed stiffly to it and sat down.

'If you had suffered less, I would have made you answer for more,' said the Brig. 'But vengeance and hatred are barren things—as you have discovered.'

David dropped his eyes to the floor.

'I will not pursue them further, despite the dictates of my heart, for that is what I am condemning in you. You are a violent young man, and violence is the pleasure of fools and only the last resort of wise men. The only excuse for it is to protect what is rightfully yours—any other display of violence is abuse. You abused the power I gave you—and in doing it you killed my son, and brought my country to the verge of war.'

The Brig stood up from his desk, and he crossed to the window and looked down into the garden. They were both silent while he stroked his moustache and remembered his son.

At last the Brig sighed heavily and turned back into the room.

'Why do you come to me?' he asked.

'I wish to marry your daughter, sir.'

'You are asking me—or telling me?' the Brig demanded, and then without waiting for an answer returned to his desk and sat down. 'If you abuse this also—if you bring her pain or unhappiness, I will seek you out. Depend upon it.'

David stood up and settled the cloth cap over his gross head, pulling the brim well down.

'We would like you to be at the wedding. Debra asked that particularly—for you and her mother.'

The Brig nodded. 'You may tell her that we will be there.'

The synagogue at Jerusalem University is a gleaming white structure, shaped like the tent of a desert wanderer, with the same billowing lines.

The red-bud trees were in full bloom and the wedding party was larger than they had planned, for apart from the immediate family there were Debra's colleagues from the university, Robert and some of the other boys from the squadron, Ella Kadesh, Doctor Edelman the baby-faced eye surgeon who had worked on Debra, Aaron Cohen and a dozen others.

After the simple ceremony, they walked through the university grounds to one of the reception rooms that David had hired. It was a quiet gathering with little laughter or joking. The young pilots from David's old squadron had to leave early to return to base, and with them went any pretence of jollity.

Debra's mother was still not yet fully recovered, and the prospect of Debra's departure reduced her to quiet grey weeping. Debra tried without success to comfort her.

Before he left, Dr Edelman drew David aside.

'Watch for any sign of atrophy in her eyes, any cloudiness, excessive redness—any complaints of pain, headaches—'

'I will watch for it.'

'Any indications, no matter how trivial—if you have any doubts, you must write to me.'

'Thank you, doctor.'

They shook hands. 'Good luck in your new life,' said Edelman.

Through it all Debra showed iron control, but even she at last succumbed and she, her mother, and Ella Kadesh all broke down simultaneously at the departure barrier of Lod Airport and hung round each other's necks, weeping bitterly.

The Brig and David stood by, stiff and awkward, trying to look as though they were not associated with the weeping trio, until the first warning broadcast gave them an excuse for a brief handshake and David took Debra's arm and drew her gently away.

They climbed the boarding ladder into the waiting Boeing without looking back. The giant aircraft took off and turned away southwards, and as always the sensation of flight soothed David; all the cares and tensions of these last few days left on the earth behind and below, he felt a new lightness of the spirit—excitement for what lay ahead.

He reached across and squeezed Debra's arm.

'Hello there, Morgan,' he said, and she turned towards him and smiled happily—blindly.

It was necessary to spend some time in Cape Town before they could escape to the sanctuary of Jabulani in the north.

David took a suite at the Mount Nelson Hotel, and from there he was able to settle the numerous issues that had piled up in his absence.

The accountants who managed his trust funds demanded ten days of his time and they spent it in the sitting-room of the suite, poring over trust documents and accounts.

In two years his income had grossly exceeded his spending, and the unused portion of his income had to be re-invested. In addition the third trust fund would soon pass to him and there were formalities to be completed.

Debra was hugely impressed by the extent of David's wealth.

'You must be almost a millionaire,' she said in a truly awed voice, for that was as rich as Debra could imagine.

'I'm not just a pretty face,' David agreed, and she was relieved that he could talk so lightly about his appearance.

Mitzi and her new husband came to visit them in their suite. However, the evening was not a success. Although Mitzi tried to act as though nothing had changed, and though she still called him 'warrior', yet it was apparent that she and her feelings had altered.

She was heavily pregnant and more shapeless than David would have thought possible. It was half-way through the evening before David realized the true reason for all the reserve. At first he thought that his disfigurement was worrying them, but after Mitzi had given a half-hour eulogy of the strides that Cecil was making at Morgan Group and the immense trust that Paul Morgan had placed in him, Cecil had asked innocently, 'Are you thinking of joining us at the Group? I'm sure we could find something useful for you to do–ha, ha!'

David could assure them quietly.

'No, thank you. You won't have to worry about me, Cecil, old boy. You take over from Uncle Paul with my blessing.'

'Good Lord, I didn't mean that.' Cecil was shocked, but Mitzi was less devious.

'He really will be very good, warrior, and you never were interested, were you?'

After that evening they did not see the couple again, and Paul Morgan was in Europe, so David fulfilled his family obligations without much pain or suffering and he could concentrate on the preparations for the move to Jabulani.

Barney Venter spent a week with them in choosing a suitable aircraft to handle the bush airstrip and yet give David the type of performance he enjoyed. At last they decided on a twin-engined Piper Navajo, a six-seater with two big 300-h.p. Lycoming engines and a tricycle undercart, and Barney walked around it with his hands on his hips.

'Well, she's no Mirage.' He kicked the landing-wheel and then checked himself and glanced quickly at David's face.

'I've had enough of Mirages,' David told him. 'They bite!'

On the last day David drove out with Debra to a farm near Paarl. The owner's wife was a dog breeder and when they went down to the kennels one of her labrador pups walked directly to Debra and placed a cold nose on her leg as he inhaled her, scent. Debra squatted and groped for his head and after fondling for a few moments she in her turn leaned forward and sniffed the pup's fur.

'He smells like old leather,' she said. 'What colour is he?'

'Black,' said David. 'Black as a Zulu.'

'That's what we'll call him,' said Debra. 'Zulu.'

'You want to choose this one?' David asked.

'No,' Debra laughed. 'He chose us.'

When they flew northwards the next morning the pup was indignant at being placed in the back seat and with a flying scrambling leap he came over Debra's shoulder and took up position in her lap, which seemed to suit them both very well.

'It looks like I have competition,' David muttered ruefully.

From the brown plateau of the high veld, the land dropped away steeply down the escarpment to the bush veld of southern Africa.

David picked up his landmark on the little village of Bush Buck Ridge and the long slim snake of the Sabi River as it twisted through the open forests of the plain. He altered course slightly northwards and within ten minutes he saw the low line of blue hills which rose abruptly out of the flat land.

'There it is, ahead of us,' David told Debra and his tone was infectious. She hugged the dog closer to her and leaned towards David.

'What does it look like?'

The hills were forested with big timber, and turreted with grey rock. At their base the bush was thick and dark. The pools glinted softly through the dark foliage. He described them to her.

'My father named them "The String of Pearls", and that's what they look like. They rise out of the run-off of rain water from the sloping ground beyond the hills. They disappear just as suddenly again into the sandy earth of the plain,' David explained as he circled the hills, slowly losing height. 'They are what give Jabulani its special character, for they provide water for all the wild life of the plain. Birds and animals are drawn from hundreds of miles to the Pearls.' He levelled out and throttled back, letting the aircraft sink lower. 'There is the homestead, white walls and thatch to keep it cool in the hot weather, deep shaded verandas and high rooms—you will love it.'

The airstrip seemed clear and safe, although the windsock hung in dirty tatters from its pole. David circled it carefully before lining up for the landing, and they taxied towards the small brick hangar set amongst the trees. David kicked on the wheel brakes and cut the engines.

'This is it,' he said.

Jabulani was one of a block of estates that bounded the Kruger National Park—the most spectacular nature reserve on earth. These estates were not productive, in that they were unsuitable for the growth of crops and few of them were used for grazing of domestic animals; their immense value lay in the unspoiled bush veld and the wild life—in the peace and space upon which wealthy men placed such a premium that they would pay large fortunes for a piece of this *Lebensraum*.

When David's grandfather had purchased Jabulani he had paid a few shillings an acre, for in those days the wilderness was still intact.

It had been used as a family hunting estate down the years, and as Paul Morgan had never shown interest in the veld, it had passed to David's father and so to David.

Now the eighteen thousand acres of African bush and plain, held as freehold land, was a possession beyond price.

Yet the Morgan family had made little use of it these last fifteen years. David's father had been an enthusiastic huntsman, and with him most of David's school holidays had been spent here. However, after his father's death, the visits to Jabulani had become shorter and further apart.

It was seven years since the last visit, when he had brought up a party of brother officers from Cobra Squadron.

Then it had been immaculately run by Sam, the black overseer, butler and game ranger.

Under Sam's management there had always been fresh crisp linen on the beds, highly polished floors, the exterior walls of the buildings had been snowy white and the thatch neat and well-tended. The deep-freeze had been well stocked with steak and the liquor cupboard filled—with every bottle accounted for.

Sam ran a tight camp, with half a dozen willing and cheerful helpers.

'Where is Sam?' was the first question David asked of the two servants who hurried down from the homestead to meet the aircraft.

'Sam gone.'

'Where to?' And the answer was the eloquent shrug of Africa. Their uniforms were dirty and needed mending, and their manners disinterested.

'Where is the Land-Rover?'

'She is dead.'

They walked up to the homestead and there David had another series of unpleasant surprises.

The buildings were dilapidated, looking forlorn and neglected under their rotting black thatch. The walls were dingy, grey-brown with the plaster falling away in patches.

The interiors were filthy with dust, and sprinkled with the droppings of the birds and reptiles that made their homes in the thatch.

The mosquito gauze, that was intended to keep the wide verandas insect-free, was rusted through and breaking away in tatters.

The vegetable gardens were overgrown, the fences about them falling to pieces. The grounds of the homestead itself were thick with rank weed, and not only the Land-Rover had died. No single piece of machinery on the estate—water pump, toilet cistern, electricity generator, motor vehicle—was in working order.

'It's a mess, a frightful mess,' David told Debra as they sat on the front step and drank mugs of sweet tea. Fortunately David had thought to bring emergency supplies with them.

'Oh, Davey. I am so sorry, because I like it here. It's peaceful, so quiet. I can just feel my nerves untying themselves.'

'Don't be sorry. I'm not. Those old huts were built by Gramps back in the twenties—and they weren't very well built even then.' David's voice was full of a new purpose, a determination that she had not heard for so long. 'It's a fine excuse to tear the whole lot down, and build again.'

'A place of our own?' she asked.

'Yes,' said David delightedly. That's it. That's just it!'

They flew into Nelspruit, the nearest large town, the following day. In the week of bustle and planning that followed they forgot their greater problems. With an architect they planned the new homestead with care, taking into consideration all their special requirements—a large airy study for Debra, workshop and office for David, a kitchen laid out to make it safe and easy for a blind cook, rooms without dangerous split levels and with regular easily learned shapes, and finally a nursery section. When David described this addition Debra asked cautiously, 'You making some plans that I should know about?'

'You'll know about it, all right,' he assured her.

The guest house was to be separate and self-contained and well away from the main homestead, and the small hutment for the servants was a quarter of a mile beyond that, screened by trees and the shoulder of the rocky kopje that rose behind the homestead.

David bribed a building contractor from Nelspruit to postpone all his other work, load his workmen on four heavy trucks and bring them out to Jabulani.

They began on the main house, and while they worked David was busy resurfacing the airstrip, repairing the water pumps and such other machinery as still had life left in it. However, the Land-Rover and the electricity generator had to be replaced.

Within two months the new homestead was habitable, and they could move. Debra set up her tape recorders beneath the big windows overlooking the shaded front garden, where the afternoon breeze could cool the room and waft in the perfume of the frangipani and poinsettia blooms.

While David was completely absorbed in making Jabulani into a comfortable home, Debra made her own arrangements.

Swiftly she explored and mapped in her mind all her immediate surroundings. Within weeks she could move about the new house with all the confidence of a person with normal sight and she had trained the servants to replace each item of furniture in its exact position. Always Zulu, the labrador pup, moved like a glossy black shadow beside her. Early on he had decided that Debra needed his constant care, and had made her his life's work.

Quickly he learned that it was useless staring at her or wagging his tail, to attract her attention he must whine or pant. In other respects she was also slightly feeble-minded, the only way to prevent her doing stupid things like falling down the front steps or tripping over a bucket left in the passage by a careless servant was to bump her with his shoulder, or with his nose.

She had fallen readily into a pattern of work that kept her in her workroom until noon each day, with Zulu curled at her feet.

David set up a large bird bath under the trees outside her window, so the tapes she made had as a background the chatter and warble of half a dozen varieties of wild birds. She had discovered a typist in Nelspruit who could speak Hebrew, and David took the tapes in to her whenever he flew to town for supplies and to collect the mail, and he brought each batch of typing back with him for checking.

They worked together on this task, David reading each batch of writing or correspondence aloud to her and making the alterations she asked for. He made it a habit of reading almost everything, from newspapers to novels, aloud.

'Who needs braille with you around,' Debra remarked, but it was more than just the written word she needed to hear from him. It was each facet and dimension of her new surroundings. She had never seen any of the myriad birds that flocked to drink and bathe below her window, though she soon recognized each individual call and would pick out a stranger immediately.

'David, there's a new one, what is it? What does he look like?'

And he must describe not only its plumage, but its mannerisms and its habits. At other times he must describe to her exactly how the new buildings fitted into their surroundings, the antics of Zulu the labrador, and supply accurate descriptions of the servants, the view from the window of her workroom—and a hundred other aspects of her new life.

In time the building was completed and the strangers left Jabulani, but it was not until the crates from Israel containing their furniture and other possessions from Malik Street arrived that Jabulani started truly to become their home.

The olive-wood table was placed under the window in the workroom.

'I haven't been able to work properly, there was something missing–' Debra ran her fingers caressingly across the inlaid ivory and ebony top '–until now.'

Her books were in shelves on the wall beside the table, and the leather suite in the new lounge looked very well with the animal-skin rugs and woven wool carpets.

David hung the Ella Kadesh painting above the fireplace, Debra determining the precise position for him by sense of touch.

'Are you sure it shouldn't be a sixteenth of an inch higher?' David asked seriously.

'Let's have no more lip from you, Morgan, I have to know exactly where it is.'

Then the great brass bedstead was set up in the bedroom, and covered with the ivory-coloured bedspread. Debra bounced up and down on it happily.

'Now, there is only one thing more that is missing,' she declared.

'What's that?' he asked with mock anxiety. 'Is it something important?'

'Come here.' She crooked a finger in his general direction. 'And I'll show you just how important it is.'

During the months of preparation they had not left the immediate neighbourhood of the homestead, but now quite suddenly the rush and bustle was over.

'We have eighteen thousand acres and plenty of four-footed neighbours–let's go check it all out,' David suggested.

They packed a cold lunch and the three of them climbed into the new Land-Rover with Zulu relegated to the back seat. The road let naturally down to the String of Pearls for this was the focal point of all life upon the estate.

They left the Land-Rover amongst the fever trees and went down to the ruins of the thatched summer house on the bank of the main pool.

The water aroused all Zulu's instincts and he plunged into it, paddling out into the centre with obvious enjoyment. The water was clear as air, but shaded to black in the depths.

David scratched in the muddy bank and turned out a thick pink earthworm. He threw it into the shallows and a dark shape half as long as his arm rushed silently out of the depths and swirled the surface.

'Wow!' David laughed. 'There are still a few fat ones around. We will have to bring down the rods. I used to spend days down here when I was a kid.'

The forest was filled with memories and as they wandered along the edge of the reed banks he reminisced about his childhood, until gradually he fell into silence, and she asked:

'Is something wrong, David?' She had grown that sensitive to his moods.

'There are no animals.' His tone was puzzled. 'Birds, yes. But we haven't seen a single animal, not even a duiker, since we left the homestead.' He stopped at a place that was clear of reeds, where the bank shelved gently. 'This used to be a favourite drinking place. It was busy day and night–the herds virtually lining up for a chance to drink.' He left Debra and went down to the edge, stooping to examine the ground carefully. 'No spoor even, just a few kudu and a small troop of baboon. There has not been a herd here for months, or possibly years.'

When he came back to her she asked gently, 'You are upset?'

'Jabulani without its animals is nothing,' he muttered. 'Come on, let's go and see the rest of it. There is something very odd here.'

The leisurely outing became a desperate hunt, as David scoured the thickets and the open glades, followed the dried water courses and stopped the Land-Rover to examine the sand beds for signs of wild life.

'Not even an impala,' he was worried and anxious. 'There used to be thousands of them. I remember herds of them, silky brown and graceful as ballet dancers, under nearly every tree.'

He turned the Land-Rover northwards, following an overgrown track through the trees.

'There is grazing here that hasn't been touched. It's lush as a cultivated garden.'

A little before noon they reached the dusty, corrugated public road that ran along the north boundary of Jabulani. The fence that followed the edge of the road was ruinous, with sagging and broken wire and many of the uprights snapped off at ground level.

'Hell, it's a mess,' David told her, as he turned through a gap in the wire on to the road, and followed the boundary for two miles until they reached the turn-off to the Jabulani homestead.

Even the signboard hanging above the stone pillars of the gateway, which David's father had fashioned in bronze and of which he had been so proud, was now dilapidated and hung askew.

'Well, there's plenty of work to keep us going,' said David with a certain relish.

Half a mile beyond the gates the road turned sharply, hedged on each side by tall grass, and standing full in the sandy track was a magnificent kudu bull, ghostly grey and striped with pale chalky lines across the deep powerful body. His head was held high, armed with the long corkscrew black horns, and his huge ears were spread in an intent listening attitude.

For only part of a second he posed like that, then, although the Land-Rover was still two hundred yards off, he exploded into a smoky blur of frantic flight. His great horns laid along his back as he fled through the open bush in a series of long, lithe bounds, disappearing so swiftly it seemed he had been only a fantasy, and David described it to Debra.

'He took off the very instant he spotted us. I remember when they were so tame around here that we had to chase them out of the vegetable garden with sticks.'

Again he swung off the main track and on to another overgrown path, on which the new growth of saplings was already thick and tall. He drove straight over them in the tough little vehicle.

'What on earth are you doing?' Debra shouted above the crash and swish of branches.

'In this country when you run out of road, you just make your own.'

Four miles farther on, they emerged abruptly on to the fire-break track that marked the eastern boundary of Jabulani, the dividing line between them and the National Park which was larger than the entire land area of the state of Israel, five million acres of virgin wilderness, three hundred and eighty-five kilometres long and eighty wide, home of more than a million wild animals, the most important reservoir of wild life left in Africa.

David stopped the Land-Rover, cut the engine and jumped down. After a moment of shocked and angry silence he began to swear.

'What's made you so happy?' Debra demanded.

'Look at that—just look at that!' David ranted.

'I wish I could.'

'Sorry, Debs. It's a fence. A game fence!'

It stood eight feet high and the uprights were hardwood poles thick as a man's thigh, while the mesh of the fence was heavy gauge wire. 'They have fenced us off. The National Park's people have cut us off! No wonder there are no animals.'

As they drove back to the homestead David explained to her how there had always been an open boundary with the Kruger National Park. It had suited everybody well enough, for Jabulani's sweet grazing and the perennial water of the pools helped to carry the herds through times of drought and scarcity.

'It's becoming very important to you, this business of the wild animals.' Debra had listened silently, fondling the labrador's head, as David spoke.

'Yes, suddenly it's important. When they were here, I guess I just took them for granted—but now they are gone, well, now they are very important,' he laughed abruptly and bitterly. 'I wonder how often that's been said in Africa—now they are gone it's suddenly important.'

They drove on for a mile or two without speaking and then David said with determination, 'I'm going to get them to pull that fence out. They can't cut us off like that. I'm going to get hold of the head warden, now, right away.'

David remembered Conrad Berg from his childhood when he had been the warden in charge of the southern portion of the park, but not yet the chief. There was a body of legend about the man that had been built up over the years, and two of these stories showed clearly the type of man he was.

Caught out in a lonely area of the reserve after dark with a broken-down truck, he was walking home when he was attacked by a full-grown male lion. In the struggle he had been terribly mauled, half the flesh torn from his back and the bone of his shoulder and arm bitten through. Yet he had managed to kill the animal with a small sheath knife, stabbing it repeatedly in the throat until he hit the jugular. He had then stood up and walked five miles through the night with the hyena pack following him expectantly, waiting for him to drop.

On another occasion one of the estate owners bounding the park had poached one of Berg's lions, shooting it down half a mile inside the boundary. The poacher was a man high in government, wielding massive influence, and he had laughed at Conrad Berg.

'What are you going to do about it, my friend? Don't you like your job?'

Doggedly, ignoring the pressure from above, Berg had collected his evidence and issued a summons. The pressure had become less subtle as the court date approached, but he had never wavered. The important personage finally stood in the dock, and was convicted. He was sentenced to a thousand pounds' fine or six months at hard labour.

Afterwards he had shaken Berg's hand and said to him, 'Thank you for a lesson in courage,' and perhaps this was one of the reasons Berg was now chief warden.

He stood beside his game fence where he had arranged over the telephone to meet David. He was a big man, broad and tall and beefy, with thick heavily muscled arms still scarred from the lion attack, and a red sunburned face.

He wore the suntans and slouch hat of the Park's service, with the green cloth badges on his epaulets.

Behind him was parked his brown Chevy truck with the Park Board's emblem on the door, and two of his black game rangers seated in the back. One of them was holding a heavy rifle.

Berg stood with his clenced fists on his hips, his hat pushed back and a forbidding expression on his face. He so epitomized the truculent male animal guarding its territory that David muttered to Debra, 'Here comes trouble.'

He parked close beside the fence and he and Debra climbed down and went to the wire.

'Mr Berg. I am David Morgan. I remember you from when my father owned Jabulani. I'd like you to meet my wife.'

Berg's expression wavered. Naturally he had heard all the rumours about the new owner of Jabulani; it was a lonely isolated area and it was his job to know about these things. Yet he was unprepared for this dreadfully mutilated young man, and his blind but beautiful wife.

With an awkward gallantry Berg doffed his hat, then realized she would not see the gesture. He murmured a greeting and when David thrust his hand through the fence he shook it cautiously.

Debra and David were working as a team and they turned their combined charm upon Berg, who was a simple and direct man. Slowly his defences softened as they chatted. He admired Zulu, he also kept labradors and it served as a talking-point while Debra unpacked a Thermos of coffee and David filled mugs for all of them.

'Isn't that Sam?' David pointed to the game ranger in the truck who held Berg's rifle.

'Ja.' Berg was guarded.

'He used to work on Jabulani.'

'He came to me of his own accord,' Berg explained, turning aside any implied rebuke.

'He wouldn't remember me, of course, not the way I look now. But he was a fine ranger, and the place certainly went to the bad without him to look after it,' David admitted before he went into a frontal assault. 'The other thing which has ruined us is this fence of yours.' David kicked one of the uprights.

'You don't say?' Berg swished the grounds of his coffee around the mug and flicked it out.

'Why did you do it?'

'For good reason.'

'My father had a gentleman's agreement with the Board, the boundary was open at all times. We have got water and grazing that you need.'

'With all respects to the late Mr Morgan,' Conrad Berg spoke heavily, 'I was never in favour of the open boundary.'

'Why not?'

'Your daddy was a *sportsman*.' He spat the word out, as though it were a mouthful of rotten meat. 'When my lions got to know him and learned to stay this side of the line—then he used to bring down a couple of donkeys and parade them along the boundary—to tempt them out.'

David opened his mouth to protest, and then closed it slowly. He felt the seamed scars of his face mottling and staining with a flush of shame. It was true, he remembered the donkeys and the soft wet lion skins being pegged out to dry behind the homestead.

'He never poached,' David defended him. 'He had an owner's licence and they were all shot on our land.'

'No, he never poached,' Berg admitted. 'He was too damned clever for that. He knew I would have put a rocket up him that would have made him the first man on the moon.'

'So that's why you put up the fence.'

'No.'

'Why then?'

'Because for fourteen years Jabulani has been under the care of an absentee landlord who didn't give a good damn what happened to it. Old Sam here–' he motioned at the game ranger in the truck '–did his best, but still it became a poacher's paradise. As fast as the grazing and water you boast of pulled my game out of the Park, so they were cut down by every sportsman with an itchy trigger finger. When Sam tried to do something about it, he got badly beaten up, and when that didn't stop him somebody put fire into his hut at night. They burned two of his kids to death–'

Daved felt his very soul quail at the thought of the flames on flesh, his cheeks itched at the memory.

'I didn't know,' he said gruffly.

'No, you were too busy making money or whatever is your particular form of pleasure,' Berg was angry. 'So at last Sam came to me and I gave him a job. Then I strung this fence.'

'There is nothing left on Jabulani–a few kudu, and a duiker or two–but otherwise it's all gone.'

'You are so right. It didn't take them long to clean it out.'

'I want it back.'

'Why?' Berg scoffed. 'So you can be a sportsman like your daddy? So you can fly your pals down from Jo'burg for the weekend to shoot the shit out of my lions?' Berg glanced at Debra, and immediately his red face flushed a deep port-wine colour. 'I'm sorry, Mrs Morgan, I did not mean to say that.'

'That's perfectly all right, Mr Berg. I think it was very expressive.'

'Thank you, ma'm.' Then he turned furiously back to David. 'Morgan's Private Safari Service, is that what you are after?'

'I would not allow a shot fired on Jabulani,' said David.

'I bet–except for the pot. That's the usual story. Except for the pot, and you've got the battle of Waterloo being fought all over again.'

'No,' said David. 'Not even for the pot.'

'You'd eat butcher's beef?' Berg asked incredulously.

'Look here, Mr Berg. If you pull your fence out, I'll have Jabulani declared a private nature reserve–'

Berg had been about to say something, but David's declaration dried the words, and his mouth remained hanging open. He closed it slowly.

'You know what that means?' he asked at last. 'You place yourself under our jurisdiction, completely. We'd tie you up properly with a lawyer's paper and all that stuff: no owner's licence, no shooting lions because they are in cattle area.'

'Yes. I know. I've studied the act. But there is something more. I'd undertake to fence the other three boundaries to your satisfaction, and maintain a force of private game rangers that you considered adequate–all at my own expense.'

Conrad Berg lifted his hat and scratched pensively at the long sparse grey hairs that covered his pate.

'Man,' he said mournfully, 'how can I say no to that?' Then he began to smile, the first smile of the meeting. 'It looks like you are really serious about this then.'

'My wife and I are going to be living here permanently. We don't want to live in a desert.'

'Ja,' he nodded, understanding completely that a man should feel that way. The strong revulsion that he had originally felt for the fantastic face before him was fading.

'I think the first thing we should work on is these poachers you tell me about. Let's snatch a couple of those and make a few examples,' David went on.

Berg's big red face split into a happy grin.

'I think I'm going to enjoy having you as a neighbour,' he said, and again he thrust his hand through the fence. David winced as he felt his knuckles cracking in the huge fist.

'Won't you come to dinner with us tomorrow night? You and your wife?' Debra asked with relief.

'It will be a mighty great pleasure, ma'm.'

'I'll get out the whisky bottle,' said David.

'That's kind of you—' said Conrad Berg seriously, 'but the missus and I only drink Old Buck dry gin, with a little water.'

'I'll see to it,' said David just as seriously.

Jane Berg was a slim woman of about Conrad's age. She had a dried-out face, lined and browned by the sun. Her hair was sunbleached and streaked with grey, and, as Debra remarked, she was probably the only thing in the world that Conrad was afraid of.

'I'm talking, Connie,' was enough to halt any flow of eloquence from her huge spouse, or a significant glance at her empty glass sent him with elephantine haste for a refill. Conrad had a great deal of trouble finishing any story or statement, for Jane had to correct the details during the telling, while he waited patiently for an opportunity to resume.

Debra chose the main course with care so as not to give offence, beefsteaks from the deep freeze, and Conrad ate four of them with unreserved pleasure although he spurned the wine that David served.

'That stuff is poison. Killed one of my uncles,' and stayed with Old Buck gin, even through the dessert.

Afterwards they sat about the cavernous fireplace with its logs blazing cheerfully and Conrad explained, with Jane's assistance, the problems that David would face on Jabulani.

'You get a few of the blacks from the tribal areas coming in from the north—'

'Or across the river,' Jane added.

'Or across the river, but they are no big sweat. They set wire snares mostly, and they don't kill that much—'

'But it's a terribly cruel way, the poor animals linger on for days with the wire cutting down to the bone,' Jane elaborated.

'As I was saying, once we have a few rangers busy that will stop almost immediately. It's the white poachers with modern rifles and hunting lamps—'

'Killing lamps,' Jane corrected.

'—killing lamps, they do the real damage. They finished off all your game on Jabulani in a couple of seasons.'

'Where do they come from?' David asked, his anger was rising again, the same protective anger of the shepherd that he had felt as he flew the skies of Israel.

'There is a big copper mine fifty miles north of here at Phalabora, hundreds of bored miners with a taste for venison. They would come down here and blaze away at every living thing–but now it's not worth the trip for them. Anyway they were just the amateurs, the weekend poachers.'

'Who are the professionals?'

'Where the dirt road from Jabulani meets the big national highway, about thirty miles from here–'

'At a place called Bandolier Hill,' Jane supplied the name.

'–there is a general dealer's store. It's just one of those trading posts that gets a little of the passing trade from the main road, but relies on the natives from the tribal areas. The person who owns and runs it has been there eight years now, and I have been after him all that time, but he's the craftiest bastard–I'm sorry, Mrs Morgan–I have ever run into.'

'He's the one?' David asked.

'He's the one,' Conrad nodded. 'Catch him, and half your worries are over.'

'What's his name?'

'Akkers. Johan Akkers,' Jane gave her assistance, the Old Buck was making her slightly owl-eyed, and she was having a little difficulty with her enunciation.

'How are we going to get him?' David mused. 'There isn't anything left on Jabulani to tempt him–the few kudu we have got are so wild, it wouldn't be worth the effort.'

'No, you haven't got anything to tempt him right now, but about the middle of September–'

'More like the first week in September,' Jane said firmly with strings of hair starting to hang down her temples.

'–the first week in September the marula trees down by your pools will come into fruit, and my elephants are going to visit you. The one thing they just can't resist is marula berries, and they are going to flatten my fence to get at them. Before I can repair it a lot of other game are going to follow the jumbo over to your side. You can lay any type of odds you like that our friend Akkers is oiling his guns and drooling at the mouth right this minute. He will know within an hour when the fence goes.'

'This time he may get a surprise.'

'Let's hope so.'

'I think–' David said softly '–that we might run down to Bandolier Hill tomorrow to have a look at this gentleman.'

'One thing is for sure–' said Jane Berg indistinctly, '–a gentleman, he is not.'

The road down to Bandolier Hill was heavily corrugated and thick with white dust that rose in a banner behind the Land-Rover and hung in the air long after they had passed. The hill was rounded and thickly timbered and stood over the mean metalled highway.

The trading post was four or five hundred yards from the road junction, set back amidst a grove of mango trees with their deep green and glistening foliage. It was a type found all over Africa–an unlovely building of mud brick with a naked corrugated iron roof, the walls plastered thickly with posters advertising goods from tea to flashlight batteries.

David parked the Land-Rover in the dusty yard beneath the raised stoop. There was a faded sign above the front steps:

'Bandolier Hill General Dealers'.

At the side of the building was parked an old green Ford one-ton truck with local licence plates. In the shade of the stoop squatted a dozen or so potential customers, African women from the tribal area, dressed in long cotton print dresses, timeless in their patience and their expressions showing no curiosity about the occupants of the Land-Rover. One of the women was suckling her infant with an enormously elongated breast that allowed the child to stand beside her and watch the newcomers without removing the puckered black nipple from his mouth.

Set in the centre of the yard was a thick straight pole, fifteen feet tall, and on top of the pole was a wooden structure like a dog kennel. David exclaimed as from the kennel emerged a big brown furry animal. It descended the pole in one swift falling action, seemingly as lightly as a bird, and the chain that was fastened to the pole at one end was, at the other, buckled about the animal's waist by a thick leather strap.

'It's one of the biggest old bull baboons I've ever seen.' Quickly he described it to Debra, as the baboon moved out to the chain's limit, and knuckled the ground as he made a lesiurely circle about his pole, the chain clinking as it swung behind him. It was an arrogant display, and he ruffled out the thick mane of hair upon his shoulders. When he had completed the circle, he sat down facing the Land-Rover, in a repellently humanoid attitude, and thrust out his lower jaw as he regarded them through small brown, close-set eyes.

'A nasty beast,' David told Debra. He would weigh ninety pounds, with a long dog-like muzzle and a jaw full of yellow fangs. After the hyena, he was the most hated animal of the veld—cunning, cruel and avaricious, all the vices of man and none of his graces. His stare was unblinking and, every few seconds, he ducked his head in a quick aggressive gesture.

While all David's attention was on the baboon, a man had come out of the store and now leaned on one of the pillars of the veranda.

'What can I do for you, Mr Morgan?' he asked in a thick accent. He was tall and spare, dressed in slightly rumpled and not entirely clean khaki slacks and open-neck shirt, with heavy boots on his feet and braces hooked into his pants, crossing his shoulders.

'How did you know my name?' David looked up at him, and he was of middle age with close-cropped greying hair over a domed skull. His teeth were badly fitting with bright pink plastic gums and his skin was drawn over the bones of the cheeks, and his deep-set eyes gave him a skull-like look. He grinned at David's question.

'Could only be you, scarred face and blind wife—you the new owner of Jabulani. Heard you built a new house and all set to live there now.'

The man's hands were huge, out of proportion to the rest of his rangy body, they were clearly very powerful and the lean muscles of his forearms were as tough as rope.

He slouched easily against the pillar and took from his pocket a clasp knife and a stick of black wind-dried meat—the jerky of North America, boucan of the Caribbean, or the biltong of Africa—and he cut a slice as though it were a plug of tobacco, popping it into his mouth.

'Like I asked—what can we do for you?' he chewed noisily, his teeth squelching at each bite.

'I need nails and paint.' David climbed out of the Land-Rover.

'Heard you did all your buying in Nelspruit.' Akkers looked him over with a calculated insolence, studying David's ruined face with attention. David saw that his deep-set eyes were a muddy green in colour.

'I thought there was a law against caging or chaining wild animals.' Akkers had roused David's resentment almost immediately, and the needle showed in his tone. Akkers began to grin again easily, still chewing.

'You a lawyer—are you?'

'Just asking.'

'I got a permit—you want to see it?'

David shook his head, and turned to speak to Debra in Hebrew. Quickly he described the man.

'I think he can guess why we are here, and he's looking for trouble.'

'I'll stay by the car,' said Debra.

'Good.' David climbed the steps to the veranda.

'What about the nails and paint?' he asked Akkers.

'Go on in,' he was still grinning. 'I got a nigger helper behind the counter. He will look after you.'

David hesitated and then walked on into the building. It smelled of carbolic soap and kerosene and maize meal. The shelves were loaded with cheap groceries, patent medicines, blankets and bolts of printed cotton cloth. From the roof hung bunches of army surplus boots and greatcoats, axe-heads and storm lanterns. The floor was stacked with tin trunks, pick handles, bins of flour and maize meal and the hundreds of other items that traditionally make up the stock of the country dealer. David found the African assistant and began his purchase.

Outside in the sunlight Debra climbed from the Land-Rover and leaned lightly against the door. The labrador scrambled down after her and began sniffing the concrete pillars of the veranda with interest where other dogs before him had spurted jets of yellow urine against the white-washed plaster.

'Nice dog,' said Akkers.

'Thank you.' Debra nodded politely.

Akkers glanced quickly across at his pet baboon, and his expression was suddenly cunning. A flash of understanding passed between man and animal. The baboon ducked its head again in that nervous gesture, then it rose from its haunches and drifted back to the pole. With a leap and bound it shot up the pole and disappeared into the opening of its kennel.

Akkers grinned and carefully cut another slice of the black biltong.

'You like it out at Jabulani?' he asked Debra, and at the same time he offered the scrap of dried meat to the dog.

'We are very happy there,' Debra replied stiffly, not wanting to be drawn. Zulu sniffed the proffered titbit, and his tail beat like a metronome. No dog can resist the concentrated meat smell and taste of biltong. He gulped it eagerly. Twice more Akkers fed him the scraps, and Zulu's eyes glistened and his soft silky muzzle was damp with saliva.

The waiting women in the shade of the veranda were watching with lively interest now. They had seen this happen before with a dog, and they waited expectantly. David was in the building, out of sight. Debra stood blind and unsuspecting.

Akkers cut a larger piece of the dried meat and offered it to Zulu, but when he reached for it he pulled his hand away, teasing the dog. With his taste for biltong now firmly established, Zulu tried again for the meat as it was offered. Again it was pulled away at the last moment. Zulu's black wet nose quivered with anxiety, and the soft ears were cocked.

Akkers walked down the steps with Zulu following him eagerly, and at the bottom he showed the dog the biltong once more, letting him sniff it. Then he spoke softly but urgently, 'Get it, boy,' and threw the scrap of biltong at the base of the baboon's pole. Zulu bounded forward, still slightly clumsy on his big puppy paws, into the circle of the chain where the baboon's paws had beaten the earth hard. He ran on under the pole and grubbed hungrily for the biltong in the dust.

The bull baboon came out of his kennel like a tawny grey blur and dropped the fifteen feet through the air; his limbs were spread and his jaws were open in a snarl like a great red trap, and the fangs were vicious, long and yellow and spiked. He hit the ground silently, and his muscles bunched as they absorbed the shock and hurled the long lithe body feet first at the unsuspecting pup. The baboon crashed into him, taking him on the shoulder with all the weight of his ninety pounds.

Zulu went down and over, rolling on his back with a startled yelp, but before he could find his feet or his wits, the baboon was after him.

Debra heard the pup cry, and started forward, surprised but not yet alarmed.

As he lay on his back, Zulu's belly was unprotected, sparsely covered with the silken black hair, the immature penis protruding pathetically, and the baboon went on to him in a crouching leap, pinning him with powerful furry legs as he bowed his head and buried the long yellow fangs deep into the pup's belly.

Zulu screamed in dreadful agony, and Debra screamed in sympathy and ran forward.

Akkers shot out a foot as she passed him and tripped her, sending her sprawling on her hands and knees.

'Leave it, lady,' he warned her, still grinning. 'You'll get hurt if you interfere.'

The baboon locked its long curved eye teeth into the tender belly, and then hurled the pup away from it with all the fierce strength of its four limbs. The thin wall of the stomach was ripped through, and the purple ropes of the entrails came out, hanging festooned in the baboon's jaws.

Again the disembowelled pup screamed, and Debra rolled blindly to her feet.

'David!' she cried wildly. 'David—help me!'

David came out of the building running; pausing in the doorway he took in the scene at a glance and snatched up a pick handle from the pile by the door. He jumped off the veranda, and in three quick strides he had reached the pup.

The baboon saw him coming and released Zulu. With uncanny speed, he whirled and leapt for the pole, racing upwards to perch on the roof of the kennel, his jowls red with blood, as he shrieked and jabbered, bouncing up and down with excitement and triumph.

David dropped the pick and gently lifted the crawling crippled black body. He carried Zulu to the Land-Rover and ripped his bush jacket into strips as he tried to bind up the torn belly, pushing the hanging entrails back into the hole with his fist.

'David, what is it?' Debra pleaded with him, and as he worked he explained it in a few terse Hebrew sentences.

'Get in,' he told her and she clambered into the passenger seat of the Land-Rover. He laid the injured labrador in her lap, and ran around to the driver's seat.

Akkers was back at the doorway of his shop, standing with thumbs hooked into his braces, and he was laughing. The false teeth clucked in the open mouth as he laughed, rocking back and forth on his heels.

On its kennel the baboon shrieked and cavorted, sharing its master's mirth.

'Hey, Mr Morgan,' Akkers giggled, 'don't forget your nails!'

David swung round to face him, his face felt tight and hot, the cicatrice that covered his cheeks and forehead was inflamed and the dark blue eyes blazed with a terrible anger. He started up the steps. His mouth was a pale hard slit, and his fists were clenched at his sides.

Akkers stepped backwards swiftly and reached behind the shop counter. He lifted out an old double-barrelled shotgun, and cocked both hammers with a sweep of his thick bony thumb.

'Self defence, Mr Morgan, with witnesses,' he giggled with sadistic relish. 'Come one step closer and we will get a look at your guts also.'

David paused at the top of the steps, and the gun—held in one huge fist—pointed at his belly.

'David hurry—oh, please hurry,' Debra called anxiously from the Land-Rover, with the weakly squirming body of the pup in her lap.

'We'll meet again.' David's anger had thickened his tongue.

'That will be fun,' said Akkers, and David turned away and ran down the steps.

Akkers watched the Land-Rover pull away and swing into the road in a cloud of dust, before he set the shotgun aside. He went out into the sunlight, and the baboon scrambled down from its pole and rushed to meet him. It jumped up on to his hip and clung to him like a child.

Akkers took a boiled sweet from his pocket and placed it tenderly between the terrible yellow fangs.

'You lovely old thing,' he chuckled, scratching the high cranium with its thick cap of grey fur and the baboon squinted up at his face with narrow brown eyes, chattering softly.

Despite the rough road surface, David covered the thirty miles back to Jabulani in twenty-five minutes. He skidded the vehicle to a halt beside the hangar, and ran with the pup in his arms to the aircraft.

During the flight Debra nursed him gently in her lap, and her skirts were sodden with his dark blood. The pup had quieted, and except for an occasional whimper now lay still. Over the W/T David arranged for a car to meet them at Nelspruit airfield and forty-five minutes after take-off they had Zulu on the theatre table in the veterinary surgeon's clinic.

The veterinary surgeon worked with complete concentration for over two hours at repairing the torn entrails and suturing the layers of abdominal muscle.

The pup was so critically injured, and infection was such a real danger, that they dared not return to Jabulani until it had passed. Five days later when they flew home with Zulu still weak and heavily strapped but out of danger, David altered his flight path to bring them in over the trading store at Bandolier Hill.

The iron roof shone like a mirror in the sun, and David felt his anger very cold and hard and determined.

'The man is a threat to us,' he said aloud. 'A real threat to each of us, and to what we are trying to build at Jabulani.'

Debra nodded her agreement, stroking the pup's head and not trusting herself to speak. Her own anger was as fierce as David's.

'I'm going to get him,' he said softly, and he heard the Brig's voice in his memory.

'The only excuse for violence is to protect that which belongs to you.'

He banked steeply away and lined up for his approach to the the landing-strip at Jabulani.

Conrad Berg called again to sample the Old Buck gin, and to tell David that his application to have Jabulani declared a private nature reserve had been approved by the Board and that the necessary documentation would soon be ready for signature.

'Do you want me to pull the fence out now?'

'No,' David answered grimly. 'Let it stand. I don't want Akkers frightened off.'

'Ja,' Conrad agreed heavily. 'We have got to get him.' He called Zulu to him and examined the scar that was ridged and shaped like forked lightning across the pup's belly. 'The bastard,' he muttered, and then glanced guiltily at Debra. 'Sorry, Mrs Morgan.'

'I couldn't agree more, Mr Berg,' she said softly, and Zulu watched her lips attentively when she spoke—his head cocked to one side.

Like all young things, he had healed cleanly and quickly.

The marula grove that ran thickly along the base of the hills about the String of Pearls came into flower.

The boles were straight and sturdy, each crowned with a fully rounded, many-branched head of dense foliage, and the red flowers made a royal show.

Almost daily David and Debra would wander together through the groves, down the rude track to the pools, and Zulu regained his strength on these leisurely strolls which always culminated in a swim and a lusty shaking off of water droplets, usually on to the nearest bystander.

Then the green plum-shaped fruits that covered the female marulas thickly began to turn yellow as they ripened, and their yeasty smell was heavy on the warm evening breeze.

The herd came up from the Sabi, forsaking the lush reed beds for the promise of the marula harvest. They were led by two old bulls, who for forty years had made the annual pilgrimage to the String of Pearls, and there were fifteen breeding cows with calves running at heel and as many adolescents.

They moved up slowly from the south, feeding spread out, sailing like ghostly grey galleons through the open bush, overloaded bellies rumbling. Occasionally a tall tree would catch the attention of one of the bulls and he would place his forehead upon the thick trunk and, swaying rhythmically as he built up momentum, he would strain suddenly and bring it crackling and crashing down. A few mouthfuls of the tender tip leaves would satisfy him, or he might strip the bark and stuff it untidily into his mouth before moving on northwards.

When the reached Conrad Berg's fence the two bulls moved forward and examined it, standing shoulder to shoulder as though in consultation, fanning their great grey ears, and every few minutes picking up a large pinch of sand in their trunks to throw over their own backs against the worrisome attention of the stinging flies.

In forty years they had travelled, and knew exactly all the boundaries of their reserve. As they stood there contemplating the game fence, it was as though they were fully aware that its destruction would be a criminal act, and injurious to their reputations and good standing.

Conrad Berg was deadly serious when he discussed 'his' elephants sense of right and wrong with David. He spoke of them like schoolboys who had to be placed on good behaviour, and disciplined when they transgressed. Discipline might take the form of driving, darting with drugs, or formal execution with a heavy rifle. This ultimate punishment was reserved for the incorrigibles who raided cultivated crops, chased motor-cars or otherwise endangered human life.

Sorely tempted, the two old bulls left the fence and ambled back to the breeding herd that waited patiently for their decision amongst the thorn trees. For three days the herd drifted back and forth along the fence, feeding and resting and waiting—then suddenly the wind turned westerly and it came to them laden with the thick, cloyingly sweet smell of the marula berries.

David parked the Land-Rover on the firebreak road and laughed with delight.

'So much for Connie's fence!'

For reasons of pachyderm prestige, or perhaps merely for the mischievous delight of destruction, no adult elephant would accept the breach made by another.

Each of them had selected his own fence pole, hard wood uprights embedded in concrete, and had effortlessly snapped it off level with the ground. Over a length of a mile the fence was flattened, and the wire mesh lay across the firebreak.

Each elephant had used his broken pole like a tightrope, to avoid treading on the sharp points of the barbed wire. Then once across the fence they had streamed in a tight bunch down to the pools to spend a night in feasting, an elephantine gorge on the yellow berries, which ended at dawn when they had bunched up into closer order and dashed back across the ruined fence into the safety of the Park—perhaps pursued by guilt and remorse and hoping that Conrad Berg would lay the blame on some other herd.

However, the downed fence provided ready access for many others who had long hankered after the sweet untouched grazing and deep water holes.

Ugly little blue wildebeest with monstrous heads, absurdly warlike manes and curved horns in imitation of the mighty buffalo. Clowns of the bush, they capered with glee and chased each other in circles. Their companions the zebra were more dignified, ignoring their antics, and trotted in businesslike fashion down to the pools. Their rumps were striped and glossy and plump, their heads up and ears pricked.

Conrad Berg met David at the remains of his fence, climbing out of his own truck and picking his way carefully over the wire. Sam, the African ranger, followed him.

Conrad shook his head as he surveyed the destruction, chuckling ruefully.

'It's old Mahommed and his pal One-Eye, I'd know that spoor anywhere. They just couldn't help themselves—the bastards—' He glanced quickly at Debra in the Land-Rover.

'That's perfectly all right, Mr Berg,' she forestalled his apology.

Sam had been casting back and forth along the soft break road and now he came to where they stood.

'Hello, Sam,' David greeted him. It had taken a lot of persuasion to get Sam to accept that this terribly disfigured face belonged to the young *nkosi* David who he had taught to track, and shoot and rob a wild beehive without destroying the bees.

Sam saluted David with a flourish. He took his uniform very seriously and conducted himself like a guardsman now. It was difficult to tell his age, for he had the broad smooth moonface of the Nguni—the aristocratic warrior tribes of Africa—but there was a frosting of purest white on the close-curled hair of his temples under the slouch hat, and David knew he had worked at Jabulani for forty years before leaving. The man must be approaching sixty years of age.

Quickly he made his report to Conrad, describing the animals and the numbers which had crossed into Jabulani.

'There is also a herd of buffalo, forty-three of them,' Sam spoke in simple Zulu that David could still follow. 'They are the ones who drank before at Ripape Dam near Hlangulene.'

'That will bring Akkers running—the sirloin of a young buffalo makes the finest biltong there is,' Conrad observed dryly.

'How long will it be before he knows the fence is down?' David asked, and Conrad fell into a long rapid-fire discussion with Sam that lost David after the first few sentences. However, Conrad translated at the end.

'Sam says he knows already, all your servants and their wives buy at his store and he pays them for that sort of information. It turns out that there is bad blood between Sam and Akkers. Sam suspects him of arranging to have him beaten, on a lonely road on a dark night. Sam was in hospital three months—he also accused Akkers of having his hut fired to drive him off Jabulani.'

'It adds up, doesn't it?' David agreed.

'Old Sam is dead keen to help us grab Akkers—and he has a plan of action all worked out.'

'Let's hear it.'

'Well, as long as you are in residence at Jabulani Akkers is going to restrict his activities to night poaching with a killing lamp. He knows every trick there is and we will never get him.'

'So?'

'You must tell your servants that you are leaving for two weeks, going to Cape Town on business. Akkers will know as soon as you leave and he will believe he has the whole of Jabulani to himself—' For an hour more they discussed the details of the plan, then they shook hands and parted.

As they drove back to the homestead they emerged from the open forest into one of the glades of tall grass, and David saw the brilliant white egrets floating like snow flakes over the swaying tops of golden grass.

'Something in there,' he said and cut the engine. They waited quietly until David saw the movement in the grass, the opening and closing at the passage of heavy bodies. Then three egrets, sitting in a row, moved slowly towards him, borne on the back of a concealed beast as it grazed steadily forward.

'Ah, the buffalo!' David exclaimed as the first of them appeared, a great black bovine shape. It stopped as it saw the Land-Rover on the edge of the trees and it regarded them intently from beneath the wide spread of its horns, with its muzzle lifted high. It showed no alarm for these were Park animals, almost as tame as domestic cattle.

Gradually the rest of the herd emerged from the tall grass. Each in turn scrutinized the vehicle and then resumed feeding once more. There were forty-three of them, as Sam had predicted, and amongst them were some fine old bulls standing five and a half feet tall at the shoulder and weighing little less than 2000 lb. Their horns were massively bossed, meeting in the centre of the head and curving downwards and up to blunt points, with a rugged surface that became polished black at the tips.

Crawling over their heavy trunks and thick short legs were numbers of ox-peckers, dull-plumaged birds with scarlet beaks and bright beady eyes. Sometimes head down they scavenged for the ticks and other blood-sucking body vermin in the folds of skin between the limbs. Occasionally one of the huge beasts would snort and leap, shaking and swishing its tail, as a sharp beak pried into a delicate portion of its anatomy, under the tail or around the heavy dangling black scrotum. The birds fluttered up with hissing cries, waited for the buffalo to calm down and then settled again to their scurrying and searching.

David photographed the herd until the light failed, and they drove home in the dark.

Before dinner David opened a bottle of wine and they drank it together on the stoop, sitting close and listening to the night sounds of the bush—the cries of the night birds, the tap of flying insects against the wire screen and the other secret scurrying and rustling of small animals.

'Do you remember once I told you that you were spoiled, and not very good marriage material?' Debra asked softly, nestling her dark head against his shoulder.

'I'll never forget it.'

'I'd like to withdraw that remark formally,' she went on, and he moved her gently away so that he could study her face. Sensing his eyes upon her she smiled, that shy little smile of hers. 'I fell in love with a little boy, a spoiled little boy, who thought only of fast cars and the nearest skirt—' she said, '—but now I have a man, a grown man,' she smiled again, 'and I like it better this way.'

He drew her back to him and kissed her, their lips melded in a lingering embrace before she sighed happily and laid her head back upon his shoulder. They were silent for a while before Debra spoke again.

'These wild animals—that mean so much to you—'

'Yes?' he encouraged her.

'I am beginning to understand. Although I have never seen them, they are becoming important to me also.'

'I'm glad.'

'David, this place of ours—it's so peaceful, so perfect. It's a little Eden before the fall.'

'We will make it so,' he promised, but in the night the gunfire woke him. He rose quickly, leaving her lying warm and quietly sleeping, and he went out on the stoop.

It came again, faintly on the still night, distance muting it to a small unwarlike popping. He felt his anger stirring again, as he imagined the long white shaft of the killing lamp, questing relentlessly through the forest until it settled suddenly upon the puzzled animal, holding it mesmerized in the beam, the blinded eyes glowing like jewels, making a perfect aiming point in the field of the telescopic rifle sight.

Then suddenly the rifle blast, shocking in the silence, and the long licking flame of the muzzle flash. The beautiful head snapping back at the punch of the bullet and the soft thump of the falling body on the hard earth, the last spasmodic kicking of hooves and again the silence.

He knew it was useless to attempt pursuit now, the gunman would have an accomplice in the hills above them ready to flash a warning if any of the homestead lights came on, or if an auto engine whirred into life. Then the killing lamp would be doused and the poacher would creep away. David would search the midnight expanse of Jabulani in vain. His quarry was cunning and experienced in his craft of killing, and would only be taken by greater cunning.

David could not sleep again. He lay awake beside Debra, and listened to her soft breathing—and at intervals to the distant rifle fire. The game was tame and easily approached, innocent after the safety of the Park. It would run only a short distance after each shot, and then it would stand again staring without comprehension at the mysterious and dazzling light that floated towards it out of the darkness.

David's anger burned on through the night, and in the dawn the vultures were up. Black specks against the pink dawn sky, they appeared in ever-increasing numbers, sailing high on wide pinions, tracing wide swinging circles before beginning to drop towards the earth.

David telephoned Conrad Berg at Skukuza Camp, then he and Debra and the dog climbed into the Land-Rover, warmly dressed against the dawn chill. They followed the descent of the birds to where the poacher had come on the buffalo herd.

As they approached the first carcass, the animal scavengers scattered—slope-backed hyena cantering away into the trees, hideous and cowardly, looking back over their misshapen shoulders, grinning apologetically—little red jackal with silvery backs and alert ears, trotting to a respectful distance before standing and starting back anxiously.

The vultures were less timid, seething like fat brown maggots over the carcass as they squawled and squabbled, fouling everything with their stinking droppings and loose feathers, leaving the kill only when the Land-Rover was very close and then flapping heavily up into the trees to crouch there grotesquely with their bald scaly heads out-thrust.

There were sixteen dead buffalo, lying strung out along the line of the herd's flight. On each carcass the belly had been split open to let the vultures in, and the sirloin and fillet had been expertly removed.

'He killed them just for a few pounds of meat?' Debra asked incredulously.

'That's all,' David confirmed grimly. 'But that's not bad—sometimes they'll kill a wildebeest simply to make a fly whisk of its tail, or they'll shoot a giraffe for the marrow in its bones.'

'I don't understand.' Debra's voice was hopeless. 'What makes a man do it? He can't need the meat that badly.'

'No,' David agreed. 'It's deeper than that. This type of killing is a gut thing. This man kills for the thrill of it, he kills to see an animal fall, to hear the death cry, to smell the reek of fresh blood—' his voice choked off, 'this is one time you can be thankful you cannot see,' he said softly.'

Conrad Berg found them waiting beside the corpses, and he set his rangers to work butchering the carcasses.

'No point in wasting all that meat. Food there for a lot of people.'

Then he put Sam to the spoor. There had been four men in the poaching party, one wearing light rubber-soled shoes and the others bare-footed.

'One white man, big man, long legs. Three black men, carry meat, blood drip here and here.'

They followed Sam slowly through the open forest as he parted the grass with his long thin tracking staff, and moved towards the unsurfaced public road.

'Here they walk backwards,' Sam observed, and Conrad explained grimly.

'Old poacher's trick. They walk backwards when they cross a boundary. If you cut the spoor while patrolling the fence you think they have gone the other way—leaving instead of entering—and you don't bother following them.'

The spoor went through the gap in the fence, crossed the road and entered the tribal land beyond. It ended where a motor vehicle had been parked amongst a screening thicket of wild ebony. The tracks bumped away across the sandy earth and rejoined the public road.

'Plaster casts of the tyre tracks?' David asked.

'Waste of time.' Conrad shook his head. 'You can be sure they are changed before each expedition, he keeps this set especially and hides it when it's not in use.'

'What about spent cartridge shells?' David persisted.

Conrad laughed briefly. 'They are in his pocket, this is a fly bird. He's not going to scatter evidence all over the country. He picks up as he goes along. No—we'll have to sucker him into it.' And his manner became businesslike. 'Right, have you selected a place to stake old Sam out?'

'I thought we would put him up on one of the kopjes, near the String of Pearls. He'll be able to cover the whole estate from there, spot any dust on the road, and the height will give the two-way radio sufficient range.'

After lunch David loaded their bags into the luggage compartment of the Navajo. He paid the servants two weeks' wages in advance.

'Take good care.' He told them. 'I shall return before the end of the month.'

He parked the Land-Rover in the open hangar with the key in the ignition facing the open doorway, ready for a quick start. He took off and kept on a westerly heading, passing directly over Bandolier Hill and the buildings amongst the mango trees. They saw no sign of life, but David held his course until the hill sank from view below the horizon, then he came around on a wide circle to the south and lined up for Skukuza, the main camp of the Kruger National Park.

Conrad Berg was at the airstrip in his truck to meet the Cessna, and Jane had placed fresh flowers in the guest room. Jabulani lay fifty miles away to the north-west.

It was like squadron 'Red' standby again, with the Navajo parked under one of the big shade trees at the end of the Skukuza airstrip, and the radio set switched on, crackling faintly on the frequency tuned to that of Sam's transmitter, as he waited patiently on the hill-top above the pools.

The day was oppressively hot, with the threat of a rainstorm looming up out of the east, great cumulus thunderheads striding like giants across the bushveld.

Debra and David and Conrad Berg sat in the shade of the aircraft's wing, for it was too hot in the cockpit. They chatted in desultory fashion, but always listening to the radio crackle, and they were tense and distracted.

'He is not going to come,' said Debra a little before noon.

'He'll come,' Conrad contradicted her. 'Those buffalo are too much temptation. Perhaps not today–but tomorrow or the next day he'll come.'

David stood up and climbed in through the open door of the cabin. He went forward to the cockpit.

'Sam,' he spoke into the microphone. 'Can you hear me?'

There was a long pause, presumably while Sam struggled with radio procedure, then his voice, faint but clear: 'I hear you, *Nkosi*.'

'Have you seen anything?'

'There is nothing.'

'Keep good watch.'

'*Yebho, Nkosi*.'

Jane brought a cold picnic lunch down to the airstrip, they ate heartily despite the tension, and they were about to start on the milk tart, when suddenly the radio set throbbed and hummed. Sam's voice carried clearly to where they sat.

'He has come!'

'Red standby–Go! Go!' shouted David, and they rushed for the cabin door, Debra treading squarely in the centre of Jane's milk tart before David grabbed her arm and guided her to her seat.

'Bright Lance, airborne and climbing,' David laughed with excitement and then memory stabbed him with a sharp blade. He remembered Joe hanging out there at six o'clock but he shut his mind to it and he banked steeply on to his heading, not wasting time in grabbing for altitude but staying right down at tree-top level.

Conrad Berg was hunched in the seat behind them, and his face was redder than usual–seeming about to burst like an over-ripe tomato.

'Where is the Land-Rover key?' he demanded anxiously.

'It's in the ignition–and the tank is full.'

'Can't you go faster?' Conrad growled.

'Have you got your walkie-talkie?' David checked him.

'Here!' It was gripped in one of his huge paws, and his double-barrelled ·450 magnum was in the other.

David was hopping the taller trees, and sliding over the crests of higher ground with feet to spare. They flashed over the boundary fence and ahead of them lay the hills of Jabulani.

'Get ready,' he told Conrad, and flew the Navajo into the airstrip, taxiing up to the hangar where the Land-Rover waited.

Conrad jumped down at the instant that David braked to a halt, then he slammed the cabin door behind him and raced to the Land-Rover. Immediately David opened the throttle and swung the aircraft around, lining up for his take-off before the Navajo had gathered full momentum.

As he climbed, he saw the Land-Rover racing across the airstrip, dragging a cloak of dust behind it.

'Do you read me, Connie?'

'Loud and clear,' Conrad's voice boomed out of the speaker, and David turned for the grey ribbon of the public road that showed through the trees, beyond the hills.

He followed it, flying five hundred feet above it, and he searched the open parkland.

The green Ford truck had been concealed from observation at ground level, again in a thicket of wild ebony, but it was open from the sky. For Akkers had never thought of discovery coming from there.

'Connie, I've got the truck. He's stashed it in a clump of ebony about half a mile down the bank of the Luzane stream. Your best route is to follow the road to the bridge, then go down into the dry river bed and try and cut him off before he gets to the truck.'

'Okay, David.'

'Move it, man.'

'I'm moving.' David saw the Land-Rover's dust above the trees, Conrad must have his foot down hard.

'I'm going to try and spot the man himself—chase him into your arms.'

'You do that!'

David started a long climbing turn towards the hills, sweeping and searching, up and around. Below him the pools glinted and he opened the throttles slightly, seeking altitude to clear the crests.

From the highest peak, a tiny figure waved frantically.

'Sam,' he grunted. 'Doing a war dance.' He altered course slightly to pass him closely, and Sam stopped his imitation of a windmill and stabbed with an extended arm towards the west. David acknowledged with a wave, and turned again, dropping down the western slopes.

Ahead of him the plain spread, dappled like a leopard's back with dark bush and golden glades of grass. He flew for a minute before he saw a black mass, moving slowly ahead of him, dark and amorphous against the pale grass. The remains of the buffalo herd had bunched up and were running without direction, desperate from the harrying they had received.

'Buffalo,' he told Debra. 'On the run. Something has alarmed them.' She sat still and intent beside him, hands in her lap, staring unseeingly ahead.

'Ah!' David shouted. 'Got him—with blood on his hands!'

In the centre of one of the larger clearings lay the black beetle-body of a dead buffalo, its belly swollen and its legs sticking out stiffly as it lay on its side.

Four men stood around it in a circle, obviously just about to begin butchering the carcass. Three of them were Africans, one with a knife in his hand.

The fourth man was Johan Akkers. There was no mistaking the tall gaunt frame. He wore an old black Fedora hat on his head, strangely formal attire for the work in which he was engaged, and his braces criss-crossed his tan-coloured shirt. He carried a rifle at the trail in his right hand, and at the sound of the aircraft engines he swung round and stared into the sky, frozen with the shock of discovery.

'You swine. Oh, you bloody swine,' whispered David, and his anger was strong and bright against the despoilers.

'Hold on!' he warned Debra, and flew straight at the man, dropping steeply on to him.

The group around the dead buffalo scattered, as the aircraft bore down on them, each man picking his own course and racing away on it, but David selected the lanky galloping frame with the black hat jammed down over the ears and sank down behind him. The tips of his propellers clipped the dry grass, as he swiftly overtook the running Akkers.

He was set to fly into him, driven by the unreasoning anger of the male animal protecting his own, and he lined up to cut him down with the spinning propeller blades.

As David braced himself for the impact Akkers glanced back over his shoulder, and his face was muddy grey with fright, the skull eyes dark and deeply set. He saw the murderous blades merely feet from him, and he threw himself flat into the grass.

The Navajo roared inches over his prone body, and David pulled it round in a steep turn, with the wing-tip brushing the grass. As he came round he saw that Akkers was up and running, and that he was only fifty paces from the edge of the trees.

David levelled out, aimed for the fugitive again but realized that he could not reach him before he was into the trees. Swiftly he sped across the clearing, but the lumbering figure drew slowly closer to the timber line and as he reached the sanctuary of a big leadwood trunk, Akkers whirled and raised the rifle to his shoulder. He aimed at the approaching aircraft; although the rifle was unsteady in his hands the range was short.

'Down,' shouted David, pushing Debra's head below the level of the windshield, and he pulled open the throttles and climbed very steeply away.

Even above the bellow of the engines David heard the heavy bullet clang into the fuselage of the aircraft.

'What's happening, David?' Debra pleaded.

'He fired at us, but we've got him on the run. He'll head back for his truck now, and Conrad should be there waiting for him.'

Akkers kept under cover of the trees, and circling above him David caught glimpses of the tall figure trotting purposefully along his escape route.

'David, can you hear me?' Conrad's voice boomed suddenly in the tense cockpit.

'What is it, Connie?'

'We've got trouble. I've hit a rock in your Land-Rover and knocked out the sump. She's had it, pouring oil all over the place.'

'How the hell did you do that?' David demanded.

'I was trying a short cut.' Conrad's chagrin carried clearly over the ether.

'How far are you from the Luzane stream?'

'About three miles.'

'God, he'll beat you to it,' David swore. 'He's two miles from the truck and going like he's got a tax collector after him.'

'You have not seen old Connie move yet. I'll be there waiting for him,' Berg promised.

'Good luck,' David called, and the transmission went dead.

Below them Akkers was skirting the base of the hills, his black hat bobbing along steadily amongst the trees. David kept his starboard wing pointed at him and the Navajo turned steadily, holding station above him.

Other movement caught David's eye on the open slope of the hill above Akkers. For a moment he thought it was an animal, then with an intake of breath he realized that he was mistaken.

'What is it?' Debra demanded, sensing his concern.

'It's Sam, the damned fool. Connie told him not to leave his post—he's unarmed—but he's haring down the slope to try and cut Akkers off.'

'Can't you stop him?' Debra asked anxiously, and David didn't bother to answer.

He called Conrad four times before there was a reply. Conrad's voice was thick and wheezing with the effort of running.

'Sam is on to Akkers. I think he's going to confront him.'

'Oh God damn him,' groaned Conrad. 'I'll kick his black ass for him.'

'Hold on,' David told him, 'I'm going around for a closer look.'

David saw it all quite plainly, he was only three hundred feet above them when Akkers became aware of the running figure on the slope above him. He stopped dead, and half-lifted the rifle; perhaps he shouted a warning but Sam kept on down, bounding over the rocky ground towards the man who had burned his children to death.

Akkers lifted the rifle to his shoulder and aimed deliberately, the rifle jumped sharply, the barrel kicking upwards at the recoil and Sam's legs kept on running while his upper torso was flung violently backwards by the strike of the heavy soft-nosed bullet.

The tiny brown-clad body bounced and rolled down the slope, before coming to a sprawling halt in a clump of scrub.

David watched Akkers reload the rifle, stooping to pick up the empty cartridge shell. Then he looked up at the circling aircraft above him, David may have been mistaken but it seemed the man was laughing–that obscene tooth-clucking giggle of his–then he started off again at a trot towards the truck.

'Connie,' David spoke hoarsely into his handset, 'he just killed Sam.'

Conrad Berg ran heavily over the broken sandy ground. He had lost his hat and sweat poured down his big red face, stinging his eyes and plastering the lank grey hair down his forehead. The walkie-talkie set bounced on his back, and the butt of the rifle thumped rhythmically against his hip.

He ran with grim concentration, trying to ignore the swollen pounding of his heart and the torture of breath that scalded his lungs. A thorn branch clawed at his upper arms, raking thin bloody lines through his skin, but he did not break the pattern of his run.

He turned his red and streaming face to the sky and saw David's aircraft, circling ahead of him and slightly to his left. That marked for him Akkers' position–and it was clear that Conrad was losing ground in his desperate race to head off the escape.

The radio set on his back buzzed, but he ignored the call, he could not halt now. To break his run would mean he would only slump down exhausted. He was a big heavy man, the air was hot and enervating, and he had run three miles through loose and difficult going–he was almost finished. He was burning the last of his reserves now.

Suddenly the earth seemed to fall away under him, and he pitched forward and half-slid–half-rolled–down the steep bank of the Luzane stream, to finish lying on his back in the white river sand, clean and grainy as sugar. The radio was digging painfully into his flesh and he dragged it out from under him.

Still lying in the sand he panted like a dog, blinded by sweat and he fumbled the transmit button of the set.

'David–' he croaked thickly, 'I am in the bed of the stream–can you see me?'

The aircraft was arcing directly overhead now, and David's answer came back immediately.

'I see you, Connie, you are a hundred yards down-stream from the truck. Akkers is there, Connie, has just reached the truck, he'll be coming back down the river bed at any moment.'

Painfully, gasping, choking for breath, Conrad Berg dragged himself to his knees–and at that moment he heard the whirr and catch and purr of an engine. He unstrapped the heavy radio and laid it aside, then he unslung his rifle, snapped open the breech to check the load, and pulled himself to his feet.

Surprised at the weakness of his own massive body, he staggered into the centre of the river bed.

The dry river bed was eight feet deep with banks cut sheer by flood water, and it was fifteen feet wide at this point, and the floor was of smooth white sand, scattered with small water-rounded stones no bigger than a baseball. It made a good illegal access road into Jabulani, and the tracks of Akkers' truck were clearly etched in the soft sand.

Around a bend in the stream Conrad heard the truck revving and roaring as it came down a low place in the bank into the smooth bed.

Conrad stood squarely in the middle of the river bed with the rifle held across his hip, and he fought to control his breathing. The approaching roar of the truck reached a crescendo as it came skidding wildly around the bend in the stream, and raced down towards him. Showers of loose sand were thrown out from under the spinning rear wheels.

Johan Akkers crouched over the steering wheel, with the black hat pulled down to his eyebrows, and his face was grey and glistening with sweat, and he saw Conrad blocking the river bed.

'Stop!' Conrad shouted, hefting the rifle. 'Stop or I shoot!'

The truck was swaying and sliding, the engine screamed in tortured protest. Akkers began to laugh, Conrad could see the open mouth and the shaking shoulders. There was no slackening in the truck's roaring, rocking charge.

Conrad lifted the rifle and sighted down the stubby double barrels. At that range he could have put a bullet through each of Johan Akkers' deep-set eyes, and the man made no effort to duck or otherwise avoid the menace of the levelled rifle. He was still laughing, and Conrad could clearly see the teeth lying loosely on his gums. He steeled himself with the truck fifty feet away, and racing down upon him.

It takes a peculiar state of mind before one man can deliberately and cold-bloodedly shoot down another. It must either be the conditioned reflex of the soldier or law-enforcement officer, or it must be the terror of the hunted, or again it must be the unbalanced frenzy of the criminal lunatic.

None of these was Conrad Berg. Like most big strong men, he was essentially a gentle person. His whole thinking was centred on protecting and cherishing life—he could not pull the trigger.

With the truck fifteen feet away, he threw himself aside, and Johan Akkers swung the wheel wildly, deliberately driving for him.

He caught Berg a glancing blow with the side of the truck, hurling him into the earthen bank of the stream. The truck went past him, slewing out of control. It hit the bank farther down the stream in a burst of earth and loose pebbles, swaying wildly as Akkers fought the bucking wheel. He got it under control again, jammed his foot down on the accelerator and went roaring on down the river bed, leaving Conrad lying in the soft sand below the bank.

As the truck hit him, Conrad felt the bone in his hip shatter like glass, and the breath driven from his lungs by the heavy blow of metal against his rib cage.

He lay in the sand on his side and felt the blood well slowly into his mouth. It had a bitter salt taste, and he knew that one of the broken ribs had pierced his lung like a lance and that the blood sprang from deep within his body.

He turned his head and saw the radio set lying ten paces away across the river bed. He began to drag himself towards it and his shattered leg slithered after him, twisted at a grotesque angle.

'David,' he whispered into the microphone, 'I couldn't stop him. He got away,' and he spat a mouthful of blood into the white sand.

David picked the truck up as it came charging up the river bank below the concrete bridge of the Luzane, bounced and bumped over the drainage ditch and swung on to the road. It gathered speed swiftly and raced westwards towards Bandolier Hill and the highway. Dust boiled out from behind the green chassis, marking its position clearly for David as he turned two miles ahead of it.

After crossing the Luzane the road turned sharply to avoid a rocky outcrop, and then ran arrow-straight for two miles, hedged in with thick timber and undulating like a switchback, striking across the water shed and the grain of the land.

As David completed his turn he lowered his landing gear, and throttled back. The Navajo sank down, lined up on the dusty road as though it was a landing-strip.

Directly ahead was the dust column of the speeding truck. They were on a head-on course, but David concentrated coldly on bringing the Navajo down into the narrow lane between the high walls of timber. He was speaking quietly to Debra, reassuring her and explaining what he was going to attempt.

He touched down lightly on the narrow road, letting her float in easily, and when she was down he opened the throttles again, taking her along the centre of the road under power but holding her down. He had speed enough to lift the Navajo off, if Akkers chose a collision rather than surrender.

Ahead of them was another hump in the road, and as they rolled swiftly towards it the green truck suddenly burst over the crest, not more than a hundred yards ahead.

Both vehicles were moving fast, coming together at a combined speed of almost two hundred miles an hour, and the shock of it was too much for Johan Akkers.

The appearance of the aircraft dead in the centre of the road, bearing down on him with the terrible spinning discs of the propellers was too much for nerves already run raw and ragged.

He wrenched the wheel hard over, and the truck went into a broadside dry skid. It missed the port wing-tip of the Navajo as it went rocketing off the narrow road.

The front wheels caught the drainage ditch and the truck went over, cartwheeling twice in vicious slamming revolutions that smashed the glass from her windows and burst the doors open. The truck ended on its side against one of the trees.

David shut the throttles and thrust his feet hard down on the wheel brakes, bringing the Navajo up short.

'Wait here,' he shouted at Debra, and jumped down into the road. His face was a frozen mask of scar tissue, but his eyes were ablaze as he sprinted back along the road towards the wreckage of the green truck.

Akkers saw him coming, and he dragged himself shakily to his feet. He had been thrown clear and now he staggered to the truck. He could see his rifle lying in the cab, and he tried to scramble up on to the body to reach down through the open door. Blood from a deep scratch in his forehead was running into his eyes blinding him, he wiped it away with the back of his hand and glanced around.

David was close, hurdling the irrigation ditch and running towards him. Akkers scrambled down from the battered green body, and groped for the hunting knife on his belt. It was eight inches of Sheffield steel with a bone handle, and it had been honed to a razor edge.

He hefted it under-handed, in the classical grip of the knife-fighter and wiped the blood from his face with the palm of his free hand.

He was crouching slightly, facing David, and the haft of the knife was completely covered by the huge bony fist.

David stopped short of him, his eyes fastened on the knife, and Akkers began to laugh again. It was a cracked falsetto giggle, the hysterical laughter of a man driven to the very frontiers of sanity.

The point of the knife weaved in the slow mesmeric movement of an erect cobra, and it caught the sunlight in bright points of light. David watched it, circling and crouching, steeling himself, summoning all the training of paratrooper school, screwing up his nerve to go in against the naked steel.

Akkers feinted swiftly, leaping in, and when David broke away, he let out a fresh burst of high laughter.

Again they circled, Akkers mouthing his teeth loosely, sucking at them, giggling, watching with those muddy green eyes from their deep, close-set sockets. David moved back slowly ahead of him, and Akkers drove him back against the body of the truck, cornering him there.

He came then, flashing like the charge of a wounded leopard. His speed and strength were shocking, and the knife hissed upwards for David's belly.

David caught the knife hand at the wrist, blocking the thrust and trapping the knife low down. They were chest to chest now, face to face, like lovers, and Akkers' breath stank of unwashed teeth.

They strained silently, shifting like dancers to balance each other's heaves and thrusts.

David felt the knife hand twisting in his grip. The man had hands and arms like steel, he could not hold him much longer. In seconds it would be free, and the steel would be probing into his belly.

David braced his legs and twisted sideways. The move caught Akkers off-balance and he could not resist it. David was able to get his other hand on to the knife arm, but even with both hands he was hard put to hold on.

They swayed and shuffled together, panting, grunting, straining, until they fell, still locked together, against the bonnet of the truck. The metal was hot and smelled of oil.

David was concentrating all his strength on the knife, but he felt Akkers' free hand groping for his throat. He ducked his head down on his shoulders, pressing his chin against his chest but the fingers were steel hard and powerful as machinery. They probed mercilessly into his flesh, forcing his chin up, and settling on his throat, beginning to squeeze the life out of him.

Desperately David hauled at the knife arm, and found it more manageable now that Akkers was concentrating his strength on strangling him.

The open windscreen of the truck was beside David's shoulder, the glass had been smashed out of it, but jagged shards of it still stood in the metal rim, forming a crude but ferocious line of saw-teeth.

David felt the fingers digging deep into his throat, crushing the gristle of his larynx and blocking off the arteries that fed his brain. His vision starred and then began to fade darkly, as though he were pulling eight G's in a dogfight.

With one last explosive effort David pulled the knife arm around on to the line of broken glass, and he dragged it down, sawing it desperately across the edge.

Akkers screamed and his strangling grip relaxed, back and forth David sawed the arm, slashing and ripping through skin and fat and flesh, opening a wound like a ragged-petalled rose, hacking down into the nerves and arteries and sinews so that the knife dropped from the lifeless fingers and Akkers screamed like a woman.

David broke from him and shoved him away. Akkers fell to his knees still screaming and David clutched at his own throat massaging the bruised flesh, gasping for breath and feeling the flow of fresh blood to his brain.

'God Jesus, I'm dying. I'm bleeding to death. Oh sweet Jesus, help me!' screamed Akkers, holding the mutilated arm to his belly. 'Help me, oh God, don't let me die. Save me, Jesus, save me!'

Blood was streaming and spurting from the arm, flooding the front of his trousers. As he screamed his teeth fell from his mouth, leaving it a dark and empty cave in the palely glistening face.

'You've killed me. I'll bleed to death!' he screamed at David, thrusting his face towards David. 'You've got to save me—don't let me die.'

David pushed himself away from the truck and took two running steps towards the kneeling man, then he swung his right leg and his whole body into a flying kick that took Akkers cleanly under the chin and snapped his head back.

He went over backwards and lay still and quiet, and David stood over him, sobbing and gasping for breath.

For purposes of sentence Mr Justice Barnard of the Transvaal division of the Supreme Court took into consideration four previous convictions—two under the wildlife conservation act, one for aggravated assault, and the fourth for assault with intent to do grievous bodily harm.

He found Johan Akkers guilty of twelve counts under the Wildlife Conservation Act, but considered these as one when sentencing him to three years at hard labour without option of a fine, and confiscation of firearms and motor vehicles used in commission of these offences.

He found him guilty of one count of aggravated assault, and sentenced him to three years at hard labour without option.

The prosecutor altered one charge from attempted murder to assault with intent to do grievous bodily harm. He was found guilty as charged on this count, and the sentence was five years' imprisonment without option.

On the final charge of murder he was found guilty and Justice Barnard said in open court:

'In considering sentence of death on this charge, I was obliged to take into account the fact that the accused was acting like an animal in a trap, and I am satisfied that there was no element of premeditation—'

The sentence was eighteen years' imprisonment, and all sentences were to run consecutively. They were all confirmed on appeal.

As Conrad Berg said from his hospital bed with one heavily plastered leg in traction, and a glass of Old Buck gin in his hand, 'Well, for the next twenty-eight years we don't have to worry about that bastard—I beg your pardon, Mrs Morgan.'

'Twenty-nine years, dear,' Jane Berg corrected him firmly.

In July the American edition of *A Place of Our Own* was published, and it dropped immediately into that hungry and bottomless pool of indifference wherein so many good books drown. It left not a sign, not a ripple of its passing.

Bobby Dugan, Debra's new literary agent in America, wrote to say how sorry he was—and how disappointed. He had expected at least some sort of critical notice to be taken of the publication.

David took it as a personal and direct insult. He ranted and stormed about the estate for a week, and it seemed that at one stage he might actually journey to America to commit a physical violence upon that country—a sort of one-man Vietnam in reverse.

'They must be stupid,' he protested. 'It's the finest book ever written.'

'Oh, David!' Debra protested modestly.

'It is! And I'd love to go over there and rub their noses in it,' and Debra imagined the doors of editorial offices all over New York being kicked open, and literary reviewers fleeing panic-stricken, jumping out of skyscraper-windows or locking themselves in the women's toilets to evade David's wrath.

'David my darling, you are wonderful for me,' she giggled with delight, but it had hurt. It had hurt very badly. She felt the flame of her urge to write wane and flutter in the chill winds of rejection.

Now when she sat at her desk with the microphone at her lips, the words no longer tumbled and fought to escape, and the ideas no longer jostled each other. Where before she had seen things happening as though she were watching a play, seen her characters laugh and cry and sing, now there was only the dark cloud banks rolling across her eyes—unrelieved by colour or form.

For hours at a time she might sit at her desk and listen to the birds in the garden below the window.

David sensed her despair, and he tried to help her through it. When the hours at the desk proved fruitless he would insist she leave it and come with him along the new fence lines, or to fish the big blue Mozambique bream in the deep water of the pools.

Now that she had completely learned the layout of the house and its immediate environs, David began to teach her to find her way at large. Each day they would walk down to the pools and Debra learned her landmarks along the track; she would grope for them with the carved walking-stick David had given her. Zulu soon realized his role in these expeditions, and it was David's idea to clip a tiny silver bell on to his collar so that Debra could follow him more readily. Soon she could venture out without David, merely calling her destination to Zulu and checking him against her own landmarks.

David was busy at this time with the removal of Conrad's game fence, as he was still laid up with the leg, and with building his own fences to enclose the three vulnerable boundaries of Jabulani. In addition there was a force of African rangers to recruit and train in their duties. David designed uniforms for them, and built outposts for them at all the main access points to the estate. He flew into Nelspruit at regular intervals to consult Conrad Berg on these arrangements, and it was at his suggestion that David began a water survey of the estate. He wanted surface water on the areas of Jabulani that were remote from the pools, and he began studying the feasibility of building catchment dams or sinking boreholes. His days were full and active, and he became hard and lean and sunbrowned. Yet always there were many hours spent in Debra's company.

The 35-mm. colour slides that David had taken of the buffalo herd before Johan Akkers had decimated it, were returned by the processing laboratory and they were hopelessly inadequate. The huge animals seemed to be standing on the horizon, and the ox-peckers on their bodies were tiny grey specks. This failure spurred David, and he returned from one trip to Nelspruit with a 600-mm. telescopic lens.

While Debra was meant to be working, David set up his camera beside her and photographed the birds through her open window. The results were mixed. Out of thirty-six exposures, thirty-five could be thrown away, but one was beautiful, a grey-headed bush shrike at the moment of flight, poised on spread wings with the sunlight catching his vivid plumage and his sparkling eye.

David was hooked by the photography bug, and there were more lenses and cameras and tripods, until Debra protested that it was a hobby which was completely visual, and from which she was excluded.

David had one of his inspirations of genius. He sent away for pressings of June Stannard's bird song recordings—and Debra was enchanted. She listened to them intently, her whole face lighting with pleasure when she recognized a familiar call.

From there it was a natural step for her to attempt to make her own bird recordings, which included the tinkle of Zulu's silver bell, the buzz of David's Land-Rover, the voices of the servants arguing in the kitchen yard—and faintly, very faintly, the chatter of a glossy starling.

'It's no damned good,' Debra complained bitterly. 'I wonder how she got hers so clear and close.'

David did some reading, and built a parabolic reflector for her. It did not look particularly lovely, but it worked. Aimed at a sound source it gathered and directed the sound waves into the microphone.

From the window of Debra's study they became more adventurous and moved out. He built permanent and comfortable hides beside the drinking places at the pools, and when his rangers reported a nesting site of an interesting bird species, they would built temporary blinds of thatch and canvas—sometimes on tall stilts—where David and Debra spent many silent and enjoyable hours together, shooting film and catching sound. Even Zulu learned to lie still and silent with his bell removed on these occasions.

Slowly they had begun to build up a library of photographs and recordings of a professional standard—until at last David plucked up sufficient courage to send to *African Wild Life Magazine* a selection of a dozen of his best slides. Two weeks later, he received a letter of acceptance, with a cheque for a hundred dollars. This payment represented a return of approximately one-twentieth of one per cent of his capital outlay on equipment. David was ecstatic, and Debra's pleasure almost as great as his. They drank two bottles of Veuve Clicquot for dinner, and under the spell of excitement and champagne their love-making that night was particularly inventive.

When David's photographs were published in *Wild Life* accompanied by Debra's text, they reaped an unexpected harvest of letters from persons of similar interest all over the world, and a request from the editors for a full-length, illustrated article on Jabulani, and the Morgans' plans for turning it into a game sanctuary.

Debra made a lovely model for David's photographs that he compiled for the article, and she also worked with care on the text—while David fed her ideas and criticism.

Debra's new book lay abandoned, but her disappointment was forgotten in the pleasure of working together.

Their correspondence with other conservationists provided them with sufficient intellectual stimulus, and the occasional company of Conrad Berg and Jane satisfied their need for human contact. They were still both sensitive about being with other people, and this way they could avoid it.

The *Wild Life* article was almost complete and ready for posting, when a letter arrived from Bobby Dugan in New York. The editor of *Cosmopolitan* magazine had chanced upon one of the few copies of *A Place of Our Own* in circulation. She had liked it, and the magazine was considering serialization of the book—possibly linked with a feature article on Debra. Bobby wanted Debra to let him have a selection of photographs of herself, and four thousand words of autobiographical notes.

The photographs were there, ready to go to *Wild Life,* and Debra ran through the four thousand words in three hours with David making suggestions, some helpful and some bawdy.

They sent off the tape and pictures in the same post as the article to *Wild Life*. For nearly a month they heard nothing more about it and then something happened to drive it from their minds.

They were in the small thatch and daub hide beside the main pool, sitting quietly and companionably during a lull in the evening activity. David had his camera tripod set up in one of the viewing windows and Debra's reflector was raised above the roof of the hide, daubed with camouflage paint and operated by a handle over her head.

The water was still and black, except where a surface-feeding bream was rising near the far reed banks. A flock of laughing doves was lining up with a chittering troop of spotted guinea fowl at the water's edge, sipping water and then pointing their beaks to the sky as they let it run down their throats.

Suddenly David took her wrist as a cautionary signal, and by the intensity of his grip she knew that he had seen something unusual and she leaned close against him so that she could hear his whispered descriptions, and with her right hand she switched on the recorder and then reached up to aim the reflector.

A herd of the rare and shy nyala antelope were approaching the drinking place timidly, clinging until the last possible moment to the security of the forest. Their ears were spread, and their nostrils quivered and sucked at the air, huge dark eyes glowing like lamps in the gloom.

There were nine hornless females, delicate chestnut in colour, striped with white, dainty-stepping and suspicious, as they followed the two herd bulls. These were so dissimilar from their females as though to belong to a different species. Purplish black, and shaggy with a rough mane extending from between the ears to the crupper. Their horns were thick and corkscrewed, tipped with cream, and between their eyes was a vivid white chevron marking.

Advancing only a step at a time, and then pausing to stare with the limitless patience of the wild, searching for a hint of danger, they came slowly down the bank.

They passed the hide so closely that David was afraid to press the trigger of his camera lest the click of the shutter frighten them away.

He and Debra sat frozen as they reached the water; Debra smiled happily as she picked up the soft snort with which the lead bull blew the surface before drinking, and the liquid slurping with which he drew his first mouthful.

Once they were all drinking David aimed and focused with care, but at the click of the shutter the bull nearest him leapt about and uttered a hoarse, throbbing alarm bark. Instantly the entire herd whirled and raced away like pale ghosts through the dark trees.

'I got it! I got it!' exulted Debra. 'Wow! He was so close, he nearly burst my eardrums.'

The excitement on Jabulani was feverish. Nyala antelope had never been seen on the estate before, not even in David's father's time, and all steps were taken to encourage them to remain. The pools were immediately placed out of bounds to all the rangers and servants, lest the human presence frighten the herd off before they had a chance to settle down and stabilize their territory.

Conrad Berg arrived, still using a stick and limping heavily as he would for the rest of his life. From the hide he watched the herd with David and Debra, and then back at the homestead he sat before the log fire, eating prime beef steak and drinking Old Buck while he gave his opinion.

'They aren't from the Park, I shouldn't think. I would have recognized a big old bull like that if I'd ever seen him before—they have probably sneaked in from one of the other estates—you haven't got the south fence up yet, have you?'

'Not yet.'

'Well, that's where they have moved from—probably sick of being stared at by all the tourists. Come up here for a bit of peace.' He took a swallow of his gin. 'You're getting a nice bit of stuff together here, Davey—another few years and it will be a real show-place. Have you got any plans for visitors—you could make a good thing out of this place, like they have at Mala-Mala. Five-star safaris at economy prices—'

'Connie, I'm just too damn selfish to want to share this with anybody else.'

The distractions and the time had given Debra an opportunity to recover from the American failure of *A Place of Our Own,* and one morning she sat down at her desk and began working again on her second novel. That evening she told David:

'One of the blocks I have had is that I hadn't a name for it. It's like a baby—you have to give it a name or it's not really a person.'

'You have got a name for it?' he asked.

'Yes.'

'Would you like to tell me?'

She hesitated, shy at saying it to some other person for the first time. 'I thought I'd call it—*A Bright and Holy Thing,*' she said, and he thought about it for a few moments, repeating it softly.

'You like it?' she asked anxiously.

'It's great,' he said. 'I like it. I really do.'

With Debra once more busy on her novel it seemed each day was too short for the love and laughter and industry which filled it.

The call came through while David and Debra were sitting around the barbecue in the front garden. David ran up to the house when the telephone bell insisted.

'Miss Mordecai?' David was puzzled, the name was vaguely familiar.

'Yes. I have a person-to-person call from New York for Miss Debra Mordecai,' the operator repeated impatiently, and David realized who she was talking about.

'She'll take it,' he said, and yelled for Debra. It was Bobby Dugan, and the first time she had heard his voice.

'Wonder girl,' he shouted over the line. 'Sit down, so you don't fall down. Big Daddy has got news for you that will blow your mind! *Cosmopolitan* ran the article on you two weeks ago. They did you real proud, darling, full-page photograph—God, you looked good enough to eat—'

Debra laughed nervously and signalled David to put his ear against hers to listen.

'—the mag hit the stands Saturday, and Monday morning was a riot at the book stores. They were beating the doors down. You've caught the imagination of everybody here, darling. They sold seventeen thousand hardback in five days, you jumped straight into the number five slot on the *New York Times* bestseller list—it's a freak, a phenomenon, a mad crazy runner—darling, we are going to sell half a million copies of this book standing on our heads. All the big papers and mags are screaming for review copies—they've lost the ones we sent them three months ago. Doubleday are reprinting fifty thousand—and I told them they were crazy—it should have been a hundred thousand—it's only just starting—next week will see the west coast catch fire and they'll be screaming for copies across the whole country—' There was much more, Bobby Dugan riding high, shouting his plans and his hopes, while Debra laughed weakly and kept saying, 'No! I can't believe it!' and 'It's not true!'

They drank three bottles of Veuve Clicquot that night, and a little before midnight Debra fell pregnant to David Morgan.

'Miss Mordecai combines superb use of language and a sure literary touch with the readability of a popular bestseller,' said the *New York Times*.

'Who says good literature has to be dull?' asked *Time*, 'Debra Mordecai's talent burns like a clean white flame.'

'Miss Mordecai takes you by the throat, slams you against the wall, throws you on the floor and kicks you in the guts. She leaves you as shaken and weak as if you had been in a car smash,' added the *Free Press*.

Proudly David presented Conrad Berg with a signed copy of *A Place of Our Own*. Conrad had finally been prevailed upon to drop the 'Mrs Morgan' and call Debra by her given name. He was so impressed with the book that he had an immediate relapse.

'How do you think of those things, Mrs Morgan?' he asked with awe.

'Debra,' Debra prompted him.

'She doesn't think of them,' Jane Berg explained helpfully. 'It just comes to her—it's called *inspiration*.'

Bobby Dugan was correct, they had to reprint another fifty thousand copies.

It seemed as though the fates, ashamed of the cruel pranks they had played upon them, were determined to shower Debra and David with gifts.

As Debra sat at her olive-wood table, growing daily bigger with her child, once again the words flowed as strongly and as crystal clear as the spring waters of the String of Pearls. However, there was still time to help David with the illustrated publication he was compiling on the birds of prey of the bushveld, and to accompany him on the daily expeditions to different areas of Jabulani, and to plan the furnishings and the layout of the empty nursery.

Conrad Berg came to her secretly to enlist her aid in his plan to have David nominated to the Board of the National Parks Committee. They discussed it in length and great detail. A seat on the Board carried prestige and was usually reserved for men of greater age and influence than David. However, Conrad was confident that the dignity of the Morgan name combined with David's wealth, ownership of Jabulani, demonstrated interest in conservation and his ability to devote much time to the affairs of the Board would prevail.

'Yes,' Debra decided. 'It will be good for him to meet people and get out a little more. We are in danger of becoming recluses here.'

'Will he do it?'

'Don't worry,' Debra assured him, 'I'll see to it.'

Debra was right. After the initial uneasiness of the first meeting of the Board, and once the other members became accustomed to that dreadful face and realized that behind it was a warm and forceful person, David gathered increasing confidence with each subsequent journey to Pretoria where the Board met. Debra would fly up with him and while they were at their deliberations she and Jane Berg shopped for the baby and the other items of luxury and necessity that were not readily come by in Nelspruit.

However, by November Debra was carrying low and she felt too big and uncomfortable to make the long flight in the cockpit of the Navajo, especially as the rains were about to break and the air was turbulent with storm cloud and static and heavy thermals. It would be a bumpy trip, and she was deeply involved in the last chapters of the new book.

'I'll be perfectly all right here,' she insisted. 'I've got a telephone and I have also got six game rangers, four servants and a fierce hound to guard me.'

David argued and protested for five days before the meeting and agreed only after he had worked out a timetable.

'If I leave here before dawn I'll be at the meeting by nine, we'll be finished by three and I can be back here by six-thirty at the latest,' he muttered. 'If it wasn't the budget and financial affairs vote, I would cut it—tell them I was sick.'

'It's important, darling. You go.'

'You sure now?'

'I won't even notice you're not here.'

'Don't get too carried away by it,' he told her ruefully. 'I might stay just to punish you.'

In the dawn the thunderheads were the colour of wine and flame and ripe fruit, fuming and magnificent, towering high above the tiny aircraft, high above the utmost ceiling of which it was capable.

David flew the corridors of open sky alone and at peace, wrapped in the euphoria of flight which never failed for him. He altered course at intervals to avoid the mountainous upsurges of cloud; within them lurked death and disaster, great winds that would tear the wings from his machine and send the pieces whirling on high, up into the heights where a man would perish from lack of oxygen.

He landed at Grand Central where a hire car was waiting for him, and spent the journey into Pretoria reading through the morning papers. It was only when he saw the meteorological prediction of a storm front moving in steadily from the Mozambique channel that he felt a little uneasy.

Before he entered the conference-room he asked the receptionist to take a telephone call to Jabulani.

'Two-hour delay, Mr Morgan.'

'Okay, call me when it comes through.'

When they broke for lunch he asked her again.

'What happened to my call?'

'I'm sorry, Mr Morgan. I was going to tell you. The lines are down. They are having very heavy rainfall in the low veld.'

His vague uneasiness became mild alarm.

'Would you call the meteorological office for me, please?'

The weather was down solid. From Barberton to Mpunda Milia and from Lourenço Marques to Machadodorp, the rain was heavy and unrelenting. The cloud ceiling was above twenty thousand feet and it was right down on the ground. The Navajo had no oxygen or electronic navigational equipment.

'How long?' David demanded of the meteorological officer. 'How long until it clears?'

'Hard to tell, sir. Two or three days.'

'Damn! Damn!' said David bitterly, and went down to the canteen on the ground floor of the government building. Conrad Berg was at a corner table with two other members of the Board, but when he saw David he jumped up and limped heavily but urgently across the room.

'David,' he took his arm, and his round red face was deadly serious. 'I've just heard—Johan Akkers broke jail last night. He killed a guard and got clean away. He's been loose for seventeen hours.'

David stared at him, unable to speak with the shock of it.

'Is Debra alone?'

David nodded, his face stiff with scar tissue, but his eyes dark and afraid.

'You'd better fly down right away to be with her.'

'The weather—they've grounded all aircraft in the area.'

'Use my truck!' said Conrad urgently.

'I need something faster than that.'

'Do you want me to come with you?'

'No,' said David. 'If you aren't there this afternoon, they won't approve the new fencing allocations. I'll go on my own.'

Debra was working at her desk when she heard the wind coming. She switched off her tape recorder and went out on to the veranda with the dog following her closely.

She stood listening, not sure of what she was hearing. It was a soughing and sighing, a far-off rushing like that of a wave upon a pebble beach.

The dog pressed against her leg and she squatted beside him, placing one arm around his neck, listening to the gathering rush of the wind, hearing the roar of it building up swiftly, the branches of the marula forest beginning to thrash and rattle.

Zulu whimpered, and she hugged him a little closer.

'There, boy. Gently. Gently,' she whispered and the wind struck in a mighty squalling blast, crashing through the tree-tops, tearing and cracking the upper branches.

It banged into the insect screen of the veranda with a snap like a mainsail filling, and unsecured windows and doors slammed like cannon shots.

Debra sprang up and ran back into her workroom, the window was swinging and slamming, dust and debris boiling in through it. She put her shoulder to it, closing it and securing the latch, then she ran to do the same to the other windows and bumped into one of the house servants.

Between them they battened down all the doors and windows.

'Madam, the rain will come now. Very much rain.'

'Go to your families now,' Debra told them.

'The dinner, madam?'

'Don't worry, I'll make that,' and thankfully they streamed away through the swirling dust to their hutments beyond the kopje.

The wind blew for fifteen minutes, and Debra stood by the wire screen and felt it tugging and whipping her body. Its wildness was infectious, and she laughed aloud, elated and excited.

Then suddenly the wind was passed, as swiftly as it had come, and she heard it tearing and clawing its way over the hills above the pools.

In the utter silence that followed the whole world waited, tensed for the next onslaught of the elements. Debra felt the cold, the sudden fall in temperature as though the door to a great ice-box had opened and she hugged her arms and shivered; she could not see the dense dark cloud banks that rolled across Jabulani, but somehow she sensed their menace and their majesty in the coldness that swamped her.

The first lightning bolt struck with a crackling electric explosion that seemed to singe the air about her, and Debra was taken so unawares that she cried out aloud. The thunder broke, and seemed to shake the sky and rock the earth's very foundations.

Debra turned and groped her way back into the house, locking herself into her room, but walls could not diminish the fury of the rain when it came. It drummed and roared and deafened, battering the window panes, and striking the walls and doors, pouring through the screen to flood the veranda.

As overpowering as was the rainstorm, yet it was the lightning and the thunder that racked Debra's nerves. She could not steel herself for each mighty crack and roar. Each one caught her off balance, and it seemed that they were aimed directly at her.

She crouched on her day bed, clinging to the soft warm body of the dog for a little comfort. She wished she had not allowed the servants to leave, and she thought that her nerve might crack altogether under the bombardment.

Finally she could stand it no longer. She groped her way into the living-room. In her distress she had almost lost her way about her own home, but she found the telephone and lifted it to her ear.

Immediately she knew that it was dead, there was no tone to it but she cranked the handle wildly, calling desperately into the mouthpiece, until finally she let it fall and dangle on its cord.

She began to sob as she stumbled back to her workroom, hugging the child in her big belly, and she fell upon the day bed and covered her ears with both hands.

'Stop it,' she screamed. 'Stop it, oh please God, make it stop.'

The new national highway as far as the coal-mining town of Witbank was broad and smooth, six lanes of traffic, and David eased the hired Pontiac into the fast lane and went flat, keeping his foot pressed down hard. She peaked out at a hundred and thirty miles an hour, and she sat so solid upon the road that he hardly needed to drive her. His mind was free to play with horror stories, and to remember Johan Akkers' face as he stood in the dock glaring across the Court Room at them. The deep-set muddy eyes, and the mouth working as though he were about to spit. As the warders had led him to the stairs down to the cells he had pulled free and shouted back.

'I'm going to get you, Scarface,' he giggled. 'If I have to wait twenty-nine years—I'm going to get you,' and they took him away.

After Witbank the road narrowed. There was heavy traffic and the bends had dangerous camber and deceptive gradients. David was able to concentrate on keeping the big car on the road, and to drive the phantoms from his mind.

He took the Lydenburg turn off, cutting the corner of the triangle, and the traffic thinned out to an occasional truck. He was able to go flat out again, and race along the edge of the high escarpment. Then suddenly the road turned and began its plunge down into the low veld.

When he emerged from the Erasmus tunnel David ran into the rain. It was a solid grey bank of water that filled the air and buffeted the body of the Pontiac. It flooded the road, so David had difficulty following its verge beneath the standing sheets of water, and it swamped the windshield, so that the efforts of the wipers to clear it were defeated.

David switched on his headlights and drove as fast as he dared, craning forward in his seat to peer into the impenetrable blue-grey curtains of rain.

Darkness came early in the rain, beneath the lowering black clouds, and the wet road dazzled him with the reflections of his own headlights, while the fat falling drops seemed as big as hail stones. He was forced to moderate his speed a little more, creeping down the highway towards Bandolier Hill.

In the darkness he almost missed the turning, and he reversed back to it, swinging on to the unmade surface.

It was slushy with mud, puddled and swampy, slippery as grease. Again he was forced to lower his speed. Once he lost it, and slid broadside into the drainage ditch. By packing loose stones under the wheels and racing the engine he pulled the Pontiac out and drove on.

By the time he reached the bridge over the Luzane stream, he had been six hours at the wheel of the Pontiac, and it was a few minutes after eight o'clock in the evening.

As he reached the bridge the rain stopped abruptly, a freak hole in the weather. Directly overhead the stars showed mistily, while around them the cloud banks swirled, turning slowly, as though upon the axis of a great wheel.

David's headlights cut through the darkness, out across the mad brown waters to the far bank a hundred yards away. The bridge was submerged under fifteen feet of flood water, and the water was moving so swiftly that its waves and whirlpools seemed sculptured in polished brown marble, and the trunks of uprooted trees dashed downstream upon the flood.

It seemed impossible that the bed of this raging torrent had been the narrow sandy bed in which Johan Akkers had run down Conrad with the green Ford truck.

David climbed out of the Pontiac and walked down to the edge of the water. As he stood there he saw the level creeping up perceptibly towards his feet. It was still rising.

He looked up at the sky, and judged that the respite in the weather would not last much longer.

He reached his decision and ran back to the Pontiac. He reversed well back on to the highest ground and parked it off the verge with the headlights still directed at the river edge. Then, standing beside the door, he stripped down to his shirt and underpants. He pulled his belt from the loops of his trousers and buckled it about his waist, then he tied his shoes to the belt by their laces.

Barefooted he ran to the edge of the water, and began to feel his way slowly down the bank. It shelved quickly and within a few paces he was knee-deep and the current plucked at him, viciously trying to drag him off-balance.

He poised like that, braced against the current, and waited, staring upstream. He saw the tree trunk coming down fast on the flood, with its roots sticking up like beseeching arms. It was swinging across the current and would pass him closely.

He judged his moment and lunged for it. Half a dozen strong strokes carried him to it and he grasped one of the roots. Instantly he was whisked out of the beams of the headlight into the roaring fury of the river. The tree rolled and bucked, carrying him under and bringing him up coughing and gasping.

Something struck him a glancing blow and he felt his shirt tear and the skin beneath it rip. Then he was under water again, swirling end over end and clinging desperately to his log.

All about him the darkness was filled with the rush and threat of crazy water, and he was buffeted and flogged by its raw strength, grazed and bruised by rocks and driftwood.

Suddenly he felt the log check and bump against an obstruction, turning and swinging out into the current again.

David was blinded with muddy water and he knew there was a limit to how much more of this treatment he could survive. Already he was weakening quickly. He could feel his mind and his movements slowing, like a battered prize fighter in the tenth round.

He gambled it all on the obstruction which the log had encountered being the far bank, and he released his death-grip on the root and struck out sideways across the current with desperate strength.

His overarm stroke ended in the trailing branches of a thorn tree hanging over the storm waters. Thorns tore the flesh of his palm as his grip closed over them, and he cried out at the pain but held on.

Slowly he dragged himself out of the flood and crawled up the bank, hacking and coughing at the water in his lungs. Clear of the river, he fell on his face in the mud and vomited a gush of swallowed water that shot out of his nose and mouth.

He lay exhausted for a long while, until his coughing slowed and he could breathe again. His shoes had been torn from his belt by the current. He dragged himself to his feet and staggered forward into the darkness. As he ran, he held his hand to his face, pulling the broken thorns from the flesh of his palm with his teeth.

Stars were still showing overhead and by their feeble light he made out the road, and he began to run along it, gathering strength with each pace. It was very still now, with only the dripping of the trees and the occasional far-out mutter of thunder to break the silence.

Two miles from the homestead, David made out the dark bulk of something on the side of the road, and it was only when he was a few paces from it that he realized it was an automobile—a late model Chevy. It had been abandoned, bogged down in one of the greasy mudholes that the rains had opened.

The doors were unlocked and David switched on the interior and parking lights. There was dried blood on the seat, a dark smear of it, and on the back seat was a bundle of clothing. David untied it quickly and recognized immediately the coarse canvas suiting as regulation prison garb. He stared at it stupidly for a moment, until the impact of it struck him.

The car was stolen, the blood probably belonging to the unfortunate owner. The prison garb had been exchanged for other clothing, probably taken from the body of the owner of the Chevy.

David knew then beyond all possible doubt that Johan Akkers was at Jabulani, and that he had arrived before the bridge over the Luzane stream had become impassable—probably three or four hours previously.

David threw the prison suiting back into the car, and he began to run.

Johan Akkers drove the Chevy across the Luzane bridge with the rising waters swirling over the guard rail, and with the rain teeming down in blinding white sheets.

The muddy water shoved at the body of the car, making steering difficult, and it seeped in under the doors, flooding the floorboards and swirling about Akkers' feet; but he reached the safety of the far bank and raced the engine as he shot up it. The wheels spun on the soft mud, and the Chevy skidded and swayed drunkenly in the loose footing.

The closer he drew to Jabulani the more reckless he became in his haste.

Before his conviction and imprisonment, Akkers had been a twisted and blighted creature, a man of deep moods and passionate temper. Feeling himself rejected and spurned by his fellow men he had lived in a world of swift defensive violence, but always he had kept within the bounds of reason.

However, during the two years that he had laboured and languished within prison walls, his anger and his lust for vengeance had driven him over that narrow boundary.

Vengeance had become the sole reason for his existence, and he had rehearsed it a hundred times each day. He had planned his prison break to give himself three days of freedom—after that it did not matter. Three days would be enough.

He had infected his own jaw, running a needle poisoned with his excreta deeply into the gum. They had taken him to the dental clinic as he had planned. The guard had been easily handled, and the dentist had co-operated with a scalpel held to his throat.

Once clear of the prison, Akkers had used the scalpel, vaguely surprised by the volume of blood that could issue from a human throat. He had left the dentist slumped over his steering-wheel on a plot of waste ground and, with his white laboratory gown over his prison suit, he had waited at a set of traffic lights.

The shiny new Chevy had pulled up for a red light and Akkers had opened the passenger door and slid in beside the driver.

He had been a smaller man than Akkers, plump and prosperous-looking, with a smooth pale face and soft little hairless hands on the steering-wheel. He had obeyed meekly Akkers' instruction to drive on.

Akkers had rolled his soft white body, clad only in vest and shorts, into a clump of thick grass beside a disused secondary road and pulled the grass closed over him, then he had beaten the first road block out of the city area by forty minutes.

He stayed on the side roads, picking his way slowly eastwards. The infection in his jaw had ached intolerably despite the shot of antibiotics the dentist had given him, and his crippled claw of a hand had been awkward and clumsy on the gear lever—for the severed nerves and sinews had never knitted again. The hand was a dead and insensate thing.

Using the caution of a natural predator and helped by the news flashes on the radio, he had groped his way carefully through the net that was spread for him, and now he was on Jabulani and he could restrain himself no longer.

He hit the mud hole at forty and the Chevy whipped and spun, slewing her back end deep into the mud and high-centring her belly on the soft ooze.

He left her there and went on swiftly through the rain, loping on long legs. Once he giggled and sucked at his teeth, but then he was silent again.

It was dark by the time he climbed the kopje behind Jabulani homestead. He lay there for two hours peering down into the driving rain, waiting for the darkness. Once night fell, he could see no lights, and he began to worry, there should have been lights burning.

He left the kopje and moved cautiously through the darkness down the hill. He avoided the servants' quarters, and went through the trees to the landing-strip.

He ran into the side of the hangar in the dark and followed the wall to the side doorway.

Frantically he spread his arms and felt for the aircraft that should be here—and when he realized that it was not he let out a groan of frustration.

They were gone. He had planned and schemed in vain, all his desperate striving was in vain.

Growling like an animal, he smashed the fist of his good hand against the wall, enjoying the pain of it in his frustration, and his anger and his hatred was so strong that it shook his body like a fever, and he cried out aloud, a formless animal cry without coherence or sense.

Suddenly the rain stopped. The heavy drum of it upon the iron roof of the hangar ceased so abruptly that Akkers was distracted. He went to the opening and looked out.

The stars were swimming mistily above him, and the only sound was the gurgle and chuckle of running water and the dripping of the trees.

There was the glimmering of light now, and he saw the white walls of the homestead shine amongst the trees. He could do damage there, Akkers realized. He could find there some outlet for his terrible frustration. There was furniture to smash, and the thatch would burn—if lit from inside, the thatch would burn even in this weather.

He started towards the homestead through the dark sodden trees.

Debra woke in the silence. She had fallen asleep in the midst of the storm, perhaps as a form of escape.

Now she groped for the warm comforting body of the dog but he was gone. There was a patch of warmth on the bed beside her where he had lain.

She listened intently and there was nothing but the soft sounds of water in the guttering and far-off the growl of thunder. She remembered her earlier panic and she was ashamed.

She stood up from the bed and she was shivering with the cold in her loose, free-flowing dark blue maternity blouse, and the elastic-fronted slacks that were adjustable to her expanding waistline. She felt with her toes and found the light ballet pumps on the stone floor and pushed her feet into them.

She started towards her dressing-room for a sweater, then she would make herself a cup of hot soup, she decided.

Zulu started barking. He was outside in the front garden. Clearly he had left the house through the small hinged doorway that David had built especially for him in the veranda wall.

The dog had many barks, each with a different meaning which Debra understood.

A self-effacing woof, that was the equivalent of the watchman's 'Ten o'clock on a June night—and all's well.'

Or a longer-drawn-out yowl, that meant, 'There is a full moon out tonight, and the wolf's blood in my veins will not allow me to sleep.'

A sharper, meaningful bark, 'Something is moving down near the pumphouse. It may be a lion.'

And then there was an urgent clamouring chorus, 'There is dire danger threatening. Beware! Beware!'

It was the danger bark now, and then growling through closed jaws as though he were worrying something.

Debra went out on to the veranda and she felt the puddled rainwater soaking through her light shoes. Zulu was harrying something in the front garden, she could hear the growling and scuffling, the movement of bodies locked in a struggle. She stood silently, uncertain of what to do, knowing only that she could not go out to Zulu. She was blind and helpless against the unknown adversary. As she hesitated she heard clearly the sound of a heavy blow. It cracked on bone, and she heard the thump of a body falling. Zulu's growls were cut off abruptly, and there was silence. Something had happened to the dog. Now she was completely alone in the silence.

No, not silence. There was the sound of breathing—a heavy panting breath.

Debra shrank back against the veranda wall, listening and waiting.

She heard footsteps, human footsteps coming through the garden towards the front door. The footsteps squelched and splashed in the rain puddles.

She wanted to call out a challenge, but her voice was locked in her constricted throat. She wanted to run, but her legs were paralysed by the sound of the intruder climbing the front steps.

A hand brushed against the wire screening, and then settled on the handle, rattling it softly.

At last Debra found her voice. 'Who is that?' she called, a high panicky cry that ran out into the night silence.

Instantly the soft sounds ceased. The intruder was frozen by her challenge. She could imagine whoever it was standing on the top step, peering through the screening into the darkness of the veranda, trying to make her out in the gloom. Suddenly she was thankful for the dark blouse and black slacks.

She waited motionlessly, listening, and she heard a little wind shake the tree-tops, bringing down a sudden quick patter of droplets. A hunting owl called down near the dam. She heard the thunder murmur bad-temperedly along the hills, and a nightjar screeched harshly from amongst the poinsettia bushes.

The silence went on for a lóng time, and she knew she could not stand it much longer. She could feel her lips beginning to quiver and the cold and fear and the weight of the child were heavy upon her bladder, she wanted to run—but there was nowhere to run to.

Then suddenly the silence was broken. In the darkness there was the sound of a man giggling. It was shockingly close and clear, and it was a crazy sound. The shock of it seemed to clutch at her heart and crush the air from her lungs.

Her legs went weak under her, beginning to shake, and the pressure on her bladder was intolerable—for she recognized the sound of that laughter, the sick insane sound of it was graven upon her mind.

A hand shook the door handle, jerking and straining at it. Then a shoulder crashed into the narrow frame. It was a screen door—not built to withstand rough treatment. Debra knew it would yield quickly.

She screamed then, a high ringing scream of terror, and it seemed to break the spell which held her. Her legs would move again, and her brain would work.

She whirled and ran back into her workroom, slamming the door and locking it swiftly.

She crouched beside the door, thinking desperately. She knew that as soon as he broke into the house Akkers need only switch on a light. The electricity generator would automatically kick in on demand, and in the light he would have her at his mercy. Her only protection was darkness. In the darkness she would have the advantage, for she was accustomed to it.

She had heard the nightjar and the owl calling so she knew that night had fallen, and it was probable that the rain cloud still blanketed moon and stars. Darkness was out there in the forest. She must get out of the house, and try to reach the servants' quarters.

She hurried through the rooms towards the rear of the house, and as she went she thought of a weapon. The firearms were locked in the steel cabinet in David's office—and the key was with him. She ran through to the kitchen and her heavy walking-stick was in its place by the door. She grasped it thankfully and slipped open the door catch.

At that moment she heard the front door crash open, with the lock kicked in, and she heard Akkers charge heavily into the living-room. She closed the kitchen door behind her and started across the yard. She tried not to run, she counted her steps. She must not lose her way. She must find the track around the kopje to the servants' hutments.

Her first landmark was the gate in the fence that ringed the homestead. Before she reached it she heard the electricity generator throb to life in the power house beyond the garages. Akkers had found a light switch.

She was slightly off in her direction and she ran into the barbed-wire fence. Frantically she began to feel her way along it, trying for the gate. Above her head she heard the buzz and crackle of the element in one of the arc lamps that lined the fence and could flood the gardens with light.

Akkers must have found the switch beside the kitchen door, and Debra realized that she must be bathed in the light of the arcs.

She heard him shout behind her, and knew that he had seen her. At that moment she found the gate, and with a sob of relief she tore it open and began to run.

She must get out of the light of the arcs, she must find the darkness. Light was mortal danger, darkness was sanctuary.

The track forked, left to the pools, right to the hutments. She took the right-hand path and ran along it. Behind her she heard the gate clank shut. He was after her.

She counted as she ran, five hundred paces to the rock on the left side of the path that marked the next fork. She tripped over it, falling heavily and barking her shins.

She rolled to her knees, and she had lost the walking-stick. She could not waste precious seconds in searching for it. She groped for the path and ran on.

Fifty paces and she knew she was on the wrong fork. This path led down to the pumphouse—and she was not familiar with it. It was not one of her regular routes.

She missed a turn and ran into broken ground. She stumbled on until rank grass wrapped about her ankles and brought her down again, falling heavily on her side so that she was winded.

She was completely lost, but she knew she was out of the arc lights now. With luck she was shielded by complete darkness—but her heart was racing and she felt nauseous with terror.

She tried to control her gulping, sobbing breath, and to listen.

She heard him coming then, pounding footsteps that rang clearly, even on the rain-soaked earth. He seemed to be coming directly to where she lay, and she shrank down against the wet earth and she pressed her face into her arms to hide her face and muffle her breathing.

At the last moment his blundering footsteps passed her closely, and ran on. She felt sick with relief, but it was premature for abruptly the footsteps ceased and he was so close she could hear him panting.

He was listening for her, standing close beside where she lay in the grass. They stayed like that during the long slow passage of minutes. For Debra it seemed an eternity of waiting—broken at last by his voice.

'Ah! There you are,' he giggled, 'there you are. I can see you.'

Her heart jumped with shock, he was closer than she had thought. Almost she jumped up and began to run again—but some deeper sense restrained her.

'I can see you hiding there,' he repeated, giggling and snickering. 'I've got a big knife here, I'm going to hold you down and cut—'.

She quailed in the grass, listening to the awful obscenities that poured from his mouth. Then suddenly she realized that she was safe here. She was covered by the night and the thick grass, and he had lost her. He was trying to panic her, make her run again and betray her position. She concentrated all her attention on remaining absolutely still and silent.

Akkers' threats and sadistic droolings ended in silence again. He listened for her with the patience of the hunter, and the long minutes dragged by.

The ache in her bladder was like a red-hot iron, and she wanted to sob out loud. Something loathsome crawled out of the wet grass over her arm. Her skin prickled with fresh horror at the feel of multiple insect feet on her skin, but she steeled herself not to move.

The thing, scorpion or spider, crawled across her neck and she knew her nerves would crack within seconds.

Suddenly Akkers spoke again. 'All right!' he said, 'I'm going back to fetch a flashlight. We'll see how far you get then. I'll be back soon—don't think you'll beat old Akkers. He's forgotten more tricks than you'll ever learn.'

He moved away heavily, noisily, and she wanted to strike the insect from her cheek and run again, but some instinct warned her. She waited five minutes, and then ten. The insect moved up into her hair.

Akkers spoke again out of the darkness near her. 'All right, you clever bitch. We'll get you yet,' and she heard him move away. This time she knew he had gone.

She brushed the insect from her hair, shuddering with horror. Then she stood up and moved quietly into the forest. Her fingers were stiff with cold on the fastenings of her slacks, but she loosened them and squatted to relieve the burning ache in her lower belly.

She stood up again and felt the child move within her body. The feel of it evoked all her maternal instincts of protection. She must find a safe place for her child. She thought of the hide by the pools.

How to reach them? For she was now completely lost. Then she remembered David telling her about the wind, the rain wind out of the west, now reduced to an occasional light air, and she waited for the next breath of it on her cheek. It gave her direction. She turned her back to the next gust and set off steadily through the forest with hands held out ahead to prevent herself running into one of the trunks. If only she could reach the pools, she could follow the bank to the hide.

As the cyclonic winds at the centre of the storm turned upon their axis, so they swung, changing direction constantly and Debra followed them faithfully, beginning a wide aimless circle through the forest.

Akkers raged through the brightly lit homestead of Jabulani, jerking open drawers and kicking in locked cupboard doors.

He found the gun cabinet in David's office, and ransacked the desk drawers for keys. He found none, and giggled and swore with frustration.

He crossed the room to the built-in cupboard unit. There was a sealed-cell electric lantern on the shelf with a dozen packets of shotgun shells. he took down the lantern eagerly and thumbed the switch. The beam was bright white, even in the overhead lights—and he sucked his teeth and chuckled happily.

Once more he ran into the kitchen, pausing to select a long stainless-steel carving knife from the cutlery drawer before hurrying across the yard to the gate and along the path.

In the lantern beam, Debra's footprints showed clearly in the soft earth with his own overlaying them. He followed them to where she had blundered off the path, and found the mark of her body where she had lain.

'Clever bitch, he chuckled again and followed her tracks through the forest. She had laid an easy trail to follow, dragging a passage through the rain-heavy grass and wiping the droplets from the stems. To the hunter's eye it was a clearly blazed trail.

Every few minutes he paused to throw the beam of the lantern ahead of him amongst the trees. He was thrilling now to the hunter's lust, the primeval force which was the mainspring of his existence. His earlier set-back made the chase sweeter for him.

He went on carefully, following the wandering trail, the aimless footprints turning haphazardly in a wide circle.

He stopped again and panned the lantern beam across the rain-laden grass tops, and he saw something move at the extreme range of the lamp, something pale and round.

He held it in the lantern beam, and saw the woman's pale strained face as she moved forward slowly and hesitantly. She went like a sleep-walker, with arms extended ahead of her, and with shuffling uncertain gait.

She was coming directly towards him, oblivious of the light which held her captive in its beam. Once she paused to hug her swollen belly and sob with weariness and fear.

The legs of her trousers were sodden with rain water and her flimsy shoes were already torn, and as she hobbled closer he saw that her arms and her lips were blue and shivering with the cold.

Akkers stood quietly watching her coming towards him, like a chicken drawn to the swaying cobra.

Her long dark hair hung in damp ropes down her shoulders, and dangled in her face. Her thin blouse was wet also with drops fallen from the trees, and it was plastered over the thrusting mound of her belly.

He let her come closer, enjoying the fierce thrill of having her in his power. Drawing out the final consummation of his vengeance–hoarding each moment of it like a miser.

When she was five paces from him he played the beam full in her face, and he giggled.

She screamed, her whole face convulsing, and she whirled like a wild animal and ran blindly. Twenty paces before she ran headlong into the stem of a marula tree.

She fell back, collapsing to her knees and sobbed aloud, clutching at her bruised cheek.

Then she scrambled to her feet and stood shivering, turning her head and cocking it for the next sound.

Silently he moved around her, drawing close and he giggled again, close behind her.

She screamed again and ran blindly, panic-stricken, witless with terror until an ant-bear hold caught her foot and flung her down heavily to the ground, and she lay there sobbing.

Akkers moved leisurely and silently after her, he was enjoying himself for the first time in two years. Like a cat he did not want to end it, he wanted it to last a long time.

He stooped over her and whispered a filthy word, and instantly she rolled to her feet and was up and running again–wildly, sightlessly, through the trees. He followed her, and in his crazed mind she became a symbol of all the thousand animals he had hunted and killed.

David ran barefooted in the soft earth of the road. He ran without feeling his bruised and torn skin, without feeling the pounding of his heart nor the protest of his lungs.

As the road rounded the shoulder of the hill and dipped towards the homestead he stopped abruptly, and stared panting at the lurid glow of the arc lights that floodlit the grounds and garden of Jabulani. It made no sense that the floodlights should be burning, and David felt a fresh flood of alarm. He sprinted on down the hill.

He ran through the empty, ransacked rooms shouting her name–but the echoes mocked him.

When he reached the front veranda he saw something moving in the darkness, beyond the broken screen door.

'Zulu!' He ran forward. 'Here, boy! Here, boy! Where is she?'

The dog staggered up the steps towards him, his tail wagged a perfunctory greeting, but he was obviously hurt. A heavy blow along the side of his head had broken the jaw, or dislocated it, so that it hung lopsided and grotesque. He was still stunned, and David knelt beside him.

'Where is she, Zulu? Where is she?' The dog seemed to make an effort to gather its scattered wits. 'Where is she, boy? She's not in the house. Where is she? Find her, boy, find her.'

He led the labrador out into the yard, and he followed gamely as David circled the house. At the back door Zulu picked up the scent on the fresh damp earth. He started resolutely towards the gate, and David saw the footprints in the floodlights, Debra's and the big masculine prints which ran after them.

As Zulu crossed the yard, David turned back into his office. The lantern was missing from its shelf, but there was a five-cell flashlight near the back. He shoved it into his pocket and grabbed a handful of shotgun shells. Then he went quickly to the gun cabinet and unlocked it. He snatched the Purdey shotgun from the rack and loaded it as he ran.

Zulu was staggering along the path beyond the gates, and David hurried after him.

Johan Akkers was no longer a human being, he had become an animal. The spectacle of the running quarry had roused the predator's single-minded passion to chase and drag down and kill—yet it was seasoned .with a feline delight in torment. He was playing with his wounded dragging prey, running it when he could have ended it, drawing it out, postponing the climax, the final consuming thrill of the kill.

The moment came at last, some deep atavistic sense of the ritual of the hunt—for all sport killing has its correct ceremony—and Akkers knew it must end now.

He came up behind the running figure and reached out to take a twist of the thick dark hair in the crippled claw of his hand, wrapping it with a quick movement about his wrist and jerking back her head, laying open the long pale throat for the knife.

She turned upon him with a strength and ferocity he had not anticipated. Her body was hard and strong and supple, and now that she could place him she drove at him with the wild terror of a hunted thing.

He was unprepared, her attack took him off-balance, and he went over backwards with her on top of him, and he dropped the knife and the lantern into the grass to protect his eyes, for she was tearing at them with long sharp nails. He felt them rip into his nose and cheek, and she screeched like a cat—for she was also an animal in this moment.

He freed the stiff claw from the tangle of her hair, and he drew it back, holding her off with his right hand—and he struck her. It was like a wooden club, stiff and hard and without feeling. A single blow with it had stunned the labrador and broken his jaw. It hit her across the temple, a sound like an axe swung at a tree trunk. It knocked all the fight out of her, and he came up on his knees, holding her with his good hand and with the other he clubbed her mercilessly, beat her head back and across with a steady rhythm. In the light of the fallen lantern, the black blood spurted from her nose, and the blows cracked against her skull, steady and unrelenting. Long after she was still and senseless he continued to beat her. Then at last he let her drop, and he stood up. He went to the lantern and played the beam in the grass. The knife glinted up at him.

There is an ancient ceremony with which a hunt should end. The culminating ceremony of the gralloch, when the triumphant huntsman slits open the paunch of his game, and thrusts his hand into the opening to draw out the still-warm viscera.

Johan Akkers picked the knife out of the grass and set down the lantern so the beam fell upon Debra's supine figure.

He went to her and, with his foot, rolled her on to her back. The dark black mane of sodden hair smothered her face.

He knelt beside her and hooked one iron-hard finger into the front of her blouse. With a single jerk he ripped it cleanly open, and her big round belly bulged into the lantern light. It was white and full and ripe with the dark pit of the navel in its centre.

Akkers giggled and wiped the rain and sweat from his face with his arm. Then he changed his grip on the knife, reversing it so the blade would go shallow, opening the paunch neatly from crotch to rib cage without cutting into the intestines, a stroke as skilful as a surgeon's that he had performed ten thousand times before.

Movement in the shadows at the edge of the light caused him to glance up. He saw the black dog rush silently at him, saw its eyes glow in the lantern light. He threw up his arm to guard his throat and the furry body crashed into him. They rolled together, with Zulu mouthing him, unable to take a grip with his injured jaws.

Akkers changed his grip on the hilt of the carving knife and stabbed up into the dog's rib cage, finding the faithful heart with his first thrust. Zulu yelped once, and collapsed. Akkers pushed the glossy black body aside, pulling out the knife and he crawled back to where Debra lay.

The distraction that Zulu had provided gave David a chance to come up.

David ran to Akkers, and the man looked up with the muddy green eyes glaring in the lantern light. He growled at David with the long blade in his hand dulled by the dog's blood. He started to come to his feet, ducking his head in exactly the same aggressive gesture as the bull baboon.

David thrust the barrels of the shotgun into his face and he pulled both triggers. The shot hit solidly, without spreading, tearing into him in the bright yellow flash and thunder of the muzzle blast, and it took away the whole of Akkers' head above the mouth, blowing it to nothingness. He dropped into the grass with his legs kicking convulsively, and David hurled the shotgun aside and ran to Debra.

He knelt over her and he whispered, 'My darling, oh my darling. Forgive me, please forgive me. I should never have left you.' Gently he picked her up and holding her to his chest, he carried her up to the homestead.

Debra's child was born in the dawn. It was a girl, tiny and wizened and too early for her term. If there had been skilled medical attention available she might have lived, for she fought valiantly. But David was clumsy and ignorant of the succour she needed. He was cut off by the raging river and the telephone was still dead, and Debra was still unconscious.

When it was over he wrapped the tiny little blue body in a clean sheet and laid it tenderly in the cradle that had been prepared for her. He felt overwhelmed by a sense of guilt at having failed the two persons who needed him.

At three o'clock that afternoon, Conrad Berg forced a passage of the Luzane stream with the water boiling above the level of the big wheels of his truck, and three hours later they had Debra in a private ward of the Nelspruit hospital. Two days later she became conscious once more, but her face was grotesquely swollen and purple with bruises.

Near the crest of the kopje that stood above the homestead of Jabulani there was a natural terrace, a platform which overlooked the whole estate. It was a remote and peaceful place and they buried the child there. Out of the rock of the kopje David built a tomb for her with his own hands.

It was best that Debra had never felt the child in her arms, or at her breast. That she had never heard her cry or smelled the puppy smell of her.

Her mourning was therefore not crippling and corrosive, and she and David visited the grave regularly. One Sunday morning as they sat upon the stone bench beside it, Debra talked for the first time about another baby.

'You took so long with the first one, Morgan,' she complained. 'I hope you've mastered the technique.'

They walked down the hill again, put the rods and a picnic basket into the Land-Rover and drove down to the pools.

The Mozambique bream came on the bite for an hour just before noon and they fought over the fat yellow wood grubs that David was baiting. Debra hung five, all around three pounds in weight, and David had a dozen of the big blue fish before it went quiet and they propped the rods and opened the cold box.

They lay together on the rug beneath the outspread branches of the fever trees, and drank white wine cold from the icebox.

The African spring was giving way to full summer, filling the bush with bustle and secret activity. The weaver birds were busy upon their basket nests, tying them to the bending tips of the reeds, fluttering brilliant yellow wings as they worked with black heads bobbing. On the far bank of the pool a tiny bejewelled kingfisher sat his perch on a dead branch above the still water, plunging suddenly, a speck of flashing blue to shatter the surface and emerge with a silver sliver wriggling in his outsize beak. Hosts of yellow and bronze and white butterflies lined the water's edge below where they lay, and the bees flew like golden motes of light to their hive in the cliff, high above the quiet pools.

The water drew all life to it, and a little after noonday David touched Debra's arm.

'The nyala are here—' he whispered.

They came through the grove on the far side of the pool. Timid and easily spooked, they approached a few cautious steps at a time before pausing to stare about them with huge dark eyes, questing muzzles and widespread ears; striped and dainty and beautiful they blended with the shadows of the grove.

'The does are all belly now,' David told her. 'They'll be dropping their lambs within the next few weeks. Everything is fruitful.' He half-turned towards her and she sensed it and moved to meet him. When the nyala had drank and gone, and a white-headed fish eagle circled high above them on dark chestnut wings, chanting its weird and haunting cry, they made love in the shade beside the quiet water.

David studied her face as he loved her. She lay beneath him with her eyes closed, and her dark hair spread in a shiny black sheet upon the rug. The bruise on her temple had faded to soft yellow and palest blue, for it was two months since she had left hospital. The white fleck of the grenade scar stood out clearly against the pale bruising. The colour rose in Debra's cheeks, and the light dew of perspiration bloomed across her forehead and upper lip and she made little cooing sounds, and them whimpered softly like a suckling puppy.

David watched her, his whole being engorged and heavy with the weight of his love. From above them an errant beam of sunlight broke through the canopy of leaves and fell full upon her upturned face, lighting it with a warm golden radiance so that it seemed to be the face of a madonna from some medieval church window. It was too much for David and his love broke like a wave, and she felt it and cried out. Her eyes flew wide, and he looked down into their gold-flecked depths. The pupils were huge black pools but as the sunlight struck full into them they shrank rapidly to black pinpoints.

Even in the extremity of his love, David was startled by the phenomenon, and long afterwards when they lay quietly together she asked, 'What is it, David? Is something wrong?'

'No, my darling. What could possibly be wrong?'

'I feel it, Davey. You send out the strongest signals—I am sure I could pick them up from half-way around the world.'

He laughed, and drew away from her almost guiltily. He had imagined it perhaps, a trick of the light, and he tried to dismiss it from his mind.

In the cool of the evening he packed up the rods and the rug and they strolled back to where he had parked and they took the firebreak road home, for David wanted to check the southern fence line. They had driven for twenty minutes in silence before Debra touched his arm.

'When you are ready to tell me about whatever is bugging you—I'm ready to listen,' and he began talking again to distract both her and himself, but a little too glibly.

In the night he rose and went to the bathroom. When he returned he stood for many seconds beside their bed looking down at her dark sleeping shape. He would have left it then, but at that moment a lion began roaring down near the pools. The sound carried clearly through the still night across the two miles that separated them.

It was the excuse that David needed. He took the five-cell flashlight from his bedside table and shone it into Debra's face. It was serene and lovely, and he felt the urge to stoop and kiss her, but instead he called.

'Debra! Wake up, darling!' and she stirred and opened her eyes. He shone the beam of the flashlight full into them and again, unmistakably, the wide black circles of the pupils contracted.

'What is it, David?' she murmured sleepily, and his voice was husky as he replied.

'There is a lion holding a concert down near the pools. Thought you might want to listen.' She moved her head, averting her face slightly, almost as though the powerful beam of the flashlight was causing discomfort, but her voice was pleased.

'Oh yes. I love that big growly sound. Where do you suppose this one is from?'

David switched out the flashlight and slipped back into bed beside her.

'Probably coming up from the south. I bet he has dug a hole under the fence you could drive a truck through.' He tried to speak naturally as they reached for each other beneath the bedclothes and lay close and warm, listening to the far-away roaring until it faded with distance as the lion moved back towards the reserve. They made love then, but afterwards David could not sleep and he lay with Debra in his arms until the dawn.

Still it was a week before David could bring himself to write the letter:

Dear Dr Edelman,

    We agreed that I should write to you if any change occurred in the condition of Debra's eyes, or her health.

    Recently Debra was involved in unfortunate circumstances, in which she was struck repeated heavy blows about the head and was rendered unconscious for a period of two and a half days.

She was hospitalized for suspected fracture of the skull, and concussion, but was discharged after ten days.

This occurred about two months ago. However, I have since noticed that her eyes have become sensitive to light. As you are well aware, this was not previously the case, and she has showed no reaction whatsoever until this time. She has also complained of severe headaches.

I have repeatedly tested my observations with sunlight and artificial light, and there can be no doubt that under the stimulus of a strong light source, the pupils of her eyes contract instantly and to the same degree as one would expect in a normal eye.

It now seems possible that your original diagnosis might have to be revised, but–and I would emphasize this most strongly–I feel that we should approach this very carefully. I do not wish to awaken any false or ill-founded hope.

For your advice in this matter I would be most grateful, and I wait to hear from you.

Cordially yours,
David Morgan

David sealed and addressed the letter, but when he returned from the shopping flight to Nelspuit the following week, the envelope was still buttoned in the top pocket of his leather jacket.

The days settled into their calmly contented routine. Debra completed the first draft of her new novel, and received a request from Bobby Dugan to carry out a lecture tour of five major cities in the United States. *A Place of Our Own* had just completed its thirty-second week on the *New York Times* bestseller list–and her agent informed her that she was 'hotter than a pistol'.

David said that as far as he was concerned she was probably a lot hotter than that. Debra told him he was a lecher, and she was not certain what a nice girl like herself was doing shacked up with him. Then she wrote to her agent, and refused the lecture tour.

'Who needs people?' David agreed with her, knowing that she had made the decision for him. He knew also that Debra as a lovely, blind, bestselling authoress would have been a sensation, and a tour would have launched her into the superstar category.

This made his own procrastination even more corrosive. He tried to re-think and rationalize his delay in posting the letter to Dr Edelman. He told himself that the light-sensitivity did not mean that Debra could ever regain her vision; that she was happy now, had adjusted and found her place and that it would be cruel to disrupt all this and offer her false hope and probably brutal surgery.

In all his theorizing he tried to make Debra's need take priority, but it was deception and he knew it. It was special pleading, by David Morgan, for David Morgan–for if Debra ever regained her sight, the delicately balanced structure of his own happiness would collapse in ruin.

One morning he drove the Land-Rover alone to the farthest limits of Jabulani and parked in a hidden place amongst camel thorn trees. He switched off the engine and, still sitting in the driving-seat, he adjusted the driving-mirror and stared at his own face. For nearly an hour he studied the ravaged expanse of inhuman flesh, trying to find some redeeming feature in it–apart from the eyes–and at the end he knew that no sighted woman would ever be able to live close to that, would ever be able to smile at it, kiss and touch it, to reach up and caress it in the critical moments of love.

He drove home slowly, and Debra was waiting for him on the shady cool stoop and she laughed and ran down the steps into the sunlight when she heard the Land-Rover. She wore faded denims and a bright pink blouse, and when he came to her she lifted her face and groped blindly but joyously with her lips for his.

Debra had arranged a barbecue for that evening, and although they sat close about the open fire under the trees and listened to the night sounds, the night was cool. Debra wore a cashmere sweater over her shoulders, and David had thrown on his flying jacket.

The letter lay against his heart, and it seemed to burn into his flesh. He unbottoned the leather flap and took it out. While Debra chatted happily beside him, spreading her hands to the crackling leaping flames, David examined the envelope turning it slowly over and over in his hands.

Then suddenly, as though it were a live scorpion, he threw it from him and watched it blacken and curl and crumple to ash in the flames of the fire.

It was not so easily done, however, and that night as he lay awake, the words of the letter marched in solemn procession through his brain, meticulously preserved and perfectly remembered. They gave him no respite, and though his eyes were gravelly and his head ached with fatigue, he could not sleep.

During the days that followed he was silent and edgy. Debra sensed it, despite all his efforts to conceal it—and she was seriously alarmed, believing that he was angry with her. She was anxiously loving, distracted from all else but the need to find and cure the cause of David's ills.

Her concern only served to make David's guilt deeper.

Almost in an act of desperation they drove one evening down to the String of Pearls, leaving the Land-Rover they walked hand in hand to the water's edge. They found a fallen log screened by reeds and sat quietly together. For once neither of them had anything to say to each other.

As the big red sun sank to the tree-tops and the gloom thickened amongst the trees of the grove, the nyala herd came stepping lightly and fearfully through the shadows.

David nudged Debra, and she turned her head into a listening attitude and moved a little closer to him as he whispered.

'They are really spooky this evening, they look as though they are standing on springs and I can see their muscles trembling from here. The old bulls seem to be on the verge of a nervous breakdown, they are listening so hard their ears have stretched to twice their usual length, I swear. There must be a leopard lurking along the edge of the reed bed—' he broke off, and exclaimed softly, 'oh, so that's it!'

'What is it, David?' Debra tugged at his arm insistently, her curiosity spurring her.

'A new fawn!' David's delight was in his voice. 'One of the does has lambed. Oh God, Debra! His legs are still wobbly and he is the palest creamy beige—' He described the fawn to her as it followed the mother unsteadily into the open. Debra was listening with such intensity, that it was clear the act of birth and the state of maternity had touched some deep chord within her. Perhaps she was remembering her own dead infant. Her grip on his arm tightened, and her blind eyes seemed to glow in the gathering dusk—and suddenly she spoke. Her voice low, but achingly clear, filled with all the longing and sadness which she had suppressed.

'I wish I could see it,' she said. 'Oh God! God! Let me see. Please, let me see!' and suddenly she was weeping; great racking sobs that shook her whole body.

Across the pool the nyala herd took fright, and dashed away among the trees. David took Debra and held her fiercely to his chest, cradling her head, so her tears were wet and cold through the fabric of his shirt—and he felt the icy winds of despair blow across his soul.

He re-wrote the letter that night by the light of a gas lamp while Debra sat across the room knitting a jersey she had promised him for the winter and believing that he was busy with the estate accounts. David found that he could repeat the words of the original letter perfectly and it took him only a few minutes to complete and seal it.

'Are you working on the book tomorrow evening?' he asked casually, and when she told him she was, he went on. 'I have to nip into Nelspruit for an hour or two.'

David flew high as though to divorce himself from the earth. He could not really believe he was going to do it. He could not believe that he was capable of such sacrifice. He wondered whether it was really possible to love somebody so deeply that he would chance destroying that love for the good of the other—and he knew that it was, and as he flew on southwards he found that he could face it at last.

Of all persons, Debra needed her vision, for without it the great wings of her talent were clipped. Unless she could see it, she could not describe it. She had been granted the gift of the writer, and then half of it had been taken from her. He understood her cry, 'Oh God! God! Let me see. Please, let me see,' and he found himself wishing it for her also. Beside her need his seemed trivial and petty, and silently he prayed.

'Please God, let her see again.'

He landed the Navajo at the airstrip and called the taxi and had it drive him directly to the Post Office, and wait while he posted the letter and collected the incoming mail from the box.

'Where now?' the driver asked as he came out of the building, and he was about to tell him to drive back to the airfield when he had inspiration.

'Take me down to the bottle store, please,' he told the driver and he bought a case of Veuve Clicquot champagne.

He flew homewards with a soaring lightness of the spirit. The wheel was spinning and the ball clicking, nothing he could do now would dictate its fall. He was free of doubt, free of guilt—whatever the outcome, he knew he could meet it.

Debra sensed it almost immediately, and she laughed aloud with relief, and hugged him about the neck.

'But what *happened*?' she kept demanding. 'For weeks you were miserable. I was worrying myself sick—and then you go off for an hour or two and you come back humming like a dynamo. What on earth is going on, Morgan?'

'I have just found out how much I love you,' he told her, returning her hug.

'Plenty?' she demanded.

'Plenty!' he agreed.

'That's my baby!' she applauded him.

The Veuve Clicquot came in useful. In the batch of mail that David brought back with him from Nelspruit was a letter from Bobby Dugan. He was very high on the first chapters of the new novel that Debra had airmailed to him, and so were the publishers; he had managed to hit them for an advance of $100,000 dollars.

'You're rich!' David laughed, looking up from the letter.

'The only reason you married me,' agreed Debra. 'Fortune hunter!' but she was laughing with excitement, and David was proud and happy for her.

'They like it, David.' Debra was serious then. 'They *really* like it. I was so worried.' The money was meaningless, except as a measure of the book's value. Big money is the sincerest type of praise.

'They would have to be feeble-minded not to like it,' David told her, and then went on. 'It just so happens that I have a case of French champagne with me, shall I put a bottle or ten on the ice?'

'Morgan, man of vision,' Debra said. 'At times like this, I know why I love you.'

The weeks that followed were as good then as they had ever been. David's appreciation was sharper, edged by the storm shadows on the horizon, the time of plenty made more poignant by the possibility of the drought years coming. He tried to draw it out beyond its natural time. It was five weeks more before he flew to Nelspruit again, and then only because Debra was anxious to learn of any further news from her publishers and agent, and to pick up her typing.

'I would like to have my hair set, and although I know we don't really need them, David, my darling, we should keep in touch with people—like once a month—don't you think?'

'Has it been that long?' David asked innocently, although each day had been carefully weighed and tallied, the actuality savoured and the memory stored for the lean times ahead.

David left Debra at the beauty salon, and as he went out he could hear her pleading with the girl not to 'put it up into those tight little curls and plaster it with lacquer' and even in the anxiety of the moment, David grinned for he had always thought of the hairstyle she was describing as 'Modern Cape Dutch' or 'Randburg Renaissance'.

The postbox was crammed full and David sorted quickly through the junk mail and picked out three letters from Debra's American agent, and two enveloped with Israeli stamps. Of these one was addressed in a doctor's prescription scrawl, and David was surprised that it had found its destination. The writing on the second envelope was unmistakable, it marched in martial ranks, each letter in step with the next, and the high strokes were like the weapons of a company of pike men, spiky and abrupt.

David found a bench in the park under the purple jacaranda trees, and he opened Edelman's letter first. It was in Hebrew, which made deciphering even more difficult.

Dear David,

Your letter came as a surprise, and I have since studied the X-ray plates once more. They seem unequivocal, and upon an interpretation of them I would not hesitate to confirm my original prognosis—

Despite himself, David felt the small stirrings of relief.

—However, if I have learned anything in twenty-five years of practice, it is humility. I can only accept that your observations of light-sensitivity are correct. Having done so, then I must also accept that there is at least partial function of the optic nerves. This presupposes that the nerve was not completely divided, and it seems reasonable to believe now that it was only partially severed, and that now—possibly due to the head blows that Debra received—it has regained some function.

The crucial question is just how great that recovery is, and again I must warn you that it may be as minimal as it is at the present time, when it amounts to nothing more than light sensitivity without any increase to the amount of vision. It may, however, be greater, and it is within the realms of possibility that with treatment some portion of sight may be regained. I do not expect, however, that this will amount to more than a vague definition of light or shape, and a decision would have to be made as to whether any possible benefit might not be outweighed by the undesirability of surgery within such a vulnerable area.

I would, of course, be all too willing to examine Debra myself. However, it will probably be inconvenient for you to journey to Jerusalem, and I have therefore taken the liberty of writing to a colleague of mine in Cape Town who is one of the leading world authorities on optical trauma. He is Dr Reuben Friedman and I enclose a copy of my letter to him. You will see that I have also despatched to him Debra's original X-ray plates and a clinical history of her case.

I would recommend most strongly that you take the first opportunity of presenting Debra to Dr Friedman, and that you place in him your complete confidence. I might add that the optical unit of Groote Schuur Hospital is rightly world-renowned and fully equipped to provide any treatment necessary—they do not restrict their activities to heart transplants!

I have taken the liberty of showing your letter to General Mordecai, and of discussing the case with him—

David folded the letter carefully. 'Why the hell did he have to bring the Brig into it, talk about a war horse in a rose garden—' and he opened the Brig's letter.

Dear David,

Dr Edelman has spoken with me. I have telephoned Friedman in Cape Town, and he has agreed to see Debra.

For some years I have been postponing a lecture tour to South Africa which the S.A. Zionist Council has been urging upon me. I have today written to them and asked them to make the arrangements.

This will give us the excuse to bring Debra to Cape Town. Tell her I have insufficient time to visit you on your farm, but insist upon seeing her.

I will give you my dates later, and expect to see you then—

It was in typical style, brusque and commanding, presupposing acquiescence. It was out of David's hands now. There was no turning back, but there was still the chance that it would not work. He found himself hoping for that—and his own selfishness sickened him a little. He turned over the letter and on the reverse he drafted a dummy letter from the Brig setting out his plans for the forthcoming tour. This was for Debra, and he found faint amusement in aping the Brig's style, so that he might read it aloud to Debra convincingly.

Debra was ecstatic when he read it to her and he experienced a twinge of conscience at this deceit.

'It will be wonderful seeing him again, I wonder if Mother will be coming out with him—?'

'He didn't say, but I doubt it.' David sorted the American mail into chronological order from the post marks, and read them to her. The first two were editorial comment on *Burning Bright* and were set aside for detailed reply—but the third letter was another with hard news.

United Artists want to film *A Place of Our Own* and were talking impressively heavy figures for the twelve-month option against an outright purchase of the property and a small percentage of the profits. However, if Debra would go to California and write the screenplay, Bobby Dugan felt sure he could roll it all into a quarter-million-dollar package. He wanted her to weigh the fact that even established novelists were seldom asked to write their own screenplays—this was an offer not to be lightly spurned, and he urged Debra to accept.

'Who needs people?' Debra laughed it away quickly, too quickly—and David caught the wistful expression before she turned her head away and asked brightly, 'Have you got any of that champagne left, Morgan? I think we can celebrate—don't you?'

'The way you're going, Morgan, I'd best lay in a store of the stuff,' he replied, and went to the gas refrigerator. It foamed to the rim of the glass as he poured the wine, and before it subsided and he had carried the glass to her, he had made his decision.

'Let's take his advice seriously, and think about you going to Hollywood,' he said, and put the glass in her hand.

'What's to think about?' she asked. 'This is where we belong.'

'No, let's wait a while before replying—'

'What do you mean?' She lowered the glass without tasting the wine.

'We will wait until—let's say, until after we have seen the Brig in Cape Town.'

'Why?' She looked puzzled. 'Why should it be different then?'

'No reason. It's just that it is an important decision—the choice of time is arbitrary, however.'

'Beseder!' she agreed readily, and raised the glass to toast him. 'I love you.'

'I love you,' he said, and as he drank he was glad that she had so many roads to choose from.

The Brig's arrangements allowed them three more weeks before the rendezvous in Cape Town, and David drew upon each hour to the full, anticipating his chances of expulsion from their private Eden.

They were happy days and it seemed that nature had conspired to give them of her best. The good rains fell steadily, always beginning in the afternoon after a morning of tall clouds and heavy air filled with static and the feel of thunder. In the sunset the lightning played and flickered across the gilt cloud banks, turned by the angry sun to the colour of burnished bronze and virgins' blushes. Then in the darkness as they lay entwined, the thunder struck like a hammer blow and the lightning etched the window beyond the bed to a square of blinding white light, and the rain came teeming down with the sound of wild fire and running hooves. With David beside her, Debra was unafraid.

In the morning it was bright and cool, the trees washed sparkling clean so that the leaves glinted in the early sun and the earth was dark with water and spangled with standing pools.

The rains brought life and excitement to the wild things, and each day held its small discoveries—unexpected visitations, and strange occurrences.

The fish eagles moved their two chicks from the great shaggy nest in the mhobahoba at the head of the pools and taught them to perch out on the bare limb that supported it. They sat there day after day, seeming to gather their courage. The parent birds were frenetic in their ministrations, grooming their offspring for the great moment of flight.

Then one morning, as he and Debra ate breakfast on the stoop, David heard the swollen chorus of their chanting cries, harsh with triumph, and he took Debra's hand and they went down the steps into the open. David looked up and saw the four dark shapes spread on wide wings against the clear blue of the sky—and his spirit soared with them in their moment of achievement. They flew upwards in great sweeping circles, until they dwindled to specks and vanished, gone to their autumn grounds upon the Zambezi River, two thousand miles to the north.

There was, however, one incident during those last days that saddened and subdued them both. One morning, they walked four miles northwards beyond the line of hills to a narrow wedge-shaped plain on which stood a group of towering leadwood trees.

A pair of martial eagles had chosen the tallest leadwood as their mating ground. The female was a beautiful young bird but the male was past his prime. They had begun constructing their nest on a high fork, but the work was interrupted by the intrusion of a lone male eagle, a big young bird, fierce and proud and acquisitive. David had noticed him lurking about the borders of the territory, carefully avoiding overflying the airspace claimed by the breeding pair, choosing a perch on the hills overlooking the plain and gathering his confidence for the confrontation he was so clearly planning. The impending conflict had its particular fascination for David and his sympathy was with the older bird as he made his warlike show, screeching defiance from his perch upon the high branches of the leadwood or weaving his patrols along his borders, turning on his great wings always within the limits of that which he claimed as his own.

David had decided to walk up to the plain that day, in order to choose a site for the photographic blind he planned to erect overlooking the nest site, and also in curiosity as to the outcome of this primeval clash between the two males.

It seemed more than chance that he had chosen the day when the crisis was reached.

David and Debra came up through the gap in the hills and paused to sit on an outcrop of rock overlooking the plain, while they regained their breath. The battlefield was spread below them.

The old bird was at the nest, a dark hunched shape with white breast and head set low on the powerful shoulders. David looked for the invader, sweeping the crests of the hills with his binoculars, but there was no sign of him. He dropped the binoculars to his chest and he and Debra talked quietly for a while.

Then suddenly David's attention was attracted by the behaviour of the old eagle. He launched suddenly into flight, striking upwards on his great black pinions, and there was an urgency in the way he bored for height.

His climb brought him close over their heads, so that David could clearly see the cruel curve of the beak and the ermine black splashes that decorated the imperial snow of his breast.

He opened the yellow beak and shrieked a harsh challenge, and David turned quickly in the old fighter pilot's sweep of sky and cloud. He saw the cunning of it immediately. The younger bird had chosen his moment and his attack vector with skill beyond his years. He was towering in the sun, high and clear, a flagrant trespasser, daring the old eagle to come up at him and David felt his skin crawl in sympathy as he watched the defender climb slowly on flogging wings.

Quickly, and a little breathlessly, he described it to Debra and she reached for his hand, her sympathy with the old bird also.

'Tell me!' she commanded.

The young bird sailed calmly in waiting circles, cocking his head to watch his adversary's approach.

'There he goes!' David's voice was taut, as the attacker went wing over and began his stoop.

'I can hear him,' Debra whispered, and the sound of his wings carried clearly to them, rustling like a bush fire in dry grass as he dived on the old bird.

'Break left! Go! Go! Go!' David found he was calling to the old eagle as though he were flying wingman for him, and he gripped Debra's hand until she winced. The old eagle seemed almost to hear him, for he closed his wings and flicked out of the path of the strike, tumbling for a single turn so that the attacker hissed by him with talons reaching uselessly through air, his speed plummeting him down into the basin of the plain.

The old bird caught and broke out of his roll with wings half-cocked, and streaked down after the other. In one veteran stroke of skill he had wrested the advantage.

'Get him!' screamed David. 'Get him when he turns! Now!'

The young bird was streaking towards the tree-tops and swift death, he flared his wings to break his fall, turning desperately to avoid the lethal stoop of his enemy. In that moment he was vulnerable and the old eagle reached forward with his terrible spiked talons and without slackening the searing speed of his dive he hit the other bird in the critical moment of his turn.

The thud of the impact carried clearly to the watchers on the hill and there was a puff of feathers like the burst of explosives, black from the wings and white from the breast.

Locked together by the old bird's honed killing claws, they tumbled, wing over tangled wing, feathers streaming from their straining bodies and then drifting away like thistledown on the light breeze.

Still joined in mortal combat, they struck the top branches of one of the leadwood trees, and fell through them to come to rest at last in a high fork as an untidy bundle of ruffled feathers and trailing wings.

Leading Debra over the rough ground David hurried down the hill and through the coarse stands of arrow grass to the tree.

'Can you see them?' Debra asked anxiously, as David focused his binoculars on the struggling pair.

'They are trapped,' David told her. 'The old fellow has his claws buried to the hilt in the other's back. He will never be able to free them and they have fallen across the fork, one on either side of the tree.'

The screams of rage and agony rang from the hills about them, and the female eagle sailed anxiously above the leadwood. She added her querulous screeching to the sound of conflict.

'The young bird is dying.' David studied him through the lens, watching the carmine drops ooze from the gaping yellow beak to fall and glisten upon the snowy breast, like a dying king's rubies.

'And the old bird—' Debra listened to the clamour with face upturned, her eyes dark with concern.

'He will never get those claws loose, they lock automatically as soon as pressure is applied and he will not be able to lift himself. He will die also.'

'Can't you do something?' Debra was tugging at his arm. 'Can't you help him?'

Gently he tried to explain to her that the birds were locked together seventy feet above the earth. The bole of the leadwood was smooth and without branches for the first fifty feet of its height. It would take days of effort to reach the birds, and by then it would be too late.

'Even if one could reach them, darling, they are two wild creatures, fierce and dangerous, those beaks and talons could tear the eyes out of your head or rip you to the bone—nature does not like interference in her designs.'

'Isn't there anything we can do?' she pleaded.

'Yes,' he answered quietly. 'We can come back in the morning to see if he has been able to free himself. But we will bring a gun with us, in case he has not.'

In the dawn they came together to the leadwood tree. The young bird was dead, hanging limp and graceless, but the old bird was still alive, linked by his claws to the carcass of the other, weak and dying but with the furious yellow flames still burning in his eyes. He heard their voices and twisted the shaggy old head and opened his beak in a last defiant cry.

David loaded the shotgun, snapping the barrels closed and staring up at the old eagle. 'Not you alone, old friend,' he thought, and he lifted the gun to his shoulder and hit him with two charges of buckshot. They left him hanging in tatters with trailing wings and the quick patter of blood slowing to a dark steady drip. David felt as though he had destroyed a part of himself in that blast of gunfire, and the shadow of it was cast over the bright days that followed.

These few days sped past too swiftly for David, and when they were almost gone he and Debra spent the last of them wandering together across Jabulani, visiting each of their special places and seeking out the various herds or individual animals almost as if they were taking farewell of old friends. In the evening they came to the place amongst the fever trees beside the pools, and they sat there until the sun had fallen below the earth in a splendour of purples and muted pinks. Then the mosquitoes began whining about their heads, and they strolled back hand in hand and came to the homestead in the dark.

They packed their bags that night and left them on the stoop, ready for an early start. Then they drank champagne beside the barbecue fire. The wine lifted their mood and they laughed together in their little island of firelight in the vast ocean of the African night—but for David there were echoes from the laughter, and he was aware of a sense of finality, of an ending of something and a new beginning.

When they took off from the landing-strip in the early morning, David circled twice over the estate, climbing slowly, and the pools glinted like gunmetal amongst the hills as the low sun touched them. The land was lush with the severe unpromising shade of green, so different from that of the lands of the northern hemisphere, and the servants stood in the yard of the homestead, shading their eyes and waving up at them, their shadows lying long and narrow against the ruddy earth.

David came around and steadied on course.

'Cape Town, here we come,' he said, and Debra smiled and reached across to lay her hand upon his leg in warm and companionable silence.

They had the suite at the Mount Nelson Hotel, preferring its ancient elegance and spacious palmy gardens to the modern slabs of glass and concrete upon the foreshore and the rocks of Sea Point. They stayed in the suite for two days, awaiting the Brig's arrival, for David had grown unaccustomed to humanity in its massed and unlovely multitudes, and found the quick inquisitive glances and murmurs of pity that followed him hard to stomach.

On the second day the Brig arrived. He knocked on the door of the suite and then entered with his aggressive and determined stride. He was lean and hard and brown, as David remembered, and when he and Debra had embraced, he turned to David and his hand was dry and leathery—but it seemed that he looked at David with a new calculation in the fierce warrior eyes.

While Debra bathed and dressed for the evening, he took David to his own suite and poured whisky for him without asking his preference. He gave David the glass and began immediately to discuss the arrangements he had made.

'Friedman will be at the reception. I will introduce him to Debra and let them talk for a while, then he will be seated next to her at the dinner-table. This will give us the opportunity to persuade Debra to undergo an examination later—'

'Before we go any further, sir,' David interrupted, 'I want your assurance that at no time will it ever be suggested to her that there is a possibility of Debra regaining her sight.'

'Very well.'

'I mean, at no time whatsoever. Even if Friedman determines that surgery is necessary, it must be for some other reason than to restore sight—'

'I don't think that is possible,' the Brig snapped angrily. 'If matters go that far, then Debra must be told. It would not be fair—'

It was David's turn for anger, although the frozen mask of his features remained immobile, the lipless slit of mouth turned pale and blue eyes glared.

'Let me determine what is fair. I know her as you never can, I know what she feels and what she is thinking. If you offer her a chance of sight, you will create for her the same dilemma in which I have been trapped since the possibility first arose. I would spare her that.'

'I do not understand you,' the Brig said stiffly. The hostility between them was a tangible essence that seemed to fill the room with the feel of thunder on a summer's day.

'Then let me explain,' David held his eyes, refusing to be brow-beaten by this fierce and thrusting old warrior. 'Your daughter and I have achieved an extraordinary state of happiness.'

The Brig inclined his head, acknowledging. 'Yes, I will accept your word for that—but it is an artificial state. It's a hot-house thing, reared in isolation—it has no relation to the real world. It's a dream state.'

David felt his anger begin to shake the foundations of his reason. He found it offensive that anybody should speak of Debra and his life in those terms—but at the same time he could see the justification.

'You may say so, sir. But for Debra and me, it is very real. It is something of tremendous value.'

The Brig was silent now.

'I will tell you truly that I thought long and hard before I admitted that there was a chance for Debra, and even then I would have hidden it for my own selfish happiness—'

'You still do not make sense. How can Debra regaining her sight affect you?'

'Look at me,' said David softly, and the Brig glared at him ferociously, expecting more, but when nothing further came his expression eased and he did look at David—for the first time truly seeing the terribly ravaged head, the obscene travesty of human shape—and suddenly he thought on it from David's side, whereas before he had considered it only as a father.

His eyes dropped and he turned to replenish his whisky glass.

'If I can give her sight, I will do it. Even though it will be an expensive gift for me, she must take it.' David felt his voice trembling. 'But I believe that she loves me enough to spurn it, if she were ever given the choice. I do not want her ever to be tortured by that choice.'

The Brig lifted his glass and took a deep swallow, half the contents at a gulp.

'As you wish,' he acquiesced, and it may have been the whisky, but his voice sounded husky with an emotion David had never suspected before.

'Thank you, sir.' David set down his own glass, still untasted. 'If you'll excuse me, I think I should go and change now.' He moved to the door.

'David!' the Brig called to him and he turned back. The gold tooth gleamed in the dark bristly patch of moustache, as the Brig smiled a strangely embarrassed but gentle smile.

'You'll do,' he said.

The reception was in the banquet-room at the Heerengracht Hotel, and as David and Debra rode up together in the elevator she seemed to sense his dread, for she squeezed his arm.

'Stay close to me tonight,' she murmured. 'I'll need you,' and he knew it was said to distract him and he was grateful to her. They would be a freak show, and even though he was sure most of the guests had been prepared, yet he knew it would be an ordeal. He leaned to brush her cheek with his.

Her hair was loose and soft, very dark and glossy—and the sun had gilded her face to gold. She wore a plain green sheath that fell in simple lines to the floor, but left her arms and shoulders bare. They were amongst and smooth, with the special lustre of the skin highlighting the smooth flow of her flesh.

She wore little make-up, a light touch on the lips only, and the serene expression of her eyes enhanced the simple grace of her carriage as she moved on his arm, giving David just that courage he needed to face the crowded room.

It was an elegant gathering, women in rich silks and jewellery, the men dark-suited, with the heaviness of body and poise which advertises power and wealth—but the Brig stood out amongst them, even in a civilian suit, lean and hard where they were plump and complacent—like a falcon amongst a flock of pheasants.

He brought Reuben Friedman to them and introduced them casually. He was a short heavily built man, with a big alert head seeming out of proportion to his body. His hair was cropped short and grizzled to the round skull, but David found himself liking the bright bird eyes and the readiness of his smile. His hand was warm, but dry and firm. Debra was drawn to him also, and smiled when she picked up the timbre of his voice and the essential warmth of his personality.

As they went in to dinner, she asked David what he looked like, and laughed with delight when he replied.

'Like a koala bear,' and they were talking easily together before the fish course was served. Friedman's wife, a slim girl with horn-rimmed spectacles, neither beautiful nor plain, but with her husband's forthright friendly manner, leaned across him to join the conversation and David heard her say,

'Won't you come to lunch tomorrow? If you can stand a brood of squalling kids.'

'We don't usually—' Debra replied, but David could hear her wavering, and she turned to him.

'May we—?' and he agreed and then they were laughing like old friends, but David was silent and withdrawn, knowing it was all subterfuge and suddenly oppressed by the surging chorus of human voices and the clatter of cutlery. He found himself longing for the night silence of the bushveld, and the solitude which was not solitude with Debra to share it.

When the master of ceremonies rose to introduce the speaker, David found it an intense relief to know the ordeal was drawing to a close and he could soon hurry away with Debra to hide from the prying, knowing eyes.

The introductory speech was smooth and professional, the jokes raised a chuckle—but it lacked substance, five minutes after you would not remember what had been said.

Then the Brig rose and looked about him with a kind of Olympian scorn, the warrior's contempt for the soft men, and though these rich and powerful men seemed to quail beneath the stare, yet David sensed that they enjoyed it. They derived some strange vicarious pleasure from this man. He was a figure-head—he gave to them a deep confidence, a point on which their spirits could rally. He was one of them, and yet apart. It seemed that he was a storehouse of the race's pride and strength.

Even David was surprised by the power that flowed from the lean old warrior, the compelling presence with which he filled the huge room and dominated his audience. He seemed immortal and invincible, and David's own emotions stirred, his own pulse quickened and he found himself carried along on the flood.

'—but for all of this there is a price to pay. Part of this price is constant vigil, constant readiness. Each of us is ready at any moment to answer the call to the defence of what is ours—and each of us must be ready to make without question whatever sacrifice is demanded. This can be life itself, or something every bit as dear—'

Suddenly David realized that the Brig had singled him out, and that they were staring at each other across the room. The Brig was sending him a message of strength, of courage—but it was misinterpreted by others in the gathering.

They saw the silent exchange between the two men, and many of them knew that David's terrible disfigurement and Debra's blindness were wounds of war. They misunderstood the Brig's reference to sacrifice, and one of them began to applaud.

Immediately it was taken up, a smattering here and there amongst the tables, but quickly the sound rose—became thunder. People were staring at David and Debra as they clapped, other heads turned towards them. Chairs began to scrape as they were pushed back and men and women came to their feet, their faces smiling and their applause pounding, until it filled the hall with sound and they were all standing.

Debra was not sure what it was all about, until she felt David's desperate hand in hers and heard his voice.

'Let's get out of here—quickly. They are all staring. They are staring at us—'

She could feel his hand shaking and the strength of his distress at being the subject of their ghoulish curiosity.

'Come, let's get away.' And she rose at his urging with her heart crying out in pain for him, and followed him while the thunder of applause burst upon his defenceless head like the blows of an enemy and their eyes wantonly raked his ravaged flesh.

Even when they reached the sanctuary of their own suite, he was still shaking like a man in fever.

'The bastard,' he whispered, as he poured whisky in a glass and the neck of the bottle clattered against the crystal rim. 'The cruel bastard—why did he do that to us?'

'David.' She came to him groping for his hand. 'He didn't mean it to hurt. I know he meant it well, I think he was trying to say he was proud of you.'

David felt the urge to flee, to find relief from it all within the sanctuary of Jabulani. The temptation to say to her 'Come' and lead her there, knowing that she would do so instantly, was so strong that he had to wrestle with it, as though it were a physical adversary.

The whisky tasted rank and smoky. It offered no avenue of escape and he left the glass standing upon the counter of the private bar and turned instead to Debra.

'Yes,' she whispered into his mouth. 'Yes, my darling,' and there was a woman's pride, a woman's joy in being the vessel of his ease. As always she was able to fly with him above the storm, using the wild winds of love to drive them both aloft, until they broke through together into the brightness and peace and safety.

David woke in the night while she lay sleeping. There was a silver moon reflecting from the french windows and he could study her sleeping face, but after a while it was not sufficient for his need and he reached across gently and switched on the bedside lamp.

She stirred in her sleep, coming softly awake with small sighs and tumbling black hair brushed from her eyes with a sleep-clumsy hand, and David felt the first chill of impending loss. He knew he had not moved the bed when he lit the lamp, what had disturbed her he knew beyond doubt was the light itself—and this time not even their loving could distract him.

Reuben Friedman's dwelling proclaimed his station in the world. It was built above the sea with lawns that ran down to the beach and big dark green melkhout trees surrounding the swimming-pool, with an elaborate Cabana and barbecue area. Marion Friedman's horde of kids were especially thinned out for the occasion, probably farmed out with friends, but she retained her two youngest. These came to peer in awe at David for a few minutes, but at a sharp word from their mother they went off to the pool and became immersed in water and their own games.

The Brig had another speaking engagement, so the four adults were left alone, and after a while they relaxed. Somehow the fact that Reuben was a doctor seemed to set both David and Debra at their ease. Debra remarked on it, when the conversation turned to their injuries and Reuben asked solicitously,

'You don't mind talking about it?'

'No, not with you. Somehow it's all right to bare yourself in front of a doctor.'

'Don't do it, my dear,' Marion cautioned her. 'Not in front of Ruby anyway—look at me, six kids, already!' And they laughed.

Ruby had been out early that morning and taken half a dozen big crayfish out of the crystal water, from a kelp-filled pool in the rocks which he boasted was his private fishing-ground.

He wrapped them in fresh kelp leaves and steamed them over the coals until they turned bright scarlet and the flesh was milk white and succulent as he broke open the carapaces.

'Now, if that isn't the finest spring chicken you have ever seen—' he crowed as he held up the dismembered shellfish, '—you all bear witness that it's got two legs and feathers.'

David admitted that he had never tasted poultry like it and as he washed it down with a dry Cape Riesling he found it was no terrible hardship to reach for another. Both he and Debra were enjoying themselves, so that it came as a jolt when Reuben at last began on the real purpose of their meeting.

He was leaning across Debra to refill her wine glass, when he paused and asked her.

'How long is it since your eyes were last checked out, my dear?' and gently he placed his hand under her chin and tilted her face to look into her eyes. David's nerves snapped taut, and he moved quickly in his chair, watching intently.

'Not since I left Israel—though they took some X-rays when I was in hospital.'

'Any headaches?' Ruby asked, and she nodded. Ruby grunted and released her chin.

'I suppose they could strike me off, drumming up business, but I do think that you should have periodic checks. Two years is a long time, and you have foreign matter lodged inside your skull.'

'I hadn't even thought about it.' Debra frowned slightly and reached up to touch the scar on her temple. David felt his conscience twinge as he joined actively in the conspiracy.

'It can't do any harm, darling. Why not let Ruby give you a going over while we are here? Heaven knows when we will have another opportunity.'

'Oh, David—' Debra disparaged the idea. 'I know you are itching to head for home—and so am I.'

'Another day or two won't matter, and now that we have thought about it, it's going to worry us.'

Debra turned her head in Ruby's direction. 'How long will it take?'

'A day. I'll give you an examination in the morning, and then we'll shoot some X-ray plates in the afternoon.'

'How soon could you see her?' David asked, his voice unnatural for he knew that the appointment had been arranged five weeks previously.

'Oh, I'm sure we could fit her in right away—tomorrow—even if we have to do a little juggling. Yours is a rather special case.'

David reached across and took Debra's hand. 'Okay, darling?' he asked.

'Okay, David,' she agreed readily.

Ruby's consulting-rooms were in the Medical Centre that towered above the harbour and looked out across Table Bay to where the black south-easter was hacking the tops from the waves in bursts of white, and shrouding the far shores of the bay in banks of cloud as grey as wood smoke.

The rooms were decorated with care and taste: two original landscapes by Pierneef and some good carpets, Samarkand and a gold-washed Abedah—even Ruby's receptionist looked like a hostess from a Playboy Club, without the bunny ears and tail. It was clear that Dr Friedman enjoyed the good things of life.

The receptionist was expecting them, but still could not control the widening of her eyes and the shocked flight of colour from her cheeks as she looked at David's face.

'Dr Friedman is waiting for you, Mr and Mrs Morgan. He wants you both to go through, please.'

Ruby looked different without his prosperous paunch bulging over the waistband of a bathing costume, but his greeting was warm as he took Debra's arm.

'Shall we let David stay with us?' he asked Debra in mock conspiracy.

'Let's,' she answered.

After the usual clinical history which Ruby pursued relentlessly, he seemed satisfied and they went through into his examination-room. The chair looked to David to be identical to a dentist's, and Ruby adjusted it for Debra to lie back comfortably while he made a physical examination, directing light through the pupils deep into the body of each eye.

'Nice healthy eyes,' he gave his opinion at last, 'and very pretty also, what do you say, David?'

'Smashing,' David agreed, and Ruby sat Debra upright while he attached electrodes to her arm and swung forward a complicated-looking piece of electronic equipment.

'ECG,' David guessed, and Ruby chuckled and shook his head.

'No—it's a little invention of my own. I'm quite proud of it, but in reality it's only a variation on the old-fashioned lie-detector.'

'Question time again?' Debra asked.

'No. We are going to flash lights at you, and see just what sort of subconscious reaction you have to them.'

'We know that already,' Debra told him, and they both heard the edge in her voice now.

'Perhaps. It's just an established routine we work to.' Ruby soothed her, and then to David. 'Stand back here, please. The lights are pretty fierce, and you don't want to be looking into them.'

David moved back and Ruby adjusted the machine. A roll of graph paper began running slowly under a moving stylus which settled almost immediately into a steady rhythmic pattern. On a separate glass screen a moving green dot of light began to repeat the same rhythm, leaving a fading trail across the screen like the tail of a comet. It reminded David of the interceptor radar screen on the instrument panel of a Mirage jet. Ruby switched out the top lights, plunging the room into utter darkness, except for the pulsing green dot on the screen.

'Are we ready now, Debra? Look straight ahead, please. Eyes open.'

Soundlessly a brilliant burst of blue light filled the room, and distinctly David saw the green dot on the screen jump out of its established pattern, and for a beat or two it went haywire, then settled again into the old rhythm. Debra had seen the light flash, even though she was unaware of it; the pulse of light had registered on her brain and the machine had recorded her instinctive reaction.

The play with light went on for another twenty minutes while Ruby adjusted the intensity of the light source and varied the transmissions. At last he was satisfied, and turned the top lights up.

'Well?' Debra demanded brightly. 'Do I pass?'

'There's nothing more I want from you,' Ruby told her. 'You did just great, and everything is the way we want it.'

'Can I go now?'

'David can take you to lunch, but this afternoon I want you at the radiologist's. My receptionist arranged it for 2.30, I believe, but you had best check with her.' Neatly Ruby countered any attempt of David's to get him alone.

'I shall let you know as soon as I have the X-ray results. Here, I'll write down the radiologist's address.' Ruby scribbled on his prescription pad and handed it to David.

'See me *alone* tomorrow 10 a.m.'

David nodded and took Debra's arm. He stared at Ruby a moment trying to draw some reaction from him, but he merely shrugged his shoulders and rolled his eyes in a music-hall comedian's gesture of uncertainty.

The Brig joined them for lunch in their suite at the Mount Nelson, for David still could not endure the discomfort of the public rooms. The Brig drew upon some hidden spring of charm, as though sensing that his help was needed, and he had both of them laughing naturally with stories of Debra's childhood and the family's early days after leaving America. David was grateful to him, for the time passed so quickly that he had to hurry Debra to her appointment.

'I am going to use two different techniques on you, my dear–' David wondered what it was about her that made all males over forty refer to Debra as though she were twelve years old. 'First of all we will do five of what we call police mug shots, front, back, sides and top–' The radiologist was a red-faced, grey-haired man with big hands and heavy shoulders like a professional wrestler. 'We aren't even going to make you take your clothes off–' he chuckled, but David thought he detected a faint note of regret. 'Then after that, we are going to be terribly clever and take a continuous moving shot of the inside of your head. It's called tomography. We are going to clamp your head to keep it still and the camera is going to describe a circle around you, focused on the spot where all the trouble is. We are going to find out everything that's going on in that pretty head of yours–'

'I hope it doesn't shock you too much, doctor,' Debra told him, and he looked stunned for a moment, then let out a delighted guffaw, and later David heard him repeating it to the sister with gusto.

It was a long tedious business, and afterwards when they drove back to the hotel, Debra leaned close to him and said, 'Let's go home, David. Soon as we can?'

'Soon as we can,' he agreed.

David did not want it that way, but the Brig insisted on accompanying David on his visit to Ruby Friedman the following morning. For one of the very few times in his life David had lied to Debra, telling her he was meeting with the Morgan Trust accountants, and he had left her in a lime-green bikini lying beside the hotel swimming pool, brown and slim and lovely in the sunlight.

Ruby Friedman was brusque and businesslike. He seated them opposite his desk and came swiftly to the core of the business.

'Gentlemen,' he said. 'We have a problem, a hell of a problem. I am going to show you the X-ray plates first to illustrate what I have to tell you–' Ruby swivelled his chair to the scanner and switched on the book-light to bring the prints into high relief. 'On this side are the plates that Edelman sent me from Jerusalem. You can see the grenade fragment.' It was stark and hard edged, a small triangular shard of steel lying in the cloudy bone structure. 'And here you can see the track though the optic chiasma, the disruption and shattering of the bone is quite evident. Edelman's original diagnosis–based on these plates, and on the complete inability to define light or shape–seems to be confirmed. The optic nerve is severed, and that's the end of it.' Quickly he unclipped the plates, and fitted others to the scanner. 'All right. Now here are the second set of plates, taken yesterday. Immediately notice how the grenade fragment has been consolidated and encysted.' The stark outline was softened by the new growth of bone around it. 'That is good, and expected. But here in the channel of the chiasma we find the growth of some sort that leaves itself open to a number of interpretations. It could be scarring, the growth of bone chips, or some other type of growth either benign or malignant.' Ruby arranged another set of plates upon the scanner. 'Finally, this is the plate exposed by the ·technique of tomography, to establish the contours of this excrescence. It seems to conform to the shape of the bony channel of the chiasma, except here–' Ruby touched a small half-round notch which was cut into the upper edge of the growth, '–this little spot runs through the main axis of the skull, but is bent upwards in the shape of an inverted U. It is just possible that this may be the most significant discovery of our whole examination.' Ruby switched off the light of the scanner.

'I don't understand any of this,' the Brig's voice was sharp. He did not like being bludgeoned by another man's special knowledge.

'No, of course.' Ruby was smooth. 'I am merely setting the background for the explanations that will follow.' He turned back to the desk, and his manner changed. He was no longer lecturing, but leading with authority.

'Now as to my own conclusions. There can be absolutely no doubt that certain function of the optic nerve remains. It is still conveying impulses to the brain. At least a part of it is still intact. The question arises as to just how much that is, and to what extent that function can be improved. It is possible that the grenade fragment cut through part of the nerve—severing five strands of a six-strand rope, or four or three. We do not know the extent, but what we do know is that damage of that nature is irreversible. What Debra may be left with is what she has now–almost nothing.'

Ruby paused and was silent. The two men opposite him watched his face intently, leaning forward in their seats.

'That is the dark side–if it is true, then Debra is for all practical purposes blind and will remain that way. However, there is another side to the question. It is possible that the optic nerve has suffered little damage, or none at all, please God–'

'Then why is she blind?' David asked angrily. He felt baited, driven by words, goaded like the bull from so long ago. 'You can't have it both ways.'

Ruby looked at him, and for the first time saw beyond that blank mask of scarred flesh and realized the pain he was inflicting, saw the hurt in the dark eyes, blue as rifle steel.

'Forgive me, David. I have been carried away by the intriguing facts of this case, seeing it from my own academic point of view rather than yours, I'm afraid. I will come to it now without further hedging.' He leaned back in his chair and went on speaking. 'You recall the notch in the outline of the chiasma. Well, I believe that is the nerve itself, twisted out of position, kinked and pinched like a garden hose by bone fragments and the pressure of the metal fragment so that it is no longer capable of carrying impulses to the brain.'

'The blows on her temple–?' David asked.

'Yes. Those blows may have been just sufficient to alter the position of the bone fragments, or of the nerve itself, so as to enable the passage of a minimal amount of impulse to the brain–like the garden hose, movement could allow a little water to pass through but still hold back any significant flow, but once the twist is straightened the full volume of flow would be regained.'

They were all silent then, each of them considering the enormity of what they had heard.

'The eyes,' the Brig said at last. 'They are healthy?'

'Perfectly,' Ruby nodded.

'How could you find out—I mean, what steps would you take next?' David asked quietly.

'There is only one way. We would have to go to the site of the trauma.'

'Operate?' David asked again.

'Yes.'

'Open Debra's skull?' The horror of it showed only in his eyes.

'Yes,' Ruby nodded.

'Her head—' David's own flesh quailed in memory of the ruthless knife. He saw the lovely face mutilated and the pain in those blind eyes. 'Her face—' His voice shook now. 'No, I won't let you cut her. I won't let you ruin her, like they have me—'

'David!' The Brig's voice cracked like breaking ice, and David sank back in his chair.

'I understand how you feel,' Ruby spoke gently, his voice in contrast to the Brig's. 'But we will go in from behind the hairline, there will be no disfigurement. The scar will be covered by her hair when it grows out, and the incision will not be very large anyway—'

'I won't have her suffer more.' David was trying to control his voice, but the catch and break were still in it. 'She has suffered enough, can't you see that—'

'We are talking about giving her back her sight,' the Brig broke in again. His voice was hard and cold. 'A little pain is a small price to pay for that.'

'There will be very little pain, David. Less than an appendectomy.' Again they were silent, the two older men watching the younger in the agony of his decision.

'What are the chances?' David looked for help, wanting the decision made for him, wanting it taken out of his hands.

'That is impossible to say.' Ruby shook his head.

'Oh God, how can I judge if I don't know the odds?' David cried out.

'All right. Let me put it this way—there is a possibility, not probability, that she may regain a useful part of her sight.' Ruby chose his words with care. 'And there is a remote possibility that she may regain full vision or almost full vision.'

'That is the best that can happen.' David agreed. 'But what is the worst?'

'The worst that can happen is there will be no change. She will have undergone a deal of discomfort and pain to no avail.'

David jumped out of his chair and crossed to the windows. He stared out at the great sweep of bay where the tankers lay moored and the far hills of the Tygerberg rose smoky blue to the brilliant sky.

'You know what the choice must be, David.' The Brig was ruthless, allowing him no quarter, driving him on to meet his fate.

'All right,' David surrendered at last, and turned back to face them. 'But on one condition. One on which I insist. Debra must not be told that there is a chance of her regaining her sight—'

Ruby Friedman shook his head. 'She must be told.'

The Brig's moustache bristled fiercely. 'Why not? Why don't you want her to know?'

'You know why.' David answered without looking at him.

'How will you get her there—if you don't explain it to her?' Ruby asked.

'She has been having headaches—we'll tell her there is a growth—that you've discovered a growth—that it has to be removed. That's true, isn't it?'

'No.' Ruby shook his head. 'I couldn't tell her that. I can't deceive her.'

'Then I will tell her,' said David, his voice firm and steady now. 'And I will tell her when we discover the result after the operation. Good or bad. I will be the one who tells her—is that understood? Do we agree on that?'

And after a moment the two others nodded and murmured their agreement to the terms David had set.

David had the hotel chef prepare a picnic basket, and the service bar provided a cool bag with two bottles of champagne.

David craved for the feeling of height and space, but he needed also to be able to concentrate all his attention on Debra, so he reluctantly rejected the impulse to fly with her—and instead they took the cableway up the precipitous cliffs of Table Mountain, and from the top station they found a path along the plateau and followed it, hand in hand, to a lonely place upon the cliff's edge where they could sit together high above the city and the measureless spread of ocean.

The sounds of the city came up two thousand feet to them, tiny and disjointed, on freak gusts of the wind or bouncing from the soaring canyons of grey rock—the horn of an automobile, the clang of a locomotive shunting in the train yards, the cry of a muezzin calling the faithful of Islam to pray, and the distant shrilling of children released from the classroom—yet all these faint echoes of humanity seemed to enhance their aloneness and the breeze out of the south-east was sweet and clean after the filthy city air.

They drank the wine together, sitting close while David gathered his resolve. He was about to speak when Debra forestalled him.

'It's good to be alive and in love, my darling,' she said. 'We are very lucky, you and I. Do you know that, David?'

He made a sound in his throat that could have been agreement, and his courage failed him.

'If you could, would you change anything?' he asked at last, and she laughed.

'Oh, sure. One is never absolutely content until and unless one is dead. I'd change many small things—but not the one big thing. You and I.'

'What would you change?'

'I would like to write better than I do, for one thing.'

They were silent again, sipping the wine.

'Sun is going down fast now,' he told her.

'Tell me,' she demanded, and he tried to find words for the colours, that flickered over the cloud banks and the way the ocean shimmered and dazzled with the last rays of gold and blood—and he knew he could never tell it to her. He stopped in the middle of a sentence.

'I saw Ruby Friedman today,' he said abruptly, unable to find a gentle approach, and she went still beside him in that special way of hers, frozen like a timid wild thing at the scent of some fearful predator.

'It's bad!' she said at last.

'Why do you say that?' he demanded quickly.

'Because you brought me here to tell me—and because you are afraid.'

'No,' David denied it.

'Yes. I can feel it now, very clearly. You are afraid for me.'

'It's not true,' David tried to reassure her. 'I'm a little worried, that's all.'

'Tell me,' she said.

'There is a small growth. It's not dangerous—yet. But they feel something should be done about it—' He stumbled through the explanation he had so carefully prepared, and when he ended she was silent for a moment.

'It is necessary, absolutely necessary?' she asked.

'Yes,' he told her, and she nodded, trusting him completely–then she smiled and squeezed his arm.

'Don't fret yourself, David, my darling. It will be all right. You'll see, they can't touch us. We live in a private place where they can't touch us.' Now it was she who was striving to comfort him.

'Of course it will be all right.' He hugged her to him roughly, slopping a little wine over the rim of his glass.

'When?' she asked.

'Tomorrow you will go in, and they'll do it the following morning.'

'So soon?'

'I thought it best to have it over with.'

'Yes. You are right.'

She sipped her wine, withdrawn, fearful, despite her brave show.

'They are going to cut my head open?'

'Yes,' he said, and she shuddered against him.

'There is no risk,' he said.

'No. I'm sure there isn't,' she agreed quickly.

He woke in the night with the instant knowledge that he was alone, that she was not curled warm and sleeping beside him.

Quickly he slipped from the bed and crossed to the bathroom. It was empty and he padded to the sitting-room of the suite and switched on the lights.

She heard the click of the switch and turned her head away, but not before he had seen the tears glowing on her cheeks like soft grey pearls. He went to her quickly.

'Darling,' he said.

'I couldn't sleep,' she said.

'That's all right.' He knelt before the couch on which she sat, but he did not touch her.

'I had a dream,' she said. 'There was a pool of clear water and you were swimming in it, looking up at me and calling to me. I saw your dear face clearly, beautiful and laughing–' David realized with a jolt in his guts that she had seen him in her dream as he had been, she had seen the beautiful dream-David, not the monstrous ravaged thing he was now. 'Then suddenly you began to sink, down, down, through the water, your face fading and receding–' Her voice caught and broke, and she was silent for a moment. 'It was a terrible dream, I cried out and tried to follow you, but I could not move and then you were gone down into the depths. The water turned dark and I woke with only the blackness in my head. Nothing but swirling mists of blackness.'

'It was only a dream,' he said.

'David,' she whispered. 'Tomorrow, if anything happens tomorrow–'

'Nothing will happen,' he almost snarled the denial, but she put out a hand to his face, finding his lips and touching them lightly to silence them.

'Whatever happens,' she said, 'remember how it was when we were happy. Remember that I loved you.'

The hospital of Groote Schuur sits on the lower slopes of Devil's Peak, a tall conical peak divided from the massif of Table Mountain by a deep saddle. Its summit is of grey rock and below it lie the dark pine forests and open grassy slopes of the great estate that Cecil John Rhodes left to the nation. Herds of deer and indigenous antelope feed quietly in the open places and the south-east wind feathers the crest with a flying pennant of cloud.

The hospital is a massive complex of brilliant white buildings, substantial and solid-looking blocks, all roofed in burnt red tiles.

Ruby Friedman had used all his pull to secure a private ward for Debra, and the sister in charge of the floor was expecting her. They took her from David and led her away, leaving him feeling bereft and lonely, but when he returned to visit her that evening she was sitting up in the bed in the soft cashmere bedjacket that David had given her and surrounded by banks of flowers which he had ordered.

'They smell wonderful,' she thanked him. 'It's like being in a garden.'

She wore a turban around her head and, with the serene golden eyes seeming focused on a distant vision, it gave her an exotic and mysterious air.

'They have shaved your head.' David felt a slide of dismay, he had not expected that she must also sacrifice that lustrous mane of black silk. It was the ultimate indignity, and she seemed to feel it also, for she did not answer him and instead told him brightly how well they were treating her, and what pains they were taking for her comfort.'You'd think I was some sort of queen,' she laughed.

The Brig was with David, gruff and reserved and patently out of place in these surroundings. His presence cast restraint upon them and it was a relief when Ruby Friedman arrived. Bustling and charming, he complimented Debra on the preparations she had undergone.

'Sister says that you are just fine, all nicely shaved and ready. Sorry, but you aren't allowed anything to eat or drink except the sleeping pill I've prescribed.'

'When do I go to theatre?'

'We've got you down bright and early. Eight o'clock tomorrow. I am tremendously pleased that Billy Cooper is the surgeon, we were very lucky to get him, but he owes me a favour or two. I will be assisting him, of course, and he'll have one of the best surgical teams in the world backing him up.'

'Ruby, you know how some women have their husbands with them when they are confined—'

'Yes.' Ruby looked uncertain, taken aback by the question.

'Well, couldn't David be there with me tomorrow? Couldn't we be together, for both our sakes, while it happens?'

'With all due respects, my dear, but you are not having a baby.'

'Couldn't you arrange for him to be there?' Debra pleaded, with eloquent eyes and an expression to break the hardest heart.

'I'm sorry,' Ruby shook his head. 'It's completely impossible—' then he brightened. 'But I tell you what. I could get him into the students' room. It will be the next best thing, in fact he would have a better view of the proceedings than if he were in theatre. We have closed-circuit television relayed to the students' room and David could watch from there.'

'Oh, please!' Debra accepted immediately. 'I'd like to know he was close, and that we were in contact. We don't like being parted from each other, do we, my darling?' She smiled at where she thought he was, but he had moved aside and the smile missed him. It was a gesture that wrenched something within him.

'You will be there, David, won't you?' she asked, and though the idea of watching the knife at work was repellent to him, he forced himself to reply lightly.

'I'll be there,' and he almost added, 'always', but he cut off the word.

This early in the morning there were only two others in the small lecture-room with its double semi-circular rows of padded chairs about the small television screen, a plump woman student with a pretty face and shaggy-dog hairstyle and a tall young man with a pale complexion and bad teeth. They both wore their stethoscopes dangling with calculated nonchalance from the pockets of their white linen jackets. After the first startled glance they ignored David, and they spoke together in knowing medical jargon.

'The Coop's doing an exploratory through the parietal.'

'That's the one I want to watch–'

The girl affected blue Gauloises cigarettes, rank and stinking in the confined room. David's eyes felt raw and gravelly for he slept little during the night, and the smoke irritated them. He kept looking at his watch, and imagining what was happening to Debra during these last minutes–the undignified purging and cleansing of her body, the robing, and the needles of sedation and antisepsis.

The slow drag of minutes ended at last when the screen began to glow and hum, the image shimmered and strobed then settled down into a high view of the theatre. The set was in colour, and the green theatre gowns of the figures moving around the operating-table blended with the subdued theatre green walls. Height had foreshortened the robed members of the operating team and the muttered and disjointed conversation between the surgeon and his anaesthetist was picked up by the microphones.

'Are we ready there yet, Mike?'

David felt the sick sensation in the pit of his stomach, and he wished he had eaten breakfast. It might have filled the hollow place below his ribs.

'Right,' the surgeon's voice sharpened as he turned towards the microphone. 'Are we on telly?'

'Yes, doctor,' the theatre sister answered him, and there was a note of resignation in the surgeon's voice as he spoke for the unseen audience.

'Very well, then. The patient is a twenty-six-year-old female. The symptoms are total loss of sight in both eyes, and the cause is suspected damage or constriction of the optic nerve in or near the optic chiasma. This is a surgical investigation of the site. The surgeon is Dr William Cooper, assisted by Dr Reuben Friedman.'

As he spoke, the camera moved in on the table and with a start of surprise David realized that he had been looking at Debra without knowing it. Her face and the lower part of her head were obscured by the sterile drapes that covered all but the shaven round ball of her skull. It was inhuman-looking, egglike, painted with Savlon antiseptic that glistened in the bright, overhead lights.

'Scalpel please, sister.'

David leaned forward tensely in his seat, and his hands tightened on the armrests, so the knuckles turned white, as Cooper made the first incision drawing the blade across the smooth skin. The flesh opened and immediately the tiny blood vessels began to dribble and spurt. Hands moved in the screen on the television, clad in rubber so that they were yellow and impersonal, but quick and sure.

An oval flap of skin and flesh was dissected free and was drawn back, exposing the gleaming bone beneath, and again David's flesh crawled as though with living things, as the surgeon took up a drill that resembled exactly a carpenter's brace and bit. His voice continued its impersonal commentary, as he began to drill through the skull, cranking away at the handle as the gleaming steel bit swiftly through the bone. He pierced the skull with four round drill holes, each set at the corners of a square.

'Peri-osteal elevator, please, sister.'

Again David's stomach clenched as the surgeon slid the gleaming steel introducer into one of the drill holes and manœuvred it gently until its tip reappeared through the next hole in line. Using the introducer, a length of sharp steel wire saw was threaded through the two holes and lay along the inside of the skull. Cooper sawed this back and forth and it cut cleanly through the bone. Four times he repeated the procedure, cutting out the sides of the square, and when he at last lifted out the detached piece of bone he had opened a trapdoor into Debra's skull.

As he worked David's gorge had risen until it pressed in his throat, and he had felt the cold glistening sheen of nauseous sweat across his forehead, but now as the camera's eye peered through the opening he felt his wonder surmount his horror, for he could see the pale amorphous mass of matter, enclosed in its tough covering membrane of the dura mater that was Debra's brain. Deftly Cooper incised a flap in the dura.

'We have exposed now the frontal lobe, and it will be necessary to displace this to explore the base of the skull.'

Working swiftly, but with obvious care and skill, Cooper used a stainless steel retractor, shaped like a shoe horn, to slide under the mass of brain and to lift it aside. Debra's brain—staring at it, David seemed to be looking into the core of her being, it was vulnerable and exposed, everything that made her what she was. What part of that soft pale mass contained her writer's genius, he wondered, from which of its many soft folds and coils sprang the fruitful fountain of her imagination, where was her love for him buried, what soft and secret place triggered her laughter and where was the vale of her tears? Its fathomless mystery held him intent as he watched the retractor probe deeper and deeper through the opening, and slowly the camera moved in to peer into the gaping depths of Debra's skull.

Cooper opened the far end of the dura mater and commented on his progress.

'We have here the anterior ridge of the sphenoid sinus, note this as our point for access to the chiasma—'

David was aware of the changed tone of the surgeon's voice, the charging of tension as the disembodied hands moved slowly and expertly towards their goal.

'Now this is interesting, can we see this on the screen, please? Yes! There is very clearly a bone deformation here—'

The voice was pleased, and the two students beside David exclaimed and leaned closer. David could see soft wet tissue and hard bright surfaces deep in the bottom of the wound, and the necks of steel instruments crowding into it, like metallic bees into the stamen of a pink and yellow bloom. Cooper scratched through to the metal of the grenade fragment.

'Now here we have the foreign body, can we have a look at those X-ray plates again, sister—'

The image cut quickly to the X-ray scanner, and again the students exclaimed. The girl puffed busily on her stinking Gauloise.

'Thank you.'

The image cut back to the operating field, and now David saw the dark speck of the grenade fragment lodged in the white bone.

'We will go for this, I think. Do you agree, Dr Friedman?'

'Yes, I think you should take it.'

Delicately the long slender steel insects worried the dark fragment, and at last with a grunt of satisfaction it came free of its niche, and Cooper drew it out carefully. David heard the metallic ping as it was dropped into a waiting dish.

'Good! Good!' Cooper gave himself a little encouragement as he plugged the hole left by the fragment with beeswax to prevent haemorrhage. 'Now we will trace out the optic nerves.'

They were two white worms, David saw them clearly, converging on their separate trails to meet and blend at the opening of the bony canal into which they disappeared.

'We have got extraneous bone-growth here, clearly associated with the foreign body we have just removed. It seems to have blocked off the canal and to have squeezed or severed the nerve. Suggestions, Dr Friedman?'

'I think we should excise that growth and try and ascertain just what damage we have to the nerve in that area.'

'Good. Yes, I agree. Sister, I will use a fine bone-nibbler to get in there.'

The swift selection and handling of the bright steel instruments again, and then Cooper was working on the white bone growth which grew in the shape of coral from a tropical sea. He nibbled at it with the keen steel, and carefully removed each piece from the field as it came away.

'What we have here is a bone splinter that was driven by the steel fragment into the canal. It is a large piece, and it must have been under considerable pressure, and it has consolidated itself here—'

He worked on carefully, and gradually the white worm of the nerve appeared from beneath the growth.

'Now, this is interesting.' Cooper's tone altered. 'Yes, look at this. Can we get a better view here, please?' The camera zoomed in a little closer, and the focus realigned. 'The nerve has been forced upwards, and flattened by pressure. The constriction is quite obvious, it has been pinched off—but it seems to be intact.'

Cooper lifted another large piece of bone aside, and now the nerve lay exposed over its full length.

'This is really remarkable. I expect that it is a one in a thousand chance, or one in a million. There appears to be no damage to the actual nerve, and yet the steel fragment passed so close to it that it must have touched it.'

Delicately, Cooper lifted the nerve with the blunt tip of a probe.

'Completely intact, but flattened with pressure. Yet I don't suspect any degree of atrophy, Dr Friedman?'

'I think we can confidently expect good recovery of function.' Despite the masked features, the triumphant attitude of the two men was easily recognized, and watching them, David felt his own emotions at war. With a weight upon his spirits he watched Cooper close up, replacing the portion of Debra's skull that he had removed, and once the flap of scalp was stitched back into place there was little external evidence of the extent and depth of their penetration. The image on the screen changed to another theatre where a small girl was to receive surgery for a massive hernia, and the fickle interest of the watching students changed with it.

David stood up and left the room. He rode up in the elevator and waited in the visitors' room on Debra's floor until the elevator doors opened again and two white uniformed male nurses trundled Debra's stretcher down the corridor to her room. She was deadly pale, with dark bruised-looking eyes and lips, her head swathed in a turban of white bandages. There was a dull brown smear of blood on the sheets that covered her and a whiff of anaesthetic hung in the corridor after she was gone.

Ruby Friedman came then, changed from theatre garb into an expensive light-weight grey mohair suit and a twenty-guinea Dior silk tie. He looked tanned and healthy, and mightily delighted with his achievement.

'You watched?' he demanded, and when David nodded he went on exuberantly, 'It was extraordinary.' He chuckled, and rubbed his hands together with glee.

'My God, something like this makes you feel good. Makes you feel that if you never do another thing in your life, it was still worthwhile.' He was unable to restrain himself any longer and he threw a playful punch at David's shoulder. 'Extraordinary,' he repeated, drawing it out into two words with relish, rolling the word around his tongue.

'When will you know?' David asked quietly.

'I know already, I'll stake my reputation on it!'

'She will be able to see as soon as she comes around from the anaesthetic?' David asked.

'Good Lord, no!' Ruby chuckled. 'That nerve has been pinched off for years, it's going to take time to recover.'

'How long?'

'It's like a leg that has gone to sleep when you sit wrongly. When the blood flows back in, it's still numb and tingling until the circulation is restored.'

'How long?' David repeated.

'Immediately she wakes, that nerve is going to start going crazy, sending all sorts of wild messages to the brain. She's going to see colours and shapes as though she is on a drug binge, and it's going to take time to settle down–two weeks to a month, I would guess–then it will clear, the nerve will have recovered its full and normal function and she will begin having real effective vision.'

'Two weeks,' David said, and he felt the relief of a condemned man hearing of his reprieve.

'You will tell her the good news, of course.' Ruby gave another buoyant chuckle, shaped up to punch David again and then controlled himself. 'What a wonderful gift you have been able to give her.'

'No,' David answered him. 'I won't tell her yet, I will find the right time later.'

'You will have to explain the initial vision she will experience, the colour and shape hallucinations, they will alarm her.'

'We will just tell her that it's the normal after-effect of the operation. Let her adjust to that before telling her.'

'David, I–' Ruby began seriously, but he was cut off by the savage blaze of blue in the eyes that watched him from the mask of scarred flesh.

'I will tell her!' The voice shook with such fury, that Ruby took a step backwards. 'That was the condition, I will tell her when I judge the time is ripe.'

Out of the darkness a tiny amber light glowed, pale and far off, but she watched it split like a breeding amœba and become two, and each of those split and split again until they filled the universe in a great shimmering field of stars. The light throbbed and pulsed, vibrant and triumphant, and it changed from amber to brightest purest white like the sparkle from a paragon diamond, then it turned to the blue of sunlight on a tropical ocean, to soft forest greens and desert golds—an endless cavalcade of colours, changing, blending, fading, flaring in splendour that held her captive.

Then the colours took shape, they spun like mighty Catherine wheels, and soared and exploded, showered down in rivers of flame that burst again into fresh cascades of light.

She was appalled by the dimensions of shape and colour that engulfed her, bewildered by the beauty of it and at last she could bear it no longer in silence and she cried out.

Instantly there was a hand in hers, a strong hard familiar hand, and his voice, dearly beloved, reassuring and firm.

'David,' she cried with relief.

'Quietly, my darling. You must rest.'

'David. David.' She heard the sob in her own voice as new torrents of colour poured over her, insupportable in their richness and variety, overwhelming in their depth and range.

'I'm here, my darling. I'm here.'

'What's happening to me, David? What's happening?'

'You are all right. The operation was a success. You are just fine.'

'Colours,' she cried. 'Filling my whole head. I've never known it like this.'

'It's the result of the operation. It shows that it was a success. They removed the growth.'

'I'm frightened, David.'

'No, my darling. There is nothing to be afraid of.'

'Hold me, David. Hold me safe.' And in the circle of his arms the fear abated, and slowly she learned to ride the oceanic waves and washes of colour, came gradually to accept and then at last to look upon them with wonder and with intense pleasure.

'It's beautiful, David. I'm not frightened any more, not with you holding me. It's wonderful.'

'Tell me what you see,' he said.

'I couldn't. It's impossible. I couldn't find the words.'

'Try!' he said.

David was alone in the suite, and it was after midnight when the call that he had placed to New York came through.

'This is Robert Dugan, to whom am I speaking?' Bobby's voice was crisp and businesslike.

'It's David Morgan.'

'Who?'

'Debra Mordecai's husband.'

'Well, hello there, David.' The agent's voice changed, becoming expansive. 'It's sure nice to talk to you. How is Debra?' It was obvious that Dugan's interest in David began and ended with his wife.

'That's why I am calling. She's had an operation and she's in hospital at the moment.'

'God! Not serious, is it?'

'She's going to be fine. She'll be up in a few days and ready for work in a couple of weeks.'

'Glad to hear it, David. That's great.'

'Look here, I want you to go ahead and set up that script-writing contract for *A Place of Our Own*.'

'She's going to do it?' Dugan's pleasure carried six thousand miles with no diminution.

'She'll do it now.'

'That's wonderful news, David.'

'Write her a good contract.'

'Depend on it, boyo. That little girl of yours is hot property. Playing hard to get hasn't done her any harm, I tell you!'

'How long will the script job last?'

'They'll want her for six months,' Dugan guessed. 'The producer who will do it is making a movie in Rome right now. He'll probably want Debra to work with him there.'

'Good,' said David. 'She'll like Rome.'

'You coming with her, David?'

'No,' David answered carefully. 'No, she'll be coming on her own.'

'Will she be able to get by on her own?' Dugan sounded worried.

'From now on she'll be able to do everything on her own.'

'Hope you are right,' Dugan was dubious.

'I'm right.' David told him abruptly. 'One other thing. That lecture tour, is it still on?'

'They are beating the door down. Like I said, she's hotter than a pistol.'

'Set it up for after the script job.'

'Hey, David boy. This is the business. Now we are really cooking with gas. We are going to make your little girl into one very big piece of property.'

'Do that,' said David. 'Make her big. Keep her busy, you hear. Don't give her time to think.'

'I'll keep her busy.' Then as though he had detected something in David's voice. 'Is something bugging you, David? You got some little domestic problem going there, boy? You want to talk about it?'

'No, I don't want to talk about it. You just look after her. Look after her well.'

'I'll look after her,' Dugan's tone had sobered. 'And David—'

'What is it?'

'I'm sorry. Whatever it is, I'm sorry.'

'That's okay.' David had to end the conversation then, immediately. His hand was shaking so that he knocked the telephone from the table and the plastic cracked through. He left it lying and went out into the night. He walked alone through the sleeping city, until just before the morning he was weary enough to sleep.

The streams of colour settled to steady runs and calmly moving patterns, no longer the explosive bursts of brightness that had so alarmed her. After the grey shifting banks of blindness that had filled her head like dirty cotton wool for those long years, the new brightness and beauty served to buoy her spirits, and after the main discomfort of her head surgery had passed in the first few days, she was filled with a wondrous sense of well-being, a formless optimistic expectation, such as she had not experienced since she was a child anticipating the approach of a long-awaited holiday.

It was as though in some deep recess of her subconscious she was vaguely aware of the imminent return of her sight. However, the knowledge seemed not to have reached her conscious mind. She knew there was change, she welcomed her release from the dark and sombre dungeons of nothingness into the new brightness, but she did not realize that there was more to come, that after colour and fantasy would follow shape and reality.

Each day David waited for her to say something that might show that she had realized that her sight was on the way back; he hoped for and at the same time dreaded this awareness—but it did not come.

He spent as much of each day with her as hospital routine would allow, and he hoarded each minute of it, doling out time like a miser paying coins for a diminishing hoard. Yet Debra's ebullient mood was infectious, and he could not help but laugh with her and share the warm excitement as she anticipated her release from the hospital and their return together to the sanctuary of Jabulani.

There were no doubts in her mind, no shadows across her happiness, and gradually David began to believe that it would last. That their happiness was immortal and that their love could survive any pressure placed upon it. It was so strong and fine when they were together now, carried along by Debra's bubbling enthusiasm, that surely she could regain her sight and weather the first shock of seeing him.

Yet he was not sure enough to tell her yet, there was plenty of time. Two weeks, Ruby Friedman had told him, two weeks before she would be able to see him and it was vitally important to David that he should extract every grain of happiness that was left to him in that time.

In the lonely nights he lay with the frantic scurryings of his brain keeping him from sleep. He remembered that the plastic surgeon had told him there was more they could do to make him less hideous. He could go back and submit to the knife once more, although his body cringed at the thought. Perhaps they could give Debra something less horrifying to look at.

The following day he braved the massed stares of hundreds of shoppers to visit Stuttafords Departmental Store in Adderley Street. The girl in the wig department, once she had recovered her poise, took him into a curtained-off cubicle and entered into the spirit of finding a wig to cover the domed cicatrice of his scalp.

David regarded the fine curly head of hair over the frozen ruins of his face, and for the first time ever he found himself laughing at it, although the effect of laughter was even more horrifying as the tight lipless mouth writhed like an animal in a trap.

'God!' he laughed. 'Frankenstein in drag!' and for the sales girl who had been fighting to control her emotions this was too much. She broke into hysterical giggles of embarrassment.

He wanted to tell Debra about it, making a joke of it and at the same time prepare her for her first sight of his face, but somehow he could not find the words. Another day passed with nothing accomplished, except a few last hours of warmth and happiness shared.

The following day Debra began to show the first signs of restlessness. 'When are they going to let me out, darling? I feel absolutely wonderful. It's ridiculous to lie in bed here. I want to get back to Jabulani—there is so much to do.' Then she giggled. 'And they've had me locked up here ten days now. I'm not used to convent life, and to be completely honest with you, my big lusty lover, I am climbing the wall–'

'We could lock the door,' David suggested.

'God, I married a genius,' Debra cried out delightedly, and then later. 'That's the first time it ever happened for me in Technicolor. I think I could get hooked on that.'

That evening Ruby Friedman and the Brig were waiting for him when he returned to his suite, and they came swiftly to the reason for their visit.

'You have already left it too long. Debra should have been told days ago,' the Brig told him sternly.

'He is right, David. You are being unfair to her. She must have time to come to terms, latitude for adjustment.'

'I'll tell her when I get the opportunity,' David muttered doggedly.

'When will that be?' the Brig demanded, the gold tooth glowing angrily in its furry nest.

'Soon.'

'David,' Ruby was placatory, 'it could happen at any time now. She has made strong and vigorous progress, it could happen much sooner than I expected.'

'I'll do it,' said David. 'Can't you stop pushing me? I said I'll do it–and I will. Just get off my back, won't you.'

'Right.' The Brig was brisk now. 'You've got until noon tomorrow. If you haven't told her by then, I'm going to do it.'

'You're a hard old bastard, aren't you,' David said bitterly, and anger paled the Brig's lips and they could see the effort he made to force it down.

'I understand your reluctance,' he spoke carefully. 'I sympathize. However, my first and only concern is for Debra. You are indulging yourself, David. You are wallowing in self-pity, but I am not going to allow that to hurt her more. She has had enough. No more delay. Tell her, and have done.'

'Yes,' David nodded, all the fight gone out of him. 'I will tell her.'

'When?' the Brig persisted.

'Tomorrow,' said David. 'I will tell her tomorrow morning.'

It was a bright warm morning, and the garden below his room was gay with colour. David lingered over breakfast in his suite, and he read all of the morning papers from end to end, drawing out the moment to its utmost. He dressed with care afterwards, in a dark suit and a soft lilac shirt, then, when he was ready to leave, he surveyed his image in the full-length mirror of the dressing-room.

'It's been a long time–and I'm still not at ease with you,' he told the figure in the mirror. 'Let's pray that somebody loves you more than I do.'

The doorman had a cab ready for him under the portico, and he settled in the back seat with the leaden feeling in his stomach. The drive seemed much shorter this morning, and when he paid off the cab and climbed the steps to the main entrance of Groote Schuur, he glanced at his wrist-watch. It was a few minutes after eleven o'clock. He was hardly aware of the curious glances as he crossed the lobby to the elevators.

The Brig was waiting for him in the visitors' room on Debra's floor. He came out into the corridor, tall and grim, and unfamiliar in his civilian clothes.

'What are you doing here?' David demanded, it was the ultimate intrusion and he resented it fiercely.

'I thought I might be of help.'

'Good on you!' said David sardonically, making no effort to hide his anger.

The Brig let the anger slide past him, not acknowledging it with either word or expression as he asked mildly, 'Would you like me to be with you?'

'No.' David turned away from him as he spoke. 'I can manage, thank you,' and he set off along the corridor.

'David!' the Brig called softly, and David hesitated and then turned back.

'What is it?' he asked.

For a long moment they stared at each other, then abruptly the Brig shook his head. 'No,' he said. 'It's nothing,' and watched the tall young man with the monstrous head turn and walk swiftly towards Debra's room. His footsteps echoed hollowly along the empty corridor, like the tread of a man upon the gallows steps.

The morning was warm with a light breeze off the sea. Debra sat in her chair by the open window, and the warm air wafted the scent of the pine forests to her. Resinous and clean-smelling, it mingled with the faint whiff of the sea and the kelp beds. She felt quiet and deeply contented, even though David was late this morning. She had spoken to Ruby Friedman when he made his rounds earlier, and he had teased her and hinted that she would be able to leave in a week or so, and the knowledge rounded out her happiness.

The warmth of the morning was drowsy, and she closed her eyes subduing the strong rich flow of colour into a lulling cocoon of soft shades which enfolded her, and she lay on the downy edges of sleep.

David found her like that, sitting in the deep chair with her legs curled sideways under her and her face side-lit by the reflected sunlight from the window. The turban of white bandages that swathed her head was crisp and fresh and her gown was white as a bride's, with cascades of filmy lace.

He stood before her chair studying her with care, her face was pale, but the dark bruises below her eyes had cleared and the set of her full lips were serene and peaceful.

With infinite tenderness he leaned forward and laid his open hand against her cheek. She stirred drowsily, and opened eyes that were honey brown and flecked with bright flakes of gold. They were beautiful, and vague, misty and sightless—then suddenly he saw them change, the look of them was sharp and aware. Her gaze focused, and steadied. She was looking at him—and seeing him.

Debra was roused from the warm edge of sleep by the touch upon her cheek, as light as the fall of an autumn leaf. She opened her eyes to soft golden clouds, then suddenly like the morning wind slashing away the sea mist, the clouds rolled open and she looked beyond to the monster's head that swam towards her, a colossal disembodied head that seemed must arise from the halls of hell itself, a head so riven with livid lines and set with the bestial, crudely worked features of one of the dark hosts, that she flung herself back in her chair, cringing away from the terror of it, and she lifted her hands to her face and she screamed.

David turned and ran from the room, slamming the door behind him, his feet pounded down the passage and the Brig heard him coming and stepped into the corridor.

'David!' He reached out a hand to him, to hold him back, but David struck out at him wildly, a blow that caught him in the chest throwing him back heavily against the wall. When he regained his balance, and staggered from the wall clutching his chest, David was gone. His frantic footsteps clattered up from the well of the stairs.

'David!' he called, his voice croaking. 'Wait!' But he was gone, his footsteps fading, and the Brig let him go. Instead he turned and hurried painfully down the corridor to where the hysterical sobs of his daughter rang from behind the closed door.

She looked up from her cupped hands when she heard the door open, and wonder dawned through the terror in her eyes.

'I can see you,' she whispered, 'I can see.'

He went to her quickly and took her in the protective circle of his arms.

'It's all right,' he told her awkwardly, 'it's going to be all right.'

She clung to him, stifling the last of her sobs.

'I had a dream,' she murmured, 'a terrible dream,' and she shuddered against him. Then suddenly she pulled away.

'David,' she cried, 'where is David? I must see him.'

The Brig stiffened, realizing that she had not recognized reality.

'I must see him,' she repeated, and he replied heavily, 'You have already seen him, my child.'

For many seconds she did not understand, and then slowly it came to her.

'David?' she whispered, her voice catching and breaking. 'That was David?'

The Brig nodded, watching her face for the revulsion and the horror.

'Oh dear God,' Debra's voice was fierce. 'What have I done? I screamed when I saw him. What have I done to him? I've driven him away.'

'So you still want to see him again?' the Brig asked.

'How can you say that?' Debra blazed at him. 'More than anything on this earth. You must know that!'

'Even the way he is now?'

'If you think that would make any difference to me—then you don't know me very well.' Her expression changed again, becoming concerned. 'Find him for me,' she ordered. 'Quickly, before he has a chance to do something stupid.'

'I don't know where he has gone,' the Brig answered, his own concern aroused by the possibility which Debra had hinted at.

'There is only one place he would go when he is hurt like this,' Debra told him. 'He will be in the sky.'

'Yes,' the Brig agreed readily.

'Get down to Air Traffic Control, they'll let you speak to him.' The Brig turned for the door and Debra's voice urged him on.

'Find him for me, Daddy. Please find him for me.'

The Navajo seemed to come around on to a southerly heading under its own volition. It was only when the sleek, rounded nose settled on course, climbing steadily upwards towards the incredibly tall and unsullied blue of the heavens that David knew where he was going.

Behind him, the solid flat-topped mountain with its glistening wreaths of cloud fell away. This was the last of the land, and ahead lay only the great barren wastes of ice and cruel water.

David glanced at his fuel gauges. His vision was still blurred but he saw the needles registering a little over the half-way mark on the dials.

Three hours' flying perhaps, and David felt a chill relief that there was to be a term to his suffering. He saw clearly then how it would end down there in the wilderness below the shipping lanes. He would continue to bore for height, climbing steadily until at last his engines starved and failed. Then he would push the nose down into a vertical dive and go in hard and fast, like the final suicide stoop of a maimed and moribund eagle. It would be over swiftly, and the metal fuselage would carry him down to a grave that could not be as lonely as the desolation in which he now existed.

The radio crackled and hummed into life. He heard Air Traffic snarl his call sign through the static crackle, and he reached for the switch to kill the set—when the well-remembered voice stayed his hand.

'David, this is the Brig.' The words and the tone in which they were spoken transported him back to another cockpit in another land.

'You disobeyed me once before. Don't do it again.'

David's mouth tightened into a thin colourless line and again he reached for the switch. He knew they were watching him on the radar plot, that they knew his course, and that the Brig had guessed what he intended. Well, there was nothing they could do about it.

'David,' the Brig's voice softened, and some sure instinct made him choose the only words to which David would listen. 'I have just spoken to Debra. She wants you. She wants you desperately.'

David's hand hovered over the switch.

'Listen to me, David. She needs you—she will always need you.'

David blinked, for he felt tears scalding his eyes once more. His determination wavered.

'Come back, David. For her sake, come back.'

Out of the darkness of his soul, a light shone, a small light which grew and spread until it seemed to fill him with its shimmering brightness.

'David, this is the Brig.' Again it was the voice of the old warrior, hard and uncompromising. 'Return to base immediately.'

David grinned, and lifted the microphone to his mouth. He thumbed the transmit button, and spoke the old acknowledgement in Hebrew.

'Beseder! This is Bright Lance leader, homeward bound,' and he brought the Navajo around steeply.

The mountain was blue and low on the horizon, and he let the nose sink gradually towards it. He knew that it would not be easy—that it would require all his courage and patience, but he knew that in the end it would be worth it all. Suddenly he needed desperately to be alone with Debra, in the peace of Jabulani.

THE DIAMOND HUNTERS

His flight had been delayed for three hours at Nairobi, and despite four large whiskies he slept only fitfully until the intercontinental Boeing touched down at Heathrow. Johnny Lance felt as though someone·had thrown a handful of grit in each eye, and his mood was ugly as he came through the indignity of Customs and Immigration into the main hall of the international terminus.

The Van Der Byl Diamond Company's London agent was there to meet him.

'Pleasant trip, Johnny?'

'Like the one to hell,' Johnny grunted.

'Good practice for you.' The agent grinned. The two of them had seen some riotous times together.

Reluctantly Johnny grinned back at him.

'You got me a room and a car?'

'Dorchester—and Jag.' The agent handed over the car keys. 'And I've got two first-class seats reserved on tomorrow's nine o'clock flight back to Cape Town. Tickets at the hotel reception desk.'

'Good boy.' Johnny dropped the keys into the pocket of his cashmere overcoat and they started for the exit. 'Now where is Tracey van der Byl?'

The agent shrugged. 'Since I wrote to you she has dropped out of sight. I don't know where you can start looking.'

'Great, just great!' said Johnny bitterly as they came out into the car park. 'I'll start with Benedict.'

'Does the Old Man know about Tracey?'

Johnny shook his head. 'He's a sick man. I didn't tell him.'

'Here's your car.' The agent stopped by the pearl-grey Jaguar. 'Any chance of a drink together?'

'Not this trip, sorry.' Johnny slipped in behind the wheel. 'Next time.'

'I'll hold you to that,' said the agent and walked away.

It was almost dark by the time Johnny crossed the Hammersmith flyover in the moist smoky grey of the evening, and he lost himself twice in the maze of Belgravia before he found the narrow mews behind Belgrave Square and parked the Jaguar.

The exterior of the flat had been lavishly redecorated since his last visit, and Johnny's mouth twisted. He might not be so hot at earning the stuff—but our boy Benedict certainly was a dab hand at spending it.

There were lights burning and Johnny hit the door knocker half a dozen lusty cracks. It echoed hollowly about the mews, and in the silence that followed Johnny heard the whisper of voices from behind the curtains, and a shadow passed quickly across the window.

Johnny waited three minutes in the cold, then he stepped back into the middle of the mews.

'Benedict van der Byl,' he bellowed. 'I'll give you a count of ten to get this door open. Then I'll kick the bloody thing down.'

He drew breath and bellowed again.

'This is Johnny Lance – and you know I mean it.'

The door opened almost immediately. Johnny pushed his way through it, not glancing at the man who held it, and started for the lounge.

'Dammit, Lance. You can't go in there.' Benedict van der Byl started after him.

'Why not?' Johnny glanced back at him. 'It is a Company flat – and I'm the General Manager.'

Before Benedict could reply, Johnny was through the door.

One of the girls picked up her clothing from the floor and ran naked into the bedroom passage. The other pulled a full-length caftan over her head and glared at Johnny sulkily. Her hair was in wild disorder, fluffed out into a grotesque halo of stiff curls.

'Nice party,' said Johnny. He glanced at the movie projector on the side table, and then at the screen across the room. 'Films and all.'

'Are you the fuzz?' demanded the girl.

'You've got an infernal cheek, Lance.' Benedict van der Byl was beside him, tying the belt of his silk dressing-gown.

'Is he fuzz?' the girl demanded again.

'No,' Benedict assured her. 'He works for my father.' With the statement he seemed to gather self-assurance, drawing himself up to his full height and smoothing his long dark hair with one hand. His voice regained its polish and lazy inflection. 'Actually, he is Daddy's messenger boy.'

Johnny turned to him, but he addressed the girl without looking at her.

'Beat it, girlie. Follow your friend.'

She hesitated.

'Beat it!' Johnny's voice crackled like a bush fire, and she went.

The two men stood facing each other. They were the same age, in their early thirties – both tall, both dark-haired – different in every other way.

Johnny was big in the shoulders and lean across the hips and belly, his skin polished and browned by the desert sun. The line of his heavy jawbone stood out clearly, and his eyes seemed still to seek far horizons. His voice clipped and twanged with the accents of the other land.

'Where is Tracey?' he asked.

Benedict lifted one eyebrow in a pantomime of arrogant surprise. His skin was pale olive, unstained by sunlight for it was months since he had last visited Africa. His lips were very red, as though they had been painted, the classical lines of his features were blurred by flesh. There were soft little pouches under his eyes, and a plumpness beneath the silk dressing-gown that suggested he ate and drank often and exercised infrequently.

'My dear chap, what on earth makes you think I know where my sister is? I haven't seen her for weeks.'

Johnny turned away and crossed to one of the paintings on the far wall. The room was hung with good original South African artists – Alexis Preller, Irma Stern and Tretchikoff – an unusual mixture of techniques and styles, but someone had convinced the Old Man they were sound investments.

Johnny turned back to face Benedict van der Byl. He studied him as he had the paintings, comparing him with the clean young athlete he had been a few years before. A clear mental image in his mind pictured Benedict moving with leopard grace across the green field of play under the packed grandstands, turning smoothly beneath the high floating arc of the ball to gather it neatly, head high, and break back in field to open the line for the return kick.

'You're getting fat, Laddy Buck,' he said softly, and Benedict's anger stained his cheeks dull red.

'Get out of here,' he snapped.

'In a minute–tell me about Tracey first.'

'I've told you–I don't know where she is. Whoring it up around Chelsea, I expect.'

Johnny felt his own anger surge fiercely, but his voice remained level.

'Where is she getting the money, Benedict?'

'I don't know–the Old Man–'

Johnny cut him short. 'The Old Man is keeping her on an allowance of ten pounds a week. From what I hear she's throwing more than that around.'

'Christ, Johnny,' Benedict's tone became conciliatory, 'I don't know. It's not my business. Perhaps Kenny Hartford is–'

Again Johnny interrupted impatiently. 'Kenny Hartford is giving her nothing. That was part of the divorce agreement when they split up. Now I want to know who is subsidizing her trip to oblivion. How about it, big brother?'

'Me?' Benedict was indignant. 'You know there is no love wasted between us.'

'Must I spell it out?' Johnny asked. 'All right, then. The Old Man is dying–without losing his horror of all weakness and sin. If Tracey turns into a drug-soaked little tramp–then there's a good chance that our boy Benedict will come back into full favour. It would be a good gamble on your part to lay out a few thousand now, to send Tracey to hell. Cut her off completely from her father–and all those nice fat millions.'

'Who said anything about drugs?' Benedict blustered.

'I did.' Johnny stepped up to him. 'You and I have a little unfinished business. It would give me intense pleasure to take you to pieces and see what makes you work.'

He held Benedict's eyes for long seconds, then Benedict looked down and fiddled with the cord of his dressing-gown.

'Where is she, Benedict?'

'I don't know, damn you!'

Johnny moved softly across to the movie projector and picked up a reel of film from the table beside it. He peeled off a few feet of celluloid from the reel and held it up to the light.

'Pretty!' he said, but the line of his mouth tightened with disgust.

'Put that down,' snapped Benedict.

'You know what the Old Man thinks about this sort of thing, don't you, Benedict?'

Suddenly Benedict went pale.

'He wouldn't believe you.'

'Yes, he would.' Johnny tossed the reel on the table and turned back to Benedict. 'He believes me because I've never lied to him.'

Benedict hesitated, wiped his lips nervously with the back of his hand.

'I haven't seen her for two weeks. She was renting a place in Chelsea. Stark Street. No. 23. She came to see me.'

'What for?'

'I lent her a couple of pounds,' Benedict muttered sulkily.

'A couple of pounds?' Johnny asked.

'All right, a couple of hundred. After all, she is my sister.'

'Damn decent of you,' Johnny lauded him. 'Write down the address.'

Benedict crossed to the leather-topped writing desk and scribbled on a card. He came back and handed the card to Johnny.

'You like to think you're big and dangerous, Lance.' His voice was pitched low but it shook with fury. 'Well, I'm dangerous too—in a different sort of way. The Old Man can't live for ever, Lance. When he's gone I'm coming after you.'

'You frighten the hell out of me.' Johnny grinned at him, and went down to the car.

The traffic was solid in Sloane Square as Johnny eased the Jaguar slowly down towards Chelsea. There was plenty of time to think; to remember how close they had been—the three of them. He and Tracey and Benedict.

Running together as wild young things with the endless beaches and mountains and sun-washed plains of Namaqualand as their playground. That was before the Old Man made the big strike on the Slang river, before there was money for shoes. When Tracey wore dresses made from flour sacks sewn together, and they rode to school each day, all three of them bare-back on a single pony like a row of bedraggled little brown sparrows on a fence.

He remembered how the long sun-drenched weeks while the Old Man was away were spent in laughter and secret games. How they climbed the *kopje* behind the mud-walled shack each evening and looked towards the north across the limitless land, flesh-coloured and purple in the sunset, searching for the wisp of dust in the distance that would mean the Old Man was coming home.

Then the almost painful excitement when the dusty, rackety Ford truck with its mudguards tied on with wire was suddenly there in the yard, and the Old Man was climbing down from the cab, a sweat-stained hat on the back of his head and the dust thick in the stubble of his beard, swinging Tracey squealing above his head. Then turning to Benedict, and lastly to Johnny. Always in that order—Tracey, Benedict, Johnny.

Johnny had never wondered why sometimes he was not first. It was always that way. Tracey, Benedict, Johnny. The same way as he had never wondered why his name was Lance and not van der Byl. Then it had come to an end suddenly, the whole brightly sunlit dream of childhood was gone and lost.

'Johnny, I'm not your real father. Your father and mother died when you were very young.' And Johnny had stared at the Old Man in disbelief.

'Do you understand, Johnny?'

'Yes, Pa.'

Tracey's hand groped for his beneath the table top like a little warm animal. He jerked his own hand away from it.

'I think you'd better not call me that any more, Johnny.' He could remember the exact tone of the Old Man's voice, neutral, matter of fact, as it splintered the fragile crystal of his childhood to fragments. The loneliness had begun.

Johnny accelerated the Jaguar forward and swung into the King's Road. He was surprised that the memory hurt so intensely—time should have mellowed and softened it.

His life from then on had become a ceaseless contest to win the Old Man's approval—he dare not hope for his love.

Soon there were other changes, for a week later the old Ford had come roaring unexpectedly out of the desert in the night, and the barking of the dogs and the Old Man's shouted laughter had brought them, sleepy-eyed, tumbling from their bunks.

The Old Man had lit the Petromax lamp and sat them on the kitchen chairs about the scrubbed deal table. Then with the air of a conjurer he had laid something that looked like a big lump of broken glass on the table.

The three sleepy children had stared at it solemnly, not understanding. The harsh glare of the Petromax was captured within the crystal, captured, repeated, magnified and thrown back at them in fire and blue lightning.

'Twelve carats—' gloated the Old Man. 'Blue-white and perfect, and there is a cartload where that came from.'

After that there were new clothes and motor cars, the move to Cape Town, the new school and the big house on Wynberg Hill—but always the contest. The contest that did not earn the Old Man's approval as it was designed to do, but earned instead Benedict van der Byl's jealousy and hatred. Without his drive and purpose, Benedict could not hope to match Johnny's achievements in the classroom and on the sports field. He fell far behind the pace that Johnny set—and hated him for it.

The Old Man did not notice for he was seldom with them now. They lived alone in the big house with the thin silent woman who was their housekeeper, and the Old Man came infrequently and for short periods. Always he seemed tired and distracted. Sometimes he brought presents for them from London and Amsterdam and Kimberley, but the presents meant very little to them. They would have liked it better had it stayed the way it was in the desert.

In the void left by the Old Man the hostility and rivalry between Johnny and Benedict flourished to such proportions that Tracey was forced to choose between them. She chose Johnny.

In their loneliness they clung to each other.

The grave little girl and the big gangling boy built together a castle against the loneliness. It was a bright secure place where the sadness could not reach them—and Benedict was excluded from it.

Johnny swung the Jaguar out of the line of traffic into old Church Street, down towards the river in Chelsea. He drove automatically and the memories came crowding back.

He tried to recapture and hold the castle of warmth and love that he and Tracey had built so long ago, but instantly his mind leapt to the night on which it had collapsed.

One night in the old house on Wynberg Hill Johnny had come awake to the sound of distant weeping. He had gone barefooted in his pyjamas, following that heart-rending whisper of grief. He was afraid, fourteen years old and afraid in the dark house.

Tracey was weeping into her pillow and he had stooped over her.

'Tracey. What is it? Why are you crying?'

She had jumped up, kneeling on the bed, and flung both arms about his neck.

'Oh, Johnny. I had a dream, a terrible dream. Hold me, please. Don't go away, don't leave me.' Her whisper was still thick and muffled with tears. He had gone into her bed and held her until at last she slept.

Every night after that he had gone to her room. It was innocent and completely childlike, the twelve-year-old girl and the boy who was her brother, in fact if not in name. They held each other in the bed, and whispered and laughed secretly until sleep carried them both away.

Then suddenly the castle was blasted by the bright electric glare of the overhead light. The Old Man was standing in the door of the bedroom, and Benedict was behind him in his pyjamas dancing with excitement and chanting triumphantly.

'I told you, Pa! I told you so!'

The Old Man was shaking with rage, the bush of grey hair standing erect like the mane of a wounded lion. He had dragged Johnny from the bed, and struck away Tracey's clinging hands.

'You little whore,' he bellowed, holding the terrified boy easily with one hand and leaning forward to strike his daughter in the face with his open hand. Leaving her sobbing, face down on the bed, he dragged Johnny down the passages to the study on the ground floor. He threw him into the room with a violence that sent him staggering against the desk.

The Old Man had gone to the rack and taken out a light Malacca cane. He came to Johnny and, taking a handful of his hair, threw him face down over the desk.

The Old Man had beaten him before, but never like this. Mad with rage the Old Man's blows had been unaimed, some fell across Johnny's back.

Yet in the agony it was deadly important to the boy that he should not cry out. He bit through his lip so the taste of blood was salt and copper in his mouth. He must not hear me cry! And he choked back the moans feeling his pyjama trousers hanging heavy and sodden with blood.

His silence served only as a goad to the Old Man's fury. Flinging the cane aside, he pulled the boy upright and attacked him with his hands. Slamming Johnny's head from side to side with full, open-handed blows that burst in Johnny's skull with blinding flashes of light.

Still Johnny kept on his feet, clinging to the edge of the desk. His lips broken and swollen and his face bloated and darkening with bruises, until at last the Old Man was driven far beyond the borders of sanity. He bunched his fist and drove it into Johnny's face—and with a wonderful sense of relief Johnny felt the pain go out in a warm flood of darkness.

Johnny heard voices first. A strange voice:

'—As though he's been savaged by a a wild beast. I'll have to inform the police.'

Then a voice he recognized. It took him a little time to place it. He tried to open his eyes but they seemed locked tight, his face felt enormous, swollen and hot. He forced the fat lids of his eyes back and recognized Michael Shapiro, the Old Man's secretary. He was talking quietly to the other man.

There was the smell of antiseptic and the doctor's bag lay open on the table beside the bed.

'Listen, Doctor. I know it looks bad—but hadn't you better talk to the boy before you stir up the police?'

They both looked towards the bed.

'He's conscious.' The doctor came to him quickly. 'What happened to you, Johnny? Tell us what happened. Whoever did this to you will be punished—I promise you.'

The words were wrong. Nobody must ever punish the Old Man.

Johnny tried to speak but his lips were stiff and swollen. He tried again.

'I fell,' he said. 'I fell. Nobody! Nobody! I fell down.'

When the doctor had gone Mike Shapiro came and stood over him. His Jewish eyes were dark with pity, and something else—anger perhaps, or admiration. 'I'm taking you to my house, Johnny. You will be all right now.'

He stayed two weeks under the care of Michael Shapiro's wife, Helen. The scabs came away, the bruises faded to a dirty yellow, but his nose stayed crooked with a lump at the bridge. He studied his new nose in the mirror, and liked it. It made him look like a boxer, he thought or a pirate, but it was many months before the tenderness passed and he could finger it freely.

'Listen, Johnny, you are going to a new school. A fine boarding-school in Grahamstown.' Michael Shapiro tried to sound enthusiastic. Grahamstown was five hundred miles away. 'In the holidays you'll be going to work in Namaqualand—learning all about diamonds and how to mine them. You'll enjoy that, won't you?'

Johnny had thought about it for a minute, watching Michael's face and reading in it his shame.

'I won't be going home again then?' By home he meant the house on Wynberg Hill. Michael shook his head.

'When will I see—' Johnny hesitated as he tried to find the right words, '—when will I see them again?'

'I don't know, Johnny,' Michael answered him honestly.

As Michael had promised it was a fine school.

On his first Sunday after the church service, he had followed the other boys back to their classroom for the session of compulsory letter-writing. The others had immediately began dashing off hasty scribbles to their parents. Johnny sat miserably until the master in charge stopped at his desk.

'Aren't you going to write home, Lance?' he asked kindly. 'I'm sure they'll all want to hear how you are.'

Johnny picked up his pen obediently, and puzzled over the blank writing-pad.

He wrote at last:

Dear Sir,

    I hope you will be pleased to hear that I am now at school. The food is good, but the beds are very hard.

    We go to church every day and play rugby football.

Yours faithfully,
Johnny.

From then until he left school and went up to university three years later, he wrote every week to the Old Man. Every letter began with the same salutation and went on, 'I hope you will be pleased to hear—' There was never a reply to any of these letters.

Once each term he received a typewritten letter from Michael Shapiro setting out the arrangements that had been made for the school holidays. Usually these involved a train journey hundreds of miles across the Karroo to some remote village in the vast dry wasteland, where a light aircraft belonging to Van Der Byl Diamonds was waiting to fly him still deeper into the desert to one of the Company's concession areas. Again as Michael Shapiro had promised he learned about diamonds and how to mine them.

When the time to move on to university arrived, it was completely natural that he chose to take a degree in Geology.

During all that time he was an outcast from the van der Byl family. He had seen none of them–not the Old Man, nor Tracey, nor even Benedict.

Then, in one long eventful afternoon, he saw all three of them. It was his final year at university. His degree was a certainty. He had headed the lists at every examination from his first year onwards. He had been elected the senior student of Stellenbosch University, but now there was a further honour almost within his grasp.

In ten days' time the national selectors would announce the rugby team to meet the New Zealand All Black touring team–and Johnny's place at flank forward was as certain as his degree in Geology.

The sporting press had nicknamed Johnny 'Jag Hond' after that ferocious predator of the African wilds, the Cape hunting dog; an animal of incredible stamina and determination that savages its prey on the run. The nickname had stuck fast, and Johnny was a favourite of the crowds.

In the line-up of the team from Cape Town University was another crowd-pleaser whose place in the national side to meet the All Blacks seemed equally assured. From his position at full back Benedict van der Byl dominated the field of play with a grace and artistry that was almost godlike. He had grown tall and wide-shouldered, with long powerful legs and dark brooding good looks.

Johnny led the visiting team out onto the smooth green velvet field, and while he jogged and flexed his back and shoulders he looked up at the packed stands seeking assurance that the high priests of rugby football were all there. He saw Doctor Danie Craven sitting with the other selectors in the privileged position below the Press enclosure. While in front of the Doctor, leaning back to exchange a few words with him, sat the Prime Minister.

This meeting between the two universities was one of the high spots of the rugby season, and the *aficionados* travelled thousands of miles to watch it.

The Prime Minister smiled and nodded, then leaned forward to touch the shoulder of the big white-headed figure that sat in the row below him.

Johnny felt an electric tingle run up his spine as the white head lifted and looked directly at him. It was the first time he had seen the Old Man in the seven years since that terrible night.

Johnny lifted his arm in salute, and the Old Man stared at him for long seconds before he turned away to speak with the Prime Minister.

Now the drum majorettes came out in ranks onto the field. White-booted, dressed in Cape Town University colours with short swinging skirts and tall hats, they high-stepped and paraded, lovely young girls flushed with excitement and exertion.

The roar of the crowd drummed with the blood in Johnny's ears, for Tracey van der Byl was leading the first rank. He knew her instantly, despite the passage of years in which she had grown to young womanhood. Her legs and arms were sun-bronzed and her dark hair hung glossily to her shoulders. She cavorted and kicked and stamped, shouting the traditional cheers, jiggling her firm young bottom with innocent abandon while the crowds screamed and writhed, beginning already to work themselves into an hysterical frenzy. Johnny watched Tracey. He stood completely still in the thunderous uproar. She was the most beautiful woman he had ever seen.

Then the show was over, the drum majorettes retreating back through the stadium entrance, and the home team trotted onto the field.

The presence of the Old Man and Tracey added intensity to the glare of hatred that Johnny turned on the tall white-clad figure that fell back to take control of the Cape Town back field.

Benedict van der Byl reached his position and turned. From inside his calf-length sock he took a comb and ran it through his dark hair. The crowd bellowed and whistled, loving this little theatrical gesture. Benedict returned the comb to his sock and posed with one hand on his hip, his chin lifted arrogantly as he surveyed the opposition.

Suddenly he intercepted Johnny's glare, and the pose altered as he dropped his eyes and shuffled his feet a little.

The whistle fluted, and play began. It was everything the crowds had hoped for, a match that would long be remembered and gloated over. Massive panzer offensives by the forwards, long probing raids by the backs with the oval ball flickering from hand to hand, until a bone-jarring tackle smashed the carrier to the turf. Hard and fast and clean play swung from side to side, a hundred times the crowd came up on its feet as one, eyes and mouths wide in screaming unbearable tension, to sink back with a groan as the ball was held by a desperate defence within inches of the goal line.

No score and three minutes of play left, Cape Town attacking from a set scrummage, driving through a gap in the defence and then putting the ball in the air with a long raking pass, taken cleanly by the Cape Town wing without a break in his stride. His feet twinkled across the green turf, and again the crowd came up with a gasp.

Johnny hit him low, just above the knee, with his shoulder. The two of them rolled together out of the field of play lifting a puff of white lime from the line and the crowd groaned and sank back.

While they waited to receive the throw, Johnny whispered hoarse orders. His gold and maroon jersey was soaked with sweat, and blood from a grazed hip stained his white shorts.

'Get it back fast. Don't run with it. Give it to Dawie. Kick high and deep, Dawie.'

Johnny leaped high to the flight of the thrown ball, with a bunched fist he punched it back accurately into Dawie's hands, at the same moment twisting his body to block the attackers.

Dawie fell back two paces and kicked. The power of the kick swung his right foot above his head, and the impetus flung him forward to put his forwards 'on side'.

The ball climbed slowly, flying like a dart with no wobble or roll in the air, reaching the zenith of its trajectory high over mid-field, then floating back to earth.

Twenty thousand heads followed its flight, a hush had fallen over the field—and in the unnatural silence Benedict van der Byl was drifting back deep into his own territory, anticipating the drop of the ball with deceptively unhurried strides, yet timing it with the precision of the gifted athlete.

The ball slotted neatly into his arms, and he began moving lazily infield to open his angle for the return kick. Still a tense throbbing mesmeric hush hung over the field, Benedict van der Byl was at the focus of attention.

'Jag Hond!' A single voice in the crowd alerted them, and twenty thousand heads swung downfield.

'Jag Hond!' A roar now. Johnny was well clear of the pack, arms pumping and legs churning as he bore down on Benedict. It was a futile effort, he could not hope to intercept a player of Benedict's calibre from such long range, yet Johnny was burning the last of the physical reserves in that charge. His face was a sweat-shining mask of determination, and clods of torn grass flew from under his savagely driving boots.

Then something happened which was unaccountable, almost past belief. Benedict van der Byl glanced round and saw Johnny. He broke his stride, two clumsy shuffling paces, and tried to pivot away deeper into his own ground. All the assurance had gone from his body, all the skill and grace. He tripped and stumbled, almost fell and the ball popped out of his hands, bouncing awkwardly.

Benedict scrambled after it, groping blindly, looking back over his shoulder. Now on his face was an expression of naked terror. Johnny was very close. Grunting at each stride like a gut-shot lion, massive shoulders already bunching for the strike, his lips drawn back into a murderous parody of a grin.

Benedict van der Byl dropped to his knees and covered his head with both arms, cringing down on to the green turf.

Johnny swept past him without a check, stooping easily in his run to gather the bouncing ball.

When Benedict uncovered his head and, still kneeling, looked up, Johnny stood ten yards away between the goal posts watching him. Then deliberately Johnny placed the ball between his feet to complete the formality of the touchdown.

Now, as if by agreement, both Johnny and Benedict looked towards the main grandstand. They saw the Old Man rise from his seat and make his way slowly through the ecstatic crowds towards the exit.

The day after the match, Johnny went back into the desert.

He was down in the bottom of a fifteen-foot prospect trench that had been dug across the grain of the country rock. It was oppressively hot in the confines of the trench and Johnny was stripped to a skimpy pair of khaki shorts, his sun-browned muscles oily with sweat, but he worked steadily at his sampling. He was establishing the contours and profile of an ancient marine terrace that the ages had buried beneath the sand. It was here on the bedrock that he expected to find the thin layer of diamond-bearing gravel.

He heard the jeep pull up at ground level above him, and the crunch of footsteps. Johnny straightened up and held his aching back muscles.

The Old Man stood at the edge of the trench and looked down at him. He held a folded newspaper in his hand. This was the first time Johnny had seen him at close range in all the years, and he was shocked at the change. The mass of bushy hair was so white, and his features were folded and creased like those of a mastiff, leaving the big hooked nose standing like a hillock from his face. But there was no wasting or deterioration in his body, and his eyes were still that chilling enigmatic blue.

He dropped the newspaper into the trench and Johnny caught it, still staring up at the Old Man.

'Read it!' said the Old Man. The paper was folded to the sports page, and the headline was thick and bold.

JAG HOND IN. VAN DER BYL OUT.

The shock was as delicious as the plunge into a mountain stream. He was in—he would carry the gold and green, and wear the leaping springbok on his blazer pocket.

He looked up, proud and happy, standing bare-headed in the sun waiting for the Old Man to speak.

'Make up your mind,' said the Old Man softly. 'do you want to play ball—or work for Van Der Byl Diamonds? You can't do both.' And he walked back to the jeep and drove away.

Johnny cabled his withdrawal from the team to the Doctor personally. The storm of outraged protest and abuse in the national Press, and the hundreds of viperous letters Johnny received accusing him of cowardice and treachery and worse made him thankful for the sanctuary of the desert.

Neither Johnny nor Benedict had ever played the game again. Thinking about it, even at this remove of time, Johnny felt the sting of disappointment. He had wanted that green and gold badge of honour so very deeply. Brusquely he pulled the Jaguar off the road and scanned the street map of London and found Stark Street tucked away off the King's Road. He drove on remembering how it had been after the Old Man had taken it from him. The agony of mind had been scarcely endurable.

His companions in the desert were Ovambo tribesmen from the north, and a few of those taciturn white men that the desert produces, as hardy and uncompromising as her vegetation or her mountain ranges.

The deserts of the Namib and the Kalahari are amongst the loneliest places on earth, and the desert nights are long. Not even the day's unremitting physical labour could tire Johnny sufficiently to drug his dreams of a lovely girl in a short white skirt and high boots—or an old white-headed man with a face like a granite cliff.

Out of those long days and longer nights came solid achievements to stand like milestones marking the road of his career. He brought in a new diamond field, small but rich, in country which no one else had believed would yield diamonds. He pegged a uranium lode which Van Der Byl Diamonds sold for two and a half millions, and there were other fruits from his efforts almost as valuable if not as spectacular.

At twenty-five, Johnny Lance's name was whispered in the closed and forbidding walls of the diamond industry as one of the bright young comers.

There were approaches—a junior partnership in a firm of consulting geologists, field manager for one of the struggling little companies working marginal ground in the Murderers' Karroo. Johnny turned them down. They were good offers, but he stayed on with the Old Man.

Then the big Company noticed him. A century ago the first payable pipe of 'blue ground' in Southern Africa was discovered on a hard scrabble farm owned by a Boer named De Beer. Old De Beer sold his farm for £6,000, never dreaming that a treasure worth £300,000,000 lay beneath the bleak dry earth. The strike was named De Beers New Rush, and a horde of miners, small businessmen, drifters, chancers, rogues and scoundrels moved in to purchase and work minute claims, each the size of a large room.

From this pretty company of fortune's soldiers two men rose high above the others, until between them they owned most of the claims in De Beers New Rush. When these two, Cecil John Rhodes and Barney Barnato, at last combined their resources, a formidable financial enterprise was born. From such humble beginnings the company has grown to awesome respectability and dignity. Its wealth is fabled, its influence immeasurable, its income is astronomical. It controls the diamond supply to the world. It controls also mineral concessions over areas of Central and Southern Africa which total hundreds of thousands of square miles, and its reserves of unmined precious and base minerals cannot be calculated. Small diamond companies are allowed to co-exist with the giant until they reach a certain size—then suddenly they become part of it, gobbled up as a tiger shark might swallow any of its pilot fish who become too large and daring. The big Company can afford to buy the best prospects, equipment—and men. It reached out one of its myriad tentacles to draw in Johnny Lance. The price they set on him was twice his present salary, and three times his future prospects.

Johnny turned it down flat. Perhaps the Old Man did not notice, perhaps it was mere coincidence that a week later Johnny was promoted Field Manager of Beach Operation. The nickname that went with the job was 'King Canute'.

Van Der Byl Diamonds had thirty-seven miles of beach concession. The tiny ribbon of shoreline, one hundred and twenty feet above high-water mark, and one hundred and twenty feet below low-water mark. Inland the concession belonged to the big Company. It had purchased the land, a dozen vast ranches, simply to obtain the mineral rights. The sea concession, territorial up to waters twelve miles off shore, belonged to them also. Granted to them by Government charter twenty years before. But Van Der Byl Diamonds had the Admiralty strip—and it was 'King Canute's' job to work it.

The sea-mist came smoking in like ground pearl dust off the cold waters of the Benguela current. From out of the mist bank the high unhurried swells marched in towards the bright yellow sands and the tall wave-cut cliffs of Namaqualand.

The swells peaked up sharply as they felt the land. Their crests trembled and turned luminous green, began to dissolve in plumes of wind-blown spray, arched over and slid down upon themselves in the roar and rumble of white water.

Johnny stood on the driver's seat of the open Land-Rover. He wore a sheepskin jacket against the chill of the dawn mist, but his head was bare and his dark hair fluttered nervously against his forehead in the wind.

His heavy jaw was thrust forward, and his hands in the pockets of the sheepskin jacket were balled into fists. He scowled aggressively as he measured the height and push of the surf. With his crooked nose he looked like a boxer waiting for the gong.

Suddenly with an awkward angry movement he jerked his left hand from his pocket and looked down at the dial of his wrist watch. Two hours and three minutes to low tide. He pushed his fist back into his pocket, and swivelled quickly to look at his bulldozers.

There were eleven of them, big bright yellow D8 Caterpillars, lined up along the high-water mark. The operators sat goggled and tense in their high stern seats. They were all watching him anxiously.

Beyond them, standing well back, were the earth-loaders. They were ungainly, pregnant-looking machines with swollen bellies, and heavily lugged tyres that stood taller than a man. When the time came they would rush in at thirty miles an hour, drop a steel blade beneath their bellies and scrape up a fifteen-ton load of sand or gravel, race back inland and drop their load, turn and rush back for another gargantuan bite cut of the earth.

Johnny was steeling himself, judging the exact moment in which to hurl a quarter of a million pounds' worth of machinery into the Atlantic Ocean, in the hope of recovering a handful of bright pebbles.

The moment came, and Johnny spent half a minute of precious time in scrutinizing his preparations before committing himself to action.

Then 'GO!' he shouted into his loudhailer and windmilled his right arm in the unmistakable command to advance.

'Go!' he shouted again, but his voice was lost. Even the sound of the wild surf was lost in the bull bellow of the diesels. Lowering their massive steel blades, a chorus line of steel monsters, they crawled forward.

Now the golden sand curled before the scooped blades, like butter from the knife. It built up before the monstrous machines, becoming a pile and then a high wall. Thrusting, pulling back, butting, worrying, the bulldozers swept the wall of sand forward. The arms of the operators pumping the handles of the controls like mad barmen drawing a thousand pints of beer, the diesels roaring and muttering and roaring again.

The wall of sand met the first low push of sea water up the beach and smothered it. In seeming astonishment and uncertainty the sea pulled back, swirling and creaming before the advancing dyke of sand.

The bulldozers were performing a complicated but smoothly practised ballet now. Weaving and crossing, blades lifting and falling, backing and advancing, all under the supervision of the master choreographer, Johnny Lance.

The Land-Rover darted back and forward along the edge of the huge pit that was forming, with Johnny roaring orders and instructions through the electric loud-hailer.

Gradually a sickle-shaped dyke of sand was thrown out into the sea, while behind it the bulldozer blades cut down, six, ten, fifteen feet through the loose yellow sand.

Then suddenly they hit the oyster line, that thin layer of fossilized oyster shell that so often covers the diamond gravels of South West Africa.

Johnny saw the change in the character of his pit, saw the shell curling from the blades of the bulldozers.

With half a dozen orders and hand signals he had his 'dozers flatten a ramp at each end of his pit, to give the earthloaders access. Then he ordered them away to hold the dyke against the sea.

He glanced at his watch. 'One hour thirteen minutes,' he muttered. 'We're running tight!'

Quickly he checked his pit. Two hundred yards long, fifteen feet deep, the overburden of sand stripped away, the oyster line showing clean and white in the sun, the bulldozers clear of the pit bottom—fighting back the sea.

'Right,' he grunted. 'Let's see what we've got.'

He turned to face the two earthloaders waiting expectantly above the high-water mark.

'Go in and get it!' he shouted, and gave the windmill arm signal.

Nose to tail the earthloaders roared forward, swinging wide at the head of the pit, then swooping down the ramp and dashing along the bottom. They scooped up a load of shell and gravel without checking their speed and went bellowing up the far ramp, swinging again to race up and deposit their load below the cliff, but above the high-water mark.

Round they went, and round again, chasing their tails, while the bulldozers held back the sea which was now becoming angry—sending its cohorts to skirmish along the dyke, seeking a weak place to attack.

Johnny glanced at his watch.

'Three minutes to low water,' he spoke aloud, and grinned. 'We're going to make it–I think!'

He lit a cigarette, relaxing a little now. He dropped into the driving seat and swung the Land-Rover up the beach, parking it beyond the mountain of gravel that the earth loaders were building.

He climbed out and took up a handful of the gravel.

'Lovely!' he whispered. 'Oh sweet! Sweet!'

It was right. All the signs were good. In the single handful he identified a small garnet, and a larger lump of agate.

He scooped another handful.

'Jasper,' he gloated. 'And banded ironstone!'

All these stones were the team-mates of the diamond, you found them together.

The shape was right also, the stones polished round and shiny as marbles, not flattened like coins which would mean they had washed in only one direction. Round stones meant a wave action zone–a diamond trap!

'We've hit a jewel box–I'll take Lysol on that!'

From thirty-seven miles of beach Johnny had picked a two-hundred yard stretch, and hit it right on the nose. A choice not by luck, but by careful study of the configuration of the coastline, aerial photographs of the wave patterns and bottom contours of the sea, an analysis of the beach sands, and finally by that indefinable 'feel' for ground that a good diamond man has.

Johnny Lance was mightily delighted with himself as he climbed back into the Land-Rover. The earthloaders had scraped the gravel down to bed-rock. Their job was finished, and they pulled out of the pit and stood with panting exhausts beside the enormous pile of gravel they had recovered.

'Bottom boys!' roared Johnny, and the patient army of Ovambo tribesmen who had been squatting about the beach came swarming down into the pit. Their job was to sweep and clean the pit bottom, for a high proportion of the diamonds would have worked their way down through the gravel into the crevices and irregularities of the bed-rock.

The sea changed its mood, furious at the brutal rape of its beaches it came hissing and tearing at the sand dyke. The tide was making now, and the bulldozers had to redouble their efforts to keep it out.

In the pit the Ovambos worked in a frenzy of activity, sparing only an occasional apprehensive glance for the wall of sand that held the Atlantic at bay.

Now Johnny was tensing up again. If he pulled them out early he would be leaving diamonds down there, if he left them in too late he might drown machinery–and men.

He cut it fine, just a fraction too fine. He pulled the bottom boys out with the sea beginning to break over the dyke, and to seep through under it.

Then he began to pull out his bulldozers, ten of them out–one still coming infinitely slowly, waddling across the wide bottom of the empty pit.

The sea broke through, it broke simultaneously in two places and came boiling into the pit in a waist-high wave.

The bulldozer operator saw it, hesitated one second, then his spirit failed him and he jumped down from his machine; abandoning it to the sea he sprinted ahead of the wave, making for the steep nearest side of the pit.

'Bastard!' swore Johnny as he watched the operator scramble to safety. 'He could have made it.' But his anger was against himself also. His decision to withdraw had been too long delayed, that was £20,000 worth of machinery he had sacrificed to the sea.

He slammed the Land-Rover into gear, and put her to the pit. She went off the edge like a ski jump, falling fifteen feet before she hit the bottom, but her fall was cushioned by the slope of sand and she sprang forward bravely to meet the rush of sea water.

It broke over the bonnet, slewing the vehicle viciously, but Johnny fought her head round and kept her going towards the stranded bulldozer.

The engine of the Land-Rover had been sealed and waterproofed against just such an emergency, and now she ploughed forward throwing a sheet of water to each side. But her forward rush faltered as the green water poured over her.

Now suddenly the entire sand dyke collapsed under the white surf and the Atlantic took control. The tall wave of green water that raced across the pit hit the Land-Rover, upending her, throwing Johnny into the jubilant frothing water, while the Land-Rover rolled over on her back, pointing all four wheels to the sky in surrender.

Johnny went under but came up immediately. Half swimming, half wading, battered by the boisterous sea, he struggled on towards the yellow island of steel.

The sea struck him down, and he went under again. Found his feet for a moment, then had them cut from under him once more.

Then suddenly he had reached the bulldozer and was dragging himself up over the tracks to the driver's seat. He was coughing and vomiting sea water, as he reached the controls.

The bulldozer sat immovable, held down by her own twenty-six tons of dead weight on to the hard bed-rock of the pit. Although the sea burst over her, and swirled through her tracks, it could not move her.

Through eyes blurred and swimming with salt water and his own tears, Johnny briefly checked the gauges on the instrument panels. She had oil pressure and engine revs, and high above his head the exhaust pipe chugged blue smoke.

Johnny coughed again. Vomit and sea water shot up his throat in a scalding jet, but he pushed the throttle wide and threw in both clutch levers.

Ponderously the great machine ground forward, almost contemptuously shouldering the sea aside, her tracks solidly gripping the bed-rock.

Johnny looked about him quickly. The sand ramps at each end of the pit were washed away. The sides were sheer now, and behind him the sea was rushing unimpeded into the pit.

A wave broke over his head, and Johnny shook the water from his hair like a spaniel and looked around with mounting desperation for an avenue of escape.

With a shock of surprise he saw the Old Man. He had thought him to be four hundred miles away in Cape Town, but here he was on the edge of the pit. The white hair shone like a beacon.

Instinctively Johnny swung the bulldozer towards him, crawling through the turbulent waters towards him.

The Old Man was directing two of the other bulldozers, reversing them as close as he dared to the lip of the bank of sand, while from the service truck parked below the cliff a line of Ovambos came staggering down the beach with the heavy tractor tow chain over their shoulders. They shuffled bow-legged under the tremendous weight of the chain, sinking ankle deep into the sand with each step.

The Old Man roared at them, urging them on, but the words were lost in the thunder of diesel engines and the ranting of the wind and the sea. Now he turned back to Johnny.

'Get her in close,' the Old Man yelled through cupped hands. 'I'll bring the end of the chain down to you!'

Johnny waved an acknowledgement, then grabbed at the controls as the force of the next wave pushed even the giant tractor off its line, and Johnny felt the diesel falter for the first time—the water had found its way through the seals at last.

Then he was under the high bank of yellow sand that towered twenty feet above him and he scrambled forward over the engine bonnet to meet the Old Man.

The Old Man was poised on the lip of the pit with the end of the chain draped in a loop over both shoulders. He was stooped beneath its weight, and when he stepped forward the sand crumpled away beneath him and he came sliding and slipping down the steep incline, buried waist deep, the great chain snaking after him.

Judging the rush of the sea, Johnny jumped down to help him. Together, battered by the sea, they dragged the chain to the bulldozer.

'Fix it on to the blade arm,' grunted the Old Man, and they got a double turn of chain around the thick steel arm.

'Shackle!' Johnny snapped at him, and while the Old Man untied the length of rope which secured the steel shackle around his waist, Johnny looked up at the cliff of sand that hung over them.

'Christ!' he said softly, the sea was attacking it—and now it was soft and trembling above them, ready to collapse and smother them.

The Old Man passed him the huge shackle, and Johnny began with numbed hands to secure the end of the chain. He must pass the thick case-hardened pin through two links and then screw it closed. It was a herculean task under these conditions, with the surf bursting over his head, the drag of the sea on the chain, and the cliff of sand threatening to fall on them at any moment. From twenty feet above them Johnny's foreman was watching anxiously, ready to pass the word to the two waiting bulldozers to throw their combined weights on the chain.

The thread of the pin caught, half a dozen turns would secure it, he would have finished the job by the time the word was passed to the 'dozer operators.

'Okay,' he nodded and gasped at the Old Man. 'Pull!'

The Old Man lifted his head and bellowed up the bank.

'Pull!'

The foreman acknowledged with a wave.

'Okay.' And his head disappeared behind the bank as he ran back to the bulldozers, and at that moment the surf swung the chain. A movement of a few inches, but enough to catch Johnny's left index finger between two of the links.

The Old Man saw his face, saw his struggling to free himself.

'What is it?'

Then the water sucked back, for a moment, and he saw what had happened. He waded forward to help—but from above them came the throaty roar of the diesels and the chain began running away, snaking and twisting up the bank like a python.

The Old Man reached Johnny and caught him about the shoulders to steady him. They braced themselves in horror, staring at the captive hand.

The chain jerked taut, severing the finger cleanly in a bright burst of scarlet, and Johnny reeled back into the Old Man's arms. The great yellow bulk of the bulldozer was dragged relentlessly down on top of them, threatening to crush them both, but using the next break and push of the sea the Old Man dragged Johnny clear—and they were carried sideways along the bank, tumbled helplessly by the strength of the water out of the bulldozer's path.

Johnny clutched his injured hand to his chest, but it hosed a bright stream of blood that discoloured the water about them. His head went under and salt water shot down his throat into his lungs. He felt himself drowning, the strength oozing out of him.

He surfaced again, and through bleary eyes saw the glistening wet bulldozer half-way up the sand bank. He felt the Old Man's arms about his chest and he went under again relaxing as the darkness closed over his eyes and brain.

When the darkness cleared from his eyes, he was lying on the dry sand of the beach and the first thing he saw was the Old Man's face above him, furrowed and pouched, his silver white hair plastered across his forehead.

'Did we get her out?' Johnny asked quickly.

'Ja,' the Old Man answered. 'We got her out.' And he stood up, walked to the jeep, and drove away, leaving the foreman to tend to Johnny.

Johnny grinned at the memory, and lifting his left hand off the driving-wheel of the Jaguar he licked the shiny stump of his index finger.

'It was worth a finger,' he murmured aloud, and still searching for road signs he drove on slowly.

He smiled again comfortably, shaking his head with amusement as he remembered his hurt and disappointment when the Old Man had walked away and left him lying on the beach. He had not expected the Old Man to fall on his shoulders sobbing his gratitude and begging forgiveness for all the years of misery and loneliness—but he had expected something more than that.

After a two-hundred mile round jeep-journey through the desert night to the nearest hospital where they had trimmed and bound the stump, Johnny was back at the workings the next day in time to watch the first run of gravel from the beach.

In his absence, the gravel had been screened to sieve off all the over-size rock and stone, then it had been puddled through a tank of silicon mud to float off all the material with a specific gravity less than 2·5, then finally what was left had been run through a ball mill—a long steel cylinder containing steel balls the size of a baseball. The cylinder revolved continually and the steel balls crushed to powder all substance softer than 4 on Mohs hardness scale.

Now there was a residue, a thousandth part of the gravel they had won from the sea. In this remainder would be the diamonds—if diamonds there were.

When Johnny arrived back at the shed of galvanized iron and wood on the cliff above the beach that housed his separation plant, he was still half groggy from the anaesthetic and lack of sleep.

His hand throbbed with the persistence of a lighthouse, his eyes were reddened and a thick black stubble covered his jaws.

He went to stand beside the grease table that filled half the shed. He was swaying a little on his feet, as he looked around at the preparations. The massive bin at the head of the table was filled with the concentrated diamond gravels, the plates greased down, and his crew was standing ready.

'Let's go!' Johnny nodded at his foreman, who immediately threw in the lever that set the table shaking like an old man with palsy.

The table was a series of steel plates, each slightly inclined and thickly coated with dirty yellow grease. From the bin at the head of the shuddering table a mixture of gravel and water begun to dribble, its consistency and rate of flow carefully regulated by the foreman. It spread all over the greased table like spilled treacle, dropping from one plate to the next, and finally into the waste bin at the end of the table.

A diamond is unwettable, immerse it in water, scrub it–but it comes out dry. A coat of grease on a steel plate is also unwettable, so wet gravel and sea shell will slide over it and keep moving across the agitating, sloping table.

But a diamond when it hits grease sticks like a half-sucked toffee to a woollen blanket.

In the excitement and anxiety of the moment Johnny felt his weariness recede, even the pain in his stump was muted by it. His eyes and whole attention were fastened on that glistening yellow sheet of grease.

The little stuff under a carat in weight, or the industrial black diamond and boart would not be visible on the table; the agitation was too rapid–blurring with speed, and the flow of loose material would disguise them.

So complete was his absorption that it was some seconds before he was aware of a presence beside him. He glanced up quickly.

The Old Man was there, standing with the wide stance and tension-charged attitude that was his own special way.

Johnny was acutely conscious of the Old Man's bulk beside him–and he felt the first flicker of alarm. What if this was a barren run? He needed diamonds now–as he had never needed anything in his life. He scanned the blurring plates of yellow grease, seeking the purchase price that could buy back the Old Man's esteem. The speckled gravel flowed imperturbably across the plates, and Johnny felt a flutter of panic.

Then from across the table the foreman let out a whoop, and pointed.

'Thar she blows!'

Johnny's eyes darted to the head of the table. There beneath the outlet from the bin, half buried in the thick grease by its own weight, anchored solidly while the worthless gravel washed past it, was a diamond.

A big fat five-carat thing, that glowed sulky and yellow, like a wild animal resenting its captivity.

Johnny sighed softly and darted a sideways glance at the Old Man. The Old Man was watching the table without expression, and though he must have been conscious of Johnny's scrutiny, he did not look up. Johnny's eyes were dragged irresistibly back to the table.

By some freakish chance, the next diamond fell from the bin directly onto the one already anchored in the grease.

When diamond strikes diamond it bounces like a golf ball off a tarmac road.

The second diamond, a white beauty the size of a peach pip, clicked loudly as it struck the other then spun head high in the air.

Both Johnny and the foreman laughed involuntarily with delight at the beauty of that twinkling drop of solid sunlight.

Johnny reached across the table with his good hand, and snatched it out of the air. He rubbed it between his fingers–revelling in the soapy feel of it, then turned and offered it to the Old Man.

The Old Man looked at the diamond, nodded in acknowledgement. Then he pulled back the cuff of his coat and checked his wrist watch.

'It's late. I must get back to Cape Town.'

'Won't you stay for the rest of the run, sir?' Johnny realized his tone was too eager. 'We could have a drink together afterwards.' He remembered after he had spoken, that the Old Man abhorred alcohol.

'No.' The Old Man shook his head. 'I have to get back by this evening.' Now he looked steadily into Johnny's eyes. 'You see, Tracey is getting married tomorrow afternoon and I must be there.'

Then he smiled, watching Johnny's face, but nobody could ever guess the meaning of a smile on the Old Man's lips—for it never showed in his eyes.

'Didn't you know?' he asked, still smiling. 'I thought you had received an invitation.' And he went out of the shed to where his jeep stood in the bright sunshine waiting to take him out to the aircraft landing-strip among the sand dunes.

The pain in his injured hand, and the Old Man's words denied Johnny the sleep he so desperately needed, but it was two o'clock in the morning before he threw back his blankets and lit the lamp beside his camp bed.

'He said I had been invited—and, by God, I'll be there.'

He drove through the night, and the next morning. The first two hundred miles were on desert tracks of sand and stone, then he reached the metalled highway in the dawn and turned south across the great plains and over the mountains. It was noon before he saw the squat blue silhouette of Table Mountain on the skyline dwarfing the city that huddled beneath it.

He checked in at the Vineyard Hotel, and hurried to his room to bath and shave and change into a suit.

The grounds of the old house were crowded with expensive automobiles, and the overflow was parked along both sides of the street outside, but he found a space for the dusty Land-Rover. He walked up through the white gates and across the green lawns.

There was a band playing in the house, and a hubbub of voices and laughter drifted out through the windows of the ballroom.

He went in through the side door. The passages were thronged with guests, and he made his way amongst them seeking a familiar face in the groups of loud-voiced gesticulating men and giggling women. At last he found one.

'Michael.' And Michael Shapiro looked round, recognized him and letting the conflicting emotions of pleasure, surprise and alarm show clearly on his face.

'Johnny. It's good to see you.'

'Is the ceremony over?'

'Yes, and the speeches also—thank God.' He took Johnny's arm and led him aside. 'Let me get you a glass of champagne.' Michael hailed a waiter and put a crystal glass into Johnny's hand.

'Here's to the bride,' Johnny murmured and drank.

'Does the Old Man know you are here?' Michael came out with the question that was burning his mouth, and when Johnny shook his head, Michael's expression became thoughtful.

'What's he like, Michael, Tracey's husband?'

'Kenny Hartford?' Michael considered the question. 'He's all right, I suppose. Nice-looking boy, plenty of money.'

'What's he do for a crust of bread?'

'His daddy left him the whole loaf—but to fill in the time he does fashion photography.' And Johnny pulled down the corners of his mouth.

Michael frowned. 'He's all right, Johnny. The Old Man picked him carefully.'

'The Old Man?' Johnny's jaw thrust out.

'Of course, you know him—he wouldn't leave an important decision like that to anybody else.'

Johnny finished his champagne in silence, and Michael watched his face anxiously.

'Where is she? Have they left yet?'

'No.' Michael shook his head. 'They're still in the ballroom.'

'Thanks, Michael. I think I'll go and wish luck to the bride.'

'Johnny.' Michael caught hold of his elbow. 'Don't do anything stupid—will you?'

Johnny stood at the head of the marble staircase that led down into the ballroom. The floor was crowded with dancing couples and the music was loud and merry. The bridal party sat at a raised table across the floor.

Benedict van der Byl saw Johnny first. His face flushed and he leaned quickly to whisper to the Old Man, then began to rise from his seat. The Old Man placed a restraining hand on Benedict's shoulder, and smiled across the room at Johnny.

Johnny went down the stairs and made his way through the dancers. Tracey had not seen him. She was talking to the silky-faced young man who sat beside her. He had wavy blond hair.

'Hello, Tracey.' She looked up at Johnny and caught her breath. She was more beautiful than he remembered.

'Hello, Johnny.' Her voice was almost a whisper.

'May I dance with you?' She was pale now, and her eyes went to the Old Man, not to her new husband. The gleaming white bush of hair nodded slightly, and Tracey stood up.

They made one circuit of the dance floor before the band stoppped playing. Johnny had planned a hundred different things to say to her, but he was dumb until the music ended and the opportunity was passing.

Hurriedly now in the few seconds that were left Johnny told her:

'I hope you will be happy, Tracey. But if you ever need help—ever—I will come, I promise you that.'

'Thank you.' Her voice was husky, and for a moment she looked like the little girl who had cried in the night. Then he took her back to her husband.

The promise had been made five years ago, and now he had come to London to honour it.

Number 23 Stark Street was a neat double-storied cottage with a narrow front. He parked outside it. It was dark now and lights burned on both floors. He sat in the parked Jaguar, suddenly reluctant to go farther. Somehow he knew that Tracey was here, and he knew it would not be pretty. For a moment he recaptured the image of her as a lovely young woman in a wedding dress of white satin, then he climbed out of the Jaguar and went up the steps to the front door. He reached for the bell before he noticed with surprise that the door was ajar. He pushed it open and walked into a small sitting-room furnished with feminine taste.

The room had been hastily ransacked, one of the curtains was spread on the floor and on it were piled books and ornaments. Pictures had been taken down from the walls and stacked ready for removal.

Johnny picked up one of the books, and opened the cover. On the fly leaf was a handwritten name. 'Tracey van der Byl'. He dropped it back on the pile as he heard footsteps on the stairs from the floor above.

A man came down the stairs. He was dressed in soiled green velvet trousers, sheepskin boots, and shabby frock coat of military cut frogged with tarnished gold braid. He was carrying an armful of women's dresses.

He saw Johnny and stopped nervously, his pink lips opened in vacant surprise but his eyes were beady and bright under the thatch of lank blond hair.

'Hello,' Johnny smiled pleasantly. 'Are you moving out?' And he drifted quietly closer to the man on the stairs and stood looking up at him.

Suddenly from the floor above a low wail echoed down the stairs. It was an eerie sound, without passion or pain, as though steam were escaping from a jet, only just recognizable as human. Johnny went rigid at the sound, and the man on the stairs glanced nervously over his shoulder.

'What have you done to her?' Johnny asked softly, without menace.

'No. Nothing! She's on a trip. A bad trip.' The man's denial was frantic. 'It's her first time on acid.'

'So you're cleaning the place out, are you?' Johnny asked mildly.

'She owes me plenty. She can't pay. She promised—and she can't pay.'

'Oh,' said Johnny. 'That's different. I thought you were hitting the place.' He reached into his overcoat and brought out his wallet, riffling the wad of banknotes. 'I'm a friend of hers. How much does she owe you?'

'Fifty nicker.' The man's eyes sparkled when he saw the wallet. 'I gave her credit.'

Johnny counted off ten fivers, and held them out. The man dropped the bundle of clothing over the banisters and came eagerly down the last few stairs.

'Did you sell her the stuff—the acid?' Johnny asked, and the man stopped a pace from him, his expression stiffening with suspicion.

'Oh, for God's sake.' Johnny grinned. 'We are not children—I know the score.' He offered the banknotes. 'Did you get the stuff for her?'

The man grinned back at him weakly, and nodded as he reached for the money. Johnny's free hand snapped closed on the thin wrist and he swung him off his feet, forcing his wrist up between his shoulder-blades.

Johnny stuffed the money into his pocket, and marched him up the stairs.

'Let's go and have a look, shall we?'

There was a mattress on the iron bedstead covered with a grey Army blanket. Tracey sat cross-legged on the blanket. She wore only a thin cotton slip and her hair hung lank and lustreless to her waist. Her arms crossed over her chest were thin and white as sticks of chalk. Her face also was pale, the skin translucent in the light of the electric bulb. She was rocking gently back and forth and wailing softly, her breath steaming in the icy cold room.

It was her eyes that shocked Johnny the most. They seemed to have expanded to an enormous size, and beneath each was a dark bruised-looking smear. The pupils of the eyes were distended and glittery with the same adamant sheen as uncut diamonds.

The big glittery green eyes fastened on Johnny and the man in the doorway, and the wail rose abruptly to a shriek. The shriek died away, and she bowed forward and buried her face in her hands covering her eyes.

'Tracey,' said Johnny softly. 'Oh God, Tracey!'

'She'll be all right,' the man whimpered and twisted in his grip. 'It's the first time—she'll be all right.'

'Come.' Johnny dragged him out of the room, and pushed the door closed with his foot. He held him against the wall, and his face was set and pale, his eyes merciless—but he spoke quietly, patiently as though he was explaining to a child.

'I'm going to hurt you now. I'm going to hurt you very badly. Just as badly as I can without killing you. Not because I enjoy it, but because that girl is a very special person to me. In the future when you think about giving poison to another girl—I want you to remember what I did to you tonight.'

Johnny held him with his left hand against the wall and he used his right hand, punching up under the ribs at an angle to tear the stomach muscles. With three or four blows he was too high, and he felt ribs crack and snap under his fist.

When he stepped back the man sagged slowly face forward, and Johnny caught him cleanly in the mouth snapping his teeth off at the gums, splitting his lips open like the petals of a rose. The man had made a lot of noise. Johnny looked into Tracey's room to make sure she had not been disturbed, but she was still bowed forward, rocking rhythmically on her haunches.

He found the bathroom and dampened his handkerchief to wipe the blood off his hands and the front of his overcoat. He came out into the passage again and stooped over the unconscious body to check the pulse. It was strong and regular, and he felt a lift of relief as he dragged the man's face out of the puddle of his own vomit and blood to prevent him drowning.

He went through to Tracey and, despite her frantic struggles, wrapped her in the greasy Army blanket and carried her down to the Jaguar.

She quietened down and lay like a sleeping child in the back seat while he tucked the blanket round her, then he went back into the house and phoned 999, giving the address and hanging up immediately.

He left Tracey in the car outside the Dorchester, while he went in to speak to the reception clerk. Within minutes Tracey was in a wheelchair on her way up to the two-bedroom suite on the second floor. The doctor was there fifteen minutes later.

After the doctor had gone Johnny bathed, and carrying a tumbler of Chivas Regal in one hand he went into Tracey's room and stood by her bed. Whatever the doctor had given her had put her out cleanly. She lay gaunt and pale—yet with a strangely fragile beauty that seemed enhanced by the bruised discoloration of her eye sockets.

He stooped to brush the hair from her cheek, and her breath was light and warm on his hand. He felt such an infinity of tenderness for her then as he had never known for any other person, he was amazed by the strength of it.

He stooped over her and gently brushed her lips with his own. Her lips were dry and flaky white, and their touch was harsh as sandpaper.

Johnny straightened up and went to the armchair across the room. He sank into it wearily, and sipped the whisky, feeling its warmth spread from his belly and untie the knots in his muscles. He watched the pale ruined face on the pillows.

'We are in a hell of a mess, you and I,' he spoke aloud, and felt anger again. For long minutes it was undirected, but slowly it jelled and found an object to focus on.

For the first time in his life he was angry with the Old Man.

'He has brought you to this,' he said to the girl on the bed. 'And me—'

The reaction was swift, his loyalty was a thing grown part of his existence. Always he had trained himself to believe that the Old Man's machinations were just and wise—even if at times the justice and wisdom were hidden from him. Mortal man does not doubt the omnipotence of his gods.

Sickened by his own treachery, he began to examine the Old Man's motives and actions under the bright light of reason.

Why had the Old Man sent Michael Shapiro to fetch him out of the desert?

'He wants you in Cape Town, Johnny. Benedict didn't measure up. The Old Man has given him the London Office, it's a form of exile. He's picked you to take over the Company,' Michael explained. 'Tracey is out of the way. She and her husband are in London also. I guess the Old Man thinks it's safe to have you back in Cape Town now.'

Michael watched Johnny's undisguised joy and went on slowly.

'I'm speaking out of turn, perhaps. Mr van der Byl is a strange man. He's not like other people. I know how you feel about him, I've watched it all, you know—but listen, Johnny, you can go anywhere on your own now. There are a lot of other companies that want you—' But he had seen the expression on Johnny's face, and stopped '—okay, Johnny. Forget I ever said it. I only spoke because I like you.'

Thinking on it now, there had been substance in Michael's warning. Certainly he was General Manager of Van Der Byl Diamonds, but he was no nearer to the Old Man than he had ever been. He lived under the mountain but the mountain was remote and he had not been able to scale the lowest slopes.

He had found the city as lonely as the desert, and he was ripe for the first attractive woman who set her snares for him.

Ruby Grange was tall and slim with hair the colour they call 'Second Cape' in a diamond, like sunlight through a crystal glass of champagne.

He wondered now at his own naïvety. That he should be so easily misled, and should have rushed so headlong into her web. After the wedding she had revealed herself, exposing the deeply calculating greed, the driving hunger for flattery and material possessions which was her main-spring, and her complete absorption with herself—Johnny had not been able to believe it. For months he fought off the growing certainty until it could be denied no longer, and he looked with chilled dismay on the shallow selfish little creature he had married.

He had withdrawn from her and flung all his energies into the Company.

This, then, was his life and he saw that it was an empty thing, hollowed out by the Old Man's hand.

For the first time his mind skirted the idea that it was a carefully calculated and sadistic revenge for the innocent action of a half-grown boy.

As though it were an escape from thoughts too dreadful to be borne, he fell asleep in the chair and the glass fell from his hand.

Jacobus Isaac van der Byl sat in a leather chair before the X-ray viewer. Fear had blasted the granite of his features, leaving them cracked and sagging, recognizable but subtly altered below the gleaming white mane.

Fear was in his eyes also, moving below the surface like slimy water creatures in the pale blue pools. With the fear chilling and numbing his limbs he watched the cloudy and swirling images on the screen.

The specialist was talking softly, impersonally as though he were lecturing one of this classes.

'—enveloping the thymus here, and extending beyond the trachea.'

The point of his gold pencil followed the ghostly outline on the screen. The Old Man swallowed with an effort. it seemed to be swelling in his throat as he listened, and his voice was hoarse and blurred to his own ears.

'You will operate?' he asked, and the specialist paused in his explanation. He glanced at the surgeon across the desk. The exchange was as guilty as that of conspirators.

The Old Man swivelled his chair and faced the surgeon.

'Well?' he demanded harshly.

'No.' The surgeon shook his head apologetically. 'It's too late. If only you had—'

'How long?' The Old Man overrode his explanation.

'Six months, not more.'

'You are certain?'

'Yes.'

The Old Man's chin sank onto his chest and he closed his eyes. There was complete silence in the room, they watched him with professional pity and interest as he reached his own personal acceptance of death.

At last the Old Man opened his eyes and stood up slowly. He tried to smile but his lips would not hold the shape.

'Thank you, gentlemen,' he croaked in this new rough voice. 'Will you excuse me, please. There are many things to arrange now.'

He went down to where the Rolls waited at the entrance. He walked slowly, shuffling his feet and the chauffeur came to him quickly, but the Old Man shrugged away his helping hands and climbed into the back seat of the car.

Michael Shapiro was waiting for him in the study of the big house. He saw the change in him immediately and jumped up from his chair. The Old Man stood in the doorway, his body seemed to have shrunk.

'Six months,' he said. 'They gave me six months.' He went to his desk and sat in the chair behind it.

'After all the money they've taken from me.' He said it as though he had expected to buy off death, and they had tricked him. He closed his eyes again, and when he opened them there was a glint of cunning in them, even his face had a pinched foxy look to it.

'Where is he? Is he back yet?'

'Yes, the Boeing got in at nine this morning. He's at the office now.' Michael was shocked, it was the first time he had seen the Old Man without the mask.

'And the girl?' He had not called her 'daughter' since the divorce.

'Johnny has her in a private nursing-home.'

'Worthless slut,' said the Old Man softly, and Michael stilled the protest before it reached his lips. 'Get your pad. I want you to take something down.' The Old Man chuckled hoarsely. 'We'll see!' he said, making it sound like a threat. 'We'll see!'

Johnny's doctor was waiting at Cape Town airport.

'Take her, Robin. Dry her out, and fatten her up. She's up to her gills with drugs and she probably hasn't eaten for a month.'

Tracey showed her first spark of spirit.

'Where do you think—'

'Into a nursing-home.' Johnny anticipated her questions. 'For as long as is necessary.'

'I'm not—'

'Oh, yes, you bloody well are.' He took her arm, and Robin grabbed the other. They walked her, still protesting weakly to the car park.

'Thanks, Robin, Old Soldier, give her the full workout.'

'I'll send her back to you like new,' Robin promised and drove away. Johnny took a few moments to look at the massive squat silhouette of the mountain—his own private home-coming ceremony. Then he fetched the Mercedes from the airport garage, and hesitated between home or the office, decided he was not up to an interrogation from Ruby and chose the office. He kept a clean shirt and shaving tackle in his private bathroom there.

They descended on him like a tribe of man-eating Amazons as he came in through the glass doors into the lusciously furnished and carpeted reception area of Van Der Byl Diamonds head office.

The two pretty little receptionists began yipping joyfully in chorus.

'Oh, Mr Lance, I have a whole sheaf of messages—'

'Oh, Mr Lance, your wife—'

Trying not to run he made it to within ten feet of his own door, when the Old Man's secretary popped out of ambush from behind the frosted-glass panel.

'Mr Lance, where on earth have you been? Mr van der Byl has been asking—'

Which alerted Lettie Pienaar, his own secretary.

'Mr Lance, thank goodness you're back.'

Johnny stopped and held up his hands in an attitude of surrender.

'One at a time, ladies. There is enough to go round—don't panic.'

Which broke the reception team into a quivering jelly of giggles, and sent the Old Man's watchdog back behind her panel sniffing disgustedly.

'Which is the most important, Lettie?' he asked as he went to his desk and flipped through his mail, shrugged out of his coat and began stripping tie and shirt as he headed for his bathroom.

They shouted at each other through the open door of the bathroom, as Johnny shaved quickly and showered, Lettie bringing him up to date on every aspect of Company and domestic business.

'Mrs Lance has phoned regularly. She called me a liar when I told her you were at Cartridge Bay.' Lettie was silent a moment, then as Johnny came out of the bathroom she asked, 'By the way, where have you been?'

'Don't *you* start that.' Johnny stood over the desk, and began flipping through the accumulated papers. 'Get my wife on the phone, please—no, hold it. Tell her I'll be home at seven.'

Lettie saw she had lost his attention, and she stood and went out. Johnny settled down behind his desk.

Van Der Byl Diamonds was a sick company. Despite Johnny's protests the Old Man had been drawing off its reserves and feeding them into his other ventures—the property-developing company, the clothing factory, Van Der Byl fisheries, the big irrigation scheme on the Orange river—and now the cupboard was almost bare.

The beach concessions were reaching the end of a short but glorious life. They were starting to work break-even ground. The Old Man had sold the Huib Hoch concession to the big Company for a quick profit—but the profit had been just as quickly transferred out of Johnny's control.

There was only one really fat goose left in his pen, and it wasn't laying eggs yet.

Eighteen months earlier Johnny had purchased two offshore diamond grounds from a company which had died in attempting to work them. It had been strangled by its own inefficiency.

Taking diamonds from the sea is about eight times more expensive than working them from a dry open-cast. One must dredge the gravel from the wild and unpredictable waters of the Skeleton Coast, load it into dumb barges, tow the barges to a safe base, off-load it and then begin the recovery process—or rather, that was the method the defunct company had attempted.

Johnny had dreamed up, and then ordered a vessel which was completely self-contained. It could lie out at sea, suck up the gravel and process it, spilling the waste gravel back into the sea as rapidly as it was sucked aboard. It was fitted with a sophisticated recovery plant that was completely computerized and contained within the ocean-going hull. It needed only a small crew, and it could work in all weather conditions short of a full tornado.

The *Kingfisher* was lying at Portsmouth dockyards rapidly nearing completion. Her trials were scheduled for early August.

Financing the building of this vessel had been a nightmare for Johnny. The Old Man had been unhelpful, when he wasn't being downright obstructive. He never discussed the venture without that little smile twitching at his lips. He had restricted Van Der Byl Diamonds' monetary involvement in the project so severely that Johnny had been forced to raise two millions outside the Company.

He had found the money, and the Old Man had smiled again.

Kingfisher should have been lying on the grounds three months ago, sucking up diamonds. The whole financial structure of the scheme was based on her completion on schedule, but *Kingfisher* was running six months behind and now the foundations were shivering.

Sitting at his desk Johnny was working out how to shore up the whole edifice and keep it from collapsing before he could get *Kingfisher* working. The creditors were rumbling and creaking, and Johnny had only his own enthusiasm and reputation left to keep them quiet.

Now he must ask them to defer their interest payments for another three months. He picked up the telephone.

'Get me Mr Larsen at Credit Finance,' he said, steeling himself as he did so, jutting out his jaw and thrusting one bunched fist into his coat pocket.

At five o'clock he stood up from his desk and went to the cabinet. He poured three fingers of whisky and went back to lower himself wearily into his swivel chair. He felt no elation at having won another reprieve, he was too tired.

The unlisted telephone on his desk rang and he picked it up.

'Lance,' he said.

'How was London?' he recognized the voice instantly, feeling no surprise that the Old Man knew about his journey. The Old Man knew everything. Before he could answer the hoarse croak came again, 'Come up to the house—now!' And the receiver clicked dead.

Johnny looked at the whisky in his hand regretfully and set it down untouched. The Old Man would smell it and smile.

Cloud was blowing over the mountain, and the setting sun turned it to the colour of tangerine and peaches. The Old Man stood at the window and watched the cloud cascade down into the valley, dispersing as it fell.

He turned from the window as Johnny entered the study and instantly Johnny was aware that something momentous had taken place in his absence.

He glanced quickly at Michael Shapiro for a cue, but Michael's grey-streaked head was bowed over the papers he held on his lap.

'Good evening,' Johnny addressed the Old Man.

'Sit there.' The Old Man indicated the Spanish leather chair opposite his desk.

'Read it,' the Old Man ordered Michael, and Michael cleared his throat and patted the papers into a neat square before he began.

The Old Man sat with his eyes on Johnny's face. It was a candid, intimate scrutiny, but Johnny felt no discomfort under it. It was almost as though the Old Man's eyes were caressing him.

Mike Shapiro read intelligently, bringing out the meaning of the involved and convoluted legal phrases. The document was the Old Man's Last Will and Testament, and it took twenty minutes for Mike to complete the reading of it. When he had finished there was silence in the room, and the Old Man broke it at last.

'Do you understand?' he asked. There was a gentleness about him that there had never been before. He seemed to have shrunk, the flesh withering on his bones and leaving them dry and light—like the sun-dried bones of a long dead seabird.

'Yes, I understand.' Johnny nodded.

'Explain it to us simply, not in your lawyer's gobbledy-gook, just to be certain,' the Old Man insisted, and Mike began to speak.

'Mr van der Byl's private estate, with the exception of his shares in Van Der Byl Diamond Co Ltd, after taxes and expenses, is placed in Trust for his two children, Tracey—'

The Old Man interrupted impatiently, swatting Mike's words out of the air as though they were flies.

'Not that. The Company. Tell him about the shares in the Company.'

'Mr van der Byl's shares in the Company are to be divided equally between you and the two van der Byl children, Tracey—'

Again the Old Man interrupted.

'He knows their names, dammit.'

It was the first time ever that either of them had heard him swear. Mike grinned ruefully at Johnny, as though asking for his sympathy, but Johnny was intent on the Old Man, studying his face, feeling the deep satisfying thrill swelling within his chest.

A third share in Van Der Byl Diamonds was no great fortune—nobody knew that better than Johnny.

However, by placing Johnny's name on the list with Tracey and Benedict—he had made him his own. This was what he had worked for all these years. The declaration was public, an acknowledgement to the world.

Johnny Lance had a father at last. He wanted to reach out and touch the Old Man. His chest felt swollen, tight with emotion. Behind his eyelids was a slow soft burning. Johnny blinked.

'This is—' His voice was ragged, and he coughed. 'I just don't know how to tell you—'

The Old Man interrupted him impatiently, silencing him with an imperious gesture, and he croaked at Mike.

'Now read him the codicil to the Will. No, don't read it. Explain it to him.'

Michael's expression changed; he looked down at his papers as he spoke, as though reluctant to meet Johnny's eyes. He cleared his throat unnecessarily and shifted in his seat.

'"By the codicil to the Will, dated the same date, and duly signed by Mr van der Byl the bequest of shares in Van Der Byl Diamond Co Ltd to JOHN RIGBY

LANCE, is made conditional on the issue by the said JOHN RIGBY LANCE of a personal guarantee for the debts of the company, including the present loan account and amounts outstanding to tributary companies for royalties and options.'''

'Christ,' said Johnny, stiffening in his chair and turning to stare incredulously at the Old Man. The tightness in his chest was gone. 'What are you trying to do to me?'

The Old Man dismissed Mike Shapiro quietly, without even looking at him. 'I'll call you when I want you.' And when he had gone he repeated Johnny's question.

'What am I trying to do to you?' he asked. 'I am trying to make you responsible for debts totalling about two and a half million Rand.'

'No creditor would come to me for half a million, I would be hard pressed to raise ten thousand on my personal account.' Johnny shook his head irritably, the whole thing was nonsensical.

'There is one creditor who could come to you, and subject you to the full process of law. Not to receive payment in cash—but in personal satisfaction. He would smash you—and delight in doing so.'

Johnny's eyes narrowed disbelievingly. 'Benedict?'

The Old Man nodded. 'For once Benedict will hold the top cards. He won't be able to dislodge you from the management of the Company, because Tracey will support you as she always has done—but he will be able to watch every move you make from his seat on the Board of Directors. He will be able to hound you, bring you and the Company down without suffering financial loss himself. And when you fall—you know better than to expect mercy from him. You will be devoured by the ogre you have created.'

'Created?' Johnny's voice was shocked. 'What do you mean?'

'You turned him into what he is now. You broke his heart, made him weak and useless—'

'You are crazy.' Johnny came to his feet. 'I have never done anything to Benedict. It was he who—'

But the Old Man's husky croak brushed aside Johnny's protests. 'He tried to run with you—but could not. He gave up, became small and vicious. Oh, I know about the way he is—how you made him.'

'Please, listen to me. I did not—'

But the Old Man went on remorselessly. 'Tracey also, you have ruined her life. You enslaved her, in your sin—'

'That night!' Johnny shouted at him. 'You never let me explain. We never—'

Now the Old Man's voice was a whiplash.

'Silence!' And Johnny could not defy him, the habit was too deeply engrained. The Old Man was trembling, his eyes glittering with passion. 'Both my children! You have plagued me and my family. My son is a weak-willed drifter, trying to hide his hurt in a hunt for pleasure. I have given him the instruments to destroy you, and when he does so perhaps he will become a man.'

The Old Man's voice was strained now, rusty and painracked. He swallowed with an effort, his throat convulsing—but there was no softening of the glitter in his eyes.

'My daughter also, tortured by her lust. A lust which you awakened—she also seeks an escape from her guilty passion. Your destruction will be her release.'

'You're wrong,' Johnny cried out, half in protest, half in entreaty. 'Please let me explain—'

'This is how it will work. I have made you vulnerable, linking you to a crippled and foundering enterprise. This time we will be rid of you.' He stopped to pant quickly, like a running dog. His breathing was strangled, harsh-sounding. 'Benedict will cut you down, and Tracey will have to watch you go. She cannot help you, her inheritance is carefully tied up, she has no control of the capital. Your only hope is the *Kingfisher*. The *Kingfisher* will turn into a vampire and suck your life blood! You asked why I was systematically transferring the assets of Van Der Byl Diamonds to my other companies? Well, now you know the answer.'

Johnny's lips moved. He was very pale. His voice came out small and whispery.

'I could refuse to sign the guarantee.'

The Old Man smiled bleakly, a drawing back of the lips that was without warmth or humour.

'You will sign it.' His voice was wheezy. 'Your pride and conceit will not let you do otherwise. You see, I know you. I've studied you all these years. But if you refuse to sign the guarantee, I will still have smashed you. Your shares will go to Benedict. You will be out. Out! Gone! We will be finished with you at last.' Then his voice dropped, 'But you will sign, I know it.'

Involuntarily Johnny lifted his hands towards the Old Man, a gesture of supplication. 'In all this time. When I stayed with you, when I—' His voice went husky and dried up. 'Did you never feel anything for me—anything at all?'

The Old Man sat up in his chair. He seemed to regain his bulk and he began to smile. He spoke quietly now, he did not have to shout.

'Get out of my nest, cuckoo. Get out and fly!' he said.

Slowly Johnny's expression changed, the line of his jaw hardened, thrusting out aggressively. His shoulders went back. He pushed his hands into his pockets, balling his fists into bony hammers.

He nodded once in understanding.

'I see.' He nodded again, and then he started to grin. It was an unconvincing grin, that twisted his mouth out of shape, and left his eyes dark and haunted.

'All right, you mean old bastard, I'll show you.'

He turned and walked from the room without looking back.

The Old Man's expression lit in deep satisfaction. He chuckled, then his breath caught. He began to cough, and the pain ripped his throat with a violence that left him clinging weakly to the edge of his desk.

He felt the crab of death move within his flesh, sinking its claws more deeply into his throat and lungs—and he was afraid.

He called out in his pain and fear, but there was nobody in the old house to hear him.

Kingfisher was launched in August and ran her trials in the North Sea. Benedict was aboard, by the Old Man's express command. With a vessel of such complexity, and of such revolutionary design, it would have been a miracle had she functioned perfectly. August that year was not the month for miracles. At the end of the trials Johnny had compiled a list of twenty-three modifications that were necessary.

'How long?' he asked the representative of the shipyard.

'A month.' The reply was hesitant.

'You mean two,' said Benedict and laughed out loud. Johnny looked at him thoughtfully, he guessed that the Old Man had spoken to him.

'I'll tell you something, Johnny.' Benedict was still laughing. 'I'm glad this cow isn't my dream of paradise.'

Johnny froze. Those words were the Old Man's, repeated parrot fashion. It was all the confirmation he needed.

Johnny flew back to Cape Town to find his creditors on the verge of mutiny. They wanted to sell out, and take the loss.

Johnny spent two whole precious days on Larsen's wine farm at Stellenbosch calming his fears. When Fifi Larsen twenty years younger than her husband, squeezed Johnny's thigh under the lunch table he knew it would be all right—for another two months.

During the next hectic, strength-sapping week of arguments and negotiations, Johnny made time to see Tracey.

She had been out of the nursing-home for a month now, staying with friends on a small farm near Somerset West.

When Johnny climbed out of the Mercedes, and Tracey came down from the stoep to greet him, he had his first real lift of pleasure in a long time.

'God,' he said. 'You look great.'

She was dressed in a cotton summer dress with open sandals on her feet. Her friends were away for the day, so they walked through the orchards. He studied her openly, noticing how her cheeks and arms had filled out and the colour had come back into them. Her hair was bright and springing with lights in the sun, but there were still the dark smears under her eyes, and she smiled only once when he picked a sprig of peach blossoms for her. She seemed to be afraid of him, and unsure of herself.

At last he faced her and placed his hands on her shoulders. 'All right. What's eating you?'

It came out in a quick staccato rush of words.

'I want to thank you for coming to find me. I want to explain why I was—like that. In that state. I don't want you to believe—well, bad things about me.'

'Tracey, you don't have to explain to me.'

'I want to. I must.' And she told him, not looking at his face, twisting and tearing the blossoms in her hands.

'You see, I didn't understand, I thought all men were like that. Not wanting, I mean not doing it—' She broke off and started again. 'He was kind, you understand. And there were lots of parties and friends around all the time, every night. Then he wanted to go to London—for his career. There was not enough scope here. Even then I didn't know. Well, I knew he had lots of men friends and that some of them were different—but . . . Then I went to his studio and found them, and they laughed. Kenny and the boy twined together like snakes. "But you must have known," he said. Something just snapped in my head, I felt spoiled, dirty and horrible and I wanted to die. There was nobody to go to and I didn't want anybody—I just wanted to die.' She stopped and stood waiting for him to speak.

'Do you still want to die?' he asked gently, and she looked up startled and shook her shining hair.

'I don't want you to die either.' And suddenly they were both laughing. After that it was good between them and they talked with all the strangeness gone until it was almost dark.

'I must go,' Johnny said.

'Your wife?' she asked, the laughter fading.

'Yes. My wife.'

It was dark when Johnny went through the front door of the new split-level ranch type in Bishopscourt which was his house but not his home; the telephone was ringing. He picked up the receiver.

'Johnny?'

'Hello Michael.' He recognized the voice.

'Johnny, get up here to the old house right away.'Michael Shapiro's voice was strained.

'Is it the Old Man?' Johnny asked anxiously.

'No talk—just come, quickly!'

The curtains were drawn, and a log fire roared on the stone hearth. But the Old Man was cold. The coldness was deep inside him where the flames could not warm it. His hands shook as he picked sheets of paper from the open document box, glanced at them and then dropped them into the fire. They exploded into orange flame, then curled and blackened to ash. At last the box was empty but for a thick wad of multi-coloured envelopes bound together with a ribbon. He loosened the knot, picked out the first envelope, and slipped from it a single sheet of writing paper.

Dear Sir.
   I hope you will be pleased to hear that I am now at school. The food is good but the beds are very hard—

He dropped both envelope and letter on the fire and selected another. One at a time he read and then burned them

—that I have been selected to play for the first fifteen—

Sometimes he smiled, once he chuckled.

—I was top in all subjects except history and religious teaching. I hope to do better next—

When there was one envelope left he held it a long time in his blue-veined bony hands. Then with an impatient flick of his wrist he threw it onto the fire and reached up to the mantelpiece to pull himself to his feet. As he stood he looked into the gilt-framed mirror above the fireplace.

He stared at his reflection, mildly surprised by the change that the last few weeks had wrought in his appearance. His eyes had lost the sparkle of life, fading to a pale dirty brownish blue—the colour of putrefaction. They bulged from the sockets, in the glassy startled stare which is peculiar to the later stages of terminal cancer.

The watery feeling of limb, and the coldness were not the result of the pain-killing drugs, he knew. Nor was the shuffling feet-dragging gait with which he crossed the thick Bokhara carpet to the stinkwood desk.

He looked down at the oblong leather case with its brass-bound corners, and he coughed, a single flesh-tearing bark. He caught at the desk to steady himself, waiting for the pain to pass before he sprang the catch on the case and laid the lid back.

His hands were quite steady as he took the barrel and butt section of the Purdey Royal twelve-bore shotgun from the case and fitted them together.

He died the way he had lived—alone.

'God, how I hate black.' Ruby Lance stood in the centre of the bedroom floor, staring at the clothing laid out on the double bed. 'It makes me look so washed out.'

She swung her head from side to side, setting the champagne-coloured cascade of her hair swinging. She turned and moved lazily across the room to the tall mirrors. She smiled at herself, a languid slanting of the eyes, and then she spoke over the shoulder of her own image.

'You say that Benedict van der Byl has arrived from England?'

'Yes,' Johnny nodded. He sat slumped in the chair beside his dressing-room door, pressing his fingers into his eyes.

Ruby came up on her toes, pulling in her stomach and pushing forward her small hard breasts.

'Who else will be there?' she asked, cupping her hands under her breasts and squeezing out the nipples between thumb and forefinger, inspecting them critically. Johnny took his hand from his eyes.

'Did you hear me?' Ruby's voice took on a sharp admonishing note. 'I'm not talking to myself you know.'

She turned away from the mirror to face him. Standing long and slim and golden as a leopard, even her eyes had the yellow intentness of a leopard's stare. She gave the impression that at any moment she would draw her lips back in a snarl.

'It's a funeral,' he said quietly. 'Not a cocktail party.'

'Well, you can't expect me to die of sorrow. I couldn't stand him.' She crossed to the bed and picked up the pair of peach-coloured panties and rubbed the glossy material against her cheek. Then she stepped into them with two long-legged strides.

'At least I can wear something pretty under the weeds.' She snapped the elastic against her sun-gilt belly, and the almost colourless blonde curls were flattened beneath the sheer silk.

Johnny stood up slowly, and went into his dressing-room. Scornfully she called after him. 'Oh for God's sake, Johnny Lance, stop dragging that long face around as though it's the end of the world. Nobody owes that old devil a thing—he collected all his debts long before they fell due.'

They were a few minutes early, and they stood together beneath the pine trees outside the entrance to the chapel.

When the pearl-grey Rolls drew up at the gate and brother and sister stepped down and came up the paved path, Ruby could not contain her interest.

'Is that Benedict van der Byl?'

Johnny nodded.

'He's very good-looking.'

But Johnny was looking at Tracey. The change in her appearance since he had last seen her was startling. She walked like a desert girl again, straight and proud. She came directly to Johnny and stopped in front of him. She removed her dark glasses, and he could see she had been weeping, for her eyes were slightly puffy. She wore no make-up, and with dark scarf framing her face she looked like a nun. The marks that sorrow had left gave her face maturity.

'I did not think this day would ever come,' she said softly.

'No,' Johnny agreed. 'It was as though he would live for ever.'

Tracey moved a step closer to him, she reached out as if to touch Johnny's arm but her fingers stopped within inches of his sleeve. Johnny understood the gesture, it was a sharing of sorrow, an understanding of mutual loss, and an unstated offer of comfort.

'I don't think we have met.' Ruby used her sugar and arsenic tone. 'It is Miss van der Byl, isn't it?'

Tracey turned her head and her expression went flat and neutral. She replaced the dark glasses, masking her eyes.

'Mrs Hartford,' she said. 'How do you do.'

Mike Shapiro stood beside Johnny in the pew. He spoke without moving his lips, just loud enough for Johnny to catch the words.

'Benedict knows the conditions of the Will. You can expect his first move immediately.'

'Thanks, Mike.'

Johnny kept his eyes on the massive black coffin. The candlelight glinted and sparkled on the elaborate silver handles.

As yet he could find no interest for the conflict that lay ahead. That would come. Now he was too deeply involved in the passing of an era, his life had reached another point of major departure. He knew it would change, had already changed.

He looked across the aisle suddenly, his gaze drawn intuitively.

Benedict van der Byl was watching him, and at that moment the priest asked for the pallbearers.

They went to stand beside the coffin, Benedict and Johnny on opposite sides of the polished black casket among the massed display of arum lilies. They watched each other warily. It seemed to Johnny that the whole scene was significant. The two of them standing over the Old Man's corpse, facing each other, with Tracey looking on anxiously.

Johnny glanced back into the body of the church, looking for Tracey. Instead he found Ruby. She was watching them both, and Johnny knew suddenly that the board had changed more than he realized. A new piece had been added to the game.

He felt Mike Shapiro nudge him, and he stepped forward and grasped the silver handle. Between them they carried the Old Man out into the sunshine.

The handle had cut into his palm with the weight of the coffin. He went on massaging it, even after the coffin had gone down into the pit. The crude mounds of fresh earth were covered with blankets of bright green artificial grass. The mourners began to drift away, but Johnny went on standing there bareheaded. Until Ruby came to touch his arm.

'Come on.' Her voice pitched low, but stinging. 'You're making a fool of yourself.'

Benedict and Tracey were waiting under the pine trees by the churchyard gate, shaking hands and talking quietly to the departing mourners.

'You are Ruby, of course.' Benedict took her hand, smiling a little, urbane and charming. 'The flattering reports I've had of you hardly do you justice.' And Ruby glowed, seeming like a butterfly to spread her wings to the sun.

'Johnny.' Benedict turned to him, and Johnny was taken off balance by the friendly warmth of his smile and the grip of his hand. 'Michael Shapiro tells me that you have accepted my father's legacy and the conditions attached to it—you have signed the guarantee. It's wonderful news. I don't know what we would have done without you in Van Der Byl Diamonds. You are the only one

that can pull the Company through this difficult period. I want you to know I
am behind you all the way, Johnny. I intend becoming much more involved
with the Company now, giving you all the help you need.'

'I knew I could depend on you, Benedict.' Johnny accepted the challenge as
smoothly as it was thrown down. 'I think everything is going to turn out all
right.'

'We have a meeting on Monday, then I must return to London on
Thursday—but I hope you can have dinner with me before then—you and your
lovely wife, of course.'

'Thank you.' Ruby, seeing the refusal on Johnny's lips, interrupted quickly.
'We'd enjoy that.'

'You were going to refuse, weren't you?' She sat with her legs curled up
sideways under her, watching him from the passenger seat of the Mercedes
with the slanting eyes of a Persian cat.

'You're damn right.' Johnny nodded grimly.

'Why?'

'Benedict van der Byl is poison.'

'You say so.'

'Yes, I say so.'

'Could be you're jealous of him.' Ruby lit one of her gold-tipped cigarettes,
pouting the smoke through her lips.

'Good God!' Johnny gave one harsh snort of laughter, then they were silent,
both staring ahead.

'I think he's pretty dreamy.'

'You can have him.' Johnny's tone was disinterested, but her retort was
shrill.

'I could too—if I wanted to. Anyway you and that Tracey creature
mooning—'

'Cut it out, Ruby.'

'Oh my, I've said the wrong thing. The precious Mrs Hartford—'

'Cut it out, I said.' Johnny's tone was sharp.

'Little Miss Fancy Pants—God! She almost had them down for you in the
bloody graveyard—'

'Shut up, damn you.'

'Don't you swear at me.' And she lashed out at him flat-handed, leaning
forward across the seat to strike him in the mouth. His lower lip smeared
against his teeth, and the taste of blood seeped into his mouth. He took the
handkerchief from his breast pocket and held it to his mouth, steering the
Mercedes with one hand.

Ruby sat curled in her corner of the seat, puffing quickly at the cigarette.
Neither of them spoke again until he drew up in front of the double garage.
Then Ruby slipped out of the Mercedes and ran across the lawns to the front
door. She slammed it behind her, with a force that rattled the full-length glass
panel.

Johnny parked the Mercedes, closed the garage door and followed her
slowly into the house. She had kicked off her shoes on the wall-to-wall carpet
in the lounge, and run through onto the patio beside the swimming pool. She
stood barefooted staring down into the clear water, hugging herself about the
shoulders.

'Ruby.' He came up behind her, forcing the anger out of his voice with an effort, trying to keep it conciliatory. 'Listen to me–'

She spun around to face him, eyes blazing like a cornered leopard.

'Don't try and gentle talk me, you bastard. What do you think I am–your damned servant? When did I last get to do anything I wanted?'

With Ruby he had long ago realized that placation was the short cut to peace, so he was roused by the implication.

'I've never stopped you from–'

'Good! That's just fine! then you won't stop me going away.'

'What do you mean?' He was caught between shock and a sneaking sense of hope. 'Are you talking about divorce–'

'Divorce? Are you out of your little mind! I know all about the big bagful of goodies the Old Man left you in his Will. Well, little Ruby is getting her pinkies into that bag–starting right now.'

'What do you want exactly?' His voice was cold and flat.

'A new wardrobe, and a quick whip around all those nice places you go to all the time–London, Paris and the rest. That will do for a start.'

He thought for a moment, assessing how far he could stretch his overdraft; since his marriage his bank statement had seldom been typed in black. It was worth it, he decided. He could afford no distraction over the next few months. He could move faster and think quicker without having Ruby Lance sitting between his shoulder-blades–much better she should go.

'All right,' he nodded. 'If that's what you want.'

Her eyes narrowed slightly and her mouth pinched in as she studied his face.

'That was too easy,' she said. 'You want to get rid of me? Don't get any ideas, Johnny boy, you put one finger–or anything else–out of line and I'll chop it off.'

'There is a Mrs Hartford to see you, sir.' Lettie Pienaar's voice whispered through on the intercom, then just audibly she added, 'Lucky you!'

Johnny grinned. 'You're fired for insolence–but send her in before you go.'

He stood up as Tracey came in, and went around his desk to meet her. She wore a no-nonsense grey suit, with her hair scraped back from her face. She should have looked like a school marm–but she didn't.

'You've got your times mixed up, Tracey. The Directors' meeting is at two this afternoon.'

'That's a sweet greeting.' She sat down in an egg-shaped swivel chair, crossing long legs which Johnny dragged his eyes off with an effort. 'I've come looking for a job.'

'A job?' He stared at her blankly.

'Yes, a job. You know–work? Employment?'

'What on earth for?'

'Well, now that you've dragged me back from the bright lights with all the finesse of a caveman–you don't expect me to sit around until I drop dead of boredom. Besides, your tame doctor feels that good healthy employment is essential to the completion of my–ah–cure.'

'I see.' He sank back into his own chair. 'Well–what can you do?'

'Mr Lance.' Tracey widened her eyes suggestively, but made her voice prim. '–Really!'

'All right,' Johnny chuckled. 'What are your qualifications?'

'You may or may not know that I have a law degree from the University of Cape Town.'

'I didn't.'

'Also, it occurred to me that during the next few months you might need someone around whom you can trust.' She was serious now, and Johnny's smile faded also. 'Like the old days,' she added quietly. They were silent for a few seconds.

'It just so happens that we are looking for a personal assistant in our legal department.' Johnny murmured, and then softly, 'Thanks, Tracey.'

The Board Room of Van Der Byl Diamonds was furnished in soft forest colours, browns and greens. A long luxurious room that reflected the opulence of the days when the Company had been glutted with capital. But now the air was charged with a tension that crackled in the air like static electricity.

The subject of debate was the diamond recovery vessel, *Kingfisher*. The Company's last hope. Her only substantial asset, and Johnny's personal cross.

'This vessel should have been in operation nine months ago. All the estimates were based on that assumption—yet, she is still lying awaiting completion on the slips at Portsmouth.' Benedict was speaking with unconcealed relish. 'In consequence, the interest charges that are accruing put us in a position—'

'The shipyard was out on strike for a total of four months during construction—in addition they were working to rule for—' Johnny's jaw was thrust out, he was ready to fight.

'Ah! I don't think we are particularly interested in the unpredictability of the British workman—the contract should have gone to the Japanese company. Their tender was lower—'

'It would have,' grated Johnny, 'if your father had not insisted—'

'Please, let us not attempt to lay the blame at the door of a dead man.' Benedict's tone was sanctimonious. 'Let us rather try and rectify a grievous situation. When will *Kingfisher* be ready for sea?'

'On the thirteenth of September.'

'It had better be.' Benedict dropped his eyes to his notes. 'Now, this man whom you have engaged to captain the vessel—Sergio Caporetti—let us hear a little about him, please.'

'Fifteen years' experience on offshore oil-drilling vessels in the Red Sea. Three years as Captain of Atlantis Diamonds' offshore dredger operating off the West Coast. He's one of the best, no doubt about it.'

'All right.' Almost reluctantly Benedict accepted this, and consulted his notes. 'Now, we have two sea-concession areas. No 1 area off Cartridge Bay; No 2 some twenty miles north of that. Judging by your prospecting results you will elect to work No 1 area first.'

Johnny nodded, waiting for the next attack to develop. Benedict sat back in his chair.

'Atlantis Diamonds Ltd went broke working our No 1 area—what makes you think you can succeed where they failed?'

'We've been over this before,' Johnny snapped.

'I wasn't there, remember? Humour me, please. Go over it again.'

Quickly Johnny explained that Atlantis Diamonds' costs had been inflated by their method of operation. Their dredgers were not self-propelled but had to be towed by tugs. The gravel they recovered had been stored, taken into Cartridge Bay in bulk, transhipped ashore to be processed at a land-based plant. *Kingfisher* was a self-propelled and self-contained vessel. She would suck up the gravel, process it through the most sophisticated system of cyclone and X-ray equipment and dump the waste overboard.

'Our costs will be one quarter those of Atlantis Diamonds,' he finished.

'And our loan account is a mere two millions,' Benedict murmured dryly. Then he looked towards Mike Shapiro at the bottom of the table. 'Mr Secretary, please note the following motion–"That this Company proceed to sell the vessel *Kingfisher* presently building at Portsmouth. That it sells all diamond concessions at the most advantageous terms negotiable, and goes into voluntary liquidation forthwith." Have you got that?'

It was a direct frontal attack. Clearly if the motion succeeded the Company was worthless. They could not recover the price of the *Kingfisher* on a forced sale. There would be a shortfall–and Johnny had signed the guarantee. It was a straight test that Benedict was making. A setting of the lines of battle. Tracey held the balance between Johnny and Benedict. He was forcing her to declare herself.

Benedict watched her while the motion was put to the vote. He leaned forward in the padded leather chair, a slightly amused smile on the full red lips. Beautifully groomed and tailored, with the grace that wealth and position gave to a man and which cannot be counterfeited. But the clean athletic lines of his body were fractionally blurred by indulgence, and there was a little too much flesh along the line of his jaw that gave him the petulant look of a spoilt child.

Tracey voted with Johnny Lance, not hesitating a second before lifting her hand. Returning Benedict's smile levelly, and watching her brother's smile alter subtly–become wolfish, for Benedict did not like to lose.

'Very well, my darling sister. Now we know how we stand at least.' He turned easily to Johnny. 'I presume you wish me to continue with my duties in London.'

For years now Benedict had handled the London sales of the Company's stones. It was an unexacting task, which the Old Man had judged within his capabilities.

'Thank you, Benedict,' Johnny nodded. 'Now, I have a proposal to put to the meeting–"That the Directors of this Company, as a gesture of solidarity, agree to waive their rights to Directors' fees until such time as the Company's financial position is on a more sound footing."'

It was a puny counter attack, but the best he could mount at the moment.

Take-off was in the first light from Youngsfield, and Johnny swung the twin-engined Beechcraft on to a northerly heading, leaving the blue massif of Table Mountain on the left hand.

Tracey wore an anorak over her rose-coloured shirt, and the bottoms of her denim pants were tucked into soft leather boots, her dark hair caught at the nape of her neck with a leather thong.

She sat very still, looking ahead through the aircraft's windshield at the dawn-touched contours of the land ahead. At the bleak lilac and purple mountains and the great lion-coloured plains spreading down to meet the mists that hung over the cold Atlantic.

In her stillness Johnny sensed her excitement and found it infectious.

The sun exploded over the horizon, washing golden and bright over the plains, and tipping the mountains with flame.

'Namaqualand.' Johnny pointed ahead.

She laughed with excitement, like a child at Christmas, turning in the seat to face him.

'Do you remember–' She began, then stopped in confusion.

'Yes,' said Johnny. 'I remember.'

They landed before noon on a rough air-strip bulldozed out of the wilderness. There was a Land-Rover waiting to take them down to the beach to inspect the progress of the workings.

There was little remaining along the thirty-seven-mile Admiralty strip worth working. It was a clean-up and shut-down operation.

When the reigning 'King Canute' handed over the parcel of diamonds that made up the month's recovery, he was apologetic.

'You took out all the plums, Johnny. It's not like the old days.'

Johnny prodded the pathetic pile of small, low-grade stones with his forefinger.

'No, it's not,' he agreed. 'But every little bit helps.'

They climbed back into the Beechcraft and flew on northwards.

Now they passed over areas where the desert had been scratched and torn over wide areas.

The tractors had left centipede tracks in the soft earth.

'Ours?' asked Tracey.

'I wish they were. We'd have no worries then. No, all this belongs to the big Company.'

Johnny checked his watch, automatically comparing the progress of the flight to his estimates. Then he lifted the microphone from the R/T set.

'Alexandra Bay Control. This is Zulu Sugar Peter Tango Baker.'

He knew that they had him on the radar plot, and were watching him–not because they were worried about his safety, but because he was now over the Proclaimed Diamond Area of South West Africa–that vast jealously guarded tract of nothingness.

The radio crackled back at him instantly, demanding his permit number, his flight plan, querying his intentions and his destination.

Having convinced Control of his innocence, and received their permission to continue his flight, he switched off his R/T set, and grimaced at Tracey.

He felt ruffled by this small brush with Olympus. He knew that most of it was professional jealousy. He smarted under the knowledge that he was working ground that the big Company would despise as not sufficiently lucrative to bother about.

Sometimes Johnny dreamed about discovering a fault in a land title, or an error in a survey that had been casually performed seventy years previously before the value of this parched denuded earth had been realized. He imagined himself being able to claim the mineral rights to a few square miles plumb in the middle of the big Company's richest field. He shivered voluptuously at the thought, and Tracey looked at him inquiringly.

He shook his head, then this line of thought took him on to a further destination.

'Tracey, I am going to show you something.'

He banked the aircraft, crossing the coastline with its creamy lines of surf running in on the freezing white sands of the beach.

'What?' She was expectant, receptive to the new tone in his voice.

'Thunderbolt and Suicide,' he said, and she made a small grimace of incomprehension.

'There.' He pointed ahead, and through the light smoke of the sea mist she saw them show bare—white and shiny, like a pair of albino whales.

'Islands?' she asked. 'What's so special about them?'

'Their shape,' he answered. 'See how they lie like the mouth of a funnel, with a small opening between them.'

She nodded. The two islands were almost identical twins, two narrow wedges of smooth granite, each about three miles long, lying in a chevron pattern to each other—but not quite meeting at the peak. The mighty Atlantic swells bore up from the south and ran into the mouth of the funnel. Finding themselves trapped in this granite corral, the swells reared up wildly and hurled themselves on the cliffs in massive bomb-bursts of spray before streaming out in white foam through the narrow opening between the two islands.

'I can see how Thunderbolt gets its name.' Tracey eyed the wild booming surf with awe. 'But how about Suicide?'

'The old guano collectors must have called it that, after they tried landing on it.'

'Guano,' Tracey nodded. 'That accounts for the colour.'

Johnny put the Beechcraft into a shallow dive, hurtling in low over the green water. Ahead of them the seabirds rose in alarm, streaming in a long black smear into the sky, the cormorants and gannets whose excreta through the ages had painted the rocks that glaring white.

As they flashed through the gap below the level of the cliffs, Tracey exclaimed, 'There's some sort of tower there—look! In the back of the island.'

'Yes,' Johnny agreed. 'It's an old wooden gantry they used for loading the guano into the longboats.'

He pulled the Beechcraft up in a climbing turn, gaining height to look down on the two islands.

'Do you see where the surf comes through the gap? Now look beneath the surface, can you see the reefs under the water?'

They lay like long dark shadows through the green water, at right angles to the drift of white foam.

'Well, you are looking at the most beautifully designed natural diamond trap in the world.'

'Explain,' Tracey invited.

'Down there,' he pointed south, 'are the big rivers. Some of them dried up a million years ago, but not before they had spat the diamonds they carried into the sea. The tide and the wind has been working them up towards the north for all these ages. Throwing some of them back on the beach but carrying others up this way.'

He levelled the Beechcraft out and resumed their interrupted flight northwards.

'Then suddenly they run up against Thunderbolt and Suicide. They are concentrated and squeezed through the gap, then they are confronted by a series of sharp reefs across their path. They cannot cross them—they just settle down in the gullies and wait for someone to come and suck them out.'

He sighed like a man crossed in love.

'My God, Tracey. The smell of those diamonds reeks in my nostrils. I can almost see the shine of them through a hundred and sixty feet of water.'

He shook himself as though awakening from a dream.

'I've been in the game all my life, Tracey. I've got the "feel", the same as a water-diviner has. I tell you with absolute certainty there are millions of carats of diamonds lying in the crotch of Thunderbolt and Suicide.'

'What's the snag?' Tracey asked.

'The concession was granted twenty years ago to the big Company.'

'By whom?'

'The Government of South West Africa.'

'Why aren't they mining it?'

'They will—sometime in the next twenty years. They aren't in any hurry.'

They lapsed into silence, staring ahead, though once Johnny clucked his tongue irritably and shook his head—still thinking about Thunderbolt and Suicide.

To distract him Tracey asked, 'Where do they come from in the first place—the diamonds?'

'Volcanic pipes,' Johnny answered. 'There are more than a hundred known pipes in Southern Africa. Not all yield stones, but then some do. New Rush—Finsch—Dutoitspan—Bulfontein—Premier—Mwadui. Great oval-shaped treasure chests, filled with the legendary "Blue Ground"—the mother lode of the diamond.'

'There are no pipes here—surely?' Tracey turned towards him in her seat.

'No,' Johnny agreed. 'We are after the alluvial stones. Some of the ancient pipes exploded with the force of a hydrogen bomb, spraying diamonds over hundreds of square miles. Others were submarine pipes that discharged their treasure into the restless sea. Others of the more passive volcanic pipes were simply eroded away by wind and water and the diamonds were exposed.'

'Then they were washed down into the sea?' she guessed.

Johnny nodded. 'That's right. Over millions of years they were moved infinitely slowly by landslides, floods, rivers and rainwater. Where all the other pebbles and stones were abraded and worn away to nothingness—the diamonds, four hundred times harder than any other natural substance on earth, were unmarked. So at last they reached the sea and mingled with the others from the submarine pipes, to be laid down by wave action on the beaches, or finally to come up against a place like Thunderbolt and Suicide.'

Tracy opened her mouth to ask another question, but Johnny interrupted.

'Here we are. There is Cartridge Bay.' And he pushed the nose of the aircraft down slightly. It was more a lagoon than a bay. Separated from the sea by a narrow sandspit, it spread away into the treeless waste, an enormous extent of quite shallow water in tranquil contrast to the unchecked surf that burst on the sandpit. There was a deep water entrance through the sandspit, and a channel that was clearly defined in darker green from the air. The channel meandered across the lagoon to where a cluster of lonely whitewashed buildings sprang up on the edge of the desert.

Johnny banked steeply towards the buildings, and below them flocks of black and white pelican and pink flamingo rose in panic from the shadows.

Johnny landed and taxied across to the waiting Land-Rover with the white lightning insignia of Van Der Byl Diamonds painted on its side.

Lugging the cool box that contained their lunch, Johnny led Tracey to the vehicle and introduced her to his foreman. Then they climbed in and went bumping down to the buildings of the lagoon. Johnny received from his foreman a report on the progress of the work. The buildings had been abandoned by the defunct Atlantis Diamond Company. Johnny was renovating them to serve as a base for the *Kingfisher*; a rest and recreation centre for the crew, a radio centre, a refuelling depot and a workshop to handle running maintenance and repairs. In addition he was putting a jetty out into the lagoon for the converted seventy-foot pilchard trawler that would be *Kingfisher*'s service boat—acting as tender and ferry.

They ran an extensive inspection of the base. Johnny was pleased with the interest Tracey showed, and he enjoyed answering her questions for his own enthusiasm was high. It was nearly two o'clock before they had finished.

'How are the watchtowers coming?' Johnny asked.

'All up, ready and waiting.'

And suddenly Johnny had a two-edged inspiration.

'Might as well go and have a look.' He made it casual.

'Okay, I'll fetch the Land-Rover,' the foreman agreed.

'I know the way.' Johnny put him off. 'You go and get your lunch.'

'It's no trouble—' the foreman began, caught Johnny's frown, cut himself short, then glanced at Tracey. 'Yeah! Sure! Fine! Okay—here are the keys.' He handed Johnny the Land-Rover keys, and disappeared into his own quarters.

Johnny checked the grub box, and they climbed into the open Land-Rover.

'Where are we going?' Tracey asked.

'Inspect the watchtowers along the sandspit.'

'Watchtowers?'

'We've put up a line of fifty-foot wooden towers along the beach. From them we will take continual bearings on *Kingfisher* when she is working offshore. By radio we will be able at any time to give her the exact position over the bottom to within a few feet, as a check to the computer.'

'My, you are clever.' Tracey fluttered her eyelashes at him in mock admiration.

'Silly wench,' said Johnny, and let out the clutch. He swung down past the radio shack onto the hard wet sand at the edge of the lagoon; accelerating he hit second then third and they went away around the curve of the lagoon, headed towards the great yellow wind-carved dunes that lined the coast.

Tracey stood up on her seat, clutching the edge of the windscreen, and the wind snatched at her hair. She pulled the retaining thong from it, and shook it out into a shiny black flag that snapped and snaked behind her.

'Look! Look!' she cried as the flocks of startled flamingoes lurched into flight, streaming white and pink and black over the glossy silver water.

Johnny laughed with her, and swung the Land-Rover towards the dunes.

'Hold on!' he shouted, and she clung to the windscreen, shrieking in delicious terror as they flew up the steep side of a dune, spinning a cloud of sand from the rear wheels and then dropped over the crest in a stomach-churning swoop. They crossed the sandspit and hit the beach, racing along it, playing tag with the waves that shot up the sand.

Five miles up the beach Johnny parked above the high watermark and they ate cold chicken and drank a bottle of chilled white wine sitting side by side in the sand, leaning against the seat cushions from the Land-Rover. Then they went down to the edge of the sea to wash the chicken grease from their fingers.

'Yipes! It's cold.' Tracey scooped a double handful of seawater. Then she looked at Johnny and her expression became devilish.

He backed away, but not quickly enough. The icy water hit him in the chest, and he gasped.

'War!' It was their childhood cry.

Tracey whirled and went off long-legged along the beach, with Johnny pounding after her. She sensed him gaining on her, and shouted.

'It was a mistake! I didn't mean it! I'm sorry!'

At the last moment as he reached out to grip her shoulder, she jinked and ran knee-deep into the sea. Turning at bay to face him, she kicked a spray of water at him, shouting defiance and laughter.

'All right, come on then!'

Braving the flying spray, he reached her and picked her up kicking and struggling and waded out waist deep.

'No, no—please. Johnny. I give in—I'll do anything.'

At that moment a freak wave, bigger and stronger than the others, knocked Johnny's legs out from under him. They went under, and were rolled up the beach, to stagger out, completely soaked, clinging together, helpless with laughter.

They stood beside the Land-Rover trying to wring the water out of their clothing.

'Oh, you beast!' sobbed Tracey through her laughter. Her hair was a sodden mass, and drops of sea water clung in her eyelashes like dew.

Johnny took her in his arms and kissed her, and they stopped laughing.

She went loose against his chest, her eyes tightly closed and her lips, salty with sea water, opened against his.

The radio telephone in the Land-Rover beside them began to bleat fretfully, flashing its little red warning light.

They drew apart slowly, reluctantly, and stared at each other with dazed, bemused eyes.

Johnny reached into the Land-Rover, unhooked the microphone and lifted it to his lips.

'Yes?' his voice cracked. He cleared his throat and repeated, 'Yes?'

The foreman's voice was distorted and scratchy through the speaker.

'Mr Lance, I'm sorry to have—' he was clearly about to finish '—interrupted you.' But he stopped abruptly, and began again. 'It's just that I think you should know we've had a gale warning. Northerly gale building up quickly. If you want to get back to Cape Town you had better get airborne before it hits us—otherwise you could be shut in for days.'

'Thanks. We'll be back right away.' He hung up, and Tracey smiled shakily. Her voice was also husky and unnatural-sounding.

'And a damn good thing, too!'

Tracey's hair was still damp, and the borrowed polo-neck jersey swamped her. The grey trousers were also borrowed, rolled up to show her bare feet.

She sat very quietly and thoughtfully in the passenger seat of the Beechcraft. Far below them a small fishing vessel lay with a white cloud of seabirds hovering over it, and she watched it with exaggerated attention. There was a heavy feeling of restraint between them now, they could no longer meet each other's eyes.

'Pilchard trawler.' Johnny noticed her gaze.

'Yes,' said Tracey, and they were silent again.

'Nothing happened.' Johnny spoke again gruffly.

'No,' she agreed. 'Nothing happened.' Then shyly she reached out and took his hand. Lightly she rubbed the stump of his missing finger.

'Still friends?' she asked.

'Still friends.' He grinned at her with relief, and they flew on towards Cape Town.

Hugo Kramer watched the aircraft through his binoculars, balancing easily against the roll and pitch of the bridge.

'Police patrol?' asked the man at the helm beside him.

'No,' Hugo replied without lowering the glasses. 'Red and white twin Beechcraft. Registration ZA–PTB. Private aircraft, probably one of the diamond companies.'

He lowered the glasses, and crossed to the wing of the bridge. 'Anyway, we are well outside territorial waters.'

The drone of the aircraft engine faded away, and Hugo transferred his attention to the frantic activity on the deck below him.

The trawler, *Wild Goose,* lay heeled over under the weight of fish that filled her purse seine-net; at least a hundred tons of seething silver pilchards bulging the net out alongside the trawler into a round bag fifty feet across. While above it a shrieking canopy of sea birds swirled and wheeled and dived, frantic with greed.

Three of the crew on a scoop-net which hung from the overhead derrick were dipping the fish out of the net, swinging a ton of fish at each scoop over the side, and dropping them like a silver cloudburst into the trawler's hold. The donkey engine on the winch clattered harshly in time to their movements.

Hugo watched with satisfaction. He had a good crew, and although the fishing was only a cover for the *Wild Goose*–yet Hugo took pride in his Teutonic thoroughness which dictated that the cover should be as solid as possible. In any case, all profits from fishing were for his personal account. It was part of the agreement with the Ring.

He packed the binoculars carefully into their leather case, and hung them behind the chartroom door. Then he clambered swiftly down the steel ladder to deck level, moving with catlike grace despite the heavy rubber hip boots he wore.

'I'll take her for a while,' he told the man at the winch controls. He spoke in Afrikaans, but his accent was shaded with the German of South West Africa.

Wide-shouldered under the blue fisherman's jersey, he worked with smooth economic movements. His hands on the winch controls were rough and reddened by wind and sun, for his skin was too fair to weather. The skin of his face also was red, and half-boiled, peeling so there were pinky raw places on his cheeks and black scabs on his lips.

The hair that hung out under his cap was white as bleached sisal, and his eyelashes were thick and colourless, giving him a mild near-sighted look. His eyes were the palest cornflower blue, yet without being weak and watery as those of most albinos; they were slitted now, as he judged the roll and dip of the boat–engaging the clutch to meet the movement, or pulling on the drum brake.

'Skipper!' A shout from the bridge above him.

'Ja.' Hugo did not allow his attention to waver as he replied. 'What is it?'

'Gale warning! There is a northerly bluster building up.'

And Hugo grinned, pulled on the brake and shut the throttle.

'All right, clean up. Cut the purse rope, let the fish go free.'

He turned and swarmed up the ladder to the bridge, and went to his chart table.

'It will take us three hours to get in position,' he muttered aloud, leaning over the chart, then he barged out onto the wing of the bridge again to chase up his crew.

They had cut the purse rope on the net, allowing the net to fall open like a woman's skirt, and the fish were pouring out, a dark spreading stain through the gap. Two men had the pressure hose on, washing loose fish from the deck into the sea, others were slamming the hatch-covers closed.

Within forty minutes *Wild Goose* was running south under full throttle to take up her waiting station.

The diamond coast of South Western Africa lies in the belt of the Trades. The prevailing wind is the south-easter, but periodically the wind system is completely reversed and a gale comes out of the north, off the land.

It is a Sirocco-type wind like the 'Khamsin' of the Libyan desert, or the 'Simoom' of Tripoli.

It was the same searing dry wind out of the desert, filling the sky with brooding dust and sand clouds, smothering everything beneath a hellish pall like the smoke from a great battlefield.

The dust clouds were part of the design, the Ring had taken account of them when they planned the system—for the north wind lifted into the sky such a quantity of mica dust that the radar screens of the diamond security police were cluttered and confused, throwing up phantom echoes and making it impossible to pick up the presence of a small airborne object.

Turn Back Point was three miles inland, and sixty miles north of the Orange river. The name was given by the first travellers, and expressed their views on continuing a journey northwards. Those old travellers had not known that they stood in the centre of an elevated marine terrace, an ancient beach now lifted above the level of the sea, and that it was the richest prospect of an area so diamond-rich that it was to be ring-fenced, patrolled by jeep and dog and aircraft, guarded by gun and radar, a laager so secure that a man leaving it would have to submit to X-ray, and take nothing out with him but the clothes he wore.

At Turn Back Point was one of the four big separation plants where all the gravel from the big Company's working from miles around was processed. The settlement was comparatively large, with plant, workshops and stores, and accommodation for five hundred men and their families. Yet not all the Company's efforts to make it attractive and livable could alter the fact that Turn Back Point was a hell-hole in a savage and forbidding desert.

Now with the north wind blowing, what had been unpleasant before was almost unbearable. The buildings were tightly sealed, even the joints around the windows and doors were plugged with cloth or paper—and yet the red dust seeped in to powder the furniture, the desks, the bed linen, even the interior of the refrigerators, with a thin gritty film. It settled in the hair, was sugary between the teeth, clogged the nostrils—and with it came that searing heat that seemed to dry the moisture from the eyeballs.

Outside the dust was a red glittering fog which reduced visibility to a dozen yards. Men who were forced out into that choking dry soup wore dust goggles to protect their eyes, and the mica dust covered their clothing with a shiny coating that glittered even in that dun light.

Beyond the settlement a man moved now through the fog, carrying a small cylindrical object. He leaned forward into the wind, moving slowly away into the desert. He reached a shallow depression and went down into it. Setting his burden on the sand, he rested a moment. Then he knelt over the cylinder. He appeared monstrous under his leather jacket and cap, his face covered by goggles and a scarf.

The fibre-glass cylinder was painted with yellow fluorescent paint. At one end was a transparent plastic bubble which housed an electric globe, at the other end was a folded envelope of rubberized nylon material attached to the cylinder by a stainless steel coupling, and linked to the coupling was a small steel bottle of hydrogen gas. The whole assembly was eighteen inches long, and three inches in diameter. It weighed a few ounces more than fifteen pounds.

Within the cylinder were two separate compartments. The larger contained a highly sophisticated piece of transistorized electronic equipment which would transmit a homing signal, light or extinguish its lamp on long-distance radio signal command, and also at command it would control the inflow of hydrogen gas into the nylon balloon through the connecting coupling.

The smaller compartment held simply a sealed plastic container into which were packed twenty-seven diamonds. The smallest of these stones weighed fourteen carats, the largest a formidable fifty-six carats. Each of these stones had been selected by experts for colour, brilliance, and perfection. These were all first-water diamonds, and once they were cut they would fetch in the open market between seven hundred thousand and a million pounds—depending on the skill of the cutting.

There were four members of the Ring at Turn Back Point. Two of them were long service and trusted diamond sorters employed behind the guarded walls of the processing plant. They worked together, to check each other, for the Company operated a system of employee double check—which was completely useless when there was collusion. These men selected the finest stones and got them out of the plant.

The third member of the Ring was a diesel mechanic in the Company workshops. It was his job to receive and assemble the equipment which arrived concealed in a marked drum of tractor grease. He also packed the stones into the cylinder and passed it on to the man who was now kneeling out in the desert, preparing to launch the cylinder into the swirling dust fog.

His final check completed, the man stood up and went to the lip of the depression and peered out into the dust storm. At last he seemed satisfied, and hurried back to the yellow cylinder. With an incisive twist of the bevelled release ring he opened the valve on the bottle of hydrogen gas. There was a snakelike hiss, and the nylon balloon began to inflate. The folds of material crackled as they filled. The balloon lifted, eager to be gone, but the man restrained it with difficulty until the balloon was smooth and tight. He let go, and the balloon with its dangling cylinder leapt into the sky, and almost instantly was gone into the dust clouds.

The man stood with his face lifted to the dark furnace-red sky. His goggles glinted blindly, but his attitude was one of triumph, and when he turned away he walked lightly with the step of a man freshly released from danger.

'One more package,' he promised himself. 'Just one more, and I'll pull out. Buy that farm on the Olifants river, do a bit of fishing, take a shooting trip every year–'

He was still dreaming when he reached the parked Land-Rover and climbed into the driver's seat. He started the engine, switched on the headlights, and drove slowly down the track towards the settlement.

The sign on the rear of the departing Land-Rover was in white paint so that it showed clearly through the haze of red dust.

'SECURITY PATROL', it read.

Wild Goose lay on station, with her diesels throbbing softly ticking over to hold her head into the wind. Even twenty miles out at sea the wind was searing hot and the occasional splatter of spray on Hugo's face was refreshing.

He stood in the corner of the bridge where he could watch the sea and the helmsman, but he was anxious. *Wild Goose* had been lying on station for fifteen hours now, during ten of which the norther had howled dismally through her rigging.

He was always anxious at the beginning of a pick-up. There was so much that could have gone wrong, anything from a police sweep to a tiny electrical fault in the equipment.

'What time is it, Hansie?' he shouted and the helmsman glanced up at the chronometer above his head.

'Three minutes after six, skipper.'

'Dark in half an hour,' Hugo grunted disgustedly, slitted those pale-lashed eyes into the wind once more, then shrugged and ambled back into the bridge house.

He stopped at the console beside his chart table. Even to an experienced eye the machine was an ordinary 'Fish-Finder', an adaptation of the old wartime anti-submarine device, the ASDIC, to the more prosaic business of plotting the depth and position of the pilchard shoals beneath the surface.

However, this model had undergone a costly and specialized conversion. The Ring had flown an expert out from Japan to do the work.

Now the set hummed softly, its control panel lit soft green by internal light, but the sound was neutral, and the circular glass screen was blank.

'You want some coffee, Hansie?' Hugo asked the old coloured man at the wheel. His crew were handpicked, loyal and trusted. They had to be—one loud mouth could blow a multi-million pound business.

'Ja dankie, skipper.' The old man creased his weather-battered face in appreciation, and Hugo shouted down the companionway to the galley.

'Cooky, how's it for a pot of coffee?'

But the reply was lost, for at that moment the console came to life dramatically. A row of lights blinked on above the control panel, the muted hum changed to a rapid beep-beep signal, and the screen glowed ghostly green.

'She's up!' Hugo shouted his relief, and ran to the set. His first mate rushed through from his cabin behind the bridge, tucking his shirt into unbuttoned trousers, his face puckered with sleep.

'About bloody time,' he blurted, groggily.

'Take over from Hansie,' Hugo told him, and he settled into the padded seat in front of the ASDIC set.

'Right, bring her round two points to port and open her up.'

The *Wild Goose* swung her head into the sea, and her motion changed from easy swoop and glide to a crabbing butting lunge, and the spray burst over the glass of the bridge.

Sitting before the console Hugo was tracking the flight of the balloon and keeping *Wild Goose* on an interception course.

Driven by the forty-knot norther the balloon crossed the coastline, climbing swiftly to three thousand feet. Hugo manipulated the knob on the console which sent the balloon a command to release gas and maintain altitude. Her response was recorded immediately on the screen.

'Good,' Hugo whispered. 'Good girl.' Then louder. 'Bring her around a bit, Oscar—the balloon is drifting to the south.'

For twenty minutes more they butted through the swells.

'Okay,' Hugo broke the silence. 'I'm going to ditch her.' He twisted the knob clockwise slowly, expelling all the gas from the nylon balloon.

'Ja. That's it. She's down now.' He looked out of the window above the set. The dust-laden clouds had brought the night on prematurely. It was dark outside, with a low black ceiling through which no star showed.

Hugo turned his attention back to the set.

'That's it, Oscar. You're right on-course. Hold her there.'

Then he glanced across at old Hansie and another younger crewman. They were sitting patiently on the bench against the far bulkhead. Both of them were clad in full oilskins, shiny yellow plastic from head to ankle, with gumboots below that.

'Okay, Hansie,' Hugo nodded. 'You can get up into the bows. We are only a mile or so away now.'

They climbed down onto the wave-swept deck, and Hugo watched them scuttling forward between each green burst of water and crouching in the bows, both of them ducking each time another swell poured over the top of them, their yellow plastic suits showing clearly in the murky deck lights.

'I'm going to switch on now,' Hugo warned the helm. 'We should have her visual.'

'Right.' Oscar peered ahead, and Hugo flicked a switch on the panel, commanding the balloon to turn on her guide light.

Almost immediately there was a shout from Oscar.

'There she is. Dead ahead!'

Hugo jumped up and ran forward. It took a few seconds for his eyes to adjust, then he made out the tiny red firefly of light ahead of them in the vast blackness of sea and sky. It showed for a second, then was gone in the trough of the next wave.

'I'll take her.' Hugo replaced Oscar at the wheel. 'You get on the spot-light.'

The beam of the spotlight was a solid white shaft through the darkness. The fluorescent yellow paint of the cylinder glowed in the circle of the spot.

Hugo laid *Wild Goose* up wind of the cylinder, and then allowed her to drift down gently on it. Hansie and his assistant were ready with the twenty-foot boat-hook.

Delicately Hugo manœuvred down over the bobbing yellow cylinder, and grunted with satisfaction as the boat-hook slipped through the recovery ring and the cylinder was hauled in over the bows.

He watched while the two dripping oilskin-clad figures clambered back up the ladder into the wheelhouse, and laid the cylinder on the chart table.

'Good! Good!' Hugo slapped their backs heartily. 'Now go and get dry—both of you.' They climbed down the companionway, and Hugo handed the wheel over to Oscar.

'Home!' he instructed him. 'As quick as you like.' And he carried the cylinder through into his cabin.

Sitting at the fold-down table in his cabin Hugo unscrewed the lower section of the cylinder and took out the plastic container. He opened it and spilled the contents out on the table-top.

He whistled softly, and picked up the biggest stone. Although he was no expert he knew instinctively that it was a brilliant of exceptional quality. Even the roughness of its exterior could not mask the fire in its depths.

To him it was worthless, there was nowhere he could market a stone like that. There was no temptation to take it out of the Ring—all it would mean for him was fifteen years at hard labour.

The Ring was based on this mutual reliance, no one part of it could function without all the others—yet each part was self-contained and watertight. Only one man knew all its parts, and nobody knew who that one man was.

From the drawer beside him Hugo took out his tools and set them on the table. He lit the spirit stove and set the pot of paraffin wax on the gimbal above it to heat.

Then he poured the diamonds into a shiny metal can. It was the type of ordinary commercial can used for packing and preserving foodstuffs.

Balancing easily against the ship's motion, he lifted the pot from the stove, and poured the steaming liquid wax over the diamonds, filling the can to rim level.

The wax was cooled and solidified quickly, turning opaque and white. The stones were now incorporated in a cake of wax that would prevent them rattling, and would give the sealed can authentic weight.

Hugo lit a cigarette and crossed the cabin to look out into the wheelhouse. The helmsman winked at him and Hugo smiled.

He went back to the table, the can was cool enough to handle. He placed the circular lid over it, and moved to the portable Jenny bolted to a chest of drawers. Carefully he clinched the lid into place, his eyes squinting at the smoke from the cigarette that dangled from his lips.

Satisfied at last he set the sealed can on the table, while he went to where his jacket hung on the door. From the inside pocket he pulled out a manilla envelope, then from the envelope he drew a printed, colour-screened label. He came back to the bench and meticulously pasted the label around the can. On the label was a highly glamorized artist's conception of a leaping pilchard, making it look like a Scottish salmon.

'Pilchards in Tomato Sauce.' Hugo read the label aloud, as he leaned back to admire his work. 'A product of South West Africa.' He smiled with satisfaction and began packing his equipment away.

'How much?' The foreman of the fish pump called across the narrowing gap between *Wild Goose* and the jetty.

'About fifty tons,' Hugo shouted back. 'Then the norther chased us home.'

'Ja. None of the boats stayed out.' The foreman watched his gang secure the mooring ropes, and swing the hose of the vacuum pump over *Wild Goose*'s hold to begin pumping out the pilchards.

'Take over, Oscar.' Hugo picked up his jacket and cap. 'I'll be back tomorrow.' He jumped down onto the jetty and strode down towards the canning factory with its awesome stink of pilchard oil. His jacket was slung over his shoulder, one finger hooked through the tag.

He went down the alley between the boiler rooms and the fish-drying plant, across a wide yard where the bags of fish meal were piled to the height of a double-storey building. He turned in through the double doors of the cavernous warehouse filled to roof height with cardboard cartons, each stencilled with the words:

1 gross cans.	Pilchards in tomato sauce.
Consign to:	Vee Dee Bee Agencies Ltd,
	32 Bermondsey Street,
	London SE1.

He went to the cubicle that served the warehouse storeman as an office.

'Hello, Hugo. Good trip?' The storeman was Hugo's brother-in-law.

'Fifty ton.' Hugo hung his coat casually on the hook behind the door. 'I've got to take a leak,' he said, and went to the latrine across the floor of the warehouse.

He came back, and drank a cup of tea with his brother-in-law. Then he stood and said, 'Jeannie will be waiting.'

'Give her my love.'

'She don't need yours. She's going to get plenty of mine!' Hugo winked, and took his coat from the hook. It was lighter now, the can was gone from the pocket.

He went through the main gates of the harbour, exchanging a casual greeting with the customs officer, and went to the battered early model convertible in the car park.

He kissed the girl at the driving-wheel, threw his coat on the back seat and climbed in over the door.

'You drive,' he told her, grinning. 'I want both hands free.'

She squeaked and pulled his hand out of her skirts.

'Can't you wait till we get home?'

'I've been at sea five days and I'm hungry as hell.'

'You're a caution, you are.' She laughed at him and started the car.

This was Sergio Caporetti, the man Johnny had chosen to captain the *Kingfisher*. He was a round man, the same shape as a snowman. He filled the doorway of Johnny's office, and his great belly bulged into the room ahead of him. His face was round also, like a baby's—but he had beautiful dark Italian eyes fringed with thick lashes like a girl's.

'Come in, Sergio,' Johnny greeted him. 'Nice to see you.'

The Italian crossed the room deceptively quickly, and Johnny's hand was completely engulfed by the enormous hairy paw.

'So, at last we are ready,' Sergio grunted. 'Three months I sit on bum—do nothing. Look at me—' He slapped his belly with a sound like a pistol shot. '—fat! No good.'

'Well, not quite ready.' Johnny qualified the statement. He was flying Sergio and his crew over to England well ahead of time. He wanted the big Italian to have plenty of opportunity to study and get to know the revolutionary new equipment with which *Kingfisher* was fitted. Then when the vessel was ready for sea, Sergio would sail her out to Africa.

'Sit down, Sergio. Let's go over the crew list—'

When Sergio left an hour later, Johnny went as far as the lift with him.

'If you have any problems phone me, Sergio.'

'Si.' Sergio shook hands. 'Don't worry—Caporetti is in charge. All is well.'

On his way back Johnny stopped at the reception desk.

'Is Mrs Hartford in today?' he asked one of the little receptionists, and both of them replied in chorus like Tweedledum and Tweedledee.

'No, Mr Lance.'

'Has she phoned at all to say where she is?'

'No, Mr Lance.'

Tracey had disappeared. Five days now there had been no sign of her, her new office was deserted and unused. Johnny was worried and angry. He was worried that she had gone on another binge, and he was angry because he missed her.

He was scowling ferociously as he went back into his office.

'Goodness me.' Lettie Pienaar stood beside his desk with a batch of mail in her hand. 'We do look happy. Here's something to cheer you.'

She handed him a postcard with a colour picture of the Eiffel Tower. It was the first word from Ruby since she had left. Johnny read it quickly.

'Paris–' he said, '–is fun, it seems.' He tossed the card onto the desk and plunged back into the day's work.

He worked late, stopped at the steakhouse to eat, then drove back to the silent house in Bishopscourt.

The crunch of tyres on the gravel drive and headlights flashing across the bedroom wall woke him. He sat up in bed as the front-doorbell began a series of urgent peals and he switched on the bedside light. Two o'clock–Christ!

He pulled a dressing gown over his nudity and tottered down the passage, switching on lights as he went. The doorbell kept ringing.

He turned the front-door key. The door flew open and Tracey came in like a strong wind, clutching a briefcase to her chest.

'Where the hell have you been?' Johnny was suddenly fully awake, angry and relieved.

'Johnny! Johnny!' She was dancing with excitement, incoherent, her cheeks flaming and eyes shining. 'I've got them–at least, it, both of them.'

'Where have you been?' Johnny was not to be so easily sidetracked, and with an obvious effort Tracey brought her excitement under control, but she was still smiling and gave the impression of humming like an electric motor.

'Come.' She took his hand and dragged him into the lounge. 'Get yourself a large whisky and sit down,' she ordered, imperious as a queen.

'I don't want a whisky, and I don't–'

'You'll need one,' she interrupted, and went to the open liquor cabinet, poured a massive whisky into a crystal glass, squirted soda into it, and brought it back to Johnny.

'Tracey, what the hell is going on?'

'Please, Johnny. It's so wonderful, don't spoil it for me. Just sit there, please!'

Johnny sank reluctantly into the chair, and Tracey slipped the catch on her briefcase and drew out a sheaf of documents. She stood in the centre of the floor, and took up the pose of a Victorian actress.

'This–' she explained, '–is a translation from the original German of a proclamation by Governor in Council dated May 3rd 1899 and issued at Windhoek. I will leave out the preamble and go straight to the meat.'

She cleared her throat and began reading:

'In consideration of the sum of 10,000 marks which is hereby paid and received, the rights to mine, win, recover, collect or carry away all metals, whether base or precious, stones whether base, semi-precious or precious, minerals, guano, vegetation and other substances organic or inorganic for a period of Nine Hundred and Ninety-Nine years is granted to Messrs Farben, Hendryck and Mosenthal SA, Guano Merchants of 14 Bergenstrasse, Windhoek, in respect of a circular area ten kilometres in radius whose centre shall be a point situate at the highest elevation of the island lying on latitude 23° 15′ South and longitude 15° 12′ East.'

Tracey paused and looked at Johnny. He was frozen, stony-faced, staring at her with all his attention. She went on quickly, gabbling it out.

'All the old German mineral concessions and rights were ratified by the Union Parliament when the Union of South Africa took over the mandate after the Great War.'

He nodded, unable to speak. Tracey's smile kept breaking out.

'That concession still has all the force of law behind it. The grant of any subsequent rights is invalid, and although the original grant was mainly for the recovery of guano—yet it covers precious stones also.'

Again Johnny nodded, and Tracey put the document at the bottom of the sheaf of papers in her hand.

'The concession Company, Farben, Hendryck and Mosenthal SA, is still in existence. The Company's only remaining asset, apart from any long-forgotten concessions, is an old building at 14 Bergenstrasse, Windhoek.'

Tracey seemed to change the subject suddenly.

'You asked me where I have been, Johnny. Well I've been to Windhoek, and over most of the worst roads in South West Africa.

'The Farben, Hendryck and Mosenthal Company is owned by the brothers Hendryck, a couple of karakul fur farmers. They are a pair of horrible old men, and when I saw them slitting the throats of those poor little Persian lambs just to prevent the fur uncurling, well—' Tracey paused, and gulped. 'Well, I didn't explain to them about the concession. I just offered to buy the Company, and they asked twenty thousand and I said "sign", and they signed and I left them chuckling with glee. They thought they'd been terribly clever. There! It's all yours!'

Tracey handed the Agreement to Johnny and while he read it she went on.

'I made the Agreement in the name of Van Der Byl Diamonds, I signed it as a Director—I hope you don't mind.'

'Christ!' Johnny took a long deep swallow of whisky, then set the glass down and stood up.

'Mind?' he repeated. 'You bring me the concession to Thunderbolt and Suicide—and ask me if I mind.'

He reached for her, and eagerly she went to him.

'Tracey, you're wonderful.' They hugged each other ecstatically, and Johnny swung her off her feet. Without either of them planning it they were suddenly lying, still in each other's arms, on the couch. Then they were kissing, and the laughter dwindled into small murmurs and incoherent sounds.

Tracey pulled away from him at last, and slipped off the couch. She stood in the centre of the floor. Her breathing was ragged. Her hair was a dark tangle.

'Whoa! That's enough.'

'Tracey.' He started up from the couch, wild for her, but she held him at the full stretch of her arms, her hands flat on his chest, backing away in front of him.

'No, Johnny, no!' She shook her head urgently. 'Listen to me.'

He stopped. The wild look faded from his eyes.

'Look, Johnny, God knows I'm no saint, but—well, I don't want us to—well, not on a couch in some other woman's house. That's not how I want it to be.'

Benedict eased the big honey-coloured Bentley out of the traffic stream that clogged Bermondsey Street and turned into the gates of the warehouse. He parked beside the loading bank and climbed out.

As he pulled off his gloves, he glanced along the bank. Mountains of goods were stacked ready for distribution. Cases of Cape wine and spirits, canned fruit in brown cartons, canned fish, forty-gallon drums of fish oil, bundles of raw hides stiff as boards, and cases of indefinable goods–all of it the produce of Southern Africa.

Vee Dee Bee Agencies had grown out of all recognition in the ten years since Benedict had launched it.

Benedict climbed the steps to the bank three at a time, and strode down between the towering stacks of goods that reached up into the murk of the high ceiling. He walked with the assurance of a man on his own ground, the skirts of his overcoat swirling about his knees, broad-shouldered and tall. The storeman and porters greeted him deferentially as he passed, and when he entered the main office there was a stirring and whispering among the ranks of typists as though a wind had blown through a forest.

The Managing Director hurried out of his office to greet Benedict and usher him in.

'How are you, Mr van der Byl? There's tea coming now.' And he stood behind Benedict to take his coat.

The meeting lasted half an hour, Benedict reading through the weekly sales and cost reports, querying an item here, remarking on a figure with pleasure or displeasure as it deserved. Many people watching him work would have been startled. This was not the indolent playboy they thought they knew, this was a hard-eyed businessman coldly and unemotionally milking the maximum profit from his enterprise.

There would have been others who wondered where Benedict had found the capital to finance a business of this magnitude, especially if they had known that he owned the premises, and that Vee Dee Bee Agencies was by no means his only stake in the world of business. He had not received money from his father–the Old Man had not believed Benedict capable of successfully negotiating the purchase of a pound of butter.

The meeting ended, and Benedict stood up and shrugged on his overcoat, while his Managing Director went to the grey steel safe in the corner, tumbled the combination and swung the heavy door open.

'The shipment arrived yesterday,' he explained as he reached into the safe and brought out the can. 'On the SS *Loch Elsinore* from Walvis Bay.'

He handed the can to Benedict, who examined it briefly, smiling a little at the painting of the leaping fish and the lettering 'Pilchards in Tomato Sauce'.

'Thank you.' He slipped the can into his briefcase, and the Managing Director walked with him back to the Bentley.

Benedict left the Bentley in a garage in Broadwick Street, and walked through the jostle of Soho until he reached the grimy brick building behind the square. He pressed the bell opposite the card that read Aaron Cohen, Manufacturing Jeweller, and when the door opened he climbed the stairs to the top and fourth floor. Again he rang, and after a while an eye peered at him through the peephole–but the door opened almost immediately.

'Hello, Mr van der Byl. Come in! Come in!' The young doorman welcomed him in and locked the door behind him. 'Papa is expecting you!' he went on as they both looked up at the eye of the closed-circuit TV camera above the wrought-iron grille that barred the passage.

Whoever was viewing the screen was satisfied, for there was an electrical buzz and the grille swung open. The doorman led Benedict down the passage. 'You know the way. Papa is in his office.'

Benedict was in a shabby little reception room, with a threadbare carpet and a pair of chairs that looked like Ministry of Works rejects. He turned to the right-hand door and went through it into a long room that clearly occupied most of the top floor of the building.

Along one side of the room ran a narrow bench, to which were bolted twenty small lathes. Each machine ran off a belt from a central drive below the bench. The man tending the machines wore a white dust jacket, and he grinned at Benedict. 'Hello, Mr van der Byl, Papa is expecting you.' But Benedict delayed a moment to watch the operation of the saws. In the jaw of each lathe was set a diamond, and spinning against the diamond was a circular blade of phosphor bronze. As Benedict watched, the man turned back to the task of spreading a fine paste of olive oil and diamond dust onto the cutting edge of each blade—for it was not the bronze that cut. Only a diamond will cut a diamond.

'Some nice stones, Larry,' Benedict remarked, and Larry Cohen nodded.

'All of them between four and five carats.'

Benedict leaned close and examined one of the diamonds. The line of the cut was marked with Indian ink on the stone. Benedict knew what heart-searching and discussion, what examination and drawing upon the rich storehouses of experience had preceded the positioning of that ink line. It might take two days to saw through each diamond, so Benedict left the bench and moved on.

In a row down the other side of the room sat the other Cohen brothers. Eight of them. Old Aaron was a great breeder of boys. They ranged in age from nearly forty to nineteen years and there were a couple who were still in school and hadn't yet come into the business.

'How do you like this one, Mr van der Byl?' Michael Cohen looked up as Benedict approached. Michael was shaping a fine diamond, cutting it into a round using a lesser stone as a blade. A small tray beneath the lathe caught the dust from the two stones. This dust would be used later for sawing and polishing.

'A beauty,' said Benedict. These men were of the brotherhood, working with diamonds all their lives and loving them as other men love women or horses or fine paintings.

He moved on down the room, greeting each of the brothers, stopping to watch for a minute the loving care with which the elder boys, master craftsmen each of them, were cutting the precisely-angled facets that make up the perfect round brilliant. The fifty-eight facets—table, stars, pavilions and the others which endow a cut stone with its mystic 'life' and 'fire'.

Leaving them crouched over their wheels, so similar to those of a potter, he went through the door at the end of the room.

'Benedict, my friend.' Aaron Cohen came from his desk to embrace him. He was a tall thin man in his late sixties with a thick silvery-grey mane of hair, round-shouldered from years of crouching over a diamond wheel. 'I did not know you were in London, they told me you were in Cape Town. Yesterday was Ruth's birthday. If we had known–'

Benedict took the envelope from his pocket and shook twenty-seven diamonds onto the blotter of the desk.

'What do you think of those, Papa?'

'Shu! Shu!' Papa patted his own cheeks with delight, and he reached instinctively for the biggest stone.

'I should live to see such a stone!' He screwed a jeweller's *loupe* into his eye, turning to catch the natural light from the high windows, and scrutinized the diamond through the eyepiece.

'Ah, yes. There is a feather,* but small. V.V.S.I.† But we will cut through it. Yes, we will take two gems from this stone. Two perfect diamonds of ten or twelve carats each, and perhaps five smaller ones.' More than half a diamond's bulk is lost in the cutting.

'Yes! Yes! From this stone we will sell a hundred thousand pounds' worth of polished diamonds!'

Aaron crossed to the door. 'Boys! Come see! I will show you a prince among diamonds.' And his sons crowded into the office. Michael took it first and gave his opinion. 'A good stone, yes. But not of the same water as the stone we had in the last batch. You remember that octahedron crystal—'

'What you talking!' his father interrupted. 'You wouldn't know a diamond from a piece of gorgonzola cheese already!'

'He is right, Papa.' Larry joined in the discussion. 'The other stone was better.'

'So the Big Lover argues with his father! Little shiksas with skirts up around their tochis you know all about. Dancing the Watusi and the Cha-Cha. Yes! But diamonds you know from nothing.' This declaration precipitated a full-scale, family argument in which each of the brothers joined with gusto.

'Shuddup! Shuddup! Back to work all of you! Out! out!' Aaron broke up the meeting, driving his sons from the office and slamming the door behind them.

'Shu!' He looked to heaven. 'What a business! Now we can weigh the stones.'

When they had weighed and tallied the stones, and Aaron had locked them into the safe, Benedict told him:

'I am thinking of breaking up the Ring.'

Aaron froze and looked across the desk at Benedict. Between them there was always a pretence that their relationship was legitimate. They never spoke about the Ring, or where the unregistered stones came from, or how the finished gems were sent to Switzerland.

'Why?' Aaron asked carefully.

'I am a rich man now. With my father's money, and what I have made from the Ring and invested. A very rich man. I no longer need to take the risks.'

'Such problems I wish I had. But perhaps you are wise—I would not think to argue with you.'

'There will be one or two more packages. Then it will be finished.'

Aaron nodded. 'I understand,' he said. 'Like all good things it must end.'

It was a little after noon when Benedict parked the Bentley outside the mews flat off Belgrave Square. He went to shower immediately he was home. In all the years he had lived here he had never grown accustomed to London's grime-laden atmosphere, and he bathed or showered at least three times a day.

He sang in the shower, and then enveloped in a huge bath towel he left a

---

*Semi-transparent veinlike flaw.

†Very very slight imperfection.

string of damp footprints through to the lounge where he mixed a Martini, and screwed up his eyes at the first stinging taste of the drink.

The phone rang.

'Van der Byl,' he said into the mouthpiece, and then his expression changed as he listened. Quickly he put down the glass and used both hands to hold the telephone receiver.

'What on earth are you doing here?' His tone of astonishment was not faked.

'What a wonderful surprise. When can I see you? How about right now—for lunch? That's great! No, nothing I can't put off—this is a pretty special occasion, you know. Where are you staying? The Lancaster. Fine. Look, give me forty-five minutes, and I'll meet you in the Looking-Glass Room on the top floor. Yes, ten past one. God, what a delightful—I've said that already. See you in three-quarters of an hour.'

He replaced the receiver, swallowed the remains of his Martini and headed for the bedroom suite. This would make a good day into a truly memorable one, he thought, as he quickly selected a silk shirt. He looked at his reflection in the mirror and grinned.

'The ball has really started bouncing your way, Benedict,' he whispered.

She was not at the bar, nor in the Looking-Glass Room. Benedict crossed to the tall picture windows for a glimpse of one of London's finest views across Hyde Park and the Serpentine. It was a smoky blue day, and the pale sun added bronze to the autumn shades of gold and red in the park.

He turned from the windows, and she was crossing the room towards him. His stomach swooped with delight for she also was pale gold with the coppery sheen of sun on her long legs and bare arms. The grace of her carriage was as he remembered it, the precise lifting and laying down of narrow feet on the thick pile of the carpet.

He stood quite still, letting her come to him. Heads turned all across the room, for she was a splendid golden creature. Benedict knew suddenly and clearly that he wanted this woman for himself.

'Hello, Benedict,' she said, and he stepped forward to take her hand in both of his.

'Ruby Lance!' He squeezed her long fingers gently. 'It's so good to see you again.'

The use of her surname was the clue to the strength of his reaction. She belonged to the one man in the world that Benedict most envied and hated. For this reason she was infinitely desirable.

'Let us celebrate with a little drink. I think the occasion deserves at the very least a champagne cocktail.'

She sat with those long slim legs neatly crossed, leaning back in her chair, holding the stemmed glass with tapering fingers. Her hair hung straight to her shoulders, like some rare silken tapestry in white gold, and her eyes watched him with a catlike candour, a calm feline intentness that seemed to look into his soul.

'I should not have bothered you,' she said. 'But I know so few people here.'

'How long can you stay?' He brushed aside the disclaimer. 'I must cancel my other arrangements.'

'A week.' She made it sound like an offer that was subject to negotiation.

'Oh, no!' His voice was mock distressed. 'You can do better than that—we won't be able to do half what I had planned in so short a time. You can stay longer, surely?'

'Perhaps,' she agreed, and lifted the glass an inch. 'It's good to see you.'

'And you.' Benedict agreed with emphasis. They sipped the sparkling wine watching each other's eyes.

Where others must wait weeks and months Benedict went in immediately as though it were his right. A smile and a murmured word, and theatre tickets were his or the doors of fashionable restaurants opened magically.

That first night he took her to the National Theatre, then for dinner at Le Coeur de France where a very famous movie actor stopped at their table.

'Hello, Benedict. We are all going on to the yacht later for a bit of a party. Join us, won't you?' And those legendary eyes turned to Ruby. 'And bring your beautiful friend with you.'

They ate breakfast under the awning on the afterdeck of the yacht, eggs and bacon and Veuve Cliquot champagne, and watched the hubbub of dawn traffic on the wondrously smelly old Thames. Ruby was the only girl in the party without a fur to cheat the chill of the river dawn. Benedict made a mental note of the fact.

On the way home she sat with those long legs curled under her in the seat of the Bentley, still sleek and golden despite the night's exertions, but with the lightest touching of blue beneath her eyes.

'I can't remember having enjoyed an evening so much, Benedict.' She patted a tiny pink-lipped yawn. 'You're a wonderful companion.'

'Tonight again?' he asked.

'Yes, please,' she murmured.

She sensed an urgency in him, when she came down into the lobby of the Lancaster that evening. He came quickly to meet her as she stepped out of the lift, and the quiet assurance with which he kissed her cheek and took her arm surprised her.

They were silent as he snaked the Bentley through the evening traffic. Ruby realized that at the tips of her long tapered fingers, within touching distance, was a fortune such as she had never before allowed herself to dream about. She was deadly afraid. A wrong move, even a wrong word might drive that fortune beyond her grasp for ever. She would never have a chance like this again, and she was afraid to move, almost paralysed with fear. The decision she knew she would have to make very soon would be fateful. Must she counter his advance with withdrawal, or must she meet it as frankly as it was made?

She was so deeply involved with her thoughts that when the Bentley came to a standstill she looked up with surprise. They were parked in a mews outside an expensive-looking flat.

Benedict came round and opened her door, and led her without protest into the flat.

She looked about her curiously, recognizing some of the art works on display in the entrance hall. Benedict took her through into the long lounge and settled her solicitously into the tapestry-covered chair which dominated the room like a throne, and suddenly her fear was gone. She felt queenlike in her control. She knew with certainty that this would all be hers.

Benedict stood in the centre of the room, almost a petitioner in his attitude, and he began to speak. She listened quietly, her expression showing no hint of the triumphant surge of her spirits, and when he stopped to wait for her reply she did not hesitate.

'Yes,' she said.

'I will be with you when you tell him,' Benedict promised.

'It won't be necessary,' Ruby assured him. 'I can handle Johnny Lance.'

'No.' Swiftly Benedict crossed to her chair and took her hands, drawing her to her feet. 'I must be there with you. Promise me that.'

Then it came suddenly evident to Ruby that the strength of her position was unassailable. Benedict needed her not for any physical reasons—but merely because she belonged to Johnny Lance.

Looking steadily into Benedict's eyes she determined to test her intuition.

'He does not have to know about you,' she said. 'I could arrange a divorce with him.'

'He *must* know about me. That's what I want, don't you see?'

'Yes, I see.' She was secure.

'It is agreed?' He could barely conceal his anxiety.

'Yes,' she nodded. 'It's agreed.' And they smiled at each other—each completely satisfied.

'Come.' He led her almost reverently into his bedroom, and Ruby stopped in the doorway with a little cry of delight.

The double bed was a mountain of glowing fur in a score of shades ranging from soft pinkish cream, through beige and oyster, pale smoky blue to midnight and jet glossy black.

'Choose one!' he ordered her. 'To seal our bargain.'

She moved like a sleepwalker towards the bed, but as she reached the centre of the Khedive carpet Benedict called out softly.

'Wait.'

She stopped obediently and he came up behind her. She felt his hands on the back of her neck, and she lowered her chin, shaking her hair forward so that he could unhook the clasp and draw down the fastening of her dress.

She stepped out of the dress as it dropped around her ankles, then waited passively as he carefully removed her brassiere.

'Now,' he said. 'Try them on.'

In her stockings and high-heeled shoes she went to the bed, subtly emphasizing the lilt of her movements, and took up the first fur.

Benedict was sprawled in the wingback chair across the room as she glanced back at him. His face was gloating and flushed, so that his features seemed swollen and coarsened as he stared at her. She understood now that this was a form of ritual in which they were engaged. Like a victorious Roman general, Benedict was conducting his own personal triumph, reviewing the spoils and the plunder. It had no basis in sexual or physical desire, but was rather a service of worship to Benedict himself. She was the priestess of this rite.

Yet, knowing this, Ruby felt no resentment. Rather she found herself excited by the cold perversity of the pageant. As she paraded and postured, turned and swirled, and flared the skirts of a wild mink, she was very conscious of his eyes upon her body. She knew it was perfect, and his scrutiny stirred her physically for the first time in her life. She felt her blood quicken and pound, felt her heart flutter within its cage of ribs like a captive bird, and her loins tighten like a clenching fist. For her also the ritual was narcissistic—satisfying her own deep emotional need.

As she discarded each of the coats she dropped it in the centre of the floor, until there was a knee-high pile of precious fur.

At last she faced him, hugging the soft creamy cloud tightly about her body.

Then she opened her arms, and the coat also, standing on tip-toe to tighten and highlight the hard muscle in her legs and flanks.

'This one,' she whispered, and he came out of the chair, picked her up in his arms and laid her, still wrapped in mink, on the great pile of mink.

Ruby woke in the double bed to a feeling of excitement and enormous well-being such as she had not experienced since she was a schoolgirl on the first morning of a holiday.

The morning was far advanced, pale sunshine in a square shaft poured through the open window like a stage effect.

Benedict in a yellow silk dressing-gown stood beside the bed watching her with an unfathomable expression which changed immediately he realized that she was awake.

'My man has collected your luggage from the Lancaster. Your toilet things are in the bathroom, your clothing in the dressing-room.'

He sat down carefully on the edge of the bed, and leaned forward to kiss her forehead and then each cheek.

'We will breakfast when you are ready.' He sat back and watched her eyes; clearly he was waiting for her to say something important. Immediately she was on guard, wary of making a mistake, seeking a clue in his expression.

'Last night,' he asked. 'Was it as good for you, as it was for me?'

Understanding washed over her in a warm wave. He wanted assurance, a comparison between himself and Johnny Lance.

'I have never in my life—' She placed the emphasis carefully, '—experienced anything like it.'

He nodded, relieved, pleased—and stood up.

'After breakfast we will go to town.'

This morning, Edmund, Benedict's man, chauffeured the Bentley. When they alighted at the north end of Bond Street and walked arm in arm along the pavement, Edmund tailed them at a dignified crawl, steadfastly ignoring the abuse of other drivers.

The morning was cool enough for Ruby to wear her new cream mink, and the looks of admiration and envy she drew drom the other strollers delighted Benedict. He wanted to impress her, he wanted to flaunt his wealth.

'The wife of a diamond man must have diamonds.' He spoke on impulse as they came up to an expensive-looking jewellers. Ruby squeezed his arm and turned to look into the window.

'Good Lord,' Benedict laughed. 'Not here!' And Ruby looked at him with surprise.

Mockingly Benedict began reading the signs in the window

'Paradise Jewellers. A large selection of blue-white gems. Certificate of flawlessness with every diamond. Perfect flawless stones at bargain prices as advertised on TV and in the national Press. Small deposit secures your ring now. A diamond is for ever—show her you really care.'

'But they are such a well-known firm. They have branches all over the world—even in South Africa!' Ruby protested, and bridled a little as Benedict smiled patronizingly.

'Let me explain about diamonds. They are bought for two reasons by two different types of people. Firstly by rich men as investments that will not erode and can only increase in value. These men buy notable stones on the advice of experts, the best of the gem diamond production goes to them. So when

Richard Burton buys Liz a £300,000 diamond he is not being extravagant–on the contrary he is being ultra-conservative and thrifty with his money.'

'That's the kind of meanness I like,' Ruby laughed, and Benedict smiled at her honesty.

'You may find me as thrifty,' he promised.

'Go on,' she said, 'tell me more about diamonds.'

'Well, there is another type who buys diamonds. Usually just one in his life, luckily for him–and he very seldom tries to resell it again or he would get a nasty shock. This type is Joe Everybody–who wants to get married. He usually goes to somebody like Paradise Jewellers.' Benedict poked a derisive finger at the sign in the window. 'Because he has seen it on telly and can get a ring on the instalment plan. In many cases the deposit covers the dealer for the cost of the stone–the rest goes on advertising, finance charges and, of course, profit.'

'How do you know Paradise Jewellers are that type?' Ruby's attention was wide-eyes and girlish.

'You recognize them firstly by the big advertising splurge, then by their language.' Again he studied the notices in the window. '"A large Selection of blue-white gems"–of every thousand stones of jewellery quality produced only one is fine enough in colour to be termed blue-white. It is unlikely they have a large selection. "Gem" is a special term reserved for a diamond which is in every way superb. "Flawless stones at bargain prices"–the lack of flaws in a diamond is only one of many factors governing its value. As for bargain prices–there ain't no such animal. Prices are maintained at the lowest level by fierce competition among expert and canny dealers, and there are no "sales" or special prices for anyone.'

'But where should a person buy a diamond?' Ruby was impressed and dismayed despite herself.

'Not here.' Benedict chuckled. 'Come, I will show you.' And before she could protest he had taken her arm and swept her into the shop, to be greeted with enthusiasm by the manager who must have noticed Ruby's mink and the attendant Bentley, which was causing a small traffic jam outside the shop.

'Good morning, madam and sir. May I be of service to you?'

'Yes,' Benedict nodded. 'A selection of your blue-white gems. The best you have.'

'This way, please.' The manager backed away in front of them, snapping his fingers like a flamenco dancer to summon his assistants.

'Now.' Benedict turned to Ruby, as they settled down in the manager's office with a tray of diamond rings in front of them. 'You cannot examine a diamond properly in its setting.'

He selected the biggest diamond, took from his pocket a gold-plated penknife fitted with a special tool and prised open the claws of the setting to a chorus of horrified squeals from the staff.

'I will make good any damage,' he snapped, and they subsided as Benedict took the loose stone and laid it on the velvet-covered tray.

'Firstly, size. This stone is about one carat.' He looked for confirmation to the manager who nodded. 'Let us say the value of this stone is £500. Ten similar stones will be worth £5,000, right? However, a ten-carat stone may be worth as much as £75,000. So the price per carat rises sharply as the total weight of the stone increases. If I were investing I would not touch a stone under three carats.'

The staff were listening now with as much attention as Ruby.

'Next, colour,' said Benedict, and glanced at the manager. 'A sheet of clean white paper, please.'

The manager scratched in his drawer and laid a sheet of paper in front of Benedict who placed the stone upon it, bottom upwards.

'We compare the colour it "draws" from white paper in good natural light.' He looked up at the manager. 'Switch off the fluorescent lights, and open those curtains, please,'

The manager obeyed with alacrity.

'This is a matter of experience. The colour is judged by a standard. We forget about the fancy rare colours like blue and red and green, and take our top standard as blue-white. A stone so white as to appear slightly blue, after which the distinctions drop to "fine white", and "white". Then stones which "draw" a yellowish tinge which we call "Cape"–in different shades, then finally stones which "draw" a brown colour–which will reduce the value of a stone by up to eighty per cent.'

Benedict fished in his fob pocket and pulled out a guinea case which he opened.

'Every expert carries a special diamond which he uses as a gauge for colour by which to judge all other stones. This is mine.'

The staff exchanged apprehensive looks as Benedict placed a small diamond beside the other. He studied them a moment then replaced his gauge in the case.

'Second Silver Cape, I'd say,' he grunted, and the staff looked suitably abashed. 'Now we consider the stone's perfection.' He looked at the manager. 'Please lend me your *loupe*.'

'*Loupe?*' The manager was mystified.

'Yes, your jeweller's glass.'

'I–' the manager was deeply embarrassed.

'You sell diamonds–yet you do not own a *loupe*.' Benedict shook his head in disapproval. 'No matter, I have my own.'

Benedict took the glass from his inner pocket and placed it in his eye.

'Imperfections can be almost negligible–a "natural" at the girdle, or a bubble or pinpoint of carbon in the stone, on the other hand they can be gross "cracks", "clouds", "ice", or "feathers" which will ruin the value of the stone. But this one is flawless–so when the certificate of flawlessness is issued there will be no misrepresentation.' Benedict closed the glass and tucked it back into his pocket. 'However, in order to produce a flawless stone, the cut has been squeezed.'

He held up the stone between thumb and forefinger.

'The cut or "make" of a stone is the fourth and final decider in its value. The "make" should conform closely to the "ideal". This stone had been cut to exclude a flaw, and in consequence it is badly proportioned–heavy and out of round. I would prefer to see a graceful stone which includes a slight imperfection rather than a grotesque little cripple like this.'

He put the diamond down on the desk.

'The asking price by Paradise Jewellers for this stone is £500–which would be fair and correct for a gem. However, the colour is poor and although it is flawless it is of ungainly make. Its true value would be about–ah, let's see–£185 approximately.'

There was another chorus of protest from the assembled staff, led by the manager.

'I assure you sir, that all our stones have been most carefully appraised.'

'How long have you been with Paradise Jewellers?' Benedict demanded brusquely. 'Four months, isn't it?'

The manager gaped at him.

'Before that you were a salesman in the showroom of a large firm of embalmers and undertakers.'

'I, well—I mean.' The manager fluttered his hands weakly. 'How did you know that?'

'I like to know about all my employees.'

'Employees?' The manager looked stunned.

'That's correct. My name is Benedict van der Byl. I own Paradise Jewellers.'

Ruby clapped her hands and cooed her applause.

'What a bundle of surprises you are!' she exclaimed.

Benedict smiled in acknowledgement and inclined his head.

'Now,' he said, as he rose and helped Ruby to her feet. 'We will go and buy some real diamonds.'

Aaron Cohen sold them two fine white twin marquise-cut brilliants, and Ruby chose the mounting for a pair of white-gold earrings from a leather-bound catalogue.

Benedict gave Aaron his cheque for twenty thousand pounds, then turned to Ruby.

'Now,' he said. 'We'll have lunch at the Celeste Grill-room. The food is bloody awful—but the décor is stupendous. We had best phone and reserve a table—it isn't really necessary but they get terribly hurt if you don't.'

As they settled back in the lush upholstery of the Bentley, Benedict instructed the chauffeur.

'Go past Trafalgar Square, Edmund. I want to pick up the newspapers from South Africa House.'

Edmund double-parked outside the Ambassador's entrance, and the doorman recognized the car and hurried inside to fetch the bundle of newspapers.

As they pulled away around the square towards Haymarket, Benedict selected a copy of the *Cape Argus*.

'Let's see what's happening at home.' He glanced at the front page, and stiffened perceptibly.

'What is it?' Ruby leaned towards him anxiously, but he ignored her. His eyes were darting across the page like the shuttle of a loom. She saw the colour fade from his face, leaving it white and intent. He finished reading, and pushed the paper towards her. She spread the page.

VAN DER BYL DIAMONDS WIN VALUABLE CONCESSION.

APPEAL COURT SUPPORTS KAISER'S MINERAL GRANT.

LANCE GETS THUNDERBOLT AND SUICIDE.

Bloemfontein, Thursday.

In an urgent application by the Central Diamond Mines Ltd to prevent Van Der Byl Diamonds Ltd prospecting and mining a concession area off the South West African Coast, Mr Justice Tromp today dismissed the application with costs stating in his judgement: 'The original concession granted by German Imperial Decree in 1899, and subsequently ratified by Act of the Union Parliament in Act 24 of 1920 must hold good in law, and will take precedence over any subsequent grant or concession purporting to have been made by the Minister of Mines to any other party.'

The area in dispute covers 100 square kilometres surrounding two small islands lying some fifteen miles south of Cartridge Bay and five miles offshore. The islands are known as Thunderbolt Island and Suicide Island, and at the turn of the century were the site of considerable exploitation by a German Guano Company. Mr John Rigby Lance the General Manager of Van Der Byl Diamond Co Ltd, acquired the rights to the concession when he took over the inoperative guano company.

In Cape Town today Mr Lance stated: 'It's the opportunity I have waited for all my life. All indications are that Thunderbolt and Suicide will prove to be one of the richest marine diamonds fields in the world.'

Van der Byl Diamond Co has a diamond-dredging vessel nearing completion in the United Kingdom, and Mr Lance stated that he hoped to begin recovery operations off Thunderbolt and Suicide Islands before the end of the year.

Ruby lowered the paper and looked at Benedict. What she saw was an intense physical shock.

Benedict had crumpled down in the seat. Gone was all the assurance and *savoir faire*. His face was still deathly pale, but now his lips trembled and with disgust she saw that his eyes were swimming with tears. He hunched forward over his hands, shaking his head gently and hopelessly.

'The bastard,' he whispered, and his voice was soggy and muffled. 'He does it every time. I thought that I had him at last, but—Oh God, I hate him.'

He looked at her, his face soft with self-pity. 'He does it every time. Often I've thought I had him, but he just—'

She was mystified by his reaction.

'Aren't you pleased? Van Der Byl Diamonds will make millions—'

'No! No!' he cut in savagely, and then the years of hatred and frustration and humiliation began pouring out. Ruby listened quietly, slowly beginning to understand it all, marvelling at the accumulation of pain and hatred that he exposed for her. He remembered conversations from twenty years ago. Small childhood episodes, innocent remarks that had festered and rankled for a decade.

'You don't want him to succeed, is that it?' she asked.

'I want to crush him, break him, humiliate him.'

For ten seconds Ruby was silent.

'Well, what are we going to do about it?' she asked flatly.

'Nothing, I suppose.' Benedict's tone irritated her. 'He always comes out on top, you just can't—'

'Nonsense,' Ruby snapped. She was angry now. 'Let's go over it carefully, and see how we can stop him. He is only human, and you have shown me enough to prove you are a brilliant and successful businessman.'

Benedict's expression changed, becoming trusting and animated. He turned to her almost eagerly. He blinked his eyes. 'Do you really believe that?'

The bunk was too narrow, Sergio Caporetti decided, much too narrow. He would have one of the carpenters alter it today.

He lay on his back, wedged in firmly, with the blanket-covered mound of his belly blocking his view southwards. He lay and assessed his physical condition. It was surprisingly good. There was but a small blurred pain behind his eyes and the taste of stale cigars and rank wine in the back of his throat was bearable. The leaden cigars in his lower limbs alarmed him until he realized that he was still wearing his heavy fisherman's boots. He remembered one of the girls complaining about that.

He hoisted himself on one elbow, and looked at the girls. One on each side of him, jamming him solidly into the bunk, with magnificent hillocks of pink flesh. Big strong girls both of them, he had chosen them with care, neither of them an ounce under twelve stone. Sergio sighed happily–it had been a wonderful weekend. The girls were snoring, in such harmony that it might have been a rehearsed stage act. He listened to them with mild admiration for a few minutes, then crawled over the outside girl and stood in the centre of the cabin, clad only in his heavy boots. He yawned extravagantly, scratching the thick black wiry curls that covered his chest and belly, and cocked an eye at the bulkhead clock. Four o'clock on a Monday morning, but it had been a truly memorable weekend.

The table was hidden under a forest of empty wine bottles, and dirty plates. There was a congealed mass of cold spaghetti bolognaise in a dish and he picked it up. As he climbed out of the cabin on to *Kingfisher*'s bridge he was scooping up spaghetti with his fingers and cramming it into his mouth.

He stood at the rail of the bridge, a naked hairy figure in tall black boots clutching a dish of spaghetti to his chest, and looked around the dockyard.

Kingfisher was in stocks undergoing the modifications that Johnny Lance had ordered. She was standing high above the level she would attain when she was launched. Although she was a vessel of a mere 3,000 ton displacement, she appeared black and monstrous in the floodlights that illuminated the shipbuilders' yard. It was obvious from her unusual silhouette that she was designed for a special purpose. Her superstructure was situated well aft like that of an oil tanker, while her foredeck was crowded by the huge gantry which would control the dredge, and by the massive storage tanks for the compressed air.

At this hour of the morning the shipyard was deserted, and wisps and tendrils of sea mist drifted about *Kingfisher*'s bulk.

Standing fifty feet above the dry dock, still wolfing cold spaghetti, Sergio urinated over the rail–deriving a simple honest pleasure from the long arching stream and the tinkle of liquid striking the concrete far below.

He clumped back into his cabin, and looked down fondly on his two sleeping Valkyries while he finished the last of the spaghetti. Then he wiped his fingers carefully on his chest hair and called to them gently.

'Come, my kittens, my little doves, the time for play she has passed–the time for work she commences.'

With Latin gallantry he bundled them into a taxi at the dockyard gates, pressing onto each of them a lusty buss, a bank-note, a bottle of Chianti, protestations of deep affection, and the promise of another party next Friday night.

He picked his way through the dockyard jungle of machinery and buildings, lighting a long black cigar and inhaling smoke pleasurably until he came in sight of *Kingfisher* and halted with surprise and annoyance. There was a big honey-coloured Bentley parked near the gangway that led up to *Kingfisher*'s deck. He resented visits from the Company bosses, especially this one, and especially at this ridiculous hour on a Monday morning.

The hose spiralled down into greenness, and they followed it down holding hands. Tracey was still a little nervous. This was not like the Mediterranean, a warm blue friendly embrace of waters to welcome the diver–it was the wild Atlantic, coldly menacing, green and untamed. It frightened her, and Johnny's hand gave her comfort.

Their Draeger demand valves repeated their breathing in a singing metallic wheeze, and icy leaks and rivulets kept finding their way into the cuffs and neck of Tracey's rubber suit.

Sixty feet below the surface Johnny paused, and peered into the glass window of her mask. He grinned at her, his mouth distorted by the bulky mouthpiece, and she gave him a thumbs-up sign. They both looked upwards. The surface was silvered like an imperfect mirror, and the black cigar shape of the boat was lapped in strange light. The hose and anchor chain pierced the silver ceiling and hung down into the shady green depths.

Johnny pointed downwards, and she nodded. They put their heads down, pointed their flippers to the surface, and still hand in hand they paddled steadily towards the sea bed.

Tracey was aware of a crackling hissing sound now, and from out of the greenery blackness below them scudded clouds of silver bubbles twisting and writhing towards the surface. She strained her eyes downwards, following the line of the hose, and slowly out of the murk materialized the black rubber-clad forms of the two men working at the end of the hose; they appeared weird and mystical like black priests performing a satanical mass.

She and Johnny reached the sea and hung just above it, a little way off from the two men on the hose. Johnny indicated the depth gauge that he wore like a wrist watch. It showed a depth of 120 feet. Then he turned and by a hand signal showed her the direction of the reefs.

They were in a valley between these long peaked underwater ridges of black rocks, the same reefs that Tracey had seen from the air. There was a distinct pull of water as the current drifted at right angles to the direction of the reefs.

Johnny squeezed her hand, and then pulled her down. They lay on their bellies on the floor of the sea, and Johnny scooped a handful of the white sand, washed it quickly so that the smaller particles were carried away in a cloud on the current, then he showed her the coarse gravel which remained. Again he grinned, and she returned his smile.

Still leading her by the hand, he swam slowly towards the two men working on the hose, and stopped to watch them.

Attached to the end of the hose was a rigid steel pipe two inches in diameter, and twenty feet long—although now only half its length was visible above the sand bottom. The two divers were forcing it down through sand and gravel to reach bed-rock. The hose itself was attached to a compressor on the deck of the boat which was generating a vacuum in the hose and sucking up the sand and gravel as the steel pipe was forced downwards.

They were prospecting the Thunderbolt and Suicide field. Taking these two-inch samples at five-hundred-foot intervals to ascertain the depth of the water, the thickness of the overburden, and the content of the gravel beds. They were also mapping and plotting the reefs, so that by the time *Kingfisher* arrived they would have a fairly clear picture of the topography and aspect of the field. They would know where to begin dredging, and roughly what to expect when they did.

So far the results had endorsed Johnny's most optimistic expectations. There was a good thick catchment of gravel in all the gullies between the reefs. As he had expected, the heavier gravels had been laid down in the gullies closest to the gap between Thunderbolt and Suicide, and the smaller and lighter gravels had been carried farther. In some of the gullies the gravel beds were fifteen feet deep, and the types of stone present were all highly promising. He had isolated garnet, jasper, ironstone, beryl chips and titanium dust.

However, the conclusive and definite proof had also come up through that two-inch hose out of the depths. They had already pulled the first diamonds from the Thunderbolt and Suicide fields. When you considered the odds against finding a stone in a two-inch sample at five-hundred-foot centres and that payable gravel contained one part diamond in fifty million, it was exciting and encouraging that they had already recovered four diamonds. Small stones, to be sure, not one of them more than half a carat, but diamonds for all that, and some of them of excellent quality.

One of the men on the hose turned and gave Johnny a flat-handed cut-out sign. The pipe was on bed-rock. Johnny nodded and jerked a thumb upwards, and drawing Tracey with him started for the surface.

They climbed the ladder over the survey boat's counter moving clumsily under the weight of the air bottles strapped to their backs, but there were willing hands to help them aboard and strip off the heavy equipment, and unzip the clinging rubber suits.

Tracey accepted a towel gratefully from one of the crew, and while she tilted her head to dry her sodden mane of hair, she looked across half a mile of green sea to the two white whale-backed islands with their attendant clouds of sea birds. The wave bursts on the cliffs sounded like distant artillery, or far thunder.

'God, this is a wild and exciting place.' Her voice bubbled with excitement as she scrubbed at her hair. 'It makes one come alive.'

Johnny understood her feelings, it was the forbidding restless sea and the harsh land that promised danger and adventure. He was about to reply, but the two hose men came aboard at that moment, the taller of them spitting out his mouthpiece and letting it fall to his chest.

'We'll move up to the next point, if it's okay by you, Mr Lance?' The man pulled off his mask and hood, exposing white-blond hair and a sun-broiled face.

'Fine, Hugo,' Johnny agreed, and watched approvingly as Hugo Kramer gave the order to get the anchor and the hose up before taking *Wild Goose* seawards to her next prospecting point. Johnny had been reluctant to charter *Wild Goose* as the prospecting vessel and as the service boat for *Kingfisher*. He did not know Hugo Kramer, and Benedict van der Byl's insistence on the man had made his suspicious.

However, it was natural that they should use a skipper from the van der Byl fleet and Johnny was now prepared to admit he had been wrong. Kramer was an intelligent and willing worker, resourceful and trustworthy, a fine seaman who handled *Wild Goose* with all the skill it would need to bring her alongside *Kingfisher* in a heavy sea. His unfortunate physical appearance Johnny hardly noticed any more, although the original shock of that pink face, white hair and those blind-looking eyes had been considerable.

Tracey was not so charitable. The man made her uneasy. There was a wild-animal ferocity about him, a barely controlled violence. The way he looked at her sometimes made her skin prickle. He did it now; turning back from issuing his order he ran his eyes over her body. In the black silk costume her good round breasts showed at their best, and Hugo Kramer looked at them with those white-fringed bland eyes. Instinctively she covered them with the towel, and it seemed as though his lips twitched with amusement as he turned to Johnny.

'They tell me this dredger of yours is something special, Mr Lance?'

'She is, Hugo. Not like the other half-baked barges and bastardized conversions that have been tried by other companies. She's the first diamond recovery vessel designed expressly for the job.'

'What's different about her?'

'Nearly everything. Her hose is operated off a gantry on the foredeck, it goes through a well pierced through her hull.'

'What kind of hose?'

'Eighteen-inch armoured woven steel with rubber liner. We can get it down to a hundred fathoms, and it has a compensating section in it to stop it plunging with the wave action of the hull.'

'Eighteen inches is pretty big. How will you build up vacuum?'

'That's the point, Hugo. We don't suck—we blow! We evacuate water from the hose by purging it with compressed air, the inrush of water into the opening of the hose sucks in the gravel.'

'Hey, that's neat. So the deeper you work the more effective it will be!'

'Right.'

'What about the actual recovery? Are you going to have the usual screening, ball mill, and grease table arrangement?'

'That's what killed the other companies—trying to separate by the old methods. No. We've got a cyclone to start with.'

'Cyclone?'

'You know a cream separator?'

'Yeah.'

'Same principle. Just spin the gravel in a circular tank and float off everything with a specific gravity of less than 2·5. Take what is left, dry it, spread it on a conveyor belt and run it under an X-ray machine which pinpoints every single diamond. As you know, diamonds fluoresce under X-rays and they show up crisply. The X-ray machine reports the diamond to the central computer—' Johnny's voice and whole attitude was charged with enthusiasm which was impossible for his listeners to resist. Tracey was carried along with him, watching his eyes and his mouth as he talked, smiling when he smiled, her lips following his faithfully.

'This is the cyclone room,' Benedict van der Byl explained as, with a hand on her elbow, he helped Ruby Lance down off the last rung of the ladder. 'I explained to you how it worked.'

'Yes.' Ruby nodded, and looked around the room with interest. The roughly riveted and grey painted plating of *Kingfisher*'s hull formed a square metal box, in the centre of which stood the cyclone. It was also painted battleship grey, a ten-foot-high cone shaped circular tower.

'The gravel is blown in through here.' Benedict indicated the eighteen-inch pipe which entered the cyclone room through the forward bulkhead, then connected to the bottom of the cyclone. 'Up it goes.' Benedict flung his hand upwards. 'And round it goes.' He made a stirring motion. 'The heavy stuff is thrown off and led away through that.' A smaller pipe emerged from the shoulder of the cyclone and disappeared through the farther bulkhead. 'While the lighter stuff shoots out through the top and is sprayed overboard again.'

'I understand. Now, where is the weak spot?' Ruby asked.

'Come.' Benedict led her across the room, picking their way among the litter left by the workmen who still swarmed through *Kingfisher*. They reached a steel door in the bulkhead.

'Watch your head.' They ducked into a long passageway with doors at both ends. On their right hand was an enclosed tunnel that ran the length of the room.

'This is the conveyor room,' Benedict explained. 'The concentrated gravels fall through a hot air draught from an electric furnace to dry them. They are gathered on a conveyor belt, concealed in that tunnel, and carried through into the X-ray room.'

'This is where you will fit it?' Ruby asked.

'Yes. In the conveyor tunnel. It will mean moving that inspection hatch back twelve feet to give us the space.'

Ruby nodded. 'The man who will do the work—can you trust him?'

'Yes. He has worked for me before.' Benedict did not add that the same man had designed the electronic equipment for the balloons used by the Ring, and had flown out from Japan to convert the ASDIC equipment on *Wild Goose*.

'All right.' Ruby seemed satisfied. More and more she was becoming the driving force in the alliance, bolstering Benedict's resolution when he showed timidity or when he tried to evade the actions which must, in time, lead to a confrontation with Johnny Lance.

'Let's see the X-ray room.'

It was a tiny cupboard-like compartment. The floor, roof and all four walls were clad with thick sheet lead. Suspended from the roof was the X-ray machine, and under it a circular table whose surface was covered with a honeycomb-patterned stainless steel sheet.

'The concentrated gravel spills onto the table, and the table revolves under the X-ray machine which fluoresces each diamond and the computer picks it up and reports its size and exact position on the table. The computer then commands one of those—' Benedict pointed to a forest of hard plastic tubes, each attached to a metal arm, '—to swing out over the table exactly above the diamond and suck it up. The computer selects the correct diameter of tube for the size of the diamond—and, after the tube has obeyed the computer the table passes under a second X-ray machine which confirms that the diamond has been collected. If, by chance, the tube fails to suck up the stone, then the computer automatically sends the table on another circuit. If, however, the diamond is safely gathered then the waste material is scraped from the table and it swings round to pick up more gravel from the cyclone room—and repeat the whole process. The system is 100 per cent effective. Every single diamond is recovered by it. Even stones as small as sugar grains.'

'Where is the computer?' Ruby asked.

'There.' Benedict pointed through the small leaded glass window which overlooked the X-ray table. Beyond it was another small compartment. Ruby flattened her nose against the glass, and peered in. The computer occupied most of the room, a huge glossy enamelled cabinet not unlike a refrigerator despite the switches and dials. Benedict peered in beside her.

'The computer runs the entire operation. It controls the flow of compressed air into the dredger pipe, it regulates the cyclone, runs the X-ray machine and the table, it weighs and counts the diamonds recovered before depositing them in a safe, and it even navigates the *Kingfisher* and reports to the bridge her exact position over the sea bed, it checks the lubrication and temperature of the engines and power plant and on request will make a complete and immediate report of the whole or any part of the operation.'

Ruby was still peering into the computer room.

'What happens to the diamonds once they have been picked off the revolving table?' she asked.

'They are sucked through an electronic scale which weighs each stone, then they are carried through into the computer room and deposited in that safe.' Benedict pointed out the steel door set in the bulkhead. 'The safe has a time and combination lock. So the system works without a diamond being touched by human hands.'

'Let's go and talk to the Italian peasant,' suggested Ruby, and as she turned from the window Benedict slippped his arm about her shoulders and hugged her possessively.

'Not now,' snapped Ruby irritably, shrugging off his arm, and she led the way out of the X-ray compartment, passing the locked door of the computer control room opposite the door to the conveyor room. She was impressed with the ingenuity of the system—but the fact that it had been constructed by Johnny Lance made her angry.

Her loyalties had changed completely, going to the highest bidder.

Sergio Caporetti felt a small twinge of pity when he looked at Ruby Lance. So thin, and with a backside like a boy. She would be little comfort to a man on a cold night. Sergio worked the cheroot from one corner of his mouth to the other, anointing the stub with saliva in the process. Also she was cold-blooded, he decided. Sergio had a very sensitive intuition when it came to judging the temperature of a woman's passion. Cold like a snake, he decided, his pity giving way to revulsion. He repressed a small shudder as he watched her settle onto the day couch in his cabin, and cross her long golden legs precisely. Just like a snake, she would eat a man as though he were a little hopping frog. Sergio had admiration for Johnny Lance, but—he decided—not even he would be safe with a woman like this.

'You like my ship?' he asked, an attempt at friendliness. 'She is *very* fine ship.'

Sergio actually used a more forceful adjective than *very*, one that suggested *Kingfisher* was capable of procreation, and Ruby's lips curled with disgust. She ignored the question and lit a cigarette, swinging one leg impatiently, and turned her head to stare through the porthole.

Sergio was hurt by the rebuff, but he had no time to brood on it for Benedict van der Byl came to stand in the centre of the cabin with his hands clasped behind his back.

'Mr Caporetti—' he asked quietly. 'How much do you like money?'

Sergio grinned, and pushed the grubby maritime cap to the back of his head. 'I like it pretty good, I like it better than my mother—and I love my mother like my life,' he said.

'Would you like to become a rich man?' Benedict asked, and Sergio sighed wistfully.

'Si!' he nodded. 'But it is the impossible thing. There is too much *vino*, too much lovely girls, and the cards they are cruel like —' Sergio paused to find a suitable simile and glanced at Ruby, '—like a thin woman. No. Money she does not stay long, she comes and she goes.'

'What would you do for twenty-five thousand pounds?' Benedict asked.

'For twenty-five thousand—' Sergio's eyes were dark liquid and lovely as those of a dying gazelle or a woman in love '—there is nothing I will not do.'

Kingfisher sailed for Africa on October 4th. As the representative of the owners, Benedict van der Byl drove down from London to bid her *bon voyage*, and he spent an hour behind locked doors with Sergio Caporetti before the departure of the vessel.

Kingfisher made good time southwards on her first leg of the voyage, but the unscheduled delay of ten days at the islands of Las Palmas infuriated Johnny. His urgently cabled inquiries from Cape Town elicited the reply that there were teething troubles in *Kingfisher*'s engine room which were being attended to in the Las Palmas dockyards. The voyage would be resumed as soon as the repairs had been effected.

The Japanese gentleman who welcomed *Kingfisher* to Las Palmas was named Kaminikoto. This was too much for Sergio's tongue, so he called him 'Kammy'.

Sergio's crew was sent ashore with the excuse that the work on *Kingfisher* was dangerous. They were installed in the best tourist hotel and liberally supplied with intoxicating liquor. Sergio did not see them for the next ten days that he and Kammy were busy on the modifications to *Kingfisher*'s computer, and recovery equipment.

During those ten days Sergio and Kammy discovered that despite physical appearances they were brothers.

Kammy had mysterious packing-cases brought on board and they worked like furies from dawn until after dark each day. Then they relaxed.

Kammy was half Sergio's size with a face like a mischievous monkey. At all times he wore a Homburg hat. On the one occasion that Sergio saw him in his bath without his headgear he discovered that Kammy was as bald as St Peter's dome.

Kammy's abundant tastes in women were identical to Sergio's. This made the hiring of partners an easy matter, for what suited the one suited the other. Sergio took south with him fond memories of the little Japanese clad only in his Homburg hat, uttering birdlike cries of encouragement and excitement, while perched like a jockey on top of a percheron mare.

When at last Sergio shepherded his debauched crew back aboard *Kingfisher* the only obvious sign of their labours was that the inspection hatch on the conveyor tunnel had been moved back twelve feet.

'It is my best work,' Kammy told Sergio. Already he was sad at the prospect of parting. They were brothers. 'I signed my name. You will remember me when you see it.'

'You good guy, Kammy. The best!' Sergio embraced him, lifting him off his feet and kissing him heartily on each cheek while Kammy clutched desperately at his Homburg.

They left him standing on the wharf, a forlorn and solitary figure, while *Kingfisher* butted out into the Atlantic and swung away southwards.

Ruefully Johnny Lance glanced over at the mountain of empty champagne bottles beyond the barbecue pits. The bill for this little party would be in the thousands, but it was not an extravagance. The guest list included all Van Der Byl Diamond Company's major creditors and their wives, Johnny Lance was showing them all what they were getting for their money. To appear prosperous was almost as reassuring to a creditor as being prosperous. He was going to stuff them full of food and champagne, show them over the *Kingfisher* and fly them back home, hoping sincerely that they would be sufficiently impressed to stop badgering him for a while—and let him get on with the business of taking the Company out into the clear.

Tracey caught his eye. Her humorous roll of the eyes was a plea for sympathy, for she was surrounded by a pack of middle-aged bankers and financiers whom champagne had made susceptible to her charms. Johnny winked at her in reply, then glanced around guiltily to find Ruby, and was relieved that she was in deep conversation with Benedict van der Byl in a far corner of the marquee.

He made his way out of the crowd to the edge of the dune, and lit a cigarette while he looked back across Cartridge Bay.

The chartered Dakotas that had flown the guests and caterers up from Cape Town were standing on the airstrip beyond the buildings.

The marquee was situated on the crest of a sand-dune overlooking the narrow entrance to the bay. The dune had been bulldozed to accommodate the tent, the laden tables, and the barbecue pits around which white-clad servants were busy, and the spitted carcasses of three sheep and a young ox were already browning crisply and emitting a cloud of fragrant steam.

Tracey watched Johnny standing out on the edge of the dune. He looked tired, she thought. The strain of the last few months had worn him. Looking back on it now she realized that every few days had thrust a crisis upon him. The terrible worry of the court case that had won them Thunderbolt and Suicide had barely ended before Johnny had faced the delays in the construction of *Kingfisher*, the bullying of creditors, the sniping of Benedict and a hundred other worries and frustrations.

He was like a prize-fighter coming out to the bell of the last round, she thought tenderly, as she studied the profile of his face now staring out to sea. His stance was still aggressive, the big jaw pushed out and the hand with the missing finger that held the cigarette balled into a fist, but there were blue shadows under his eyes and lines of tension at the corners of his mouth.

Suddenly, there was an alertness in Johnny's attitude, he shaded his eyes with a hand before turning back towards the marquee.

'All right, everyone!' he called, stilling the babble of their voices. 'Here she comes.'

Immediately the uproar was redoubled and the whole party trooped out into the sunlight, their excitement and the shrillness of their voices enhanced by the Pommery they had been walloping back since mid-morning.

'Look! There she is!'

'Where? Where?'

'I can't see her.'

'Just to the left of that cloud on the horizon.'

'Oh yes! Look! Look!'

Tracey took a second glass of champagne from one of the waiters, and carried it across to Johnny.

'Thanks.' He smiled at her with the ease that now existed between them.

'It's taken her long enough to get here.' Tracey picked out the faraway speck on the green ocean that was *Kingfisher*. 'When will she begin working?'

'Tomorrow.'

'How long will it be before we know—well, if it has come off?'

'A week.' Johnny turned to her. 'A week to be certain, but we'll know in a day or two how it's shaping up.'

They were silent then, staring out at the gradually approaching speck. The crowd lost interest quickly and drifted back to the liquor, and the fragrant steaming platters of golden-brown meat that were coming from the barbecue pits.

Tracey broke the long friendly silence at last. She spoke hesitantly, as though reluctant to bring up a painful subject.

'How long has Ruby been back now—ten days?'

'About that,' Johnny agreed, glancing at her quickly. 'I haven't seen much of her,' he admitted. 'But she seems to be a lot more relaxed—at least she's off my back.'

'She and Benedict seem to have become very pally.' Tracey glanced across to where the other couple were now included in a boisterous circle of revellers.

'She bumped into him in London.' Johnny agreed, sounding offhand. 'She tells me they had lunch a couple of times.'

She waited for him to continue, to express some suspicion or reservation, but he seemed to have no further interest in the subject; instead he began running over the day's further arrangements with her.

'I'm relying on you to take charge of the wives when we go aboard. Keep an eye on Mrs Larsen particularly—she's up to her gills in bubbly.'

For the next two hours that it took *Kingfisher* to make her approach and enter the channel of Cartridge Bay, Johnny hardly took his eyes from her unusual silhouette. She was not a pretty vessel but the white lightning insignia of Van Der Byl Diamonds on her funnel gave her a special beauty in his eyes. As she passed below them and entered the bay, Larsen proposed a toast to her successful career, then they all descended the dune and climbed into the waiting Land-Rovers and drove round the bay to meet her. By the time they arrived *Kingfisher* had made fast alongside the jetty, and Captain Sergio Caporetti was waiting to welcome them aboard.

He stood at the head of the gangway, and sensible to the importance of the moment he was decked in his finest and best; a double-breasted suit with a cream and lilac pinstripe set off the tomato-red silk tie, but his two-tone black and white crocodile skin shoes drew attention to his large feet and his gait was that of an emperor penguin. A liberal application of a hair pomade with a penetrating smell of violets had flattened his black hair into a shiny slick, bisected by the ruler-straight line of white scalp which was his parting. However, the aroma of the pomade was at odds with the particularly stinky cheroot of a brand which Sergio reserved for weddings, funerals and other special occasions.

His beautiful gazelle eyes became passionate and dark as they lit on Fifi Larsen. Mrs Larsen's tight-fitting slacks moved as though they were full of live rabbits and her pink sweater was straining its seams. Her eyes were sparling with champagne and she giggled without apparent reason, flushing under Sergio's scrutiny.

The tour of *Kingfisher* began, Sergio Caporetti taking up an escort position directly behind Mrs Larsen. They had hardly descended the first ladder when Mrs Larsen let out a small squeak and shot about eighteen inches into the air, before coming back to earth with all her plentiful womanhood aquiver.

'My dear Fifi, whatever is wrong?' Her husband was all solicitude, while behind her Sergio Caporetti wore an expression of cherubic innocence. Johnny felt dizzy with alarm, for he had seen Sergio's great hairy paw settling comfortably onto those majestic buttocks. Mrs Fifi Larsen had been thoroughly goosed.

In relieved disbelief Johnny heard her reply, which was preceded by another giggle.

'I seem to have twisted my ankle. Perhaps there is somewhere I could sit down.'

Johnny looked around frantically for Tracey to get Mrs Larsen out of Sergio's clutching range, but before he could signal her, Fifi was limping away on Sergio Caporetti's arm, bravely declining all offers of help.

'Please don't let me spoil your fun. I'll just sit in the Captain's cabin for a few minutes.'

Quickly Johnny moved up beside the silver-haired Larsen and resolved to stay close beside him. Even if he could not prevent Fifi visiting Sergio's quarters, he was going to make good and sure that her husband didn't join the party.

'This is the explosives locker.' Johnny took Larsen's arm and led him away. 'We keep a store of plastique explosives for underwater blasting–'

Larsen's concern at his wife's injury dissolved and he became immersed in the tour of *Kingfisher*. Johnny followed the line of production for him from the moment the gravel was sucked in through the dredge.

As they left the cyclone room Johnny preceded him, holding the steel door open for Larsen.

'From the cyclone the concentrates pass through here into–' He stopped with surprise as they entered the narrow compartment beyond the cyclone.

'What's wrong, Lance?' Larsen demanded.

'No. It's nothing,' Johnny assured him. After the surprise of finding that the inspection plate in the conveyor tunnel had been moved he realized that it was as well from a security angle. Probably the marine architects had ordered the modification. 'The concentrates are carried through into the next compartment to the X-ray room. This way, please.'

As Johnny led the way to the next door he resolved to check with the architects. Larsen asked a question and he replied and the conveyor tunnel was forgotten. They went through into the X-ray room.

'He noticed it.' Benedict puffed quickly and nervously at the cigarette cupped in his hand. 'He doesn't miss a thing. The bastard.'

'He noticed it, yes. But he accepted it.' Ruby was definite. 'I know him. I was watching him. He was disturbed for a second then he rationalized it. I could almost see his mind work. He accepted it.'

They stood together on the exposed angle of *Kingfisher*'s bridge. Suddenly Ruby laughed.

'Don't look so worried,' she warned him merrily. 'We are being watched by your sister again. She's down on the foredeck. Come.'

Still smiling she led him around the angle of the bridge house, and out of sight she was immediately deadly serious again.

'That sister of yours is getting suspicious. We must keep away from each other until you tell Johnny.'

Benedict nodded.

'When are you going to tell him?' she demanded.

'Soon.'

'How soon?' Ruby would not be able to rest until it was out in the open, until Benedict had committed himself, yet she must not push him too hard.

'As soon as *Kingfisher* runs the Company under. I will pick the moment that he is beaten financially, then I will tell him. I want it to be the *coup de grâce*.'

'When will it be, Benedict darling? I am so anxious to be with you—without all this subterfuge.'

Benedict opened his mouth to reply and froze like that, his expression changing slowly into that of a man who doubts the evidence of his own eyes. He was staring over Ruby's shoulder.

Ruby turned quickly. The curtain across the Captain's porthole behind her was open a chink. She looked in upon a spectacle of such whole-hearted rubicund magnitude that it should have occurred only on Olympus between Jupiter and Juno.

In the cabin Fifi Larsen was receiving treatment for her sprained ankle.

'Well, you've got your toy now. Let's hope for all our sakes you can do something with it,' Benedict smiled pleasantly as he came across to where Johnny stood with Larsen under the great gallows-shaped gantry on the foredeck of *Kingfisher* that would raise and lower the dredging head.

'Toy, Mr van der Byl?' Larsen's white eyebrows bristled. 'Surely you have no doubts? I mean, now that you've got this Thunderbolt and Suicide concession?'

'Oh, I wouldn't say doubts, Mr Larsen. Reservations perhaps, but not really doubts. Mr Lance has been the champion of this venture. His enthusiasm has carried it—in the face of all opposition. Even that of my late father.' Benedict turned to Larsen smoothly.

'Your father opposed the scheme? I didn't know that!' Larsen was perturbed.

'Not opposed it, Mr Larsen.' Benedict smiled reassuringly. 'Not really opposed it. But you will notice that he was prepared to risk your money—not his own. That will give you some idea of how he felt.'

There was a chilled silence, before Larsen turned to Johnny.

'Well, Lance, thank you for an interesting day. Very interesting. I'll be watching your progress with attention—close attention.' And he turned away and strode to where a subdued and demure Fifi was waiting with a group of other wives.

'Thanks.' Johnny gave Benedict a bleak grin.

'Don't mention it.' Benedict smiled that charming boyish smile.

'At the end of this week I'll take that little speech of yours, roll it into a ball and ram it down your throat,' Johnny promised him softly, and Benedict's expression changed. His eyes slitted and his grin showed his teeth and tightened the soft line of his jaw.

'You're pretty slick with your mouth, Lance.'

They glared at each other, the antagonism so apparent, as elemental as a pair of rutting stags, that they were suddenly the centre of all attention. The guests stared curiously, aware of the drama but not understanding it.

Ruby started forward quickly to intervene, taking Johnny's elbow, her voice sugary.

'Oh, Benedict, do you mind if I talk to Johnny a moment? I have to know if he's returning to Cape Town with me this evening.'

She led him away, and the tension dissolved. The disappointed guests began drifting to the gangplank and filing down onto the jetty.

In the confusion of embarkation aboard the two Dakotas, Johnny managed to exchange a last word with Tracey.

'You'll stay here until you know?' she asked. He nodded.

'Good luck, Johnny. I'll pray for you,' she whispered, then followed Ruby Lance up into the fuselage of the Dakota.

Johnny watched the two big aircraft taxi down to the end of the strip, turn in succession and roar away into the purple and red sky of evening.

After they had gone it was very still, and the silence of the desert was complete. Johnny sat in the open Land-Rover and smoked a cigarette while the night came down around him.

He was uneasy, aware of a deep-down tickle of apprehension and foreboding which he could not pin down.

The last glow of sunset faded from the Western sky, and the desert stars were bright and hard and close to the earth, silvering the dome of space with the splendour that the city-dweller would never guess at.

Still Johnny hunched in the seat of the open Land-Rover trying to explore the source of his uneasiness, but with so little success that at last he must attribute it to the strain and fatigue of the last few months, his involvement with Tracey, his steadily worsening relationship with Ruby—and the latest clash with Benedict.

He flicked the stub of his cigarette away, watching morosely the explosion of red sparks as it struck the earth, then he started the Land-Rover and drove slowly down towards the jetty.

Kingfisher's lights were smeared in paths of yellow and silver across the still waters of the bay. Every porthole was lit brightly, giving her the festive air of a cruise ship.

Johnny left the Land-Rover at the head of the jetty, and walked out to her. The muted throb of her engines cheered him a little, the knowledge that the vessel was preparing for the morrow.

On deck he paused beside the gigantic compressed air tanks, each the size of a steam locomotive, and checked the pressure gauges. The needles were moving perceptibly around the dials, and his mood lightened a little.

He went up the ladder to the bridge, and into the chartroom where Sergio and Hugo were drinking coffee.

'Not my fault, Mr Lance,' Sergio began defensively. 'I am a gentleman–I cannot refuse a lady.'

'You'll dig your own grave with that spade of yours one day,' Johnny warned him grimly, as he went to the chart table and hung over it.

'Now let's get cracking.' Johnny's sense of dread lifted completely as he looked down at the large-scale Admiralty chart. The twin humps of Thunderbolt and Suicide were clearly marked. 'Hugo, have you got the prospecting schedules?'

'There, on the table.' Hugo and Sergio came to stand on each side of Johnny while he opened the bound file of typewritten sheets.

'The soundings we made differ from the Admiralty chart. We'll put in our figures, before we plot the dredging pattern.'

The three of them settled over the chart with dividers and parallel to begin marking in the path that *Kingfisher* would follow through the maze of reefs and gullies.

It was long after midnight before Johnny made his way wearily to the guest cabin below the bridge. He kicked off his shoes, lay on the bunk to rest a moment before undressing and fell into a deathlike sleep of exhaustion.

He was awakened by one of the crew with a mug of coffee and he pulled on a windbreaker before hurrying onto the bridge.

Kingfisher was just passing out through the channel of Cartridge Bay into the open sea, and Sergio grinned at him from where he stood beside the helm.

Dawn was only a lemon-coloured promise over the desert behind them, and the sea was black as washed anthracite, kicked into a chop by the small morning wind. They stood on the darkened bridge and sipped steaming coffee, cupping their hands around the enamel mugs.

Then they turned and ran south, parallel to the desert which was now touched with hot orange and violet. The sea birds were up, a flight of malgas turned to glowing darts of fire by the early sun as they winged swiftly across the bows.

With dramatic suddenness the sun came up over the horizon, and highlighted the chalk-white cliffs of Thunderbolt and Suicide far ahead so that they shone like beacons on the cold green sea. The curtains of spray that burst on the islands flashed and faded as they shot into the sky and fell again.

Wild Goose was waiting for them lying under the lee of the islands, but she came out to meet them, staggering and plunging theatrically over the short uneasy sea that hooked around the islands or boiled through the gap between them.

The radio telephone began crackling and squawking as the sighting reports from Johnny's watch towers on the shore started coming in, cross referencing to give *Kingfisher* her position over the ground. There were short exchanges between Sergio and Hugo on *Wild Goose* as they came together, and the little trawler worked in close, ready to give assistance with the laying of the cables if she were needed.

But standing in the angle of the bridge, Sergio Caporetti had the situation under his control. The grubby marine cap pushed to the back of his head and a long black cheroot stuck in the side of his mouth, he stood balanced on the balls of his feet, his eyes darting from judging the set of the sea surf to the repeater of the computer which was feeding him from his soundings and position—yet attentive to the R T reports from shore and from *Wild Goose*.

Johnny was contented with his choice of man as he watched Sergio at work. *Kingfisher* crept slowly up into the lee of Suicide Island, half a mile from the pearly white cliffs, then she hung there a moment before Sergio punched one of the buttons on her control panel.

From forward there was the harsh metallic roar of an anchor cable running out, and as *Kingfisher* backed away leaving a yellow painted buoy the size of a barrage balloon bobbing under the cliffs of Suicide so one of the massive deck winches began automatically paying out its six-inch steel cable.

Kingfisher backed and crept forward, drifted down on the current or butted up against it while she went through the laborious but delicate operation of laying her four anchors at each point of the compass. Chained above each anchor floated the huge yellow buoys, and from each buoy the steel cables led to the winches on *Kingfisher*'s deck. On instruction from the computer the winches on each quarter would pay out or reel in the cable to hold *Kingfisher* steady over the ground while she worked.

It was mid afternoon before *Kingfisher* was ready, pinned down like an insect to a board, and the computer reported that she was directly over the gully that Johnny had selected as the starting point. She had twenty-five fathoms of water under her—and then the thick bank of gravel.

'All is ready.' Sergio turned to Johnny, who had stood by quietly all this time—not interfering in the task of positioning. 'You will begin the programme now?'

'Yes.' Johnny stirred himself.

'I would like to watch,' Sergio suggested, and Johnny nodded.

'All right, come.' Sergio handed over the bridge to the helmsman and they went down to the armoured door of the computer room.

Johnny opened the lock. There were only two keys to this compartment. Johnny had one and Benedict van der Byl had the other. He had insisted on having the duplicate, and Johnny had reluctantly agreed not knowing that the key would be used in Las Palmas.

The heavy steel door swung back, and Johnny stepped over the coaming and seated himself before the console of the computer. Covered in cellophane and suspended on a clip above the keyboard of the computer were the cards containing the various programme codes.

Johnny selected the sheet headed: PRIMARY OPERATION: DREDGING AND RECOVERY, and began feeding the code into the computer, punching it on the keyboard.

'Beta, stroke, oh, oh, seven, alpha.'

And within the enamelled console, a change of sound heralded the beginning of the new programme, the hum of her reels and the click of the selectors, while on her control panel the lights blinked and flashed.

Now the computer's screen began to answer the instruction, spelling out her response like a typewriter.

> New programme.
> Primary Operation. Dredging and Recovery.
> Phase One.
> Initiate safety procedure:–
> a) Report air pressure . . . 1
> b) Report air pressure . . . 2

Johnny leaned back in the padded stool and watched the exhaustive check that the computer now made of *Kingfisher*'s equipment, typing out the results on the screen.

'What she do now?' Sergio asked curiously, as though he had never spent ten days in this compartment assisting his Japanese friend. Johnny explained the procedure briefly.

'How come you know this so good?' Sergio inquired.

'I spent a month at the Computer Company's head office in America last year while they designed this machine.'

'You the only one in the Company who can work it?'

'Mr Benedict van der Byl has done the course as well as I,' Johnny told him, then he leaned forward again. 'Now she is set.'

The screen on the computer reported itself satisfied.

> Phase One Completed.
> Initiate Phase Two.
> Lowering and siting of dredge head.

Johnny stood up. 'Okay, let's get upstairs.'

He locked the door of the computer room and followed Sergio up to the bridge.

Johnny went to stand beside the repeater screen on the bridge, which was relaying the computer's signals exactly as they were printed on the main screen in the compartment below. He could see out through the windows of the wheelhouse, and he watched the automatic response of the heavy equipment on the foredeck.

The gantry swung forward, and the steel arms picked the dredge head from its chocks, and lifted it with the armoured suction hose dangling behind it. Then the gantry swung back, and with a jerky mechanical movement lowered the head through the square opening in the deck. This well pierced the hull, and through it the hose began to snake—a monstrous black python sliding into its hole. The huge reels that held the hose revolved smoothly, as the dredge was lowered to the sea bed.

'Head on bottom.'

The computer screen reported, and the hose reels stopped abruptly.

> Phase Two Completed.
> Initiate Phase Three.
> Cyclone Revolutions 300.
> Vent dredge pump.

There was a rising high-pitched whine now, like the approach of a jet aircraft. The sound reached a peak, and steadied—and immediately another sound overlaid it. The dull bubbling roar of high-pressure air through water, a sound of such power and excitement that Johnny felt the hair on his forearms prickle erect. He stood still as a statue, his expression rapt and his lips set in a small secret smile. That sound was the culmination of two years of planning and endeavour, the sweet reward of the driving dedication that had made a dream into reality.

Suddenly he wished that Tracey were with him to share this moment, and then he knew instinctively that she had deliberately left him alone to savour his moment of triumph.

He grinned then, as he watched the thick black hose engorge and pulse with internal life, like a great artery—pumping, pumping, pumping.

In his imagination Johnny could see the rich porridgy mixture of sea water and mud and gravel that shot up the hose into the spinning cyclone, he could imagine the steel dredge head on the sea bed below the hull surging rhythmically to stir the sand and pound loose any gravel that pressure had welded into a conglomerate.

From the waste pipe over *Kingfisher*'s stern poured a solid stream of dirty yellow water mixed with the sand and gravel that had been rejected and spun out of the cyclone. It stained the green sea with a cloudy fecal discharge, like the effluent from a sewage outlet.

For three days and two nights *Kingfisher*'s pumps roared, and she inched forward along the marine gully like a fussy housewife vacuuming every speck of dust from her floor. As the third evening spread its dark cloak over her, Johnny Lance sat on the padded seat in front of the computer console. He sat forward on the stool with his elbows on his knees and his face in his hands for a full hour. He sat like that in the attitude of despair.

When he lifted his head, his face was haggard and the lines of defeat were clearly cut into his features with the cold chisel of failure.

From the meagre recovery of small diamonds that *Kingfisher* had made in the last three days it was clear beyond reasonable doubt that despite all the indications of Thunderbolt and Suicide field would not support the running costs of the vessel let alone cover the overheads, or the interest charges and capital repayments on the loan account.

Van Der Byl Diamond Company was finished—and Johnny Lance was financially ruined beyond any possibility of ever finding redemption.

It remained only for the jackals to assemble and squabble over the carcass. Sergio Caporetti leaned over the railing of the bridge, blowing long streamers of blue cheroot smoke from mouth and nostrils to help foul a morning which was already thick and grey with sea-fret. The islands of Thunderbolt and Suicide were blanketed by the mist, but the surf broke against their hidden cliffs like distant artillery and the sea birds' voices were plaintive and small as lost souls in the void.

Wild Goose came bustling up out of the mist, swinging in under *Kingfisher*'s side to hover there under power with two of her crew fending off.

Hugo Kramer stuck his white blond head out of the wheelhouse window, and shouted up at the deck.

'Okay, boss. Come on!'

Sergio watched the tall figure on *Kingfisher*'s deck rise and look around like a man walking from sleep. Johnny Lance lifted his head and looked up at the bridge, and Sergio noticed that he was unshaven, a new beard darkened his jaw and emphasized its prominence. He looked as though he had not slept, and he hunched into the wind-breaker with the collar turned up against the mist. He did not smile, but lifted one hand in farewell salute to Sergio—who noticed incongruously that the index finger was missing from the hand. Somehow, that pathetic little detail struck Sergio. He was sorry, truly sorry. But there is always a loser in every game, and twenty-five thousand pounds is a lot of money.

'Good luck, Johnny.'

'Thanks, Sergio.' Johnny went to the rail lugging his briefcase and swung it; he dropped swiftly down the steel rungs set in *Kingfisher*'s hull and jumped the narrow gap of surging water to *Wild Goose*'s deck.

The trawler's engine bellowed, and she pulled away, rounding on to a course for Cartridge Bay. Johnny Lance stood on her open deck looking back at *Kingfisher*.

'He's a good guy.' Sergio shook his head with regret.

'He's a boss,' the helmsman grunted. 'No boss is any good.'

'Hey, you! I am also a boss,' Sergio challenged him.

'Like I said.' The helmsman suppressed a grin.

'I kiss your mother,' Sergio insulted him with dignity, then changed the subject. 'I go below now, take over.'

Sergio opened the door to the control room with the duplicate key. He closed the door behind him, seated himself at the console and took from his pocket a sheet of paper headed: KAMINIKOTO SECONDARY RECOVERY PROGRAMME.

Ten minutes later he came out of the control room and locked the door.

'Kammy, I love you,' he chuckled as he closed off the water-tight doors that isolated this deck from the one above. He wound the locking bars into position to ensure that he was not interrupted by one of his own crew.

From the tool cupboard on the bulkhead he selected a pair of set spanners and went through into the conveyor room. It took him twenty minutes to unscrew the heavy, deeply threaded bolts that secured the hatch. It had been designed to resist easy entry—a deterrent to casual investigation, but at least

Sergio could lift the steel plate off its seating.

He eyed the small square opening with distaste, and reflexively sucked in his pendulous belly. The hatch had not been designed to afford passage to a man of his dimensions.

He took off his cap and jacket and hung them on the cock of one of the pipes, then he ground out his cheroot under his heel and brushed back the hair from his forehead with both hands, checked that his flashlight was in his pocket, and committed himself to the hatch.

He wriggled and kicked, and grunted and built up a heavy sweat for five minutes before he had squeezed through into the conveyor belt tunnel. He squatted on his haunches, panting heavily and flashed his torch along the tunnel. Above his head the conveyor belt carrying the gravel ran smoothly, but the residual heat from the driers made it unbearably hot. He began to crawl rapidly to the end of the tunnel.

From the inside it was impossible to tell, without measuring, that the conveyor belt tunnel was shorter by twelve feet than the external length.

The end of the tunnel was false, and beyond it was a secret cubicle only just large enough to house Kaminikoto's equipment through which all the gravel passed on its journey to the X-ray room.

The Japanese genius for miniaturization was demonstrated by the equipment in this secret cubicle. It was an almost exact copy of the sorting equipment in the main X-ray compartment—except that it had been scaled down to one tenth of the size without affecting its efficiency; in addition, this miniature plant could discriminate in the diamonds it selected. It would not allow a stone over four carats to pass through, and it screened out fixed percentages of the smaller stones—allowing only a proportion of the smaller and less valuable diamonds to proceed through into the main X-ray room.

It was an amazing piece of electrical engineering, but Sergio was unimpressed as he lay on his side in the cramped hot tunnel and began laboriously to unscrew another smaller plate in the false bulkhead.

At last it was open, and he reached through the opening; after a few seconds of fiddling and groping and heavy breathing he brought out a stainless steel cup with a capacity of about two pints. There were clamps on the cup to hold it in position below the chute under Kaminikoto's machine.

The metal cup was heavy, and Sergio placed it carefully on the deck beside him before propping himself on an elbow and shining the flashlight into the cup. His expression changed, and he groped in the cup and took something out of it, stared at it a moment then dropped it back.

'By the blood of all the martyrs!' he gasped with shock, and then immediately contrite for his blasphemy he crossed himself awkwardly with the hand holding the flashlight. Then again he shone the torch into the cup, and shook his head in disbelief. Quickly he pulled a canvas drawstring bag from his pocket, and lying on his side he carefully poured the contents of the cup into the bag, drew the string tight and stuffed it back into his pocket where it made a big hard bulge on his hip like a paper sack of rock-candy. He clamped the stainless steel cup back into position, screwed the cover plate over the opening, and backed away down the tunnel on hands and knees.

He very badly needed a cheroot.

Four hours later Hugo Kramer shinned up the ladder onto *Kingfisher*'s deck while his helmsman took the trawler down to leeward to wait for him.

Sergio shouted down from the bridge.

'Johnny he has gone?'

'Ja!' Hugo shouted back. 'He should almost be in Cape Town by now. That Beechcraft is a fast plane.'

'Good.'

'How did it go with you?' Hugo countered.

'Come up—I'll show you.'

Sergio led him into his cabin behind the bridge and locked the door carefully. Then he went to each of the portholes and drew the curtains across them, before crossing to his desk and switching on the reading lamp.

'Sit down.' Sergio indicated the chair opposite the desk. 'You want a drink, or something?'

'Come on,' Hugo grated impatiently. 'Stop mucking around, let's have a look.'

'Ah!' Sergio looked at him sadly. 'You Germans, you are always in too much hurry. You cannot rest, enjoy life—'

'Cut the crap!' Hugo's pale eyes were on his face, and Sergio was suddenly aware that this man was dangerous, like a tiger-shark. Coldly dangerous, without malice or passion. Sergio was surprised he had not noticed it before. I must be careful with this one, he thought, and he unlocked the drawer of his desk and took out the canvas bag.

He loosened the drawstring and poured the diamonds onto the blotter. The smallest was the size of a match head—perhaps point one of a carat, and the poorest quality was black and granular-looking, ugly little industrial stones, for Kammy had been careful not to take out only the best and so distort the *Kingfisher*'s recovery as to arouse suspicion. There were hundreds of these tiny crystals and chips which would fetch a few pounds in the industrial market; but there were other stones in the full range of quality and shapes and sizes—as big as green peas, or as marbles, and a few bigger than that. Some of them were perfect octahedron crystals, others water-worn, chipped or amorphous in shape.

They formed a dully glittering pile in the centre of the blotter, in all perhaps five hundred diamonds, yet all of these were dwarfed by one single stone that lay in the centre of the pile, rising out of it the way Mount Everest rises from her foothills.

There are freak diamonds so large or unusual that they become legend. Diamonds who have their own names and whose histories are recorded and invested with romance. The great 'paragons'—stones of the first water whose cut and finish weight exceed one hundred metric carats.

Africa has produced many of them: the *Jonker Diamond*, a 726-carat rough cut to a brilliant of 125 carats that hangs about the throat of the Queen of Nepal; the *Jubilee Diamond*, a superb 245-carat cushion of unearthly fire fashioned out of 650-carat rough—then the biggest of them all, a monstrous rough stone of 3,106 carats, the *Cullinan* which yielded not one, but two paragons. The *Great Star of Africa* at 530 carats and the *Cullinan 11* at 317 carats. Both these stones grace the Crown Jewels of England.

Now on Sergio Caporetti's desk lay a rough stone which would add yet another paragon to the list.

'Have you weighed it?' asked Hugo, and Sergio nodded.

'How much?'

'Three hundred and twenty carats,' Sergio said softly.

'Jesus!' whispered Hugo, and Sergio crossed himself quickly to dissociate from the use of names.

Reverently Hugo Kramer leaned forward and picked up the big diamond. It filled the palm of his hand, the cleavage plane that formed its base was smooth and clean as an axe-stroke. There were bigger diamonds in history, but this diamond had a special feature which would set it in a niche of its own and endow it with peculiar value.

Its colour was the serene blue of a high summer sky.

This stone could pay half the total bill for *Kingfisher*'s construction—if it were ever used for that purpose.

Hugo replaced the blue diamond on the desk and lit a cigarette without taking his eyes from it.

'This field—it is bigger—richer, far richer than we had guessed.'

Sergio nodded.

'In three days we have taken diamonds that I hoped to see once in five years,' Hugo went on as he began picking out the larger diamonds from the pile and laying them in a line across the desk-top in approximate order of size, while Sergio opened his desk drawer and took out a box of his special occasion cheroots.

'We must tell the boss,' Hugo decided. He began arranging the diamonds in a neat circle about the big Blue, thinking deeply. 'He must know how rich it is before he talks to Lance. He must make arrangements. He will know what to do—he's a clever one.'

'What about these?' Sergio indicated the treasure on the desk. 'Are you going to take them off?'

Hugo hesitated. 'No,' he decided. 'We could never get rid of this big Blue through the usual channel, it is too big, too distinctive. We will keep it aboard. When the boss takes over the Company again—then we will just declare it all nice and legal. No trouble.' He stood up. 'Look after them. I must hurry if I am to get a message to Cape Town in time.'

'The Company bears my father's name, Mr Larsen. It's as simple as that.' Benedict's voice was husky with emotion, and he looked down at his hands. 'I have a duty to my father's memory.'

'My boy, well—' Larsen came to lay his hand on Benedict's arm. 'Well, I just don't know what to say. Honour is a rare and precious thing these days.' With his free hand he was groping almost frantically for the bell on the desk behind him. He must get this signed up solid before the youngster changed his mind.

'I tried to warn you, Mr Larsen. My father and I never had any faith in this marine recovery scheme. Lance pushed it through—'

'Yes, quite so,' Larsen agreed, and turned to his assistant who came into the office at the trot in response to the bell. 'Ah, Simon. The Van Der Byl Diamond loan. Will you have an agreement made out immediately—Mr van der Byl will take over the capital amounts, and the out-standing interest as well.' By rolling his eyes Larsen tried to convey to his assistant the deadly urgency of the situation. The young man understood and fifteen minutes later laid the Agreement on Larsen's desk. Larsen unscrewed the cap of his pen and handed it to Benedict.

Larsen and three of his young men ushered Benedict out through the glass doors of the bank and across the pavement to where the Rolls stood in the reserved parking bay in Adderley Street.

Benedict settled into the back seat, acknowledged the bank official's farewells, and tapped on the chauffeur's window. As they pulled away, Ruby Lance slipped her hand through his arm and squeezed it.

'Did you get it?' she asked.

Benedict grinned happily. 'I frightened five years' growth out of old Larsen. He almost broke his neck in the hurry to give it to me.'

'Now you've got it all.' Ruby snuggled a little closer to him on the soft leather upholstery. Benedict nodded, and checked his watch.

'The meeting is set for fifteen minutes' time. I'll go up the front way, but I want you to go up in the private lift from the basement garage, and wait in my office. We will be in the Board Room. I will ring you at the right moment.'

The Rolls picked its way slowly down around the Heerengracht and double-parked outside the building. The chauffeur came to open the door, but before he alighted Benedict smiled into Ruby's face.

'This will be one of the high moments of my life,' he said softly. 'This time I've got the bastard cold.'

'I'll be waiting for you,' Ruby said, and he climbed out of the Rolls. He waited until it had turned into the entrance ramp of the basement garage, then he crossed the pavement into the main lobby of the skyscraper. He strode to the elevator with long eager strides, and his mouth kept pulling into a small excited smile.

The Board Room was set high, and the picture windows looked up at the great squat mountain, whose sheer cliffs dropped directly to the wooded slopes up which the first buildings of the city straggled.

Johnny Lance stood at the head of the table. He had lost weight in the last few days, so that his shoulders appeared bony and gaunt under the white silk shirt. He had discarded his jacket, and pulled the knot of his tie down an inch. The bones of his cheeks and jaw made harsh angles that were accentuated and not softened by the deep shades of fatigue that darkened his eyes. His hands were thrust deep into his pockets, and he spoke without reference to the sheaf of paper that lay on the table before him.

'Our working costs are as close as dammit to a hundred pounds an hour; right Mike?' And Michael Shapiro nodded. 'Well, we worked the Suicide main gully for sixty-six hours, and we recovered a princely 200 carats of the lousiest pile of junk I've ever seen. If we get a thousand quid for the lot we'll be doing well. This for an expenditure of six and a half thousand.'

Johnny paused, and looked around the table. Michael Shapiro was doodling on his note pad with fierce concentration, Tracey van der Byl was pale, her eyes never left Johnny's face and her expression ached with pity and helpless compassion; Benedict van der Byl was looking out of the window at the mountain, he was slumped comfortably in his chair, smiling a little and listening politely.

'The Suicide main gully is one of the five most likely parts of the entire concession. It's no good, so the rest of the field may be useless. We have the two other concessions, the original fields, to try. However, it will take three or four days to get *Kingfisher* moved up the coast.' Johnny paused, and Benedict swivelled his chair, still with the small smile on his lips.

'The interest payments fall due on the 30th—three days' time. Where are you going to find one hundred and fifty thousand Rand?'

'Yes,' Johnny nodded. 'I think I can persuade Larsen to extend for a few weeks; he will bloody well have to if he wants to protect his—'

'Hold on,' Benedict murmured. 'Larsen has got nothing to do with it.'

Johnny was silent, watching him warily. 'Explain,' he invited.

'I've taken over the loan from Larsen,' Benedict told him. 'I'm not interested in extending.'

'Larsen wouldn't have negotiated without warning me.' Johnny was stricken, his disclaimer was wrung from him in pain.

'Shapiro?' Benedict turned to Michael Shapiro for confirmation.

'Sure, Johnny. It's true. I've seen the documents.'

'Thanks, Michael.' Johnny's voice was bitter with accusation. 'Thanks for letting me know.'

'He showed me a few minutes before the meeting, Johnny. I swear I didn't know.' Michael's expression was distressed.

'Right.' Benedict straightened up in his chair, his voice was brisk. 'Let's get down to first principles. You've ruined my father's Company, Lance—but, thank God, I may be able to retrieve the situation. Call it sentiment or what you like, but I want your shares—and yours.' He turned to Tracey and nodded at her.

'No,' said Tracey sharply.

'Right.' Benedict smiled at her. 'Then I'm going to hammer Johnny Lance for his full obligations. That way I get the Company anyway, but I'll make damn sure he remains an unrehabilitated bankrupt for the rest of his life.'

Tracey lifted her hand to her throat, and turned her eyes to Johnny. Waiting for him to set a lead. There was a long stark silence, then Johnny Lance dropped his eyes.

'I've still got three days.' His voice was gruff and tired.

'Three days you have.' Benedict grinned coldly. 'And you're welcome to them.'

Johnny picked up his papers and put them under one arm; he took his jacket off the back of the chair and swung it over his shoulder.

'Wait,' ordered Benedict.

'What for?' Johnny's grin was twisted. 'You've had your fun.'

Benedict lifted the receiver of the telephone on the table and dialled swiftly.

'Come through, please, darling.' He spoke into the mouthpiece and smiled at Johnny as he hung up. Then as the door opened he went to meet Ruby Lance, and kissed her on the mouth. The two of them stood, arm in arm, and looked at Johnny.

'The Company is not the only thing I've taken from you,' Benedict said softly.

'I want a divorce.' Ruby looked steadily into Johnny's face. 'Benedict and I are going to get married.'

They were all watching Johnny, and they saw him flinch. He looked from one face to the other, then his mouth tightened and his forehead furrowed.

Tracey saw his anger mounting, and her eyes flicked to Benedict's face. He was leaning forward expectantly, his lips quivering with expectation, his eyes alight with triumph. Tracey wanted to scream out a warning to Johnny, stop him falling into the trap that Benedict had set so carefully.

Johnny took a pace forward, coming up onto the balls of his feet. He was about to make his defeat total and ineradicable. Then Benedict spoiled it for himself, he goaded once more.

'Game, set and match, Johnny Lance,' he crowed.

The effort of will that Johnny made to recover his reason was not shown on his face, he made the step forward seem natural and he continued towards the door.

'The house is in your name, of course, Ruby, so would you please send my things down to the Tulbagh Hotel,' he asked quietly.

He stopped in front of the couple and spoke to Ruby.

'You'll want to protect your reputation, of course, so I'll not sue for aldultery. We'll call it desertion.'

'You're eating your guts out,' jeered Benedict. 'Lance can't keep his woman. Van der Byl took her away from him. Go on, sue for adultery—let the world hear it.'

'As you wish,' Johnny agreed.

And he walked out of the Board Room to the elevators.

Johnny flopped onto the bed fully dressed, and rubbed his closed eyes with his finger-tips. He felt confused and off-balance, the edge of his mind which usually slashed quickly and incisively through a problem was dulled. This problem was so multiplied and tangled that he felt like a man in a thicket of African ebony trying to cut his way out with a blunt machete.

Without opening his eyes he groped for the telephone, and the girl on the hotel switchboard downstairs answered. He gave her a number in Kimberley.

'Person to person, Mr Ralph Ellison.'

'Fifteen minutes' delay, Mr Lance,' the girl told him.

'Okay,' Johnny replied. 'Ask room service to send me up a Chivas Regal and soda.' He suddenly needed liquor, something to dull the pain. 'Make that a double, honey—no, make it two doubles.'

He had drained both glasses by the time his Kimberley call came through.

'Ralph?' Johnny spoke into the receiver.

'Johnny, how nice of you to call.' There was an echo like distant laughter beneath those cool ambassadorial tones in Ralph Ellison's voice and Johnny knew instantly that the word was out. Damn it, he was slow—of course Benedict would have blocked him.

'Are you still interested in a deal on the Thunderbolt and Suicide Concession?' Johnny loosed a despairing long-range shot.

'Of course, you know we are always interested,' Ralph replied.

'The price is two million.' Johnny lost interest and lay back on the bed, closing his eyes again. He knew Ralph was having his revenge—you didn't take this boy to court and win without sowing yourself a minefield to retreat over.

'Two million,' Ralph murmured. 'Now that's a little high—for a field that's yielding 200 carats of small industrial diamonds per 10,000 loads, that's definitely on the high side. Of course we wouldn't want that battleship of yours either—we are not starting our own navy.' Ralph chuckled juicily. 'We could talk around fifty to a hundred grand—no more than that, Johnny.'

'Okay, Ralph.' Johnny spoke wearily. 'Thanks all the same. We'll have a drink together sometime.'

'Any time, Johnny,' Ralph agreed. 'Any time at all. You call me.'

Johnny dropped the receiver back on its hook and looked at the ceiling. He had heard that a gunshot wound was numb at first—he felt numb now. All the energy had seeped out of him, he had lost direction.

The telephone shrilled and he picked it up. The girl on the switchboard asked politely:

'Are you finished, Mr Lance?'

'Yes,' said Johnny. 'You might say that.'

'Is there anything else you require?' The girl sounded puzzled.

'Yes, honey, send up the hemlock.'

'I beg your pardon?'

'Two more big fat whiskies, please.'

He drank them in the bath, and while he dried himself the doorbell tinkled. He wound the bath towel round his waist and went through to open the door.

Tracey stepped into the bedroom and closed the door behind her. They stood looking at each other for a long moment. Her eyes were big and dark, reflecting his agony faithfully.

'Johnny—' Her voice was husky, and she reached out and laid the palm of her hand on his chest. His shoulders sagged, and he moved close to her, his forehead sinking onto her shoulder. He sighed, a ragged broken exhalation of breath.

'Come,' she said, and led him to the bed. Leaving him there she went to the windows and closed the curtains.

It was warm and safe in the half dark of the curtained room, and they held each other as they had done long years before. Clinging together, so their breathing mingled, and it was not necessary to speak.

When they became lovers it seemed that they had waited all their lives for that moment.

Afterwards he lay with her in his arms and he felt strength flowing back into him, drawing it from her. When he sat up in the bed the bemused, almost dazed expression had gone. His jaw was out and his eyes were bright.

'We've still got three days,' he said.

'Yes.' She sat up beside him. 'Go, Johnny. Go quickly, don't waste another moment.'

'I'll pull *Kingfisher* out of the main gully. I'll find those diamonds. They are there. I *know* they are there. I'll take her right down into the jaws of Thunderbolt and Suicide, I'll find those bloody diamonds—damned if I won't.' He swung his legs off the bed, reached for his clothes, glancing at his wristwatch as he did so. 'Four o'clock. I can get to Cartridge Bay a few minutes after dark. Will you call the communications office, ask them to radio Cartridge Bay and have a flare set for me, and *Wild Goose* standing by to run me out?'

'I'll phone them from here. Then I'll take a bath—you go on. Don't waste time.' Tracey nodded eagerly, and Johnny let his eyes drop down over her body. He reached out and touched one big white breast almost diffidently.

'You are beautiful—I hate to go.'

'It will all be here, waiting for you, when you get back.'

'It wasn't the way I'd planned it. It wasn't good the way I'd dreamed about it.' Benedict paced angrily over the floor of the Old Man's study, swinging towards the windows and pausing to stare at the mountain across the valley.

'You hurt him. You crushed him.' Ruby moved restlessly in her chair across the room from him, curling her long golden legs defensively under her, sitting like a cat in the big chair. She was worried, and it showed in the tiny crows' feet at the corners of her eyes and the way she held her lips pursed. She should have anticipated this reaction from him, she should have known that his moment of triumph could never match his anticipation of it—and that revenge must always be followed by sour distaste and a feeling of disappointment. She realized that her safest course was to leave him alone now, she should never have returned with him to the old house on Wynberg Hill. She stood up.

'Darling.' She crossed to him. 'I'm going home now. I want to pack his clothes and get rid of them. I want to wipe out every memory of him. From now on it's you and I–together.'

She stretched up to kiss him, but Benedict turned his face away.

'Oh! So you're going, are you?' His expresssion was petulant, his lips pouting spitefully.

'We're both tired, darling. Let us both rest a while– and I'll come back later this evening.'

'So now you're giving the orders, are you?' He laughed nastily.

'Darling–'

'And cut out all the darlings. We pulled a deal and it didn't work out. You were meant to be a club to break his skull–and do you know something? He didn't give a damn. I was watching him, he was pleased–yes! He was bloody well delighted to get rid of you.'

'Benedict–' She stepped back.

'Listen.' He stepped close to her, and pushed his face towards hers. 'If you're so bloody anxious to go, why don't you bloody well go–and keep going. If he doesn't want you–then I sure as hell don't want you either.'

'Benedict,' she whispered. The colour faded from her face, leaving it washed white as beach sand. She stared at him in horror, as her dreams began to fall into ruins around her. 'You don't mean that.'

'I don't? Is that so?' He threw back his head and laughed again. 'Listen, you got some nice diamonds and a mink coat. You got a big house in Bishopscourt–now, that's pretty good pay for a whore.'

'Benedict–' She gasped at the insult, but he wasn't listening.

'I proved I could have you, didn't I? I proved I could take you away from him–and that's what it was all about. Now, why don't you go on home like a good girl.'

'The machine. I know about that thing in *Kingfisher*.' It was a mistake. Until then she still had a chance. His face changed shape and the blood flooded into it. His voice when he spoke was unsteady, thick with rage for his lips seemed to have swollen.

'Try it,' he whispered back at her. 'Go on, try it. They'll give you fifteen years. You're in it as deep as I am. Think about it–fifteen years in a woman's prison, my beauty. And think about this also–' He showed her his hand, holding it like a blade before her eyes. 'I'll kill you. I swear before God, I'll kill you with my bare hands. You know I'll do it–you know enough about me now.'

She backed away from him, and he followed her still holding his hand at her throat.

'You've been paid. Now get out.'

A few seconds longer she stood before him, and he was not too far gone in rage to see the fear in her eyes mingle with something else that made her eyes slit and drew her lips back to show the little white teeth.

'All right,' she said. 'I'll go.' And she walked from the room, stepping daintily, the long yellow hair swinging against her shoulders.

Ruby drove slowly for her vision was blurred with her tears. Twice other drivers hooted at her but she kept both hands clenched on the wheel and stared ahead, following the De Waal Drive around the lower slopes of the mountain.

Before she reached the University she swung off the road and drove up through the pine forests until she reached the car park behind the Cecil Rhodes Memorial. She left the car and walked down onto the wide paved terrace below the Greek columns and stone steps where the mounted statue eternally searched the horizon with one hand lifted to shade his eyes.

She went to the parapet and looked across to the far blue mountains of the Helderberg. She hugged herself about the shoulders for the wind through her silk summer dress was as cold as her misery.

Now the tears broke over her lids and slid down her cheeks to fall unheeded onto the silken front of her dress. They were the tears of self-pity, but also the tears of an anger as searing cold as dry ice.

'The swine,' she whispered through lips that trembled. Near her two young students sitting on the parapet, kicking their legs over the drop beneath them and hugging each other in the abandon of first love, turned to glance at her.

The boy whispered to the girl, and she giggled in unthinking cruelty—but looked away as Ruby directed a long venomous glare at her. Then in embarrassment the couple scrambled off the parapet and moved away, leaving her alone.

Never for one moment did she consider standing aside, Benedict's threats meant nothing—her only concern was to take the action which would injure him most severely. The consequences to herself were not part of her calculations. She wanted only to select the swiftest and most terrible vehicle of retribution. As the dark clouds that fogged her reason slowly cleared, the means came to her readily.

Johnny was staying at the Tulbagh Hotel.

She turned and ran back to her car, the long yellow banner of her hair floating behind her like the pennant at the tip of a cavalry lance. She drove fast until she hit the downtown rush-hour crowds. The tears dried on her face as she crawled, fuming with impatience, along the slow river of traffic.

It was after five when she parked in a loading zone outside the entrance to the Tulbagh and ran into the lobby.

'What room is Mr Lance in?' she demanded of the girl at the desk.

'Mr Lance checked out an hour ago.' Curiously the girl examined Ruby's ruined make-up.

'Did he say where he was going?' Ruby snapped at her, feeling the sickening slide of disappointment within her.

'No, madam.' The girl shook her head. 'But he was in a hurry.'

'Damn! Damn!' Ruby swore bitterly. She turned from the desk undecided where next to look. Perhaps Johnny had gone back to the office.

Across the lobby the elevator doors slid open and Tracey Hartford stepped out. Even in her impatience Ruby recognized in the glow that seemed to emanate from her that Tracey was a girl freshly risen from the bed of the man she loved. There was not a vestige of doubt in Ruby's mind as to the identity of that man.

The shock of it paralysed her for a moment. Then she felt the urge to cross the floor and claw that smug smile from Tracey's face. She fought it down, and instead, she stepped into her path as Tracey started for the glass outer doors.

'Where is Johnny?' she demanded, and Tracey came up short. Her little gasp of guilt confirmed Ruby's suspicion.

'Where is he, damn you!' Ruby's voice was pitched low but brittle with emotion.

'He's not here.' Tracey recovered herself, quickly masking her expression.

'Where has he gone? I must see him.'

'He's flown up to Cartridge Bay.'

'When did he leave? It's important—terribly important.'

'An hour ago. He'll be airborne already.'

'Can you get a message to him?' In her impatience Ruby caught Tracey's wrist, holding her in a grip that marked the skin.

'I can radio him—' Tracey pulled her hand free.

'No,' Ruby cut in quickly. She could not have her message shouted across the ether for all to hear. 'Can you follow him—charter a plane?'

Tracey shook her head. 'They won't fly to an unscheduled airfield after dark.'

'Then you must follow him—by car. You must drive up there.'

'Why?' Tracey stared at her, puzzled by this strange insistence, noticing the dried tears and the wild look in Ruby's eyes. 'It's an eight-hour drive.'

'I'll tell you. Can we use Johnny's room?'

Tracey hesitated, remembering the unmade bed. Then the hotel manager came into the lobby and Tracey turned to him with relief.

The Beechcraft bucked suddenly and dropped a wing, instinctively Johnny corrected the lunge with stick and rudder then glanced quickly at his instrument panel for an explanation. There was none to be found there, so he looked over the wing and for the first time noticed the dust on the great plains below him; it was moving low against the earth in long streamers like mist, and the setting sun turned it to mauve and old gold. With a prickle of alarm he scanned the horizon ahead, and saw it coming down from the north like a great moving range of blue mountains. Even as he watched it, it rolled across the low sun, turning it into a sullen red orb. The light in the cockpit changed to a weird glow as though the door to a furnace had been thrown open.

Again the Beechcraft crabbed awkwardly as another gust of high wind hit her, and at the same moment the radio crackled and came alive.

'Zulu Sugar Peter Tango Baker this is Alexandra Bay Control, come in please.'

The voice of the controller was almost unintelligible with storm static. Johnny reached for the transmit switch of the radio, then stopped his hand. He thought quickly. He could guess they were trying to reach him to cancel his flight approval. That was a big norther boiling down out of the desert. They would abort his flight, and divert him out of the path of the storm.

He checked his wrist watch. Twenty minutes' flying time to Cartridge Bay. No—he was flying full into the eye of the wind, say twenty-five or thirty minutes. Quickly he searched the coast on his port side and saw the long white lines of surf stretched ahead into the thickening purple gloom. The coast was still clear, it might stay that way for another thirty minutes.

'Zulu Sugar Peter Tango Baker this is Alexandra Bay. I say again—come in. Come in. Zulu Sugar Peter Tango Baker.' The agitation in the controller's voice came through over the static.

There was a fair chance of getting in to Cartridge Bay, racing the storm and winning. He could edge out to the westward and come in from the sea, pick up *Kingfisher*'s riding lights as a beacon and sneak in under the leading edge of the dust clouds. If he missed he could turn and run with the wind for home. The radio was hissing and crackling angrily now, the controller's voice sometimes lost in the interference, sometimes coming through strongly.

'–Cancelled. I say again: your flight approval is cancelled. Do you read me, Zulu Sugar Peter Tango Baker. Come in, please.–Beaufort force seven.–visibility in the storm area–I say again, there is nil visibility in–'

The norther would roar for days now and with it would blow away his last chance of working the gap at Thunderbolt and Suicide.

Johnny switched off the radio, cut off contact with Control and immediately it was strangely quiet in the cockpit. He settled himself down into the bucket seat, and eased open the throttles, watching the needles creep up around the dials of the rev counters.

Now he was down to an altitude of three hundred feet and the Beechcraft was leaping about like a hooked marlin. He was flying her on instruments for outside the cockpit it was completely dark. He could not see his own wing-tips, but above him the stars still showed. He was riding the vanguard of the storm, and the dust clouds were ahead, racing to meet him and blanket the flare path at Cartridge Bay.

Every few seconds he darted a quick glance ahead, hoping to pick up the lights, then his eyes flew back to the instrument panel.

'Now,' he thought grimly. 'It should be now. I should be over the grounds. Thirty seconds more and I'll know I've missed her.'

He looked up again, and there was *Kingfisher* dead ahead. All her lights were ablaze, a burning beacon of hope in the darkness. She appeared to be riding easily, for the wind had not yet had time to thrash the sea into a frenzy.

He flashed over her, seeming to graze her superstructure in passing, and now he was searching anxiously for the glow of the flare path on the land beyond.

It came up as a patch of lesser darkness in the absolute blackness of the night. He steadied on course towards it, watching it change to a long double line of oil-burning flares that smoked and fluttered in the wind.

He flew her in fast, high above the stall and the shock of touchdown threatened to tear the undercarriage off her. Then he was jolting and trundling down the earthen runway with the flares flashing past his wingtips.

'Lance, old man,' he murmured thankfully, 'that was a very shaky do!'

The wind hum against the body of the car, and the snarl of rubber on tarmac as the Mercedes snaked through the bends of the twisting mountain road were sounds to match the racing of Tracey's blood and the hammer of her heart.

She drove with an inspired abandon, watching the bends leap at her out of the darkness, sensing the massive crags and cliffs that hung over the road and blotted out half the night sky.

The silver sheet of Clanwilliam Lake reflected the stars, and then was left behind. Down from the mountains she went and over the Olifants River to make a brief fuel stop at Vanrynsdorp and scan the road map anxiously in the light of the gasoline pumps. She read with a sinking feeling the mileage figures printed along the little red ribbon of the road, and knew that for her each mile would be multiplied by her own urgency.

Then once more behind the wheel she faced the vast emptiness of Namaqualand–and sent the Mercedes flying across it.

'–There is some type of machine, I don't know how it works, but it filters out the diamonds. Benedict had it installed at Las Palmas–'

The headlights were puny little white shafts, and the road a long blue smear that went on endlessly. Tracey lit a cigarette with one hand, hearing Ruby's voice again in her ears.

–There is one diamond amongst them. He called it "The Big Blue". Benedict says it's worth a million–'

Tracey was not sure she believed it. It was the enormity of the treachery and deceit that she could not accept.

'–The Italian, the Captain, be careful of him. He works for Benedict. The other one also–Hugo–they are all in it. Warn Johnny.'

Benedict! Weak, spoilt Benedict, the playboy, the spendthrift. Could he have planned and carried this through?

A gust of wind hit the car from the side, taking her unawares, pushing the Mercedes off the tar onto the gravel. Tracey fought to hold the skid. Dust and gravel roared out in a cloud from under the wheels. Then she was back on the road, hurtling northwards.

'Warn Johnny! Warn Johnny!'

Benedict van der Byl sat in his father's chair, in his father's house, and he was alone. His loneliness ate deep into the fibres of his whole being.

Before him on the stinkwood desk stood a crystal glass and a decanter. The brandy was no comfort, its warmth in his throat and belly seemed only to accentuate the icy cold of his loneliness. His fantasy showed him as a hollow man. He thought of himself as a husk, filled only with the cold of melancholia.

He looked about the room with its dark panelled wood-work and he smelled the musty dead smell. He wondered how many times his father had sat in this chair alone and lonely. Lonely and afraid as the cancer ate him alive.

He stood up and moved listlessly about the room, touching the furniture as if he were trying to communicate with the man who lived and died here. He moved across and stood in front of the curtained windows. The rug was new. It replaced the other that they had been unable to clean.

'The Old Man had the right idea.' He spoke aloud, his voice sounding strange in his own ears.

Then on an impulse he crossed quickly to the cupboard that flanked the massive stone fireplace, and tried the door. It was locked.

Without passion he stood back and kicked in the panel. The wood splintered and he kicked again, smashing the door from its hinges.

The oblong leather case was on the top shelf, and he took it down and carried it to the desk. He sprang the catches and laid back the lid.

He lifted out the blue metalled double barrels of the Purdey Royal, and the gun oil was greasy on his hands.

'Jacobus Isaac van der Byl.' He read aloud the name in gold inlay set into the steel among the engraved pheasants and gundogs.

He smiled then.

'The old devil.' He shook his head smiling as though at some private joke, and began slowly to assemble the shotgun. He weighed it in his hands, feeling the sweet pure balance of the weapon.

'The old bastard made his own decisions.' And still smiling he carried the gun across to the new carpet. He placed it butt down between his feet with the barrels pointed at the ceiling and leaning slowly forward he opened his mouth and placed the muzzles between his lips, then reaching farther down he placed a thumb on each trigger and pushed them simultaneously.

'Click! Click!'

The firing pins fell on the empty chambers, and Benedict straightened up and wiped the taste of gun oil from his lips. He grinned again.

'That's the way he did it. Both barrels in the back of the throat. What a cure for tonsils?' he chuckled, and glanced across at the shattered cupboard door. The square packets of cartridges were on the second shelf.

He tucked the gun under his arm and went to the cupboard again, moving more purposefully now. He snatched down a packet of SSG and broke it open. Suddenly his hands were shaking and the fat red cartridges spilled onto the floor. He stooped and picked up two of them.

With mounting excitement and dread he broke open the shotgun and slipped the cartridges into the blank eyes of the breeches. They slid home against the seating with a solid double thunk, and he hurried back to the spot in front of the window.

His eyes were bright and his breathing quick as he pushed the safety catch onto 'Fire' and placed the butt between his feet once more.

He took the muzzles in his mouth again, in an obscene soul kiss and reached down for the triggers. They were cold and oily. He caressed them lightly, feeling the fine grooving in the curves of metal, thrilling to the touch and feel of them as he had never thrilled to the feel of a woman's body.

Then abruptly he stood up again. He was gasping for breath.

Unsteadily he carried the weapon back to the desk and laid it on the dark polished wood.

As he poured brandy into the crystal glass his eyes were fastened with perverse fascination on the beautiful glistening weapon.

The steam had fogged the mirrored walls of the bathroom, so her image was dewed and misty. Ruby Lance dried herself slowly with one of the thick fluffy towels. She was in no hurry; she wanted Tracey to have a start of at least four hours on her journey to Cartridge Bay. With a deep narcissistic pleasure she noticed in the mirror how her whole body glowed with soft pink highlights from the hot water of the bath.

Wrapping herself in the towel she went through into the dressing-room and picked up one of the silver-backed brushes began stroking it through her hair, moving across to the open wardrobe to select a dress for the occasion. It must be something special, perhaps the unworn full-length Louis Feraud of daffodil satin.

Still undecided she went back to seat herself at the dressing-table and began the complicated ritual of applying her make-up. She worked with meticulous care until at last she smiled at her reflection with satisfaction.

She dropped the towel, went back to the wardrobe, and stood slim and naked before it. Pouting slightly with concentration she decided against the Feraud. Then suddenly she smiled, and reached for Benedict's mink.

She wrapped herself in the pale cloud of fur, fluffing up the collar to frame her face. It was perfect. Just the fur and a pair of golden slippers, pale gold, a perfect match for her hair.

Now suddenly she was eager to go. She ran from the house to where her car was parked in the driveway.

She switched off the headlights as she turned into the driveway that curved up to where the old house crouched on the top of Wynberg Hill. The whisper of the engine was unobtrusive and blended with the whimper of the night breeze in the chestnut trees that flanked the driveway.

She parked in the courtyard, and saw that Benedict's Rolls was still in the garage and a light burned in the window of the study, a yellow oblong behind the curtains. The front door was open. Her slippered feet made no sound along the gloomy passages, and when she tried the door to the study it swung open readily. She stepped into the room, and closed the door behind her. She stood with her back to the dark panelled wood. A single shaded lamp lit the room dimly.

Benedict sat behind the desk. The room was heavy with the smell of cigar smoke and brandy fumes. He had been drinking. His face was flushed, and the top button of his shirt was undone. On the desk in front of him lay a shot-gun. Ruby was surprised at the presence of the weapon, it disconcerted her and the words she had prepared were forgotten.

Benedict looked up at her. His eyes were slightly unfocused; and he blinked slowly. Then he grinned; it twisted his mouth and his voice when he spoke was slurred.

'So you've come back.'

Instantly her hatred returned in full flood. But she kept her face impassive. 'Yes,' she agreed. 'I've come back.'

'Come here.' He swivelled his chair to the side of the desk. Ruby did not move, she leaned back against the door.

'Come here.' Benedict's voice was stronger now, and suddenly Ruby smiled and obeyed.

She stood in front of him, huddled in the fur.

'Kneel down,' commanded Benedict, and she hesitated.

'Down!' his voice crackled. 'Down, damn you!'

Ruby sank to her knees in front of him, and he straightened up in the chair. She knelt in front of him in the attitude of submission, with her head forward so the golden hair hung like a curtain over her face.

'Say it,' he gloated. 'Ask me to forgive you.'

Slowly she lifted her face and looked up at him. She spoke softly.

'Tracey left for Cartridge Bay at five-thirty this evening.'

Benedict's expression changed.

'She has a start of four hours—she is halfway there already.'

He stared at her with his lips parting, soft and red and slack.

'She is going to Johnny,' Ruby went on. 'She knows about the thing in *Kingfisher*. She knows about the big blue diamond.'

He began to shake his head in disbelief.

'By dawn tomorrow Johnny will know also. So you see, my darling, you have lost again—haven't you? You can never beat him, can you, Benedict? Can you, my darling?'

Her voice was rising, ringing with triumph.

'You?' he croaked. 'You?'

And she laughed, nodding her head in agreement, unable to speak through her laughter.

Benedict lunged clumsily out of the chair, his hands going for her throat. She went over backwards with him on top of her. Her laughter died gurgling in her throat.

They rolled together on the floor. Benedict's hands locked on her neck, his voice rising in a scream of fury and despair. Her long legs kicking and thrashing, clawing at his face and hands, she fought him with the strength of a cornered animal.

They rolled back suddenly and Benedict's head struck the solid leg of the desk with a crack that jarred his whole body. His grip on her throat loosened and she tore herself free with fresh breath hissing into her open mouth. She rolled away from him and in one fluid movement gained her feet, reeling back from him with the front of the mink torn open and her hair tangled across her face.

Benedict dragged himself up the desk onto his knees. He was still screaming, a high keening note without form or coherence, as Ruby spun away from him and stumbled to the door.

Blinded by her own hair, fighting for strangled breath, she fumbled for the door handle with her back turned to him

Benedict reached up and lifted the shotgun off the desk. Still kneeling beside the desk he held the weapon across his hip. The recoil was a liquid pulsing jolt in his hands and the muzzle blast was thunderous in the confines of the room, the long yellow flame lighting the scene like a photographer's flash-bulb.

The heavy charge caught Ruby in the small of her back. At that range there was no spread of shot and it went through spine and pelvis in a solid shattering ball. It tore out through the front of her belly, spinning her sideways along the wall. She slid down into a sitting position, facing him with the mink flared open about her.

On his knees Benedict swung the gun to follow her fall and he fired the second barrel; again the brief thunder and flame of the muzzle blast flashed across the room.

At even closer range than the first charge it struck her full in her beautiful golden face.

Benedict stood in the garage with his forehead pressed against the cold metal of the Rolls-Royce. The shotgun was still in his hands, and his pockets were crammed with cartridges that he had picked up from the floor before leaving the study.

He was shivering violently, like a man in high fever.

'No!' he moaned to himself, repeating the single negative over and over again, leaning against the big car.

Abruptly he gagged, remembering the carnage he had created. Then he retched, still leaning against the Rolls, bringing up the brandy mingled with his horror.

It left him pale and weak, but steadier. Through the open window he threw the gun onto the back seat of the Rolls, and climbed shakily into the driver's seat.

He sat there bowed over the steering-wheel, and now his instinct of self-preservation took hold of him.

It seemed to him there was but one avenue of escape still open to him. *Wild Goose* had the range to take him across an ocean—South America perhaps, and there was money in Switzerland.

He started the Rolls and reversed out of the garage, the spin of tyres against concrete burning blue smoke into the beams of the headlights.

The Mercedes crawled through the thick sand, the headlights probing ineffectually into the bright orange fog of dust that whipped endlessly over the track ahead. The hot gritty wind buffeted the car, rocking it on its suspension.

Tracey sat forward in the driver's seat peering ahead through eyes that felt raw and swollen with fatigue and mica dust.

From the main road to the coast this jeep track was the only land access to Cartridge Bay. It was a hundred miles of tortuous trail, made up of deep sandy ruts and broken stone where it crossed one of the many rocky ridges.

The radiator of the Mercedes was boiling furiously, over-heating in the searing wind and the slogging low-gear grind through thick sand. In places Tracey followed the track only by driving through gaps in the stunted knee-high growth of desert bush. Every few minutes a tumbleweed, driven by the wind, would blow across the track like a frightened furry animal.

At times she was sure she had missed a turning and was now grinding aimlessly out into the desert, then reassuringly the twin ruts would show up in the lights ahead of her. Once she did drive off the road, and immediately the Mercedes came to a gentle standstill with its rear wheels spinning helplessly in the soft sand. She had to climb out of the cab and, with her bare hands, scoop away the sand from behind the wheels and stuff bundles of tumbleweed into the depressions to give the wheels purchase. She almost wept with relief when the Mercedes pulled back sluggishly onto the trail again.

The slow dawn broke through the dustclouds and Tracey switched off the headlights and drove on until suddenly, and quite unexpectedly, she reached Cartridge Bay. The depot buildings loomed suddenly before her, and she left the Mercedes and ran to the living quarters. The foreman opened the door to her insistent hammering, and stared at her in astonishment before ushering her in. Tracey cut off his questions with her own.

'Where is *Wild Goose*?'

'She took Mr Lance out to *Kingfisher*, but she's back now lying at the jetty.'

'Hugo Kramer—the Captain?'

'He's aboard, holed up in his cabin.'

'Thanks.' Tracey left him, pushed the door open against the wind and ran out into the storm.

Wild Goose lay at her moorings, secured by heavy lines to the bollards, but fidgeting and fretting at the push of the wind. There was a gangplank laid to her deck, and lights showed at her portholes. Tracey went aboard.

Hugo Kramer came to the doorway of his cabin in a suit of rumpled striped pyjamas. Tracey pushed past him.

'You took Lance out to *Kingfisher*?' she accused him, her voice sharp and anxious.

'Yes.'

'You idiot, didn't you realise there was something up? Good God, why otherwise would he fly in through this weather?'

Hugo stared at her, and instinctively she knew that what Ruby had told her was true.

'I don't know what you're talking about,' he blurted.

'You'll know all right when we are all sitting behind bars—we'll have fifteen long years to think about it. Lance has tumbled to it, you fool, I've got to stop him. Take me out to *Kingfisher*.'

He was confused—and afraid.

'I know nothing about—' Hugo started again.

'You're wasting time.' Brusquely Tracey brushed his protests aside. 'Take me out to *Kingfisher*.'

'Your brother—where is he? Why didn't he come?'

Tracey had anticipated the question. 'Lance beat him up—badly. He's in hospital. He sent me.'

Suddenly Hugo was convinced.

'*Gott!*' he swore. 'What are we going to do? This storm–I may be able to get you out there, but I won't be able to leave *Wild Goose*. My crew can't handle her in this sea. What can you do on your own?'

'Get me out there,' said Tracey. 'Get me aboard *Kingfisher* and you can come back. The Italian, Caporetti, he and I will take care of Lance. In this storm a man can be washed overboard very easily.'

'Ja.' Hugo's face lit with relief.'That's it. The Italian!' And he reached for his oilskins hanging on the bulkhead. As he pulled them on over his pyjamas he looked at Tracey with new respect.

'You,' he said. 'I didn't know you were in it.'

'Did you think my brother and I would stand by and let a stranger take our birthright from us?'

Hugo grinned. 'You're a cool one, I'll say that for you. You had me fooled.' And he went out onto the bridge.

Johnny Lance and Sergio Caporetti stood shoulder to shoulder on *Kingfisher*'s bridge. The ship was taking the big green seas over the bows, solid walls of water, and the wind whipped spray that spattered the armoured glass windows of the bridge house.

Kingfisher had slipped her moorings the previous evening, leaving the big yellow buoys floating on their anchor cables and she was working free of her fetters. She was on computer navigation, holding her position over the ground against the swells and the wind by use of her engine and rudder.

'She is no good.' Sergio spoke morosely. 'We come too close to the rocks. I get sick in my heart looking at them.'

The dust clouds did not carry this far out to sea despite the vicious screeching of the wind. The visibility was a mile or more, quite enough to show the brooding twin hulks of Thunderbolt and Suicide. The storm-crazed swells burst against them, throwing white spray two hundred feet into the gloomy sky, then surging back to expose the gleaming white rock.

'Hold her,' growled Johnny. Twice during the night they had changed position, each time edging down closer on the gap between the two islands. *Kingfisher* was battling gamely to hold her ground against the insidious sucking current that added its pull to that of the swell and the wind.

Johnny was not attempting to work any one of the gullies extensively, he wanted only to sample as much of the field as possible in the time that was left to him. The storm would not stop him–for *Kingfisher* was constructed to work in worse weather than this. Her compensating hose section was keeping the dredge-head on the bottom despite the lift and fall of her hull.

'Calm down, Sergio.' Johnny relented a little. 'The computer is foolproof.'

'The goddamned computer she no got eyes to see those rocks. Me, I got eyes–and it gives me a sick heart.'

Twice during the night Johnny had gone down into the control room and ordered the computer to report its recovery of diamonds. Each time the reply had been consistent–not a single stone over four carats, and precious few of any others.

'I'm going through to the plot. Watch her,' Johnny told Sergio, and staggering against the pitch and roll he went through the door behind the bridge.

He paused beside the repeater screen of the computer, and at a glance saw that *Kingfisher* was holding her primary operation and all departments were running normally. He passed the screen and leaned over the chart table.

The large scale chart of the South West African coast between Luderizt and Walvis Bay was pinned down on the board. The *Wild Goose* soundings were pencilled in, and the pattern of *Kingfisher*'s sweeps were carefully plotted around the islands of Thunderbolt and Suicide.

Johnny picked up a pair of dividers and stared moodily at the chart. Suddenly a surge of anger rose in him against those two names. They had promised so much and delivered so little.

He stared at the names Thunderbolt and Suicide printed in italics among the maze of soundings, and his anger turned to blind red hatred.

With the points of the dividers he slashed at the chart, ripping the thick linen paper once, and twice, in a ragged cross-shaped tear.

This small act of violence dissipated his anger. He felt embarrassed, it had been a petty childish gesture. He tried to smooth the edges of the tear, and through the gap he felt another loose scrap of paper which someone had slipped under the chart. He probed a finger through the tear in the chart and wormed the scrap out. He glanced at the scribbled title and the lines of figures and numbers that followed.

The sheet was headed: 'KAMINIKOTO SECONDARY RECOVERY PROGRAMME.'

He studied it, puzzled by the title but recognizing the numbers as a computer programme. The writing was in Sergio Caporetti's pointed continental style. The easiest way to resolve the mystery was to ask Sergio. Johnny started back for the bridge.

'Boss,' Sergio called anxiously, as Johnny stepped through the door. 'Look!'

He was pointing ahead into the eye of the wind. Johnny hurried to his side, the paper crumpled and forgotten in his hand

'*Wild Goose*.' Sergio identified the small craft that was staggering and plunging towards them out of the gloom.

'What the hell is he doing here?' Johnny wondered aloud. *Wild Goose* was lost for long seconds behind the walls of green sea, then again she was lifted high into unnatural prominence, showing the red lead of her bottom as she rode the crests; water poured from her scuppers, before she shot down the steep slope of the next wave to bury her nose deep in frothing water. She came down swiftly on the wind, rounding to and beginning to edge in under *Kingfisher*'s counter.

'What the hell is he playing at?' Johnny protested, and then in disbelief he saw a slim figure dart from *Wild Goose*'s wheelhouse and run to the side nearest *Kingfisher*.

'It's Tracey,' shouted Johnny.

She reached the rail just as another swell burst over the bows and smothered her. Johnny expected to see her washed away, but she was still there clinging to the rail.

Thrusting the page of paper into his pocket, Johnny went out through the wing of the bridge and swarmed down the steel ladder to the deck, jumping the last ten feet and running the instant he landed.'

He reached the side and looked down on the drowned-kitten figure of Tracey.

'Go back,' he yelled. 'Go back. Don't try it.'

She shouted something that was lost in the next smother of spray, and when it cleared he saw her poising herself to jump the gap of surging water between the two vessels.

He flung himself over *Kingfisher*'s side and climbed swiftly down the steel rungs.

He was still ten feet above her as she gathered herself for the leap.

'Go back,' he shouted desperately.

She jumped, missed her hold and fell into the murderous stretch of water between the hulls. Her head bobbed below Johnny, and he was aware of the next swell bearing down on them. It would throw *Wild Goose* against the steel cliff of *Kingfisher*, crushing Tracey between them.

Johnny went down those last ten feet and hanging outwards by one arm he got his other arm around her, and with a heave that crackled in his muscles and joints he plucked her from the water just as the two vessels dashed together with a crunching impact that tore splinters from *Wild Goose*'s planking, and left a smear of alien paint on *Kingfisher*'s steel plating.

Wild Goose swung away, and with her diesels bellowing went bucking off into the wind.

With puddles of sea water forming around her feet from her sodden clothing, Tracey stood in the centre of *Kingfisher*'s guest cabin. Her dark hair was plastered down her face and neck, and she was shivering so violently from shock and the icy water that she could not talk. Her teeth chattered together, and her lips were blue with cold.

Desperately she was trying to form words, her eyes never leaving Johnny's face.

Quickly he stripped off her clothing and throwing one towel around her shoulders he began roughly to chafe warmth back into her with another.

'You little idiot,' he berated her. 'Are you stark staring bloody mad?'

'Johnny,' she gasped through her chattering teeth.

'Christ—that was so close,' he snarled at her as he knelt to rub her legs.

'Johnny, listen.'

'Shut up and dry your hair.'

Humbly she obeyed him, her shivers became controllable as he crossed to the locker and found a thick jersey which he pulled over her head. It hung almost to her knees.

'Now,' he said, taking her roughly by the shoulders. 'What the hell is this all about?'

And she told him in a rush of words that poured out like water from a broken dam. Then she burst into tears and stood there forlornly in the voluminous jersey with her damp hair dangling about her shoulders, sobbing as though her heart was breaking.

Johnny took her in his arms.

For a long minute Tracey revelled in his warmth and strength, but she was the first to pull away.

'Do something, Johnny,' she implored him, her voice still thick with tears. 'Stop them. You mustn't let them get away with it.'

He went back to the locker, and while he ransacked it for clothing that might fit her, Johnny's mind was racing over the story she had told him.

He watched her pull on a pair of blue serge trousers and tie them at the waist with a length of cord. She folded back the cuffs and tucked them into thick woollen socks, before thrusting her feet into a pair of seaboots that were only a few sizes too large for her.

'Where do we start?' she asked, and he remembered the sheet of paper. He fished it out of his pocket and flattened it on the table beside the bunk. Quickly he ran his eyes over the columns of figures. His first guess was right—it *was* a computer programme.

'Stay here,' he ordered Tracey.

'No.' Her response was immediate, and he grinned.

'Listen, I'm just going up onto the bridge to keep them busy there. I'll come back for you, I promise. You won't miss anything.'

'How is she, boss?' Sergio Caporetti's concern was genuine. Johnny realised that he must be worrying himself into a frenzy trying to guess the reason for Tracey's arrival.

'She is pretty shaken up,' Johnny answered.

'What she want—that was big chance she takes. Nearly fish food.'

'I don't know,' Johnny said. 'I want you to take over up here. Keep *Kingfisher* working. I'm going to get her to bed—I'll let you know what it's all about as soon as I find out.'

'Okay, boss.'

'Oh, and Sergio—keep an eye on those rocks. Don't let her drift down any closer.'

Johnny chose a powerful incentive to keep Sergio up on the bridge.

Johnny left him and went below, stopping only at the guest cabin.

'Come on.'

Tracey followed him, lurching unsteadily with *Kingfisher*'s antics in the high sea.

Two decks down they reached the computer control room and Johnny unlocked the heavy steel door, then locked it again behind them.

Tracey wedged herself against the bulkhead and watched as Johnny seated himself at the console and clipped the rumpled sheet into the board.

Reading from the sheet he typed the first line of figures on the keyboard. Immediately the computer registered a protest.

'Operator error,' it typed back. Johnny ignored its denial and typed the second line. This time it was more emphatic.

'No procedure. Operator error.'

And Johnny typed the next line of figures. He guessed that whoever had stored this programme in the computer's memory would have placed a series of blocks to prevent accidental discovery. Again the denial flashed back at him.

'Operator error.'

And Johnny muttered, 'Thrice before the cock crows,' striking an incongruously biblical note in the tense atmosphere of the control room.

He typed the last line of figures and the denial faded from the screen. The console clicked like a monstrous crab, then suddenly it started to print again.

'Kaminikoto Secondary Recovery Programme.
Installed October 1969. At Las Palmas by
Hideki Kaminikoto. Doctor Of Science.
Tokyo University.

The little Japanese had been unable to resist autographing his masterpiece. Tracey and Johnny crouched over the screen, staring at it with awful fascination as the computer began spelling out its report. It began with the number of hours worked, and the weight of gravel processed during that time.

Next it reported the weight of concentrates recovered from the cyclone and finally, in a series of columns, it printed out the weights and sizes of all the diamonds won from the sea. The Big Blue showed up in the place of honour, and wordlessly Tracey touched the figure 320 with a forefinger. Johnny nodded grimly.

The computer ended by giving a grand total of carats recovered, and Johnny spoke for the first time.

'It's true,' he said softly. 'It doesn't seem possible—but it is.'

The click and hum of the computer ceased, and the screen went blank.

Johnny straightened up in the chair.

'Where would they put it?' he asked himself, as he ran quickly over the line of recovery. He stood up from the chair and peered through the leaded glass peephole into the X-ray room. 'It must be this side of the cyclone, this side of the drier—' He was speaking aloud. '—Between the drier and the X-ray room.'

Then there bobbed to the surface of memory the modification in design which he had meant to query, but which he had forgotten.

'The inspection plate on the conveyor tunnel!' He punched his fist into his palm. 'They moved the inspection plate! That's it! It's in the conveyor tunnel.'

His hands were frantic with haste as he unlocked the steel door of the control room.

Sergio Caporetti paced his bridge like a captive bear, puffing so furiously on his cheroot that sparks flew from its tip. The wind howled hungrily around the wheelhouse, and the swells still marched in from the north.

Suddenly he reached a decision and turned to the helmsman.

'Watch those goddamn rocks—watch them good.'

The helmsman nodded and Sergio shambled through the chartroom to his own cabin. He locked the door behind him, and crossed to his desk. Fumbling with his keys he opened the bottom drawer of his desk and reaching under the pile of cheroot packets he brought out the canvas bag.

Weighing it thoughtfully in his hand, he looked about the cabin for a more secure hiding-place. Through the canvas he could feel the nutty irregular shape of the stones.

'That Johnny, he is a clever bastard,' he muttered. 'It better be a good place.'

Then he reached a decision. 'Best place where I can watch them all a time.'

He opened his jacket and stuffed the bag into his inside pocket. He buttoned the jacket and patted the bulge over his heart

'Fine!' he said. 'Good!' And stood up from the desk. He hurried back, unlocking the door into the chartroom, and headed for the bridge. He stopped in the middle of the chartroom and his head swung towards the repeater screen of the computer. The buzzer was going like a rattlesnake, and the red bulb that warned of a new procedure was blinking softly.

Fearfully Sergio approached the screen and stooped over it. A single glance was enough, and he rushed from it to the chart table. He saw the cross-shaped tear in the chart.

'Mary Mother!'

He ripped back the thick crackling paper and searched under it. He stepped back from the table and hit himself across the chest.

'Fool!' he said. 'Idiot!' He spent ten seconds in self-castigation, then he looked about for a weapon. The locking handle of the cabin was a twelve-inch steel bar with a heavy head. He pulled out the pin and worked it loose. He slipped it into the waistband of his trousers.

'I'm going below,' he told the helmsman curtly, and clambered down the companionway. Swiftly he moved through the ship, balancing easily to her roll and pitch.

When he reached the lowest deck he became more stealthy, creeping silently forward. Now he carried the steel bar in his right hand. Every few paces he stopped to listen, but *Kingfisher*'s hull was groaning and popping as she worked in the swells.

He could hear no other sound. He crept up to the door of the control room and cautiously peered through the small armoured glass window. The control room was empty. He tried the handle, and found it locked.

Then he heard voices—from the open doorway of the conveyor room behind him. Quickly he crossed to it and flattened himself against the jamb.

Johnny's voice came muffled and indistinct:

'There's another hatch in here. Get me a half-inch spanner from the tool cupboard.'

'What's a half-inch spanner look like?'

'It's a big one. The size is stamped on it.'

Sergio glanced one-eyed around the door jamb. The cover was off the inspection hatch in the conveyor tunnel, and Tracey's head was thrust into the opening. It was clear that Johnny Lance was in there, and that he had found the secret compartment.

Tracey drew her head out of the hatch, and Sergio ducked back and looked down the passageway. The tool cupboard was bolted to the bulkhead under the stairs from the deck above. He turned and darted around the corner of the passageway.

Tracey came out of the conveyor room, and went to the cupboard. She opened the doors on the glittering array of tools, each clipped securely into its rack.

While she stood before the cupboard, completely absorbed in her search for a half-inch spanner, Sergio came from around the corner and crept up silently behind her.

He lifted the steel bar over his shoulder and came up on his toes, poised to strike.

Tracey was muttering softly to herself, head bowed slightly, handling the spanners—and Sergio knew the blow would crush her skull.

He closed his mind to the thought, and aimed carefully at the base of her skull. He started the blow, and then checked it. For a second that seemed to last for a long time he remained frozen. He couldn't do it.

With an exclamation of satisfaction Tracey found what she was searching for. As she turned away from the cupboard Sergio shrank back behind the angle of the bulk-head, and Tracey hurried back into the conveyor room.

'I've got it, Johnny,' she shouted into the hatch.

'Bring it to me. Hurry, Tracey. Sergio will be getting suspicious,' he shouted back, and Tracey hitched up her voluminous trousers and wriggled into the hatch.

On hands and knees she crawled up beside him. It was cramped and hot in the narrow tunnel. He took the spanner from her.

'Hold the flashlight.' She took it from him, holding the beam on the panel while he unscrewed the retaining bolts and lifted off the cover.

Lying on his side he peered into the opening.

'There's a container of sorts,' he grunted, and reached in. For a minute he struggled with the clamps, then slowly he lifted out the stainless steel cup.

At that moment *Kingfisher* reared and plunged to a freak wave and the cup slipped from Johnny's fingers, and from it spilled the diamonds. They cascaded over both of them, a glittering shower of stones of all sizes and colours. some lodged in Tracey's damp hair, the rest rolled and bounced and scattered about them, catching the light from the torch and throwing it back in splinters of sunshine.

'Yipes!' gasped Tracey and laughed at Johnny's whoop of triumph.

Lying side by side they scrabbled and snatched at the treasure scattered around them.

'Look at this one,' exulted Tracey.

'And this.' They were crazy with excitement, hands filled with diamonds. They hugged each other and kissed ecstatically, laughing into each other's mouths.

Johnny sobered first, 'Come on. Let's get out of here.'

'What about the diamonds?'

'Leave them. There'll be plenty of time later.'

They crawled backwards down the tunnel, still laughing and exclaiming, and one after the other emerged into the conveyor room. while they straightened their clothing, and regained their breath, Tracey asked, 'What now?'

'First thing is to get young Sergio safely under lock and key, his crew also.' Johnny's face hardened. 'The bloody bastards,' he added angrily.

'Then?' Tracey asked.

'Then we'll pull up the hose, and sail *Kingfisher* back into Cartridge Bay. Then we'll call up the police on the radio. There's going to be an accounting with the whole gang of the bastards—your darling brother included.'

Johnny started for the door, asking as he crossed the deck:

'Why did you close the door, Tracey?'

'I didn't,' she replied as she hurried after him, and Johnny's expression changed. He ran to the heavy steel door and threw his weight on it. It did not move, and he swung round to face the door that led into the cyclone room.

It was closed also. He charged across the room and grabbed the handle, heaving at it with all his strength.

He stood back at last, and looked wildly about the long narrow cabin. There was no other opening, no hatch or porthole—nothing except the tiny square peephole in the centre of the steel door that led into the cyclone room beyond. The peephole was covered with three-inch armoured glass that was as strong as the steel that surrounded it. He looked through it.

The tall cyclone reached from floor to roof, dominating the room. Beyond it the steel pipe that carried the gravel from the sea bed pierced the roof from the deck above, but the cyclone room was deserted.

Johnny sobered first. 'Come on. Let's get out of here.'

'We've got problems,' he said.

After closing and locking both the doors that led into the conveyor room, Sergio climbed quickly back to his bridge. The helmsman looked at him curiously.

'How's the lady?'

'Fine,' Sergio snapped at him. 'She's safe.' And then with unnecessary violence, 'Why you no mind your own business, hey? You think you Captain for this ship?'

Startled, the helmsman quickly transferred his attention back to the storm which still raged lustily about them. Sergio began to pace up and down the bridge, balancing easily and instinctively to her exaggerated motion. His smooth baby face was crumpled into a massive scowl, and he puffed on one of his cheroots. With all his soul Sergio Caporetti was lamenting his involvement in this business. He wished that he had never heard of *Kingfisher*. He would have traded his hopes of a life hereafter to be sitting on the seafront at Ostia, sipping *grappa* and watching the girls go by.

Impulsively he pulled open the storm doors at the angle of the bridge and went out onto the exposed wing. The wind buffeted him and set his soft hair dancing and flickering.

From inside his jacket he pulled the canvas bag.

'This is the trouble,' he muttered, looking at the bag in his hand. 'Bloody little stones.'

He threw back his arm like a baseball pitcher, set to hurl the bag out into that hissing green sea below him, but again he could not make the gesture. Swearing quietly to himself, he stuffed the stones back into his jacket, and went back into the wheelhouse.

'Call the radio operator,' he ordered, and the helmsman reached quickly for the voice tube.

The radio operator reached the bridge still owl-eyed with sleep and buttoning his clothing.

'Get on to *Wild Goose*,' Sergio told him.

'I won't be able to raise her in this,' the man protested, glancing out at the storm.

'Call her.' Sergio stepped towards him threateningly. 'Keep calling until you get her.'

Wild Goose staggered and wallowed through the turbulence at the entrance to Cartridge Bay, then fought her way into the sanctuary of the channel.

Hugo relaxed perceptibly. It had been a long hard run back from Thunderbolt and Suicide. Yet there was an uneasy feeling that still persisted. He hoped that the girl was able to handle Lance. He was a tough cooky that Lance, he wished that he had been able to go along with her and make sure of the business. Fifteen years was one hell of a long time—he would be almost fifty years old at the end of it.

Hugo followed the channel markers that appeared like milestones out of the dust clouds, until ahead he made out the loom of the jetty and the depot buildings.

There was a figure on the jetty, crouched beside the mountain of dieseline drums. With a prickle of alarm, Hugo strained his eyes in the bad visibility.

'Who the hell is it?' He puzzled aloud. The figure straightened and came forward to stand on the edge of the jetty. Bareheaded, dressed in rumpled dark business suit, the man carried a shotgun in one hand—and it was another few seconds before Hugo recognized him.

'Christ! It's the boss!' Hugo felt alarm flare in his stomach and chest, it tightened his breathing.

Benedict van der Byl jumped down onto the deck of *Wild Goose* at the moment she touched the jetty.

'What happened?' Benedict demanded as he barged into the wheelhouse.

'I thought you were in hospital,' Hugo countered.

'Who told you that?'

'Your sister.'

'You've seen her? Where is she?'

'I took her out to *Kingfisher*. Like you said. She went out to deal with Lance.'

'Deal with Lance! She's with him, you idiot, she's not with us. She knows the whole deal. Everything!'

'She told me—' Hugo was appalled. But Benedict cut him short.

'The whole thing's blown up. We've got to clear out. Get your crew to load those drums of dieseline into the hold. How are your water tanks?'

'Full.'

'Food?'

'We are stocked up.'

'For how long?'

'Three weeks—at a push, four.'

'Thank God for that.' Benedict looked relieved. 'This storm will blow another three days—we'll have that much start. They'll never find us in this. By the time it clears we'll be well on our way.'

'Where to—Angola?'

'God no! We have to get well clear. South America.'

'South America!'

'Yes—we can do it, carrying extra fuel.'

Hugo was silent a moment, becoming accustomed to the idea.

'We can do it,' Benedict repeated.

'Yes.' Hugo nodded. 'We can do it,' he agreed thoughtfully. For the first time he examined Benedict closely. He saw that he was in an emotional and physical mess, his bloodshot eyes were sunk into deep plum-coloured hollows, dark new beard covered his jowls, and there was a gaunt hunted look to him—like some fugitive animal.

He was filthy with dust, and there was a streak of something that could have been dried vomit down the front of his jacket.

'But, what do we do when we get there?' For the first time since he had known Benedict he felt in control. This was the time to deal, to make bargains.

'We'll get ashore on some deserted spot, and then we split up and disappear.'

'What about money?' Hugo spoke carefully. He glanced down at the shotgun. Benedict's hands were fidgety and restless on the weapon.

'I've got money.'

'How much?' Hugo asked.

'Enough.' Benedict blinked cautiously.

'For me also?' Hugo prodded him, and Benedict nodded.

'How much for me?' Hugo went on.

'Ten thousand.'

'Pounds?'

'Pounds,' Benedict agreed.

'That's not enough.' Hugo shook his head. 'I'll need more than that.'

'Twenty.' Benedict increased his bid, but he knew he was playing from weakness into strength. Ruby was lying mutilated in his study, the net was probably being spread for him already.

'Fifty,' said Hugo decisively.

'I haven't that much.'

'Who are you kidding, Buster!' Hugo snorted. 'You've been stacking it away for years.'

Benedict let the barrels of the shotgun swing towards Hugo's belly suggestively.

'Go ahead,' Hugo grinned at him, screwing up his pale albino eyes. 'That'll leave you to paddle this canoe—you want to try it? You'd pile her up on the bar at the entrance—that's how far you'd get.'

Benedict swung the barrels aside.

'Fifty,' he agreed.

'Right!' Hugo spoke briskly. 'Let's get the hell out of here.'

Wild Goose was clear of the land, and of the towering blinding dust clouds. The following seas came sweeping up under her stern urging her on her westward flight, while the high-pitched shriek of the wind in her rigging cried to her to hasten.

'Why don't you get down below and grab some sleep?' Hugo said. He found Benedict's restless haunting presence in the crowded wheelhouse disconcerting.

Benedict ignored the suggestion. 'Switch on the radio,' he said.

'What for? You'll get nothing on the set.'

'We are out of the dust,' Benedict replied. 'We might pick up a police message.'

The image of Ruby was so clear in his mind. He wanted to know if they'd found her yet. He felt his gorge rising again. That head—oh God—that head! He crossed quickly to the radio set and switched it on.

'They won't be in on us yet,' said Hugo, but Benedict was manipulating the dials—searching the tortured radio waves. The static wailed and gibbered and shrieked like a maniac.

'Turn it off,' snapped Hugo, and at that moment a voice cut in on them.

'—*Wild Goose*,' said the voice from the loudspeaker quite clearly. Benedict crouched eagerly over the set, his hands were busy on the dials, and Hugo came up beside him.

'—Come in, *Wild Goose*. This is *Kingfisher*. I repeat, come in *Wild Goose*—'

Benedict and Hugo looked at each other. 'Don't answer,' said Hugo, but he made no move to intervene as Benedict lifted the microphone off its hook.

'*Kingfisher*, this is *Wild Goose*.'

'Stand by, *Wild Goose*.' The answer came back immediately. 'Stand by for Captain Caporetti.'

'*Wild Goose* standing by.'

Hugo caught Benedict's shoulder and his voice was angrily uncertain:

'Leave it, don't be a fool.'

Benedict shrugged off the hand, and Sergio's voice boomed out of the speaker.

'This is Caporetti—who dat?'

'No names,' Benedict cautioned him. 'Where are your guests?'

'They safe—battened down nicely.'

'Safe? Are you certain? Both of them safe?'

'Si. I have them safe and sure.'

'Stand by.' Benedict crouched over the set, and his mind was racing. Johnny Lance was in his power. This was the last chance he would ever have. Plans began to form, gelling quickly in his mind.

'The diamonds. Caporetti has the diamonds. That big Blue is worth a million on its own,' said Hugo. 'If Caporetti has taken care of the others—it would be worth the risk.'

'Yes.' Benedict turned to him, he had been puzzling how he could make Hugo turn back. He had forgotten the diamonds. 'It would be worth it,' he agreed.

'Just a quick pass alongside *Kingfisher*—pick up Caporetti with the diamonds and we'd be on our way.'

'I have to go aboard.' Benedict qualified the suggestion.

'Why?' Hugo asked.

'Wipe out the reel on the computer that carries the programme—it's got the Jap's name on it. They could trace him. I paid him on my Swiss bank. They'll find the account.'

Hugo hesitated. 'No killing—or anything like that. We've got enough trouble without that.'

'You think I'm crazy?' Benedict demanded.

'Okay, then,' Hugo agreed.

'*Kingfisher*.' Benedict spoke into the microphone. 'We are coming to you. I'll be coming on board to finalize matters.'

'Fine.' Through the static they could hear the relief in Sergio's voice. 'I'll be standing by.'

It took nearly two hours for *Wild Goose* to slug her way back to where *Kingfisher* lay beneath the ghostly white shapes of Thunderbolt and Suicide, and it was after midday before Hugo began manœuvring *Wild Goose* into the big ship's lee.

'Don't waste time,' Hugo cautioned Benedict. 'The sooner we get on our way—the better for all of us.'

'I'll be about half an hour,' Benedict answered. 'You lay off and wait for us.'

'Are you taking that bloody shotgun?' Benedict nodded.

'What for?' But Benedict did not reply, he looked up at the sky. The sun was merely a luminous patch of silver light through the ceiling of sea-fret and wind-driven mist, and still the storm hunted hungrily across the sea.

'It will slow you up on the ladder.' Hugo harped on the shotgun. He wanted very much to part Benedict from it, he wanted it over the side—for its presence aboard would prejudice the plans that Hugo had been forming during the last few hours—plans that took into account the ready market for diamonds in South America, and the undesirability of sharing the proceeds with two partners.

'I'll take it.' Benedict tightened his grip on the stock of the weapon. Without it he would feel naked and vulnerable—and it was part of his own private plans for the future. Benedict's brain had also been busy during the last two hours.

'Suit yourself.' Hugo resigned himself to Benedict's refusal; there would be an opportunity later, during the long passage across the Southern Atlantic. 'You better get up for'ard.'

This time Hugo's approach was neatly executed; in a lull between the colossal swells he touched *Wild Goose*'s bows to the steel side of the factory ship. Benedict stepped across the gap and was up the landing ladder and standing at *Kingfisher*'s rail before the next wave came marching down on them.

He waved Hugo off, then hanging onto the rail, made his way aft to *Kingfisher*'s bridge works.

'Where is Lance?' he demanded of Sergio the moment he stepped onto the bridge, but Sergio glanced significantly at the inquisitively listening helmsman and led Benedict through into his cabin.

'Where is Lance?' Benedict repeated the moment the door was locked.

'He and your sister they are in the conveyor room.'

'The conveyor room?' Benedict was incredulous.

'Si. They find out about Kammy's machine. They open the hatch and go inside. I close both doors. Lock them good.'

'They are in there now?' Benedict asked to gain time to reconstruct his plans.

'Si. Still there.'

'All right.' Benedict reached his decision. 'Now listen, Caporetti, this is what we are going to do. The whole thing has blown up on us. We are going to wipe out as much of the evidence against us as possible, then we are clearing out. We are going to run for South America in *Wild Goose*. You have got the diamonds—haven't you?'

'Si.' Sergio patted the breast of his jacket.

'Give them to me.' Benedict held out his hand, and Sergio grinned.

'I tink I look after them. They keep my heart warm.'

A frown of annoyance narrowed Benedict's eyes, but he let the moment pass.

'All right.' His tone was still friendly. 'Now, what you have to do is get down to the control room and wipe out Kaminikoto's programme. Get his name off that reel. He showed you how to do that?'

'Si.' Sergio nodded.

'How long will it take?'

'Half an hour, not longer,' Sergio answered, and Benedict checked his wrist watch that this would give him time enough to do what he had to do.

'Good! Get cracking.'

'Boss.' Sergio hesitated at the cabin door. 'What about my boys, my crew? They good boys, no trouble for them?'

'They're clean,' Benedict pointed out irritably. 'I'll get them together now, and explain that you have to go ashore. They can keep *Kingfisher* hove to waiting for you to come back. After the storm blows out they are bound to radio base and find out we have disappeared. They'll be all right.'

Sergio nodded his satisfaction.

'I'll call them all to the bridge now. You talk to them.'

The five crew members were gathered on *Kingfisher*'s bridge, and Sergio had disappeared down below.

'Any of you speak English?' Benedict demanded, and two of them affirmed that they did.

'Right,' Benedict addressed them. 'You will have been wondering about all the coming and going in this weather. I want you all to be ready to leave the ship. I want you to get all your valuables—now!'

Quickly they translated to the others, who looked apprehensively at Benedict. He was a strange wide-eyed figure with the shotgun tucked under his arm.

'Right—let's go.' And there was no dissent from any of them as they trooped to the companionway.

Benedict followed them along the passage-way towards the crew quarters, and glanced quickly at his wrist watch. Seven minutes had elapsed. He looked at the men ahead of him.

The backs of their heads formed a solid target. He had shot guineafowl like that in Namaqualand when they were on the ground running away from him in a thick file, down on one knee and aim for the thickest of heads, knocking down half the flock with both barrels.

He knew he could take all five of these men with two shots. Just let them get a little farther ahead so the shot could be spread. But he remembered Ruby and his stomach heaved. The other was just as sure.

'Stop!' he commanded as the five men came level with the paint store. They obeyed and turned back to face him. Now he held the shotgun so that there was no mistaking its menace. They stared at the gun fearfully.

'Open that door.' He pointed at the paint store. Nobody moved.

'You.' Benedict picked on one of those who spoke English. Like a man in a trance he went to the steel door and spun the locking handle. He pulled the door open.

'In!' Eloquently Benedict gestured with the shotgun. Reluctantly the five of them filed into the small windowless cubicle, and Benedict slammed the door on them. He spun the lock, throwing all his weight on the handle to set it.

Now he had a clear field, and his wrist watch gave him another twenty minutes. He hurried for'ard, he wanted to keep well clear of the control room and Sergio Caporetti.

Using the forward companionway he dropped down to the working deck, fumbling out his duplicate set of keys.

WARNING. EXPLOSIVES. NO UNAUTHORIZED ENTRY.

He unlocked the door, and lying the shotgun flat on the deck he lifted a twenty-five pound drum of plastique down from its rack.

In his haste he tore a fingernail on the lid of the drum, but hardly felt the pain. He uncoiled a six-foot length of the soft dark toffee-coloured material and slung it around his neck. Next he selected a cardboard box of pencil time fuses. He read the label.

'Fourteen-minute delay. That's about right.'

Blood from his torn nail left brown blotches on the cardboard as he took four of the pencils from the box, picked up the shotgun and hurried aft. The jet engine whine of the cyclone mounted deafeningly as he came closer to it.

Tracey was curled on the bare steel plating of the deck with Johnny's jacket folded under her head. She was in a fatigue-drugged sleep, so deep as to be almost deathlike.

Every few minutes Johnny interrupted his restless patrol of the conveyor room to stand over her and look down on her unconscious form. His worried expression softened a little each time he studied her pale lovely face. Once he stooped over her and tenderly lifted a strand of dark hair from her cheek, before resuming his pacing up and down the narrow cabin.

Each time he reached the door of the conveyor room he glanced through the tiny windows. The glass had resisted his attempts to smash it with one of the spanners. He wanted to open the window to call for help, but his efforts had not marked the thick armoured glass.

There was no way out of the cabin. Johnny had tried every possible outlet. The apertures for the conveyor system were guarded at one end by the furnace, and at the other by moving machinery which would ferociously chew to tatters anyone who became entangled in it. They were caged securely, and Johnny paced his cage.

Again he stopped before the peephole, but this time he flung himself at the door with clenched fists. The steel plate smeared the skin from his knuckles as he hammered on it and the pain sobered him. He pressed his face to the glass and through it watched Benedict van der Byl enter the conveyor room and, without glancing at the window, cross to the cyclone.

Benedict laid aside the shotgun he carried and for a moment stood looking up at the thick steel pipe that carried the gravel down from the deck pumps above. As he lifted the thick rope of plastique from around his neck, Johnny knew exactly what he was going to do.

He watched him in fascination as Benedict mounted the steel ladder up the side of the cyclone. Hanging with one hand to the ladder, Benedict reached out with the other and clumsily tied the rope of plastique around the gravel pipe. It hung there like a necklace about the throat of some obscene prehistoric monster.

'You bastard! You murdering bloody swine!' Johnny shouted, and again he beat on the steel door with his fists. But the thickness of the door and the whine of the cyclone drowned his voice. Benedict showed no sign of hearing him—but Tracey sat up and looked about her blearily. Then she came to her feet and staggering to the roll and pitch of the ship she went to Johnny and pressed her face to the window beside her.

Benedict was sticking the time pencils into the soft dark explosive. He used all four fuses, taking no chances on a misfire.

'What's he doing?' Tracey asked after she had recovered from the surprise of recognizing her brother.

'He's going to cut the pipe, and let *Kingfisher* pump herself full of gravel.'

'Sink her?' Tracey's voice was sharp with alarm.

'She'll pump water and gravel into herself at pressures that will tear away all the inner bulkheads.'

'This one?' Tracey patted the steel plate.

'It'll pop like a paper bag. God, you have no idea of the power in those pumps.'

'No.' Tracey shook her head. 'He's my brother. He won't do it, Johnny. He couldn't murder us.'

'By the time he's finished—' Johnny contradicted her grimly, '—*Kingfisher* will by lying in 200 feet of water. Her hull will be packed so tightly with gravel that it will be like a block of cement. We, and everything in her, including his little machine, will be so flattened as to be unrecognizable. It would cost millions to salvage *Kingfisher*—and no one will care that much.'

'No, not Benedict.' Tracey was almost pleading. 'He's not that bad.'

Johnny interrupted her brusquely. 'He could get away with it. It's a good try—his best chance. Encase all the evidence against him in concrete, and bury it deep.'

'No, Benedict.' Tracey was watching her brother as he climbed down the cyclone ladder and picked up the shotgun. 'Please, Benedict, don't do it.'

Almost as if he had heard her, Benedict turned suddenly and saw the two faces at the window. The shock of guilt held him rigid for a moment, as he stared at them—Tracey's pale lips forming words he could not hear, Johnny's eyes burning with accusation.

Benedict dropped his eyes, he made a gesture that was indecisive, almost pathetic. He looked up at the fused and charged rope of explosive—and then he grinned. a sardonic twitching of the lips, and he stumbled out of the cyclone room and was gone.

'He'll come back,' whispered Tracey. 'He won't let it happen.'

'I wouldn't bet on that—if I were you,' said Johnny.

Benedict reached *Kingfisher*'s rail and clung to it. He looked out to where *Wild Goose* bobbed and hung on the swells. He saw Hugo's face as a white blob behind the wheelhouse window, but as the little trawler began closing in for the pick-up Benedict waved it away. He glanced at his watch again, then looked back anxiously at the bridge.

The long minutes dragged by. Where the hell was the Italian? Benedict could not leave him—not while he still had that diamond; not while he could stop the dredge pumps and release the prisoners locked below.

Again Benedict checked his watch, twelve minutes since he had set the time pencils. He must go back and find Caporetti. He started back along the rail, and at that moment Sergio appeared on the wing of the bridge. He shouted a question at Benedict that was lost in the wind.

'Come on!' Frantically Benedict beckoned to him. 'Come on! Hurry!'

With another last look about the bridge, Sergio ran to the ladder and climbed down to deck level.

'Where my boys?' he shouted at Benedict. 'Why nobody at the con? What you do with them?'

'They are all right,' Benedict assured him. He had turned to the rail and was signalling *Wild Goose* to come alongside.

'Where they?' Sergio demanded. 'Where my boys?'

'I sent them to—' Benedict's reply was cut off as *Kingfisher*'s deck jarred under their feet. The explosion was a dull concussion in her belly, and Sergio's jaw hung open. Benedict backed away from him along the rail.

'Filth!' Sergio's jaw snapped closed, his whole body appeared to swell with anger.

'You kill them, dirty pig. You kill my boys. You kill Johnny—the girl.'

'Keep away from me.' Benedict braced himself against the rail, leaving both hands free to use the gun.

Not even Sergio would advance into the deadly blank eyes of those muzzles. He paused uncertainly.

'I'll blow your guts all over the deck,' Benedict warned him, and his forefinger was hooked around the trigger.

They stared at each other, and the wind fluttered their hair and tore at their clothing.

'Give me those diamonds,' Benedict commanded, and when Sergio stood unmoving, he went on urgently, 'Don't be a hero, Caporetti. I can gun you down and take them anyway. Give them to me—and our deal is still on. You'll come with us. I'll get you out of here. I swear it.'

Sergio's expression of outrage faded. A moment longer he hesitated.

'Come on Caporetti. We haven't got much time.' It may have been his imagination, but to Benedict it seemed that *Kingfisher*'s action in the water had altered, she was sluggish to meet the swells and her roll was more pronounced.

'Okay,' said Sergio, and began unbuttoning his jacket. 'You win. I give you.'

Benedict relaxed with relief, and Sergio thrust his hand into his jacket and stepped towards him. He grasped the canvas bag by its neck, and brought it out held like a cosh.

Sergio was close to him, too close for Benedict to swing the shotgun onto him. Sergio's expression became savage, his intentions blazed in his dark eyes as he lifted the canvas bag and poised himself to deliver a blow at Benedict's head, but he had not reckoned with the extraordinary reflexes of the natural athlete he was facing.

As Sergio launched the blow, Benedict rolled his shoulders and head away from it, lifting the butt of the shotgun as a guard. Sergio's wrist struck the seasoned walnut, and he grunted with the pain. His fingers opened nervelessly and the canvas bag flew from his grip, glanced off Benedict's temple and flew on down the deck, sliding to stop against one of the compressed air tanks thirty feet away.

Benedict danced back, dropping the barrels of the shotgun until Sergio looked into the muzzles.

'Hold it, you bastard,' Benedict snarled at him. 'You've made your choice. Now let's see what your guts look like.'

Sergio was hugging his injured wrist to his belly, crouching over it. Benedict was backing away to where the bag lay against the tank. His face was flushed and hectic with anger, but he kept darting side glances at the canvas bag.

At that moment *Kingfisher* took another wave over her bows, and the water came swooshing down the deck, picking up the bag and washing it towards the scuppers.

'Look out!' Sergio shouted. 'The bag! It's going.'

Benedict lunged for it, sprawling full length. With his free hand he grabbed the sodden canvas as it was disappearing over the side. But he was thirty feet away from Sergio, and he still held the shotgun in his other fist. Sergio could not hope to reach him without getting both charges of the buckshot in his belly.

Instead Sergio spun round and sprinted back along the deck towards the bridge.

Benedict was on his knees frantically stuffing the bag of diamonds into the side pocket of his jacket and shouting after Sergio.

'Stop! Stop or I'll shoot!'

Sergio did not look back nor check his run, and Benedict had the bag in his pocket and now both hands were free. He lifted the shotgun, and tried to balance himself against *Kingfisher*'s wallowing motion as he aimed.

At the shot, Sergio stumbled slightly but kept on running. He reached the ladder and went up it.

Again Benedict aimed, and the shotgun clapped dully in the wind. This time a spasm of pain shuddered through Sergio's big body, and he froze on the ladder.

Benedict fumbled in his pocket for fresh shells, but before he could reload Sergio had begun climbing again. Benedict broke the gun and thrust the shells into the breech. He snapped the gun closed and looked up just as Sergio disappeared through the storm doors—and the two shots that Benedict loosed after him merely pockmarked the paintwork and starred the glass of the wheelhouse. 'The stupid bastard.' Hugo watched from the wheelhouse of *Wild Goose*. 'He's gone berserk.'

Hugo had heard the explosion and seen the shooting.

'Fifteen years is enough—but not the rope as well.'

He swung the wheel and *Wild Goose* sheered in towards *Kingfisher*'s side. Peering through the spray and salt-smattered windows, he saw Benedict drag himself to his feet and start after Sergio along the deck.

Hugo snatched the electric loudhailer from its bracket and pulled open the side window of the wheelhouse, holding the hailer to his lips.

'Hey! You stupid bastard, have you gone mad? What the hell you doing?'

Benedict glanced down at the trawler, then ignored it to give all his attention to reloading the gun. He kept going back along the deck, following Sergio to finish him off.

'You'll get us all strung up, you fool,' Hugo called through the loudhailer. 'Leave him. Let's get out of here.'

Benedict kept scrambling and slipping towards *Kingfisher*'s bridge.

'I'm leaving—now! Do you hear me? You can stew in your own pot. I'm getting out.'

Benedict checked and looked down at the trawler. He shouted and pointed at the bridge. Hugo caught one word: 'Diamonds.'

'All right, friend! Do what you like—I'll see you around,' Hugo hailed, and hit the trawler's throttle wide open. The roar of the diesels and the churning of her propeller convinced Benedict.

'Hugo! Wait! Wait for me, I'm coming.' He scampered back to the ladder and started down it.

Hugo throttled back and brought *Wild Goose* in neatly under the ladder.

'Jump!' he shouted through the hailer, and obediently Benedict jumped to hit the foredeck heavily. The shotgun flew from his hands to fall into the water alongside. Benedict cast one longing glance after the gun, then crawled to his feet and limped back to the wheelhouse.

Already *Wild Goose* was plunging away into the wind, but as Benedict entered the wheelhouse Hugo turned on him with his pink albino face set in a snarl of rage.

'What the hell have you done, you bastard? You lied to me. What was that explosion?'

'Explosion—I don't know. What explosion?'

Hugo hit him a stinging open-handed blow across the cheek.

'We agreed no killing—and you put us all on the spot.' Hugo's attention was focused completely on Benedict who had backed into the farthest corner of the wheelhouse. He massaged the dark red finger marks that stained his cheek.

'You set scuttling charges in *Kingfisher*—didn't you, you dirty son of a bitch? God, I hate to think what you've done with Lance and the girl.'

Outside the storm was nearing its climax. A rain squall swept down on *Wild Goose*—sure sign that the wind must soon drop.

Automatically Hugo switched on the rotating wipers to clear the rain from the screen, as he continued to harangue Benedict.

'I saw you trying to murder the Italian. Christ! What for? He's one of us! Am I next on your list?'

'He had the diamonds,' mumbled Benedict. 'I was trying to get them from him.'

And Hugo's expression changed; he turned away from the wheel and stared at Benedict.

'You haven't got the diamonds? Is that what you're saying?' His tone was almost hurt.

'I tried—he wouldn't—'

And Hugo left the wheel and was across the wheelhouse like a white leopard. He grabbed the front of Benedict's coat, and screamed into his face.

'You left the diamonds! You stick my head in a noose—and I get nothing out of it.'

He was trembling with rage and his pale eyes bulged from their sockets.

Looking into those eyes Benedict realized his own danger. In the time it had taken him to leave *Kingfisher*'s deck and reach the wheelhouse of the trawler he had decided to let Hugo think that Sergio still had the diamonds. Squeamish as Hugo appeared to be about drowning Johnny and Tracey, despite his repeated demands for 'No Killing', Benedict knew intuitively that Hugo had no intention of splitting a million pounds' worth of diamonds with him.

Once Hugo was certain that Benedict had the stones on board, Benedict knew there was no chance that he would reach South America alive.

The crossing might take weeks, the crew of the trawler were in Hugo's pay and loyal only to him. Benedict must sleep, and they would take him in the night.

On the other hand, of course, Benedict had no intention of splitting a million pounds' worth of diamonds with Hugo Kramer. He let his voice whine as he cringed in Hugo's grip.

'I tried. Sergio had them. He wouldn't—that's why I shot him.'

Hugo drew back his hand to slap Benedict again. Benedict twisted slightly, and drove his knee into Hugo's crutch, sending him staggering back across the wheelhouse, clutching himself between the legs and whimpering with the pain.

'Right, Kramer,' Benedict spoke softly. 'That's a little lesson for you. Behave yourself, and you'll get your fifty grand on the other side of the Atlantic.'

They stared at each other. Hugo Kramer weak and pale with agony, Benedict standing tall and arrogant again.

'Treat me gently, Kramer. I'm your meal-ticket. Remember it.'

Hugo gaped at him. The positions had reversed so swiftly. He pulled himself upright and his voice was thick with agony, but humble.

'I'm sorry, Mr van der Byl, I lost my temper. It's been a hell of a —'

'Skipper! Ahead!' The warning was shouted by the coloured crewman, Hansie.

Hugo stumbled to the untended wheel, and peered out into the storm.

Wild Goose was shooting down another slope of green water, and just ahead of her bows Hugo saw one of the huge yellow buoys that *Kingfisher* had laid down and then abandoned. It was held captive in the trough of the swells by the anchor cable. The cable was drawn as tight as a rod of steel across the trawler's bows, lifted just above the surface of the water; shivering drops of water flew from it under the tension of the buoy's drag.

'Oh God!' Hugo spun the wheel and threw *Wild Goose*'s engine into reverse—but she was racing down the swell, and her speed was unchecked as the cable scraped harshly along her keel.

Then came the harsh banging and clattering of the drive shaft as the cable fouled the propeller—followed by a crack as the shaft snapped. *Wild Goose*'s engine screamed into overrev as the load was lifted from it.

Hugo shut the throttle, and there was silence in the wheelhouse. *Wild Goose* swung beam on to the seas which came boiling in over her deck. Without her propeller she was transformed from a husky little sea creature to a piece of driftwood at the mercy of each current and the whim of the wind.

Hugo's head swung slowly until he was looking down-wind to where the massive shapes of Thunderbolt and Suicide just showed through the rain squall.

'Cover your ears—tight!' Johnny Lance pressed Tracey against the bulkhead as far from the cyclone room as they could get. 'There are twenty-five pounds of plastique in there—it will blow like a volcano. He will have used a short fuse, fourteen minutes. We won't have long to wait.'

Johnny set Tracey's shoulders squarely against the steel plating, and crouched over her—trying to shield her with his own body.

They stared into each other's eyes, teeth clenched, the heels of their palms jammed hard over their ears and they cowered away from the blast that must come.

The minutes passed, the longest minutes of Tracey's life. She could not have borne them without screaming hysteria except for that big hard body covering her—even with it she felt her fear mounting steadily during the molasses drip of time.

Suddenly the air lunged at her, driving the breath from her lungs. Johnny was thrown heavily against her. The blast sucked at her eardrums, and burst in her head so that bright lights flashed across her vision and she felt the steel plates heave under her shoulders.

Then her head cleared, and although her eardrums buzzed and sang, she found with a leaping relief that she was still alive.

She reached out for Johnny, but he was gone. In panic she groped, then opened her eyes. He was lurching down the long conveyor room, and when he reached the locked door at the far end he pressed his face to the peephole.

The fumes of the explosion still filled the cyclone room, a swirling bluish fog, but through them Johnny could make out the shambles that was the aftermath.

The huge cyclone had been torn from its mountings, and now sagged against the far bulkhead—crushed. It was worth only a single glance before Johnny froze into rigidity at the true horror.

The gravel pipe had been severed cleanly just below its junction with the upper deck. It protruded for six feet, but now the force of the jet through it was flickering and whipping it about as though it were not steel but a rubber garden hose.

The jet was a solid eighteen-inch column, a pillar of brown mud and yellow gravel and sea water that beat against the steel plates of the hull with a hollow drumming roar.

In the few seconds since the explosion the cyclone room was already half-filled with a slimy shifting porridge that rushed from wall to wall with the movement of the ship. If was like some monstrous jelly fish which each second gathered weight and srength.

Tracey reached Johnny's side and he placed his arm around her shoulders. She looked through the armoured glass and he felt her body stiffen.

At that moment the yellowish monster spread over the window, obscuring it completely. Johnny felt the first straining of the steel plates under his hands. They fluttered and bulged, then began to protest aloud at the intolerable pressure. A seam started, and a fine jet of filthy water hissed from the gap and soaked icily through Johnny's jersey.

'Get back.' Johnny dragged Tracey away from the squeaking, groaning bulkhead. Back along the narrow conveyor room they stumbled, moving with difficulty for the deck beneath their feet was slanting as *Kingfisher* began to lean under the increasing weight in her belly.

Still holding Tracey, he reached the locked door and resisted the futile desire to attack it with his bare hands. Instead he forced his brain to work, tried to anticipate the sequence of events that would lead to the final destruction of *Kingfisher*—and all those aboard her.

Benedict had left the other entrance to the cyclone room wide open. Already that viscous mass of mud and water must be spreading rapidly through the lower levels of the hull, following always the avenue of least resistance—finding the weak spots and bursting through them.

If the walls of the conveyor room held against the pressure, the rest of the hull would be filled and they would be enfolded in the tentacles of that great yellow monster—a small bubble of air trapped within it and taken down with it when it returned to the depths from which it had come.

Would the bulkheads of the conveyor room hold? The answer came almost immediately in the squeal of metal against metal, and the crackle of springing rivets.

The monster had found the weak spot, the aperture through the drying furnace into the conveyor, ripping away the fragile baffles, bursting through the furnace in a cloud of steam, it gushed into the conveyor room bringing with it the sewage stench of deep-sea mud.

Kingfisher made another sluggish roll, so different from her usual spry action, and the mud came racing down the tunnel in a solid knee-high wall.

It slammed both of them back against the steel door with a shocking strength, and the feel of it was cold and loathsome as something long dead and putrefied.

Kingfisher rolled back and the mud slithered away, bunched itself against the far bulkhead then charged at them again.

Waist-deep it struck them, and tried to suck them back with the next roll.

Tracey was screaming now, nerves and muscles reaching their breaking-point. She was clinging to Johnny, coated to the waist in stinking ooze, her eyes and mouth wide open in terror as she watched the mud building up for its next assault.

Johnny groped for some hold to anchor them. They must keep on their feet to survive that next rush of mud. He found the locking handle of the door and braced himself against it, holding Tracey with all his strength.

The mud came again, silently, murderously. It burst over their heads and punched them with stunning force against the plating.

Then it sucked back once more, and left them down on their knees, anchored only by Johnny's grip on the locking handle.

Tracey was vomiting the foul mud and it filled her ears and eyes and nostrils, clogging them so that it bubbled at her breathing.

Johnny could feel her weakening in his arms, her struggles becoming more feeble as she tried to regain her feet.

His own strength was going. It needed his last reserve to drag them both upright.

The locking handle turned in his fingers, spinning open. The steel door against which he was braced fell away, so that he staggered backwards without support but still clutching Tracey.

There was just a moment to recognize the big, reassuring bulk of Sergio Caporetti beside him and feel an arm like the trunk of a pine tree steady him before the rush of mud down the conveyor room hit them and knocked all three of them down, sending them swirling and rolling end over end before its strength dissipated in the new space beyond the conveyor room door.

Johnny pulled himself up the bulkhead. He had lost Tracey. Dazed but desperate he looked for her, mumbling her name.

He found her swilling aimlessly in the waist-deep mud, floating on her face. He took a handful of muddy-hair and lifted her face out, but the mud had hold of his legs, pulling him off balance as it surged back and forth.

'Sergio. Help!' he croaked. 'For God's sake, Sergio.'

And Sergio was there, lifting her like a child in his arms and wading to the ladder that led to the deck above. The mud knocked Johnny down again, and when he surfaced Sergio was climbing steadily up the ladder.

Despite the mud and water that blurred Johnny's eyesight, he could see that Sergio's wide back, from shoulders to hips, was speckled with dozens of punctures as though he had been stabbed repeatedly with a knitting needle. From each tiny wound oozed droplets of blood that spread like brown ink on the blotting-paper of his sodden jacket.

At the head of the companionway Sergio turned, still holding Tracey in his arms; he stood like a Colossus looking down at Johnny wallowing and slipping in the mud below.

'Hey, Lance—go switch off your bloody machine. She drown my ship. I sail her myself now—the right way. No bloody fancy machine.'

Johnny steadied himself against the bulkhead and called up at him:

'Sergio, what happened to Benedict van der Byl, where is he?'

'I think he go with *Wild Goose*—but first he shoot the hell out of me, not half. Fix your machine, no time for talk.'

And he was gone, still carrying Tracey.

Another rush of mud carried Johnny down the flooded passage and threw him against the door to the control room. Already his body seemed to be one aching bruise, and still the battering continued as he tried to unlock and open the control room door.

At last, using the suck of the mud to help him, he yanked it open and went in with a burst of yellow slime following him and flooding the compartment shoulder deep.

Clinging to the console of the computer he reached up and punched the master control buttons.

'Dredge Stop.'

'Dredge engines Stop.'

'Main engines manual.'

'Navigation system manual.'

'All programme abort.'

Instantly the roar from the severed dredge pipe, which had echoed through the ship during all their strivings, dwindled as though some vast waterfall had dried. Then there was silence. Though only comparative silence, for the hull still groaned and squeaked at the heart-breaking burden it now carried and the mud slopped and thudded against the plating.

Weak and sick, Johnny clung to the console. He was shivering with cold, and every muscle in his body felt bruised and strained.

Suddenly the ship changed her motion, heaving under his feet like a harpooned whale as she swung broadside to the storm. Johnny roused himself with alarm.

The journey back through the flooded passages to the companionway was an agony of mind and body—for *Kingfisher* was now behaving in a strange and unnatural way.

The scene that awaited Johnny as he dragged himself onto the bridge chilled his soul as the icy mud had chilled his body.

Thunderbolt and Suicide lay less than a furlong off *Kingfisher*'s starboard quarter. Both islands were wreathed in sheets of spray that fumed from the surf that was breaking like cannon-fire on the cliffs.

The maniacal flute of the wind joined with the drum of the surf to produce a symphony fit for the halls of Hell, but above this devil's music Sergio Caporetti bellowed, 'We got no power on port main engine.'

Johnny turned to him. Sergio was hunched over the wheel, and Tracey lay on the deck at his feet like a discarded doll.

'The water she kill port main.' Sergio was pumping the engine telegraph. Then abandoning the effort, he looked over the side.

The reeking white cliffs were closer now, much closer—as though you could reach out a hand to them. The ship was drifting down rapidly on the wind.

Sergio spun the wheel to full port lock, trying to bring *Kingfisher*'s head round to meet the sea and the wind. She was rolling as no ship was ever meant to roll, hanging over at the limit of each swing, so that the wheelhouse windows seemed but a few feet from the crests of the green waves. She hung like that as though she meant never to come upright again. Then sluggishly, reluctantly, she swung back, speeding up as she reached the perpendicular and the great mass of mud and water in her hull shifted and slammed her over on her other side, pinning her like that for eternal seconds before she could struggle upright again for the cycle to be repeated.

Sergio held the wheel at full lock, but still *Kingfisher* wallowed down towards the cliffs of Thunderbolt and Suicide. The wind had her the way a dog carries a bone in its teeth. Under half power and with her decks awash *Kingfisher* could not break that grip.

Johnny was a helpless spectator, held awe-bound so he could not break away even to succour Tracey who was still lying on the deck. He saw everything with a super-natural clarity—from the dribbling little shot holes in Sergio's back, to the ponderous irresistible rush of the white water up the cliffs that loomed so close alongside.

'She no answer helm. She too sick.' Sergio spoke now in conversational tones which carried with surprising clarity through the uproar of the elements. 'All right then. We go the other way. We take the gap.'

For a moment Johnny did not understand, then he saw it. *Kingfisher*'s bows were coming up to the narrow opening between the two islands.

A passage less than a hundred yards wide at its narrowest point, where the vicious cross currents met head on and leapt fifty feet into the air as they collided. Here the surface was obscured by a thick froth of spindrift that heaved and humped up as though the ocean were fighting for breath under the thick cream-coloured blanket.

'No.' Johnny shook his head, staring at that hideous passage. 'We won't make it, Sergio. We won't do it.'

But already Sergio was spinning the wheel from lock to lock, and unbelievably *Kingfisher* was responding. Helped now by the wind she came around slowly, seeming to brush her bows across the white cliff of Thunderbolt, and she steadied her swing and aimed at the gap. It was then Johnny saw it for the first time.

'Christ, there's a boat dead ahead!'

The steep swells had hidden it up to that moment, but now she bobbed up on a crest. It was a tiny trawler, flying in a dirty scrap of canvas as a staysail at her stubby mast, and struggling piteously in the granite jaws of Thunderbolt and Suicide.

'*Wild Goose!*' roared Sergio, and he reached for the handle of the foghorn that hung above his head.

'Now we have some fun.' And he yanked the handle. The croaking bellow of the foghorn echoed off the cliffs that were closing on either side of them.

'Kill my boys—hey? Shoot me—hey? Trick me—hey? Now I trick you— but good!' Sergio punctuated his triumphant yells with blasts on the foghorn.

'Christ, no! You can't do it!' Johnny caught ungently at the big Italian's shoulder, but Sergio struck his hand away and steered directly for the trawler as it lay full in the narrow passage.

'I give him plenty warning.' Sergio sent another blast echoing off the cliffs. 'He no give me warning when he shoot me—the bastard.'

There was a group of men on the trawler's foredeck. Johnny could see that they were manhandling an inflatable escape raft, a thick mattress of black rubber, towards the nearest side of the trawler. But now they were frozen by the bellow of *Kingfisher*'s foghorn. They stood looking up at the tall cliff of steel that bore down on them. Their faces were pale blobs in the gloom.

'Sergio. It's murder. Turn away, damn you, you can miss them. Turn away!' Again Johnny lunged across the wheelhouse and grabbed at the wheel.

Sergio swung a backhanded blow that cracked against Johnny's temple and sent him reeling half-stunned against the storm doors.

'*Who* Captain for this bloody ship!' There was blood on Sergio's lips, the shout had torn something inside him.

Kingfisher's bows were lifting and swinging down like an executioner's axe over the trawler. They were close enough now for Johnny to recognize the men on the trawler's deck— but only one of them held his full attention.

Benedict van der Byl cowered against the trawler's rail, gripping it with both hands. His hair fluttered, soft and dark, in the wind. His eyes were big dark holes like those of a skull in the bone-white face, and his lips a pink circle of terror.

Then suddenly the trawler disappeared under *Kingfisher*'s massive bows, and immediately after that came the splintering crunching sound of her timbers shattering. *Kingfisher* bore down on the passage between the cliffs without a check in her speed.

Johnny fumbled with the catch of the storm doors, and the wind tore it open. He staggered out onto the exposed wing of the bridge and reached the rail.

He stood there with the storm clawing at his clothing and looked down at the wreckage that dragged slowly along *Kingfisher*'s hull, and then was left behind.

There were human heads bobbing among the wreckage, and the wash from

Kingfisher's propeller pushed them towards the cliffs of Suicide.

A wave picked up one of the men and carried him swiftly onto the cliff, sweeping him high and then swirling back to leave the body stranded on that smooth white slope of granite.

The man was still alive, Johnny saw him clawing at the smooth rock with his bare fingers, trying to drag himself above the reach of the sea.

It was Hugo Kramer; even through the fog of spray there was no mistaking that head of pale hair and the lithe twisted body.

The next wave reached up and dragged him back over the rock, tearing the nails from his hooked fingers as he tried to find a hold.

He was swirled and flung about in the turbulence below the cliff before another wave lifted him and hurled him onto the granite. One of his legs was broken at the knee by the force of the impact and the lower part of the leg spun loosely like the blade of a windmill as the water tugged at it.

Once again Hugo was left stranded but now he made no movement. His arms were flung wide, and his leg stuck out at a grossly unnatural angle from the knee.

Then from among these mighty waves there rose up a mass of green water which dwarfed all the others.

It reared up with slow majesty and hung poised over the granite cliff before it fell on Hugo's broken body with a boom that seemed to shake the very rock.

When the giant wave drew back, the cliff was washed clean. Hugo was gone.

The same wave that destroyed him came down the passage between the cliffs and, in contrast to its treatment of Hugo Kramer, it was tender as a mother as it lifted *Kingfisher* and carried her out into the open sea beyond the reach of those cruel cliffs.

Looking back into the gap between the islands, the last trace that Johnny saw of the *Wild Goose* was the black rubber escape raft tossing and leaping high on the turmoil of broken water and creamy spindrift.

'They'll have no use for that,' he said aloud. He searched for a sight of any survivors, but there was none. They were chewed to pulp in the jaws of Thunderbold and Suicide, and swallowed down into the cold green maw of the sea.

Johnny turned away and went back into the wheelhouse. He lifted Tracey from the deck and carried her through to Sergio's cabin.

As he laid her on the bunk he whispered to her, 'I'm glad. I'm glad you didn't see it, my darling.'

At midnight the wind still howled about the ship, hurling sheets of solid rain against the windows of the bridge. Forty minutes later the wind had veered through a hundred and eighty degrees and become a light south-easterly air. The black sky opened like a theatre curtain, and the full moonlight burst through so brightly as to pale the stars. Though the tall black swells still marched in martial ranks from the north, the gentle wind was soothing and lulling them.

'Sergio, you must rest now. I will take the con. Let Tracey dress your back.'

'You take the con!' Sergio snorted scornfully. 'I save the ship—and you sink her for me. Not bloody likely.'

'Listen, Sergio. We don't know how badly you are hurt. You are killing yourself.'

The same argument spluttered and flared intermittently during the long night hours while Sergio clung stubbornly to the helm and coaxed the labouring vessel back towards Cartridge Bay. He insisted on detouring far out to sea to avoid the islands, so that when the bright dawn broke, the land was only a low brown line on the horizon and the mountains of the interior were a distant blue.

An hour after dawn Johnny made radio contact with the very agitated operator at Cartridge Bay.

'Mr Lance, we've been trying to raise you since yesterday evening.'

'I've been busy.' Despite his fatigue Johnny grinned at his own understatement. 'Now, listen to me. We are coming into Cartridge Bay. We'll be there in a couple of hours. I want you to have a doctor, Doctor Robin Sutherland, flown up from Cape Town—also I want you to have the police standing by. I want somebody from both the Diamond police and the Robbery and Murder squad—have you got that?'

'The police are here already, Mr Lance. They are looking for Mr Benedict van der Byl. They found his car here—they have a warrant . . .' The operator's voice broke off and Johnny heard the mumble of background voices, then—'Mr Lance, are you there? Stand by to speak to Inspector Stander of the CID.'

'Negative!' Johnny cut in on the transmission. 'I'm not talking to anybody. He can wait until we get into the Bay. Just you have Doctor Sutherland ready. I've got a badly wounded man on board.'

Johnny leaned over the radio set and shut off the main switch, then he stood and made his way slowly back to the bridge. Every muscle in his body felt stiff and bruised, and he was groggy with tiredness, but he took up the argument with Sergio where they had left off.

'Now listen to me, Sergio. You must lie down, You can take us in over the bar; but now you must get an hour or two's rest.'

Still Sergio would not relinquish the wheel, but he consented to strip to the waist and let Tracey examine his back.

In the expanse of white muscle were little black holes each set in its own purple bruise. Some of the holes had sealed themselves with black clotted blood, from others fluid still oozed—clear or pink in colour—and there was a faint sweetish smell from the wounds.

Johnny and Tracey exchanged worried looks before Tracey reached into the first aid box and set to work.

'How she look, Johnny?' Sergio's jovial tone was belied by his face which was a lump of bread dough touched with greenish blue hues.

'Depends if you like your meat rare.' Johnny matched his tone, and Sergio chuckled but cut it short with a wince.

Johnny put a cheroot between Sergio's lips and held a match for him. As Sergio puffed the tip into a glow, Johnny asked casually, 'What made you change your mind?' And Sergio looked up at him quickly, guiltily, through the cloud of cheroot smoke.

'You had us cold. You could have got away with it—perhaps,' Johnny persisted quietly. 'What made you come back?'

'Listen, Johnny. Me, I've done some damned awful bloody things—but I never killed a man or a woman—ever. He said no killing. Fine, I go alone. Then I hear the plastique blow. I know you two in conveyor room. I think the hell with it. Now, I climb off the wagon—but she's going too fast. I get bum full of buckshot.'

They were silent for a while. Tracey was absorbed in patching the shot-wounds with adhesive tape.

Johnny broke the silence. 'Was there a big diamond, Sergio? A big blue diamond?'

'Si.' Sergio sighed. 'Such a diamond as you will never see again.'

'Benedict had it?'

'Si. Benedict had it.'

'Did he have it on him?'

'In his coat. He put it in his coat pocket.'

Tracey stepped back. 'That's all we can do for now,' she murmured and caught Johnny's eye, shaking her head slightly and frowning with worry. 'The sooner we get him to a doctor the happier I'll be.'

A little before noon Sergio took *Kingfisher* in through the entrance to Cartridge Bay, handling the mud-filled ship with all the aplomb of the master mariner, but as they approached the first turning in the channel he sagged gently to the deck and the wheel spun out of his hands.

Before Johnny could reach the helm, *Kingfisher* had yawned wearily across the channel. She had so little way on her that when she went up on the sandbank there was only a small jolt and she listed over a few degrees.

Johnny pulled the engine telegraph to 'STOP'.

'Help me, Tracey.' He stooped over Sergio and took him under the armpits. Tracey grasped his ankles. Half dragging, half carrying, they got him through to his cabin and laid him on his bunk.

'Hey, Johnny. Sorry, Johnny.' Sergio was mumbling. 'First time I put ship on bank—ever! Idiot! So close— then *wap*! Sorry, hey, Johnny.'

The motor launch left the jetty and came down the channel towards the sandbank on which *Kingfisher* lay stranded. The launch was crowded, and the whine of the outboard engine raised a storm of water fowl into a whirlwind of frightened wings.

As it drew closer Johnny recognized some of the occupants. Mike Shapiro and with him Robin Sutherland, but there were also two uniformed policemen and another person in civilian clothes who stood up in the launch as it came within hail and cupped his hands about his mouth.

'I am a police officer. I have a warrant for the arrest of Benedict—'

Mike Shapiro touched the man's arm, and spoke softly to him. The officer hesitated and glanced up at Johnny again, before nodding agreement and settling back onto his seat.

'Robin, get up here as quick as you can,' Johnny shouted down at the launch, and when Robin came over the side Johnny hustled him towards the bridge, but Mike Shapiro hurried after them.

'Johnny, I must talk to you.'

'It can wait.'

'No, it can't.' Mike Shapiro turned to Tracey. 'Won't you take care of the doctor, please? I must speak to Johnny before the police do.'

Mike led Johnny down the deck and offered him a cigarette, while the three policemen hovered at a discreet distance.

'Johnny, I have some dreadful news. I want to break it to you myself.'

Johnny visibly braced himself. 'Yes?'

—'It's about Ruby—'

Johnny made his statement to the police inspector in *Kingfisher*'s guest cabin. It took two hours for him to relate the full story, and during that time one of the uniformed policemen discovered the crew locked in the paint store below decks. They were half poisoned with paint fumes but able to make their statements to the police.

The inspector kept them waiting in the next-door cabin while he finished his interrogation of Johnny.

'Two more questions for now, Mr Lance. In your opinion was the collision between the two ships accidental or deliberate?'

Jonny looked into the steel-grey eyes and lied for the first time.

'It was unavoidable.'

The inspector nodded and made a note on his pad.

'Last question. The survivors from the trawler, what were their chances?'

'In that storm they had none. There was no hope of effecting a rescue with *Kingfisher* almost disabled, and considering the condition of the surf in the passage between the islands.'

'I understand.' The inspector nodded. 'Thank you, Mr Lance. That is all for the present.'

Johnny left the cabin and went quickly to the upper deck. Tracey and Robin were still working over Sergio's bunk, but Robin looked up and came immediately to Johnny as he stood in the doorway.

'How is he, Robin?'

'He hasn't a chance,' Robin replied, keeping his voice low. 'One lung has collapsed, and there appear to be perforations of the bowel and intestine. I suspect a massive peritonitis. I can't move him without risking a secondary haemorrhage.'

'Is he conscious?'

Robin shook his head. 'He's going fast. God knows how he has lasted this long.'

Johnny moved across to the bunk and placed his arm about Tracey's shoulders. She moved closer to him and they stood looking down at Sergio.

His eyes were closed, and a dark pelt of new beard covered the lower part of his face. His breathing sawed and hissed loudly in the quiet cabin, and the fever lit bright spots of colour in his cheeks.

'You magnificent old rogue.' Johnny spoke softly, and Sergio's eyed blinked open.

Quickly Johnny stooped to him.

'Sergio. Your crew—your boys are safe.'

Sergio smiled. He closed those dark gazelle eyes, then opened them again and whispered painfully, 'Johnny, you give me a job when I come out of prison?'

'They won't have you in prison—you'd lower the tone of the place.'

Sergio tried to laugh. He managed one strangled chuckle, then he came up on his elbows in the bunk with his eyes bulging, his mouth gaping for breath. He coughed once, a harsh tearing sound, and the blood burst from his lips in thick black clots and a bright red spray of droplets.

He fell back on the pillows, and was dead before Robin reached his side.

Tracey was asleep in the bedroom next door. Robin had sedated her heavily enough to keep her that way for the next twelve hours.

Johnny lay naked on the narrow bunk in the second guest room of the Cartridge Bay depot, and when he switched on the bedside lamp his wrist watch showed the time as 2.46 in the morning.

He looked down at his own body. The bruises were dark purple and hot angry red across his ribs and flanks from where the mud had battered him against rough steel plating. He wished now that he had accepted the sleeping pills Robin had offered him, for the ache of his body and the whirl of his thoughts had kept him from sleep all that night.

His mind was trapped on a nightmare roundabout, revolving endlessly the two deaths which Benedict van der Byl must answer for in the dark places to which he had surely gone.

Ruby and Sergio. One he had seen die, the other he could imagine in all its gruesome detail.

Johnny sat up and lit a cigarette, seeking a distraction from the tortured images with which his over-excited brain bombarded him.

He tried to concentrate on reviewing the practical steps that would be necessary to clear up the aftermath of these last disastrous days.

He had spoken that evening by radio to Larsen, and received from him a promise of complete financial support during the time it would take to clear the mud from *Kingfisher*'s hull and recover the diamonds in the conveyor tunnel, and to tide over the period of salvage and repair before the dredger was ready to begin once more harvesting the rich fields of Thunderbolt and Suicide.

A salvage team would fly in tomorrow to begin the work on *Kingfisher*. He had cabled IBM requesting engineers to check out the computer for water damage.

Six weeks, Johnny estimated, before *Kingfisher* was ready for sea.

Then his unruly imagination leapt suddenly ahead to Ruby's funeral. It was set for Tuesday next week. Johnny rolled restlessly on his bunk, trying to shut his mind against the thoughts that assaulted it—but they crowded forward in a dark host.

Ruby, Benedict, Sergio, the big blue diamond.

He sat up again, stubbed out his cigarette and reached across to switch out the bedside lamp.

He froze like that, as a new thought pressed in on him. He heard Sergio's voice in his memory.

'Such a diamond as you will never see again.'

Now he felt the idea come ghosting along his spine so that the hair at the nape of his neck and on his forearms prickled with excitement.

'The Red Gods!' he exclaimed, almost shouting the name. And again Sergio's voice spoke.

'In his coat. He put it in his coat pocket.'

Johnny swung his legs off the bunk, and reached for his clothes. He felt the pounding of his heart beneath his fingers as he buttoned his shirt. He pulled on slacks and sweater, tied the laces of his shoes and snatched up a sheepskin jacket as he ran from the room.

He was shrugging on the jacket as he entered the deserted radio room and switched on the lights. He crossed quickly to the chart table and pored over it.

He found the name on the map, and repeated it aloud. 'The Red Gods.'

North of Cartridge Bay the coast ran straight and featureless for thirty miles, then abruptly the line of it was broken by the out-thrust of red rock, poking into the sea like an accuser's finger.

Johnny knew it well. It was his job to find and examine any such natural feature that might act as a barrier to the prevailing inshore currents. At such a place diamonds and other seaborne objects would be thrown ashore.

He remembered the red rock cliffs carved by wind and sea into the grotesque natural statues which gave the place its name, but more important he remembered the litter of ocean debris on the beaches beneath the cliff. Driftwood, waterlogged planking, empty bottles, plastic containers, scraps of nylon fishing-net corks—all of it cast overboard and carried up by the current to be deposited on this promontory.

He ran his finger down the chart and held it on the dots of Thunderbolt and Suicide. He read the laconic notation over the tiny arrows that flew from the islands towards the stark outline of the Red Gods.

'Current sets South South-West. 5 knots.'

Above the chart table the depot keys hung on their little cuphooks, each labelled and numbered.

Johnny selected the two of them marked GARAGE and LAND-ROVER.

The moon was full and high. The night was still and without a trace of wind. Johnny swung the double doors of the garage open and switched on the parking lights of the Land-Rover. By their glow he checked out the vehicle; petrol tank full, the spare five-gallon cans in their brackets full, the can of drinking-water full. He dipped his finger into the neck of the water containers and tasted it. It was clean and sweet. He lifted the passenger seat and checked the compartment beneath it. Jack and tyre spanner, first aid kit, flashlight, signal rockets and smoke flares, water bottle, canvas groundsheet, two cans of survival rations, tow-rope, tool kit, knapsack, knife and compass. The Land-Rover was equipped to meet any of the emergencies of desert travel.

Johnny climbed behind the wheel and started the engine. He drove quietly and slowly past the depot building, not wanting to awaken those sleeping inside, but when he hit the firm sand at the edge of the lagoon he switched on the headlights and gunned the engine.

He cut across the sand dunes at the entrance to the bay, and swung northwards onto the beach. The headlights threw solid white beams into the sea mist, and startled sea birds rose on flapping ghost wings before the rush of the Land-Rover.

The tide was out and the exposed beach was hard and shiny wet, smooth as a tarmac road. He drove fast, and the white crabs were blinded by the headlights and crunched crisply beneath the tyres.

The dawn came early, silhouetting the mystic shapes of the dunes against the red sky.

Once he startled a strand wolf, one of the brown hyenas which scavenged this bleak littoral. It galloped, hunch-shouldered, in hideous panic for the safety of the dunes. Even in his urgency Johnny felt a stir of revulsion for the loathsome creature.

The cold damp rush of the wind into his face refreshed Johnny. It cooled the gritty feeling of his eyes, and eased the throb of sleeplessness in his temples.

The sun burst over the horizon, and lit the Red Gods five miles ahead with all the drama of stage lighting. They glowed golden red in the dawn, a procession of huge half-human shapes that marched into the sea.

As Johnny drove towards them the light and shadow played over the cliffs and he saw a hundred-foot tall figure of Neptune stooping to dip his flowing red beard into the sea, while a monstrous hunchback with the head of a wolf pranced beside him. Ranks of Vestal Virgins in long robes of red rock jostled with the throng of weird and fantastic shapes. It was eerie and disquieting.

Johnny curbed his fancy and turned his attention to the beaches at the foot of the cliffs.

What he saw started his skin tingling again, and he pressed the accelerator flat against the floor-boards, racing across the wet sand to where a white cloud of sea birds circled and dived and hopped about something that lay at the water's edge.

As he drove towards them a gull flew across the front of the Land-Rover. A long ribbon of something wet and fleshy dangled from its beak, and the gull gulped at it greedily in flight. Its crop was distended and engorged with food.

The sea birds scattered raucously and indignantly as the Land-Rover approached, leaving a human body lying in the centre of an area of sand that was dappled by the prints of their webbed feet, and fouled with dropped feathers and excreta.

Johnny braked the Land-Rover and jumped out. He took one long look at the body, then turned away and braced himself against the side of the vehicle.

His gorge rose in a hot flood of nausea, and he gagged it back.

The body was nude but for a few sodden tatters of clothing and a sea boot still laced onto one foot. The birds had attacked every inch of exposed flesh—except for the scalp. The face was unrecognizable. The nose was gone, the eye sockets were empty black holes. There were no lips to cover the grinning teeth.

Above this ruined face the shock of colourless albino hair looked like a wig placed there as an obscene and tasteless joke.

Hugo Kramer had made the long voyage from Thunderbolt and Suicide to the Red Gods.

Johnny took the canvas groundsheet from under the passenger seat of the Land-Rover. Averting his eyes from the task, he wrapped the corpse carefully, tied the whole bundle with lengths of rope cut from the tow line, then laboriously dragged it up the beach well above the high-water mark.

The thick canvas would keep off the birds, but to make doubly certain Johnny collected the driftwood and planking that was scattered thickly along the high-water line and piled it over the corpse.

Some of the planking was freshly broken and the paint on it was still bright and new. Johnny guessed this was part of the wreckage of *Wild Goose*.

He went back to the Land-Rover, and drove on towards the Red Gods which lay only a mile ahead.

The sun was well up by now, and already its heat was uncomfortable. As he drove he struggled out of the sheepskin jacket without interrupting his search of the beach ahead.

He was looking for another gathering of seagulls, but instead he saw a large black object stranded in the angle formed by the red stone cliffs.

He was fifty yards from if before he realized what it was.

He felt his stomach jar violently and then clench at the shock.

It was a black rubber inflatable life raft—and it had been dragged up the beach *above the high-water line.*

As he climbed out of the Land-Rover Johnny felt his legs trembling beneath him, as though he had just climbed a mountain. The hard knotted sensation in his chest shortened his breathing.

He went slowly towards the raft, and there was a story to read in the soft sand.

The smooth drag mark of the raft, and the two sets of footprints. One set made by bare feet, broad, stubby-toed and with flattened arches, the prints of a man who habitually went barefooted.

These tracks had been made by one of the coloured crew of *Wild Goose*, Johnny decided, dismissed them and turned his whole attention to the other set of footprints.

Shod feet, long and narrow, smooth leather soles; the imprints were sharp edged suggesting new shoes little worn, the length of the stride and the depth of prints were those of a tall heavily-built man.

Johnny realized with mild surprise that his hands were shaking now, and even his lips quivered. He was like a man in high fever; light-headed, weak and shaking. It was Benedict van der Byl. He knew it with complete and utter certainty. Benedict had survived the maelstrom of Thunderbolt and Suicide.

Johnny balled his fists, squeezing hard and he thrust out his jaw, tightening his lips. Still the hatred washed over his mind in dark hot waves.

'Thank God,' he whispered. 'Thank God. Now I can kill him myself.'

The footprints had churned the sand all about the raft. Beside them lay a thick piece of planking which had been used as a lever to rip the emergency water container and the food locker from the floor-boards of the raft.

The food locker had been ransacked and abandoned. They would be carrying the packets of iron rations in their pockets to save weight, but the water container was gone.

The two sets of prints struck out straight for the dunes. Johnny followed them at a run and lost them immediately in the shifting wind-blown sands of the first dune.

Johnny was undismayed. The dunes persisted for only a thousand yards or so, then gave way inland to the plains and salt flats of the interior.

He ran back to the Land-Rover. He had his emotions under control again. His hatred was reduced to a hard indigestible lump below his ribs, and he contemplated for a few seconds lifting the microphone of the Land-Rover's R/T set and calling Cartridge Bay.

Inspector Stander had the police helicopter parked on the landing-strip behind the depot buildings. He could be here in thirty minutes. An hour later they would have Benedict van der Byl.

Johnny dismissed the idea. Officially Benedict was dead, drowned. No one would look for him in a shallow grave in the wastes of the Namib desert.

The crewman with him would be a complication; but he could be bribed and frightened or threatened. Nothing must stand in the path of his vengeance. Nothing.

Johnny opened the Land-Rover's locker and found the knife. He went back to the raft and stabbed the blade through the thick material at a dozen places. The air hissed from the holes, and the raft collapsed slowly.

Johnny bundled it into the back of the Land-Rover. He would bury it in the desert; there must be no evidence that Benedict had come ashore.

He started the engine, engaged the four-wheel drive, and followed the spoor to the foot of the dunes.

He picked his way through the valleys and across the knife-backed ridges of sand.

As he descended the last slope of the dunes he felt the oppressive silence and immensity of the land enfold him. Here, only a mile from the sea, the moderating influence of the cold Benguela did not reach.

The heat was appalling. Johnny felt the sweat pricking from the pores of his skin and drying instantly in the lethal desiccating air.

He swung the Land-Rover parallel to the line of the dunes and crawled along at walking speed, hanging over the side of the vehicle and searching the ground. The bright specks of mica in the sand bounced the heat of the sun into his face.

He cut the spoor again where it came down off the dunes and went away on it, headed arrow straight at the far line of mountains which were already receding into the blue haze as the heat built up towards noon.

Johnny's progress was a series of rushes where the spoor ran true, broken by halts and painstaking casts on the rocky ridges and areas of broken ground. Twice he left the Land-Rover to work the spoor through difficult terrain, but across one of the flat white salt pans he covered four miles in as many minutes. The prints were strung like the beads of a necklace, cut clearly through the glistening crust of salt.

Beyond the pan they ran into a maze of black rocks, riven by gullies, and guarded by the tall misshapen monoliths.

In one of the gullies he found Hansie, the little old coloured crewman from Wild Goose. His skull had been battered in with the blood-caked rock that lay beside him. The blood had dried slick and shiny, and Hansie stared with dry eyeballs at the merciless sky. His expression was of mild surprise.

The story of this new tragedy was written in the sandy bottom of the gully. In an area of milling, confused prints the two men had argued. Johnny could guess that Hansie had wanted to turn back for the coast. He must have known that the road lay beyond the mountains, a hundred miles away. He wanted to abandon the attempt, try for the coast and Cartridge Bay.

The argument ended when he turned his back on Benedict, and returned on his old tracks.

There was a depression in the sand from which Benedict had picked up the rock and followed him.

Standing over Hansie, and looking down at that pathetic crushed head, Johnny realized for the first time that he was following a maniac.

Benedict van der Byl was insane. He was no longer a man, but a raging demented animal.

'I will kill him,' Johnny promised the old white woolly head at his feet. There was no need for subterfuge now.

If he caught up with Benedict and did it, no court in the world would question but that it was self-defence. Benedict had placed himself beyond the laws of man.

Johnny took the deflated rubber raft and spread it over Hansie. He anchored the edges of the rubber sheet with rocks.

He drove on into the dancing, shimmering wall of heat with a new mood on him; murderous, elated expectation. He knew that at this moment in time he was part animal also, corrupted by the savagery of the man he was hunting. He wanted payment in full from Benedict van der Byl in his own coin. Life for life, and blood for blood.

A mile farther on he found the water container. It had been flung aside violently, skidding across the sand with the force of its rejection; the water had poured from its open mouth, leaving a dried hollow in the thirsty earth.

Johnny stared at it in disbelief. Not even a maniac would condemn himself to such a horrible ending.

Johnny went across to where the five-gallon brass drum lay on its side. He picked it up and shook it, there was the sloshy sound of a pint or so of liquid in it.

'God!' he whispered, awed and feeling a twinge of pity despite himself. 'He won't last long now.'

He lifted the container to his lips and sucked a mouthful. Immediately his nostrils flared with disgust, and he spat violently, dropping the can and wiping at his lips with the back of his hand.

'Sea water!' he mumbled. He hurried to the Land-Rover and washed out his mouth with sweet water.

How the contamination had occured he would never know. The raft might have lain for years in *Wild Goose* without its stores being checked or renewed.

From that point onwards Benedict must have known he was doomed. His despair was easy to read in the blundering footsteps. He had started running, with panic driving him. Five hundred yards farther on he had fallen heavily into the bed of a dry ravine, and lain for a while before dragging himself up the bank.

Now he had lost direction. The spoor began a long curve to the northwards, running again. It came round full circle, and where it crossed itself, Benedict had sat down. The marks of his buttocks were unmistakable. He must have controlled his panic here because once more the spoor struck out with determination towards the mountains.

However, within half a mile he had tripped and fallen. Now he was staggering off course again, drifting southwards. Once more he had fallen, but there he had lost a shoe.

Johnny picked it up and read the printed gold lettering on the inner sole. 'BALLY OF SWITZERLAND. SPECIALLY MADE FOR HARRODS. That's our boy Benedict, all right. Forty-guinea black kid,' he muttered grimly, and climbed back into the Land-Rover. His excitement was climaxing now. It would be soon, very soon.

Farther on Benedict had wandered down into the bed of an ancient watercourse, and turned to follow it. His right foot was lacerated by razor flints in the river bed, and at each pace he had left a little dab of brown crumbly blood. He was staggering like a drunkard.

Johnny zigzagged the Land-Rover through the boulders that choked the watercourse. The gully deepened, and spiky cockscomb ridges of black rock hedged it in on either hand. The air in the watercourse was a heavy blanket of heat. It seared the throat, and dried the mucus in Johnny's nostrils brick hard. A small noon breeze came off the mountains, a sluggish stirring of the heavy air, that provided no relief but seemed only to heighten the bite of the sun and the suffocating oppression of the air.

Scattered along the river bed were bushes of stunted scrub. Grotesque little plants, crippled and malformed by the drought of years.

From one of the bushes ahead of the Land-Rover a monstrous black bird flapped its wings lethargically. Johnny screwed up his eyes, uncertain if it was reality or a mirage of the heat and the tortured air.

Suddenly the bird resolved itself into the jacket of a dark blue suit. It hung in the thorny bushes, the breeze stirring the folds of expensive cloth.

'In his coat. He put it in his coat pocket.'

With eyes only for the jacket, recklessly he pressed down the accelerator and the Land-Rover surged forward. Johnny did not see the knee-high boulder of ironstone in his path. He hit it at twenty miles an hour, and the Land-Rover stopped dead with the squeal of tearing metal. Johnny was flung forward against the steering-wheel, the impact driving the breath from his lungs.

He was still doubled up with the pain of it, wheezing for breath, as he hobbled to the jacket and snatched it out of the bush.

He felt the heavy drag of the weighted pocket.

Then the fat canvas bag was in his hands, the contents crunched nuttily as he tore at the drawstring. Nothing else in the world felt like that.

'Such a diamond as you will never see again.'

The drawstring was knotted tightly. Johnny ran back to the Land-Rover. Frantically he scrabbled in the seat locker and found the knife. He cut the drawstring and dumped the contents of the bag onto the bonnet of the Land-Rover.

'Oh God! Oh sweet God!' he whispered through cracked lips. His eyesight blurred, and the big blue diamond glowed mistily, distorted by the tears that flooded his vision.

It was a full minute before he could bring himself to touch it. Then he did so reverently—as though it were a sacred relic.

Johnny Lance had worked all his life to take a stone such as this.

He held it in both hands and sank down into the scrap of shade beside the body of the Land-Rover.

It was another five minutes before the hot cloying smell of engine oil reached the conscious level of his mind.

He turned his head and saw the slowly spreading pool of it beneath the Land-Rover chassis. Quickly he rolled onto his stomach and, still clutching the diamond, crawled under the vehicle. The ironstone boulder had shattered the engine sump. The Land-Rover had belched its lifeblood into the hot sand of the river bed.

He wriggled out from under the body of the Land-Rover and leaned against the front tyre. He looked at his wrist watch and was surprised to see it was already a few minutes after two o'clock in the afternoon.

He was surprised also at the conscious effort it required to focus his eyes on the dial of the watch. Two days and two nights without sleep, the unremitting emotional strain of those days and nights, the battering his body had taken, the long hours in the heat and the soul-corroding desolation of this lunar landscape—all these had taken their toll. He knew he was as light-headed as in the first stages of inebriation, he was beginning to act irrationally. That sudden reckless charge down the boulder-strewn river bed, which had wrecked the Land-Rover, was a symptom of his present instability.

He fondled the great diamond, touching the warm smooth surface to his lips, rubbing it softly between thumb and forefinger, changing it from hand to hand, while every fibre of his muscles and the very marrow of his bones cried out for rest.

A soft and treacherous lethargy spread through his body and reached out to numb his brain. He closed his eyes for a moment to shut out the glare, and when he opened them again with an effort the time was four o'clock. He scrambled to his feet. The shadows in the gully were longer, the breeze had dropped.

Although he moved with the stiffness of an old man, the sleep had cleared his mind and while he wolfed a packet of biscuits spread with meat paste and washed it down with a mugful of lukewarm water he made his decision.

He buried the canvas bag of rough diamonds in the sand beneath the Land-Rover, but he could not bring himself to part with the big Blue. He buttoned it securely into the back pocket of his slacks. Into the light knapsack from the seat locker he packed the two-pint water bottle, the first aid kit, a small hand-bearing compass, two of the smoke flares and the knife. He checked his pockets for his cigarette-lighter and case.

Then without another glance at the radio set on the dashboard of the Land-Rover he turned away and hobbled up the gully on the spoor of Benedict van der Byl.

Within half a mile he had walked the stiffness out of his body, and he lengthened his stride, going well now. The hatred and hunger for vengeance which had died to smouldering ash since he had found the diamonds, now flared up again strongly. It gave power to his legs and sharpened his senses.

The spoor turned abruptly up the side of the gully and he lost it on the black rock of the ridge, but found it again on his first cast.

He was closing fast now. The spoor was running across the grain of the land, and Benedict was clearly weakening rapidly. He had fallen repeatedly, crawled on bloody knees over cruel gravel and rock, he had blundered into the scrub bushes and left threads of his clothing on the hooked red-tipped thorns.

Then the spoor led out of the ridges and scrub into another area of low orange-coloured sandhills and Johnny broke into a trot. The sun was sliding down the sky, throwing blue shades in the hollows of the dunes and the heat abated so that Johnny's sweat was able to cool him before drying.

Johnny was intent on the staggering footprints, beginning to worry now that he would find Benedict already dead. The signs were those of a man in extreme distress, and still he was driving himself on.

Johnny did not notice the other prints that angled in from the dunes and ran parallel to those of Benedict, until they closed in again and began overlaying the human prints.

Johnny stopped and went down on one knee to examine the broad dog-like pug marks.

'Hyena!' He felt the sick little flutter of revulsion in his stomach as he spoke. He glanced around quickly and saw the other sets of prints out on the left.

'A pair of them! They've smelt the blood.'

Johnny began to run on the spoor now. His skin crawled with what he knew could happen when they caught up with a helpless man. The filthiest and most cowardly animals in Africa, but with jaws that could crunch to splinters the thigh bone of a full-grown buffalo, and their thick stubby fangs were coated with such a slime of bacteria from a diet of putrid carrion that their bite was as deadly as that of a black mamba.

'Let me be in time; please God, let me find him in time.'

He heard it then. From beyond the crest of the next dune. The horror of the sound stopped him in mid-stride. It was a shrill giggling gibbering cry that sobbed into silence.

Johnny stood listening, panting wildly from his run.

It came again. The laughter of demons, excited, blood-crazy.

'They've got him.'

Johnny flung himself at the soft slope of sand. He reached the crest and looked down into the saucer-shaped arena formed by the crescent of the dune.

Benedict lay on his back. His white shirt was open to the waist. The blue trousers of his suit were ripped and shredded, exposing his knees. One foot was a bloody lump of sock and congealed dirt.

The pair of hyenas had trampled a path in the sand around his body. They had been circling him for hours, while greed overcame their cowardice.

One hyena sat ten feet from him, squatting obscenely with its flat snakelike head lowered between humped shoulders. Brown and shaggy, spotted with darker brown, its round ears pricked forward, its black eyes sparkling with greed and excitement as it watched its mate.

The other hyena stood with its front paws on Benedict's chest. Its head lowered, and its jaws were locked into Benedict's face. It was leaning back, bracing its paws on his chest, tugging viciously as it sought to tear off a mouthful of flesh. Benedict's head was jerking and twitching as the hyena worried it. His legs were kicking weakly, and his hands fluttered on the sand like maimed white birds.

The flesh of his face tore. Johnny heard it distinctly in the utter silence of the desert evening. It tore with the soft sound of silk—and Johnny screamed.

Both hyenas bolted at the scream, scrambling over the far crest of the dune in horrible clownish panic, leaving Benedict lying with a bloody mask for a face. Looking down at that face Johnny knew he could not kill him now, perhaps could never have killed him. He could not revenge himself on this broken thing with its ruined face and twisted mind.

He dropped onto his knees beside him, and loosened the flap of the knapsack with clumsy fingers.

Benedict's one ear and cheek were hanging over his mouth in a thick flap of torn flesh. The teeth in the side of his jaw were exposed and the blood dribbled and spurted in fine needle jets.

Johnny tore the paper packaging off an absorbent dressing and with it pressed the flap back into place, holding it there with the full pressure of his spread fingers. The blood soaked through the dressing, but it was slowing at the pressure.

'It's all right, Benedict. 'I'm here now. You'll be all right,' he whispered hoarsely as he worked. With his free hand he stripped the packaging off another dressing, and substituted it neatly for the sodden one. He maintained the pressure on the clean dressing while he lifted Benedict's head and cradled it in his lap.

'We'll just dry this bleeding up, then we'll give you a drink.' He reached into the first aid kit for a piece of cotton wool and tenderly began to clean the blood and sand from Benedict's nostrils and lips. Benedict's strangled breathing eased a little but still whistled through the black lips. His tongue was swollen, filling his mouth like a fat purple sponge.

'That's better,' Johnny muttered. Still without relaxing pressure on the compress dressing, he got the screw top off the water bottle. Holding his thumb over the opening to regulate the flow, he let a drop of water fall into the dark dry pit of a mouth.

After another ten drops he propped the water bottle in the sand, and massaged Benedict's throat gently to stimulate the swallowing reflex. The unconscious man gulped painfully.

'That's my boy,' Johnny encouraged him, and began again feeding him a drop at a time, crooning softly as he did it.

'You're going to be all right. That's it, swallow it down.'

It took him twenty minutes to administer half a pint of the warm sweet water, and by then the bleeding was negligible. Johnny reached into the kit again and selected two salt and two glucose tablets. He placed them in his own mouth and chewed them to a smooth thin paste, then he bent over the mutilated face of the man he had sworn to kill and pressed his own lips against Benedict's swollen dry lips. He injected the solution of salt and glucose into Benedict's mouth, then straightened up and began again dripping the water.

When he had given Benedict another four tablets and half the contents of the water bottle, he stoppered it and returned it to the knapsack. He soaked the compress with bright yellow acriflavine solution, and bandaged it firmly into place. This was a more difficult task than he had anticipated and after a few abortive attempts he passed the bandage under the jaw and over the eyes, swathing Benedict's head completely except for the nose and mouth.

By this time the sun was on the horizon. Johnny stood up and stretched his back and shoulders as he watched the splendid gold and red death of another desert day.

He knew he was delaying his next decision. He reckoned it was five miles to where he had abandoned the Land-Rover in the gully. Five miles of hard going, a round trip of four hours—probably five in the dark. Could he leave Benedict here, get back to the vehicle, radio Cartridge Bay, and return to him?

Johnny swung round and looked up at the dunes. There was his answer. One of the hyenas was squatting on the top of a dune watching him intently. Hunger and the approach of night had made it unnaturally bold.

Johnny shouted an obscenity and made a threatening gesture towards it. The hyena jumped up and loped over the back of the ridge.

'Moon rise at eight tonight. I'll rest then—and we'll go in the cool,' he decided and lay down on the sand beside Benedict. The lump in his back pocket prodded him, and he took the diamond out and held it in his hand.

In the darkness the hyenas began to cackle and shriek, and when the moon rose it silhouetted their evil shapes on the ridge above the saucer.

'Come on Benedict. We're going home. There are a couple of nice policemen who want to talk to you.' Johnny lifted him into a sitting position, draped Benedict's arm over his shoulder and came up under him in a fireman's lift.

Johnny stood like that a moment, sinking ankle deep into the soft sand, dismayed at the dead weight of his burden.

'We'll rest every thousand paces,' he promised himself, and began plodding up the dune, counting softly to himself, but knowing that he would not be able to perform that lift again without a rock shelf or some support, against which to brace himself. He had to make it out of the sandhills in one go.

'—Nine hundred and ninety nine. One thousand.' He was counting in his mind only. Husbanding his strength, bowed under the weight, his shoulders and back locked in straining agony, the sand hampering each pace. 'Another five hundred. We'll go another five hundred.'

Behind him padded the two hyenas. They had gobbled the bloody dressing that Johnny had left in the saucer, and the taste of blood was driving them hysterical.

'Right. Just another five hundred.' And Johnny began the third count, and then the fourth, and the fifth.

Johnny felt the drip, drip on the back of his legs. Benedict's head-down position had restarted the bleeding, and the hyenas warbled and wailed at the smell.

'Nearly there, Benedict. Stick it out. Nearly there.'

The first cluster of moon-silver rocks floated towards them and Johnny reeled in amongst them and collapsed face forward. It was a long time before he had regained enough strength to shift Benedict's weight off his shoulders.

He readjusted Benedict's bandages, and fed him a mouthful of water which he swallowed readily. Then Johnny washed down a handful of salt and glucose tablets with two carefully rationed swallows from the water bottle. He rested for twenty minutes by his watch, then using one of the rocks as an anchor he got Benedict across his shoulder again and they went on.

Johnny rested every hour for ten minutes. At one o'clock in the morning they finished the last of the water, and at two o'clock Johnny knew beyond all possibility of doubt that he had missed the watercourse and that he was lost.

He lay against a slab of ironstone, numb with fatigue and despair, and listened to the cackling chorus of death among the rocks nearby. He tried to decide where he had gone wrong. Perhaps the watercourse curved away and he was now moving parallel to it, perhaps he had already crossed it without having recognized it. That was possible, he had heard of others stumbling blindly across a tarmac road without realizing it.

How many ridges had they climbed and descended? He could not remember. There was a place where he had stumbled into a shrub thorn and ripped his legs. Perhaps that was the watercourse.

He crawled across to Benedict.

'Brace up, bucko. We're going back.'

Johnny fell for the last time a little before dawn. When he rolled his head and squinted sideways at his wrist watch it was light enough to read the dial. The time was five o'clock.

He closed his eyes and lay for a long time, he had given up. It had been a good try—but it hadn't worked. In an hour the sun would be up. Then it was finished.

Something was moving near him, soft and stealthy-footed. It was of no interest, he decided. He just wanted to lie here quietly, now that it was finished.

Then he heard the sniffing, the harsh sniffing of a hungry dog. He opened his eyes. The hyena was ten feet away, watching him. Its bottom jaw hung open, and the pink tongue lolled loosely from the side of its mouth. He could smell it, a stink like an animal cage at the zoo, dung and offal and rotting carrion.

Johnny tried to scream, but no sound came from his mouth. His throat was closed, and his tongue filled his mouth. He struggled onto his elbows. The hyena drew back, but without the ludicrous panic of before. Leisurely it trotted away, and then turned to face him again from a distance of twenty yards. It grinned at him, slurping the pink tongue into its mouth as it gulped saliva.

Johnny dragged himself to where Benedict lay, and looked down at him.

Slowly the blind bandaged head turned towards him, the black lips moved.

'Who's there?' A dry husky whisper. Johnny tried to answer but his voice failed him again. He hawked and chewed painfully, working a trace of moisture into his mouth. Now that Benedict was conscious Johnny's hatred flared again.

'Johnny,' he croaked. 'It's Johnny.'

'Johnny?' Benedict's hand came up and he touched the bandages over his eyes.

'What?'

Johnny reached across, lying on his side, and untied the knot at Benedict's temple. He peeled the bandages from his eyes, and Benedict blinked at him. The light of dawn was stronger now.

'Water?' Benedict asked.

Johnny shook his head.

'Please.'

'None.'

Benedict closed his eyes and then opened them, staring in terror at Johnny.

'Ruby!' Johnny whispered. 'Sergio! Hansie!'

A spasm of guilt twisted Benedict's face, and Johnny leaned closer to him to hiss a single word into his ear.

'Bastard!'

Johnny rested on his elbows, swallowing thickly, then he spoke again.

'Up!' He crawled behind Benedict and pushed and dragged him into a sitting position.

'Look.'

Twenty yards away the two hyenas sat expectantly, leering idiotically and bright-eyed with impatience.

Benedict began to tremble. He made a mewing whimpering sound. Johnny worked him slowly backwards until he had him propped against a rock.

He rested again, leaning on the rock beside Benedict.

'I'm going,' he whispered. 'You stay.'

Benedict made that mewing sound again, shaking his head weakly, staring at the two slobbering animals ahead of him.

Johnny slung the knapsack about his neck. He closed his eyes and called upon the last reserves of his strength. With a heave he got to his knees. Darkness and bright lights obscured his vision. They cleared and he heaved again and he was on his feet. His knees buckled and he grabbed at the rock to steady himself.

'Cheerio!' he whispered. 'Have fun!' And he went lurching and staggering away into the wilderness of black rock.

Behind him the mewing whimper rose to a bubbling scream.

'Johnny. Please, Johnny.'

Johnny closed his mind to that cry, and staggered on.

'Murder!' screamed Benedict. The accusation checked Johnny. He leaned against another rock for support, and looked back.

Benedict's face was convulsed, and a thin line of bloody froth rimmed his lips. The tears were pouring unashamedly down his cheeks to soak into the blood and antiseptic-stained bandages.

'Johnny. My brother. Don't leave me.'

Johnny pushed himself away from the rock. He swayed and almost fell. Then he staggered back to Benedict and slipped down into a sitting position beside him.

From the knapsack he took out the knife and laid it on his lap. Benedict was sobbing and moaning.

'Shut up. Damn you!' whispered Johnny.

The sun was well up now. It was burning directly into Johnny's face. He could feel the skin of his cheeks stretching to bursting-point. The veils of darkness kept passing over his vision, but he blinked them away. The flutter of his eyelids was the only movement he had made in the last hour.

The hyenas closed in. They were pacing nervously back and forth in front of where Johnny and Benedict sat. Now one of them stopped and stretched its neck out, sniffing eagerly at Benedict's blood-clotted foot, creeping inch by inch closer.

Johnny stirred and the creature jumped back, bobbing its head ingratiatingly, grinning as if in apology.

The time had come to fall back on their last line of defence. Johnny hoped he had not left it too late. He was very weak. His eyes and ears were tricking him, his vision jumped and blurred and there was a humming sound in the silence as though the desert was an orchard filled with bees. He spun the cog-wheel of his cigarette lighter and the flame lit. Carefully he applied it to the fuse of the smoke flare, and it spluttered and caught.

Johnny lobbed the flare towards the hyenas, and as the clouds of pink smoke spewed out, they fled in shrieking terror.

An hour later they were back. Slinking out of the rocks, cautious again. Johnny saw them only in flashes, between the bursts of darkness in his head. The insect drone in his ears was louder, it was confusing, making it difficult for him to think clearly.

It took him ten minutes to light the second flare. His throw was so weak that the flare pitched only a few inches beyond his own feet. The pink smoke spread over them.

Johnny felt the blood humming in his ears as the swirling pink clouds engulfed him. The sulphurous bite of the smoke in his throat choked him. The sound in his ears became a drumming roar, a rushing clattering hissing bellow. Then there was a wild wind in the stillness of the desert. Miraculously the smoke cloud was ripped away by the wind.

Johnny looked up into the sky from which the great wind came. Twenty feet above him, hanging on the glistening dragon-fly wing of its rotor, was the police helicopter.

Tracey's face was framed in the cabin window of the helicopter. He saw her lips form his name before he fainted.

